THE CHART OF
TOMORROWS

DISCARD

ALSO BY CHRIS WILLRICH

The Scroll of Years

The Silk Map

A Gaunt and Bone Novel

THE CHART OF TOMORROWS

CHRIS WILLRICH

an imprint of **Prometheus Books**
Amherst, NY

Published 2015 by Pyr®, an imprint of Prometheus Books

The Chart of Tomorrows: A Gaunt and Bone Novel. Copyright © 2015 by Chris Willrich. All rights reserved. No part of this publication may be reproduced, stored in a retrieval system, or transmitted in any form or by any means, digital, electronic, mechanical, photocopying, recording, or otherwise, or conveyed via the Internet or a website without prior written permission of the publisher, except in the case of brief quotations embodied in critical articles and reviews.

This is a work of fiction. Characters, organizations, locales, and events portrayed in this novel either are products of the author's imagination or are used fictitiously.

Cover illustration by © Kerem Beyit
Cover design by Nicole Sommer-Lecht

Inquiries should be addressed to

Pyr
59 John Glenn Drive
Amherst, New York 14228
VOICE: 716–691–0133
FAX: 716–691–0137
WWW.PYRSF.COM

19 18 17 16 15   5 4 3 2 1

Library of Congress Cataloging-in-Publication Data

Willrich, Chris, 1967-
    The chart of tomorrows : a Gaunt and Bone novel / Chris Willrich.
        pages ; cm
    ISBN 978-1-63388-058-0 (softcover) -- ISBN 978-1-63388-059-7 (ebook)
    I. Title.

PS3623.I57775C48 2015
813'.6—dc23

                                                                    2015001966

Printed in the United States of America

In memory of Jane Eades, Georgia Grytness, and Anne Rohweder

CONTENTS

Imago Bone's Notes on People, Places, and Things . . .   9

Prologue: Ash-Lad   17

Chapter 1: Mechanisms   37
Chapter 2: Otherfolk   51
Chapter 3: Runemark   61
Chapter 4: Storm   71
Chapter 5: Huginn   83
Chapter 6: Rubblewrack   95
Chapter 7: Muninn   106
Chapter 8: Jokull   122
Chapter 9: A Journey to Kantenjord   139
Chapter 10: Skalagrim   149
Chapter 11: Chroniclers   159
Chapter 12: Escape   165
Chapter 13: Torfa   174
Chapter 14: Changelings   183
Chapter 15: A Journey to Kantenjord, Continued   202
Chapter 16: Straits   212
Chapter 17: Ruin   219
Chapter 18: Skrymir   225
Chapter 19: Draug   237
Chapter 20: Wolves   244
Chapter 21: A Journey to Kantenjord, Continued   251
Chapter 22: Pyres   266
Chapter 23: Chooser   282
Chapter 24: Seter   287
Chapter 25: Council   292

Chapter 26: War   306
Chapter 27: Fossegrim   316
Chapter 28: Siege   324
Chapter 29: Sisterhood   329
Chapter 30: Larderland   337
Chapter 31: A Journey to Kantenjord, Continued   348
Chapter 32: Champions   364
Chapter 33: Fates   373
Chapter 34: Reunion   379
Chapter 35: Portals   389
Chapter 36: Queens   407
Chapter 37: Hearts   420
Chapter 38: A Journey to Kantenjord, Continued   439
Chapter 39: Gambit   447
Chapter 40: Yesterday   458
Chapter 41: Tomorrow   473
Chapter 42: Today   487
Chapter 43: Chosen   522
Chapter 44: The Middle   524
Chapter 45: Peace   526
Chapter 46: Summit   528

Acknowledgments   539

About the Author   541

IMAGO BONE'S NOTES ON PEOPLE, PLACES, AND THINGS BECAUSE HE IS GETTING OLDER AND HIS MEMORY IS TAXED

A-Girl-Is-A-Joy: Also, Joy Snøsdatter, Joy. Daughter of Snow Pine. Chosen to be the Runethane, champion of the Bladed Isles. It might have gone easier for her if she hadn't.

A Tumult of Trees on Peculiar Peaks: Also known as the Scroll of Years. A landscape painting that either contains or accesses a pocket dimension of accelerated time. You see, Gaunt? I can use magical jargon too.

Aile: A headwoman of the Vuos people. I heard of her much later, yet somehow I feel she belongs here.

Alder: A former wizardly apprentice, my comrade at the Gull-Jarl's steading.

Alfhild: A human raised as one of the fey uldra-folk. A princess of the uldra, no less. It seems to have affected her mind.

All-Now, the: Mirabad term for the compassionate creator of the universe.

Anansi: An exploratory ship from Kpalamaa.

Arngrimur Townflayer: One of the Nine Wolves. You may notice a theme in their names.

Arnulf Pyre-Maker: One of the Nine Wolves.

Ash-lad, or Askelad: A peasant hero from folktales.

Aughatai: Jewelwolf's horse. There was something very wrong with that horse.

Beinahruga: Cairn.

Bone: A fool. No, that's not all. An old fool.

Brambletop: A young woman of Larderland. It hurts to think of her now.

Breakwing Island: A troll-inhabited island beside Spydbanen.

Cairn: A Chooser of the Slain.

changeling: A troll or uldra child, left in place of a kidnapped human child.

Chart of Tomorrows, The: The Winterjarl's protean book, full of cryptic passages and alarming maps.

Chooser of the Slain: An agent of the old gods of the Bladed Isles.

Claymore: A troll.

Clifflion: Grand Khan of the Karvaks.

Corinna: Princess, later queen, of Soderland. I was never sure where we stood with her, but I was always sure she was in charge.

Crypttongue: A magic sword Gaunt wielded for a time. I hate magic swords.

Deadfall: A sapient magic carpet. Before I met it, those words would not have seemed frightening.

Dolma: An exiled warrior of Xembala. For a time she helped my son. I am grateful.

Draug: A spirit creature found upon the sea and within the Straits of Tid. Draugar can take the forms of dead folk you've known.

Draugmaw: An unnatural, gigantic maelstrom. It has Draugar in it.

Einar Bringer of Wailing: One of the Nine Wolves.

Eldshore, the: A slowly crumbling but still mighty continental empire.

Erik Glint: A foamreaver and Larderman.

Eshe: Priestess, wanderer, warrior, spy. Possibly our employer.

eventyr: Fairy tales.

Everart: Rabble-rouser of Soderland. Quite good at it.

Fiskegard: Independent-minded islands founded by fishermen, nominally part of Oxiland, periodically filled with itinerant workers. I came from a family of fishermen, and the scent was like home.

Five Fjords: A shaky alliance of the towns of Lillefosna, Vestvjell, Vesthall, Grimgard, and Regnheim.

Floki: A slaver.

Foamreaver: Can be a seafarer, trader, raider, or all of them together.

Freidar: An old tavernkeeper and Runewalker. Husband of Nan. Kind to Innocence, he was a good companion when we sailed aboard *Leaping Bison*.

Gamellaw: A region governed by old laws under which steadings are the unit of civilization, not nations. Takes in Svardmark from the Morkskag to the Chained Straits, and all of Spydbanen.

Garmsmaw Pass: A mountain pass connecting Garmstad territory to northern Svardmark.

Garmstad: A town and territory allied to Soderland.

Gaunt: What I call Persimmon when we're about our errands. The other half of my mind.

Gissur Mimurson: An Oxiland chieftain.

Gold-Jarl, or Gull-Jarl: Ruler of the small country of Gullvik.

Grawik: The steading of Ottmar Bloodslake.

Great Chain of Unbeing: A huge artifact absorbing the power of the dragons whose immense bodies gave form to the Bladed Isles.

Grunndokk: A town paying tribute to the Gull-Jarl.

Gullvik: Name of a town and a small domain in Svardmark.

Gunlaug: An overseer at the Gull-Jarl's steading.

Haboob: An efrit, a spirit of the desert.

Hakon: The retired king of Soderland.

Harald the Far-Traveled: Chieftain of the Laksfjord region.

Havtor: A slave in the Gull-Jarl's steading. May his name be honored.

Haytham ibn Zakwan ibn Rihab: Inventor and gentleman of Mirabad, daring to combine natural philosophy and magic. He gave the world ballooning. I might regret that, had I never flown.

Heavenwalls: Vast fortifications of Qiangguo—and beyond!—which somehow channel the land's vital breath.

Hekla: Huginn Sharpspear's companion. I think she was more formidable than he.

Huginn Sharpspear: A chieftain, lawyer, and tale-teller of Oxiland.

Imago: What Persimmon calls me, amid the least or greatest dangers.

Inga: She was half of the duo responsible for Peersdatter and Jorgensdatter's *Eventyr*. A mighty fighter, and brave.

Innocence Gaunt: Our son.

Ironhorn: A Karvak general.

Ivar Garm: Lord Mayor of Garmstad Town.

Jaska: A girl who turned Innocence's head in Oxiland.

Jegerhall: The steading of Arnulf Pyre-Maker.

Jewelwolf: Wife of the Grand Khan and a powerful leader in her own right. As if that wasn't enough to make me nervous, also knowledgeable in magic. Sister of Steelfox.

Jokull Loftsson: Strongest of the Oxiland chieftains.

Jotuncrown: A settlement of humans in thrall to the troll-jarl in the Trollberg.

Joy: What we all called A-Girl-Is-A-Joy.

Katta, called the Mad: One of many names for the wandering monk of the Undetermined whom we knew. A big-hearted person, though I think he regarded me as a miscreant. Truly I have no idea why.

Kantenings: The humans of the Bladed Isles, excepting the Vuos, who stand apart.

Kantenjord: It means something like "Edge-lands." Outsiders know it better as the Bladed Isles.

Karvak Realm: The empire of the Grand Khan.

Karvaks: The mightiest nomads of the steppes.

Klarvik: A town in Soderland.

Kolli the Cackling: One of the Nine Wolves.

Kollr: A young follower of the old gods in Oxiland, whom Innocence befriended.

Kpalamaa: A mighty realm of the South. If Qiangguo is not the world's most advanced nation, it is this.

Laksfjord: A surprisingly pleasant community near the Morkskag.

Langfjord: The steading of Kolli the Cackling.

Lardermen: Elite group of foamreavers, who made their name bringing supplies past a blockade.

Leaftooth: Head monk of the Peculiar Peaks.

Liron Flint: Explorer, treasure hunter, friend.

Loftsson's Hall: Steading of Oxiland's most powerful chieftain, with many allied folk nearby.

Lysefoss: A settlement beside a spectacular waterfall. I'd have appreciated it more if we hadn't been running for our lives.

Malin: She was half of the duo responsible for Peersdatter and Jorgensdatter's *Eventyr*. A brave soul. An unusual mind.

Meteor-Plum: The guardian of the Scroll of Years sometimes goes by this name.

Mirabad: Name for both a great city and the caliphate it commands. Once its power made the world tremble; its wealth and learning still make the world envious.

Morkskag, the: The haunted forest that divides "civilized" Svardmark from the Gamellaw.

Mossbeard: A troll.

Muggur Barrow-Friend: One of the Nine Wolves.

Muninn Crowbeard: Once a foamreaver styled "Surehand." He changed, more than once.

Nan: An old tavernkeeper and Runewalker. Wife of Freidar. Those two were kind to Innocence and did as much as anyone could to protect their homeland. I, a selfish man, am in awe.

Nine Smilodons: The Karvak soldier we traveled with for a time.

Nonyemeko: Captain of *Anansi*.

Northwing: A taiga shaman in service to Steelfox. Powerful as friend or enemy. I would know.

Numi: A Swan-church novitiate whom Innocence befriended.

Ostoland: A heavily wooded island, of somewhat insular folk.

Ottmar Bloodslake: One of the Nine Wolves.

Oxiland: A volcanic realm, and some associated islands, in Kantenjord's northwest. A bleak country, settled by stubborn people with notions of democracy. Clearly they are mad. It's tempting to join them.

Painter of Clouds: Swanlings use this term for what Mirabad's people call the All-Now; they got the name from the People of the Brush.

Peersdatter and Jorgensdatter's *Eventyr*: A surprisingly useful book of folktales.

Peik: A boy from Klarvik, by his own account absolutely the most truthful person that this or any other world has known.

Persimmon: See Gaunt. She is the one who should be writing this down; she has the gift for words. But she forgets little and doesn't see the need. She remembers the time I did this, and the time I did that, and the other thing. And yet she is still with me.

Qiangguo: A vast realm of the East. If Kpalamaa is not the world's most advanced nation, it is this.

Qurca: Steelfox's peregrine falcon, bonded to her spirit.

Rafnar Dragon-Axe: One of the Nine Wolves.

Ragnar: Half-brother of Corinna of Soderland.

Red Mirror: A Karvak soldier.

Roisin: A Swanling priestess. A fine person, surely, but a little too cozy with slavers.

Rolf: A young Swanling of Oxiland, whom Innocence befriended.

Rubblewrack: A troll, or so she appeared.

Runethane, or Runemarked Queen or King: The one who commands the energies of the Great Chain of Unbeing.

Runewalkers: Traditional mages of Kantenjord. Their power derives from tracings of mystic runes. Some of their tracings are enormous.

Ruvsa: Pirate queen of Larderland.

Schismglass: A magic sword, akin to Crypttongue but antagonistic.

Skalagrim the Bloody: One of the Nine Wolves. I'll say no more about him.

Skrymir Hollowheart: Lord of trolls in Spydbanen and, effectively, everywhere else.

Skyggeskag, the: An elder forest in Soderland, cousin to the Morkskag.

Snow Pine: Once known as Next-One-a-Boy or simply Next One. A bandit of Qiangguo and a companion to Persimmon and me. Our best friend.

Smokecoast: The largest settlement of Oxiland.

Soderland: Strongest and richest of the local kingdoms, principalities, chiefdoms, and what-have-yous. Therefore, the biggest target.

Splintrevej: Maze-like scattering of islands in the heart of Kantenjord.

Spydbanen: The northeastern of Kantenjord's main islands, and home to its most violent jarls, including the troll-jarl. The Vuos people live in its extreme north.

Steelfox: A princess of the Karvak Realm, determined to conquer the Earthe in the memory of her father, the first Grand Khan. Even with all that in mind, I liked her.

Storfosna: A town in Soderland.

Stormhamn: A town in Soderland.

Sturla's Steading: The home of Huginn and Hekla.

Styr Surturson: An Oxiland chieftain.

Surtfell: The great volcano of Oxiland.

Svanstad: The capital of Soderland and largest city in the Bladed Isles.

Svardmark: Kantenjord's largest island, home to what passes for its civilized lands.

Swan Goddess: The deity said to have sacrificed herself to save the world. Accounted the daughter of the Painter of Clouds.

Swanisle: An island nation, closer to the continent than are the Bladed Isles. Gaunt's homeland. Legend has it it's the petrified body of the Swan Goddess. I am not weighing in on this.

Swanling: The Kantenings call the Swan Goddess's followers this.

Tlepolemus: A fellow far-traveled adventurer who became a Larderman.

Torfa: Jokull Loftsson's wife. By report, an exemplar of Kantening ferocity.

Trollberg, the: The troll mountain-fortress beside Jotuncrown.

uldra: A varied nonhuman folk who sometimes dwell underground and sometimes in other worlds entirely.

Undetermined, the: An enlightened being venerated in the East.

Varmvik: A town in Soderland.

Vatnar: An important churchman of Oxiland.

Vinderhus: A whaling community in Oxiland.

Vuos: A human community distinct from the Kantenings. They herd reindeer and have shamanistic beliefs.

Vuk: A man of the Wagonlords on the continent, my comrade at the Gull-Jarl's steading.

Walking Stick: An itinerant official of Qiangguo. Also a wulin warrior, capable of esoteric combat moves. A good ally, and a bad enemy, to have. He's been both.

Wiglaf: A legendary warrior, whose fate was tied up with the swords Crypt-tongue and Schismglass. I don't envy him.

Winterjarl, the: Harbinger of Fimbulwinter and Ragnarok, or so we thought.

Wormeye: A troll.

Xembala: A paradisiacal eastern land, a source of ironsilk. There are times I'd like to be there.

Yngvarr Thrall-Taker: One of the Nine Wolves. He surprised us at the end.

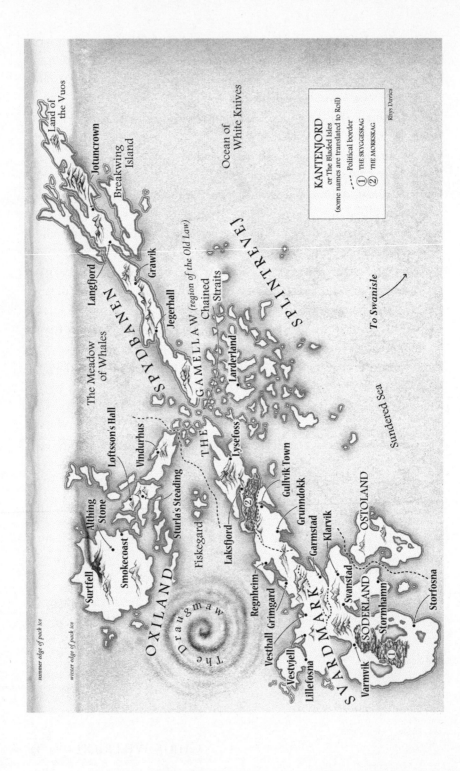

summer edge of pack ice

winter edge of pack ice

Land of
the Vuos

Jotuncrown

Breakwing
Island

Ocean of
White Knives

Grawik

Langfjord

SPYDBANEN

Jegerhall

The Meadow
of Whales

THE GAMELLAW *(region of the Old Law)*

Chained
Straits

SPLINTREVEJ

Loftsson's Hall

Vindurhus

Larderland

Lysefoss

Althing
Stone

Sturla's steading

Gullvik Town

Fiskegard

Grumdokk

Laksfjord

Garmstad

OXILAND

Surtfell

Smokecoast

Regnheim

Klarvik

OSTOLAND

The Draugmaw

Vesthall Grimgard

Svanstad

Sundered Sea

Vestvjell

SVARDMARK

SODERLAND

Storfosna

Lillefosna

Varnvik

Stormhamn

To Swanisle

KANTENJORD
or The Bladed Isles
(some names are translated to Roil)

----- Political border
① THE SKYGGESKAG
② THE MORKSKAG

Rhys Davies

PROLOGUE

ASH-LAD

The Lardermen fished the castaway from the sea's gray clutches in a place where no island rose and no wreckage lay. The maelstrom that men named the Draugmaw was not so far from that place, yet it was strange to find no broken remnant of the boy's vessel.

"There now," said the captain, not unkindly. "You're warm and safe, drinking my aquavit and eating the finest Larderman gruel. Who might you be?"

"Deadfall," the ashen-faced lad muttered between shivers and sips and bites, looking around the deck in fear. "Deadfall." The boy, who looked no older than thirteen, seemed to spy little to cheer him. The sky of fading summer was a billowing tapestry of white and gray, shading to black. The pirates below were a rough-looking bunch to be sure, scowling below the black flag of the skull and crossed meat cleavers.

"Anyone make anything of that?"

"That's southern talk," said the mate. "The part I can make out anyway. Something about death and falling. I don't think he's from Kantenjord at all."

"Death. Falling. A boy from nowhere. This is ill-omened. I had a dream, you see. A girl riding a narwhal whispered to me to come here. . . . It wasn't far off our course. But I do not like this."

The captain was a man of the Swan, and his once-yearly confessions in Svanstad were long and specific and left the unlucky priests in their boxes as pale as the snows of the Trollberg. Yet he bore around his neck both the silver token of the Swan and its opposite number, the iron axe of the heathen god Torden. For the Swan's mercy was a great prize, but in the Bladed Isles with its troll-haunted ways it paid to remember the lore of the grandfathers.

"We sail to Fiskegard," the captain said. "The fishermen there can take him in. I trust you'll remember, lad, the kindness of Captain Erik Glint." For something cold as a troll's seeing-well told Erik Glint he'd be hearing from this boy again. That indeed they all would.

Now, Fiskegard was a forbidding place even in Haymonth, craggy gray peaks rising sheer from the sea like monstrous arrowheads. The island was grim, but the waters were a sea-giant's purse of silver fish, and many men sailed to Fiskegard for the winter spawning, earning themselves coin for the year and the local lords a surplus they could sell across the Bladed Isles. Already a few knarrs nosed into the harbors bearing hardscrabble men, who peered at the notices in taverns like the Raven's Perch, known to the likes of the prince of Soderland, and the Pickled Rat, known to the likes of the Lardermen.

Thus Erik Glint tugged the boy his crew now called Askelad, the Ashen Lad, up the creaking, barnacled stairs of the Rat and into the squinting regard of Freidar the Wayfarer and Nan Henricksdatter, the proprietors.

"This lad speaks the Roil speech of the South," the captain told them, "and a bit of Kantentongue we've taught him on the way. He's a hard worker."

Old Freidar favored Askelad with a whisker-fringed frown like a cleft framed by new-fallen snow. "You're not selling him, are you, Erik?"

"Do you think I'm Yngvarr the Thrall-Taker or some such swine? You know me, Freidar."

"He is from far away, I think."

Askelad bowed with cold courtesy.

"Aye, from the South," Erik agreed.

"No," said Nan, as wizened as her husband. "Farther." Upon her red vest lay a bronze brooch, half-hidden by a coiling lock of gray hair. It had the shape of three sinuous dragons, their necks intertwined in fierce conflict. She smiled at Askelad and asked him in Roil, "Who are your people? Where is your home?"

Askelad had been taciturn aboard ship, and he startled Erik with an eloquent answer the captain couldn't quite follow. "My mother was a poet, and my father a thief. I was raised by monks, and by a warrior-scholar whom I hated in the flesh and revere in memory. My home is lost among the mountains of the known world's heart. I left it months and years ago, and bitterly now do I recall my exile. My only friend in the wider world was a rug. The thing I hate most is innocence, and the thing I miss most is joy. When can I start?"

"Son of a poet, you say," said Freidar, scratching his chin.

Nan turned to the captain. In Kantentongue she said, "A suspicious woman might mistrust him."

"He worked his passage, Nan," said Erik, "never complained. Help him out, for me. Remember when Soderland tried to annex Fiskegard and block-aded your harbor. Who was it brought you victuals?"

"You," said Nan.

"And when the cod-catch was sparse and hungry fishermen troubled your sleep, who kept you supplied?"

"You," said Freidar. "But when the lad turns out to be the lost son of the North Wind, and that one comes screeching to blow down our tavern, who gets the bill?"

"Me," said Erik with a nod. "Of course, I'll be halfway to Kpalamaa then."

So it was settled. Before the Lardermen cleared the harbor, Askelad was clearing tables. He cooked and carried and tended the fire. And late by fire-light, he learned Kantentongue. As Harvestmonth approached, Freidar and Nan took turns sacrificing sleep to ensure their hire could speak to the fish-ermen.

Freidar's lessons soon had Askelad reading Huginn Sharpspear's *Younger Sagas*. "Oxiland's is the oldest dialect of these islands," the old man explained, "preserving root-words that appear all over."

"These islands are small," Askelad said. His red hair seemed a cousin of the firelight. His nimble hands passed over a map of the archipelago. "Perhaps no more than three thousand *li* along the longest path. How can you have so many dialects?"

"Three thousand what?"

"Sorry, I should say rast? Or mil? One thousand mil. So many little king-doms and lordships!"

"Little?"

"I don't mean to offend, Freidar."

The tavernkeeper rubbed his eyes. "What lands are you familiar with, boy, that you think all the Bladed Isles so tiny?"

"I don't think I have the language to explain. Yet. So what did Eilifur Ice-Gaze do after the witch-woman tricked Wiglaf Sword-Slave into wooing his beloved, and Eilifur raised his blade Crypttongue against him?"

"You read and tell me, Askelad."

"*Eldur og sorg*. Fire and woe."

"You skipped ahead."

And thus on Freidar's nights for teaching, Eilifur Ice-Gaze and his ilk loved and fought their way toward doom, and in the nights between Nan used myths for the same purpose.

"And so, Askelad, the warring tribes of gods spat berry-juice into the vat to seal their pact of peace."

"They what?"

Nan smiled. "That's not the half of it. After the berry-juice and god-spit had swirled around a while, it gave birth to a new god."

"It what?"

"The god of knowledge. Kantenjord had a god of knowledge." Nan giggled. "He could answer any question, on any subject. A wonderful thing. So much wisdom he had. Naturally someone drowned him in the vat so they could take the magic juice."

"Aiya—crazy! I mean, Uff da? These legends are insane. I say this as one who knows the story of the philosopher who thought he might really be a dreaming butterfly, and of the tale of the peasant who married a snake."

"I might like to hear those sometime, Askelad. Well, I think sometimes Huginn's *Elder Sagas* make more sense when you're drunk."

"May I find out, Nan? No? All right, then. . . . So, the mead of drowned Knowledge was the making of skalds . . . Skalds?"

"Poets. Bards, you might say."

"My mother . . . she was a bard, once."

"Tell me about her. What has become of her?"

"I haven't seen her since the day an angry power slapped her from the sky. Nan, I'm sorry . . . *Beklager*. I do not think I can continue tonight."

Nan worried after Askelad, but in the gray of the next morning he was nowhere to be found.

She confided in Freidar, who answered, "Sometimes I think he carries a doom great as any in the sagas. That is why I taught him of Eilifur, of Wiglaf, the rest. To tease out his story. Or prepare him for his fate. He knows more than he'll say, that much is sure."

"I think he dwelled far to the east, Freidar. Farther than the Eldshore or the wild forests or the steppe. I think something bad happened to his parents there. As to how he ended up here . . ."

"He will tell us, or not. But I think Erik brought us trouble."

"I'm sure of it. But I like the lad."

"As do I." Freidar clutched the edge of the first of four shields hanging from the tavern wall. "Four sons, Nan."

"Don't speak of it."

"War. Sickness. Falling. Drowning. It still hurts."

"Then don't speak of it, Freidar. Nor of how Erik knew exactly how we'd feel."

Freidar sat and pounded a table. "He knew also we're Runewalkers. That we might be able to fight Askelad's doom, if it comes to that."

She sat beside him, wrapped an arm around him. "We gave all that up."

"Ah, Nan." He squeezed her hand. "As long as you're here, I won't worry."

"Be glad of what we have, Freidar. And that for a while we've another boy to care for."

"Glad is a fit feeling for day's end, when we know at last what the light's wrought."

As the sun struck a golden road upon the eastern waves, the one they called Askelad scaled a sea-cliff, shrieking gulls his only company. He'd avoided the other children of the island. They knew him, of course, for he was a trifle young to stand among the men of the fishing shacks, hauling and drying stockfish. And he knew the children, though he was a little old to run amongst them. They gave each other stares and a wide berth. He needed no company that lacked wings.

He was more at home with things that flew.

He reached the cliff top and collapsed in a blast of cold wind. He clutched his Kantenjord cloak. At last he stood, the dark cloth flapping like a torn sail.

"I am Innocence!" he bellowed to the steel-gray sea, with dawn still a newborn thing to his left, rays thin and tentative as the legs of a colt. To his right the infinite blade of the sea clove blue-black armor of storms. "I'm chosen of the chi of the Heavenwalls! Commander of the vital breath of Qiangguo! Master of Deadfall! I need no mother, no father! I am power, and this is my world!"

The gulls winged warily, and he raised his hand to call upon the wind.

It became no more fierce, no more cold, than before.

He lowered his hand. It became a fist as it fell.

"Why have you abandoned me? I did not want you, but you chose me. You cannot just discard me on this barbarian rock!" The wind had nothing to say beyond its continual groan. Innocence backed away and folded his arms. "Where are you, Deadfall? You saved me. You may be an evil thing, but I don't want you dead."

He stayed there, amid the raw sounds of wind and surf and birdscreech, until he risked vexing his employers. The master of the world had to get to work.

As he descended he noticed a dark winged shape, angling closer. He hurried. In Freidar and Nan's tales the three great islands of Kantenjord were in fact the greatest of arkendrakes, mineralized long ago. Oddly enough, the tales had it that younger, mobile dragons avoided these lands, for if a young dragon fell under the influence of a dreaming elder, madness might result. He didn't know what the shape was. But it was darker than a seagull—

He dropped the last ten feet, stumbled, rolled, and ran.

He remembered his mother's voice, like something in a dream. *Your father was a great climber and runner, a master acrobat and a survivor. Oh, and he stole things sometimes.*

Something screeched past him, something much faster than he.

He froze upon the rambling path, between tiny wildflowers and little granite islands in the grass. The thing rushed ahead, converged with its shadow upon the path, and revealed itself as a peregrine falcon.

It did not alight but spun midair and rushed toward him, golden belly flashing with the brightening dawn, wings gray like the western sea. Somehow its wide, dark eyes were full of recognition. The feeling was mutual.

He had seen it before, on a day that haunted his thoughts.

"Get away! I want nothing from that time! I don't need you, or them! Go!" He clapped his hands together, and thunder cracked.

The boy fell to his knees, deafened by sound and shock. When his senses returned, the falcon had gone. He searched the sky for wings and the ground for feathers. Nothing.

"I have power yet," he said to his stinging hands. He ran to the village, head down, feeling as though dark eyes followed him the whole way.

Two weeks later the knarr *Swan-road* arrived ahead of an early snowstorm, and the Pickled Rat bustled with old hands and new arrivals. Among the fresh fishermen was an unexpected visitor, a Swan priestess in a cloak of silver-gray whom Freidar and Nan offered a booth. "Are you visiting Mentor Ulf up at the church, then?" Freidar asked.

"My plans are uncertain," the priestess answered. "Except for the aquavit."

"Coming right up!"

The one called Askelad, now navigating Kantentongue with dispatch if not grace, cocked his head at the cloaked woman. He was starting to detect accents, and hers struck an odd note. It was not, he thought, of Oxiland, Svardmark, or Spydbanen, or any other nook of the Bladed Isles. It sounded closest to that of Swanisle, the nearest foreign land and home to some of Fiskegard's winter workers.

And my mother's land, he thought. But there was a lilt to it that spoke of somewhere farther off. As he studied her, neglecting the flow of cups, she turned and studied him back. She was not young, perhaps in her forties, yet with youthful mischief in her expression. She was dark brown in the way of folk from Kpalamaa and other great lands of the distant South. Her hair, what he could see of it under the hood, was a lively tangle, and dark freckles made her weathered face look impish. Yet there was a hardness in the set of her jaw. Something about her made him think of daggers and monsters, but also laughter and marvels.

As he'd grown comfortable with the language of his benefactors, he'd acquired a certain swagger that amused the fishermen. But it was all gone now. *I've been found* was his first thought, though by whom and for what he didn't know.

He busied himself with this or that and skirted that corner; and perhaps he'd inherited some of his father's stealth, for he appeared to avoid the priestess's attention until nightfall. He whirled here and there on currents of ale, mead, brandy, aquavit, hovering at times in a vortex of talk:

They say there's been more fires on the troll-mounts, up Spydbanen way—

They've talked down that rebellion in Soderland for now—

Hear tell of the Nine Wolves? Been killing folk beside the roads—

Princess Corinna and Prince Ragnar, they've got their work cut out for them—

The talk circled round and round like a raven waiting for something to die, and all the good gossip was in time rent and digested, with only the offal of old rumors and tired grudges to chew between sips. Yet snow and chill discouraged the clientele from tromping to their whistling shacks. Innocence was tired, but Freidar and Nan weren't about to close shop. When he dared glance toward the priestess she beckoned him closer . . . but he was rescued by a fisherman who called for stories.

"Let's hear marvel-tales, Askelad! Let's hear eventyr!"

He pretended not to have noticed the priestess and leapt onto a table. Men laughed and cheered, and now a hush came upon the Pickled Rat as he began, "Hear now the tale of Impossible Paal." He'd learned it from a pamphlet come lately out of Ostoland, called simply *Eventyr*, or fairy tales, compiled by two women combing the villages for stories. He'd loved them at once.

He told how lazy Paal tricked a king into thinking Paal's kettle could boil by itself, leading the king to embarrassment; and how Paal tempted him into thinking Paal's flute could restore the dead to life, leading the king to murder; and how Paal fooled him into thinking Paal had leapt off a cliff into an undersea paradise, leading the king to death—and Paal's claiming all his lands. As the poor fishermen laughed at the pranking and slaughtering of the mighty, the priestess stood and walked closer to the table, and so he launched into another story, of how the North Wind scattered the flour a poor boy was carrying, and how the boy marched right up to the North Wind's home to demand restitution. And so it went, as tale after tale, plucky ordinary folk got the better of the wise, the mighty, and the supernatural.

At last he ran out of such fare and, racking his brains, spun a chilling account of a man who raced an evil sea-spirit, a Draug, across the stormy ocean in a confrontation that could only end with shipwreck and death. He'd heard this story only once, and he embellished it by letting the man escape with the help of a merciful water-dragon.

"I've never heard it like that," said a man doubtfully.

"I think I did hear it told that way," the boy replied. "Once. In eastern parts."

"Dragons don't live in the sea," another man objected.

"They can if they want to," said the Swan priestess, drawing stares. "You've lived in places where that's true, haven't you, lad?"

"Tell us!" a fisherman said.

"Yeah, Askelad," said another. "We never hear tell about yourself."

There was general agreement, amid some knocking of mugs upon tables. Someone passed him an ale, which made self-confession more reasonable. Wiping foam from his lips, he began.

THE TALE OF THE BOY, THE SCROLL, AND THE MAGIC CARPET

East of the sunrise, far beyond the Eldshore and the Wheelgreen and the Ruby Waste, there was a land of wisdom and grace, where sages fashioned works of wonder. One such was a scroll-painting of strange peaks, ones even more jagged and spindly than those of Fiskegard, wreathed in forest and wrapped in cloud.

Had the painting only been beautiful, it would have been enough. But it was also a thing of magic. Gaze upon the mountains, or clutch the scroll, and you might find yourself drawn into another world, where the timeless mountains speared an infinite sky. A great wizard-king made the scroll to be a haven, and it had yet another peculiar property. Time flowed differently within the scroll than within our world. The relationship was a fluid thing, but time inside the scroll always flowed faster, so that hours outside might be days inside.

Once a boy and a girl were abandoned within the scroll. Their parents did something foolish—bringing a male Western dragon to an island that was really a sleeping, female Eastern dragon. The dragons' mutual desire destroyed that island with fire and earthquake, and the kids could only survive inside the scroll. The parents were supposed to come back. They never did.

I'll translate the kids' names as Innocence and A-Girl-Is-A-Joy. In some ways they were very different. The boy's parents came from the West of the world, the girl's from the East. He liked battling; she liked exploring. He was quick with the spoken word, she with the calligrapher's brush. But after their parents disappeared, they were inseparable. Their only other companions were monkish sorts full of lofty thoughts. So they chased each other around the monastery and up and down the rainy mountain. They discovered and built up and destroyed enough kingdoms to fill Peersdatter and Jorgensdatter's *Eventyr*. Such was childhood. Yet their orphanage in the mountains did not come free. There was among the monks a warrior who went by the name Walking Stick. He drilled the children endlessly.

Now, when I say warrior, you might imagine a fierce-eyed fellow with a spear and roundshield, helmet and byrnie. Or maybe in a more southern style, with plate armor and longsword and a shield like a kite, and if his gaze is fierce, his helmet conceals it. But you would have it wrong. This warrior has no armor, just a robe, and he bears no weapon, and his eyes are serene as tidepools. You laugh. You wouldn't if you fought him. They say the heathen All-Father bade men always keep a weapon within reach, but this man is his own weapon. His body is as tough as wood and as flexible as grass. He knows hundreds of ways to strike, throw, jump, grapple, trip. He knows the vital breath that flows within each person, and the thirty-six key paralytic points. And he can use his own vital breath to leap walls and walk across treetops.

Again you laugh! You wouldn't if you trained with him. He was convinced that Innocence had a great power within him, and a destiny, and that only endless toil would make his fate a good one. As for A-Girl-Is-A-Joy, well, there are those who think women incapable of being warriors. Walking Stick wasn't one of them. She might have been happier if he had been. Miles on miles of running upon the mountain, hours on hours of hard labor in the temple, and thousands on thousands of mock battles in the gardens. I'm not even going to repeat the lectures! For "the superior person speaks softly and acts boldly," and "what is done needs no declaration, what is finished needs no protest, what is past needs no blame," and "life spawns, the seasons pass and return, yet does Heaven say a word?" Perhaps you now have a sense of his speech; I will speak of it no more.

Save for this, Innocence longed to escape his teacher. And the day came when he met the agent of his escape.

In a desert city between East and West, a work was fashioned, perhaps as wondrous as the scroll. It was a magic carpet flowing with the colors of the sands and the mountains, with the image of a volcano at its heart. Like others of its kind, it was made to fly, though sometimes it did so badly. Unlike others, it was also made to snatch power away from those who possessed it. The wizard's apprentice judged its purpose evil, and he stealthily changed its weaving, hoping to alter its fate. Thus the carpet became a divided thing, torn between good and evil. Perhaps that more than anything is why it sought the boy.

The carpet was attuned to power and sought out Innocence within the scroll. It told him of many things, of the outside world, of monsters and wizards, of armies and kings—of power. And Innocence made a rash decision and left the scroll, flying away upon the carpet.

How they explored! No boy roaming the countryside beside his dog could have been more eager than this lad wandering the Earthe with his magic carpet. The things they saw! The Moon Pit with its eerie shining minerals, remnants of the lost satellites of past ages. Splendid Amberhorn upon the Midnight Sea, a whole decadent civilization retired to a single city and countryside. Loomsberg with its waterwheels and alchemical engines. It was in the eccentric air of Loomsberg that the pair hit on the plan of exploring the moon—the silver moon, the last moon, place of mountains and gray plains and ice. Why go to the moon? Because forbidding as it was, it looked safer than the sun.

And so they rose to that strange orb. They had no guarantee that the world's air extended all the way to the moon, and for a time it seemed they could never reach it. For Innocence, shivering in the great cold of that pale-blue altitude, began to fall unconscious. The carpet made one last effort and found itself in a dark expanse. Fearing it had killed its companion, it tried to dive for the Earthe—but it found itself snared by an attractive force exerted by the silver sphere overhead.

Together they crashed upon a frosty plain of gray dust. The moon, it turned out, had its own air, thin as that of a high mountain peak but enough to restore Innocence to himself. Yet they could not celebrate. The strange land beckoned, but there was little chance of the boy staying healthy in the cold and thin air. As peculiar pale creatures crept over the horizon, reminiscent of lobsters fashioned of white mushrooms, they tried to fly.

It did not work.

They were trapped upon the moon.

Innocence had little time to act. He had to draw upon the strange power that lived within him, an innate ability to manipulate the vital breath of the land. But that power was tied to a single part of the Earthe. Did he dare try to tap the power of the moon? He had little choice.

And the carpet helped him, for siphoning power was part of its purpose. Together they absorbed the strange magic of the moon.

I . . . how to describe it? The moon is beloved of poets and thieves. And of lovers. And in that moment it seemed no accident that those on the edge of life revered the moon; for love, and a zest for life, flowed into Innocence.

Also, power.

They rose from the moon in a cloud of dust, strange fungus-things clawing and chittering in their wake. Their triumph was to be short-lived. Escaping the pull of the moon, they entered the region of darkness, and as the cold ravaged Innocence's skin and the absence of atmosphere seared his lungs, light swirled within his vision and awareness ebbed.

Once, he awoke with the knowledge that they fell at great speed toward the Earthe, and that the carpet was shielding Innocence from a great heat birthed by their plunge through the atmosphere. He caught a glimpse of jagged islands, their mountains goring the clouds, then a stormy sea. They hit; their flame was quenched. So was thought.

How Innocence survived is a blurry matter. It seems he must have used the power to stay afloat and keep his body warm, but the events are as a dream. When the Lardermen found him, the carpet was nowhere to be seen.

In pride Innocence had flown too close to the moon and was nearly destroyed. He was now a simple serving boy. So, if it's fated, he will remain.

In the silence that followed, the priestess took his hand and said, "This one's practically given a confession, I'd better shrive him." There was uneasy laughter at that, which even Nan and Freidar joined, and there was no help for it but to be led into the booth.

"You are forgiven of course," the priestess said as they sat, "but you have brought great danger on yourself, Innocence Gaunt."

Almost he ran. But there was truly nowhere to run upon Fiskegard. "How do you know me?" he asked. "And who are you?"

"Weeks ago there was a boy of Fiskegard who overheard a young man on a sea-cliff yell to the wind, 'I am innocent!' He told his mother, who told another, and the chain of tellings eventually reached the ear of one who is paid to report unusual doings to us."

"Us?"

Her gaze did not waver. "That needn't concern you. Let's say there are those who keep an eye out, for threats to peace."

"What sort of threats?"

She smiled. There was something cold in it. "You start with two questions and stretch them like sailcloth into more. I'll say what I'll say. I am Eshe of the Fallen Swan, an itinerant priestess. I serve as other priestesses do, but I have a larger duty too. And I seek out interesting people who might serve the cause of peace."

"Like me?"

"And your parents. I can reunite you, Innocence."

"If I wanted that, I wouldn't be here."

"It does not sound as if you want to be here. And you have just informed a whole crowd of migrant fishermen what you are."

He looked over his shoulder. A couple of drinkers looked back at him through the haze.

He returned his gaze to the priestess, uncertain what to make of her. "What am I, then . . . Eshe, is it? My mother spoke of a priestess named Eshe, though I don't remember much."

"I remember your parents. Looking at you, I knew you at once for their son. You have your mother's intellect, your father's contrariness. But any gifts from them are dwarfed by the gift of Qiangguo's Heavenwalls. You are power, Innocence. The kind of power that wizards and warlords will want to claim."

"And you want to claim me instead?"

She raised a hand. "Hardly. I might want to employ you someday. But most of all I want you and your parents somewhere safe. Where you won't become the trigger for a war."

Innocence laughed. "You think very highly of me."

"I know the eye of a storm when I see it."

"I am my own man, priestess. Let me be."

"All right. For now. I will stay with the village priest and argue about the liturgical calendar to keep myself warm. But I will be back."

"Do what you want. You have no hold on me." He hesitated. "My parents . . . they are both alive?"

Eshe studied him as she rose. She nodded. "So my sources tell me."

"Are they looking for me?"

"I suspect so. They are heading west, haphazardly, aboard a frequently crashing flying craft. It may be many months before they reach you."

"That is as it will be." He spoke as a Kantening might, but as he rose, he bowed in the manner of Qiangguo, remembering how Walking Stick had taught him to respect his elders. Eshe surprised him by bowing likewise, with no self-consciousness, here in a room of the Outer World.

As she exited the Rat, Eshe glanced at the sky and back into the room. "I think this may be a break in the weather," she told them all.

A number of men took her advice and returned to their homes or shacks. Before long the Rat was sufficiently emptied that Nan and Freidar made noises about closing up, and their ward was too occupied with plates and bowls, mugs and knives, to worry about Eshe of the Fallen Swan. Below the surface of his thoughts, however, memories shifted like horses that had fallen asleep beneath the snow.

At some point Nan steered him to his straw-covered shelf by the stove. She covered him in a blanket. He tumbled into the deep sleep of cold nights.

He dreamed he hovered over the jagged contours of Fiskegard, the island and the snowfall patchily illuminated by a cloud-veiled moon. He floated far above the sea, yet the sound of surf beat in his ears like slow thunder. Looking around he saw translucent waves glowing silver all around him, as though a second ghost-ocean had manifested far above the first. He could still see the ordinary world, but this spectral sea stretched wide all around. Its waves slammed into some unseen headland, scattering into starry droplets.

"Aiya," he swore. "What is this place?"

He did not expect anyone to answer, but someone did.

"You drift within the Straits of Tid."

He saw a ghostly beast like a dolphin with a horn such as unicorns were said to possess. The horn resembled an icicle and the body a patch of star-speckled darkness. Upon it rode a young woman in battle gear. She bore a spear and roundshield and wore a byrnie of gleaming steel. Her helmet was a round cap with a spectacle guard masking much of her face, though he saw her braided red hair and the icy blue of her eyes. She looked older than him, sixteen perhaps, though her voice had a hint of childish laughter in it that made him wonder.

Dreaming—if such he was—made him bold. "That's not very informative," he said. "And if I ask you your name, will you say you are the Rider of Zot or the Guardian of Zed or the Slayer of Zeep?"

"Tid means 'time,'" she said. "You drift upon the edge of the Straits of Time, where its waters wash the rocks of the present. And I have taken the name Beinahruga, though you can call me Cairn."

"Charmed."

"And you?"

"You may call me Askelad. Nan has told me of the Choosers of the Slain, who swoop down from divine Vindheim and carry off the spirits of the valiant dead. Though I thought that was just a story. Are you one of them?" He looked this way and that, as an uneasy thought came to him. "Am I dead?"

Cairn laughed. The sound seemed to reverberate off the unseen headlands of present time. "Do you think yourself valiant, Askelad?"

He laughed too. "The Sage Emperor has said that a superior man should avoid violence and heedlessness, that he be sincere, and that he be polite. Would a Chooser of the Slain pick such a one?"

"You never know."

"So you are a Chooser?"

"The All-Father has said that a rash tongue sings mischief, O Askelad, if that's what you want to call yourself. I would like to keep my nature to myself for now. What you should know is that I have been waiting for you. You have the power to explore the Straits of Tid. There are certain sites in Kantenjord where the energies of the sleeping dragons distort space and time. Fractures in the fabric of reality, rent in the days when the arkendrakes fought one another. In those places it's possible to send one's dream-form into other realms. Or, with sufficient power, to go there bodily. The Pickled Rat is built upon one such site."

"Do Freidar and Nan know of this?"

"They suspect. They know many things they haven't told you of."

"What do you want from me?"

"Learn—and beware!"

She gestured with her spear, and it was as though a gale rose up. He was washed upon the waves through clouds and snow, then rain and sun, speeding across the seas.

They seemed now to float above rugged day-lit straits, where two jutting headlands lofted above a small, barren island. A titanic metal chain wrapped around each promontory, linking them to the island in the straits' midst, itself enmeshed in the links. Runes the size of horses glowed upon the links.

"What is it?" Innocence asked.

"Behold the Great Chain of Unbeing. Forged by the Vindir, great lords now thought of as gods, it drains the energies of the arkendrakes, keeping them docile, unable to resume their ancient conflict. A third length of the Chain plunges into unseen depths, sending excess power deep into the Earthe. The Chain has an intelligence of its own, and from time to time it claims a champion. This time it has chosen your friend, A-Girl-Is-A-Joy. She bears the mark of the Chain upon her hand."

Innocence looked across the seas, past an archipelago of thousands of craggy islands and skerries, out to the East.

"You are thinking of another mighty construct," said Cairn. "The Heavenwalls of Qiangguo. They too draw power from dragons. They too chose a champion—you."

"I have never understood why. I'm no son of Qiangguo. By accident I was raised as one, but the blood of that land doesn't flow in my veins. I'm much closer to the folk of Kantenjord! And why did this Chain choose Joy? She is a daughter of Qiangguo! It makes no sense."

"You are right to wonder, Innocence. Humans have wrought these mighty works to empower themselves. But they did not anticipate that those tools would conspire with each other."

"Conspire? How? Why?"

Cairn laughed and raised her spear.

The sun vanished again, and reappeared, many times, throwing the ocean into light and casting it into darkness. And now land—green coast, misty forest, looming mountains, and forest again, and pale-green grass stretching forever.

Below him lay an astonishing sight. At the southern edge of a great influx of the sea, upon the snow-covered grasses of the steppe, there stood thousands of tents and tens of thousands of men, nearly that number in horses, a hundred ships on wheels, and scores of balloons ready for flight.

He drifted down toward the horde, and suddenly a falcon crossed his vision, the same that had stalked him weeks earlier. Somehow it picked out a single individual on the ground and dove toward her. He fell too, drawn along in the bird's wake.

He seemed to hover above the ground in the midst of armored nomads, as the bird alighted upon the wrist of a woman. She was a noble of the remote East, dark hair proudly worn high and shiny with a coating of animal fat; yet she was no ornamental figurehead. He took note of her muscular figure, even hidden as it was by a thickly draped, sky-blue robe. More than that, he took note of an imperiously eager look to her gaze.

"Meat!" she called, and the language was none he knew, yet somehow within this dreamscape he understood her. "Meat for my falcon! And summon the khatun. Tell her I have interesting news."

Soon the bird was snapping down chunks of flesh, and out of the crowd came a similarly dressed woman, a little younger than the first, though her hair was piled and coiled more elaborately, and yellow makeup emphasized her brow. Her smile worried the unseen boy. "I am here, elder sister. I hope you are ready to define 'interesting.'"

"Qurca has returned. He's found the one I sought."

The younger sister's eyes narrowed. "You are sure?"

"I've seen the image in my bird's mind."

"Where is he?"

I'm right here, he thought, but tried not to think it too loudly.

"In the Bladed Isles," the elder sister said.

The younger sister nodded. "What the locals call Kantenjord. 'The Edge-lands.' I know it. I have allies and spies there. This is auspicious. The Great Khan's council is even now debating how to apply a pincer campaign against the Eldshore. The northern route is clear. The southern prospects are murky. But thanks to you, sister, there is another way." The younger sister gestured at the fleet of balloons. "Your inventions can carry a force across the waters. We can subdue the primitive island-dwellers and have a base for harrying the Eldshore from the west."

"Not my inventions. They are the work of Haytham ibn Zakwan—"

"It is charming how you wish to credit outlanders. Yes, ibn Zakwan's craft can carry a force to a new stronghold, and over the months of winter we can build up an army. The Westerners fear a winter campaign, as we do not. Yes. We can conquer the Bladed Isles by spring and assault the Eldshore in summer."

The elder smiled a trace. "You may be overconfident. And how does finding Innocence Gaunt suddenly make the Bladed Isles a good target?"

"As I said, I have allies there." The younger gestured toward two soldiers, who led forward her horse. "Not all of them human. One of them will know how to use the boy's power to our advantage. And I have you. You have yet to regain the khan's full confidence."

The elder sister's smile vanished, and her face darkened with anger as her falcon rose and shrieked. Meanwhile the younger sister's horse sniffed, whinnied, and bucked. The invisible wanderer did not understand the animals' behavior, but it worried him. The elder sister said, "Our mother sided with me in our dispute over Xembala."

"And her word carried great weight," said the younger sister, grabbing the reins. "Nevertheless, my husband is the Grand Khan. He agreed you were justified in your actions, arranging trade with the Xembalans rather than conquest. But nonetheless you undercut me."

"It was you who subverted my mission."

"Calm, calm, Aughatai," said the younger sister to the horse, but Innocence thought the words were equally meant for the elder. "Hunt down this Innocence Gaunt for me, Steelfox. I know you mean to inform his parents, whom you lent your inventor ibn Zakwan and your shaman Northwing. I do not wish you to break your word. Tell them. But surely a Karvak princess will be a more formidable huntress than a pair of lunatics from the world's edge. Join my invasion of Kantenjord. And bring Innocence to me, that I might honor the chosen of the Heavenwalls."

"Control him, you mean."

"And if that is the price of peace between us? One boy's future in exchange for your rightful, unblemished place in our father's empire?"

The elder sister, Steelfox, did not reply.

Jewelwolf's horse was snorting and shaking now. It lurched toward the spot where the unseen wanderer felt himself to be. He began to shiver.

"Aughatai, what has gotten into you!" cried Jewelwolf. "What do you see?"

The horse got loose and charged the invisible boy. Soldiers shouted.

Cairn! he tried to shout. *Help—*

So you see, "Askelad," came the voice of the Chooser, *you can't escape the burden of your name, nor your power. I leave you with a riddle. It may have practical value one day. If you should meet your future self, what is the most important question you can ask?*

And in his straw bed in the Bladed Isles, Innocence Gaunt woke with a start.

CHAPTER 1

MECHANISMS

"Imago Bone! You've gone too far this time!"

"You speak to one, Persimmon Gaunt, who's stolen a bath from a pond beside the Forbidden City! Who's claimed a treasure map from the mummies of the Desert of Hungry Shadows! Who has a book overdue from the Goblin Library! You speak to me of too far?"

"Fine! You disable the bronze automatons!"

"You are doing far better at that than I ever could. And meanwhile I have a most interesting ancient artifact to ponder—"

"Get up here, Bone!"

"Of course! You and the alchemical fire are most persuasive. . . ."

The thief Imago Bone nonetheless found it difficult to abandon the marvelous view. He dangled by a rope from Haytham ibn Zakwan's balloon, seeing the snowy moonlit expanse of the city of Amberhorn in a way he never had before. Certainly not earlier this evening when he and the explorer Liron Flint had been skulking through its alleys and across its rooftops to reach the great domed Basilica of the Logos. Nor when they'd raced through the Aisle of Illuminations, with its enchanted icons with golden eyes ready to entrance, terrify, or burn unwelcome visitors. Least of all when they'd scrambled out the great bell tower of the basilica, with stolen treasures in Bone's sack.

Now the basilica—and the hippodrome, and the forum, and the Epiphanic Baths—shrank below him, engulfed by thousands of square-shaped, dark-roofed abodes, by the waters of the Midnight Sea, and by the snowfall so kindly arranged by the shaman Northwing.

Oh, yes, and by the gouts of fiery liquid spewed by bronze statues in the city center.

Bone knew the Amberhornish prided themselves on their vomitoriums, but he hadn't known they'd turned their own sky into one. That last blast was close enough to warm his face. Best to scramble up. Flint had wisely disappeared inside already.

Stuffing his chief treasure into his bag (where his minor treasures already lay) Bone scurried up the rope into the capacious gondola of the balloon, fashioned to resemble a nomadic tent, or ger. As he did so an arrow sang out through the flap as Persimmon Gaunt shot back at an automaton. There was dull concussion far below and a louder clang as the bronze construct toppled.

"I knew those fire-gems from Anoka were worth the price," she told him as he tumbled inside. "They're tricky to attach. But one shot through the mouth, and it interacts nicely with the caustic blood of those things."

"I concede. Hopefully this will recover the dent in our finances."

"Hmph. If we survive this. Welcome back, Bone."

"A pleasure to be home, Gaunt."

Blazing light flared outside the ger once again, complement to the magical fire in the brazier inside, and Bone got a fresh look at "home." Cozy would have been a charitable way of describing the crowded gondola, especially with seven people aboard. The framework was bamboo, encased in a shell of felt. The brazier, inscribed with arcane symbols, lay at the center beneath a gap in the ceiling. Supernatural flame danced upward from the brazier from time to time, its light glinting upon the various implements and supplies hanging from the ceiling—pots, pans, spyglasses, sextants, maps, dried meats and fruits, water-flasks, flatbreads, herbs, tea, and the like. Underfoot, around the edges, were things it would be more awkward to find falling upon you— knives, swords, axes, bottles of wine. At the edges, too, were curtains one could pull to create a fragile sense of privacy.

A fresh blast, and Bone had a fleeting wish for that privacy, for he thought the illumination complemented his wife's tangle of auburn hair over tanned skin, her fierce gaze, and the tattoo upon her right cheek, a rose caught in a spider's web. She wore a blue deel, a long-sleeved coat of the nomadic Karvaks. She looked almost like a Karvak herself in that moment, magic sword (thankfully) in a sheath on her back, bow in her hands, her whole being focused on bringing down another foe. She was ever-changing. And ever Gaunt.

"I suggest, man," said the fellow readying an arrow on the opposite side of the opening from Gaunt, "you stop staring at your wife and show us what you've found." The wandering monk known to Bone as Mad Katta glanced his way. Bone was never sure if Katta actually saw him or not. The black-robed, umber-skinned Eastern holy man was blind—Bone didn't doubt it—but he possessed the power to perceive evil. The worse Bone got, in theory, the better chance Katta had to notice him. Katta had never actually said Bone was perceptible to him, but every time the monk turned his way, the thief wondered. And just now he'd robbed a church. . . .

Katta turned back to the open air, cocked his head, and loosed an arrow. A clang rewarded him. "Alas," he said, "I didn't connect with the thing's maw."

"So you can see them?" Bone asked.

"No," Katta said, "they're merely very loud. They're unthinking constructs, not evil." He turned to Bone and smiled. "Unlike some humans."

"Um," said Bone.

"Hey! Stop letting him tease you, Bone," a new voice cut in. "If you're done fooling around, how about you show us this thing that'll save our asses."

That was Snow Pine, former bandit of Qiangguo, student of the Eastern philosophy of the Forest, warrior, widow, and—tone aside—friend. Her piercing brown-eyed gaze turned away, with a swish of dark hair, for she was busy cutting loose sandbag ballasts from mountings at the gondola's bamboo-ringed portholes. "You too, Liron," she said, glancing at the tall treasure hunter who lay gasping on the bamboo deck of the gondola. "You boys had a big night on the town, but if we catch fire—"

"All right, all right!" Liron Flint was up at once. He joined Snow Pine in cutting loose more sandbags. "It's just a new experience to me—plundering the living," Flint said, stealing a kiss from her. "Invigorating!"

"Watch out," Snow Pine said. "Bone's rubbing off on you. Maybe, Gaunt, it's a mistake to let our men off the leash."

"Come now," Bone said, fumbling through his treasure sack, looking for the magic lamp. "Flint helped plan this! Haytham wanted the lamp, but stealing the Antilektron Mechanism was Flint's idea. Aha!" Bone pulled out a dented, tarnished brass oil lamp.

"I'll admit to a fascination with the device," Flint said, glancing at Bone's open bag and the corroded bronze assemblage of gears within. "It was as though a voice whispered in my ear, saying, 'Take the thing. Its destiny lies with you.'"

"I hear that voice often," Bone said.

"This one was very specific," Flint said, "like a muse, a young woman . . ."

"Excuse me?" said Snow Pine.

"Well, it doesn't matter now!" Flint said, patting the ancient machinery. "We have it! We so often think our ancestors more primitive than we, yet time and again their works belie this. The Mechanism shows how the ancient folk of the Midnight Sea could calculate the motions of the stars, without relying on gods or magic."

Gaunt called out, still firing arrows, "I see why it's interesting to Flint, and why it will be valuable to the clockwork masters of Loomsberg. But, Bone, you said the owners had no idea of either artifact's value! So why are we about to burn alive?"

"Well," Bone confessed, as he grabbed a cloth and rubbed at the lamp. "I might have nabbed a golden goblet or two, some coins of the imperial past, a pearl necklace with an impressive dolphin motif. . . ."

"Ye gods, Bone, just because you can steal a thing . . ."

"Funds, Gaunt! We will need portable wealth if we're to brave the mad North. They are not much for banknotes there."

"And I need portable patience to brave the mad Bone," Gaunt said. "Not to mention altitude. Bad enough if they hit the ger, but if they catch the envelope, we're going to have an interesting time."

"Bone," said Katta, putting down his bow and rising, a set of metal charms jingling around his neck, "how about I consider that lamp?" The thief passed him the lamp and the cloth. "Yes," Katta said. "I'm sensing something within the metal. A presence. Powerful. A bit evil." He polished the lamp in a graceful, methodical way. It irked Bone that Katta made even cleaning seem mystical. "Ah."

As if on cue, an inhuman voice keened through the lamp's metal. The words were in the tongue of Mirabad, which Bone could recognize but not understand.

Now a sixth person in the ger spoke up. He was a tall, brown man in a white robe and an orange, two-wrap turban, with thick mustachios that seemed almost as lively as his voice. He answered the lamp in kind. Bone was only able to make out the balloon's inventor's announcement of his own name, Haytham ibn Zakwan ibn Rihab.

"Yes!" rang out the voice of the lamp. "Yes, O ibn Zakwan! Your humble efrit, Haboob of the Hundred Horrors, can speak in whatever tongue you wish, be it the musical speech of Mirabad or the uncouth babble of the Eldshore. He can speak in the language of fishes or of birds. He knows the speech of the Leviathan Lords of aeons past, and of the otterwights of the opposite face of the Earthe. He has heard the songs of the Iron Moths and the poetry the stars whisper to each other when men believe they sleep."

"Ha!" snarled the seventh human in the gondola. "Has he heard the dying screams of people plunging into an ocean? Or of them burning alive? Either fate is close at hand." The speaker was a person of Mad Katta's ethnicity, though worlds apart in temperament—forceful where he was affable, practical where he was philosophical. An unadorned face glared from a hooded, furred hunter's coat. The only decoration that the shaman Northwing indulged was a set of metal charms similar to Katta's. In bearing Northwing seemed male to Bone, yet he knew Northwing was physically female. At first glance it was easy to assume the two were bickering lovers, yet each preferred their own sex for bed-mates. Well, the world was complicated, gods knew. Beyond all that, North-wing would declare no gender at all, something Bone gathered was a tradition for shamans of this sort. He-she-they (or just Northwing) condescended to Katta, who'd given up being a shaman to become a wandering monk. Katta didn't seem to take it personally. Northwing looked down on everyone.

"The suncrow feather," the shaman said, "is nearly extinguished, and thanks to Gaunt's poor haggling it's our last! I'm keeping us aloft by lashing the winds against us, but it won't work for long! If the fire-blasts unleashed by Bone's harebrained scheme don't get us, the ocean will."

"Excuse me," Bone said, "it was also Flint and ibn Zakwan's harebrained scheme."

The shaman ignored him, as did the efrit. "How can Haboob of the Har-rowing Howls help you, O dulcet-toned one?"

"Keep us aloft!" Northwing said.

"Ah, but you see, such an act will require that Haboob be released from his imprisonment, that he may gather his full powers from the aether. Now, the standard contract since time immemorial is for three requests, which I encourage you to word carefully. . . ."

Gaunt called out, still shooting arrows, "I can help you word it, Haytham! But it had better be fast."

Haytham smiled. "Oh, I don't think that will be necessary. Katta, could you drop the lamp into the brazier?"

"The brazier?" asked Katta. "Are you sure that's wise?"

"At this altitude, my friend, wisdom is a relative concept," Haytham said. "Please proceed."

"Wait!" the efrit called from the lamp. "What do you mean to do?"

The deed was done. The magic lamp tumbled and clanked into the magical brazier, to contact the eldritch fire. The lamp began to glow with the redness of newly forged metal.

"Do you seek to thwart the traditional contract by applying torture?" boomed the efrit. "Have you fallen from the ways of the Testifier of the All-Now?"

"Have you not, O efrit?" Haytham asked.

"Long ago did I learn religion and bend my knee, or the bodiless entity equivalent! My titles, such as Haboob of the Horrid Howls, were obtained in ancient times. I would be better known as Haboob the Herald of Hilarity, but I have been unable to demonstrate my change of heart, trapped as I was in this rapidly heating lamp."

"So, too, am I a devotee of the Testifier and his holy book," Haytham said. "I will not torture, nor cheat, nor do violence save at the most urgent need. I am a man of knowledge, and that scholarship has led me to you. Hear me, O efrit, primal creature of the universe! I sent my friends to Amberhorn to find you, for I believe we can help each other. I ask for no wishes, but a year of simple service. Your lamp is now within a brazier that empowers this flying craft. It is currently fueled by a magical feather that is nearly consumed. In the past it was empowered by demons, but it has developed a flaw that allows an intelligent entity to escape. And in truth I do not wish to treat with demons any longer. But if you consent to power my *Al-Saqr* for one year, I will release you from the lamp."

"To be trapped within a brazier?"

"Ah, but from the brazier you can perceive all that we perceive, from high above the ground. You will see many far places, O Haboob. Surely that is better than your dark hovel. But! If you prefer, we will drop you again among the Amberhornish, in whose basilica you languished as a curiosity."

"Your offer intrigues me. Very well, man of knowledge! I consent. One year."

Even as the efrit spoke, Gaunt shouted, "The envelope—I think they've hit it!"

"It'll catch fire!" Snow Pine said.

Haytham snatched an iron poker and jabbed at the lamp's lid. "I release you, Haboob."

What rose from the brazier struck Bone as the most dignified and majestic pillar of smoke the world over. It rose nearly the full height of the ger, and tendrils of it tickled the opening overhead. The top of the smoke column gave an impression of wind-blown curly hair. Below that, persistent eddies in the cloud suggested a wise yet imperious face. Extensions of the cloud farther down implied two folded arms, and a curving tendril sketched a sheathed scimitar. The hem of a sooty robe seemed to flutter at the level of the brazier's rim.

Blazing eyes like torchlit rubies narrowed, as the efrit Haboob faced them all. "It seems my engagement with you may be shorter than expected, for my contract will not survive your death, O wise Haytham ibn Zakwan."

"Bone," Haytham said, "do what you can with the fire. Haboob, you will not harm him or anyone in this crew."

"As you wish," said the efrit, as Bone grabbed a waterskin from the ceiling and shimmied up a rope to the roof opening. Although nearing fifty, Haytham's voice normally had an eager, boyish quality. But not where the safety of his balloon was concerned. In such matters he was as stern as any sea-captain. Bone never considered doing anything but heading out to brave wind, fire, and the potential of a precipitous fall.

"Snow Pine," he heard Haytham saying, "The scroll. I need Walking Stick . . ."

Just as Bone was leaving the ger, Bone saw Snow Pine pull a rolled-up landscape painting of the Far East from her Karvak deel. She bowed her head against it, her lips murmuring.

But he did not have time to watch the result. Now he was on the gondola's roof, grabbing a rope leading to the gas envelope. The gas in question was merely hot air, not some exotic concoction from Haytham's experiments (which was good, since he'd seen such gases explode) but an envelope fire was still perilous, as it could ruin the canvas beyond repair.

What was burning so far was a tiny stretch of rope and a bamboo fastening, so Bone had hopes of quenching it. A few more inches . . . he twined himself with his legs, opened the flask, and splashed. But at the last moment a fresh spark hit the balloon, the constructs' aim perhaps enhanced by the bright spot already there. His aim thrown off, Bone failed to extinguish the first small fire, and a second tiny light appeared upon the canvas itself.

Desperately he removed his deel and smothered the first fire, but he could not reach the second.

A blur of motion passed him.

The thief looked up to see a most bizarre sight, even for the career of Imago Bone. A black-robed man stood upon the envelope far from any rope, his body angled nearly sideways, in defiance of gravity. In the moonlight, embroidered white, spindly insects gleamed upon the black, except in one spot, over the man's heart, where there was only darkness. As for the rest, Bone could only make out a bald head and a moustache as straight and severe as Haytham's was coiled. He could envision the scowl perfectly well, however.

"You people!" Walking Stick snapped in the tongue of distant Qiangguo, even as he splashed water upon the envelope. The spark went out, but a fresh attack lit a few more. "You persist in wrecking everything while I'm away. Toss me that coat if you're done with it!"

Bone, who knew both the language and the polite forms of address Walking Stick was ignoring, answered, "It's quite windy, Master Walking Stick! This foolish young one's feeble throw may go wild!"

"Quit the sarcasm, greatest second-story man of the Spiral Sea! You know full well I can catch anything you can throw!"

Bone tossed the smoking deel, doing his best. As promised the wind sucked it almost out of reach, and as promised Walking Stick snagged it with a sweeping kick. The elite wulin warrior of Qiangguo commenced tackling the sparks as though it were a clumsy foe, shouting, "I know also that I'm younger than you, thief, for all that an enchantment kept you youthful!"

"Those years are done!" Bone reminded him, as he struggled to shift guide ropes and help the wulin. "Decrepitude is surely on its way!"

"Never assume you'll receive the status of old age, Bone! It must be earned! And many things may cut your life short! Fire, for example . . ."

"They just hit the other side. . . ."

Just as Bone was beginning to bellow for an emergency landing, however, the efrit below took action.

Fire whipped out of the gondola's opening, and Bone's first assumption was that Haboob had decided to end his service early. Yet when the magical flames hit the natural ones, the latter flowed into the former, leaving only smoke behind.

"My," Bone said.

"Indeed," Walking Stick said. "Whatever Haytham has arranged, I approve." He grunted. "Conditionally. They appear to have stopped shooting at us. However, I hear several tiny leaks."

Bone, who prided himself on his hearing, said, "I do not."

"You are not of the wulin."

"Well, if they're tiny we'll still escape."

"You will not escape laboring with patchwork and tar."

"I never said I would!" Bone protested. "If I'm older than you, why do you always make me feel younger?"

"It takes care and attention to remain old at heart."

And so they labored, and Gaunt came out to help, this time with safety ropes and admonishments. "Don't let him taunt you, Bone. Gravity has been out to get you for many years."

"Gravity and you, O wife," he said.

"I've only tripped you a few times, O husband, and only when you've deserved it." Gaunt smiled down at the receding firelights of Amberhorn; Bone noticed them raising dimmer and dimmer glints in her auburn hair.

"We'll find him, Persimmon," he said.

"We will, Imago, we will," she said, not looking at him.

The silence was broken by a new face rising out of the gondola's opening.

"What are you doing? Where are we going? Is the battle over? Were there really giant fire-breathing automata?"

"Joy!" Snow Pine's voice was calling from inside the ger. "Get down from there!"

Liron Flint was saying, "Go easy on her; it's only natural that she be curious—"

"You are not her parent," Snow Pine said. "How like a man to barge in."

A-Girl-Is-A-Joy, daughter of Snow Pine, called into the gap, "I was just. Trying. To. Take. A. Look!"

Joy was twelve years old, as far as anyone knew (for time was a peculiar thing within the Scroll of Years.) She was a match in appearance for Snow Pine, with dark hair she chose to wear longer than her mother preferred. Yet there was something in her determined-looking jaw and her cocksure smile that reminded Bone of Snow Pine's late husband, the bandit Flybait.

"You must listen to your mother, student!" Walking Stick said.

"See?" Snow Pine called. "Walking Stick agrees."

"He's a man who just 'barged in. . . .'" grumbled Flint.

"He is her teacher," Snow Pine told Flint.

"She only likes him right now because he agrees with her!" Joy said. "Flint's right!"

"And you're only siding with Flint because he agrees with you!" Snow Pine replied.

Look at me, look at me, busily patching the balloon, Bone thought. He began to whistle.

Gaunt swept her leg, pretending to trip him. "Joy, let me answer your questions quickly, and then you should return to the ger. Yes, there were fire-breathing automata, but the battle is over. That is why we're patching the balloon. We are now headed northeast, away from the Retired Empire of Amberhorn and toward the Homunculus Mountains. We are seeking the clockwork city of Loomsberg, where we might sell the artifact we've stolen."

Bone coughed.

"Which Bone stole," Gaunt said.

"Mm?" said Bone.

She rolled her eyes. "Which the great and legendary and astonishingly modest Imago Bone stole. Is that sufficient?"

"Well—"

She kicked him. Gently. She didn't want him to fall. Probably.

"But then we're looking for Innocence?" Joy said.

Bone had to remind himself that the girl had known their son longer, subjectively, than they ever had. She missed the only friend her age she'd ever known. "We're always looking, Joy," he said. "We have been since we accidentally led Kindlekarn to that sleeping Eastern dragon in the isles of Penglai, far beyond Qiangguo's shores. But yes, the rumors said the flying carpet headed into the northern provinces of the Eldshore—rough country where we'll have to watch our step."

"As opposed to the safe, carefree places we've visited so far," Gaunt said.

"From there," Bone continued, "he might go into the tundra, but at least we've experience with that region. Beyond that he either has to backtrack or go on to the *Bladed Isles*. Which seems unlikely as they're far from land. We will find him, sooner or later."

Hearing the words Bladed Isles, Joy lifted her right hand from the bamboo frame of the gondola opening and spread it wide, revealing the strange markings upon her palm.

Brown like birthmarks, they nonetheless resembled the interweaving of three lengths of chain, in a pattern resembling the letter Y in Roil. Tiny runic letters accompanied the chains, like little angular travelers on corrugated roads. The marks had not always been so detailed, but over time it had come to be so.

Bone knew Snow Pine was very worried for her daughter.

"Perhaps," Joy said eagerly, "if we get close to there, we can ask someone why Bladelander runes appeared on my hand."

"It seems a reasonable question," Gaunt said after a pause.

Snow Pine's silence had the weight of a blizzard.

"Okay, fine," Joy said in a rush. "Now I'm going to talk to the efrit!"

Bone whistled the sound of Snow Pine's sputtering from his ears. But he could not whistle away the arrival of Walking Stick between him and Gaunt.

"You must tell her," the wulin warrior said. "And her mother."

"You are certainly one for giving orders," Gaunt said.

"We have only guesses," Bone said, touching Gaunt's hand.

"Suppositions," Gaunt said. "False speculation could only harm those two."

Walking Stick said, "It could not harm them more than ignorance could. I have done enough here. Join me in the scroll when you're ready. We must speak more and consult the *Chart*."

With that, Walking Stick left them alone.

"Oh, yes, sir," Gaunt said with only Bone and the sky for witness, "indeed, sir. I'll have words for you then." Bone thought it best not to pursue the matter.

Repairs done, Gaunt and Bone were reluctant to let the moment go. They called down that Haboob could heat the air, and as fire flared below they were alone after a fashion, in the clouds. The land below was inhabited, and they saw scattered firelights from villages and farms. Fleeting scents of cook fires and manure met their noses, followed by tree sap and algae as they passed into less-settled country. The moonlight allowed them to perceive the sheen of rivers crossing this region between mountains and sea. Gaunt said, "We may be the first people to perceive these lands from above, Bone. I can cover a town with my hand! There is nothing beneath my feet."

"Innocence may have seen it," Bone said, "when he passed this way."

"Perhaps. Ah, Bone. Our worries are so ordinary at their core, so absurd in how they play out. My little boy, half-grown. Lost on a magic carpet. Other mothers might scold their boys for climbing trees."

"Did he ever climb trees?"

"Oh, he tried to. He wasn't quite big enough. But boulders. Statues. Walls. Monks. Whatever he could find."

"That pleases me." He paused. "We'll find him."

"I wish I had your certainty. And what will we say when we do?"

"Perhaps, 'Hello! Let's try this again. We're your parents and we love you.' How's that?"

"Direct, Bone. Somewhat naive. But there's something to be said for direct. But what if he tells us to go to the lowest of hells?"

"Then we leave him alone, if he's safe. If he's not, we improvise."

"How can we leave alone a thirteen-year-old boy?"

"Many a thirteen-year-old has managed in the world. I was not much older when I sought my fortune."

She touched his shoulder. "And is your life then the kind you'd want for your son?"

"That," he said, squeezing her hand, "is a dark question for such a moonlit night."

"And what life can we offer him after?"

"That one may be darker still. . . . What is that?"

They had seen no birds at this altitude, but Bone had the distinct impression that one was winging toward them.

"Could it be?" Gaunt said. "It couldn't be . . . it is! It's Lady Steelfox's falcon."

"Qurca?" Bone said, feeling as if the air was suddenly thinner.

"Qurca. Qurca! We are here!"

The peregrine falcon landed upon Gaunt's outstretched arm, and she winced, but pain was clearly irrelevant to her now. "Bone, there's a message."

Bone had visions of the tiny paper flying away on a high-altitude gust. "Let's go below," he said, heart pounding. "Qurca may want a little food. I'll bet he's come a long way, eh? Ha, ha." His voice sounded lunatic in the moonlight. Carefully they returned to the gondola and explained what had happened. Walking Stick and Joy had returned to the scroll, but the others gathered around. Even Haboob seemed interested.

The note was written in Roil, the language of the Eldshore and much of the West. It read:

He is in the Bladed Isles, upon the one called Fiskegard. Tell Northwing and Haytham to join me there. The Fox.

"Swan's Blood," Gaunt said when he'd read it aloud. "The Bladed Isles. Farther even than we'd thought."

"What does he think he's doing there?" Bone said. "That's no place for a . . . well, anyone. Barbaric, piratical . . . what are you smiling at, Flint?"

"Well, you, a thief," said the explorer, "outraged at a den of pirates and brigands. There's a bit of irony in that."

"In my line there's considerably less blood."

"Ah, my friend, but less glory, they might say," Haytham put in.

"They're welcome to the glory," Bone said, "especially if they leave their gold unguarded."

"That's the spirit," Gaunt said. To Haytham she asked, "Can *Al-Saqr* get us there?"

"Can the mosquito make the lion's eye bleed?" replied the inventor.

Northwing coughed. "*Al-Saqr* can get you there, if I direct the wind." The shaman paused. "And I will. Of course I must return to my liege. Qurca's arrival is a reminder how long we've been away from Steelfox, Haytham."

"Of course!" said Haytham. "I would be literally lost without you, Northwing. Ah, such an adventure lies ahead of us, worthy of Layali of the Tales. We shall brave the northern seas, albeit with a stop in Loomsberg to sell the Antilektron Mechanism." His hands played gingerly upon the edges of the brazier, the smoky form of the efrit favoring him with a cold stare from blazing eyes. "I am being justly compensated, and the journey is interesting. We will likely part ways once I find my patron Steelfox, of course—"

"But tell me about these Bladed Isles," Snow Pine interrupted, "and why they have such a bad reputation."

"They make the Karvaks look genteel," Bone said.

"They raided my homeland for over a century," Gaunt said. "To the degree they've stopped, it's because they've interbred with us so much we're all kin, and half of them have adopted my island's religion. But we remember—the dragon-prowed vessels slicing the sea, the warriors who would prey on help-less monasteries, their blood sacrifices and their fury."

"They sound like a challenge," Mad Katta mused. "Souls that could benefit from the healing words of the Undetermined."

"Good luck with that," Bone said.

"But they've changed somewhat, no?" Flint asked. "They're still known for piracy, but not quite the same degree of brutality, eh?"

"In a long life of thieving," Bone said, "wherein I've heard much of their gold, I've gone nowhere near them. Make of that what you will. I trust a peaceful Bladelander as much as I trust a complacent shark."

"They are perhaps no worse in their slaughter than any other land," Gaunt mused. "But they are more proud of it."

"What's your son doing with them, then?" Snow Pine wondered. "With all his power, will the Bladed Isles make him into someone really dangerous?"

Gaunt and Bone hesitated.

"There's an age, I think," Gaunt said, "when a young man likes to test himself against danger and trouble. Those are lands where it's easy to do so. I worry what they will do to him, in more ways than one."

"But who knows?" Bone said. "He may be having the time of his life."

CHAPTER 2

OTHERFOLK

Innocence had only just stoked the stove in the dark of the morning when the beautiful girls with cow's tails came out of nowhere. Groggy, he had trouble understanding where they'd come from or resisting them when they, giggling, dragged him toward the crack in the wall behind the stove.

There had been a few women in the Pickled Rat the night before, but he would have remembered these, surely? He was starting to notice girls in a manner that made his breathing go strange, and a few of the village beauties were haunting his head in a way that made him feel a little giddy, and guilty. These, now, seemed a few years older than him. Their golden tresses framed bright, mischievous eyes and swirled above colorful rustic costumes he hadn't seen since the cold weather came, long vests of red or blue stretched over tight blouses of white, short dark skirts with floral or checkered patterns that swished above graceful legs. (Were there no stockings? Weren't these young ladies cold? What did he see swishing back there, not quite in sight?)

"Um," he said, "I . . . well, it's just . . . perhaps . . . so . . ."

"Shh," said one girl, two fingers landing on his lips for a moment like a butterfly seeking nectar. "Don't spoil it by talking." She instantly seemed the wisest person that had ever lived. Innocence could not help but think these tight-fitting, short-skirted versions of the village costumes were more fetching than those he'd seen previously. He could not help grinning as the fingertips left his lips. He could not help thinking it was a foolish grin. The thought didn't wipe the grin away. Hands were starting to touch him in interesting ways, retreating suddenly with redoubled laughter, returning with mock shyness.

But always they moved toward the wall.

Now the Very Wise Girl's fingers were back, this time with a bit of bread between them. He hadn't seen where it had come from. She pushed it into his mouth and pressed her lips against his ear. "A little morsel," she purred, "before dessert." Innocence ate, even as some internal voice warned him this all might be too good to be true. The bread tasted like flatbread at first but then became sweet, like one of those potato pancakes all rolled up with sugar or jam; what were they called, lefse? He felt like he was falling. In love? Down a well? Were the sensations similar?

Now he realized the warning voice wasn't internal at all, it was Freidar, with Nan beside him, and the first was armed with a sword and the second with a book and, oddly enough, a small fragment of steel.

The girls were yanking him now and shrieking in a way that wasn't laughter, and he saw that they had cow's tails. He remembered from Peersdatter and Jorgensdatter's *Eventyr* that this was worrisome.

"Um—" He tried resisting, but something in the sweetness of the bread was making him drowsy. And he still felt enrapt by the girls' beauty. It was as if his whole boyish existence, all his pride and learning and struggles, had at last been granted meaning. And the meaning was simply to please girls in every way he could.

"Shut up," said Very Wise Girl, who now sounded Very Cross. "You're ours now, fair and square. They can't save you."

It was cold water on a fire. He blinked and understood his danger. He struggled, but his body was drugged and weak. Yet Innocence thought for a moment that she was wrong, for Freidar and Nan looked menacing and gigantic. Suddenly the moment passed, as he realized that the stove looked gigantic too, and the chairs and tables, and the vast wooden cliff of the wall.

It was he and the girls who were now mouse-sized, and the crack behind the stove assumed the proportions of a cavern entrance as they dragged him into the dark.

They were underground, moving through blackness; they were tiny, scuffling through a tunnel fit for rats. But that was not the whole story. The world felt strange. The deeper down they traveled, the more squeezed Innocence felt. There was a sense of disorientation that was strangely familiar, though he could not place it. Then as they emerged into a realm of eerie lights of many colors, Innocence's memory returned to him with such force that he almost spoke of it to his captors.

But when he looked at his nearest captors in the bizarre lighting, hit by blues and reds and yellows flashing from all directions, he did not see young women. He beheld great spherical tangles of yarn comparable to his own size, taking on whatever primary color was lighting them most strongly, their ends flayed in several directions like those of many-armed sea creatures. Only Very Wise Cross Girl still appeared human.

The tentacles that touched him still felt like hands, and indeed the points of contact split into five smaller tendrils resembling fingers. It was that small detail, after everything else, that finally made Innocence yelp and close his eyes. His screech was unbecoming for either a bold man of Kantenjord's tales or a superior man of Qiangguo's classics.

When he opened his eyes again, all the girls were girls again, though Innocence eyed their swishing cow's tails with fresh alarm. Only Very Wise Cross Girl lacked one. Her companions giggled at his discomfort, while she said, "Now you've spied the uldra-girls sideways, as we entered our world."

"Your world? Are we beyond Earthe?" For he'd remembered the sensation that reminded him of the feeling of moments before. It had been somewhat like the transition between the Scroll of Years and the world of his parents.

"Not outside, but it's a good guess. We're more inside, you see. Not just under the ground but between the folds of reality's skein. Welcome to the steading of Sølvlyss."

By now Innocence's eyes had adjusted enough that he could appreciate the cavern before them. He couldn't trust his conceptions of size anymore, but it appeared to be a space miles across, with a jagged ceiling thousands of feet overhead, misty with small clouds. That he could appreciate the view at all was the work of immense outcroppings of crystal scattered upon walls and ceiling, each shining region blazing with its own primary color. Where the colors met in proximity, mixed hues appeared, and thus the cavern seemed painted by an exuberant artist obsessed with rainbows.

Under his feet was not stone but soil, covered in golden grass. The meadow filled the cavern, interrupted by hills of the shining crystal, by several shimmering streams, and by a rocky hill in the distance, rising beside the cavern's far wall. Upon these heights stood a turreted castle whose construction seemed to be all of silver, giving an impression of gigantic cups, coins, and blades. A drawbridge shaped like a vast dagger jabbed across from a tunnel in the rock, crossing a turbulent stream.

Innocence didn't feel drugged any longer and thus lacked that explanation for what he saw. He lurched away from the girls' clutches, and they let him go, evidently feeling he was thoroughly trapped. Looking back, he had to agree: the tunnel behind them had disappeared.

"Very well," he said, in what he hoped was a firm, proud voice. "You've got me. What do you want with me?"

There commenced more of the discomfiting giggling, but "Earl Morksol wants you," said the tail-less girl, the only one who'd yet spoken any words.

"I suppose he's in the castle?" Innocence managed to say. "Lead on."

They laughed at that too. He forced a smile on his face and walked along with false merriment.

Here and there the girls waved at farmers and shepherds. A few were cow's-tailed women, but most were different varieties of the hidden folk. The majority were slight, slender humanoids with translucent skin, through which could be viewed peculiar organs resembling many-faceted jewels, as if in murky specimen jars. This type of folk took on the dominant color of their surroundings, and it was as though living fragments of rainbow waved them on. There were less common varieties, such as gray, wizened beings who looked as though all color had been drained away, leaving a cold core of purpose; these nodded gravely when Innocence's escorts passed. And there were others who looked like human adults but with a child's stature, with hair like lichen, bramble, or moss peeking from underneath conical hats of red, yellow, or blue.

And sometimes he apparently saw some of the inhabitants "sideways," for he spotted balls of living yarn of variable stature, from pebble-sized to boulder-sized to a hazy shape in the distance that rivaled the castle, and from which he quickly averted his eyes. When he nerved himself to look again it was gone.

Now they neared the fortress, guarded by a stream that surged and retreated and expanded again like the edge of an ocean, for all that it was but twenty feet across. Upon the dagger-shaped drawbridge stood two warriors in strange armor that appeared to be tinted glass. As they were the transparent sort of denizen, Innocence could almost see right through them. The guards asked for no explanation but pointed toward the open gate with swords embossed with swirling geometric designs, each gleaming in the land's wealth of colors.

The castle itself was filled with servants clad in the richest of silks waiting upon a handful of nobles dressed in peasant clothes. The girls greeted these latter, and soon they had an entourage escorting them into a throne room. The throne was carved from an immense dead tree, twisting in designs recalling dragons, wolves, sea serpents, and beasts harder to identify. Upon it sat one of the wizened gray folk. He wore a simple brown robe tied with a golden rope, and a wide-brimmed straw hat.

"So this is him?"

"Yes, Father," said the tail-less girl.

"Let's see his hands." Innocence's captors spread his fingers and lifted his palms for the old fellow to see. There seemed little point in resisting.

"Hm. Very well, release him." Freed, Innocence stretched his arms and clenched his fists. "So, daughter, would you have him?" said the fellow on the throne.

The girl smiled. Innocence felt conflicted feelings. "He's too young yet," she said. "He should plow a field for a while first. Four years, I think. But we could get engaged right now."

"Wise," said the lord. "Boy, what is your name?"

"I am Askelad," Innocence managed to say, bowing in the manner of Qiangguo. "What is this place? Who are you people?"

"You are in Sølvlyss, and I am Earl Morksol. We are called by the Kantenings the uldra, and by the Swanlanders and Eldshoren the delven, though on the Spiral Sea we are often the fata. Yet many will simply say 'the hidden folk.'"

On impulse, Innocence asked, "Do your people live in Qiangguo? Do some of your girls resemble foxes?"

"Qiangguo, Qiangguo . . ." The earl scratched his chin. "It seems to me we do have relations in such a land, though we are long out of touch. As for foxes . . . in adolescence we have some in-betweenness about our forms, as with my daughter's friends the dairymaids. Perhaps in the land you name, our youth are fond of foxes. We are quite variable. Once we were nearly as limited as you, when we dwelled on the opposite side of the coin that is the Earthe. But when a great catastrophe drove us into the underground places, we wandered far in darkness and learned strange talents. Bereft of light and open air, we opened passageways into realms that had both, though we had to change ourselves to suit the new environments. Even when we reached your side of the Earthe, many of us still preferred the hidden places under the skin of reality. We still have cousins who live much as you do, in singular forms, out in the open. We call them sky-delven, and they in turn call us the deep-delven, though in these isles we prefer to say 'uldra,' as the Kantenings do."

Innocence was regaining his composure. It was easier to find his words while speaking with the earl; he was free of the stammering that seemed to plague him around every young woman but A-Girl-Is-A-Joy. "But if that's all true then what do you want with me? I am human. I do not belong in these strange spaces."

"From time to time in our long existence, we become untethered from reality. Uldra and whole uldra-realms can flit into the cosmic void, and what becomes of them, none can say. Adding human presences to our lands helps guard against this. Adding human blood to our lines is effective too. It also guards against a difficulty we have with metal; the more human blood in our lineage, the better we can cope with the poison metal brings to us. You are quite mundane."

"What do you mean?"

"I mean, future son-in-law, that you are both ordinary, and that you are 'of the world,' tying us more thoroughly to the here and now."

"Future son-in-law. So . . . I am supposed to . . . marry . . . um, her." There were squeaks of suppressed hilarity nearby. "Because I'm . . . mundane."

"You both are! My adopted daughter here is a changeling, human in form, though uldra in mind. Together you can make many princes and princesses to give our realm many sources of human blood. But that's not all there is to it, boy. You have a power within you, something we've not seen in genera-tions. Power that could wake dragons. Maybe you are the Runemarked King. Maybe not. But you will remain our guest. Alfhild, do you plight your troth with this lad?"

"Yes," said the earl's daughter.

"Don't I get a say in this?" Innocence asked.

"No," was Alfhild's matter-of-fact answer.

"You are a hostage prince," said the earl, not unkindly, "but you lack a country, and there is no one to ransom you. Prepare a feast!"

Innocence got no more answers from Earl Morksol, and in the midst of the hidden folk's sudden rushing about and bellowing about icemeat and frothfish and shroombread and sweetgreens, he paradoxically found himself alone in the chaos. Even Alfhild ignored him, though her friends provided him with new peasant garb to slip over his nightclothes—white shirt and stockings, red vest, black pants, and shoes—before they too danced away in the general bustle.

They truly thought him incapable of escape. Maybe they were right. He shivered, a captive guest abducted in the dark of the morn. Would Nan and Freidar try to rescue him? Had they any notion how?

He shuffled into a corner framed by an empty suit of glass armor and a tapestry depicting a bizarre assortment of uldra forging a huge magic axe. He couldn't hope for outside escape. His guardians were helpful, but they were mortal. He needed Deadfall now, but there'd been no word of the magic carpet in all his time in Fiskegard.

Nevertheless he was supposed to have power. Earl Morksol confirmed it. It seemed unfair to be captured over a power he had no ability to use.

He grappled with his own panic, seized that feeling of unfairness, and envisioned it as an axe driven through the flesh of reality.

I am Innocence Gaunt! Chosen of the chi of the Heavenwalls! I have escaped from the Scroll of Years, the Karvaks, and the moon! Even in this mad place, I am who I am!

Where before, on Fiskegard, there was no response to his plea, here in Sølvlyss the castle rumbled and shook. Innocence felt a tingling in his skin. He did not know how to control his power, but the land responded.

He smiled.

Now the gyrating indifference of the uldra ceased, and the simply dressed nobles and beautifully garbed servants stared at him. The glass armor next to him swiveled and brought a sword to bear; for it had been inhabited the whole time by one of the translucent folk. Innocence had been too preoccupied to notice.

Innocence remembered his training. He slipped close to the glass knight, inside the reach of the sword, in the maneuver known as Sly Fox. Immediately he pivoted to perform Pinching Lobster upon the sword-arm, while employing the Grass-Cutter Kick to topple the uldra, who went down in a clatter. Innocence yanked the tapestry from the wall and covered the knight. He fled for the gate.

"How can you leave me?" demanded Alfhild, the earl's daughter. "After all we've been through together!"

"Delightful!" Innocence yelled back, nearly losing his balance on the sharp-edged moat bridge. "But I think it's too early for betrothals!" Two more glass knights stomped over from the far side, and Earl Morksol and Alfhild advanced from the nearer. He looked down at the moat and saw its waters surging as though he beheld wavetops of the deepest sea.

"You ate from my hand," said Alfhild. "It might be too early for betrothals, but it is too late for escape."

"To eat of our food," said Earl Morksol, "is to partake of our reality. You cannot leave."

"It was only a morsel," Innocence protested.

"To eat is to eat," said the earl.

"Enough," said Alfhild, advancing, enraged. She was no longer quite so fetching. "I will slap the mischief from you, boy."

Her words unlocked something within him. Like a song heard from far over the hills, he remembered being very small, and his mother telling him stories. In one of them, the daughter of the Earthe itself was trapped in an underworld, bringing her mother into a despairing winter. The daughter might have escaped for good, but she'd unthinkingly eaten a few pomegranate seeds underground. She must always return for part of the year, and thus the world had to endure the cold for a time.

But she had escaped.

If they were so sure they had him, he wondered, why were they so set on serving him a feast?

Innocence called out, "I will return to my world, even as will the spring." He leapt.

Entering the moat was like resuming his plunge from the moon into the sea. He sputtered and struggled for breath.

"You must do the honorable thing!" Morksol called down. "Does it not say in your Swan scripture that to look upon a woman with desire is morally the same as having relations with her? You have looked upon my daughter, eaten from her fingertips. You belong to her."

It's not my Swan scripture, Innocence thought, and found the strength to swim. He thought of the sage of Qiangguo who said, "Only one of virtue truly has the discernment to love and hate people for who they are." He might not be a man of virtue, but he had reason to hate, not love, his captors. Anger urged him on. He might be commencing manhood, but it would be in his own time, on his own terms.

He'd noticed that this ocean-like stream did not fully envelop the castle of Sølvlyss but had a horseshoe shape, emerging from and returning to the walls of the great cavern. And it was his hunch that it was easier to cross from this place to his own world at the cavern edges. Otherwise why wouldn't Alfhild's passageway have led directly to her father's castle?

Of course, by the same reasoning, if this border had led to Fiskegard, Alfhild would have used it. He'd probably not be returning to the Pickled Rat. No help for it.

He swam, throwing his full strength into the act, and at last reached a place where the water surged into the rock. He sensed glass knights upon the nearby shore. The current carried him into a small cave, where it battered him against an opening he could not pass. He called upon the power in him, this time not with language but with wordless rage. He stretched out his arms and shoved, willing the structure of the place to shatter.

The land shook. With desperate fury he found words. He called upon all the gods and holy ones he could think of, the Swan, Torden, the Painter of Clouds, the Celestial Emperor, the Undetermined. He murmured the name of Joy.

He screamed for his mother.

Through the rumble of an earthquake, he heard other screams as well. Above all the wailing rose the voice of Earl Morksol. "Very well! I will not accept the damage you will wreak within Sølvlyss! If you must escape down this path, escape you will! But you may find captivity was far more pleasant, young fool!"

There was a sensation as of wrestling with a fierce opponent who suddenly quits the match.

Innocence plunged into a strange darkness. Disorientation snuffed his consciousness.

When he came to, he lay soaked in his uldra-given garb beside a gigantic gray boulder, a solitary feature upon a wide brown plain of scrubland that looked nothing like either Sølvlyss or Fiskegard. Hills gave way to mountains in the distance, palomino with white snow and dark rock. A deep blue sky was similarly divided by swirls of white cloud. The wind moaned. He rose. All the feeling of power had fled him, and he leaned against the boulder, shivering, spent. He did not know where he was, when it was, or even what size he was. He could be sure of only two things.

He was his own master. And if he could not find shelter soon, he would shortly freeze to death.

CHAPTER 3

RUNEMARK

At first *Al-Saqr* raced over the lands tributary to Amberhorn and beyond into woodland borderlands of walled towns and chieftains, neither commanded by the mighty Eldshore nor the nomads of the Wheelgreen. Even with the need to zig and zag to avoid mountains and pursuit, progress was far swifter than a similar journey on foot. Yet to Gaunt it felt as though all the world crowded between them and Innocence.

On the evening of the first full day after Amberhorn, when it was clear they'd evaded the city's wrath, Gaunt joined Bone in entering the world of the Scroll of Years. Gaunt took the scroll from Snow Pine and put her hand upon Bone's.

"Say hello for me," A-Girl-Is-A-Joy said.

"You only emerged this morning," Gaunt said.

"But it's not the same morning for them."

Gaunt let the painting's power pull them inside, and the gondola of *Al-Saqr* vanished.

In the world of the scroll it was a misty daytime, not a clear rosy evening. Spindly mountains rose out of a sea of white cloud, and amid the gnarled trees of one such mountain stood the pagoda of a nameless monastery of the philosophy—or religion, or society—called the Forest. Gaunt and Bone drifted hand in hand, like two falling leaves whose stems were accidentally intertwined, until they settled onto a wide ledge beside a mountain path. A trio of leaning trees, stretching their branches into the abyss, protected them from falling into the fog. Trees on nearby mountains stretched similarly, as though beckoning.

"He is waiting," said a voice.

The speaker appeared to be a big, gray-haired man from Qiangguo dressed in a birch bark hat; a stained, tattered robe; and wooden shoes. He had the look of someone who spent many days out of doors, and probably some nights as well. As ever he looked familiar and not. While his body looked much as

Gaunt had known it, his eyes always looked as though they'd seen lifetimes pass between visits.

"Hello, Sage Painter," Gaunt said. Bone waved.

"Ah, that title belongs to one long dead," came the rumbling voice, speaking as though repeating music heard from a far-off peak. "What is the use of it? I am but his self-portrait."

"You are welcome company, friend," Bone said, "whatever you are."

"Indeed, it's good to see you," Gaunt said.

"Strange. You are each so shaped by the other. Yet until now I don't think I've ever encountered you on the same path."

Bone looked at Gaunt; she took his hand and smiled. It occurred to her he'd spent considerable time within the scroll while it lay lost in a mountain valley. "We do keep busy," Bone said. "So Walking Stick's expecting us, eh?"

"Every life has its know-it-alls, and you go now to meet one. You will find him at the top of the pagoda. Everything is up and down, right and wrong, with that one. Meantime my way lies rambling in the woods and shadows, far from trouble."

Gaunt said, "You will not join us?"

Bone said, "Surely he is still not so bad?"

"My words are all bird-chirps to him, and I don't speak his language." He clapped and chuckled. "But the mountain is large." He sighed, though his eyes retained their bright mischief. "Even so, I wish I might look at the outer world from your flying craft, see the land stretch far below, no kitchen smoke for many *li*, unknown mountains and waterfalls, cries of monkeys and roars of tigers."

"I wish there was a way to arrange it," Gaunt said. "But if we see you later I'll tell you all about the land."

"I would like that, poet. And now crazy Meteor-Plum walks his tangled way. And tangled Gaunt and Bone walk their crazy way. Farewell!"

They watched him descend the mountain path. In an unnervingly short time, he was a tiny figure. Gaunt wondered about his musings. *Al-Saqr* did get visitors from the scroll. If one wished to see the wider world, the view from a balloon offered a fine opportunity. Many of the monks accepted the invitation, though many others, including their leader Leaftooth, declined. Gaunt wondered if some of the monks were, like the self-portrait of the Sage Painter who'd created the scroll, aspects of the scroll itself and unable to leave. If so, she thought it might be impertinent to say so.

One individual who was decidedly not an aspect of the scroll was Walking Stick.

"Well, Bone, our crazy way beckons. Shall we?"

"Doesn't it ever. Let's!"

It was often bright and sunny here, but always cold, especially when the wind picked up. The path bore into shadow and out into sun, making rough lurches and plunges into icy streams. Birds conducted their endless conversations about territory, mates, bugs, and humans. More and more, wind slapped the visitors until they lost the cover of trees and beheld a monastery sheltered and perforated by a hardy grove, framed by neighboring mountains, backed by distant mountains, embellished by remote mountains.

They were welcomed by a monk and taken upstairs for tea. Walking Stick sat cross-legged in the midst of what could have been considered a solarium, except that rather than windows the chamber had crumbled portions of wall. Mountains and mists stretched in every direction.

"Ah, good," he said, rising. "Now that we can speak at our ease—"

Gaunt slapped him. Before that moment she wasn't certain what she would do. She might have spat. She might have laughed. The move was so sudden even Bone was surprised. Walking Stick surely could have blocked or evaded, but his only reaction was to narrow his eyes.

Gaunt folded her arms. "That is for my son. If you hadn't tried to abduct me when I was pregnant, none of this would have happened."

Walking Stick took a deep breath before answering. "You speak truly. Yet worse things might have happened."

"Such are the apologies of Walking Stick."

Bone said, "He has paid, in a way. He has been stuck in the scroll, unable to resume his former life."

"I dedicated myself to the education of your son," Walking Stick said.

"Taught him," Gaunt said, "in the manner of your Garden."

"Why would I not give him the best?" Walking Stick gestured toward one of the walls' ruined sections. "However, if it reassures you, know that the monks of the Forest have also instructed him. They have a . . . different approach."

Gaunt looked out at swirling clouds. She sighed. "I never thought I would say so, but perhaps it is not entirely bad you were exiled with him. He was left with few friends."

Bone said nothing.

Walking Stick bowed. "I fear he would not consider me one such. Yet I tried to make him an honorable man."

"I suppose he couldn't follow me in everything," Bone said.

"You may joke about your larcenous ways, Imago Bone. But I do hope for better for your son."

"You mean, you still hope to make him emperor of Qiangguo."

Walking Stick said, "That was long ago, from my perspective. I have dwelled with monks of the Forest. Some of their mad philosophy may be rubbing off. If Innocence Gaunt rejects the power of Qiangguo, so be it. Yet I hope to persuade him it's yet a worthy goal, to cherish and protect the greatest of the world's lands."

"He seems to have his own ideas," Gaunt said.

"He is young," Walking Stick said.

"Would that he were younger," Gaunt mused.

"Age, if accompanied by experience, is to be welcomed. I hope to become much older yet, for clearly I have much to learn. But . . . you don't mourn his maturity, do you, Persimmon Gaunt? You regret that you were not there beside him. Now he has that chance—and he has rejected you. That is not right. He is prideful, quarrelsome, insubordinate. Even you, thief, do not deserve such treatment. He dishonors you and my teaching. If only for this alone, I must seek him out."

"Is that why you wished to speak with us?" Bone said. "For our blessing to travel with us? As far as I'm concerned, you and the scroll are Snow Pine's business now."

Gaunt nodded. "We may not like you, Walking Stick, but if she tolerates you, we tolerate you. But try to abduct my son again, and . . . well. You have seen that we are determined people."

Bone took her hand.

Walking Stick said, "That is one of two reasons I wished to speak to you. I do want to find Innocence again. And I want you to find him as well. He's less likely to become a threat to Qiangguo if his parents can influence him. Such is my first reason."

"And your second?" Gaunt said.

"You have an unusual artifact in your possession, do you not?"

Without thinking about it, Gaunt found her fingers brushing the bejeweled pommel of the saber sheathed over her back. It unnerved her to find herself caressing the magical weapon. "Crypttongue? I'll have you know I prefer not to use the thing. I've released all its captured spirits."

"That is important to you, is it not? That you gain no benefit from this murderous thing. You've killed, poet. And you fear you will cross the invisible line between one who has had to kill, and one who is a killer. Or at any rate, you hope such a line exists."

"Be careful, Walking Stick," Bone said.

"And you," Walking Stick said, "you fear what you have done to her. You are a lost creature, but she had other destinies, before you lured her onto your path. You fear Crypttongue even more than Persimmon Gaunt does. For it represents everything you hope she won't become."

"Do you want the thing, then, Walking Stick?" Gaunt said, drawing the sword.

She let it clatter at her feet. In the vibration of metal against stone, she imagined she heard a keening, yearning quality.

"Why give it to me?" Walking Stick said. "It was Liron Flint's weapon before it was yours."

"Flint has many intuitions about Crypttongue," Bone said. "One is that it chooses new owners. Flint does not think it a good idea to have it back."

"Likewise," Walking Stick said, "I would not take it, even were my fighting style a match. Enough. I had reason to question your relationship to the sword, but any concerns I had are answered."

Gaunt hesitated before reclaiming and sheathing the weapon. "Are you quite satisfied?"

"No. Because that was not the artifact I was speaking of. There is a book in your possession that discusses the Bladed Isles, is there not? You acquired it in faraway Qushkent, and since traveling to the West you have kept it here, in this monastery."

Gaunt and Bone looked at each other. By wordless agreement, Gaunt told the truth. "How did you know?"

"Do not blame Abbot Leaftooth; I have been ferreting out truth on the

Empire's behalf for decades. He does not even know that I know. I've had considerable time to ask leading questions and shadow his movements. I know the book you possess is known as the *Chart of Tomorrows*, or the *Carta Postrema*, or even more colorfully as the *Drakkenskinnen*, after the origins of its bright leather."

"Then perhaps you know its danger," Gaunt said. "We still don't know who gave it to us in Qushkent, nor why, but perhaps it was meant never to be used. For if we can believe the book, it shows how to alter history."

"Causality may be an illusion," Bone said, "like free will, true love, and the perfect heist. But I prefer to live in a world where such things can at least be dreamt of."

"And if the *Chart of Tomorrows* speaks true," Gaunt said, "then the future can alter the past, and effect precede cause. Such a power dwarfs the little dangers posed by a magic sword, or an efrit, or a flying craft. That is why we brought it here for safekeeping."

"Will you respect that decision?" Bone asked. "Or will you try to make Qiangguo an empire that spans time?"

"Peace," said Walking Stick. "We need no such power. As I understand it the *Chart* spends considerable verbiage on the Bladed Isles. It is that knowledge I wish, not power over time. I need to know all I can, for A-Girl-Is-A-Joy's sake. You have seen the mark upon her hand."

"It's hard to trust you," Gaunt said, who had seen the Runemark in two places, on Joy's hand and within the *Chart of Tomorrows*.

"It's my price, then, for helping find Innocence."

"Is that how it is?" Bone said. He looked at Gaunt and shrugged.

Gaunt nodded. "Very well. Perhaps we've had our fill being the keepers of dread magical things."

Before honoring Walking Stick's request, she and Bone took full advantage of the accelerated time flow, for a night of lovemaking within the scroll would be negligible from *Al-Saqr*'s point of view. They also got drunk on rice wine and played weiqi, though Bone kept getting the rules confused with chess. Crowded as the monastery was, it was like a palace compared to the gondola of the balloon.

Refreshed, Gaunt and Bone awaited Walking Stick's return in the upper chamber. Today was as bright as yesterday had been misty, and the blazing sunlight seemed to belie any thoughts of murky islands, dragon-prowed ships, fire, and doom. Far in the distance, unreachable miles away, a coiling, green-blue female dragon soared among the Peculiar Peaks. Such were seen now and again, but never had anyone here spoken with one. It seemed the Sage Painter had put no male dragons into the world of the scroll. Mating dragons produced conflagrations. Gaunt was thankful the conflagrations of human love remained metaphorical. Mostly.

Walking Stick arrived with A-Girl-Is-A-Joy and Snow Pine.

Gaunt patted a stool beside her. Joy sat. "Walking Stick said something about a book?"

"Look here."

Gaunt showed Joy a tome bound in white leather. To see its spine and upper-left cover was to believe it a work of recent vintage, but on closer inspection it seemed weathered, damaged, ancient.

Yet the wear and tear had a peculiar aspect. Beginning from the spine and upper left the book seemed new, yet scuffing, creasing, and flaking increased as one looked toward the lower right. Flip the book over, and one would see worse afflictions moving from the lower-left corner to the upper right. The back cover was ragged and peeling. In the upper-right quadrant it was shedding a red powder resembling rust.

That much was odd in itself. But Gaunt had the strong impression that the exact pattern of ravages—a cut here, a flake there—changed each time she beheld it.

Likewise, the early leaves of the book seemed freshly penned but looked progressively aged as one turned pages. The middle section had the faded but intact look of parchment preserved in dry air. The back section was a catalog of ruin, with some pages buckled, curled, and torn, others shrunken, molded, or burnt. And as with the cover, Gaunt had the impression that the collection of strange maps and writing changed subtly each time she looked. Coastlines changed shape; little islands appeared and disappeared. Different scripts combined within the *Chart* . . . ancient runes mingled with the flowing calligraphy of Mirabad and the vertical script of the Karvaks. The proportions were ever-changing.

She had some experience with dangerous books. She feared this one.

"So what is it?" Joy said.

Gaunt opened the book to a set of writings that looked like neat collections of twigs.

Joy frowned. "Those are runes of the Bladed Isles. Walking Stick's told me enough to help me recognize them, but I can't read them. They don't use runes there anymore, he said."

Bone said, "I believe he's mostly right. This is an old book."

"I can only read some of this," Gaunt said, "and then with uncertainty. But this is the *Chart of Tomorrows*." She turned the page, and there was a map.

Joy peered closer. "What is that place?"

Walking Stick snorted. "It's a map of the world, in which the Bladed Isles are shown in detail, and everything else becomes increasingly simplified and distorted as one travels east or south. I assure you, the maps made by the Eunuch Admiral of Qiangguo are much more reliable."

The map was indeed more detailed in the West, for Gaunt could recognize the island groups there. Tiny red runes marked a spot on the Contrariwise Coast, and another at Swanisle.

Gaunt flipped to another page of runic text, then another map, this time of the Bladed Isles in the upper-left corner and Swanisle in the lower right. More places marked in red runes began appearing. The one at Swanisle was clearly in the north of that land. There were a few in the sea between, and many in and around the Bladed Isles.

"This," Gaunt said, "is a book of maps assembled by a wizard known only as the Winterjarl. Though it seems he had several coauthors. He claimed to have come from a future of infinite ice and snow, but he escaped backward through the years."

"Backward through the years?" Snow Pine put in. "What the hell does that even mean?"

"You have seen," said Walking Stick, "how time can flow at different speeds in two realms, like a rushing river beside a gentle stream. Now imagine leaving the flow of your river, backtracking along the land, and returning to the river at a place upstream. If this is possible with time, one might visit people long dead and places long vanished."

Gaunt flipped a page. Now the Bladed Isles' northernmost island, Spydbanen, was shown in detail, several red markings on its coast. "What this book claims is that a person with the proper understanding can use the marked locations to sail through time. Now, why the Winterjarl says 'sail' when many of the spots are inland, I don't know. I'm not one of the people with understanding."

"How did you get this book?" Joy said.

"Oddly enough," Bone said, "it was a gift. Someone with knowledge of us left it for us in the days when we sought the Silk Map. We do not know whom."

"A big coincidence," Snow Pine said.

"The kind of coincidence I have trouble believing," Gaunt agreed. "But that's a mystery for another time." She turned more of the pages, seeking a particular spot. Even with the changeable nature of the book, she was becoming familiar with the place she wanted. "So. There are multiple languages here, and I confess there is much I can't read. But I've made progress with the runes. The Winterjarl rambles about many aspects of the isles. Trolls. The underground uldra. The vortex of the Draugmaw. And . . ." Gaunt found the image of a hand marked with a rune resembling three intertwined lengths of chain, glossed by more runes yet.

"That's my mark!" Joy said. Her eagerness turned to accusation. "You knew this was here? Why didn't you say anything?"

"Right," Snow Pine said. "What Joy said. Why?"

"I've been unsure what the runes say," Gaunt said, looking away. "I didn't want to worry you. But it's best you know. 'The Runethane is the land's, and the land is the Runethane's. In the time of the land's need, the Runemarked King will arise and command the energies of the Great Chain of Unbeing, which captures the power of the three sleeping dragons. He who bears the Runemark will live for the land, and die for the land, and so long as the Chain remains he will never leave.'"

"And you didn't think this was something Joy should know?" Snow Pine said. "How many other magic dooms are you hiding?"

"Don't worry, Mom," Joy said with a stifled laugh. "All that applies to a 'he.' Obviously, I'll be just fine."

Bone sighed. "I'm sorry. We should have said something sooner."

Gaunt added, "But I'm still unsure of the translation."

"What about the runes on my hand?"

"I think," Gaunt said, "they say, 'Staraxe, Sunblade, Moonspear.'"

"Let me guess," Joy said, her laugh gone. "The names of dragons?"

"Possibly. And the runes weave through a representation of the Great Chain, a vast construction at the heart of the isles."

"Then that's where I have to go." There was something in Joy's face recalling misty cliffs and lonely winds. "After we find Innocence."

"You can't go," Snow Pine said. "You heard Gaunt. You'll be trapped there."

Joy raised her hand. "Maybe I'm already trapped. I have to know why that distant land chose me. Me! Teach me everything you can."

CHAPTER 4

STORM

"Smoke," Haytham said, peering through the brass spyglass.

They had approached the mountain city-state of Loomsberg on a sunny, clear winter's morning, the fields and copses of trees rushing below under a bright dusting of snow. Bone had jostled with his companions for a look out the portholes, until Haytham ordered them to take turns to preserve the ger's balance. Now he crossed his arms and rubbed his feet together beside the scornful-looking efrit. He'd been looking forward to city pleasures. And not just any city, but a wondrous place where humans, goblins, and the mountain-delven coexisted and built marvelous contraptions. Some, like the waterwheel and the windmill, could work anywhere. Others, like the steam calliope, tended to break down elsewhere, for reasons esoteric to him. Nonetheless, some of Loomsberg's stranger wonders were both portable and able to persist for months, and he'd lain awake while *Al-Saqr* shifted in the wind, thinking of marvelous items they might buy.

All that was looking increasingly problematic.

Gaunt peered out to where Haytham pointed the telescope. "The city lies there," she said, "upon a promontory, beside a gorge, washed by waterfalls."

"Look at the plain," Northwing said, stepping aside and making room for Bone.

Given what he'd heard already, Bone was not much encouraged to do so. But he looked. Far ahead in the blazing of dawn, blue-gray mountains sloped down to misty foothills, and these to snow-covered grasslands, crossed here and there by gleaming rivers. Yet for all that brightness there was a darkness upon the plain. Or rather thousands of points of darkness.

"The Wagonlords?" Bone wondered around. "Could there be so many?"

"There are many great wagons flying flags, to be sure," Haytham said. "But they are in the minority. I see also peoples unfamiliar to me, troops in golden helmets and riders on winged, two-headed beasts. I do think I recognize a troop of female archers as warriors of the Oirpata people. Fascinating. But what I am intensely familiar with are those wheeled sailing ships. And those mastodons and sabercats. And that ocean of horsemen."

"Karvaks," Snow Pine said, and made a fist.

"They've sacked Loomsberg," Bone said, his dreams of marvelous acquisitions dispersing like smoke. Also, he felt bad for the inhabitants.

"Such evil," Snow Pine said.

"Hm, I see no evil," Mad Katta mused. For a moment they all looked at the blind wanderer. "Oh, there are individuals of bad intent, for certain, though I see those everywhere I go. But no evil sorcery . . ."

"That's not what I meant," Snow Pine snapped. "Sure, from a cosmic perspective, like your Undetermined's, true evil may be a rare thing. 'Who knows what is good or bad?' the Forest monks say. All is in flux. But that's a bird's eye view. We mice of the world can't afford such a perspective. Sometimes we have to point to fire and madness and death and just say, well, hell with it—call it evil."

Katta bowed. "It's not for me to lecture you on attachment and its woes, my friend. Not while we smell the smoke of a burning city."

"The Karvaks have never come so far west," Gaunt said, "have they?"

"No," Northwing answered. "Except for guests, delegations, that sort of thing. Last I knew, they were pressing at the Mirrored Sea."

"Then it's happened," Flint said, scratching his chin. "They've attacked the West. Gaunt, Bone, Haytham—our homelands are now just as endangered as Snow Pine's." Bone noticed Flint omitted Northwing and Katta, whose land of birth was already subject to the Karvaks. "Loomsberg's a tributary to the Eldshore," Flint went on. "One would expect the emperor in Archaeopolis to respond."

"There are other factors, my friend," Haytham said. Bone observed Haytham didn't directly respond to Flint's depiction of the Karvak threat. "It's winter, and Loomsberg lies across the mountains. The Karvaks know this. It was risky to attack in winter, with its bad weather and poor forage. But this having been accomplished, consider the advantages. They are secure against a counterattack. By spring it may seem best to arrange a deal."

"Well, it's not our problem," Bone said. "If the battle's over perhaps we can land, sell the mechanism, and be off. The Karvaks have a reputation for keeping the bazaars open, no?"

"Ah, he's eager to fence his stolen goods!" Northwing said, "but it's not so simple."

Gaunt said, "We're aboard a Karvak balloon, Northwing, by permission of a Karvak princess. Your princess, in fact. With her personal representatives aboard. You really think there'll be trouble?"

Northwing said, "Do you see any banner for our patron, Haytham?"

Haytham searched, and grunted. "Alas. No. Steelfox's forces are not there."

"So you see," Northwing said, "Steelfox has respect in the Karvak Realm, but war is war. If we go there, the balloon will be confiscated, and Haytham and I will be pressed into service. The rest of you may be fine, but you'll have little hope of reaching the Bladed Isles before spring. I say we go there right away. What about you, inventor?"

"Oh very well," Haytham said. "There will be stormy seas. Barbarian women. Trolls. Fun!"

"All right, I'm convinced," Bone grumbled. "Gaunt?"

"Oh, substitute 'barbarian men' and I'm in accord." She winked and addressed the others. "This is your last chance to get off at civilization, I think. Haytham and Northwing might set you down in the foothills."

Katta said, "I go to preach to these Bladelanders . . . and to speak once again to the carpet Deadfall and understand what has happened to it. For he was a friend."

"Why does everyone," Northwing muttered, "insist on calling every personality a 'he' or a 'she'?"

Katta smiled. "Please indulge a limited man his metaphorical crutches. At any rate, I once told Deadfall I'd pay him for his service. Such a being can only truly be repaid with knowledge, and while I taught him the languages of Qiangguo and Qushkent, it seems too little. And I would like to understand his betrayal, if only for my own enlightenment."

Snow Pine said, "I think Joy and I must go there, to understand the meaning of this 'Runemark.' And she will want to see Innocence again." She turned to Flint. "And you . . . will you go to the Bladed Isles?"

"I am an explorer, my dear," he said, touching her cheek. "There are things I wish to discover."

Northwing coughed. "Well, my mistress gave me a sabbatical and now it is time to return."

Haytham nodded, "I too wish to see Steelfox again."

"Lady Steelfox," Northwing said. "Remember your station."

"Shaman, remember," Flint said, "we are not under the orders of the Karvak Realm, up here."

"Give it time," Northwing said.

Bone squinted out the porthole. "Time's something we may have little of. Balloons are rising. I count six."

"Nine," Haytham said, "if you add the three I see being readied."

Upon the ones that were already rising, Bone could make out symbols of a lion rearing up on a cliff and of a wolf with ruby eyes. "Gaunt, do you see a metallic sheen on those envelopes?"

"Swan's blood," Gaunt swore. "Haytham, we have to escape this place, now. Those balloons are made of ironsilk. They will be impervious to our arrows. We will be quite vulnerable to theirs."

"Altitude!" called out Haytham. "Drop ballast! Northwing, I request an easterly wind. Haboob, I desire hotter air—and a great deal of smoke."

As the travelers busied themselves with Haytham's instructions, the efrit raised a sketchy gray arm with a dramatic flourish. Flame blazed high and smoke filled the ger.

"Ack—" Haytham managed amid the general cacophony of hacking. "I mean—outside . . . conceal us with smoke?"

"You are very careless with your instructions, O mighty conqueror of the skies," Haboob scolded as the smoke swirled through the roof of the gondola. "You are fortunate you are not dealing with a djinn."

Soon there was no telling what lay outside. Smoke filled all the portholes.

Bone said, "Surely they know where we are, Haytham. Meanwhile we do not know where they are."

"Ah, but we do," Mad Katta said, staring down at the bamboo framework underfoot. "I did not perceive them at first, but now that they are rising, I see flickering pinpoints of negative karma. Nine in all."

"Of course!" Gaunt said. "We haven't been using demonic heat sources . . ."

"But my original design called for them," Haytham concluded, a trifle smugly, Bone thought. "And the Karvaks are still using those methods. Haboob is better, though they can't know that. With luck they'll conclude we've suffered an accident and must be abandoned."

"We are staying above them," Katta said.

Minutes passed within the strange limbo of their dark ascent. It grew very cold, rivaling the worst arctic weather Bone had endured. They shivered within their thick Karvak deels, edging as close as they dared to the brazier.

"We may not simply *appear* to be in trouble," Northwing said at last, her strained breaths manifesting as wispy clouds. "I am finding it harder to control the wind. Katta . . . errant countryman . . . do you still see the demons?"

"They are following, great shaman, but falling farther behind. . . ." Katta shivered, though he sounded less strained than Northwing. Bone was panting as though after a brisk run. "I see them crackle with rage as their quarry escapes," Katta continued. "Oh, how they would like to make our skins blister and pop. It is nauseating to contemplate their energies. It is surely accumulating me karmic merit. Merit, merit, merit. Wondrous merit."

"Is our air running thin?" Haytham wondered aloud, rubbing his forehead. "My vision is blurring. . . ."

The efrit Haboob formed a grin. It looked like a crack in the side of a blazing kiln. "I have pushed us as high into the atmosphere as I dare, mighty Haytham ibn Zakwan ibn Rihab, master of knowledge, tamer of demons, commander of the skies—"

"Short version, please."

"Your air is indeed growing thin. Those of you who are acclimated to high places will function better than the lowlanders, but all of you are suffering."

"I've scaled heights for decades," Bone complained, "and I feel absurdly dizzy. . . ." The ger seemed out of focus. Haboob was like the shadow of smoke upon water.

"He means mountain-height, Bone," Gaunt snapped, "not mansion-height."

"I dwelled for years upon the high plateau of Geam," Katta mused. "Early on, my lungs sometimes felt as though they burned. Later I adjusted."

"How special," Northwing spat. "The rest of us are lowlanders, Haytham! Diminish the heat and let us drop! If I lose consciousness we'll be at the winds' mercy, and who knows where we'll end up."

"Bone," Haytham said, "pull that black rope beside you . . . it opens an emergency flap to vent the hot air. . . ."

Bone did so, though his muscles were sluggish. His arms performed the operation like recalcitrant mules.

They dropped slowly at first, then precipitously. Bone's mind and vision cleared. Now he comprehended enough to feel truly frightened. "Haboob, how close are we to the mountains?"

"As I was about to say, O thieving assistant to the great Haytham ibn Zakwan—"

"That's greatest second-story man of the Spiral Sea."

"—we are plunging toward a narrow pass between the burning city and the lands westward. Perhaps you would like the smoke cloud dispersed—"

"Yes! Yes!" Bone thought he heard the voices of everyone in the ger, including his own. He peered out a porthole.

A dark curtain ripped aside, and gleaming glaciated peaks stabbed upward as a clutch of spears might pierce the awareness of a gnat. Northwing cursed and gestured wildly. A sudden wind forced them into a sheer-sided gorge.

For an unnerving moment Bone saw the shadow of a gigantic balloon against the western clouds, encircled by prismatic light. "Names of the dead gods . . . the Karvaks have sent some sort of monstrous craft against us. . . ."

Flint peered out and chuckled. "Fear not! What you perceive is a mountain specter." He turned and saw that Bone, Gaunt, Katta, and Snow Pine all had weapons out. (That Katta's weapon was a blessed pastry did not reduce the seriousness of his expression.) "Peace!" the explorer said. "Mountain specters are an illusion. Our shadow is cast against the clouds. It happens so often to travelers here that this range is named the Homunculus."

"Ah!" said Katta, returning his cake to a pouch. "That is why I see no demonic form ahead." He gazed backward. "Nor behind. We're safe."

"I beg to differ!" Northwing said. "The prevailing wind's easterly. Added to mine, it's carrying us through the pass like wild horses! Make peace with your deities!"

"You don't want to hear what I think of my deity right now," Flint said with a giddy laugh.

"You don't believe in him anyway," Snow Pine teased him.

"Well, in these mountains I might!"

The passage was indeed glorious. Bone's eyes drank it in. The landscape swept by at delirious speed. Glaciers blazed near at hand, and bright snow whirled down steep slopes like the ghost of desert dust. All was shining with reflected sunlight, as though sisters of the sun were frozen within the peaks.

Bone blinked in the glare, turning toward darker regions where spindly evergreens waved like weary dancers in the sharp-biting breeze. A hawk dipped and soared, feathers twitching so much in the wind it looked impossibly nervous. But Bone was the nervous one. Abruptly the weather changed, and clouds and mists pressed close at hand. Fog curdled along the pass, and rocky danger flashed into view only now and then within a sea of gray.

"Are you finding inspiration?" he asked Gaunt, for she was inscribing words onto a wax tablet.

"I must guard against overdone similes," Gaunt said, staring out a porthole, "like an angry hawk-beast protecting its eggs from the Scarlet Order of Omelet Chefs."

"That is exactly how I feel. Well, not exactly. It is spectacular." He smiled and pointed. "I believe we once had a long, beautiful interlude by that waterfall down there."

"Ah, I remember! But it was that one over there."

Bone frowned. "You're certain?"

Gaunt laughed. "If we survive, we're going to become one of those old couples who argue endlessly about their pasts."

Bone wondered where and how they'd be spending that old age. "Either way, we've passed both spots."

She squeezed his arm. "Life seems to be moving ever faster for us."

The fog fell away. Green forested hills of the Eldshore appeared below. Beyond the Eldshore lay the sea, and beyond that lay Swanisle, and the Bladed Isles. Bone felt once again he was nearing the edge of any sane map, going farther than any city-thief should go, and he feared for the group and their journey. He was glad so many others were willing to join them.

The ocean passage took three days. Gaunt was surprised by the speed of it, but with Northwing recovered and nothing but the weather to block them, progress was swift. Even while Northwing slept, they had a lucky air current. Sometimes they passed ships, but for the most part this was a lonely sea. Gaunt found little to observe in the steel-gray ocean below, so she spent considerable time within the Scroll, helping anyone who wished to struggle with the language of the Bladed Isles.

One day Bone appeared to her there. "We've arrived. You'd best bring the *Chart*."

It was late morning. *Al-Saqr* flew near a fractured ceiling of clouds pierced by spears of light. Oblong ingots of sun blazed upon a blue-green sea.

Ahead lay snowy mountains. It was as though the land, having finally risen above the sea, was eager to reach the clouds without any further ado. Rocky summits and cliffs and crags wore variegated coverings of snow. Sometimes the snow pooled like lakes; other times it followed cracks in the rocks like rivers. Purple-gray clouds drifted above the peaks, the only sign of movement upon the coast. Farther inland, a knot of even taller mountains reared beneath a gray-black storm.

Bone, Katta, Snow Pine, Flint, Haytham, Northwing, and Haboob were all silent. That was remarkable in itself.

Gaunt opened the *Chart of Tomorrows*.

"If this is accurate," she said, "that's probably the coast of Spydbanen. Those big mountains there must be the Trollfangs, the range near the town of Jotuncrown."

"Personally I think they're all big mountains," Bone said.

"We'd best turn southwest. Spydbanen is full of obstacles. On the map it looks like a mountain range with a thin skin of coastline."

"There's evil," Katta announced.

The mystic might not have been able to see everyone else's stares, but he noted the silence. "Ahead, in our direction of travel, is a large gathering of negative karma. Maybe a bit to the left. If Gaunt wishes to turn us away from that spot, I would consider it a wise precaution."

"Negative karma's not all that's there," Snow Pine said. "Look."

Gaunt looked, though in a sense she didn't need to. The flickers of lightning appearing ahead were dazzling enough to be noticed inside the ger. Gaunt counted, and when thunder boomed she estimated the source to be eight miles away. When her vision cleared, an afterimage lingered like jagged, thin rivers of light.

Flint said, "I must say! I am fascinated by this landscape, its violent cartography, its coursing energies, and its potential for destroying us!"

Snow Pine said, "Fascination, hell. We need cover, fast. Otherwise we'll be covered by lightning. Those strokes are all emanating from the mountains. But they're reaching out every time. Toward us."

Katta said, "It might be pertinent to note that I can see each of the bolts with exquisite clarity."

"Now I'm scared," Bone said.

Northwing said, "Snow Pine has the right idea. I'm cajoling the wind to blow us southwest, but if we want to be safe, we must descend."

"I'd hoped to land in a city," Haytham said mournfully, "a place with inns, baths, bazaars. Nevertheless I've begun the descent."

"Actually," the efrit Haboob began, "I've begun the descent. And you're welcome—"

Lightning strokes lit the sky to the northwest. Thunder cracked a few seconds later.

A terrifying night commenced.

From sunset to midnight, Haytham and Northwing guided them away from the mad lightning as the others labored to steer them safely through the mountains. At last the bolts diminished and receded, and the ger was once again safe after a fashion, though a frigid wind whistled all around.

"I do not know where we are," Haytham said.

"At least," Katta said, "I perceive no evil."

Northwing said, "With the lightning where it is, I think we're still headed southwest. We may not need to land after all. Though it might be a good idea."

"Not like this, my friend," Haytham said. "Not in the dark."

Gaunt looked down upon a moonlit sheen, broken by lines of waves. "I think we're somewhere over water. We may have reached the archipelago of little islands in the middle of these lands. The Splintrevej. I doubt there'd be good places to land there. But past these is the biggest island, Svardmark. There they have nations, towns, farmland."

"And lightning-wielders?" Bone said.

"Not that I've heard."

They rested as they could, though whenever Gaunt shut her eyes she was startled out of sleep by a dream of falling. Bone squeezed her hand each time; still, it was all she could do simply to doze.

Dawn found them entering another region of mountains. Northwing had circles under bloodshot eyes. "We need to land," Gaunt told them all by way of good morning. "Northwing can't go on like this."

"No," Northwing muttered, "Northwing can't. But there is no good place."

"Then let go," Katta said. "You've done much."

"Those mountains look close . . ." Northwing murmured.

Gaunt tried to listen, but another voice tugged at her ears. Impossibly, it seemed to be coming from the wind outside. She leaned against the felt, straining to hear.

Mother . . .

"Gaunt? Persimmon?" Bone was beside her. "What's wrong?"

"Do you not hear?"

"No."

Mother . . . Mother . . .

"It's Innocence, Imago. I hear him somehow. Perhaps the power he carries is letting him reach out to us. Innocence, it's me! We're looking for you. We'll be there soon. Do you hear me?"

The only response was a blast of wind.

Northwing shouted, "They found us! Whoever attacked in Spydbanen, this is their wind. They're going to slam us against those mountains."

Gaunt yelled, "Haboob, we need altitude!"

"Descend, Haboob! Altitude, Haboob!" the efrit scoffed. "Mortals. You creatures simply don't live long enough to justify all this changing of your minds—"

"Heat, O Haboob!" Haytham yelled. "In the All-One's name, heat! We need lift!"

"Yes, O imperious, regal, resplendent—"

"Not enough!" Gaunt said.

"Do we throw things out?" Bone asked, checking that his loot from Amberhorn was still in his pockets.

"Yes!" Haytham said. "There are fiery equations that govern the behavior of balloons. At the moment, lightness equals survival. Toss everything that isn't essential. Food! Weapons!"

"Thieves?" said Gaunt as she threw a crate of vegetables out the front of the ger.

"Poets?" Bone answered, tossing a huge soup kettle.

"Stop flirting, you two," Snow Pine said. She threw a pot and pan, narrowly missing Bone's head.

A bolt of blue lightning shattered the morning, turning the interior of the ger into an azure shadow play. Somehow the discharge of energy had the audacity to look cold. Ordinary daylight returned, but thunder rent the air and shook the balloon, and even the efrit twisted violently as the ger careened and the humans fell.

"The scroll—" Snow Pine called out.

"I have it," Katta said.

"How?" she said, sounding amazed.

"I heard it rustling and rolling," Katta said, returning it to her. "It is a lightweight thing, and I anticipated such a moment."

"Thank you," Snow Pine said.

"Not enough!" Haytham was saying. "Is there anything more to throw?"

"No . . ." Bone said.

Gaunt could almost see him thinking, *I've lived a long life, and sometimes a man sacrifices himself that his family, his friends, might live. If these fiery equations need to be writ upon human flesh, let it be mine.* Bone loved his own skin, but he loved her more. Gaunt looked around frantically for anything left to throw that wasn't a human being. She refused to accept any such calculation; let them all be smashed against a mountain before they sacrificed each other. But self-sacrifice was just the kind of flamboyant gesture her husband might try . . . once.

Then, "Lightweight," Snow Pine said, and spun the scroll in her hands. "Listen! Who needs to pilot this vessel?"

"I would raise my hand," Haytham said, fingers flickering a discreet distance over the sigils of the brazier, "but I am otherwise occupied."

There was a pause. "Should I spare breath, then," Northwing asked, "declaring that my will is helping keep us among the living? When lack of that breath may bring disaster?"

The next eruption of lightning was not quite as close, but there were two of them. The ger rocked like a boat.

"I understand!" Gaunt said, laughing. "Why didn't I see it? The scroll!"

"Yes!" said Snow Pine. "An army could vanish into it, and it would get no heavier. Some of us can disappear for a while, making the balloon rise. All right, then! Liron and I will go! If we don't lift enough, more should follow!" Flint took Snow Pine's hand, the one that held the scroll, and he vanished.

At the same moment lightning hit the canopy.

In the blazing concussion, the felt and bamboo that shielded Snow Pine from the elements was disintegrated. In the bloody light of sunset she fell through the gap, still clutching the scroll. Gaunt screamed and lunged after her.

She failed to catch her, and lost her own balance.

As she tumbled from the balloon, Gaunt saw Snow Pine vanish into the scroll, which fell near Gaunt's own path of descent. *Of course*, she thought. *And it's my salvation too, if I can only reach it.*

She tried twisting in the air, and her fingers inched closer as the mountain rock raced toward her.

Suddenly a blast of wind snatched the scroll away from her, whipping it like a stick caught by a hunting hound. It rushed away toward the northeast. Toward Spydbanen.

An icy slope rose up to meet her.

CHAPTER 5

HUGINN

"Tell me your name."

A madman on a horse had appeared out of nowhere, leapt off, and proceeded to seize Innocence where he lay in his comfortable spot upon the windy grassland. Innocence had just wanted to rest for a little, while he gathered his strength. He was sure he would rise again soon. The terrible cold of his aimless stumble across the plain had ended, and now a warm, peaceful feeling had come over him. All would be well except for the crazy horseman, who kept asking—

"Tell me your name!"

"Innocence . . ."

"What?"

"Innocence . . . Gaunt . . ."

"Speak up! Tell me your name!"

The man was a balding, red-bearded, stout man in a heavy robe of blue wool. Innocence could tell he was balding because he'd removed his thick cap and was stuffing Innocence's head into it.

"Innocence." He felt he should be saying "Askelad" to preserve his anonymity, but it was hard to feel concern about anything, least of all his identity. He wished the boorish Kantening would leave him alone. Instead the man was wrapping a blanket around him. It was red, woven with pictures of horses.

"Drink this." A flask was shoved against his nose. It smelled of brandy.

"I don't . . . don't feel like . . ."

"I don't give a fart! Drink it!"

It tasted of brandy too. And maybe moss. He no longer felt so comfortable. Something was wrong, but he couldn't articulate it.

"What's your name?" The man was stuffing some kind of bread in his mouth. This time Innocence didn't argue.

"Innocence."

"You're the best-named person I've ever met, Innocence. How the hell did you come to be out here, dressed for indoors? Never mind. Drink more."

"Glg. I . . . I was escaping . . ."

"I smell a good story. Never mind. You're going for a horse ride."

The man was stronger than he looked. Innocence found himself flopped upon his stomach onto the man's steed, which looked like a shaggy brown pony, so thick with fur Innocence wondered if it was part sheep. Innocence giggled. The horse whinnied.

"What's funny?" the man demanded as he tied Innocence to the horse. "You think dying of exposure is funny?"

"No, sir . . ."

"You will live to be mocked, boy, I promise you that. I will change your name and send you back in time and put you in a saga. But you will be mocked, sure as they call me Huginn Sharpspear. What is your name?"

"Innocence." The name Huginn Sharpspear was somehow familiar, but Innocence couldn't place it.

"You'll be a little less innocent now. Here we go."

The ride was bumpy, and the conviction grew in Innocence that Huginn Sharpspear was deliberately seeking the roughest ground, trying to jar all the comfort out of Innocence. He complained, and Huginn responded that he was going slowly and carefully. The man was clearly a born liar.

Every so often, if Innocence grew quiet, Huginn stopped this unseemly haste and demanded yet again to know Innocence's name, or the names of his parents, or his homeland, or his trade.

"Assistant tavernkeeper? The Pickled Rat?" Huginn laughed. "I know that place! They threw me out for singing too loud! Almost there, tavern boy, and then there'll be more brandy for you." Huginn made it sound like a threat.

Mooing, snorting, the smell of manure—they'd reached a farm. "Sturla's Steading," Huginn said as he unbound Innocence and hauled him off the horse. "Before Sturla, my father, came, it was nothing but difficult soil and a cold river. Now it's difficult soil, a cold river, and a farm." After verifying the lad could walk, albeit in a wobbly fashion, Huginn led him into a large house composed of stone, wood, and sod, carved from the side of a low, grassy hill. Windows with real glass gleamed from the thatch, and three chimneys peeked from the grass, spewing smoke. Huginn was bellowing orders and a number of men, women, and children rushed this way and that as Innocence was led into a long hall festooned with hanging fish and meats, with a hearth in its midst.

Huginn set him down near the hearth. A straw-haired woman with a strong physique, weathered face, and piercing blue eyes brought him broth. After he managed to get it down, the couple got Innocence to remove his wet clothes and put on new ones. Then came blankets and more broth, and sweet rye bread, and a bowl of something like thick, milky, soup but with honey on top. He still didn't want to eat, but the woman kept fussing at him.

"Should we not put him in the bedroom?" she asked Huginn. "There'll be a lot of commotion out here."

"He needs commotion, Hekla. He's gone soft in the head. If I didn't know better I'd say he got carried off by the hidden folk. He wasn't too far from the Moss-Stone. More likely somebody left him to die, part of a feud. I'll get a story out of it, you watch."

"Just so long as it doesn't keep you from meeting the chieftains. Winter's harsh this year. You'll have trouble traveling."

"Ah, fuss and fuss! Give me a few minutes with each and I'll win them over."

"It's not a small matter, Huginn Sharpspear, asking them to support your patrons. You need to be on your way, to have support for the Spring Assembly. Otherwise your position will be weak come summer and the Althing—"

"Plans and plans! Man is the sword, but woman is the hand that swings it. All will be well, Hekla. My benefactors will see to it. But let's speak no more of that. The boy's reviving."

It was true. Innocence felt stronger; indeed he felt aquiver from all the food. He tried to rise, but Hekla scolded him back down.

"I feel fine," he protested.

"Sometimes people get wobbly after a spell like this," Hekla said. "You stay put." She asked Huginn's favorite questions, and so he had to repeat many things about his origins. It was too late to take back "Innocence," and he thought it best not to be too detailed about his experiences with the uldra. Nevertheless, he couldn't think of a better explanation for how he'd gotten there. So in the end he said, "I don't know what happened. I went to bed in Fiskegard and woke up here, near a huge boulder."

"That settles it. The hidden folk got you. Stories say, sometimes they just grab a person and let him go, like cats toying with mice."

"So I'm still in the Bladed Isles?"

"That's an outlander name for Kantenjord, but yes. You're in Oxiland."

Innocence tried to remember what Freidar and Nan had said of that island. "Volcanoes. Plains. Wind. Farmers and ranchers. You came from the other islands so that no king or chieftain could rule over you. You have a council, the Althing, that makes decisions."

"My," Hekla said, "someone is book-learned. You might use this one when arguing the law, Huginn."

"Book-learned maybe, but not clever. Not if he was out on the plains like that."

"The uldra got him."

"Indeed?" Huginn sounded skeptical, but he added, "You'll have much to tell me, lad."

"I don't remember anything," Innocence said.

"That sometimes happens too," Hekla said.

"And sometimes," Huginn said, "inconvenient people are left to die by unscrupulous people. If you remember anything, you should tell us. I am trained in the law and have won many cases. If you have enemies, they too must submit to the law."

"Huginn Sharpspear!" Hekla said. "Can't you see he needs rest, not your antics?" Huginn made a dismissive gesture and walked back toward the entrance. Innocence made to follow him, though he still felt weak.

"Rest, boy." Hekla pushed him back down. Even though there were young people about (Innocence could sense them sneaking peeks at him when their chores brought them near) she did not seem particularly motherly. It was strange that Nan, with no children in her life, had been so gentle, while Hekla, with a whole band of them, seemed brusque and matter-of-fact. And yet. He owed Hekla, and especially Huginn, his life.

"Thank you," he said, resigning himself to the prison of blankets. "I know I could have died."

"Ah," Hekla said, "then you are becoming less of an innocent, Innocence. We pride ourselves on strength in Oxiland, but only a fool goes out there underdressed."

"Wait . . ." He hesitated, fearing a foolish question. "I know the name Huginn Sharpspear. Is he named after the author of the *Elder* and *Younger Sagas*?"

"Ha! That would amuse him. He is the author of the *Elder* and *Younger Sagas*."

"What? What is the year and day?"

She frowned. "It is the hundred and tenth year since the first Althing. The eleventh year since Princess Corinna of Soderland became queen in all but name. The year 1096 in the Eldshore calendar. The third day of Yulemonth. Why do you ask?"

"I'm relieved it's 1096. But last I knew it was the thirteenth day of Frost-month. Over half a month ago."

"It's said that time is twisted in the realms of the hidden folk. I think that's what became of you, lad, though Huginn dislikes the idea."

"There's another thing. I thought I might have traveled back into history. I just assumed Huginn Sharpspear must be long dead."

She smiled. "No, though he'd enjoy the notion. He is a born talker, that one. Talked me into many things as well. He can lead a farm, or a foamreaving band, but his great gift is arguing the law. And yet I think he's his truest self when he makes tales. His greatest fame is based on the sagas he tells from these parts, stories from these, our family's lands . . . Moss-Stone included. Yet he rejects anything with a hint of the otherworldly, always prefers the cold, human explanation."

"I heard that!" Huginn bellowed from where he stood directing farmhands near the door. "I disagree, Hekla. Human explanations are hot and bloody, and rarely will supernatural beings improve on the drama to be found there."

"Yet, you put your share of omens, magic swords, and monsters in your tales."

"One must give the people what they want." Huginn took his farm business outside.

Hekla shook her head. "A changeable, distractible man. He has always needed a woman to keep him from wandering off a cliff. Even at the brink of his great triumph."

It made Innocence uncomfortable to be this stranger's confidant. He tried to change the subject. "I thank you for your hospitality. I'll travel as soon as I can."

"Tomorrow, perhaps. You bear watching." She sighed. "Men and boys and your foolishness. Never admitting weakness. Where will you go?"

"I need to return to Fiskegard." But he doubted it as he said it. Originally he'd only planned to stay with Freidar and Nan until he'd mastered enough Kantentongue and earned enough coin to venture out on his own. He'd supposed he would seek out Deadfall and try to puzzle out his power.

"You and Huginn seem to know many things," he said. "Have you heard any rumors of strange flying things in the sky?"

Hekla looked at him sharply. "What have you heard about flying things?"

"Uh . . . I've heard of carpets that can fly through the sky."

Hekla relaxed. "No, I've heard no such story. Oh, and Huginn isn't my husband."

"Oh?" Innocence was shocked. And he was feeling overly confided in, once again.

"He is an old philanderer. He has a wife, far across the island, who will not speak to him—and who could blame her, with all his cheating? She was long gone when I met him. I accept him for all his faults, for I am a fractured soul myself, too wild for any but a wild man. None of the children about here are mine, for I can bear none. But many of them are his."

Innocence had no idea what to say to all this.

"You have seen very little of the world, have you?"

Hekla's tone, part compassion, part pity, irritated him. He answered, "I have seen the Dragonstorm at the heart of the Ruby Waste. I have beheld the waterwheels of Loomsberg and the thousand towers of Palmary. I have glimpsed the glittering guts of the Moon Pit and haunted ruin of Annylum, abandoned in the Sandboil. I have circled the spires of Mirabad and the Vault of Heaven in Archaeopolis. I have seen what I have seen."

Hekla inched back. "I do not know what to make of you. Except this. You must rest."

She left him then, and his sleep had none of the seductive warmth of his near death, but it was sleep, and he accepted it without battle.

It was decided (not without acrimony) that at first light Huginn would proceed with Innocence to the homestead of one Jokull Loftsson, beside the sea. From there, Innocence could travel by boat to Smokecoast.

"There's not much of a town at Smokecoast," Huginn explained in the dark of the morning while Innocence gobbled breakfast. "There's not much of a town anywhere in Oxiland. But there are many farms in that area, and a good anchorage. You might find a ship. Now, I'm obligated to visit Jokull for the Yule season. But it's also a political meeting. You've said you know your letters?"

"Yes," Innocence said, between bites of porridge. He also had bacon and the soupy, milky stuff he now knew to be a cheese, called skyr. He gathered this was a prosperous farm.

"Good. You can take notes, a task for which I'll pay you. You can earn a bit more doing chores after the feasting. That should get you to Smokecoast, where there'll be plenty of work for a strong back till a ship comes."

"Thank you."

The two set off before dawn, fording a river and riding north. Beyond the steading lay snow-dusted brown grass and dark mountains, and it occurred to Innocence this was a realm quite unlike his prior experiences. It did not seem whimsical, like the Peculiar Peaks, nor monumental like the Worldheart Mountains, nor hostile like the Desert of Sanguine Silence. Human habitation had barely scratched it, and where it did the results were not inspiring—like soaring Qushkent or splendid Amberhorn—but homey. Even Fiskegard had presented a soaring grace with its vaulting mountains. Regarding Oxiland was like becoming open to the void, like gazing up into the dark between the stars.

They rode the small shaggy horses of this land, and soon Innocence was envying their coats. For his part he wore a heavy cloak and thick-woven sweater that had made him perspire miserably indoors. Out here he was grateful for them. The wind whistled through the rocks of the plain in a voice that sounded lonely and grieved, and that hit his face like invisible stinging insects. He was glad of the oversized wool mittens Hekla had stuffed on him at the last minute. They made it harder to control the horse whose thick hair he envied, but he'd have trouble with frozen hands too.

Another thing he envied was Huginn's horsemanship. He'd ridden nothing before but a magic carpet. It was not good practice for horses. The Oxilanders made riding seem easy enough, but his mount sensed a novice and amused herself by tormenting him. Early on, when they traversed a boulder-filled hollow to escape the wind, the horse rambled under an outcropping and knocked Innocence off.

"That was on purpose!" Innocence accused, brushing dust away.

Huginn laughed. "I should have supplied you with stirrups, such as the steppe nomads use."

Curiosity overcame Innocence's annoyance as he climbed back on. "You know of them?"

"Do you think us all country bumpkins?" Huginn teased as he led them once again through the tumble. "I was educated at the house of Jokull Loftsson, where we are headed now. There are men more wealthy, and more powerful, than he. But among the high, there is none more learned, and more respected. The uncrowned king of Oxiland we call him, and bear in mind, boy, how we prize our freedom. It takes much to win a title such as that." He paused, as though seeing something far beyond the plain. "Much indeed."

"We seem to be taking a very meandering route to this Loftsson." Innocence was glad to escape the wind, but it did seem peculiar that they'd mostly avoided what passed for roads.

"Ah, for a lowly man this would be a long route, but for a man of station this is a shortcut. Can you untangle my riddle?"

Innocence felt fully occupied keeping warm and staying on a horse, but he forced himself to think. "You don't want to be seen. Or at least, not identified. Then you'd have to stop and talk."

"Yes. If we went as the crow flies to every farm between mine and Jokull's, we'd be an extra day. To reach him by the feast of Saint Kringa, we would have to cut every visit short. All would be offended. This way, no one has anything of me at all, but no inkling that they should have. And no one is offended."

"But we are exposed to a bitter gale," Innocence couldn't help but remark, "with no warm fires in between."

"You call this a gale? It's merely a *stinningskaldi*. I've seen a *rok* or three that would chill your blood! We won't have one of those, Swan willing, but we may see an *allhvasst* before we're done."

"You are teasing me again, as with the horse." Innocence adjusted himself, for he and the blanket had begun leaning like a tree scoured by a storm.

"Ha! Come along! We'll teach you to ride yet, lad, and the fifty words for wind."

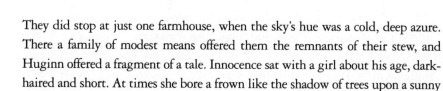

They did stop at just one farmhouse, when the sky's hue was a cold, deep azure. There a family of modest means offered them the remnants of their stew, and Huginn offered a fragment of a tale. Innocence sat with a girl about his age, dark-haired and short. At times she bore a frown like the shadow of trees upon a sunny path, and at others a grin like sunlight glinting on a newly snatched river stone.

He grew acutely aware of her and kept wondering, as Huginn spoke, if she was looking at him. He would often glance at her to check and was always disappointed, or perhaps relieved.

THE ARRIVAL OF THE VINDIR

Long ago, when the sun rose in the south and set in the north, there was a land beloved of Arthane Stormeye, chief of the gods who dwelled in the icy Surmount. In that land there were things we would recognize today: fjords and mountains, glaciers and moraines, rivers and grasslands. And too, there were people that we would recognize, people who struggled and fought and performed deeds worthy and dishonorable.

That age ended when the gods of Surmount warred with their cousins in the distant South—what is now a place beyond even the empires of the East. For their warring changed the course of the sun so that it rose and set in the places we expect today. The fair realm of Vindheim, crowned with ice, became a sun-scoured land, and in the tumult it was mostly drowned, so that only a few islands remained to mark Vindheim's passing. The gods withered, and in time Arthane himself perished; yet before these events he had placed dreams in the mind of one man, Orm, who was his son by the mortal woman Bergljot. Arthane bade Orm build vessels and depart Vindheim with all his kin.

Thus when the sun's course changed, and the seas were tormented, and the frozen lands became hot, Orm's folk sailed. Some of their ships were lost, and they mourned. But Orm had second sight, and steered them to a land that was once warm and was now cold, snow falling upon shriveling rainforest.

The Vindir landed there and forged a peace with the inhabitants, who knew the ways of the land but not the ways of cold. Together the Vindir and these Solir worked together to make this land, Kantenjord, a good place. Over generations the greatest of Vindir and Solir, like Orm's son Torden, or his wife Verden, came to be considered gods, and it is true that great champions rose among them, and others who came from across the Earthe, and some called by Orm's Choosers of the Slain from other times and places—Yngvarr the Fiery, Torfa the Vengeful, Alder of the Earthquake, and many more.

For there came to Orm one day a strange traveler, who spoke with peculiar diction. He said he had maps revealing places in Kantenjord where the right person might travel through the years to reach other times. He called himself the Winterjarl, come from a time of endless snow and ice, the time of Fimbulwinter, the age of ultimate cold and the ending of days.

The Winterjarl sojourned with the Vindir and Solir and taught them much of future days. As more peoples migrated to Kantenjord, the stories of the Vindir and Solir and their deeds became legendary. Orm and Torden and their allies and kin in their time passed away; they were accounted as gods by those who came after. And it may be that by the Winterjarl's teachings the wisdom and power of those folk can wing like ravens down the years to men of these days and in this manner aid their descendants.

There have been many dread winters between the Vindir's time and ours, and it may be that the Fimbulwinter was one of these, and that the doom the Winterjarl foretold was of the old religion and its surrender to the light of the White Swan. Or it may be that this disaster is yet to come. Either way, let us look with respect upon the old ways, for they have things to teach us, even we Swanlings, blessed as they were not.

When Huginn was done, there were other stories told by the grownups, and at some point it was decreed that younger folk should get themselves to bed. The girl showed him his place on the far end of the hearth-room.

"What is your name?" he asked.

She smiled and looked away, as if guessing a great deal from the entrails of that one sentence. "I am Jaska Torsdatter. And you?"

"Innocence Gaunt."

"A strange name."

"I've not heard the name Jaska before either."

"It's a Vuos name."

"Vuos? That is not a word I've heard before."

"The First. My mother's people were the first people of this land."

"Like the Soli?"

"The Soli were latecomers, so my mother said before she died. The Vuos were here before any others." She glanced down the hearth-room, but the adults were paying little notice. "They live in the farthest north of Spydbanen. My father met her foamreaving."

She must have understood his look of horror, for she added, "It was a trading journey, not a raid. She was his first wife, before Oddny there. He has always said he was charmed by the reindeer herders and the beauty of their icy land."

"Have you ever been there?"

"No. I don't think I will ever go."

"Why not?"

Jaska laughed a little. "Girls don't travel! Except princesses."

Innocence thought of Nan and Hekla. "That surely isn't true. Why do you believe it?"

She studied him, as if seeing a serious edge in what she'd regarded as a joke. "I will travel, just a little. To Loftsson Farm, for the feast of Saint Kringa."

"Maybe I will see you there."

"You are a servant," Jaska said, tone expressionless. "My family is not mighty like Jokull's nor famed like Huginn's. But my father has a voice in the Spring Assembly and in the Althing."

"I don't know what that means. I am . . . an orphan. But I have seen many wonders." *None more than you*, he suddenly wanted to say, but he sensed the words would squeak out of him like the voice of a new-hatched chick.

"I must go," Jaska said. "Good-night."

"Good-night."

He could not decide if it was a good night or not. He could not sleep. Something in him wanted to reach out and embrace all the embers of the fire.

He did not see Jaska in the morning. He and Huginn left in the earliest gray, for the latter hoped to reach their destination just before nightfall. Even in the gloom Huginn and the horses seemed to know their business, for all that Innocence felt himself lost.

"She is a serious one, that girl," Huginn said.

"What?" Innocence's mind seemed to return from a voyage over the sea.

"That Jaska, Tor's daughter. It's my opinion that a young man's first love should not be a serious girl. Time enough for sobriety when you're married."

Innocence forgot all Walking Stick's advice on addressing elders. "I did not ask your opinion."

"Oh, ho!" Innocence expected Huginn to take offense, but the Kantening's only further comment was a chuckle.

Strangely, Innocence's thoughts turned not to Jaska but to A-Girl-Is-A-Joy, somewhere far away. If she remained within the enchanted scroll, she would be older now than he. Perhaps years older. Even if she'd stayed within his own timeframe, even if they met again, she would be very different. The thought stabbed at him, making him feel lonelier than any remembrance of his parents.

It was a land for loneliness, he thought. It was a warmer day than yesterday, and as the sun rose, the melting snow revealed a jumbled, rough coastal country. They crossed boulder-filled streams in sight of waterfalls, and a dark volcanic cone rose in the distance. He rubbed at his forehead now and then. It tingled. Something about it itched like an old memory.

When we reach this place, the words came out of cold blue, displacing thoughts of girls and loneliness, *I will take the reins of my life.*

CHAPTER 6

RUBBLEWRACK

A Tumult of Trees on Peculiar Peaks rushed through the stormy skies to an unknown fate in a desolate land. Everyone upon the mystic mountain knew this, and everyone knew that it would take some time to reach this doom, for time ran more swiftly within the scroll than without.

When Snow Pine and Flint appeared and told their tale, the elders of the mountain gathered everyone together.

"We are in a tight spot," Walking Stick said. "It seems someone in Spydbanen wants our company. But the guardian of the scroll can help us."

The self-portrait of the sage painter, often known as Meteor-Plum, spoke. It might have been the first time he'd addressed everyone in his care.

"I can resist," he said. "But it will be a long struggle, and I may fail. If I succeed, our plunge to the ground may be violent. Be patient. Be prepared. I go now to my cave, to begin."

A-Girl-Is-A-Joy crossed her arms, trying to remain calm, remembering.

Back when the scroll had lain upon the bottom of the ocean, endless rains had little by little threatened to drown the Peculiar Peaks. The overcast skies and continual drizzle had been companions of her childhood, and it was hard to remember the more benign skies of her first couple of years.

Suddenly everything had changed. The rain had ceased, replaced by crazy windstorms that blew the clouds overhead at ridiculous speeds. If that weren't enough, later on came the great plunge, when everything in the mountains seemed much lighter. It took very little, in those days, to kick off into the air, drifting among the trees. That was great fun, until the moment when Joy had almost floated over the chasm between their peak and the next. Walking Stick had rescued her, but the momentary terror was nothing compared to the half-hour lecture he'd given her afterward.

It was in the midst of his harangue, surrounded by statues of monks in the hall who'd all looked far friendlier than Walking Stick, that Imago Bone had first entered the monastery with word of her mother.

She knew the thief as hardly any less legendary than Archer Yi, who shot nine of ten suns from the skies, or the sorcerer Hsuan Chieh, master of miniature landscapes and the art of self-shrinking. Yet she recognized him from paintings made by the guardian of this place.

Walking Stick hardly seemed less surprised. "You."

Bone bowed. "Hello, Walking Stick." He looked to her. "Hello, A-Girl-Is-A-Joy."

"You know me?" she said.

"Your mother's often spoken about you."

"My mother? Where is she?"

Bone waved an arm. "Outside. Far outside, I'm afraid. But there is at least a chance we'll be found. I will explain everything I can for the price of a cup of tea."

And so he had. He'd told of Gaunt and Bone's adventures with Snow Pine, seeking the Silk Map as the price of finding the Scroll of Years, and how at last a chance companion had been the one to do the deed, for good or for ill.

"We eventually learned the flying carpet was intelligent," Walking Stick said, nodding. "But we did not know it was a homicidal lunatic."

"It has a complicated nature," Bone said, "or so we guess. There may be hope for it yet. But I'm not an expert on weaving, magical or otherwise."

The guardian of the scroll sighed. "It was I who let your son depart the scroll with the carpet. I did not know its nature. The boy said he wished to test the waters."

"He what?"

"Many of this monastery did so from time to time," Walking Stick said, "attempting to learn if our underwater position had changed. It was hazardous, for the depth of the water could damage a person's body. Yet if the exposure was brief, the monks' arts could restore the swimmer."

"I could draw them back in before lasting harm was done," the tattered man said. "But Innocence and the carpet broke my hold. I sensed great power in the carpet . . . but too late."

Bone scowled. "You didn't think it odd that a carpet had suddenly arrived in your little world?"

"Of course we did," snapped Walking Stick. "But one expects to find danger in the form of warriors and monsters, not interior decorations."

"I counted on you to protect my son. You swore it."

Walking Stick was on his feet then. "I swore I'd put his welfare before the Empire's, and that is no small thing. But I am no god. I call myself Walking Stick, not Walking Perfection."

"You—"

"Leave him alone!" Joy shouted, and she was on her feet too, and everyone was staring at her. Well, she was making a habit of taking tigers by the tail. She lowered her head, but her words were sharp. "You, Imago Bone . . . my friend's father . . . my mother's friend and sometimes her teacher . . . you should not speak thus to Shifu Walking Stick, who has spent almost every waking hour instructing your son and me on how to carry on in the world. If Innocence has a chance of making his way out there, it is because Walking Stick has taught him the many arts." She sat down, but she folded her arms, pinning Bone with her stare.

"Student Joy," Walking Stick said mildly, "it is not your place to chastise your elders."

"But it is fair," Bone said. "You're right, Joy, and I don't mind hearing it. I forgot my manners. That ill becomes me, because I may be a guest for some time. My apologies, Walking Stick."

Walking Stick nodded.

A-Girl-Is-A-Joy looked back on that moment with a mixture of embarrassment and exhilaration, much as one who discovers she's leaped too high. It seemed to her the moment when she began to find her voice.

Bone had been right about one thing; he was indeed a guest for some time. Once the feeling of lightness ebbed, a long winter settled in. Snow fell until the peaks were white, the trees were miniature mountains, and the monastery was some giant arctic beast. Other exercises fell away as everyone labored to clear paths and unburden roofs. With that work done, Joy would burrow through the snow, creating a maze with many places to peek out and throw snowballs. She had too much fun to feel the cold, until a lack of sensation in her fingertips warned her she'd better get to the kitchen and its fire.

She'd been sitting thus, staring at the mark on her right hand, when a strange voice called across the chamber.

"Daughter? My daughter!"

And Snow Pine her mother was there, and the falling feeling was back, though this time entirely inside her stomach. Joy's memories of her mother were blurry things, like distant buildings seen through snowfall. She did have paintings, though, just as Innocence once had his. They embraced.

"Joy . . . how you've grown!"

"I'm told people do that."

"You've also grown sassy."

"My teacher is Walking Stick. You'd be sassy too!"

All that day and the next was a strange flurry of talk, words like snow-flakes, quiet and meandering on their own, but in their aggregate full of tremendous weight. The actual snowfall ended, as the scroll responded to whatever new environment it was in. A feeling of lightness returned, though not to the extent of before.

"They must have taken the scroll to the balloon," her mother said.

"Imago Bone has told us stories of balloon travel. He didn't like it."

"Bone has a tendency to fall off things."

"May I see it? The balloon?"

"I suppose you could. But you must always promise to be careful!"

"Respected and dignified Mother, I'm the one who's been safely tucked away in a scroll while you've been fighting monsters."

Snow Pine had tousled Joy's hair. "Do not attempt to be logical and rea-sonable with me, you who are worth ten thousand gold. It does not work."

Now, in the present, the falling sensation had returned. Again the Peculiar Peaks were a place of dangerous lightness. Lightning storms flashed in the distance. This time Joy stayed carefully upon the mountain but took advan-tage of the chance to practice, for all that the heavens boomed and the sky flickered.

"I think Meteor-Plum may have succeeded!" Liron Flint said as Joy and her mother sparred.

"When we land," Snow Pine said, still maintaining a fighting stance, "I will investigate."

"I'll go with you," said Liron Flint. The explorer had been agitated since he'd arrived from the balloon. Joy thought he felt guilty for abandoning his friends.

"And I," said Walking Stick, still judging the match.

"And I!" said Joy, blocking her mother's sudden attack. "I can at last be useful."

"You can be useful staying safe," said Snow Pine, tapping Joy's shoulder with her gently curved sword.

Joy ducked, ran up a tree, vaulted off, and gave her startled mother a solid kick in the shoulder. "I can be safe out there!" Joy called panting as she sprawled onto the ground.

Snow Pine regained her balance, her expression veering from scowling to thoughtful like a change of the seasons. "I can't abide the thought of losing you again," she said, rubbing her shoulder.

"I was never lost. I was always at home. It was you who were lost. I have never once been away. Let me see the world."

Snow Pine nodded. "All right. Though you may find the world no improvement on your home."

It was not. But it was still wondrous.

Joy emerged upon a snow-covered coastal plain. There were jagged mountains near at hand, but here the terrain had a gentle slope from pale grassland down to a region of splintered dark rock fringed with gray sand. Beyond surged a sea that seemed an extension of the horizon's gray clouds. Seabirds shrieked at Joy, Snow Pine, Flint, and Walking Stick, but other life was not evident.

The Peculiar Peaks of the scroll were of late just as snowy, but there the terrain was spindly, full of precarious rises, twisting trees, and meandering paths. Both this plain and the nearby peaks were novelties. The first was the widest expanse she'd ever seen from the ground. The second was a much more imposing sort of mountain than the whimsical ones of home.

And the ocean! She had not imagined such a shore before, such a feeling of lifeless presence, foaming against the coast like an exhalation. It was a calm sea, and on such a gray day it had no sparkle or reflection, yet its vast blankness kept drawing her eye.

"What do you think of this land, Shifu Walking Stick?"

Walking Stick grunted. "No obvious threats."

"An empty, foreboding place," Flint said.

"Like the edge of the world," Snow Pine said.

"I suspect that would be more interesting," Walking Stick said.

"Really?" Joy piped up, surprised at the adults. "You all don't think this is beautiful?"

"I admit it has a certain harsh attractiveness," her mentor mused, "which under other circumstances I might wish to depict in landscape painting."

"No," her mother said.

Flint scratched his chin and smiled. "I can concede that empty and foreboding can be beautiful in its own way." The smile faded. "Yet I hope that *Al-Saqr* found a more hospitable place to land."

And that it landed at all, Joy thought but decided not to say.

They searched for shelter, so that the scroll could be kept safe and a few of its occupants emerge for a while. A cold wind moaned over the white grassland. "Hey," Joy said, "how about that cave?"

"I think you've indeed found a suitable spot," Flint said. "Well done."

As they entered the cave, which bored into an escarpment with an enormous vertical opening like a keep-sized, irregular keyhole, Joy wondered if she liked Flint's attempts to be friendly with her. She understood why he did it: He was captivated by Joy's mother. Now, she liked Liron Flint, found him thoughtful and amusing. But she was not sure how her mother really felt, and sensed she should not take any side. She had no memory of her father, only paintings made by Meteor-Plum, showing a wild-eyed, friendly-looking, boyish man. Yet she felt a certain loyalty to the father she'd never known.

"This should serve as a campsite," Walking Stick said, returning from the shadows at the cave's far end. "I see no sign of animal habitation."

"That's because they know this place is too cold," Snow Pine said, stamping her feet and shaking her arms.

"Maybe you should warm up in the scroll for a bit?" Flint asked.

"I'd be teased. No, what we need is a fire."

"Hm." Walking Stick surveyed the ground beyond the cave mouth. "Yes, I think we can risk it. Wood looks to be scarce, however. I will go forage."

"I'll go as well," Snow Pine said. "I want to keep moving."

"Me too," said Joy.

"Someone should stay with the scroll," Flint said, though he sounded sad.

"Scream if there's a troll," Snow Pine said.

"That is truly unfunny," Flint said, studying the walls of the cave.

Joy blinked as they returned to the light and shivered as the wind hit them anew. The only fuel to be found was brittle scrub, but there looked to be driftwood on the beaches and dwarf trees higher up. Snow Pine suggested they divide forces; Walking Stick frowned, but studied Snow Pine and Joy and nodded. He proceeded to the beach.

"Are you going to criticize me about something?" Joy demanded as they hiked upslope.

"You must be my daughter," Snow Pine said. "You're angry with me even before I open my mouth! We simply get little time to talk. I still know you so little."

"I apologize, Mother," Joy said, her training in politeness returning. "My whole existence has been grownups instructing, correcting, criticizing. Except for Innocence."

"You miss him."

"I hope he's all right."

"From what I have heard, he has the power to survive out in the world."

"And I do not?" Joy slowed her pace and studied her Runemarked hand.

"I did not say that! Though if you do have power, I confess I'm worried about that too."

"Mother . . . this land feels familiar to me. As though I've dreamed about it. As though it's always been calling to me. And . . . I'm afraid."

Snow Pine hugged her. "Come on. Let's snap some branches. Destruction can be very satisfying."

It was. They pretended to be monsters, then swordfighters, then ancient ladies with canes, then swordfighters who were also ancient ladies with canes. Who fought monsters. It was like playing with Innocence again. The thought made her wistful, and she noticed the sun. "Maybe we should be going back?"

Snow Pine said, "We haven't gotten much wood. There's a stand of trees over there . . ."

"I'll go get some. I'm fast. You can finish up here. I'll be back soon."

"Joy—"

"I'll be fine!"

Truth was, it was a delight to run a little on her own. And she would stay in sight of her mother the whole time.

However, they'd misjudged the distance, and Joy found herself approaching the dead trees for longer than expected. Walking Stick had warned her this was a normal error for novice travelers. Knowing she'd made an error only made her more determined to wrest some good from the mistake. She forced herself forward just another five minutes, ten, fifteen. The longer the interval, the more foolish she felt, and the more determined to accomplish something to make up for the embarrassment.

The sun was distressingly high when she arrived at the copse of dead trees. The ground was covered in caked mud. A scree of boulders had fallen all around. It was a desolate place, but at last she'd found her firewood. She looked over her shoulder and saw the distant figure of Snow Pine starting to walk toward her. Expecting a scolding, she began breaking off branches.

Steel-gray clouds covered the sun, and a false twilight covered the land.

There came a great rumbling, and she feared a rockslide. The boulders were unmoving, however, as far as the eye could see . . . no. There was a collection or rocks to the north that appeared to be forming themselves into a larger shape, blocking the way back to Snow Pine.

It was like watching a collection of moths tumble toward a candle flame, only instead of singeing themselves they congealed into a larger mass, and instead of flying off they remained in that position.

Big as a barn, the humanoid figure thus formed looked this way and that.

Joy stood very still, a clutch of branches in her hand.

A long nose of granite peered from a face pale and moss-spotted, beneath hair of gray-white lichen. Mismatched slabs of obsidian might have been fist-sized eyes. The musculature of the entity would have driven Persimmon Gaunt, the amateur geologist, or Liron Flint, the armchair anatomist, to distraction. The left arm had ten smaller rocks in it, the right arm five larger ones. The left arm thus bent more smoothly, but the right arm looked to have a stronger punch. A similar mismatch prevailed with the limbs, with the left leg looking ready to stomp tall men flat, and the right looking spindly as an over-piled cairn.

Joy tiptoed behind a tree.

Nowhere on this assemblage did Joy see living tissue connecting the stones. But there was indeed living material, for a short, stubby evergreen tree twisted out of the stone-thing's back, or what she took for a back.

She did not know what manner of creature this was, but she knew she didn't want to attract its attention. Unfortunately, it lay between her and help. She would have to circle around. Carefully she set down her branches and crept away, before bursting into a run.

Her path took her into a rocky hollow that she hadn't spotted before. Sliding down a slope of sand, she faced a collection of small boulders, set in a surprisingly regular matrix. She expected she would clamber over them, using the back row to launch herself up the far slope.

She had not counted upon several piles of rock and earth behind her rising and advancing. One, composed mainly of thin granite spars, was spindly enough to make the first one seem squat. Another looked like a humanoid pile of gray dust. A third entity much resembled the first, except that pale lichen wreathed it like a sash. A fourth was a rough-looking humanoid mass of clay, with agates for eyes. And a fifth seemed an agglomeration of scores of smooth river-stones, impossibly balanced; its rockfall of a head had empty spaces for "eyes" and a "frown."

She had the impression they were all frowning as they approached her.

"Um," she said in thin hope of conversation, "hello!" She repeated herself in Kantening. "*Morn?*"

"*Nei!*" said one, and "*Slem!*" said another, their voices like stones falling into a stream.

"I don't understand," she said, her heart feeling as though a rock pounded her chest. Kantentongue phrases babbled and echoed through her thoughts, but she'd never imagined first using them on monsters. She couldn't think clearly enough to use them.

"*Jente! Dra!*" intoned another of the entities.

She thought they were commanding her to leave, and she devoutly wanted to. But she saw no path except through the garden of stones, or else back through the creatures of earth and rock.

Fear made her mind struggle for a solution. She remembered standing at a porthole of *Al-Saqr*, looking down at an expanse of red desert dappled with evening shadows. Beside her Walking Stick had been saying, "Enliven the chi within you, and you can float to the clouds, even as does this balloon."

"Can you do such a thing?" she'd challenged. "I have never seen you."

"Were I the stern disciplinarian you believe me to be, you would be smarting at your smart remark. No, I cannot truly fly, as the legendary immortals could . . . or perhaps can. Nonetheless you have seen me kick myself into the air and walk along treetops. That is the limit of my skill—but perhaps you have a small chance of surpassing me. If you work at it."

That was to goad me, she'd thought. *Never a word of praise, only a grunt if I get something right, never letting me be proud, always another level to attain. But if I attain enough, I can escape him forever, find another teacher. Or learn on my own. And Snow Pine, my mother? She can join me if she wants.*

The exchange, and her silent response, flickered through her mind in a moment, and a set of exercises uncoiled in memory like a gossamer stairway leading over the boulders. She ran and leapt.

Whereas before, the warm expression of vital breath always faded as she jumped, this time something changed. The palm of her right hand felt as though it had pressed against hot metal. Energy pulsed from the mark upon her hand and through her body. Pain wracked her, as though a series of muscles were simultaneously wrenched in the wrong direction. It was a dreadful sensation—

But she experienced it high in the air.

She landed on the slope of the hollow's far side. From there she spun, forcing herself not to yelp from the aches within her. She'd done it! She could handle anything. Even facing down five (and now she guessed their nature) trolls!

It was surprisingly easy to glean the trolls' reactions. Their stony or dusty or clay faces proved unnervingly malleable, as they all stared slack-jawed—if they could be said to have jaws—at Joy. She resisted the urge to mock. Some of her language lessons came back to her. Perhaps one of her basic phrases could help.

She raised her hands, but she was careful to keep them clenched. Something told her not to reveal the Runemark upon her right hand.

"Excuse me! I am a traveler! I do not speak Kantentongue! Do you speak Roil?" She almost said, *My friends are nearby* but thought better of it. Best to give nothing away. Was Mother walking into danger even now?

The trolls grumbled among themselves, and the one with the tree growing out of its back reappeared waving an arm and bellowing orders she couldn't follow.

And scores more trolls appeared, approaching the hollow on all sides. Joy was surrounded by these walking hunks of the Bladed Isles. She shivered but refused to show fear. The trolls did not advance farther than a few yards, but the nearest pointed at her, and then inland. Clearly, she was meant to follow.

She considered leaping out of there. Yet having tried that trick once, it seemed her body rebelled against any further esoteric uses of chi.

Her heart pounded. Perhaps by accepting capture, she could save her companions from detection. It seemed she was going to have an adventure, like her mother before her. Curiously, she smiled.

At least they hadn't tried to devour her.

Thus began A-Girl-Is-A-Joy's sojourn among the trolls.

CHAPTER 7

MUNINN

At some point in her mad, scrambling, careening slide down the icy slope, Gaunt's head met an inconvenient extrusion of rock. For a moment survival was forgotten, as she mentally flew to a distant blazing nebula upon wings of pain. When she again perceived her surroundings, she was hurtling down an icy slope with her thick Karvak deel acting as a sort of sled. Under other circumstances it might have been fun. Yet the current circumstances included a slide toward a rugged moraine of jagged rocks, itself sloping down into a beautiful, steep-sided valley blue with sheer-edged shadowed tarns, each looking eager to drown reckless poets.

Attempting to halt her descent with her hands, she couldn't find purchase. Snow sprayed behind her in a powdery flurry every time she tried. Using her feet sent her tumbling. Her stinging hands next reached for the magic sword at her belt, for she hoped to spear the snow with her blade. But she couldn't free it. She did manage to unsheathe a dagger, so she kicked and spun and stabbed.

The force of her descent sent the dagger flying wildly out of sight.

Her heart hammered. She didn't try her second dagger. Instead she kicked and squirmed, and instead of sliding to her doom on her face, she once again descended on her back.

She loosed her sword-belt, forcing her fingers to take their time. Slow unknotting, slow unknotting, but soon enough swift action—Now!

She had the sword. But she still had no leverage to draw it. So she rolled wildly and stabbed the snow with the sheathed weapon.

Now she had purchase, and when it came it surprised her, nearly ripping the sword from her hands. She clung with a howl of defiance. In that moment the whole mountain range was the enemy of Persimmon Gaunt.

She was motionless for many seconds before her body believed it. She had difficulty distinguishing the receding thunder with the pulsing of her own blood near her ears. She lay sideways on the slope, staring at snowy peaks thick with black, oblong pools of morning shadow. She looked toward her feet and saw a precipitous edge ten yards downslope.

Deep breath. You're alive. The rest is detail.

As she began digging into the snow with her remaining dagger—this time she didn't lose it—a scream broke the silence.

The source of the bloodcurdling howl moved rapidly enough to change pitch. Abruptly it ceased. By now the scream sounded familiar.

"Bone!" she called out. "Bone! Are you there?"

"Gaunt," came a weak and muffled voice. "Hello. I'm here to rescue you."

She managed to wiggle enough to look in his direction. Bone lay spread-eagled upslope, one hand clutching a rope stretching to a grappling hook far above.

"That rope," Gaunt called. "I assume it was meant to be attached to *Al-Saqr*."

"Alas! The balloon did not agree with my plan."

"It was a gallant effort! At the very worst it's allowed us a final conversation, my love."

"True, Gaunt! I propose survival as the topic of the day."

"An old classic! Now, it seems to me a rope with a hook is a very useful asset . . ."

It took a long time, during which the storm clouds dispersed and the rising sun chipped away at the shadows of the mountains, but Gaunt was able to dig in sufficiently that she could at last rest her aching arms, and meanwhile Bone managed to ascend to the hook and with its aid shift his position sideways and down, until the rope could reach Gaunt.

At last they were together, and the plan became one of shameless kissing.

"The lengths you will go to," Gaunt said, "to get me alone."

"Clever, aren't I?"

"Oh, that remains to be seen."

"Well, if we're not clever, no one will see our remains."

"What I do see, good thief, is a rocky shelf, down that way."

"Ah," he said, before tasting her lips one last time, "to business. It will be good to stand on good, solid rock."

"We'd best not delay," she sighed, noticing a sheen upon the surrounding white. "The sun's melting the upper layer of snow."

"You mean," he said, aggrieved, "this landscape is becoming *more* slippery? I already hate the Bladed Isles."

They took their time and at last stood triumphantly upon the outcropping. The sound of the wind was like the world taking generations to intone the word *hush*.

"This," Bone declared beside her, "would have been a magnificent place to die." He gestured grandly.

It was as though she really saw it for the first time, and she had to agree. The land seemed absurdly vertical, fangs of gray stone with spittle of shining ice. Here and there meadow-covered plateaus sliced the lower heights above shadowed byways of forest and gorges echoing with frothing rivers. Gaunt had seen vaster mountains at the heart of the continent, but this terrain seemed so enamored of gleaming heights and forested plunges it made her eyes blink and her neck hurt.

That wasn't all that hurt. Gaunt's head still afflicted her with swirls of pain, probably the fruits of the violent descent. She rubbed her skull gently. All her wits still seemed to be in there.

"Alone again, on the road," Gaunt said.

"It's been some time," Bone answered. "Not the road. The 'alone.'"

"Ever since we fled to the East, there've been friends. There were some terrible times. Sometimes we were apart. But there was always someone to lean on."

"I miss them too. And worry for them."

"Well," Gaunt said, "we won't find them by staying up here."

"We'll have to take this descent delicately."

"I don't feel there's anything delicate about me anymore."

"Heh. Well, we'll take it beautifully then."

"*Ja?*" came a gruff voice from beyond a pine door.

"Uh, *morn?*" said Gaunt.

There came a sound of heavy movement and the scrape and clink of weapons unsheathed or pulled from mountings.

"It's not exactly 'morning,'" Bone said, looking around at the creeping darkness. It was the second evening since their landfall. The sky was cobalt-blue overhead, and they were footsore and hungry.

"Hush," Gaunt said. "I'm trying to say 'hello.' *Morn! Unnskyld! Jeg er, um, Svanøy kylling. Hjelp?*" She again surveyed this cottage built into the side of a hill, turf merging with the roof so that the chimney peeked through grass. Smoke coiled overhead. A minute ago, it had looked homey.

The door creaked open. An old man with bloodshot eyes and a black-bladed axe glared at them. His gray beard, going white in patches, was unnervingly decorated with half a dozen interwoven bird bones.

"Goodwife," he said carefully in Roil, lowering the axe, "you must need help, if you go around saying you are a chicken from Swanisle." He peered at Bone. "This is your rooster, then?"

"I beg your pardon—" objected Bone.

"That's about right," Gaunt said.

"Come in. You do look like scrawny birds. So. Where did you come from?"

"A flying craft," Gaunt said, looking around at the cramped interior. In a way it was cousin to the ger, for tools and foodstuffs hung from various parts of the ceiling, and a hearthfire glowed at the center. The whole house smelled of smoke and stew.

A woman many seasons younger than the man, blonde with eyes like mountain pools, regarded them with dagger drawn. Two yellow-haired youths, the older bearded, the younger absurdly tall, backed away, lowering a sword on the one hand and a spear on the other.

"A flying craft?" said the old man. "Drawn by sky-goats, no doubt. Ha. Well, your business is your business. But you will pay me in talk, as you must be short on coin."

They did have some coin at that, but Gaunt reflected talk was cheaper. "I am Gaunt. This is Bone."

"The name is Muninn. Muninn the Sure-Handed, I was. But now folk call me Crowbeard."

"You don't say," Bone said.

"This is Ylva, my wife, and these are Loke and Ulf, sons of a fallen comrade, my wards. Don't mind them staring. They mean no harm. They see few outlanders. They don't speak Roil. I used to have more—and wiser—servants. But I am not what I was." He set his axe upon hooks set in the timbers. As he did so, his hands shook and firelight glinted wildly on the axe-blade.

This done, he said, "You may share our stew."

This proved a mysterious affair, a brown sludge with a crust of fat. It might have unnerved Gaunt under other circumstances but she and Bone accepted gratefully. She thought she detected beans, carrots, peas, and a hint of lamb. Perhaps she was just being optimistic. She was glad of it, though, and of the crusty old bread she used to capture the last drops.

At some point she realized she was eating so heartily, she was letting Bone do most of the talking. This was not always a good idea.

"And you have no children?" Muninn was saying.

"We . . . long for children," Bone said. "Children are much on our minds. And you?"

"All dead foamreaving. And what trade did you say you were in?"

"Oh, this and that," Bone answered.

"You are a merchant?"

"I sometimes answer to that description."

Muninn studied him. His lips parted in a smile appropriate for watching an old enemy slowly sliding off a cliff. "There is no need to hide. We are here at the edge of the Gamellaw. You may admit you've also been a foamreaver."

"That word again," Bone said. "What?"

"The Gamellaw's the region of the old laws," Gaunt broke in, "where the old gods are followed, and there are no nations as such. And as for foamreaver, he means a pirate, more or less. Though the term also means someone who raids coasts and who conducts honest trade, as the tide takes him." As she spoke, she saw silent Ylva staring at her, as though Gaunt had sprouted a tail.

"Aha!" Bone said. "No, I've never been one for—foamreaving—but rather I like to live by my wits and look for opportunities where they come. Battle and I do not agree with each other."

"You are saying," Muninn said, his expression blank, "you never fight?"

Bone waved a jagged shard of old bread like a blade. "I will fight if need be, but only then. It seems a waste of effort and bodily fluids. Sometimes the best course is to run, far and fast."

Muninn's smile was thin. "You are a Swanling, then. One who worships peace."

"I respect the Swan, but I can't claim to be one of her people. Gaunt is more devout."

"And you," Muninn asked her after a pause, glancing at Crypttongue. "Do you have a trade?"

"Sometimes I am a poet," Gaunt said.

"Ah? Do you know sagas? Praise poems? Songs of the gods?"

"The forms I know are all southern."

"Let's hear something anyway," Muninn said.

Gaunt knew she was to sing for her supper, or recite anyhow. She felt very conscious of the axe on the wall and the sword at her back. "I'll give you part of the story of Wiglaf, which is told in the Baelscaer region of County Sere, a land your people settled long since."

Crowbeard's wife stood, looked at Gaunt, and said one word. "*Skjøge.*" With that she retired for the night.

"Ignore her," Crowbeard said, and so she did. Watching the hearth-light she began:

> *Well. We've heard the deeds done by bladed barons*
> *Of Svardmark in far-sped summers, and honors*
> *The Kantenings carried far foamward.*
> *Sigemund Shield-Child, babe bobbing in a broad buckler,*
> *Foundling friendless, by fate repaid: he grew great*
> *And bold below heaven, and hale he met his end.*
> *A son he sired, a friend to his folk, sent from on high:*
> *Wayland his name, wrathful war-smith, whose swords,*
> *His mighty arms made leap like lighting,*
> *To split the swamp-bane and pierce the pool-lurk*
> *And dash the dragon witched by northern winds,*
> *Who south to County Sere soared to scour.*
> *But the hand that dealt the death-blow was not Wayland's*
> *But a cousin and comrade, Wiglaf of his warband,*
> *The only thane thereof not to falter and flee.*
> *Wayland, wounded, died with the dragon,*
> *And named Wiglaf heir to hall and home.*
> *Wielded he Schismglass, Wayland's weapon,*
> *Shining servant, stalker of souls.*

As the fire dimmed she told of Wiglaf's early adventures as a chieftain and ring-giver, generous to and beloved of heroes. Yet a darkness crept over

Wiglaf, for unlike Wayland he used his soul-taking sword rashly. In those days giants became rarer, but trolls numerous, and the uldra, as Kantenings called the delven, sometimes made war.

> And, too, raged far-northern foamreavers, bearded berserks,
> And southern charioteers, White Swan's chosen,
> And nithing knaves, bandits of the bogs,
> Cowards in conquest yet terrible in treachery.
> Against all Wiglaf warred, not the noblest, still less the strongest—
> Braver and bolder in combat and craft many were—
> Yet no man who made a life in this land knew better:
> Power will pale, and dinars deceive, youth will yield and love will leave.
> Well he knew Wayland's words, "Each must make an ending.
> So win what you will of glory ere you go. Let your name be known,
> Decked with deeds before death takes its due." So Wiglaf willed.
> But lust for life-fire claimed blade and bearer,
> And Wiglaf warred with Eilifur Ice-Gaze
> Who bore a blade wicked as Wiglaf's.

Here she finished, for it seemed the best conclusion to be had, here in the poem's first third.

"Old days," murmured Muninn, "bold days. When men sought what name they could before fate gave them fit ends. Not this straw-death." He spat the last words. His hands shook. He said more, but it was in the language of his fathers.

In the morning they passed many farms and exchanged cautious waves with many laborers, until they reached a lowland where three streams converged, birthing a marshy delta beside the high cliffs of a fjord. A pair of rune-inscribed stones heralded the beginning of a wooden track across the fen. Soon a town wall came into view—an earthen rampart, really, grass-covered and studded at intervals with wooden watchtowers.

When the guards asked their business in Gullvik Town, Gaunt tried to explain they were up from Swanisle to trade. Their leader seemed bemused by their Karvak deels and nonplussed that anyone with such bad Kantentongue could make it this far north. But he liked the look of their coin.

"That was easy," Bone said once they'd been waved through into the clomping bustle of the wooden streets. "They didn't even mind our weapons."

"Well, that's the Bladelander reputation," Gaunt said. "Ready to trade or fight with anyone."

"Let's concentrate on the first! We might as well try to sell these coats. They're wonderfully warm, but they attract attention."

"Maybe we can buy a bow," Gaunt said. "Or a fiddle," she added, as they heard a bittersweet melody from deeper in, as though played on an instrument with strings of memory and pain.

They didn't manage a bow or fiddle, but they did sell the deels for enough to get winter clothing more typical of the region and a little spare coin. Thus they set out to find lodgings and enjoy the town.

For a while they sought the source of the haunting fiddle music, but it was lost in the sights and sounds. This port was chaotic and charming, and it reeked. It wasn't just the outhouses. At times the place seemed a haven for animals, with people as an afterthought. Chickens and ducks roamed freely. Goats made agitated sounds, to which the cows seemed to voice disapproval. Ravens and seagulls were everywhere, finding much to make meals of.

"It makes sense they call it Gull-something," Bone said.

"Actually, I think the 'Gull' means gold," Gaunt said. "It's a place for business."

Many kinds of industry conspired to give the avians their beloved garbage. These were grouped by eponymous streets—Butcher Street, Parchment Street, Fishmonger Street, Gold Street, Shield Street. All this was intriguing, but they had a more immediate interest. They strolled over a bridge, past fishing children, descended onto Tavern Street, and found the least busy example of the local watering holes.

Within, all was quiet agitation. It was late afternoon, and workers were beginning to drift in. There were old men arguing with young men, in a way Gaunt was all too familiar with. To her mind the fury was false on either side; for the old truly ranted at time, and the young at fate. They should be allies against both, but time and fate tricked them and set them against each other.

"Ale and rumors?" Bone said.

"Yes, I'm feeling the need for both."

In the end they were distracted from the ale by a bottle of Eldshoren wine, and as they shared and sipped they listened to the Kantenings laughing and complaining, lamenting and contemplating.

"I hear horse thieves made off with some of Bengt Sunderson's herd, up Gamellaw way."

"Those Nine Wolves again."

"Wouldn't bet against it. Telling you, they must have allies in this land. Someone respectable."

"The Gull-Jarl'll settle it, sooner or later."

"He's not the only one with troubles. Peasants are up in arms down by Svanstad. Trouble for the princess."

"No problem of ours. We're free farmers, we are."

"They say the Lardermen are helping them."

"Someday someone's going to take an army into Splintrevej and hang the lot of those pirates."

"I won't be in it. Splintrevej is haunted. They say it's never satisfied till it drowns its victim for the year."

"There's weirder things happening than pirates and horse thieves. Old Gerta's eldest girl saw a dragon flying south. Haven't seen one of those in a while."

"What sort of dragon?" Gaunt tried to ask in Kantentongue. She got funny looks but also an answer.

"Orb Dragon."

"I've heard of many a kind of dragon," Gaunt said. "Some you might not even believe. But I've never heard of an Orb Dragon."

"By your accent, you're fresh off a ship. No matter, not everyone hereabouts believes in the Orb Dragons. They're a new thing under the sun, or an old thing newly dusted off. They fly through the air like a round clump of cloud, but with the color of the noonday sky and swifter than anything outside of a diving bird. They always seem to be bearing north, into the Gamellaw, where berserkers and trolls dwell. Some folk say they're dragons who've learned the trick of invisibility, only it doesn't always quite work. Some say they're giant dragon eggs, coming here to hatch. Some say it's a sign we're heading into Fimbulwinter, when the doom of the world will come."

"Pray pardon my lunatic friend, goodwife," said another man. "The term Orb Dragon caught on a while back, and now anything funny-looking in the skies is assumed to be one. We have to have our stories to sustain us through the winter, you see. Alcohol only goes so far! We used to have tales of people abducted and brought underground by the uldra, but now we're just as likely to hear of people swept into the sky in their nightclothes by an Orb Dragon."

"Don't you be laughing at that! A cousin of my Uncle Sten's best friend got taken by an Orb Dragon to the moon, and that man was only known to lie when sober . . ."

A scream cut the air from somewhere outside.

The talking stopped. There came a second scream. It sounded like a girl, asking to be let go.

"Shut up, thrall," Gaunt heard a man's gruff voice say in Kantentongue. "We nabbed you fair and square."

The tavern began returning to normal. Drinks were raised. Talk resumed.

"My brother!" the girl was saying. "Somebody help us! Let him go, he's too young!"

"I'll be the judge of that," Gaunt heard the man say, or so she believed. She looked into the face of one, then another, then a third patron of the tavern. The drinkers looked uneasy, but none seemed to think anything was worth stirring for.

Bone asked, "Trouble?"

"I think a pair of children are being forced into servitude."

"Ah." Bone gulped wine. "We probably shouldn't get involved."

"Most likely."

"We're getting involved, aren't we?" he said, checking his daggers.

"Yes," she said, rising.

"Nice wine," he said.

"Yes."

In a moment they burst onto the street. It wasn't hard to detect where the commotion was coming from. Two burly men with ropes were dragging along a girl and boy dressed in rags. She was perhaps nine, and he eight. Ahead of this procession was a black-bearded mountain of a man, arms as big as Gaunt's legs, with a set of scars to rival Bone's. He carried a whip, brandishing it like an army flag as they crossed the nearby bridge.

Gaunt murmured, "We cut the ropes, the children run, we run ourselves. Yes?"

"Yes. Meet you where the wooden road began?"

"It's a date."

"You want right or left?" Bone asked, cracking his knuckles.

"Left," she said, flexing her arms.

The captors seemed rather obtuse about the two outlanders striding up behind them, or perhaps they were simply unused to opposition. By now she could sense Bone preparing to dash even without a signal, and he, her. They dove in, footfalls clunking onto the bridge planks.

Daggers flashed. The ropes were not particularly thick, and Gaunt expected to cut through them in seconds; then they could flee.

What she did not expect was for the children themselves to flee, before the ropes were even cut.

"They weren't—" Bone began.

"Weren't tied." Gaunt shared an instant's panicked look with her husband. Now the huge man with the whip was laughing, and his men lunging.

Gaunt and Bone jumped off the bridge. (She took left, he took right.) They splashed and swam.

They had not yet escaped. Many men, who'd appeared to have nothing to do with the slaver party, rushed along the right-hand side. She recognized a few of them from the tavern. They threw weighted nets into the water. She saw Bone dive but could not tell if he'd evaded the nets. Down she went, seeking him. The water was unwholesome, but she found him. He was using a weight to keep himself under while he cut the netting with a dagger. She helped.

Together they swam free.

They gasped for breath in the middle of the river, diving again with shouts in their ears.

Reaching the far shore they dragged themselves up and ran through lanes and tripped over chickens and racks of lye-fish and one very stubborn goat. They did not know the layout, however, and they found a dozen ruffians facing them at the harbor. There were no adorable captive children with them. Bone's breath was coming in heaves. He'd lost wind in the river and hadn't recovered it yet. Gaunt had to give him direction.

"Throw and go?" she said.

"Yes," he said, and out came a dagger. Hers was already in hand.

She threw and caught the lead slaver in the cheek. For all the big man's intimidating appearance, his yowl suggested he'd little experience with physical pain.

Bone began his throw—

And the girl and boy they'd tried to rescue ran in front of the wounded slaver, crying out, "Father! Father!"

Bone twisted his body so that the blade dropped into the dirt; and so did he.

Down on one knee, Bone stared at the Kantenings rushing at him. Gaunt yanked him to his feet, and his wits returned.

It was too late. The slavers were enraged, and the two of them were surrounded. The children whom they'd sought to save threw mud and rocks.

Before she knew anything more, she'd drawn Crypttongue and was jabbing at their foes.

A man screamed and dropped, and one of the gems of Crypttongue's hilt glowed. She heard his voice babbling within her mind now, in incomprehensibly manic Kantentongue. She ignored him and turned to a new foe.

"Don't," Bone said. "It changes you."

"How else!"

"We'll find a way! They want our capture, not our deaths—"

He went down. They tripped and tackled him.

Absurd as the thought of beating this many foes might be, Gaunt considered it. The sword felt hungry in her hand.

Yet she hesitated, for Bone was right. She hungered to slay.

While she hesitated, Bone was kicked, jeered at, yanked to his feet, his arms roped behind him. This accomplished, the gang edged warily away from Gaunt.

"Give him back!" She looked this way and that at the bystanders, all of whom merely stared. "Swan's blood, will no one intervene? This is a kidnapping!"

A fiftyish woman in a white robe came forward, a Swan priestess with blonde hair going to white. "What is this, Yngvarr? Are your own children thrall-takers now too?" Her accent marked her as a Swanislander.

"They were necessary, Roisin," said the Kantening with the bleeding cheek. He gave Bone a kick, staring at Gaunt all the while. Bone was able to twist away from the worst of the impact, but she snarled in rage. Yngvarr said, "This man is a criminal by his own admission. And the woman's a murderer."

"I slew in self-defense!" Gaunt answered.

"You are many things, Yngvarr," Roisin said, "but you are not the law. And it is the Gull-Jarl's law that self-defense is permitted, and that no Swanling be enslaved."

A new speaker stepped forward, and Gaunt's fury brimmed over.

It was Crowbeard.

"The woman may be a Swanling," said the old warrior who'd given them shelter. "But the man is not, by his own words. Indeed, he confessed he was a ruffian. If he's not a nithing, he's something near. Thus by old ways and new, he is fit to be a thrall."

Yngvarr rolled his eyes and tossed a bag of coin at Crowbeard's feet. "Now we've paid you, old man. We'll take it from here."

Crowbeard looked suddenly confused, and stricken. "I had thought . . . instead of a fee, you might take me on a venture . . . I've proven my worth. . . ."

There was laughter at that. Yngvarr shook his head. "Take you foam-reaving? Take Muninn Surehand, maybe. But you, old one, you are Crowbeard the Palsied now. Take what you can get."

Gaunt, who cared nothing for Crowbeard's fate, gripped Roisin's shoulder. "We were betrayed."

The priestess's gaze was bleak "Are his words true? Is your man a criminal? A heathen?"

"No!" Gaunt said, envisioning her lost daggers entering Crowbeard's eyes. "He's been in church with me many times."

At once Bone said, "Swan take my life now if I lie! I follow her, and I have repented all the evil ways of my past!"

As of perhaps three seconds ago, Gaunt thought, but she had to admit he sounded sincere. She hoped she wasn't alone in that assessment.

"She does not take or give, like a servant, at our ill-considered oaths," Roisin said, sternness swelling in her voice. She removed her necklace. Alongside a silver swan pennant hung a glass disc bearing a lock of pale hair. "This is a relic of Santa Fiametta of Archaeopolis, brought here with great courage by he who founded our church yonder. Her feast day draws near. In the right hands Santa Fiametta's hair will glow to reveal the sincerity of a person's words. For only the Painter of Clouds, his daughter the Swan, and his messenger the Quenching Fire can know if one is truly a Swanling at heart; but the relic can tell me who believes their own words." Roisin cupped the glass disc in her hands and held it before one eye, the hair coiling before it. "Tell me what is in your heart, sir."

Gaunt devoutly hoped the priestess was not overly corrupt, and Bone not overly honest.

"I have done some bad deeds," he said. "I repent of them. My wife's example has urged me onto the path of the Swan. I have walked many roads, far from home. I have seen many faiths, and many un-faiths. For a time we even traveled with a Swan priestess. I have come to respect the trifold divinity the Swan represents. I will serve her faithfully."

"But have you been brushed with holy water from a consecrated feather?"

"No—have you such available?"

"Or have you been immersed in a sacred swan-pond?"

"On such a crisp day it sounds invigorating."

"Or, and it stretches my mandate to even ask, have you had a sudden conversion accompanied by voices or perhaps visual manifestations?"

"I should be so honored."

Roisin sighed. "You have said nothing false, but I have cause to question your status as an honest Swanling."

"He is willing!" Gaunt said, clutching the priestess's arm. "You heard him!"

"Willing or not, it is his current status that matters. I dislike this law, but I am not the Gull-Jarl. I cannot contest this man's servitude." The priestess looked hard at the foamreavers. "You have absolutely no claim on the woman, however, and she owes no were-gild for your man."

"We thought as much," said Yngvarr. "I will not argue. Floki was a clumsy fool anyway. Though you can come, woman, if you wish to stay with your man. You might find a posting in the same house, though you'll be a servant and he a thrall. I'll even put in a good word. They might make you a guard, heh."

There seemed no help for it. A chance to be together, however . . . that was worth much. They would puzzle out a solution.

Bone was shaking his head at her, but surely he would see reason. "Where he goes," she said, "I—"

"I repudiate her!" Bone said. "I don't even know where she came from."

She understood at once what he was doing, and just in case her gaze didn't make it clear, she strode forward and slapped him hard.

He reeled but said, "She's a madwoman! Priestess, take her away!"

"Perhaps, goodwife," said Roisin, looking pale, "you should—"

"Imago Bone," said Gaunt as the foamreavers snatched him from her grasp, "so help me, when you get free you're a dead man."

"Crazy woman! She has clearly lost her wits!" Bone narrowed his eyes at her before his captors began to beat him. He rallied long enough to say, "And her Innocence! Do you hear me? She's lost her Innocence!" Then he was bleeding and pinned.

"That much is obvious," murmured Crowbeard. But when Gaunt stared at the old foamreaver he flinched and stalked away.

"Bone!" she shouted, and before she knew it she was advancing with the sword.

A hush came over the street. Even the gulls were silent. There were many of them, but she had Crypttongue. If she gave herself fully to slaughter, to the hunger for lives, she might win Bone free. She met his gaze. She knew what he wanted: her as she was, not who she'd become after that battle. But the choice belonged to her.

One encountered many crossroads without knowing it. It was rare to see one clearly.

She lowered the sword.

"For once," said Yngvarr, looking at Gaunt in vexation and puzzlement, "the wishes of a thrall may prevail."

"Please," Gaunt said, "take me with you. Enslave me too if you must."

"Do you deny the Swan?"

Silence caught her throat.

"I thought as much," said Yngvarr. "The law is the law, woman. I can't chain you, and now I won't have you otherwise. Priestess, she's all yours."

Bone had no more words as they dragged him off, staring fish-eyed at the metal-gray skies.

"I am sorry," said Roisin.

"You are brave," said Gaunt, hand shaking, "to speak to me now."

The other backed away a step, her gaze shifting to Crypttongue. But she kept talking. "I have to be brave, sister, to work in such a place. If there is any way, short of recovering your companion, I can help . . . ask."

Almost, Gaunt backhanded the priestess with the hilt. Almost. It was a near thing. An even more difficult struggle nearly sent her steps wordlessly inland, toward the hills and an escape from these monstrous people.

She prevailed against both impulses. For she was Persimmon Gaunt, and this land would have to kill her if it meant to stop her.

Where am I? echoed the suddenly comprehensible voice of Floki the slaver in her mind. *What has—*

She sheathed the sword and silenced him. He was a problem for later.

She remembered Crowbeard, and Crowbeard's wife, and the one word she'd said to Gaunt. "Tell me," she asked Roisin, "what is the meaning of *skjøge?*"

Roisin hesitated. "It means 'harlot.' Why?"

Gaunt looked to the heavens. "I . . . will need considerable help, priestess. First. Have you any bows? And perhaps, armor?"

CHAPTER 8

JOKULL

When the sun was seeking its bloody end beyond Oxiland's main island, and the sky above was like blue-gray slate, Innocence and Huginn came to an estate beside the coast. Seven separate farmhouses stood at various spots around a bay of black sand. Huginn aimed for the largest, one thrice the size of his own, rising within a stone's throw of a grand building upon the highest hill. The hilltop construction was all of rock, with spires and vast windows of multicolored glass.

"Is that the castle of Loftsson?" Innocence asked.

"What? Ha! That is Saint Kringa's, greatest Swan-church of Oxiland, bigger even than the cathedral at Smokecoast. No, the farmhouse below is Loftsson's. Though it's no accident that the church rises so near. It was Loftsson who paid the largest share. Loftsson himself's a retired priest, and he himself will read scripture at the Mass."

"My mother followed the Swan," Innocence ventured. "Though she didn't talk about it much."

"And you do not?"

Paradoxically, honesty seemed best around Huginn, the professional liar. "No. I was raised in far Eastern ways."

Huginn scrutinized him. "Do those ways forbid courtesy at an alien religious ceremony?"

"No. Quite the contrary."

"Do those ways include human sacrifice?"

"No!"

"Then we'll have no problem, lad. Oxiland became Swanling country within living memory. Peacefully, unlike over in Svardmark. There are many here who are still quietly heathen. There is no king here commanding us to swear allegiance to crown and church. We don't make trouble for our neighbors, as long as they don't wave tokens of Torden or Orm One-Eye in the priests' faces."

"What about you? Are you . . . heathen?"

"Ha! That should be an easy question, shouldn't it? I am a Swanling raised, and I revere the light that came from the South. But my heart stirs with the winds from the North. Since I was a boy I've loved the tales of the Vindir, and the frost giants, and the trolls and uldra, and the brave men who contended with them all. My soul belongs to the Swan and her heavenly father. But that soul is heathen, Swan help me."

"That does not make a great deal of sense, Huginn."

"Don't I know it."

They descended to a true road, a pathway formed of carefully gathered and cunningly assembled flat stones. Before long a group walked upslope along the road to meet them. An elderly man in a red woolen hat, with a cloak of blue thrown over a robe of black and white, waved at them. Flanking him were a pair of swordsmen in chain byrnies.

The red-hatted man called out, "What news, old foundling?"

"Little enough, old guardian! How fares the hall?"

"We are blessed. We have enough for all and a good feast tomorrow besides. Who do you travel with?"

"This lad's called Innocence. He will act as my scribe and then is free to find employment."

"An unusual name. A southerner?"

Innocence wanted to speak, but Huginn raised a hand. "That is a long story, Jokull."

At that Jokull Loftsson smiled. "A long story from Huginn Sharpspear is a thing worth waiting for. Have you eaten?"

"But little."

"Come, then." Jokull nodded to his men. "You'll not be needed now." His guards moved at speed back toward the nearest farmhouse.

Huginn and Innocence dismounted and descended at Jokull's slower pace. For all Walking Stick's instruction on deference to the old, Innocence was hungry and impatient. It was hard not to fidget. He contented himself with staring out at the gray eastern sea as the two men talked.

"So," said Huginn. "Why does Jokull Loftsson walk with guards on his own land?"

"Why does he walk with a cane? It is prudent. There are portents. And the road is rocky."

"If there are certain stones that concern you, I would like to hear of them. A younger man might roll them out of the way."

Jokull peered intently at Innocence; Innocence pretended not to notice. Jokull sighed and said, "The creatures that folk call Orb Dragons have been sighted in Oxiland. People I know to be truthful have seen them. I do not think they are really dragons, however."

"That's good. Lesser dragons become deranged if too long in the presence of the great ones who define our land."

"It is not good. I would know what to do with a dragon. Even if we had to flee, I would know. These flying puzzles, however, I know nothing about."

"I promise this, old friend. I will uncover the truth about Orb Dragons."

"A brave promise! I'm glad to have your pledge, but I'm also glad you didn't make it at the banquet. I will keep it quiet."

"I would thunder it from yonder roof, Jokull."

"You were always too hasty, Huginn. And Torfa doesn't like anyone playing on the roof."

"Ha! I think, Innocence, this conversation is not one you need to remember. May he find his lodgings?"

"Of course. Let us speak to Torfa."

Torfa proved to be a majestic, gray-haired matriarch, sturdier than Jokull, with a voice that could boom through every corner of the farmhouse—and it was a vastly greater farmhouse than Huginn's.

Even so, she had no place for Innocence. The way she scowled at Huginn, he suspected there'd be no place for Huginn's servants even if the house were empty and the wind moaning through it. "You will proceed down the path," Torfa said, after feeding him some porridge, "taking the left-hand bend, to the red barn. That barn is assigned to male servants. You may sleep in the south-side hayloft." Innocence found all his Eastern and Western instruction at play when he bowed to this mighty woman and departed.

As he entered the smelly lodgings, it occurred to him that all the bleak, fine sentiments one encountered in the sagas were among nobles, priests, warriors, and wealthy landowners. There was little mention of grooms, maids, shepherds, carpenters, scribes. He found himself berthed with three younger servants who weren't pleased to find their shares of drafty hayloft shrinking. There was a hairy teenager named Rolf and a bald one named Kollr, who occupied opposite corners, and a boy of perhaps ten named Numi, hair cut short, who took the hinterland between. They seemed to have their ancient border disputes worked out, and Innocence was reluctant to disturb the peace.

"How about this?" he said. "I will sleep here, by the ladder."

"What if we step on you on our way to piss?" said Rolf.

"What if you fall off?" said Numi.

"What if you knock the ladder over?" said Kollr.

"Torfa herself assigned me this loft," Innocence said, "and here I will stay. The alternative is for me to sleep on a rafter. If so I will choose one above each of you for a week at a time. I believe the Yule festivities will last that long."

They stared at him. Rolf began laughing. "I must see this! Very well, southerner, bunk over my head if you wish. I sleep with a dirk in hand, so I make no promises for your safety if you fall on me."

"Sleeps with a dirk in hand?" chuckled Kollr. "Is that a kenning? Perhaps you wouldn't mind him tumbling onto you in the dark, eh?"

"Have a care," said Rolf, "my dirk is not made of words but steel." He raised a dagger for emphasis. "I have hit men farther off, and less fat, than you."

Innocence coughed. "What is a kenning?"

The boy Numi looked grateful to change the subject, more or less. "It's a poetic way of talking around a thing. A puzzle in words. The sea is the 'swan-road.' A sword is a 'friend of carrion crows.' A battle is a 'banquet of blades.'"

Kollr said, leaning back and patting his belly, "A warrior might be a 'slayer of eagles' hunger.'"

When Innocence looked puzzled, Numi explained, "Eagles can be carrion birds too. The kennings can get obscure."

Rolf sheathed his dagger and relaxed. "Old men make it a game. You could call a kenning a 'slayer of boredom.' Armed with kennings, a poet can make a simple story last for hours. What was the one Loftsson told last night? 'The visage of the something . . .'"

"'Twice the visage of the father of the axe-thrower,'" Kollr said. "That means 'blind.'"

"What?" Innocence said, sitting down cross-legged, the crisis apparently passed. (Though he must sleep on a rafter.)

"The axe-thrower is the god Torden," Kollr said.

"Heathen god, you mean," Rolf said.

"And his father is the *god* Orm," Kollr continued, while Rolf fumed and Innocence wondered if he should have sat after all. "He was one-eyed, as was his reputed father, the god Arthane Stormeye. Twice his visage would mean blind in both eyes."

"You are brave," Rolf said, "to name these men of old as gods, here in the barn of the good priest Jokull Loftsson."

Numi broke in, his voice squeaking a bit. "The Swan's ways," he said, taking an extra breath, "are ways of peace—"

"Tell that to the shade of Saint Ole," said Rolf, "who rode throughout Svardmark smashing idols."

"And look how Saint Ole died," answered Kollr, "in battle with his own countrymen."

"I should say—" Numi began.

Rolf was on his feet now. "You're good at goading, heathen, but how are you at fighting?"

"Now wait—" said Numi.

"Glad to show you," said Kollr, rising.

Innocence drew upon his chi and leapt onto a rafter.

There was sudden silence in the hayloft.

"I just wanted to see how the air was up here," said Innocence, keeping his voice relaxed. "Now, I just remembered, when they brought me in here, they told me everyone's job. I'm a scribe, see, and it's my business to remember. You, Rolf, are a groom to a fellow named Yl . . . Ylu—"

"Ylur Ymirson," said Rolf with fierce pride, demonstrating that Innocence had given him something new to be angry about.

"And you, Kollr, are a cook's assistant—"

"Chief cook's assistant," said Kollr.

"Chief cook's assistant to Styr . . . Surturson. I got that right, yes?"

"Yes, but—"

"And Numi, you are a priest of some sort, right?"

"No!" said the boy, looking around as though afraid someone might have overheard. "I'm a mere novitiate—"

"Novitiate, yes—"

"—of Blizzardmere Monastery. I'm assigned here to Abbot Vatnar's staff for the holiday, as part of my training. Vatnar is not a monastery abbot, understand, but he earns the title for leading an important church—"

"Of course, indeed, true. Now then, gentlemen, if we are going to argue religion, surely the fellow from the monastery gets as much chance to speak as the groom and the cook. Yes?"

Rolf crossed his arms and nodded. Kollr bowed in Numi's direction.

"Um," said Numi. "Yes. Now, Rolf, it says in the Swan's scripture that a divided house will fall, and a divided kingdom will become desolate. What say you about a divided hayloft?"

Rolf grunted.

"And Kollr, in the sayings of Orm it's told that a hasty tongue sings its own downfall. Am I right?"

Kollr sighed. "You are right."

"So it seems to me that we should have no talk of broken idols and fallen saints, but be glad we have a roof over our heads and good food tomorrow."

"You speak well," Kollr said.

"Aye," said Rolf.

"Thank you," said Numi, looking up at Innocence.

"I believe I will be comfortable up here," said Innocence, shifting to Rolf's side of the hayloft as planned, "if there is no fighting down there."

It was said in the classics of the Garden that the man of virtue spoke slowly and cautiously, but they had little to say of jumping onto rafters.

"He snores," Rolf groaned in the morning. "Our mystery guest has amazing balance and never once fell from his rafter. But he snores."

"Good morning," said Innocence. He dropped himself from the rafter without use of chi, so as not to show off. They all stared anyway.

"I think you owe us some explanation for your talents," Kollr said, "but not now. Now Rolf and I have to work, and Numi and you have to do whatever it is that acolytes and scribes do."

"I'm a novitiate—" began Numi.

"Yes," Kollr laughed at the red-faced Numi, hands raised. "Sorry."

"Do they feed us?" asked Innocence.

"No," Rolf said, "we must roam the plains and slay mice for our breakfast. Of course they feed us. Follow me."

They joined a throng of servants who moved through the Loftsson farmhouse like thread through a garment, and breakfast was a fine thing for all that it nearly happened on the run: bread and berries and bacon. Innocence judged this was fine fare, from the appreciative noises of the servants and thralls.

It took time for Innocence to recognize that some of the servants were not in fact free people. As the eaters dispersed to their tasks, talking and laughing, some were followed and supervised with harsher words and occasional slaps. The thralls were generally indistinguishable from the free Kantenings, but the speech of some hinted of southern lands, like his mother's.

Rolf and Kollr had already departed for their tasks in the stable and kitchen. Numi said, "Does something trouble you?"

"Are those Swanislanders?" Innocence said, gesturing toward the slaves.

"I suppose so," Numi said. An uncomfortable silence passed. "They are hard workers. I have always liked Swanislanders. Simple, honest people, close to the Earthe. With a gift for music—"

"I should find Huginn. Good-day to you."

"Wait . . . did I offend? I do not much understand you, Innocence. But I'm grateful for how you handled Rolf and Kollr."

"It was your words that did it."

"And yours. If you want employment in the church, I will vouch for you."

Despite the compliment to his speech, Innocence was full of anger that he couldn't find words for. "Thank you. I will think about that."

Numi hurried off as though he'd said something much sterner. Innocence stalked off to find Huginn, his mind grim as the volcano far off on Oxiland's main island. He found his patron laughing and jesting with two other chieftains, whom Innocence soon learned were Ylur Ymirson and Styr Surturson. "Ah!" said Huginn. "Here is my scribe, Innocence."

"How well named!" Ylur said. He was old but still fierce, with a full white beard. "For if our words are to be recorded, we'd best leave off our talk of the fine women gathered here!"

"Where is your paper and pen, boy?" Huginn said.

"I, ah . . ." Innocence said.

"It seems we have a reprieve!" said Styr, a huge red-bearded fellow with a bull-deep voice. The other men laughed, and Innocence was sent to Torfa with an affectionate slap across the shoulders from Huginn. At least, Innocence supposed, it was affectionate. He ran. He did not understand Oxilanders, or Kantenings. They seemed civilized one moment, animals the next. The Sage Emperor once said, *One cannot discourse with birds and beasts, as if they were human. Humans may be imperfect, but it is with them I must associate.* But had the Sage Emperor ever encountered men like these?

Torfa, pen and paper, Huginn, all proved to be elusive quarry, but at last he succeeded and caught up with the professional liar at a collection of boulders where Huginn regaled a group of five chieftains, now including Loftsson and a twentyish blond chieftain named Gissur Mimurson who had recently arrived. They quieted a bit when Innocence ran up, panting in the cold air, but only a bit. He sat down and arranged pen, paper, and ink. If only Walking Stick could see him now.

Innocence could not record everything, but Huginn would sometimes nod to him and say, "Please make a note of that" and "That is worth a mention," until Innocence soon was acquainted with a certain bushy-eyebrowed look that said the pen needed dipping. The discussion swirled around such matters as wine and women, funny anecdotes of the winter, and the health of family. But it also stepped upon the hard rock of border disputes between farmers, inheritance arguments, the building of new churches, the introduction of new crops. Nothing was settled, but much was weighed.

At one point Gissur Mimurson said, "Be careful, Jokull. This feast has the feel of a Spring Assembly, held before spring's even had a chance to rise and rub her hands."

"Or even an Althing," Styr Surturson agreed. "We've spoken of matters far beyond our little sphere. Others might object we're getting ahead of ourselves."

"I confess," Jokull said, "I didn't expect Huginn to bring a scribe." Here Innocence felt the regard of the Kantenings, and he did his best to imitate the great stone he wrote upon.

It had occurred to Innocence that Huginn had done him a great favor. He might have been set to work tending pigs or worse. Instead he'd been treated as an honored, educated visitor and given a post that displayed to these important folk that Innocence was worthy of employment. He didn't like thinking about this truth, for it made him feel vulnerable—he who'd once burst with the power of the Heavenwalls, who'd overflown the West on a magic carpet. But the carpet was gone, and the energies he'd once commanded were bottled within him. He must stopper his pride as well.

For now.

"But," Jokull was saying, "I did tell him in advance I wanted to plan ahead. I foresee troubled times."

Ylur Ymirson laughed at that. "You always foresee troubled times, Jokull! And yet you always swell in wealth and status."

Huginn chuckled. "There is something to be said for caution, friends. In truth, I wanted a scribe because I want a record for the assembly and the Althing. There'll be those who call us a cabal."

"We're not?" Styr said.

"No."

"No?" said Gissur.

"No," repeated Huginn. "We're looking ahead, not hatching schemes. There is much to consider this year. We haven't touched on the crazy things yet, eh, Jokull?"

Jokull said, "No." He counted on his fingers. "Orb Dragons. Earthquakes. Troll sightings. The peasant uprisings in Svardmark. The Nine Wolves. A hand's worth of worry."

Discussions of strange matters continued through the morning. Innocence heard of peculiar flying blobs, ominous shakings and eruptions, stony marauders, angry commoners, and murderous highwaymen until the shadows grew long again. Innocence was fascinated. He wracked his brains wondering what the Orb Dragons might be, whether the mountain in the distance would spout fire, whether trolls really froze in the sunlight, whom the great organizer of the rebellious peasants might be, and what made nine cruel men waylay travelers on the roads.

At last Jokull excused himself. "I must head to the church in advance of the service. Ylur, as ever I welcome you to the church, but you are welcome to the feast regardless."

Ylur nodded and clapped his hand over the axe-charm of Torden around his neck. "As ever you warm my heart, friend. I'll see you at the feast."

Jokull made a similar gesture and was off. The chieftains talked of more trifling things and began wandering off.

Huginn looked at Innocence's penmanship. "You did well . . . what is that?" He pointed at a signature Innocence had made in the upper left.

"It is a rendition of the sounds of my name," Innocence said, "in the official language of Qiangguo."

"It seems just a squiggle to me, but no matter."

"Master Huginn, I had a thought."

"Yes?"

"On the continent I have seen a flying craft that might, if one did not understand it for a human work, be taken for a strange creature."

"Indeed?"

"Yes. It is a sort of bladder filled with heated air, rising with enough determination to carry a large basket beneath."

"There are indeed many wonders in the world."

"I thought perhaps this might be the origin of the Orb Dragon stories."

"For that to be true, would that not imply visitors from the East?"

"I suppose it would."

"And you . . . you say you were raised in the East."

There was now nobody else around the boulders, though a group of travelers was descending the stone road. Innocence said, "I have no knowledge of these visitations, except what I saw long ago."

"I believe you. But it seems too great a coincidence that you arrive now."

"That is as it may be, but I have nothing to do with Orb Dragons."

Huginn stroked his beard. "We are done for now," he said, his voice deeper and more ominous than at any time before. "Go to the service and the feast, Innocence, and speak of this to no one. Be prepared to record what is said and done. I have my own thoughts on this matter."

Innocence burned to know these thoughts, but it seemed unwise to stay. He traveled to the male servants' barn, looking toward the newly arrived company. Among them was the family of Tor, Jaska's father. He could not discern Jaska herself, however.

He stretched out the walk, imagining himself battling the Nine Wolves for Jaska's safety. His desperate energy would defeat them, and she would plight her troth with him, as they said here, accepting an offer of marriage. He imagined Joy at the wedding, and confusion shredded the daydream like morning mist.

His forehead itched. He reached up and rubbed at it. He felt as though a storm was coming, although the day was clear. He walked in a daze toward the coast and stood upon a rugged, grass-covered promontory resembling the broken fingers and knuckles of a giant who'd lost a battle with Old Torden. He watched the waves rushing against the beach of black sand.

Far away there were other waves washing up on a jagged limestone coast; and beyond the trees and bushes that whispered in the warm wind from the eastern sea rose the walls and sweeping roofs of Riverclaw, where the two Heavenwalls met. Above the bustle of the capital, the Purple Forbidden City rose serene upon foundations resembling dragons' heads, and the tenders of the Windwater Garden, with its metaphorical map of the realm, looked up at a sudden breeze from the West.

Innocence took two steps backward. The vision cleared, and he saw again the cold coast. "You are still with me," he said to the East. "The power is not gone."

He reached out with hand and will and tried to shape the wind. Nothing happened.

Frustration made him kick the rock. "Why am I here, trapped in this barbaric place? Why can I not access the power? Where is Deadfall? Why is life like this?"

"Innocence?"

Innocence spun and saw that the novitiate Numi had descended from the church and was now a stone's throw away. Innocence sighed and walked toward him. *The superior man,* Walking Stick had said, *is calm and steady like the polestar, while the mean man swirls about in endless distress.* Walking Stick had despaired of making Innocence a superior man.

"Are you all right?" Numi said. "From the bell tower I saw you walking down here, and you seemed upset. What was that you were speaking? It sounded strange."

The superior man is honest and open; the mean man is furtive and afraid.

"It's the chief language of a country called Qiangguo. It's the tongue I was brought up with. I think in that language, most of the time. I didn't even realize I was speaking it."

"How many languages do you know?"

"Three. If you can count Kantentongue. I'm still working on that. Don't you have work to do? Don't let me hold you up. I'm coming back."

"I'm fast on my feet. I'm supposed to ring the bell soon. That's actually the other reason I sought you out. Turns out I'm not strong enough to squelch the ringing."

"Um, I thought you were supposed to ring it."

"I'll explain as we go." They walked. Innocence indeed had trouble keeping up with Numi. Numi said, "It's a heavier bell than I thought. I'm used to our monastery bell. I know I'll be strong enough to ring this one. But I can tell I'm not going to be able to snag the rope properly to prevent the clapper from whacking the bell again and again. The abbot likes a nice, clean sound. He likes a nice, clean everything. I don't want a drubbing. Maybe you can help me."

"You know, I grew up in a monastery. But we didn't have a bell."

"Well, all you have to do is let me ring it and then help me stop the clapper."

"Guess I haven't had anything to battle in a while. Lead on."

They entered the church, with its stained-glass windows in the outline of a rising swan on the west and a descending swan on the east. As they strode through its shadows, passing pews and acolytes, Innocence asked, "Which way is up, I wonder?"

"The stairs are over there, past the votives and the chapel."

"No, I mean which orientation of the Swan is considered the better one? Rising or falling?"

"They both represent different aspects of grace. The Swan ascending can show her on her way to quench the overbearing sun or rising from the dead after her downfall. The Swan descending may indicate the moment of her sacrifice, or her heavenly form bestowing blessings on us below. Every image of the church can be multiply determined. Such symbols are like keyholes through which stream many kinds of light, or like skeleton keys to open many kinds of doors. There is more than one kind of light, and more than one sort of door, because there is more than one kind of human, and more than one sort of worshipper."

That this boy could suddenly sound like a theologian left Innocence speechless as they climbed the belfry stairs. At the top they encountered a windy nook, a precipitous view, a large iron bell, and a scowling abbot.

"You are supposed to be here, novice," said Abbot Vatnar. The man looked to be forty, with black hair beginning to gray around the edges. His clothes were like another continent to the gray island of Numi's simple robe, a regal swirl of red and gold, with white gloves to match the silver necklace of the Swan ascending. Stern eyes narrowed beneath a gold-threaded cap. "And who is this?"

"This is Huginn Sharpspear's scribe, Father Abbot," Numi said. "I needed someone to help me with the rope." Numi gulped. "The bell is perhaps beyond my strength."

"And you sought out secular help when there are so many acolytes below."

"Beg pardon, Father Abbot, but everyone below is busy, and the scribe is not. I saw a way to resolve the problem without interrupting work."

Abbot Vatnar shut his eyes, opened them. "Commendable. In the future do not risk a delay. But I can't fault you in this case. You may proceed. Three clear rings."

They managed to get Vatnar's three rings with only a hint of a fourth, though the clapper yanked back on the rope like a wild horse. Innocence saw the crowd outside pause at their doings—their talk, their setting of tents, their preparations of food and drink, their arrangement of tables for games and horses for racing, and big rocks for the sport of stone-lifting—and turn toward the church. Innocence looked out toward the sea and beheld sea-stacks of dark, fang-like rock, and beyond them the ocean and a gray hint of other islands.

Was there something odd about the sky out there? Strange movements of tiny clouds against the path of their larger cousins?

Innocence felt Abbot Vatnar's hand on his shoulder. "I said, it is time to find a pew, lad. We thank you for your help, but this is church territory."

Innocence felt like a spy from an invading country as he bade good-bye to Numi and fled downstairs. He found a spot at the back. Here he could watch everybody as they came in.

When Jaska's family entered, she took no notice of him, though he saw her looking this way and that. He wanted to wave, but a curious silence afflicted him, some reticence born of the church and his churning stomach. He had met, and never feared, a Karvak princess, but this farm girl made him afraid of something, his own wild voice, his future, her scorn, the possibility she was really a werewolf and would eat his heart for breakfast. Something. He day-dreamed that monsters of the East, battle-mad temple lions, screeching nine-headed birds, and hopping vampires, would appear and only he, Innocence, could stop them. But for all his courage and cleverness the church would still be wrecked, with most people escaping, but he and Jaska trapped in an alcove, screened by fallen candlesticks, she holding him from primal need, he from an ancient instinct of protection, trying to silence their breaths but unable to silence their thundering hearts . . .

"Hey, this seat taken?"

"Um, no, uh, hello, Kollr."

The chef's assistant sat down, panting, dismissing Innocence's daydream of sweat and candlewax with the stench of fish. "Thanks. I like to be here near the back. Had to run to make sure. Close thing. Making sure the hakarl is ready."

"The what?"

"Oh, sure, you wouldn't know. You don't know what you're missing. It's dried fermented rotted shark meat."

"Looking forward to it."

"You bet! Not everyone buries it in the sand the right way, but Loftsson's cooks know what they're doing."

"Sounds astonishing."

"You won't forget it, trust me. Makes you strong." Kollr paused. "You might want to pinch your nose the first time."

"I'll do that."

"And down it with some aquavit."

"I'm coming to love the stuff."

"Anyway, thanks for the seat. Officially no one bothers you for being heathen, but it's best not to be too obvious."

Innocence remembered Kollr's feud with Rolf. "Do you fully participate, in here?"

"No. I don't take the sacramental rainwater and fish. There's no rule against it, but if you do that people will assume you're coming round to the Swan. Best not to disappoint them."

"Makes sense. I'll stay back here too."

"So, if you don't mind my asking, what are you then? You don't seem like someone who'd follow Kantening gods."

Innocence's religious training was of a practical bent; here is the order of Heaven, always seemed to be Walking Stick's perspective, and here is how to follow it, never mind who's in Heaven or why. The monks and the portrait of the Sage Painter had been a little more theoretical, however. "Let me think," Innocence said. "The world comes together through the tumult of opposites, light and darkness, active and passive . . ."

"Hey, that's what the skalds say too. Back before everything there was a clash of fire and ice . . ."

"Well, then out of all that there was an enormous stone egg, and out of it came a crazy giant guy named Pan-Ku . . ."

"No kidding! We have a giant named Ymir, big as the world . . ."

"Well, Pan-Ku spent thousands of years shaping the world-stuff around him, putting it into forms we know, and when he died of old age, his body formed the rest of what was needed for the Earthe. His blood became oceans and rivers, his breath became wind, his voice was thunder . . ."

"That's uncanny! Our story is exactly the same. Well, except that our giant was an evil lunatic, and he was killed by our earliest gods and chopped into bloody pieces to make the world. Our gods are kind of violent."

"I see. Well, our gods are kind of like, um, what's the word? *Guanliao* . . ."

"A whatsa?"

"In Roil you'd say they're 'bureaucrats'? They sit around in Heaven and make decrees and make sure cosmic laws are followed."

"Hey, kind of like the Althing. The stories say the Vindir would or did have talks at the base of the world-tree and figure things out. They'd argue a lot."

"Would or did?"

"Time is weird for the Vindir. Sometimes the story goes that they're mostly going to die in a huge battle against evil. Other times it's like they already died, and it all comes round again. Kind of like the Swan."

"That is different. I think the Heavenly Court just goes on and on."

"Well, like I said, our gods are violent. Lots of battles. I mean, lots of battles. The best you can hope for when you die is to go to Orm's Hall, where you get to battle every day and get brought back to life if you happen to get killed. That trains you for the day you get to fight evil and get slaughtered."

"We think that if you're virtuous for enough lifetimes, you can get a posting in Heaven. Maybe watch the cloud-horses."

"It doesn't sound that exciting."

"We make do."

By now more people had filed in, and Innocence and Kollr were loudly shushed. Mentioning clouds made Innocence remember the peculiar clouds he'd seen from the bell tower, but the thought was displaced by the singing of a choir.

He'd thought of Kantentongue as somewhat discordant, like the squawking of birds, but as the singers' voices came together, they wove a tapestry of sound that enmeshed his mind. The rituals that followed, with their use of candles, raised hands, drawings in the air, reading from thick, ancient books, had a similar effect. Part observer, part participant, Innocence found the service dreamlike.

Jokull Loftsson delivered the homily, and though Innocence had experienced no trouble following the man before, he struggled to understand him now. There was a more musical cadence to his speech and an archaic texture to the words he read from the old prayer book. It was something about the structure of the church representing important virtues. Four great pillars stood for the four books of testimony that lay at the heart of the Swan's scripture, but they also stood for the four virtues of endurance, moderation, insight, and faith. The chancel stood for both angels in the Creator's realm and the prayers that winged up to that realm. Innocence remembered Numi's multiple interpretations of the swan-shaped stained-glass windows. His mind swam with those swans. For a little while it was as though all the things he could see were symbols of things he couldn't see.

Voices from near the entrance reminded him of something else he hadn't seen.

"Where is Sharpspear going?"

"Doesn't he know he's late?"

"No time to walk on the beach. Won't he offend Loftsson?"

Something nagged at Innocence like a premonition. Was it another vision, like the one his power had given him? Just nerves at participating in an alien ceremony? Either way, he whispered apologies and rose, weaving his way through the observers standing at the back, making his way outside.

Blinking in the light, he did indeed see his patron walking toward the dark sands as though nothing of importance were going on at the church. It seemed bizarre, at odds with everything else the man had done. Innocence took a few steps Huginn's way . . . and froze.

Far out to sea, but now clearly visible, there flew a sky-blue object like an upside-down teardrop, with a much smaller gray structure hanging beneath.

"Not clouds," he murmured.

It was not alone. Several similar shapes were approaching behind the first, and all were bee-lining toward the bay, ignoring the prevailing wind.

He'd seen such a shape before. He hesitated. Should he go advise Huginn?

Huginn's words returned to him. *I promise this, old friend. I will uncover the truth about Orb Dragons.*

Far overhead he saw a circling peregrine falcon. He was sure he'd last seen it in a dream.

Speak of this to no one . . .

The superior man, when at peace, never forgets that disaster may come.

Be prepared to record what is said and done . . .

The superior man acts first, then speaks according to his actions.

Innocence acted.

He ran, but his feet carried him back into the church. There was no time to warn anyone, and who would believe the strange youth with the odd accent? And who among the mighty could he trust, if he could not trust Huginn? Even if trustworthy, they might not understand what was all too clear to Innocence. But Numi had shown him the way.

Innocence enlivened his chi and leapt through the ceremony amid shouts and screams. There was a scattering of votives. He was at the belfry stair in five steps. He could not similarly leap to the bell, and his use of such advanced techniques had tired him. Nevertheless he hurled himself upward, and though he was out of breath when he reached the rope, he coiled his hands within it and let his dead weight do the rest.

It was sloppy work, nothing like the clear tones beloved of Abbot Vatnar. But his actions were clear, if not his music.

"Invaders!" he bellowed at the priests and acolytes who rushed upstairs to stop him. "Invaders! To arms!" He let go the rope and clutched the window ledge screaming at Loftsson's guards and any heathens who might be avoiding the church. "Invaders! Look to the sea! The Orb Dragons are ships of the air! To arms! To arms!" Even as his pursuit grabbed him, the falcon screeched into the bell tower and landed upon the ledge, regarding them all.

Far below, Innocence saw Huginn Sharpspear raising his hands in greeting to the warriors of the Grand Khan.

CHAPTER 9

A JOURNEY TO KANTENJORD

(as told by Haytham ibn Zakwan, gentleman-scholar of Mirabad)

In gratitude to the compassionate Creator of the universe, who set stars to spinning and worlds to breathing, and in memory of the prophet who testified to His works, I offer this account of my sojourn in the savage country of Soderland, in the Bladed Isles. If it does not enlighten, let it at least entertain.

Knowledge, whether gained by scholarly research or the billowing crash of a sky-balloon, is never wholly useless. This is fortunate for me, for I have crashed many balloons. Prior to the particular impact I am thinking of, one that was extravagantly hard on the balloon, the crew, and a small apple orchard, *Al-Saqr* was careening along in a gale, over an otherwise picturesque winter landscape rushing below us at absurd speeds. I was about to learn a great deal.

We had survived the storm that plagued us when first we arrived in these islands, and which had cost us many of our companions. But the effort of escaping that supernatural squall had at last overwhelmed the powers of the shaman Northwing, who although heroic was only human, and who now slept exhausted upon the gondola's deck in the care of the warrior monk Katta.

We were now well south of that storm, blown into the country I hoped was Soderland, greatest realm of these isles. I had originally hoped to reach the capital of Svanstad, but by now I had little notion where we actually were.

Although we had altitude control thanks to the presence of the efrit Haboob, we could only maneuver by the expedient of testing wind direction at various heights. Prevailing winds were generally eastward at this time and ranged from brisk to bellicose. I was eager to land in any non-suicidal spot whatsoever, but not if the impact were akin to leaping from a galloping horse.

I had no desire to explore this dangerous land with a broken leg. Nevertheless, a range of mountains rose ominously to the west.

By now I had taken *Al-Saqr* so low that we'd been spotted by many of the locals. Despite the danger of the situation, there was a certain gaiety about passing over their heads, looking at the brightly painted thatched-roofed farmhouses, smelling the chimney smoke, and hearing the screeches of excited children. While many of the adults we overflew were dumbstruck, others waved, and I saluted them. They appeared a strong, tall people who sometimes put me in mind of palm trees. Their skin tended to be quite pale, their faces sometimes florid. Their hair color ranged from frosty yellow to night-black. The women tended to wear their hair long, and the men often wore beards. Their clothing was brightly colored wool, and in the chill of this morning they wore cloaks clasped with intricate metal brooches flashing reflections at me as the sun ascended.

The brooches were not the only metal in evidence. The men, and no small number of the women, seemed to feel they were naked without a weapon of some kind. That last detail returned to haunt me when I noticed we'd picked up an escort.

A growing number of men, women, and children on horseback were following us. A couple of them wore dark-blue livery, and although I'd never seen such uniforms, I knew officialdom when I saw it.

Of course the group was armed. Everybody was armed. They probably gave the babies dirks.

Katta remarked, "We have company, eh? Soldiers among them?"

Katta's resources frequently amazed me. "How did you know?" I asked him, for the blind monk remained beside Northwing within the ger.

"The balloon receives sound from the countryside quite wonderfully," Katta said. "It is easy to tell we have some twenty horses after us. Moreover, there is a regularity about some of the hoofbeats that suggests martial training."

"I fear they'll lock us up as spies."

"Look on the bright side, friend Haytham. If we are injured we'll have someone to look after us."

"You've guessed the danger?" I asked, for I had attempted to keep it from him.

"You've been dropping to the ground and changing your mind for hours now. It's your decision. But I'll remind you, sometimes the dice have to roll."

"Very well," I said. "A poet once said that a man will become bored with pleasure if he experiences it continually. I am about to slay boredom. Haboob, kindly cease heating the air. I will vent the envelope."

"Of course, O marvelous one," said the efrit. "After all, I will survive any landing."

"My heart sings for you."

One might have imagined that crashing would be a short, alarming sensation. One would be wrong. It was in fact a seemingly infinitely prolonged alarming sensation. I'd chosen a moment to descend that would take us through an orchard, hoping the trees would serve to snag the envelope and bring us to a halt. Instead we careened through the trees, snapping branches, and while the envelope was punctured, still our buoyancy and the rushing wind sent us hurtling along. The gondola shuddered absurdly as we hit ground and bounced, collided with branches, and trembled in the clutch of the spasming envelope. Katta clutched Northwing with admirable determination, gripping a bamboo support to keep them from sliding about. I was somewhat less alert and was flung to and fro, at times colliding with pots and pans, and once setting my hand upon Haboob's brazier. The efrit greeted my howls with a look of disdain.

At last the eternity of shaking came to an end. We had finally slowed enough that a particularly massive apple tree, an elder of its kind, caught the envelope in its gnarled embrace. Our ger creaked, suspended a few feet above the ground. I was bleeding from my head, but Katta and Northwing appeared to be intact. Northwing stirred and said, "What's happening?"

Squeezing my turban against my wound, I said, "I am about to claim this land in the name of the caliph."

"Perhaps I should go first," Katta said. He took a washcloth and wrapped it around my head.

"It was a joke," I said.

"Are you dizzy?"

"What would you suspect?"

"What is your name?"

"Haytham ibn Zakwan, master scholar and explorer, inventor of—"

"Good. Nevertheless, let me go first."

"Of course," Northwing said, stretching and seeking balance. "It's not as though Mad Katta's ever been chased out of any country."

"We'll all go," I said, "hands raised. Haboob, I ask that you go unseen until we next call upon you."

"And if you never return?" asked the smoky figure of the efrit.

"If a month passes without further instruction, you are free with my gratitude."

This generosity left Haboob speechless, which was in itself sufficient justification.

Thus did we set foot on the soil of Kantenjord. We had a rope ladder for such an occasion. I believe in being prepared. I was glad Katta and Northwing had gone first, however, for I stumbled on my way down and was caught between them.

And speaking of caught, we were at that point surrounded by some twenty riders, a few being the blue-clad soldiers I had noted previously. It was not difficult to understand that we were to surrender any weapons and climb a trio of horses commandeered from the farmers. Northwing and I gave up our daggers, as did Katta, but Katta successfully conveyed that his staff was a blind man's cane, and thus we had one weapon among us at least. He kept also his pack of supernaturally imbued and very tasty sweetcakes, which could in extremes be hurled against monsters with surprisingly powerful effect. I consoled myself with this accounting, as we abandoned *Al-Saqr* and rode to an unknown fate.

As fate would have it, we were within a day's ride of Svanstad. My navigation instincts had not failed me. What did fail me were my wits. I had suffered more blood loss than I reckoned on and was so eager to appear formidable that when the swooning hit me, I nearly tumbled from my horse. In moments Northwing had ridden beside me to ensure my safety. "Our mistress will be annoyed if I let you die," the shaman said.

"I love you too," I said.

I found myself a guest—or patient, or prisoner—in a nearby manor house.

Owing to the wound, I slept a great deal and was annoyed by the people who kept awakening me. Once I dreamed of the house of my mentor Abbas ibn Hayyan of Mirabad, whose workshop was one of the wonders of the world. Above the most astonishingly haphazard arrangement of beakers, flasks, and alembics glowed a dome presenting a mosaic of the heavens, split between turquoise day and onyx night, pipes from below transmitting mist to simulate clouds, metal tubes with mirrors conveying the sound and light of little alchemical explosions. The mess of Abbas's laboratory as contrasted with the glory of his ceiling made a perfect metaphor for the disorder of our lives compared with the perfection of the All-Now, though before now I had never had the nerve to express it thus.

I awakened to true sunlight and the memory of the unnatural troll-storm. My mind felt lucid as crystal. I lay in a feather bed with curtains shining with sunlight entering via windows of glass. With my wits returned, I wondered: what questions had they asked me? Questions about dragons? Although my mind was clear, my memory was not.

It occurred to me it had been some time since I prayed. I am not always a proper man, and my travels in wild regions have encouraged my eccentricity, but I do offer devotion as I can. Carefully I escaped the comforts of the bed and washed my arms, head, and feet with a nearby basin, then checked the position of the sun. I reckoned it to be midmorning, and the City of Pilgrimage as toward the back of the room. As I knelt and prayed, my thoughts cleared still more, and even as I recited verses I remembered more of what I had been asked, and what I had answered. The line of questioning had been curious, I recalled, and the voice had been a woman's. And rather memorable—

The door opened behind me. I heard the very voice from my memory cry out in alarm. Well, of course, she had checked upon her charge and found him (at that point in my devotions) on the floor.

I raised a hand. "I must request," I said in Roil, "you not interrupt me."

It seemed I was understood. I completed my acts of homage.

Rising, I found myself in the presence of a most striking woman. She was perhaps ten years my junior, in her forties, with dark-brown hair worn shoulder length and blue eyes that recalled the bright winter sky beyond the window. She wore a simple turquoise-colored dress and a silver swan pendant around her neck. A red cloak around her shoulders was attached with a brass clasp representing three intertwined dragons. Her presence was so striking, her gaze so direct and intelligent, I did not at first realize she had a slight irregularity to her shoulders, one being higher than the other.

"As I thought," she said in Roil, "you are a gentleman of Mirabad."

I smiled and bowed. She surely did not know my full reputation. "How do you know I am a gentleman?"

She smiled back. "I could say I'm a good judge of character—and I am. But I've also had reports of your craft and its possessions. There were far more books in your vessel, Haytham ibn Zakwan, than there are in this house, and this is a fine house. I wish only that I could read them all. Do not fear. They have all been brought here. Beyond that, even in a delirium you have a scholarly manner about you, an exact way of speaking."

"You have me at a disadvantage, then, Madame . . . ?"

"Sigrid Kjetilsdatter, wife of Squire Lars. Call me Sigrid. It is my house you are sleeping in."

"I'm grateful. I seem to be in good condition. You spoke of my vessel— what of *its* condition?"

"It has been extracted from the orchard and moved to this manor. Do not be alarmed, but many individuals from the city are studying it even now."

"I *am* alarmed but not surprised. I'd do no less in their place. What of my companions?"

"You are wobbling a little," the squire's wife said, gripping my arm. It was quite a strong grip. I rather liked the feeling of a woman fussing over me, and scolded myself for unworthy thoughts. She said, "Perhaps you should rest."

"Nonsense. Activity is what I need."

"Very well." She did not let go of my arm. I did not argue. I reminded myself to appear particularly feeble should the squire appear.

"Are my companions here?"

"They are guests in the city, at the Fortress."

"Forgive me, but that sounds ominous."

"I assure you it's not." She led me through the house. To my eyes it seemed a modestly appointed home, but then I am the scion of a wealthy family of glorious Mirabad of the white towers. In Kantening terms this was surely an impressive house. We descended a staircase into a grand hall marked with shields and the heads of beasts. Servants in brightly -dyed woolen clothing nodded to the house's mistress. They inspired mixed feelings in me, for while they seemed a pleasant lot they did not much seem to prize bathing, and the scent of sweat mixed with that of woodsmoke. It was a relief to pass through the oaken doors of the house and enter the snowy outdoors.

"I'm fortunate to be in such pleasant surroundings," I said, meaning it, breathing in the crisp air. "I am not so certain I'd prefer to be at your Fortress."

"The Fortress is the royal palace. Though we in Soderland have adopted the peaceful ways of the Swan, we remain a warrior people."

"A paradox."

"Not really. Many of our northern neighbors remain enamored of the old ways. If we are not strong, we inspire them into raids. Our military strength helps preserve the peace."

"I think you've merely given the paradox more detail," I said.

"Perhaps. It is a parlor game of Swanlings, to compare ourselves to the earliest worshippers—pacifistic, communal, living as though tomorrow the world would end. We cynical moderns always come up short. And yet, what fully pacifistic society can endure?"

She surprised me, this farmer's wife. "Do not ask me," I said. "Our Testifier treasured peace, but he never commanded us to abandon war."

"Indeed, at times I envy the Testifier's followers. For while your doctrines are strict they at least seem achievable. While our doctrines seem designed for angels, not flawed human beings. And yet we are never entirely condemned for failing, as long as we keep trying to roll our stone up the hill. Curious."

I looked upon her in wonder now, as our footsteps crunched snow and we passed stables, pens, henhouses, for she spoke as a philosopher. Likewise, she walked straighter and spoke more commandingly out among the elements than she had indoors. It's tempting to think of the Kantenings as ferocious due to their northern climate. Indeed, I might draw a parallel between them and the Karvaks, in the sense that both peoples must at times endure bitter cold. Such conclusions might be too pat, but she did remind me of my lady Steelfox.

I found my admiration not limited to her mind and her bearing, and began considering sinful thoughts. It seemed to me, in the poet's phrase, that she stayed the sun of beauty from darkening. As a man of modest looks, approaching old age, far from home and with little fortune, I knew I had little hope of marriage or even honest womanly companionship. Thus I allowed myself to enjoy the company of this Sigrid, though not to let my attraction show. For even though I've indulged myself sinfully on many occasions, to romance another man's wife is a garden wall I'll not climb.

"We argue much among ourselves," I ventured, "as to how uprightly to live. I myself have been condemned for moral laxness and philosophical innovation. It is one reason I took my inventions far from the Caliphate."

To see her look of sympathy was like watching the melting of snow. "You abandoned your home?"

"The desire for knowledge burned within me, hotter than a blazing tamarisk. I wanted to build my flying machines, see other lands. There are those who think that to discover new knowledge is dangerous, even disrespectful to the All-Now. As if I could reveal anything that was not ultimately the work of His hand! Year after year I moved farther from Mirabad, until in the steppes I found my great patrons." And, joying to tell my tale to such company, I briefly described my travels in the wide world, leaving out only that I still owed allegiance to a Karvak princess.

Even now, I shake my head at my own foolishness.

"I still hope one day," I told her, "to triumphantly arrive in the city of Mirabad by air."

"I wish I could see it," she said, squeezing my arm.

"Ah, you would love it. My Mirabad is a vast, circular city, perhaps eight times the scope of your Svanstad. It is a goblet of experience, brimming with people, as well as parks, palaces, gardens, promenades, and places of worship. It is a world in itself. Once it commanded a realm that shook the Earthe, but even diminished its power is considerable. Perhaps one day I'll take you—and your family—there as my guests, to repay you for your kindness."

She laughed. "I meant, I wish I could see you triumph over those who drove you out. They were fools, Haytham ibn Zakwan." She seemed to me wondrous in her self-assurance and ferocity. "You have created a thing that may change the world."

We had come to the edge of the farmstead, and I beheld an encampment. Numerous military tents surrounded a freshly painted barn, all flying flags representing a stylized white swan, bordered in indigo, upon a red field. There were soldiers in byrnies and a few men garbed in plate armor of the sort more common in Swanisle and the Eldshore.

My escort nodded to these men, and they parted for her, allowing her to enter the barn.

Within, lit by magical gems upon posts, surrounded by studious-looking men and women, was the sagging ruin of my *Al-Saqr*. The vessel's gear was neatly arranged beside one wall, and my various books and alchemical tools upon the other. In a far corner the dark brazier of Haboob stood by itself, regarded by a trio of scholarly-looking people.

One of these three noticed us and walked over, a brown-haired old woman in a nondescript gray robe.

"What news, Runewalker?" said the woman beside me.

"We're certain the brazier is the key to it all. We believe there's some sort of supernatural entity lurking in there."

"Can you isolate it?" my host said.

"With time, we believe so." This "Runewalker" turned toward my surely bemused face. "So this is our inventor," she said. "I am honored. When Soderland commands the air, it is you we must thank."

I bowed, and she returned to my brazier.

I turned to my host. "So. You intend to use my craft for purposes of your own."

"What would you do, Haytham, if an unearthly vessel crashed in your lands, a craft beyond your ken, one that might as well have arrived from another world?"

"I would study it, of course. And I would detain its occupants if I could. I would press them for information. Perhaps I would charm them with a lovely companion."

"You would be wise."

"Are you ever going to let me leave?"

"You must think us barbarians. I admit you have reason to. But fear not. We will let you go, but there will be a price."

"You are not the squire's wife."

"When did you know?"

"Only now, for certain. But you have shown a distinct lack of interest in the business of this farm and no distress as to the disruption of its routine.

Meanwhile you have flirted with me outrageously. And while I have the requisite amount of male pride, I don't believe I could so easily turn your head."

"Trust me, Haytham, if I were truly flirting with you, you would know it."

"Even learned men have trouble learning when they are truly wanted." He sighed. "And what is this price for freedom, whoever you are?"

She smiled, and the smile put me in mind of the icy peaks that had nearly destroyed our craft. "Why, once this craft is ready to fly again, you will take me with you."

In that moment I first feared the iron grip of Corinna, crown princess of Soderland.

(*This concludes the first section of* A Journey to Kantenjord)

CHAPTER 10

SKALAGRIM

"Are we not going to a slave market?" Bone asked, once he and Yngvarr's other prisoners were led beyond the town walls. In response he was swatted with a thick branch.

"Shut up," said a foamreaver. "This isn't some Oxiland Althing."

"Of course," Bone said, having no idea what that meant.

Fresh snow collected fast upon the ground. A bitter wind whipped the flakes in mad whorls as they ascended into the fjord's high country, and Bone shivered. Upon a hilltop stood a great wooden hall, bright with red pillars and golden dragons, overlooking several farms below and the town beyond.

The foamreavers stopped the line beside a cliff opposite the great rune-carved doors.

The doors opened.

"Be honored, rogue," Yngvarr told Bone in Roil, "for you are to be offered to the Gull-Jarl himself. Behold his son, Skalagrim the Bloody."

The beefy man who approached, big as the astoundingly massive Yngvarr, had a fitting epithet. He wore a red beard, a red robe over his byrnie, and a spiked mace with hints of red on the points. He inspected the slaves with a grunt, pausing now and then to poke a man's muscle or stroke a woman's chin. At all times he bore himself with a casual disdain. Bone had grown accustomed to the body language of countries far to the East. He found Skalagrim's studied insolence appalling in such an important personage. Insolence belonged to such as Imago Bone—greatest second-story man of the Spiral Sea!

As if sensing Bone's thoughts, Skalagrim hesitated beside the thief. The look he gave Bone was at first as dismissive as that of a fisherman tossing back a minnow. Bone might have made a brave remark, but not chained, not in range of that mace.

Skalagrim said something Bone could not understand but that seemed to please the foamreavers. Brief haggling commenced, obviously tilted in Skalagrim's favor. Soon Skalagrim handed over a bag and turned the slave-gang over to his men.

They were about to drag Bone past, but suddenly Skalagrim's eyes narrowed and he raised his hand. Skalagrim said something quick and incomprehensible, and Yngvarr answered something in kind. Bone could do nothing but look at Skalagrim evenly, so he did.

Skalagrim squinted. "You have self-possession," the warrior said in Roil.

"That," Bone said, "is exactly what I lack in this situation."

"But not much sense. I have a gift, you see. Ever since the dream of the shadows on the strait . . . never mind. All you need to know is, I can see into men's spirits. There is something of age and winter in your sinew. And there is a great darkness within you."

"Well, I personally wouldn't claim it's a *great* darkness," Bone said, "more of a pretty good darkness—"

Skalagrim slapped him with a mailed hand. It would have never happened had Bone not been chained. But that was little consolation for the ringing in his head and his blood dripping onto the snow.

Skalagrim grabbed Bone by the throat and shoved him to the very edge of the cliff. As Bone was still roped to the other prisoners, three of the slaves joined him in dancing at the crumbling divide between survival and cold, bloody death. A couple of people on the line screamed. Bone might have joined them, but the grip silenced his throat.

"You amuse me," Skalagrim said. "But only so much. We'll see if you last on the farms, and then we can test your other skills. But save your jests for your equals, not your masters."

They dragged Bone off.

I am a fool, he thought as they followed a winding path through the snow toward one of the farms below. Bone's swelling face testified to it. His bravado would not serve him here. He must bury it like an ill-gotten gem. He was a thrall.

No, think the word in your own tongue. Savor the meaning. "Slave."

I am not a slave! the thief in him rebelled. *This is a ridiculous accident! I am a free man.*

You are a man, said the husband and father in him. *But your condition, now, is "slave."*

They reached a large farm, hidden from view of Gullvik by the Gull-Jarl's hill. There a woman named Gunlaug greeted them and spoke for a time in Kantentongue. Then he and the others were led to a barn, where their bonds were loosened and they were offered porridge and cheese. The man next to him spoke in Roil, briefly dispersing the gloom of Bone's thoughts. "You did not understand Gunlaug."

Bone shook his head.

"We are to be well treated if we obey. If we do not, they may employ starvation, beating, isolation, and torture."

Bone grunted.

"If we try to escape and fail, we will be maimed. If we try to escape and succeed, we will be branded outlaws."

Bone shrugged.

"You may not understand the Kantentongue flavor of that word. If one is outlaw, one loses even the meager protections a thrall can enjoy. We will be in the same class as murderers. Any person can, and probably should, claim the life of an outlaw, in any manner that suits them. The Gold-Jarl might offer a reward. But in the Bladed Isles, bloodshed is its own reward."

Bone smirked.

"Now I have helped you as much as I can," the man concluded. "You have spirit, and I wished to honor that." He spoke no more.

Bone lowered his head, the mists closing once again about his brain. It was all too much.

No, it is not too much, a hard, stony voice said deep within him. *You will carry on. For fate is fickle and it can tire even of horror.*

At sunset Bone and his work gang staggered back into the barn, escorted by three armored men with axes. A haggard, straw-haired slave with a Kantening accent showed them to patches of straw and brought them stew that made Muninn Crowbeard's seem a royal feast. "The first days are the hardest," the man said. "They want to make you tired. And to see how futile escape would be. They want to make you grateful for the few comforts you get. When they're more sure of you, they'll ease up. It's not so bad after that."

That's what I'm afraid of, Bone thought, though what he said was, "Thank you."

As night fell, Bone tried to gauge the number of warriors who guarded this part of the Gull-Jarl's domain. His ears were sharp, and he tried to catch their tread, their grunts, their snatches of conversation.

But the slave-holders' methods, though simple, were effective. His skills did not matter if his body was too exhausted to employ them. Oblivion dragged him under.

He dreamed of horses. Not the fjord ponies of the farm but huge wild beasts of the Forbidden Steppe, magnificent animals of many hues, whose galloping feet never seemed to touch the grass. They had names that could be rendered as *Dawnracer Windneigh Maneshake Laughswish* or *Springjumper Wildgroan Head-toss Backkick*, though such names could only touch the shape of the horses' natures, as a cloud is only approximated by its shadow upon the steppe.

He awoke from visions of free horses of the grasslands to a reality of old straw in a smelly barn.

Bone and his gang saw to the livestock. Bone learned more about cows, chickens, geese, and pigs than he'd ever known possible. Later they were engaged in gutting, cleaning, and salting fish, and in carrying the family wash. None of it was terrible, but all of it was wearying, and none of it was chosen.

After a lunch of dry salted fish they broke stones for a new path up the hill to the Gull-Jarl's hall. This was the toughest work yet, and perversely unnecessary, as two perfectly good paths already led there.

One of the new thralls said as much, and a guard rushed to tell Gunlaug. Soon she could be seen ascending one of those perfectly good paths. The thralls were uncomfortably silent. The man who'd spoken up, a garrulous Swanislander named Alder, kept looking toward the great hall.

Presently Skalagrim descended. "One of you has questioned your betters' choice to build a new path," he said in Roil. "Let me explain the matter. Nine Wolves walk the world, men unafraid to mete out gifts and pain. Men fit for the coming Fimbulwinter, not the simpering womanish cowards who hide under the wing of the White Swan. Nine will come—I have seen it in a vision. For I am one, and you have met Yngvarr, another. The future is ours. And so there will be nine paths. But you—Alder, is it? You see the paths as unnecessary. You are a discerning fellow who likes simplicity. I will honor your thinking. You surely don't need the little fingers on each hand. They are unnecessary!"

Men seized Alder, who struggled and kicked, but they held him down, spread out his right hand as Skalagrim readied an axe.

"No!" shouted Bone. "Is this Kantening courage? This man is no outlaw! He grouses as workers grouse everywhere!"

"I was correct," Skalagrim said. "You *are* possessed of spirit. We will speak again, you and I. But interrupt me again and you will die for it. Alder, my hand is sure, but if you continue struggling you may lose all of yours. Ah, good."

Skalagrim's hand was sure. Twice.

When Bone returned to the barn, the darkness in his mind made the darkness in the sky superfluous. Alder was moaning under a blanket, hands wrapped in red-stained cloth. Bone gave Alder some of his share of food and water, and checked the bandages. Gunlaug had wrapped the maimed hands adequately, but Alder would need watching.

The one tending Alder should not be an exhausted thief.

Many things should not be.

Bone lay himself next to a whistling gap in one of the barn's floorboards. He could hear the guards converse outside and could make out the words *nithing, troll, frykt.* Then sleep took him like a falling axe.

He dreamed of horses.

A rooster crowed somewhere on the steppe. No, this wasn't the steppe, and the mouse-gap beside Bone's ear was cold, but it had done its duty and forced his eyes open early.

He pissed at the midden the slaves were instructed to use, then walked to the farmhouse in the gray half-light. Of the guard he demanded fresh bandages and water. When the nonplussed man had gone, Bone nonchalantly surveyed the steading, slowly pivoting. For once his mind was clear, and he committed every detail to his memory. This was a heist, really. It differed from the usual only in that he was stealing himself.

The guard returned with Gunlaug, who carried cloth and a kettle.

"She wanted to see," the guard said, "this thrall who worries so over other thralls."

They tended to Alder, cleaning his wounds and changing his bandages. Alder did not seem grateful to be woken and washed, but he slipped back into sleep soon enough.

Gunlaug spoke.

The young guard said, "Since you are seeing to him, you will do two shares of work. Since you have stolen Gunlaug's time, you will assist her today."

This proved to be hard work, especially as Gunlaug slapped him for failure to comprehend her mimed instructions or her Kantentongue words. *Spoken. Very. Slowly. And. Loudly.* But compared to breaking rocks it was bearable. He stoked the hearth-fires, fetched water, milked cows, fed animals, cleaned stables. In the evening he returned sore to the barn, bearing fresh cloth and water for Alder. There was an extra helping of stew and bread; the other slaves explained it was Santa Kringa's feast day, and although the Gull-Jarl did not celebrate it, Gunlaug was a Swanling and made this small gesture.

Alder was playing a game with the old Kantening slave who brought in the food. With them sat the man who'd translated Gunlaug's words when Bone first arrived. Other games were being played in other corners. The barn almost seemed festive.

"Thank you," Alder said to Bone as the thief changed the dressings. "I know you've been helping me."

"I just want to make the world less boring. There are so many more interesting ways to die, than taking fever after maiming."

"I'm not bored," Alder muttered. "Nevertheless, thanks."

"Join us if you wish," the old Kantening told Bone. "This game is winding down. Do you know it?"

"It looks a little bit like chess. Or weiqi."

"I don't know your weiqi, but this is perhaps the opposite of chess. The game is *hnefatafl*."

"Bless you."

"Ha, ha. One piece is the king. He is ringed by enemies and must escape."

"How appropriate."

"Fortunately he has friends." The old man paused, extended a hand. "The name's Havtor."

"Mine is Imago Bone." He took Havtor's hand and bowed a little also, in the Eastern manner. "I am surprised . . . well, you're a Kantening . . ."

"Ah. How does a Kantening come to be a thrall? My family's fortunes diminished when my father's ship floundered in the Draugmaw, the great maelstrom, taking him, most of his war band, and all his treasures to the deep. My mother was obliged to sell some of her children into thralldom."

"That's horrible."

Havtor shrugged. "We might have starved otherwise. The Gull-Jarl took me on, and I have never wanted. He is not so bad. His son, now . . . well, we all have things that are best not talked about." He moved a wooden warrior upon a grid, saying, "Like you and your horses."

"What?"

The big man beside them laughed. "Twice now, Imago Bone, you've cried out in the night, rambling about horses. And yet you don't remember?"

Bone scratched his chin. "I have had dreams. . . ."

"So I assumed," said the big man, "as I saw no horses in here! And I do know my horses." As if to apologize for teasing, the man shook Bone's hand. "Vuk's the name."

"You're not a Bladelander," Bone said.

"I was captured in a raid on the Mirrored Sea. My people are Wagonlords of the Wheelgreen."

"My sympathies. You must miss home."

"It haunts my dreams, like your horses. And you? Where were you taken?"

"About half a mile from here, if I'm not mistaken."

"You're joking!" Alder said.

"I wish that very much," Bone said. "My fortunes have plummeted. I made a critical mistake, one that has torn me from my wife."

"A raid gone awry?" Havtor said.

"A bad gamble?" Vuk said.

"A dalliance?" Alder said.

"I made an error of judgment in a fight. I should not have been taken."

"Ah," Vuk said. "That is indeed bitter. Well, battle has its fortunes."

"But to lose everything because of one lapse . . . I might have won that fight, at my best. But cares cloud my sight. I'm aging, it seems."

"It's said that no man can defeat Old Age," said Havtor, "if he should live long enough to face her. Even the god Torden, when he wrestled her once, found himself evenly matched."

Bone thought of Muninn Crowbeard and how he'd feared the thews of Old Age.

"I may not defeat *her*," Alder said, "but my *hnefatafl* king's escaped."

"Ah!" Havtor said. "You are not as weak as you seem!"

"Nor as defeated," Alder murmured, as Havtor set up the board for Vuk and Bone.

Vuk remarked, "Be aware the game is lopsided. It is harder to win as the king."

"I'll play that part," Bone said. "Escape suits me."

"Does it now?" Vuk said.

Bone was not as tired this night, and the sky was clear, stars and moon glittering above the snow's silver sheen. So when he woke around midnight and relieved himself at the midden, he took his time, listening. By now he was sure the standard number of guards was five.

Snow crushed behind him: a sixth. The newcomer said nothing. It was a looming sort of nothing. Someone wanted Bone afraid.

Vapor emerged from Bone in the moonlight, from above and below. "You know," he said, forcing his voice to be nonchalant, "I'd wet myself, Skalagrim, but you're just a little late." He concluded his business, hiked up his pants, and turned.

Skalagrim the Bloody stood there with his mace glinting in the moonlight. "I've had dreams of horses," said the Kantening. "They are not my dreams. I have traced them to this barn, waiting for their source to emerge. It does not wholly surprise me that it's you. I've sensed you are more than you seem."

"What am I then?"

"You're haunted by a strange wyrd, as am I. It's said my father's hall is built on the shores of the Straits of Tid. As long as I can remember I've roamed the world in my dreams, contending with others who dream as I do. One night, many of us met in dreams at the Great Chain of Unbeing, though to us it seemed as day. There we contested for the power of the Runemark. But we were surprised by new opponents that were not human . . . nine of us were forever changed. Three from Svardmark. Three from Spydbanen. Three from Oxiland. We were already strong men, but a grim power made us mighty as legends. And our eyes were opened to deeper truths of existence."

"What deeper truths?"

"Our world is a semblance, a transitory illusion. Only one thing within it is truly real."

It was strange, to hear this barbarian speaking as the warrior-priest Katta might. "Compassion?"

"Power."

"Thank you for your edifying speech. I won't criticize, as I like having pinkies. May I go?"

"Don't think you have fooled me. You are a sorcerer, or one touched by the gods. Sooner or later I'll know the truth. I have sensed *her*, skulking around you."

"What?"

"There is one who has an interest in you. She thinks she is obscured, but I have seen. And on the day she comes to your aid, I will claim her. Think of that, enchanter. The one who would rescue you will be mine."

Bone's hands clenched. Skalagrim was alone, and though the Kantening was gigantic, and armored, Bone was quick. . . .

"Yes," said Skalagrim. "I sense your hate. Rush upon me, *slave*. Reveal your true power, enchanter. I am ready."

"You have me mistaken for someone else."

"As you wish." Skalagrim backed away and gestured grandly toward the barn. "Maintain your ruse if you wish. Know that I watch you always."

Bone returned nonchalantly to the barn, whistling a tavern song from Amberhorn.

When he lay down, he heard Vuk's voice in the darkness. "When I was last outside," the Wagonlord said quietly, "I counted five bright stars among the Sisters, bunched together like a war band."

The distant star cluster called the Sisters was often used as a test of eyesight on the continent. But Bone didn't think that was what Vuk really meant.

"I might have seen six," Bone said after his nerves settled. "Though the last was perhaps a comet. Something that may or may not be there tomorrow."

Vuk grunted. There was silence. Then: "One night soon, the snowfall may be too great to see stars or moon."

"I think you're right."

"On that night, a fox may not be able to see rabbits in front of him."

"What about five foxes?" Bone asked.

"It might depend on the number of rabbits."

"You've thought more about this than I." Bone said. After some thought he added, "I had a dream in which four horses played games together and then ran free."

"I had a similar dream," Vuk said after a pause. "We will speak again."

"Soon."

They were silent, but Bone could not sleep. Could he trust Vuk, Alder, and Havtor with his plans?

The one who would rescue you will be mine.

He had little choice. Gaunt would be coming. Bone had to escape before then.

CHAPTER 11

CHRONICLERS

The trolls carried A-Girl-Is-A-Joy for miles, into rocky and desolate hills. She could tell by the illumination that the sun had risen high, but the sky remained stubbornly gray and the air only warmed a little. Any time the sun threatened to peek out from the veil of clouds, the trolls hid in some shadowed defile.

"Are you afraid of the sun?" she asked once.

"Shut up!" said more than one troll. "You speak when you're asked to speak!" So she took that as a *yes*, and shut up.

Stay calm, Joy. Your mother, your teacher, your friends, they are formidable people. They'll find you. Try not to think how many trolls there are.

For there were dozens, and every so often one or two more joined them. There were gray trolls and black trolls, white trolls and orange trolls, trolls mossy and mushroomy and brambly and bark-covered, two-headed, three-headed, no-headed, silent or gibbering or humming or monologuing rhymed poetry in an ever-changing choice of meter. There were trolls of granite and of obsidian, of quartz and of agate, of pebbly soil twisting with dead severed roots, and of smooth river stones punctured with dead bare branches.

"Where are you taking me?" she asked more than once.

She would get answers as varied as "Shut up!" "To the halls of Harrowshine!" "Silence!" "To the caves of the delven!" "Speak not!" "To the catacombs of the uldra!" "Be still!" "To the towers of Anemaratrace!"

She didn't like the sound of that. She had to escape.

The trolls had allowed her moments to relieve herself, and so this time she faked such a need. Once alone she began the slow, dancelike movements known as the Preparatory and the Commencement of the Art. She felt her body's energy reviving. She wanted to spend an hour more, but already the trolls were grumbling.

She gathered her chi, focused it into her legs, and leapt twenty paces up a hillside.

The trolls were after her immediately, with a dreadful sound of anger and recrimination.

"After her!"

"This is your fault!"

"No, it's your fault!"

"Quickly, fools!"

"It's his fault!"

"Faster!"

"She is quick!"

"Hurry! If we spend too long catching her, we may never have time to assign blame!"

The hill was treacherous. Wind-scoured, bereft of all but the hardiest scrubs, it was full of loose talus and deceptive boulders ready to dislodge at the slightest weight. She had to give her full attention to leaping from spot to spot, as each landing side slid beneath her.

The trolls were gaining.

She looked ahead to where the summit disappeared into a swirling sunlit fog. She forced herself ahead.

"The sun!"

"She seeks to reach the cruel orb!"

"Mossbeard! Claymore! I will hurl you ahead of her!"

"Why does it have to be me, Wormeye?"

"Or me?"

"You're both light enough to throw and tough enough not to break! Mostly! Hurry up!"

"But it's his fault!"

"No, it's his!"

"Shut up and be a payload!"

There came a screeching moving through the air, starting below and behind, ending ahead and above. A gray rocky troll, with eyes like blue egg-shells and a beard of green, charged downhill.

Another screech and impact revealed a gray, clay-bodied troll with eyes of schist and scraggly beach-grass for hair. It flattened like a mushu pancake when it hit but promptly popped back into a squat humanoid shape. "That hurt me, human!" it wailed, surging toward Joy. "You'll pay for that!"

"It's not my fault," Joy gasped.

"You'd make a good troll!" gloated the rocky one.

"Shut up," she told him, diving between his legs.

"A *very* good troll," said the clay one, getting in her way. "Now give up."

She responded by kicking his outstretched arm.

It was not the simple attack she'd seen the trolls pester each other with but a worthy maneuver, leg pulled back and lashing forward for maximum force at the heel.

The arm came off.

She hadn't expected that, nor the titanic wail emerging from the clay troll. Least of all she didn't expect the chorus of laughter from the other trolls.

Ha, ha! Claymore took up arms and lost an arm, tra la! A girl can beat him and so we greet him, Claymore! Arm-gore! Mighty no-more!

Claymore wept and wailed, "It's not fair! I'll clip both her arms for that!"

As Joy raced ahead of the trolls, Claymore retrieved his lost arm and carried it like a club.

But it was the rocky one who grabbed one of the loose stones and threw, clipping Joy in the leg. She toppled, and Claymore was upon her, whacking her with the fallen arm.

"Stop!" bellowed the rocky one, and stony hands grabbed her. "She is not to be hurt, not until the Chroniclers can study her!"

"She hurt me, Mossbeard!"

"Shut up and eat your arm, so you can regrow it by tomorrow."

And so they dragged her back into the procession. Miraculously Mossbeard and Claymore didn't see the Runemark, or else thought it unremarkable.

When next she had to empty her bladder, she was surrounded by glowering stony faces.

At nightfall Joy was feeling hopeless as they left the red glow of sunset behind and descended into a glittering ice cave.

Walking Stick sometimes quoted an ancient poet, saying, "'Life is thin ice, at the edge of a yawning gulf. Let us be prudent and circumspect, and kind to one another.'" Yet Joy did not feel prudent and circumspect; she felt terrified and angry. The natural ice tunnel curved upward into glittering red light, but the trolls turned right, into an ice-passage hewn sometime earlier by rocky fists.

Beyond lay a stone archway inscribed with glyphs Joy could not understand, and past it stone steps coiled down into darkness.

Joy could see nothing at first, not even walls and ceiling. All echoes vanished, and she intuited that they now entered a vast cavern. Little by little her eyes made out strange glints in the darkness—blue fires, green glows, sets of eyes in many colors—and reflections thereof, indicating spindly towers rising like crystalline renditions of pine cones, lotus flowers, thorns.

When the party of trolls had reached the bottom of the great stairway, Joy's eyes had adjusted somewhat more, and she saw they were surrounded by a peculiar crystal city. The blue fires were three great enchanted bonfires in the midst of a plaza, while the green glows emanated from huge mushrooms scattered among the streets. In the mixed blue-and-green glow, Joy became aware that many of the towers lay shattered.

The many-colored eyes stood revealed as the eyes of trolls, hundreds of them, gathered in the plaza.

Joy was unceremoniously plopped down.

"Behold!" said a troll who seemed a hulking statue of fungus-covered soil and rotting wood, with one eye that was a bole and the other a gap writhing with worms. "A human girl, spying on our territory! She was found near a grotto of unquickened trollings! She kicked off Claymore's arm! What should be her fate? Let's let the Chroniclers judge!"

Joy rose. "My name is A-Girl-Is-A-Joy! I am a traveler from a distant land! I mean no harm to you trolls! I saw no . . . trollings. I fought only to escape."

The troll-crowd parted like two, slow, sideways avalanches.

Two human figures in dark-gray cloaks stepped forward.

"Ah," said Joy. "Hello?"

The two figures pulled the hoods from their faces. Two young women, in their late teens or early twenties, stared at Joy. They seemed almost as surprised as she was. One grinned and strode forward, saying, "Hello!" The other held back, wary.

The outgoing one was a powerfully built, energetic person, a head taller than Joy and sporting an impish smile. Golden hair curled around eyes of noonday blue and a thick clouding of freckles. "Well, what have we here? Not the foamreaver or castaway I might have expected."

"I am indeed a castaway. But from farther away than you'd expect."

Turning her head, the golden-haired woman said, "I think she's all right, Malin."

The one who'd hung back was also tall but willowy, with dark hair, green eyes, and a distant expression, as though any appraisal of Joy must needs encompass every troll and the whole cavern as well. The dark-haired woman nodded to Joy nonetheless.

"I am Inga Peersdatter," the gold-haired one continued, "and this is my colleague Malin Jorgensdatter. We are folklorists."

"Folklorists?" Joy chewed on the word, looking around at the assembled trolls. "As in, you study folktales? You're serious?"

"Oh, very serious, A-Girl-Is . . ."

"Joy. You can just call me Joy."

"Joy. All this constitutes research. We have already released a few pamphlets. Our plan is to engage one of those newfangled publishers in Svanstad, get them to print a gigantic book. A collection of folktales told around Kantenjord, much like that of the Sisters Darke in the Eldshore."

"So . . . you're not prisoners?"

"Well," Inga said, "that's an awkward matter—"

"Enough talk!" boomed a voice. It was the troll formed of boulders with the obsidian eyes, the first troll Joy had seen. It seemed to Joy the voice had a slightly feminine quality, if a landslide could be considered feminine. "This human threatened a grotto of trollings! What shall be done with her?"

The one called Wormeye called out, "That is what the Chroniclers must determine, Rubblewrack. They are of her people, at least in seeming."

"Wait!" Joy called. "You keep talking about these trollings. Little trolls? I didn't see anything."

Malin spoke for the first time, "Did you find a place filled with boulders in one spot, all of similar size?"

"Yes."

Malin looked worried. "Then you stumbled on a bunch of nascent trolls. They may or may not quicken if trolls spend time telling tales, fighting, and carrying on nearby. But the potential is there. Endangering trollings makes the trolls mad."

"Not that it's hard to make them mad," Inga said.

"I didn't know!" Joy said. "Surely it's wrong to punish me for what I did not know. My teacher must despair of me, but he's said that it's better to rule by example and courtesy than by law and punishment, and that relentless control makes it difficult to govern."

"I don't understand this teaching," the troll Rubblewrack boomed, lurching toward Joy. "A troll can only rule herself."

"But I thought you had a king."

"He rules himself so well, that Skrymir Hollowheart, that we all feel a need to obey." Rubblewrack raised her fists.

"Let her be!" called Inga.

"Stop it!" shouted Malin.

"Skrymir has declared the primacy of trial by combat," said Rubblewrack. "Let this one prove its innocence by fighting me!"

Joy willed herself not to panic. She breathed in, out, concentrating on the chi flowing through her body. It was depleted, but it was there.

Hearing the name Innocence reminded her there were friends out there, family, and that she had to survive to see them again. Running had failed. Fighting would have to do. She put her hands on her hips and stared down the troll-woman.

"I will fight you, Rubblewrack," Joy said.

CHAPTER 12

ESCAPE

Persimmon Gaunt had once studied with Swanisle's bards—which was to say she'd been kicked out of her once-prosperous family's house and sent to those who could feed and tolerate her. In fact, her family had been only half-right. But she'd eaten well, for a time.

And she'd learned.

There was a tradition among bards of praising benefactors and besmirching patrons' enemies. It was said bards of old crafted spite-poems that boiled the blood and pocked the skin. Gaunt had seen no evidence of that, but she'd heard many a stinging lampoon.

She came to the house of Muninn Crowbeard armed and armored, but her best weapon had no weight.

She knew it could not truly disfigure a man, so she gripped her other new weapon—a yew bow from Swanisle, with a quiver of birchwood arrows to match—as she sang in the moonlight. Her voice was rusty, and Kantening poems surely weren't meant to be sung with bile on the lips, but one used the tools at hand.

> *By moon and sun I journeyed west*
> *My wind-borne song from Vindheim sent*
> *My poem-craft laden in bardic art*
> *With word-prow sharp to spear the heart.*
> *My praises, Sure-Hand, travel far*
> *Not only stabbing where you are,*
> *Clutching the straw of withered fame.*
> *Shall I sound your newer name?*
> *Once you sheltered my man and me,*
> *Offered kindly hospitality.*
> *I sang for our supper and our bed*
> *Of heroes brave in battles red.*

We thanked Sure-Hand at the dawn
And with his blessing we were gone,
Down to Gullvik to seek for one
Who'd help us find our missing son.
 But Muninn was not the man he'd been
When Sure-Hand hounded glory's den.
Palsy took his hand and mind
And sought the gold of slaver-kind.
 "That woman's man a heathen be,
And has no right to wander free."
So Muninn Crowbeard to Yngvarr spoke
And gave my husband to the yoke.

The door of the house opened. Gaunt readied an arrow.

Break not my spell, but listen ye:
To all I tell the treachery.
A trap they set, with mournful wails
And children dragged to slaver-sails.
 My mighty man, his own child lost
Sought their freedom at his cost.
It was a ruse—the children mocked—
The slavers meant him for the block.

Muninn Crowbeard stepped forward, axe in hand, cloak thrown over his
nightclothes and wizened frame.

Weapons screamed and shields clashed.
Within the fray his dagger flashed.
Outnumbered he, and underarmed,
He let no slaver go unharmed.
 When swords will speak, what man is free?
Who gets this point will surely see.
Men as sturdy as Orm's own ash
May fall when hungry edges clash.

Muninn's wife and wards appeared behind him, weapons raised.

O mighty Muninn, they gave him gold
For coward's ways, betrayal cold.
No more I know my husband's hand,
So praise I Crowbeard through the land.
    He asked to sail, and they laughed him off.
His coward's shivers made them scoff.
Wheezing and shaking he gave up war
His snores and farts heard shore to shore.
    So now, my friends, you've heard my stave,
How ancient coward tricked young man brave.
My words are loosed, and I have shown
How Muninn Fartsnore earns renown.

In Gaunt's mind she heard the song in Roil, but with the priestess Roisin's help she had memorized it in Kantentongue.

Crowbeard's wife said much then, the word "harlot" prominent in her speech. The wards advanced.

"I may be outnumbered," Gaunt said in Roil, "but I promise you this arrow will claim a life."

Crowbeard raised his hand, commanding the young men to halt. "You mock me," he said, "in the form of a praise-poem."

"It's said Muninn Sure-Hand was honorable. But Crowbeard is not."

"Your man didn't fight half as well as you claim."

"There is a thing," she said, "called poetic license. And you're hardly one to talk about fighting well."

"There is no dishonor in selling a knave into slavery," Crowbeard said. "Your man is a coward and a thief."

"He is no coward. But we are not talking about him. We are talking about the man who ripped a husband and father from his family, by means of a cruel trick."

"The method was not mine—"

"Is it better that you trusted in the wiles of slavers? They tricked us. Playing on our feelings for children. When we tried to save a boy and girl in trouble, we were ambushed." Gaunt laughed. "So glorious. I know there are songs about you, Muninn. Songs of Sure-Hand's valor. They will be completely forgotten, buried under the song of Muninn Fartsnore."

"I can silence the voice that sings it."

"You could try," she said, grateful for her leather armor and the round-shield at her back. "Except that I have already transcribed a dozen copies, and hired many singers, and left instructions that it be performed if I do not appear again tomorrow in Gullvik. And believe me, it is a catchy tune."

Muninn was silent. His wife began hectoring him in Kantentongue and he snarled in response. Weapons were dropped into the snow. Gaunt lowered the bow, a little.

In the stillness that followed, Muninn said, "You must want something."

"I want my husband. You will help him escape."

"What? You must know they were going to sell him to the Gull-Jarl! I would rather be known as Fartsnore than as that one's foe."

"I am not so sure. The Gull-Jarl is away now, and the man in charge is the honorless Skalagrim the Red."

"An honorless axe kills as well as a famed one."

"You spoke of a straw death before. That is surely what you're headed for. I don't think you wanted to hurt us, half so much as you wanted a place on a foamreaving ship. I think you hear death coming on the wind, and you don't fear it half as much as you fear the empty days that herald it, a whistling wind spinning the ashes of the fire." Gaunt took a chance, taking one hand from her bow, raising it to hail him. "You were somebody once. You could be again. You could be a man who raided the house of Skalagrim, who in old age walked into an adventure involving strange magics, and warriors of the distant East, and vessels that fly like ships of the old gods."

"Lies," said Muninn. But he wet his lips.

"Lies or not," Gaunt said, "you know I can sing the songs."

Once there'd been a moment when Gaunt told the bards she would rather be exiled than submit to their rules. . . .

Or when she'd seen her newborn son and spoken his name for the first time. . . .

Or when she'd told Imago Bone she would marry him after all. . . .

In none of those moments did the silence stretch farther than now, in the snow of the Bladed Isles.

"Wait here," said Muninn Crowbeard.

"This is madness," Muninn said for the third time under the moonlit boughs at the forest's edge, the third day after he'd joined her. "There are five guards at this farm, many more in the other farms and in the great hall above. This is a job for a berserker, not an old man with palsy and a madwoman."

"This madwoman also spies much snow swirling about this night," Gaunt said. "The guards will have difficulty seeing us."

"Did you witch it up somehow?"

Gaunt just smiled, for truly, what else could she do? "We'll leave the supplies here," she said, setting down her bow and removing her pack. "This is the best path into the woods, and this big tree the best . . ." she paused.

"What?"

". . . hiding spot. There's something else here, Muninn."

The old man muttered and joined her. He peered at four dark pairs of wooden planks. Each pair was accompanied by two long, straight, broken branches.

"A firewood pile?" Gaunt asked.

"Skis." Magnus spat into the snow.

"What are skis?"

"What hole did you crawl out of?"

"I fell out of the sky, remember?"

"They're skis. You put them on your feet and, ah, Torden's breath, never mind. They're probably supplies for a hunting party. Someone from the great hall might come this way."

"If these whatevers are from the hall, why do they look like junk?"

"Who can understand Skalagrim's ilk? The rescue's too risky now."

"No, this is confirmation we have a good path. We can't abandon the plan now."

"I can hardly believe we are calling this lunacy a plan. Or that I am here."

"I can, Muninn the foamreaver."

"What are you doing?"

"Moving the wood-things so pursuers won't find them."

"They are called skis, woman."

"Is this how it is in Kantenjord? Women do all the work and men correct their vocabulary?"

Muninn shared more of his vocabulary, but he helped. Then they set out.

They'd spied Bone from afar and knew which barn was his. It was near a midden and a stable. Gaunt led them toward the first, until she was within range of the second, able to see dry straw through an upper window.

She removed a set of special arrows and set them upon the snow. Next she removed a flask containing the foulest alcohol she'd found in Gullvik. The hard part was kindling it, but she had an ingenious fire-starting device from Qiangguo that served her well.

"Magic," muttered Crowbeard.

"Civilization," answered Gaunt, as her first fire arrow lit up. "You should try it sometime."

Her first shot missed and landed uselessly in the snow. The next four found their target. The stable was alight.

Shouts of alarm and quivering firelight echoed and flared in the night.

"Move," Gaunt said.

Someone in the barn had already opened the door to investigate. A wispy-haired man younger than Muninn but with a face more weathered looked out at the fire. Gaunt was surprised to see no guards but was not about to argue.

The young-old man shouted and bellowed orders into the barn. Soon, a group of thralls departed, rushing toward a group exiting the farmhouse.

The young-old man watched them go, murmuring something to someone back in the barn.

"You are mine," came a cold voice behind Gaunt.

She whirled and beheld an immense, red-bearded man in a byrnie and crimson robe, spiked mace raised.

"Skalagrim," hissed Muninn. "This witch-woman ensorcelled me. She has powers of fire and ice—"

"Oh shut up," Gaunt said, and loosed an arrow at Skalagrim the Bloody.

It pierced him in the shoulder, but the byrnie blunted the blow. Skalagrim roared and staggered, but in another moment he was upon her.

Even forewarned, his ferocity amazed her. She brought the bow up instinctively to block him, and he swatted it aside. With a twang it arced out of sight.

She dove sideways into the snow (away from Fartsnore) and drew Crypt-tongue. She rose just in time for Skalagrim's fresh lunge. She blocked the mace and edged backward, losing her footing and falling to one knee.

"Where are your powers now?" said Skalagrim, raising the mace.

"Don't believe anything Crowbeard says," Gaunt answered, drawing and throwing a dagger.

Skalagrim had good reflexes; her clear shot only grazed his cheek.

The seeping wound seemed to make him see her clearly for the first time. "You . . . you are not the one in my dreams."

"I should hope not," she muttered, scrambling backward and searching for her bow.

Listen, came the voice of Floki, the slaver whose spirit was imprisoned within Crypttongue. *I mean to pay back my former associates, who cared nothing for my blood-price. Skalagrim has a weakness. He can't abide being mocked.*

Suddenly Skalagrim staggered, for an unexpected foe had appeared.

Muninn Crowbeard stood shivering, his quivering hands gripping a bloodied axe.

Skalagrim whirled. His mace knocked Muninn aside like an old chess piece. But now Gaunt had her bow, battered but still worthy. She sheathed Crypttongue, found another arrow, and shot Skalagrim in the back.

"You!" he bellowed, spinning. "You must know about her. Tell me who she is, where she is. Is she laughing at me?"

"I should think so," Gaunt said, her cold hands seeking a new arrow. "I would."

Bellowing curses, he lunged, wild, heedless—but now a third foe leapt upon him from the barn roof.

"You!" roared Skalagrim.

"Is my name so forgettable?" the newcomer said.

"Bone!" Gaunt called out.

"That's more like it." Bone grabbed Skalagrim's beard and yanked. Gaunt did not think she dared hit Skalagrim under these circumstances, at least not with the bow. And Crypttongue would take time to redraw.

She dropped the bow and clutched the arrow, rushing forward to poke at Skalagrim's eyes.

"You!" Skalagrim told them. "Both! Will! Die!"

"They're never very original are they, Bone?"

"Not when their backs are against the wall, Gaunt."

Skalagrim roared backward and slammed himself against the barn.

"Why don't I learn to shut up?" Bone moaned from where he'd fallen off Skalagrim's back.

Skalagrim laughed and raised the mace.

Gaunt had her third surprise of the fight. The young-old thrall appeared and whacked Skalagrim with a wooden bucket from the barn. Two more thralls joined him, striking with timber and shovel. Muninn was there too, for all that his hands shook, and he shouted bloodcurdling oaths.

Skalagrim shoved them all aside and buried his mace in the stomach of the young-old thrall.

"Go!" gasped the rescuer as he fell, coughing up blood. "I regain my family's glory. . . ."

"Come," said one of the newcomers, a tall, deep-voiced man. "I will get your bow."

Gaunt was not even sure how he could have seen the bow in the moonlit snow, but she gripped her arrow in one hand and took Bone's in the other. They ran like rabbits into the snow.

"I expected—" Gaunt gasped as they reached the woods, "more guards."

"Skalagrim wasn't enough, woman?" panted Muninn.

"You shut up," she told him. "You almost betrayed us—"

"I saved you."

"That's why you're still alive."

"We didn't count on Skalagrim," Bone interrupted with heaving breaths. "But they didn't count, ugh, on my putting dung in the stew. The guards were, uh, indisposed."

"You had your own plan," Gaunt realized.

"Oh, it wouldn't have worked. Thank you."

"You're welcome."

"It may still not work," said a short Swanislander with bandaged hands. "Vuk, the skis are gone."

"The whats?" Bone said.

"You had your ploy," said the tall man, handing Gaunt her bow and joining the Swanislander beside the great tree. "We had ours. But someone has moved our gear and added their own."

"I stand guilty!" Gaunt said. "Let me show you."

Soon they had possession of two sets of gear. Gaunt got her pack on, after lightening it by giving Bone the armor pieces she'd gotten with Roisin's guilt-money, a breastplate and guards for elbows and knees.

"Thank you," he said, sounding truly impressed. "They swing heavy weapons in this country."

"Let's hear no more quibbling on how I spend our money," she said, tightening his last knot. "Or about extra weight." On that note she gave him Muninn's pack, as the Kantening had been battered by the fight.

"We have four sets," said the tall fellow named Vuk. "But Havtor has sacrificed himself. I am quick-footed and used to snow. The rest of you will ski."

"Uh," Bone said. "What will we see?"

"No, no, you will ski. You will use two planks, each attached to one foot, to slide along in the snow."

"This is so we will look especially ridiculous to Skalagrim's men when they catch us. Yes?"

"No," Vuk said, "this is so they won't catch us. Trust me."

"How do you steer?"

Muninn grabbed a pair of the long, straight branches and waved them at Bone's face. "With these."

"Ah." Bone rolled his eyes. "Gods help us, more sticks!"

"I'll show you the uses of a stick—"

"Enough," Gaunt said. "I'll try it, if you're so dubious, Bone."

"Wait," Bone said, and he glared at Muninn. "I haven't even had time to ask what the hell *he's* doing here."

"I'm here because your wife is most persuasive," Muninn said, throwing her a hard look. "I will share your adventure, to repay any debt to you."

"You will travel with us?" Bone exclaimed. "What of your wife, your wards?"

"They will get along fine without me," said Muninn. He chuckled, though it sounded rather like a gag. "Indeed, I once caught my wife getting along fine with the elder ward in the barn."

"Oh," Gaunt said.

"Ah, how can a foamreaver blame her? Her blood's still hot, and I am a palsied waste. She loves me still, I think. But when she wants me, it's a desire mixed with pity, as satisfying as cheap spirits. You like it at the hour, but it poisons you over the days. Let it rest. Let me roam."

"Indeed," Bone murmured. "Let's go."

Into the tall, deep Kantenjord woods they went.

CHAPTER 13

TORFA

Mother Earth and Father Sky, thought Lady Steelfox of the Karvak Realm, *I wander a place so dim I cannot tell black from white. I cannot distinguish colors on the horses I must ride. Help your daughter find her way.*

Steelfox had attended state gatherings before, representing her particular khanate and the Karvaks at large. She'd shared wine with the gold-bedecked Oirpata, taken tea with proud warriors of the Five Islands, broken bread in Kantening trading forts beside the Mirrored Sea. She had her power base in the taiga forest realm of the True People, whom Karvaks named the Reindeer People. She was no stranger to peculiar customs and new foods, and prided herself on a diplomatic tongue.

None of that had prepared her for the bleak, volcanic shores of Oxiland. Oxiland was mad.

The Oxilanders were even now screaming at each other like children.

"You've betrayed us, Huginn!"

"Nonsense, I've created an opportunity!"

"Did you know of this, Jokull?"

"No, Gissur. Huginn said he'd solve the mystery of the Orb Dragons."

"And have I not done so?"

"I would wipe that smile from your face with a sword-edge, Huginn, were you not under my roof."

Steelfox either had to watch them snarl or nibble at the carcass in front of her, the fermented remains of some gigantic toothy fish. There was alcohol of course, green stuff that burned the mouth. That was surely part of the problem, but she kept drinking it anyway. She wanted to skulk off to a tent.

She'd been given to believe this Jokull Loftsson was some manner of king and could treat with Steelfox on behalf of his people. Now, four days after her arrival, as she sat serenely beside him in her best blue deel, her dark hair bundled high and coated with fat, Jokull still bellowed angrily like a drunken bravo, arguing with the men named Ylur, Styr, Gissur, and Huginn—the last now revealed as one of Jewelwolf's agents. The one who was supposed to smooth everything over.

"Consider the advantages, Jokull!" Huginn was saying. "The Karvak Realm is so expansive, you could drop all of Oxiland into it and it would be lost in the grasses. With their balloons and Wind-Tamers they'll set up a trade network to beggar the routes to the Mirrored Sea or Amberhorn. No more will there be a Braid of Spice, but a Braid of Clouds! We can sell them our meats and cheeses, our walrus and narwhal ivory . . . and in return we'll have the luxuries of the East! Muslin, spices, jade, even ironsilk!"

Steelfox cleared her throat. "Gentlemen. What Huginn says is true. The world is changing. We now command the skies. The Karvaks would be glad to add Oxiland as an ally. We will be visiting these islands often."

"Don't listen to the witch-woman!" said the bellicose, red-bearded chief named Styr. "I have seen her familiar, a falcon that even now circles this steading."

At his words, Steelfox couldn't help but stretch her mind to where her bond-animal flew, keeping an eye on Innocence Gaunt.

The boy was not party to this meeting; Huginn had bidden him wait outside the great hall, in case a scribe was wanted. The falcon Qurca whirled high above Jokull's steading, watching the lad, who paced back and forth beside the wall. Light snow was falling, whirling between the pillars as Innocence scowled and trod. Steelfox did not know his mind, but she could sympathize with his mood. Important matters were being discussed, and he had no part of it.

Yet soon enough, when she could arrange it, he would be in an important talk of his own. She'd been surprised to see him here, but perhaps the hands of the gods were in it. Soon she must make her offer.

"She is under my protection as well," Jokull was saying, reminding her that dividing her attention in this way was dangerous. "Lady Steelfox. You say your people will be 'visiting.' You and your party have behaved courteously. But I've heard from our cousins along the Mirrored Sea that your people are ruthless conquerors."

"We have a reputation for bloodthirstiness," Steelfox said. She did not so much as glance at the two warriors who stood behind her in their conical helmets and armor coats, staring over the seated nobles at two of Loftsson's men, bareheaded but protected by mail shirts. "Though the same," she added, "could be said for your own people."

"Point taken. What will you do if we reject you?"

"That is not truly my decision. My sister Jewelwolf is in charge of our venture in these islands. Where conquest is the goal, she commands. Where diplomacy is desired, I will act." She tried to keep the bitterness from her voice. Steelfox was one of the best archers in the realm, but she was never accounted a war-leader, nor a baatar, a courageous combatant.

"You are refreshingly blunt," said the youngest chief, a yellow-haired man named Gissur.

"We are strange to each other," Steelfox said. "There will be much misunderstanding, even if we strive to be honest."

"I quite agree," said Gissur, giving Huginn a withering look. "So this sister of yours. She'll decide the Karvak response if the Althing rejects you?"

Steelfox frowned. She had not yet conceded the point of waiting for the Althing. "The Grand Khan, my brother-in-law, decides which countries we conquer."

"And just who," said a snowy-haired old chief named Ylur, "is currently on the menu?"

"Alas." She smiled. "That is information I could only disclose to an ally."

"Ha!" said red-haired Styr, tipping down some of the green drink. "I like you, Karvak! Though we may be enemies soon enough. I think we can guess what will happen, Ylur. Oxiland is of course lovely this time of year, but face facts, we're poor. And Spydbanen's a barbaric wilderness, even for us! The real prize is Svardmark, especially Soderland. If Corinna's realm falls, who's left? Gullvik can barely hold onto Grunndokk. Laksfjord and Lysefoss are just independent towns. The Five Fjords have some power, but it always ends up with Regnheim and Vestvjell at each other's throats, and Lillefosna, Grimgard, and Vesthall choosing sides. They can't even agree on a capital, let alone a unified defense. Garmstad and Ostoland might put up a fight, but Corinna had better watch the skies. With her gone, these Karvaks can pick the rest of Kantenjord like meat falling from an overcooked carcass."

There was silence at the table.

Jokull Loftsson's voice was subdued. "Let me guess further," he said to Steelfox. "Your terms of alliance would require placing armies on our land."

Steelfox bowed her head. "The Kantenings are accounted wise."

Ylur pounded his fist on the table. "There is no point even hammering this out. Such talk must await the Althing. The other chiefs would want our heads for even discussing this much."

As he spoke, Steelfox noted Jokull's wife, Torfa, frowning at the proceedings. Torfa and a group of female slaves had been serving them, but now the lady of the hall paused and narrowed her eyes at Steelfox. Torfa leaned over and hissed something in Jokull's ear. The uncrowned king's face reddened as though slapped, and he snapped something Steelfox couldn't follow. Torfa stiffened and exited the hall.

Well, now, Steelfox thought. *That was interesting.*

Through Qurca's eyes she saw Torfa leave the great hall and snarl at Innocence. "Your master and his witch-woman are ensorcelling our men! Well, they haven't counted on the strength of Oxiland's women! We will die before we lose our freedom!" That said, she stalked toward the main farmhouse.

This concerned Steelfox. Qurca also caught sight of some of Steelfox's own party approaching Innocence. This concerned her also.

These allies were not soldiers but three drab-robed warrior monks bearing unusual curved, serrated blades. Steelfox bit her lip. Her use of the Fraternity of the Hare was an alliance of convenience, and sometimes it seemed rather more convenient for the Fraternity. It couldn't be coincidence they approached Innocence while she was otherwise occupied.

She sent Qurca to drop upon the eaves.

But now she must focus upon the feast. All the chieftains but Huginn wanted to defer decisions till the Althing, making it clear Steelfox should attend. Huginn was saying, "Friends! You're too quick to give up your rights! Since when has the Althing decided when and how *we* can raise fighting men? Gissur! When Tryggvi of Cauldronfall slew your thrall, did you wait till summer to raise a force and demand compensation? Jokull, when Palmar of Winterfork contested your claim to the Ashblack, did you need the lawgivers to tell you to station men there? We have *always* had the right to raise troops from those sworn to us . . . and to buy the services of more. I don't see how hosting the Karvaks, if they cause no trouble, would be in principle any different."

"Ah, Huginn the lawyer has returned," Jokull said, and his tone was not unkind. Steelfox herself, annoyed as she was with the man, had to nod his way in thanks.

"Yes," Ylur said, "he could well argue that case. At the *Althing*."

The chieftains began loosing claims and counterclaims regarding the laws like so many arrows shot from horseback. Steelfox could not keep up, and so she dared listen through Qurca's ears to Innocence's conversation with the warrior-monks.

She couldn't see them from the falcon's perch, but she clearly heard Innocence say, "I've seen you somewhere."

"And I have seen you, Innocence Gaunt," said a woman's voice. "It was during a battle, and matters were confused, and soon you fled upon your flying carpet. But I know you."

"It's not my flying carpet. It's its own master."

"Where is it now?"

"I wish I knew. Last I remember we were both plunging into the sea. What is your name, why are you bothering me, and what happened to your ear?"

"I am Dolma, of the Fraternity of the Hare, now sworn to the service of Lady Steelfox of the Il-Khanate of the Infinite Sky. And I have cut off an ear so that I can hear better."

"Dolma. I don't want riddles, Dolma. I want answers."

"Such imperiousness for one so young! I gave up an ear so that it could be magically preserved and kept by our order. Anything said to it, any sound that comes its way, I will hear. In this way we may keep informed across the whole face of the Earthe. And you? What is happening to your forehead?"

"I—do not know. In the days since you arrived, people have said a pattern is growing there. Like a birthmark, only new."

Steelfox wished she could see what he described, as she hadn't managed to get close to Innocence yet. But she didn't want Dolma to notice Qurca if she could help it.

"And you fear it," Dolma said. "You fear it is connected to your power. The power of the Heavenwalls."

"I'll ask again. What do you want with me?"

"Innocence Gaunt, I hear things. I hear you are hunted and coveted. By people who might like you to be emperor of Qiangguo. By people who might like to control the emperor of Qiangguo. By people who couldn't give a fig about Qiangguo but know power when they smell it. And by things who feel any of the above, but that are not people."

"And?"

"And . . . your father was once kind to me. Maybe he just meant to use me. But I still appreciate the things he said. They helped me to find another path for myself, and the Fraternity. And if you need a friend, I would like to be that friend."

Steelfox heard the smirk in Innocence's voice. "Because you want to be friends with the emperor of Qiangguo?"

"Because I see a young person with a good heart, in a bad place. As I once was."

Inside the men were still arguing.

"I have the right to have guests, Gissur! And an army! And an army of guests!"

"Surely things are different, Huginn, when a foreign power is involved! If these were Princess Corinna's knights, would we even be talking about it?"

"Perhaps," Jokull said, "we've fueled this fire with enough alcohol. Let us have a round of toasts and resume talk tomorrow."

"A fine idea," Ylur said.

"Indeed," said Styr.

Outside, Qurca noted Torfa returning from the farmhouse with a large loaf of bread, a large knife jabbed within it. Her steps were lively through the snow.

"A last toast then," Jokull said. "To old friends and new."

Steelfox raised her mug, ready to ride into battle with the green drink once more. "Skal," she said with the others, and soon her mouth felt like the heart of the Desert of Hungry Shadows.

But outside Torfa paused to say to Innocence, "Your master is a traitor and don't think I don't know it," before stepping inside.

"What did she mean?" said Dolma, sounding concerned.

"I don't know," said Innocence, worry filling the voice that had so striven to be nonchalant. "When she came out she gave me a look to make my hair match the snow."

Torfa strode to the table with her sheath of bread.

Suddenly fearful, Steelfox rose—

Torfa seized Huginn's chair, sliding him back, making him gag on his liquor.

"These *men* are too weak to defy you, traitor," she cried. "But I shall make you look like Orm One-Eye, whom you so celebrate in your songs!"

Out came the knife from the bread, and she tried to sheathe it anew in Huginn's skull.

Gissur beside her tried to knock her aside, and the blade grazed Huginn's face. Blood sprayed. Huginn screamed.

"No!" Steelfox shouted, reaching out uselessly.

Her men misinterpreted the gesture.

Before Huginn could finish gasping, "No one attack—my word will carry," two arrows had pierced Torfa.

She dropped dead to the floor.

"Fools!" Steelfox screamed at her soldiers, who blinked at her stoically.

Armed men surrounded Steelfox and her small escort. She raised her hands, demanding that her warriors do the same.

"Torfa!" the uncrowned king was wailing, bent over her unmoving body. "My wife! Huginn, you are to blame!"

"She attacked me unprovoked—"

"Because you brought these people here." Jokull stared at Steelfox. "She acted as Kantening women will, goading us men to fight."

"She goaded me with a knife. . . ."

"Jokull," Steelfox said, aching for the man's loss and desperate to make amends. "You have my profound apology for my men's actions. They will be punished for acting without command. I myself will appear at your Althing—"

Jokull's laughter was savage and bitter. "At the Althing! No. As Huginn says, a chief may seek justice before then. I'll have the lives of all you out-landers, and yours as well, Huginn, master of lies."

"*No!*"

Innocence Gaunt stood in the doorway, the one-eared woman Dolma beside him. He was staring at Huginn, whose face was drenched in blood. He took no notice of the dead woman.

The mark that had grown upon his forehead looked like a twisting of twin dragons.

"Huginn's scribe," Jokull said. "This doesn't concern you. If you don't wish to share your master's fate, leave now."

"No, I am not 'Huginn's scribe,' barbarian scum. I am Innocence Gaunt."

He raised his hand. Steelfox saw no outward sign of power. But a winter wind blasted through the door.

It buffeted Dolma and the others of the Fraternity of the Hare, though Innocence himself stood unaffected. The wind passed him and overturned the table, scattering the Kantenings and shattering the far windows. Only Huginn and the Karvaks stood unharmed.

"Go," Steelfox said to her men, for she knew enough not to reject a miracle from Earth and Sky. "Come with us if you want," she told Huginn.

"That seems wise," Huginn muttered. "Come on, boy."

"What?" Innocence was saying, staring at the wreckage. "What have I done?"

"Saved us," said Huginn. "Don't ruin it. Move!"

Steelfox led her two soldiers and Dolma's monks, with Huginn and Innocence, to the high hill of the church, above which three of her balloons were tethered.

Evidently trouble had been spotted and conclusions drawn. The church doors were shut fast.

She was angry with herself now for bringing down only a small group. Below, maddened Kantenings, some armed and armored, ran toward the hill.

"Open up!" Huginn cried out, pounding the doors. "Sanctuary! Sanctuary!"

"No, Huginn!" the abbot called from within. "I don't know what's happened, but if Jokull's men are after you, you're not coming in."

"Pious hypocrite!" Huginn shouted back. "Boy, do that door-blasting thing again."

"I don't want to use the power again," Innocence said.

"Do you want to lose your head? That's the alternative. Trust me, I've written half the histories around here."

Innocence raised his hands. Nothing happened.

"I can't do it," he said. "It's like my chi is knotted up. . . ."

"I don't know what that means," Huginn said, "but they're going to knot up your intestines, boy."

Steelfox watched through Qurca's eyes as the Kantenings approached. They had minutes only. "I did not want to meet like this, Innocence Gaunt, but know that I will give you sanctuary. I don't want to destroy any hope of alliance. But I will not let them kill us. If you can't get us in, I will kill the Kantenings. I can do it."

"I believe it." He looked up at the church's bell tower. "I think there's another way. Even with my chi in a tangle, I think I can do this . . ."

He sprang in a way she could only believe because she saw it through two sets of eyes. Up to the roof, ascending in wild leaps toward the apex, Innocence scaled the church.

"You are fond of words," Steelfox sneered at Huginn. "Talk sense into your priest. I will do the same with your countrymen."

"Why, yes, wise and mighty Steelfox," Huginn said, clutching his face, "I do believe I will survive my wound. Thank you for your concern."

She ignored him and spoke to her guards. "Red Mirror. Nine Smilodons. Your mistake has cost us much. We have spilled blood; the scent of it is still in my nose. Men have died for less. And yet I am your leader and the ultimate responsibility is mine. I give you the chance to earn your lives."

"Yes, liege," Red Mirror told her, and Nine Smilodons said, "If you order us into fire or water, we go." Shame burned in their eyes.

They had acted, she knew, to protect her; yet they did not explain or beg. Very good.

The three Karvaks stepped forward so that all ascending the hill could see them, and in that moment it was as though her father the Universal Conqueror spoke through Steelfox.

"Kantenings of Oxiland! Because of a misunderstanding, there has been violence! I regret it! But if you do not allow us to withdraw, the bloodshed will be far greater than you can imagine. At this moment the best archers in the world have taken aim from the balloons above. Their positions are secure. You will be slaughtered before you can so much as spit at us! You make brave talk, Kantenings, and ambush people while they sit in hospitality. But we Karvaks, we make war. War on a scale you cannot comprehend. Do you want war?"

The Kantenings paused, Steelfox held her breath, and the only sound upon the hill was the dim murmur of a gently disturbed church bell.

CHAPTER 14

CHANGELINGS

Even before she'd fully believed they existed, A-Girl-Is-A-Joy would have thought battling a troll unwise. Having tangled with a couple of lightweight specimens, she would have revised it to "foolish." Actually confronted with one of the toughest of them, a boulder field brought to life, whose fists could shatter walls—as Rubblewrack was demonstrating by pulverizing fragments of crystal masonry littering the underground plaza—Joy realized a better word was "insane."

"Fight me!" Rubblewrack bellowed, her voice loud enough to raise echoes from the cavern and shimmering hums from the crystal towers.

But despite all the tricks she'd learned from Walking Stick, like the use of chi to enhance leaps and strikes and the use of mindfulness to appraise a foe, she had no chance of defeating this troll.

Except from up here.

Her initial leap had landed her on one of the many balconies facing the troll-filled plaza. Dozens of crystal shards lay beside her, for all these buildings were ancient and crumbling, or at any rate splintering. Weary though she was from the leap, she still could hurl pieces of crystal at Rubblewrack.

They didn't do the troll-woman much harm, merely scraping her stony body, but they seemed to hurt, judging by the shrieks. Enraged, she began punching the tower's base. The structure vibrated, and Rubblewrack was engulfed in a flurry of fragments, lacerating herself even more. But it seemed she could not knock the tower from its foundations. Probably.

"Hey!" Joy yelled. "You! I'm up here!"

Other trolls began laughing. The laughter of trolls was like a thousand games of stone dice happening at once.

"Fight me!" Rubblewrack stormed into the tower.

It took her some time to arrive. Joy used that period to calm her breathing, clear her mind. She did her morning exercises of life energy cultivation, her body slowly weaving to and fro, her arms making slow-motion ripples in the air, to the cacophonous laughter of trolldom below. The chi circulating through her upper body linked smoothly with the energies of her legs, hips, and waist. She was ready.

When Rubblewrack arrived at the balcony, she smiled, bowed, and leapt. Her freshly enlivened chi let her fall lightly as a leaf.

"Hey!" she called up when she arrived at the cavern floor. "I'm down here!"

The trolls laughed again, a little earthquake of mockery. It seemed to Joy the laughter injured Rubblewrack more than the shards had. The troll-woman screamed and leaped.

Rubblewrack had forgotten she could not land like a leaf.

On impact her rocky arms and legs went four separate ways, and her stony head bellowed, "Fight me!" from a boulder torso.

Joy gathered to her then all the anger she'd so carefully held in reserve. She sped forward, focused her chi in a wave moving from waist to foot, and kicked Rubblewrack's head off.

It rolled across the square and came to a stop near a crowd of chortling trolls.

"Stop laughing!" the head kept saying. "Stop laughing and get me back together!" They ignored both pleas and kicked the head back and forth among themselves.

"That was," the folklorist Inga said, running up to Joy, "astonishing." Just behind her, her colleague Malin nodded with wide eyes. Inga added, "Are you all right?"

"Yes," Joy said, a little surprised. "Is . . . Rubblewrack all right? I went a little crazy there at the end."

"Probably," Inga said. "It's very hard to kill a troll. Though that one in particular seems to have bad luck."

"Trolls think with their whole bodies," Malin said. "Their whole bodies are an idea."

Joy put the cryptic remark to one side. "Are the other trolls going to be angry?"

"Hardly!" Inga laughed, releasing nervousness so that it became a giddy sound. "You've given them great entertainment. There's nothing they find funnier than cruelty. And now that you've bested one in single combat you've gained respect. Kind of how we've gained respect by telling stories. You're still a prisoner, but you're an honored prisoner, able to live safely among the trolls as long as you don't try to escape."

Joy frowned. "Inga. Malin. I have to escape. My mother and my friends are somewhere out there. And . . ." She debated revealing her secret, but when would they be able to talk privately again? "There's this." She unfolded her right hand.

Inga and Malin gasped.

"The Runemark," Inga said.

"What do you know about it?" Joy asked.

"I know you shouldn't show it to the trolls," Inga said.

"You are the land," said Malin, "and the land is you."

"And that is why," Inga said, closing Joy's hand for her, "you shouldn't show it to the trolls. Did someone brand you? Someone who wanted to use you to gain power? Or impress people at a traveling show?"

"No," said Joy.

"She is real," Malin said.

"How can you know," Inga snapped, "when I can't? *I* have the sight. I know there's something special about her, but then I *see* something special about her. You have no unnatural senses, Malin."

"Your senses are natural in their own way," Malin said. "But yes, I see less than you. But I notice more of what I do see. I may notice more than anyone. I think about it so much, sometimes I have to go to dark places." Malin looked at the cavern floor, the eerie lights raising shifting shadows from its unevenness. "I saw the mark flash as she leapt. Others might have missed it, but not me. I see her face too. There is no mistreatment there. I don't see the harm of a branding in her eyes. She is real. And there's more, Inga. She's a girl. Think about it. What charlatan would prop up a Runemarked *Queen*? There's no precedent. She is the one. She is the land, and the land is her."

"Perhaps this is a time," Joy said, heart hammering, "when we should talk about the weather instead." For the trolls had tired of their sport with Rubblewrack, and Wormeye had delegated the hapless Claymore (whose stomach bulged from the eating of his severed arm) to reassemble the rocky champion. Meanwhile the others encircled the three humans.

"You're a worthy foe," Wormeye told Joy, "I'll grant you that. You've earned a place in my tumult. But you're still a human, and you can't be considered trollkin until Skrymir Hollowheart says you are." He squinted with his one "good" eye at Inga and Malin. "Same for you two, except that you're provisional changelings. Skrymir will have to judge your stories. It's high time we made the journey up to Jotuncrown. Skrymir wants all the tumults gathered into one terror. Mossbeard, show Joy to Rubblewrack's rooms, which she's earned. She can sleep in the ruins or fight someone else if she wants a new tower. We're only staying in Harrowshine another day anyway."

"We'll walk with her," Inga said, and Wormeye shrugged as if such human considerations were unworthy of trolldom. The crowd parted for Mossbeard, and Joy reached her lodgings.

The tower might have been spectacular once, its crystal shining here and there with purple gems that raised a dreamlike light. However, its furnishings had been largely shattered by idle troll fists. Mossbeard, grumbling, had to lead them from chamber to chamber until they found one with an intact bed and chairs. There was no mattress or cushions, just a layer of dust. Lacking a broom, Joy used her own cloak to sweep the dust into the hall; her new friends quickly helped her.

Coughing, Mossbeard muttered half-apologies and withdrew.

"Trolls!" Inga said, and the three of them laughed. The dust was hard to clear, but it was satisfying for once to have a simple problem with a simple solution.

"Do they ever clean?" Joy asked.

"Rarely," Inga said. "Sometimes the troll-women throw rocks at the men until something gets done."

"Well, I'm almost done. There. Pull up a chair. I'd offer tea if I could."

Malin laughed and took a chair. "You should try troll-coffee."

"What?"

"Let's leave that for another time," Inga said, sitting down and propping her feet on a half-shattered table. "There's a lot to say, and they might not leave us alone this way again. Joy, you're not even from Kantenjord, that's for damn sure. How did you come by the Runemark?"

"I don't know! It began manifesting after I turned twelve. I just thought it was a strange birthmark at first. But then the dreams came. Mountains. Coasts. People. I saw Kantenjord. It was as though the land called to me."

"It did," Malin said.

"We know stories, we two," Inga said. "Maybe it's fate, wyrd, plain old good luck you ran into us. We know about the Runemark. It's a connection to the Chain of Unbeing."

"I've heard about it," Joy said. "Friends of mine showed me a book, the *Chart of Tomorrows*—"

"I want friends like yours," Inga said. "What did you learn?"

"'In the time of the land's need, the Runemarked King will arise and command the energies of the Great Chain of Unbeing, which captures the power of the three sleeping dragons. He who bears the Runemark will live for the land, and die for the land, and so long as the Chain remains he will never leave.' So if I'm the Runethane," Joy said, having trouble getting the word out, it seemed so strange and apart from her, "what is the land's need right now?"

"I don't know," said Inga.

"The end," said Malin. "The Runethane fights The End, always."

"What does that mean?" Joy said.

"I'll try to tell you." And Malin's manner changed. She shut her eyes, and the hesitant young woman sat taller. Her voice became more commanding, her words more sure.

THE END

The End, for me, begins where I began—in a village that appears on no maps, called Kattsroven, on the island of Ostoland. I understand that our home village is no more roaring with sounds or blazing with images than any other place in the isles, but it shook my head so much it might as well have been Vindheim of the old gods. My family loved me, but they were troubled by my desperate need to keep sensation at bay. They urged me to talk, to look people in the eye, to say only ordinary things. As if it was clear what was ordinary! The world was drenched in wonder. How could I know the right words to say? Better to say nothing at all.

I learned to cope. I found that going deep into the forest quieted the sensory storm. It was not that the forest was without noise and light, smell and sensation—it had vast amounts of all. But the forest had an unthinking chaos to it that I could learn to anticipate. And the trees would not suddenly barge up to me and make demands. So I could be calm among them. The forest was soothing, like a friend who never judges.

Meanwhile, the shunning and violence I received from the other children made it clear I had to copy their behavior in order to survive. My parents cared very much, but they had other tasks, Mother her school, Father his smithy. They could not protect me constantly. I learned to mirror the children's statements. Often my speech was like a patchwork quilt formed of pieces of things said by others. And like a patchwork quilt it might seem crazy, but it was enough to keep the cold at bay.

But I'd have had no friends, if not for the village changeling.

She was a little older than me, part of Mother's elder class, and I rarely saw her at first. But everyone knew the story. Trolls or uldra had made off with the baby of Ulrike, Peer the priest's wife. The girl left in the baby's place was surely more than human. At eleven she was stronger than any grown man in Kattsroven and couldn't care less what anyone thought of her. The maidens mocked her and the young men fled from her. She spent her free time in the foothills setting up mannequins of stone and wood and smashing them to bits. She was dangerous, and insane, and dangerously insane.

I was scared of her like anyone else. But one day in winter when I sat in the woods calming down, I ran into her, or she ran into me. My first clue she was coming was a whistled tune. It had a sad, sweet sound to it, and I remembered it as a cow-calling tune, such as women use up in the high pastures. I remembered other times I had heard it, usually sung not whistled, most often in warmer months. I thought carefully about the tune, but not so much about how it was coming closer.

The whistling stopped.

Inga surprised me, suddenly looming over me, her breath coming out in white mist around her face, her hands clutching thick branches. It was hard to distinguish between her and a mountain, especially with a mountain behind her. The details blended together.

"What are you doing here?" she demanded.

I could not grapple with the person, the question, the immensity of it all. I found myself repeating, "What are you doing here?"

I wasn't challenging her. I was echoing, in an attempt to make sense of the words. But Inga took it as a challenge.

(Yes, you did.)

"What's it to you?" she said. "I've never bothered you! I just wanted to be sure if you needed help. You're all alone."

"You're all alone," I said.

"I like being alone. I'm the only one who understands me." She paused. "You're . . . different," she said.

"You're different."

"Hey! You're just repeating me! Are you trying to make fun of me? Are you just like all the rest?"

The entire world was suddenly a very loud Inga Peersdatter face.

It was hard to pick out words from my mind, but I knew it was very important that I do. I desperately turned my eyes away from hers, so I could think. I saw a bumpy stick in Inga's hands. "Knot," I said.

"What?"

"Not like all the rest."

"Arg!" She threw her sticks and they fell everywhere. She sat down on a rock, let out a long white breath. "You're the schoolmistress's daughter. Malin, is it? The one everyone teases. I've seen you. Why don't you punch in their faces?"

(Yes, you said that.)

The idea of punching in faces was too strange even to contemplate. Imagine if someone told you, *Is the day too hot? Punch the sun's lights out! Day too cold? Go fight the North Wind!* That's how strange Inga Peersdatter's thinking seemed to me.

But the thing that I did understand was that she felt a little sorry for me. That was the first time I had the feeling another kid felt that way. I couldn't respond in words, though. Have you ever tried to wash a cat? In those days words were cats who knew you were going to wash them. I got better at catching them, much better, but when I was ten every sentence was a struggle.

"Hey, are you lost or something?" Inga was saying. "I can get you home." She paused. "Do you hear me? Do. You. Hear. Me? I can get you *home.*"

I heard her. Each word was thunderous. I retreated to huddle near a tree.

"Arg, not this again. Now you're scared of me too! Listen, I may be a changeling, but I'm not a monster! I've never hurt anyone! Except Dad that one time. And Bjorn Janson, but Swan's blood he was asking for it, and I really did feel sorry later, mostly. And there was Poul . . . I'm not scary! Do you hear me? I'm not scary!"

I am not sure, but I think I was hugging the tree. And sounds were coming out of me. I said speaking was like washing cats. But sometimes in those days the cats would decide on their own to come rushing out of me, only I couldn't choose what message they'd bring. Sometimes they'd bring a quote from something I'd read, because a familiar pattern of words can be comforting. It was not a reply as such—but it sounded like one to Inga, because it was a salme from my mother's salmebok, a salme to calm fears.

Yea, though I make my stand in the valley of the shadow of death, I will fear no evil. The wing of the Swan shelters me. The mark of the Quenching Fire is upon my forehead. The grace of the Painter of Clouds is within me, who chose me for the canvas before the world's beginning. Light shines in the darkness, and the darkness will not overcome it. Thou art with me; thy wing and thy mark and thy grace they comfort me.

Over and over. I gripped the salme like I gripped the tree.

Tales have it that trolls and uldra fear the salmer and hate the sound of church bells. And there's something to that, for I've seen trolls react with flinches and flight. Yet it may not be heavenly power that does this but the conviction of the speaker, the faith of the bell-maker. And perhaps it's just the otherfolk's experience of woe at the hands of Swanlings.

But none of that was why Inga Peersdatter was pained. She'd lived under the same roof as salmeboks and the parish priest. She'd been to church and stood beneath the bell; and if she hardly ever went to Mass, that was because of the stares and whispers, not the church.

The salme I repeated pained Inga, but not because of any supernatural power. At last her voice came through to me, like a cry for help over the sound of a waterfall.

"I'm not evil. I'm not evil. I'm! Not! Evil!"

On the last *evil* she shattered a tree.

It took one punch. Granted, it was not a big tree. Its trunk cracked and slowly bent, its spire creaking its way down toward the forest floor, gravity gradually speeding its plunge.

Its plunge toward me.

Speechless, I heard Inga cry, "No!" and hurl herself into the falling trunk.

She snapped it away from me and collapsed with it, into a tangle of blackberry bramble. The prickles of the bushes cut up her face and hands.

"Ow," she said.

"Not evil," I said.

I rose and helped her up.

"I'm so sorry," she was saying, "I'm so sorry."

"I can get you home," I said. "Do you hear me? I can get you home. Not evil."

I got her home. She was a little out of sorts.

(Yes you were.)

Sometimes when I went out into the woods I'd get lost for a while, and before I'd learned my established paths, my parents sometimes had to come looking for me. That scared them. I still feel bad about that.

But this time was the opposite. Sometimes, when I need to, I can retrace every step I've taken that day. Isn't that strange? To want a memory may never be enough, but to need it, sometimes that gets you everything and more.

Mentor Peer and Ulrike his wife weren't always nice to Inga, but they were grateful I brought her back that day. They gave me things to eat, gravlax and bread, cheese and blackberries. That was pretty funny, to be eating blackberries after Inga fell into them. After everything that happened, I thought it was hilarious. I couldn't help laughing, and my control over my own movements wasn't as good in those days, so I think I made a big commotion.

Peer and Ulrike brought me home. Maybe it happened faster than it would have, because of the laughing. Inga had to stay put and clean up. I thought she probably hated me.

(Oh, yah, sure. Gravlax is salmon. You cure it in salt and sugar and dill. . . . Salmon? That's a fish. You do come from a long way away! Salmon are deep-sea fish, but they come inland to spawn. . . . Oh, right. The story. Sure.)

You're wondering why this story is called "The End." There's two reasons for that. The first one happened the next day. I went through my usual routines, though Mother and Father were more watchful this time. When I went to the forest, Mother came with me. I went to the same spot as the day before, and I might have drifted into my usual contemplation of the green, the breeze, the gurgle of the nearby stream, except that something was out of whack.

"What's wrong?" Mother said.

"Sticks," I said.

"Yes," Mother said, long since accustomed to cryptic answers. "There are sticks. Is there something wrong with them?"

"Yes," I said, and I began picking up the sticks Inga had scattered yesterday. There were a lot of them. I set them up in a line near where Mother sat.

"Good," she said, bemused but willing to go along. "Now that's done."

"No," I said, and commenced arranging the sticks from smallest to largest. It felt good, getting things in order.

"That is very organized," Mother said. "Now that's done."

"No," I said. "We have to get them to Inga."

Mother frowned. "The changeling? Why?"

"They belong to her."

"Does that mean you want to give her a gift?"

That was close enough. I nodded.

"Malin. You may not understand this, but Inga is not like other children."

"She is a changeling." I gathered up the sticks.

"Yes."

"And I am a changeling."

"Who told you that?"

I said nothing.

"Malin Jorgensdatter, who told you you were a changeling?"

She was making me nervous. I repeated it back to her: "Who told you you were a changeling?"

Her arms were around me. I squirmed. She said, "Listen to me. People will say what they'll say. But you are blood of my blood. I knew the stories about Inga and I sat and watched over you with a salmebok and a piece of steel from your father's forge. Even when your father thought I was being foolish and excessive, I did it, until even the craziest old wise woman agreed you were too old to be snatched away. You are my daughter. People call you 'changeling' because they do not understand that a lovely, kind human girl can also have a different sort of mind. They need a name for what you are. For them, that name is 'changeling.' But for me that name is 'Malin.'"

In their own way, those words were as disorienting for me as Inga's outburst the day before. I knew Mother was trying to free me from a word she saw as an insult. But although I could not articulate it at the time, yesterday had given me a gift. I'd overheard village kids call me a "changeling" before, and it hadn't made sense. But now that I'd spoken to Inga and learned how kind she was, the label did make sense, in a way. Perhaps "changeling" could mean "a nice kid who's different from most kids." Even if two changelings might be as different as me and Inga, night and day. It might be nice to be given a name like that, if there was someone else who had it too.

But I could not express all that. What I could express to Mother was that I needed to give Inga her sticks. At last she relented, but she wouldn't go until she'd packed up some of the lefse she'd made the night before and brought it along too.

(Oh, that's a kind of potato pancake. That didn't make sense? Joy, where are you from? Okay, the story.)

So Mother presented the priest and his wife with lefse, and I presented Inga with sticks.

"Um, thanks," she said. She hesitated. "You want to see what I do with them?" When I nodded she led me to her gallery of destruction. I can hardly imagine what the grownups talked about as their children went to a glade behind the cottage, a grassy spot with a small mannequin army.

"I like them," I said.

"Well, don't get too attached to them. They're all for smashing."

"Why do you smash things?"

"This is where I get my energy out," Inga sounded more relaxed the farther we entered the glade. She whistled her cow-calling tune. She set the sticks down beside piles of rocks and dirt alongside a stream. "These will be handy for rebuilding." She gestured grandly at two dozen things made of rock and mud and sticks, resembling the trolls of folklore. "My parents would send me back here to work off my energy. At first they set up woodpiles, but I didn't find them realistic enough. So I started painting faces on them, twining pieces of wood together to make them look more human, that sort of thing. That made it more fun to smash them."

"Why do you smash things?"

"Sometimes I get really, really mad. I mean really mad. Some people . . . well, instead of smashing them, I go up in the hills. There I find rocks that resemble faces. This one looks like Bjorn Janson." She paused, took a breath, and savagely kicked the mannequin. Stone head, rubble body, wooden arms, all fell in a heap.

"Ow," said Inga.

"Why . . . why do you smash things?"

"Why do you ask the same thing over and over?"

With others I was not able to frame answers, but somehow I found it easier to talk to Inga. "Why do you whistle the same tune over and over? I like how the words sound."

"But why does it have to be a question? Why not a rhyme, a kenning, a salme?"

"I like questions. Sometimes I forget the answers, too."

"Well, I don't like questions. I like to smash things."

"Why do you smash things?"

"Argh!" Snap went another mannequin's arm. Inga looked at the stick, chagrined. "Don't you ever want to smash things?"

"No, not really. Things change so much already. I don't want to break them. Or hurt anyone."

"I don't really want to hurt anyone, Malin. I just get mad. And even when I'm not mad, my body needs to fight. I don't know why."

"Do you feel mad now?"

"No. I feel okay. Ordinary." I couldn't tell. She looked the same to me now as when she'd punched the tree. She asked, "You sure you don't want to fight one of these guys? I'd let you."

"I don't really want to. I like looking at them, though. May I do that?"

"Sure. I'm going to fight for a while, okay?"

So I looked at Inga's opponents, while she demolished a few. Sometimes I watched what she was doing, sometimes I watched clouds, mostly I looked at the stony faces. Inga did have a knack for picking stones that looked like they had eye holes, nose, mouth, ears.

"Whew!" she said after she'd crushed a third foe. "Want anything to drink?"

"Yes."

It was about fika-time, when people often stop what they're doing to have a bite. Inga's mother and mine were talking, endless grown-woman talk about names, births, deaths, arguments, reconciliations, food. Mentor Peer had retreated to a corner of the cottage that held many books. That corner tugged at me, as though the great Godbok there had thrown a lasso around me. When we'd had milk, I could not help approaching.

"Hello, Malin," said Mentor Peer, looking up.

I nodded, my eyes moving from him to book after book.

"May I help you?"

I shook my head and kept looking at the books.

"I am preparing tomorrow's homily," Mentor Peer said.

I nodded, continuing my appraisal of his library.

Mentor Peer cleared his throat. "Inga? I am taking my coffee and notes outside. The air is nice. Perhaps you can show Malin the library."

Inga's family had many, many books. There were mostly Swan-church books of course, theology, hagiography, homilies, salmeboks, and of course the big Godbok, with its family trees written down at the front. These mostly weren't much fun for us except some of the more bloodcurdling hagiographies.

"And then," Inga read with relish, "Saint Fiametta's pagan betrothed, furious with her for distributing her rich dowry to the poor, had her denounced as a Swanling. When she refused to recant, they tried to burn her alive!"

"That's horrible," I said. "Then what?"

"The flames loved her so much, they wouldn't burn her!"

"Is that is why a girl wears candles on her head on Saint Fiametta's night?"

"Yah. So they gouged her eyes out and chopped her to pieces!"

"Yuck!" I said.

"Gross!" Inga agreed.

"It's a good thing," I said, "they only make the girl wear candles."

"Sure." Inga sighed. "Shame they'd never let me be Saint Fiametta. I'd be great. I wouldn't even wear a crown. I'd tie candles onto my hair like some berserker."

I laughed. I actually loved Saint Fiametta's night, though I doubted I'd ever get to play the part either. The very idea evoked giddiness and fear. But I marveled at the candlelit church in the hushed heart of a snowy night, the candlelit girl in its midst. Often, though, I wouldn't look at the girl but straight up at the shadows shifting on the little wooden church's ceiling. I told Inga, "You would make a very warlike saint."

"That's true. The stories I really like are about battle." She hunted through a dustier shelf of Mentor Peer's library. "Here's one from Oxiland that talks about the end of the world."

"When the Swan returns?"

"Nah, this is wicked heathen stuff. The best. Fimbulwinter. Ragnarok. Look." She opened a lamb-leather vellum codex with handwritten words in a florid hand. The words were in the Oxiland dialect, fascinating in their kinship to our Ostoland speech, and I couldn't completely follow them. Beside it was a blocky illustration of two dragons with castles and mountains on their backs, fighting. Inga said, "Listen. 'The sleeping dragons that are Spydbanen and Svardmark shall at last shatter their ancient chain and battle each other anew for the treasures of the dragon-corpse that is Oxiland. Whichever dragon wins and gorges upon the organ-jewels of Oxiland will be master of the Earthe. In that final battle the Vindheim gods will return and battle on the side of Svardmark, as will the virtuous warriors of humankind. But on the side of Spydbanen will be evil men and troll-kind, whose powers will swell so that they will be again as they were of old—frost giants vast as hills. Some uldra will be aloof, as ever, but some will take sides.'"

"So much destruction," I said.

"Yes! The two sides will be nearly evenly matched. In the end, goes the prophecy of the Winterjarl, all will be up to the Runethane. 'As in the days when Runethane Thorlak defeated the fire giants of Oxiland, or Runethane Arnwulf fought the Twin Dragons of Madrattle, or Runethane Umar fought the Draug Fleet, or Runethane Valdar wrestled the sea serpent in the Meadow of Whales, so now a Runethane unknown will again decide matters. But it is not known if he will side with the good or the evil, and it may be that he will bring about the end of all things. But even if he does not, the convulsions of the battle will slay both dragons, and smoke will rise and blot out the sun, and a great cold will come upon the world, a Fimbulwinter that will threaten all life in the world, not just in Kantenjord. And there will be only a handful of people left to populate the new world. In this way the Runemarked King will bring The End, or only by the thinnest margin prevent it.'"

That's one of two reasons this story is called "The End."

Over the next weeks I visited Inga many times, was her second in many mock battles, discussed many stories, and borrowed many books. It was a kind of Vindheim for me, as if instead of Choosers of the Slain, there were Choosers of Readers, and I had been taken out of my old life and brought to a golden library where there were things to read and discuss every day.

Eventually, however, we ran out of books. Our families were blessed with the biggest libraries in Kattsroven, but that did not amount to more than thirty books, and we'd long since exhausted our favorites.

One day I was so absorbed by rereading a translated book from the Eldshore, *The Sisters Darke Collected Eerie Folk Tales*, that I refused to play with Inga even when she came to visit. I had one of my bad moments, when the grip of the thing that fixated me was so strong, it was agony to be pulled away. I fought Inga, forgetting how powerful she was.

She raised her fist, even as Mother and Father were screaming for us to stop.

And Inga stopped, as if I'd suddenly punched her, the way she once punched the tree. There were trickles of water coming from her eyes. I heard Mother say, "Inga, she has trouble knowing what people are feeling. She is still learning." I didn't hear what else they said. I was not allowed to keep the book. I threw many things.

Inga didn't visit for a week.

When she did return, she carried not a book but a huge bag.

"What is in the bag?" I asked.

"Heads."

"Oh."

"Not real heads, silly. Come outside."

I followed her outside, and she began removing big rocks and setting them down around her haphazardly.

"Here, Malin. Look at these boulders. I gathered them from up in the mountains. I picked them because they all look kind of like heads. Now this one, I call Happy. And this one, I call Sad. And this one, he's Berserk."

"Why do you call them those names?"

"To me, they look kind of like those feelings."

"I like Berserk."

"Me too. See how big his eyes are, here and here? And his mouth, here, it's kind of like he's grinning, but really not. He's furious. Crazy mad. If you see someone like that you'd better be ready to fight or run."

"I'd rather run."

"Well, we are all different. Now, meet the other guys. Here's Mad. She's Berserk's little sister. Here's Tired, he shows up toward the end of the day, usually. And Calm, though she and I don't hang out together much. And this is Eager. He's kind of a little boy, I think, because I couldn't find a big rock for him. And this is Swan Only Knows, because sometimes I can't read people either."

I saw what she was doing. "I see what you're doing. Mother draws faces for me."

"Right. She told me. But I saw how much you liked my rocks."

I linked up her rocks with Calm on one side and Berserk on the other. (I leave the ordering of the rest as an exercise for the audience.) "Do you want to read about Ragnarok?"

"Actually, I have a suggestion," Inga said. "Since we are out of new books, and we're just village kids who can't buy more, there's only one solution."

I thought about it. "Steal books?"

"No!"

"Completely forget the books and start over?"

"No. We're going to make more."

"What do we put in them?"

"I don't know. Maybe we can make something up."

"Let's think about it," I said.

Trouble was, we couldn't come up with anything. Then Inga said, "I've got it! We'll be like the Sisters Darke. We go find people, especially old people, especially from small villages, and we ask them for their best stories."

That sounded a bit scary, and I said as much. But it also sounded like it might work, and I said that too.

"I'll do the asking," Inga said, "if you'll do the writing. You have the best handwriting in fifty miles, my father says. Please, Malin." In a more quiet voice she said, "I'm hoping I'll find out just who and what I really am, if we go asking the right questions."

I thought about that for a long time, before I said, "Okay."

And that's just what we did. Every chance we could for the next few years, we traveled our island of Ostoland, chasing down tales. We met with enough success, we wanted to head over to Svardmark to get more.

Our parents were torn, to be sure. On the one hand, we proposed wandering far from home for another year! Of course that worried them. On the other hand, both families had been worried about our futures, and our initial pamphlet had actually generated a little coin. Worse things could have happened than our becoming folklorists! As for our safety, well, Inga at sixteen was a match for most foes.

We received permission, grudgingly, to spend a year collecting tales, so long as we were wary of strange men and did not stray from the great roads.

I was indeed wary of strange men. Inga was sometimes a different story.

We also strayed from the great roads, but that too is another story. I will tell it all someday, because I've written it down in notes.

You see, I remember letters and written words in a way I don't remember spoken words. I wrote this story out so I could tell it well. When Inga and I gather tales, she's the one who gets the villagers to talk, and I'm the one who writes it all down. She can remember the stories in her head—but they change for her each time she tells them. When I write something down I remember it almost exactly. When we've gotten enough examples of the same story we talk over a combined version. Then I write it down, and I give it a number. "Katie Woodencloak" is Nineteen. "The Master Thief" is Thirty-Four. "The Charcoal Burner" is Eighty-Two.

The numbers, which are also the stories, add up. So far they add up to One Hundred and Eleven. They are always with me. They are my friends. Even the sad ones.

But this story, the one I'm telling you now, doesn't have a number. After all the stories are collected for the book, this one will go at the end. And if the book ever changes, with new stories added, this story will still move to the end.

That's the other reason this story is called "The End."

When Malin had finished, the blue bonfires outside had dimmed and turned an almost sunlike yellow.

"It's late," Inga said. "Or early, really. Troll sleep time is our daytime, but you'll have to adjust. I'll tell you that other story sometime. You'd better get your rest, because we're heading into the deep tunnels tomorrow."

"Deep tunnels?"

"We're walking from here, Brokewing Island, to Spydbanen," Malin said, "underwater."

The journey from Brokewing Island to Spydbanen took a full day, or so A-Girl-Is-A-Joy was assured. It was hard to estimate how far they traveled. The trolls made them walk for a time but eventually grew impatient with Joy and Malin's exhaustion, and carried them through the dark. (Inga seemed tireless.) The ancient uldra passage had long since lost whatever illumination its makers had given it, except in a few places where dim crystals revealed intricate bas-reliefs telling of krakens and whales and castles made of shells, in such fascinating detail that Joy wondered if the uldra had somehow perceived these features through the rock and were thus sculpting from life.

Yet for most of the journey, the only illumination came from troll-eyes. At times the silence was cut by unnerving sounds—weird keening cries echoing through layers of stone, rumbles of distant realignments of the seafloor and, once, terrifyingly, the trickle of leaking water.

"Fear not," said Wormeye, laughing at the human, the changeling, and the supposed changeling. "Lower-ranked trolls are prepared to plug up any leaks with their thumbs and then leave the thumbs behind. Isn't that right, Claymore?"

"Shut up, dread lord," came Claymore's voice. "I only just regrew this arm."

"Just in time, sounds like," Wormeye said with a chuckle.

"Even if the tunnel fills up with water," Rubblewrack said, "it will only slow us down, for we need breathe no air. If these two are really changelings, they may be able to survive. The third of course . . . well, let her try her tricks on the ocean."

Joy did not let herself be goaded. Whatever the truth of the leaking sound, they left it behind, and it bothered them no more. An hour later, however, came a thunderous noise as a section of tunnel behind them collapsed.

Please don't have been following us, Mother, Joy thought.

At last they emerged onto the surface in the crimson interval just after sunset. A cold wind blew across a region of broken hills, looking as if it might have been painted by an artist who regarded horizontal surfaces as unworthy subjects. Joy, Inga, and Malin helped each other avoid sliding their way down the rubbly ground into icy streambeds. The sea, such a looming invisible presence when they'd traversed the tunnel, was remote. Overhead reared mountains that made Joy's beloved Peculiar Peaks seem like gentle havens. Gray-black stone seemed to bleed as its snowcaps reflected the setting sun. The trolls had no difficulty in this terrain, and they whooped with delight to see the great mountains that were their kind's stronghold.

During a particularly chilling peal of laughter, Joy whispered to her companions, "Are you certain you don't want to try to run?"

"Can we outrun them?" Inga said.

"I see what you mean," Joy said, looking doubtfully at the broken gray terrain, pocked with prickly little trees. "But soon we may want to escape even more trolls, from inside a mountain. . . ."

"Sphere," said Malin.

"What?" said Joy and Inga.

"There is a sphere," Malin said, "in the sky. Coming this way. No, not exactly a sphere. Very close in shape, however. Do you have any idea what it is?"

"An Orb Dragon?" Inga said doubtfully.

Joy's eyes widened. "I know exactly what that is. Friends Peersdatter and Jorgensdatter, I am about to give you a new adventure story."

CHAPTER 15

A JOURNEY TO KANTENJORD, CONTINUED

(as penned by Katta, called the Mad)

While I hesitate to append anything to the fine calligraphy of my companion Haytham ibn Zakwan, his current preoccupation compels me to act in his stead. Indeed, I feel a duty to write for him, as he made it possible for me to write with any clarity at all.

Among Haytham's inventions is a thing he calls, I think, a *lail-qalam* or, more in the manner of northwesterly scholars, a *noctograph*. It is a box with a constrained writing window, within which are held two sheets of paper, one of the ordinary sort, the other suffused with a special ink concoction. By writing in the window with a stylus, the special paper transfers its ink neatly to the ordinary one. Haytham claims he invented the thing to enable journal entries on night journeys. I mostly believe him; it would be unlike him to invent anything solely for a friend. However, it is quite useful to me, as it allows me to make more legible notes than ever before. With its help I commence the longest account I've ever written.

In the literature of the Plateau of Geam, where I long studied, such a work would have three aspects: the "outer version," concerned with external action; the "inner version," describing the author's meditative state and other spiritual pursuits; and the "secret version," wherein the author confides one's deepest visions and miraculous experiences. Given that this account will likely never reach Geam, and may not even escape this balloon, I shall forgo the inner and secret versions, though I will comment on my mental state, and certain events may strike the reader as miraculous.

The shaman Northwing and I were loath to abandon Haytham with his head wound, but the soldiers of Soderland gave us little choice. Northwing is a powerful individual but was spent from the exertion of bringing us across the sea and surviving the troll-sent storm. I was in better shape, but my gifts are mainly in the monster-slaying line, and while the forces of Soderland were certainly intimidating, they were hardly monstrous. Thus we consented to be guests at the Fortress in Svanstad.

I cannot say the stay was unpleasant. The Fortress's exterior of orange stone may seem imposing at first, but closer up the traveler will encounter many more windows than would be prudent for a castle of war, far too many wide entrances to be truly secure. The Fortress is more a statement of power than an expression of it.

The knowledgeable reader will now wonder how I, who am blind, can have perceived all these matters. I absorb more than one might assume. I am of course alert to descriptions given by my companions, but also, even in the absence of my gift for perceiving evil (of which, much more later) I make great use of my ears, nose, and skin in considering my surroundings. It is not so much that these senses have become stronger, as that all our senses, yours, mine, and those of the dog barking down your street, are far more powerful than we can ever master. Each of your glances absorbs more information than you can truly make sense of, and thus your mind prunes the forest of perception like a brutal gardener. So, too, your ears take in an avalanche of noise, out of which your mind plucks a few rocks. It is for this reason that the Undetermined, founder of my faith, bade us to still our minds and let the perceptions wash over us, so we might better understand how thought and perception lead us into confusion.

When disease took my sight in my long-ago youth, I mourned. I might have taken up, like Northwing, the path of a taiga shaman, for I was already apprenticed as such. But in the absence of sight I could not make sense of the teachings. I know now that I might have found other means of interpreting the spirit world, but I would have had to invent all my own tricks, and at the time both I and my teacher thought this impossible. I withdrew into solitude for many days.

But though I abandoned the world, the world did not abandon me. The chirping of birds, the cool pressure of falling snow, the musk of reindeer, the taste of woodsmoke in my people's tents—these things teased me back to life.

CHRIS WILLRICH   203

I emerged from the cave of my mind a new person. The old me was gone; blind Deadfall, the new name I chose, stood in his place. Yet I was not dead, not fallen. My mind was learning to take more from my other senses, to help build a notion of my surroundings. I paid close attention to tone of voice, stride, scent of sweat in understanding others. I discerned the locations of objects from echoes, the direction of the sun from fine gradations of warmth upon my body. The process of mastering my surroundings can be slower than yours, who have sight. But I sometimes think I am less often fooled.

"It's impressive," Northwing said as we passed through the gates of the Fortress, "if you like that kind of thing. We are riding through a gate from the town proper into a courtyard."

"Yes, a stone courtyard, fenced by flat-faced buildings at least three stories high. There are many windows and doors, and a large number of soldiers awaiting us."

"Now you're just showing off," Northwing said. "Though you're right." The shaman hesitated. "Unless the place is saturated with evil . . ."

"No, I've seen no evil here. I am just acquainted with stone and sound."

"All right, well, the uniforms are blue and the walls are orange. So there."

"Thank you, Northwing."

"Don't mention it. Ah, here I think are our hosts. A man and a woman, or so I assume, both approaching middle age, bearing a family resemblance. They are not uniformed and wear garish outfits studded with pieces of meaningless metal."

"You and I wear pieces of metal," I reminded the shaman.

"Mine are not meaningless but bear the images of spirit animals. Yours do too, but of course they are meaningless in your case, since you abandoned the call of the shaman."

I am always grateful to Northwing for providing me many opportunities to enlarge my tolerance and patience. "They are meaningful to me as tokens of my past."

"How many years has it been since you left our people?"

"You were not even born."

"Are you older even than Imago Bone?"

"When I was a boy, there were still three moons in the sky. But that is another story. Let's attend to this one."

"You do the talking. You're nicer. And I'm reaching out to the local animals. I love big buildings. Always full of rats . . ."

I cannot deny that I am more sociable than Northwing. It is a trait I learned early, for a man who would explore the world blind must make friends swiftly. As the horses came to a stop I bowed in the saddle, waiting for our hosts to speak.

"Welcome," came a woman's voice, strong and somewhat amused, "to the Fortress of Svanstad. I am Princess Corinna, and this is Prince Ragnar. Please pardon the involuntary nature of your arrival. These are troubled times, and it is not every day that a flying craft crashes upon our soil. Is it suitable that we speak in Kantentongue?"

I have rendered her words as well as I can reconstruct them, though in truth I was still struggling with the language at the time. I am quick to learn languages, a skill of long practice, but I had never traveled this far. I answered, "I can speak it. I think I am better able to speak it than my companion." This was not meant as a slight of Northwing, though it was the simple truth. Rather, it might provide cover in the future. "I am Katta, a wandering monk, and this is Northwing, a shaman of the taiga."

"Come inside and be refreshed. We have much to discuss."

"May I first inquire what will happen to our friend?"

Prince Ragnar, beside her, spoke. His voice conveyed deep irritation, as though we had interrupted something he considered much more important. "He is going to rest at a farm near your craft. You will see him soon enough. Come."

So, we were prisoners, but comfortable, politely treated prisoners. I have experienced worse things. As Northwing, communing with her rats, declined to tell me anything, I tapped with my staff as we entered the Fortress, gaining a sense of stone floors and oak walls. There was a slight tinkle of crystal chandeliers overhead and a hum of metal armor on either side.

"You," Ragnar said in surprise. "You are a blind man."

"That is one of many things that I am."

"Extraordinary. I couldn't be sure before. Even now I confess I half-suspect you of acting."

"It can be difficult to prove a lack, Prince Ragnar, though I suppose I could arrange it. I hope you will not demand it, however."

"My brother is a better host than that," Princess Corinna declared. "I suspect your story is a most wonderful one, Katta, and well suited to the library."

Libraries are always tantalizing things, for gifted though I am, I cannot read the inked page. But I have had many pleasant hours in such places, listening to others recite. To have a meal there, however, was a new experience. The chamber was an upper-story room with a wooden floor and book-lined walls on three sides, with windows interrupting the stacks. The windows were open this afternoon, and breezes fluttered the tapestries upon the fourth wall. Tables wide enough to spread many volumes filled the floor, and servants shifted heavy oak chairs to accommodate four people to the accompaniment of grunts and scrapes.

Seated, we enjoyed salmon, bread, cheese, and tea. The cheese was not altogether agreeable, but the bread and tea were pleasant, and the salmon took me back to my youth.

"You may be wondering why the king is not seeing you," Princess Corinna was saying.

"I am too unacquainted with your land to wonder at such things," I said honestly.

"You are either ignorant or diplomatic," Prince Ragnar said. "As I am neither I will say it openly. The old king, our grandfather, having outlived the old queen and his mind shaken by battle, abdicated for his son after the wars of unification. The new king, Corinna's and my father, was ravaged by plague, the same plague that killed Corinna's mother the queen. As such Soderland is a kingdom in limbo, with its true king a barely conscious shell of a man, and its old king too unsteady to retake the reins."

Corinna interrupted, her tone gentle but insisting on commanding the conversation. "We were but children at the time, Katta, is it? Ragnar took command of the army, and I of the court, and we stretched our advisors to the limit. We defied all expectation by avoiding a civil war. Ragnar is my elder, you see, but he was fathered out of wedlock and cannot inherit the crown. I am a woman and thus considered by many fools to be ill suited to rulership. One day I will be queen, but that day is a long way off."

"Yet," Ragnar said, his voice harsh, "my half-sister is queen in all but title, and I am her right hand. No matter how many scheming nobles try to divide us. So there is no disrespect intended in meeting you ourselves. An audience with our father or grandfather might be . . . counterproductive."

Northwing blinked, returning to us. A rustling in one corner confirmed my guess we were now observed by rats. "No need to apologize for how you handle things," Northwing said. "You wouldn't believe how many ways people are governed. Most of them bad."

"Ah," said Corinna, "thank you, sir, Northwing . . . yes?"

"Yes," said Northwing, not trying to deny the assumption of masculinity.

"Well," Corinna said, studying us two foreign "men," "that is our strange country, and welcome to it. You are quite a mystery to us. How did you come to be here?"

"Katta can tell it better," Northwing said at once, laying a great burden on me but also the freedom to arrange it as I would.

And so I told how we befriended an inventor of Mirabad, who had flown a balloon to the steppes and landed among the Karvaks, our people's neighbors, and how later we set off to explore more of the world at Haytham's side. I pretended primitiveness and emphasized our sense of wonder at the mighty places of the West.

I had the impression Corinna and Ragnar were not quite believing in the primitiveness, and that they sensed the numerous gaping crevasses in the path of my tale. "And so you flew alone?" Ragnar asked. "No other balloons?"

"Just us," I said. "Though the Karvaks of the steppes were interested in adopting Haytham's methods."

"We may be interested ourselves," Corinna said. "Well, you must be tired. Servants will show you to your rooms. I will warn you openly that we are cautious, and until we are sure you are harmless and truthful, you will be guarded. Otherwise, you are guests of the Crown."

It was not such a bad thing, to be a guest of the Crown. We were afforded fine meals, which, although sometimes strange, were an agreeable change from tough, dry traveler's food. I normally avoid meat, but there was a paucity of vegetables in Kantenjord in the winter. To compromise I developed a taste for goat cheese.

Escorted, we were able to explore the Fortress and the city of Svanstad, which was quite a pleasant place aside from the ubiquitous odor of fish—fresh fish, dry fish, rotting fish, rotting pickled fish prepared as some mad substitute for food, and so on. We toured the Swan cathedral with its ethereal-sounding choir and the street of the traders with wares as unexpected as Mirabad coffee and Amberhorn incense. We walked along the waterfront, and Northwing described a delirious variety of ships—knarrs, longships, clinkers, caravels, galleys, plus two dhows and a sleek galleon from jungled Kpalamaa. I enjoyed the descriptions much as you might appreciate tales of imaginary creatures, for my home has long been the heart of what some Westerners call the Continent of the Young Sun, and I have rarely heard the ocean.

Back at the Fortress, Northwing and I discovered that a couple of the servants were sufficiently adventurous to share our beds, though we did our best to keep such activities quiet so as not to trip over any local taboos. We saw nothing of Corinna after the first day, but Ragnar was a compassionate if irritable keeper, pressing us for information on every land we'd seen and, I believe, poking at the gaps in our stories.

Late on the third day, much recovered, I discovered in my meditations a recurring feeling of guilt. With the session ended, I knocked on Northwing's door.

"Wait," Northwing said, and after a minute let me into her room. It, like mine, was as richly appointed as the interior of a khan's tent. I sat upon the floor, as did Northwing.

"Northwing," I said, "do you feel we should be moving on?"

"Is that what the lamb said to the slaughterer?"

I smiled. "You mistrust our hosts?"

"I've seen what's become of Haytham and the balloon, Katta. I've just now followed birds to where they've got both. He's recuperating—a guest, like us— and Princess Corinna is pressing him for information. Soon Ragnar will know our story is too thin. Haytham's much too proud of himself not to talk, and talk, and talk, especially with a striking woman hanging on his arm."

"What have they done with the balloon?"

"They are studying it, attempting to sniff out how to use it. They haven't figured out the brazier yet, but they have some sort of magic-workers on the job. We're cooked."

"Hm. I have heard from my nocturnal companion Thom that these local magic-workers, called Runewalkers, have been prophesying a great war with an army coming out of Spydbanen, the northern island. I suspect Corinna is in a hurry to turn Haytham's arts to military use. Is the vessel otherwise repaired?"

"I think so. They've patched the canvas."

"Very well," I said, "I suggest we make our exit and rescue Haytham from the wiles of good Princess Corinna."

"He may not thank you."

I shrugged. "Let's find him a less dangerous princess, somewhere in the wide world. Now, Thom told me much about secret passages hereabouts, and earlier I believe I tapped my way to finding an access point."

"My own bedmate, Hedda the head of the household staff, has promised to lend us horses whenever we want. As everyone is busy with preparations for the feast of Saint Kringa, it should be easy to sneak off."

"A pleasure working with you, Northwing."

"You're not so bad for a monk, Katta. Let's go."

As we traversed the secret corridors to a spot prearranged with Hedda, I reflected on the ethics of our actions. One the one hand, we were abusing the hospitality of royalty and playing with the hearts of others. On the other hand, we were prisoners, and we had chosen confederates who were quite willing to help us. I decided that circumstances demanded such actions but that I had acquired a karmic burden thereby. I must look for a way to repay Soderland in the future.

To repay Soderland seemed no sad thing as we rode through the back gate of the Fortress, an access that led directly out into the countryside. Leafless trees swayed and creaked, snow sliding off them in tiny avalanches. Hares padded swiftly away from our horses. Pines made a shimmering sort of sound in the breeze. The afternoon cooled, but its chill air pleased me more than the smoky closeness of the Fortress. Northwing took us swiftly across fields toward Haytham's location, as the crow flies.

We attracted stares from farmers and wayfarers, or so Northwing informed me. She'd previously told me that the occasional person of brown, black, or red hue could be found in Svanstad, but none who looked quite like ourselves.

Once away from habitation Northwing began chanting and slapping a small drum. There was something frightening about the sound. I can't claim to truly know what the shamans do, but I know Northwing was communing with mighty powers of nature, and that it was no peaceful discussion but a fierce cajoling.

Snow fell. As the sun set, it came down in waves of tiny frozen kisses on my skin. The wind swirled these so they would converge in all directions at my face.

"Sight is quite obscured," Northwing said at last, voice normal.

"I will take your word for it!" I said. We were already passing through thick drifts.

"The farm is up ahead, and I know which window to knock at. Be ready!"

I was ready, but at the first several knocks Haytham ignored us. At last I rapped with my staff. The window was simply a small opening with a thick shutter over it, which Haytham soon parted.

"Katta! Northwing!"

"What's keeping you so distracted from your own rescue?" I said.

"Uh, designs for improvements to the balloons," Haytham said.

"Love poetry for the princess," declared Northwing. "Yes, I've been spying on you."

"She *is* very striking," Haytham protested.

"I have noticed," Northwing said. "Hurry. This is our chance to escape."

"Thank you for coming for me," Haytham said, gathering his few belongings, mostly books. "Are you all right, Northwing? You seem ill."

"It's a great effort to bring the snows. We're mostly trained to bring good weather." As the shaman spoke, Katta helped Haytham climb out the window. Northwing added, "But there's more. When I opened myself to the spirits, I sensed many more of my ilk in these isles."

"Shamans?" Haytham asked.

"No, people who hate goat cheese. Of course I meant shamans! There are many, up in the north. I can't tell who, but I can detect them by the eddies they leave. Never mind, let's get to the balloon."

There were two guards by the barn of *Al-Saqr*, and they were isolated from the rest of the farm by the quiet thickness of the snowfall. Their breathing, by contrast, was loud, and their sweat pungent. Haytham and Northwing tackled one, while I employed my staff to knock out the other. I proceeded to gag his companion. We dragged both inside. Luckily no one was working at the balloon or its gear. Haytham strode over to the brazier and said, "Haboob."

The efrit billowed out of his vessel. "O mighty mariner of the air! Your sojourn on land has proven most dull for a poor, neglected efrit."

"Never mind that," Haytham said. "Are you fit to work?"

"Of course, O paragon of explorers—"

"Yes! *Yes* is a perfectly good word, short and sweet, that you could stand to learn."

"Or," sniffed the efrit, "perhaps I need a continued rest."

"Speak as you wish," sighed Haytham.

The barn, Northwing informed me, was designed for the escape of a balloon, with a heavy crank allowing the rooftop to part. I naturally took the job of opening the roof as the others piled in whatever equipment they could manage.

When the canvas was full, the others called to me—and not a minute too soon, for the soldiers of Soderland were now running toward the barn. I heard Prince Ragnar's voice among them, crying, mystifyingly, "Do not harm the princess!" I leapt into the gondola, staff ready to repel the men, wildly whacking away weapons as we rose into the night. Sometimes a blade or arrow pierced the felt. I was peculiarly happy.

"You're grinning," said Northwing.

"I enjoy travel," I said.

"So," Haytham said, "now that we've irrevocably angered the royal family of Soderland, where shall we spread cheer next?"

"Well," said a new voice, "you spoke of a companion with a Runemark. I think that sounds very interesting."

Slipping out of a curtained-off area on the far side of the gondola, Princess Corinna yawned and stretched. "It's a nice place to rest, but a terrible place to oversleep."

I could not see her at all. And I began to believe there are some perils that are no less vexing for having nothing to do with evil.

(*Here ends the second section of* A Journey to Kantenjord.)

CHAPTER 16

STRAITS

Innocence didn't know who would prevail if battle broke out between Steelfox's band on the one hand and Jokull Loftsson's enraged Kantenings on the other, but as he entered the church through the bell tower, avoiding the ropes connecting the Karvak balloons to the structure, he knew he had little time.

He shoved past acolytes and novitiates, priests and clerks. Dressed as he was, looking as he did, he inspired confusion but not alarm; nothing on the outside said *Child of the Far East Here, Collaborating with Your Enemies.*

Yet that was how they'd see him, if they knew his heart.

He made it all the way to the sanctuary before somebody recognized him.

"Innocence!" called Numi in surprise. The abbot's assistant was standing amid a knot of some twenty robed men, the abbot included, guarding the doors. Perhaps five held in white-knuckled grips things that qualified as war weapons, axes or swords. A half-dozen more had daggers, and the remainder prepared for battle with garden tools and kitchen knives. "What are you doing here?"

"Numi," Innocence said, getting his breath. "You need to let them in."

"You," said the abbot, who did not so much speak as intone. The black-robed elder swished up to Innocence. "I recognize you. You're Huginn Sharpspear's dog. What trickery is this?"

"No trickery." Innocence did not know what to say, but it was clear he couldn't simply open the doors. He followed through, with honesty. "There was an argument that got out of hand. People need time to calm down. Giving sanctuary can accomplish that. I swear they'll put down their weapons." He mostly believed it.

"They have already broken the peace," said the abbot.

"Oxilanders broke it first," Innocence said.

"Father Superior," Numi said, "I vouch for Innocence here."

"You are nearly as much a stranger to me as he is," the abbot replied. "You want me to go against the uncrowned king?"

"Does he own you, then?" Innocence snapped.

It was the wrong thing to say. The abbot's ears turned red as he bellowed for someone to tie Innocence up.

Nevertheless, although priests removed the ropes of their own robes and advanced, backed by men with axes, this was no group of warriors. Innocence realized he could outmaneuver them. He backed down the aisle of the sanctuary, trying to remain calm as a frantic pounding shook the door.

Halfway to the altar Innocence ducked left amid the pews. Some men rushed to follow, and others made to cut him off. None, however, expected him to invigorate his chi and jump onto the back of the nearest pew, leaping from there to the back of the next, and so on, taking the creaking wooden rows like stepping stones.

He jumped to the vestibule, and now there were but five people blocking his way.

In one motion he slid beneath their reach, slammed into the doors, and knocked the wooden bar aside.

His compatriots wasted no time dragging the doors ajar. He smiled.

Then it all went wrong.

"No!" cried Numi, interposing himself between Innocence and one of the armed churchmen, who sought to hack Innocence down. The cry turned into a horrifying shriek as an axe descended upon Numi's head. Innocence's smile disappeared beneath a spatter of blood and brains.

Innocence was too stunned to respond. He possessed battle reflexes, to be sure, drilled into him by Walking Stick's endless exercises. But his training had focused on individual skill.

He'd never confronted the idea of bystanders being slain, nor of men accidentally cut down by their own side.

A friend had just died in front of him, or someone who might have become a friend. It made even less sense than Torfa's death minutes earlier. In that moment, everything else unraveled. Karvak warriors rushed into the vestibule and with their swords cut down the axe-wielder, whose dying look was not one of defiance, nor fury, but confusion.

Other Kantenings, led by the abbot, tried to block the Karvak party, but Dolma and her warriors burst among them, striking with hands, feet, and daggers. Before Innocence knew it, the Kantenings were down, and Steelfox was lifting him to his feet. Blood was on her blade.

"I . . ." Innocence said. "No, no, I . . ."

She slapped him. "Return to yourself." She stared with disgust at the blood her hand had carried from his face. "Close those doors!" she commanded him and Huginn.

The professional liar did not object, nor hesitate. Innocence joined him, in a daze. Steelfox joined her people battling the men who'd previously chased Innocence, and clashes and screams echoed through the stone walls.

As the doors began groaning shut, Innocence saw a force of enraged and bellowing Kantenings charging up the hill. As they'd come directly from a banquet they were mostly unarmored, though the crowd bristled with spears, axes, swords, maces, daggers. Yet they were disorganized, frenzied, and Innocence could not think of them as fighting men. He saw instead a band of savages.

He did not think the doors would close in time.

Then death rained from the skies.

Archers shot from the safe vantage of the Karvak balloons overhead. Their speed and accuracy was such that the front of the Kantening mob fell in a heap. Confusion and shock took the remainder, who had not until now understood their peril.

The archers allowed them no time to reconsider. Even as the doors finally slammed shut, Innocence saw more Kantenings die.

Huginn returned the brace to the doors and tugged Innocence into the sanctuary. The battle there was already over. Some of Steelfox's band had fallen; Dolma now had only two companions. Blood was everywhere.

Steelfox wiped her hand within a nearby stone font. Numi's blood reddened the water.

Huginn coughed. "That is holy water. Great one."

"Blood is unclean," Steelfox said. "Its shedding offends Mother Earth and Father Sky." She looked at Innocence. "You should clean yourself as well, dragon-marked one."

"He does not understand your ways," Dolma said. "He has had a shock. The boy who was slain by the axe-wielder, he was your friend, wasn't he, Innocence? He saved you."

"Why?" Innocence said, head swimming through a blood-dark sea.

"It is the way of Kantenings," Huginn said. "Our anger boils over and scalds everyone in reach. Steelfox, it seems I may need rescue."

"You will become my vassal, then?" Steelfox said.

"I will," Huginn said, and Innocence did not even hear a pause.

"We can ascend to the balloons," Steelfox said. "This is no fortress. And I dislike being trapped."

"No," Innocence said, not knowing what he'd say before he said it. "We can't leave the dead like this."

"That is honorable," Steelfox said, "but do not your folk bury their dead? We have no time for that."

"*They* are not my people! My people, my *true* people, would clean the bodies, dress them in somber colors, and take them to a suitable tomb, a stony place where outside it is bright, green, and moist."

Huginn sighed. "There's no such place here. But there's a crypt."

"Very well," Steelfox said. "We'll take our own dead with us. Meanwhile, Innocence and Huginn, carry the dead Kantenings to this crypt. Nine Smilodons and Red Mirror, assist them."

The crypt was a wooden-walled structure that looked to be the remnant of an older church whose furnishings were carved, not sculpted. The place was eerie; Innocence thought he heard strange whispers and cries of seabirds, and the mark on his forehead tingled. The sensations seemed familiar. but he could not place them. He tried to ignore it all and focus on his task.

They brought the abbot last. As they set the man down, suddenly Innocence became dizzy.

It was as if he stood upon the Lardermen's ship *Raveneye* again, as it rolled and pitched in the cold sea, though his eyes told him he was securely underground. Then his eyes told him stranger things. The chamber appeared to fill with mist, and the ceiling seemed to have vanished, revealing not the stone sanctuary above but a starry sky. The wall beyond the wooden altar had vanished as well, and a moonlit sea washed against the room's edge.

Huginn made the sign of the Swan upon his chest. "Well, I'll screw a shark," he said.

Nine Smilodons said, "Whatever you just suggested, I beg you not do it in my presence."

"Nevertheless," his companion Red Mirror said, "this sight is full of wonder."

By these words Innocence understood the others saw what he saw. At least he hadn't gone insane. "It's the Straits of Tid."

Huginn looked at him sharply. "Boy, how do you know of such things?"

"A Chooser of the Slain told me," Innocence said simply. He heard Huginn mutter curses as Innocence stepped forward and looked out at this bizarre ocean. He did not expect to see two other locations within the silvery, starlit sea. One was an old wooden church whose soaring, angled roof panels reminded him a little of towers of the distant East. Another was a great mountain, most of whose bulk lay out of sight.

That wooden church had, just like the room Innocence stood within, a missing wall. Meanwhile the mountain had a cavern opening that looked as though a slice had been hacked away with some unimaginably huge blade.

Through the first gap he beheld his mother. Through the second he saw A-Girl-Is-A-Joy.

At first those two noticed each other, but not him.

"Joy!" he heard his mother exclaim.

"Gaunt!" came the reply.

"What—what is this? Is it a dream?"

"I do not know! I must escape—"

At that moment it seemed to Innocence that Joy's eyes found his, and she tried to speak, but suddenly a huge hand formed of stone reached out from deeper into the mountain and grabbed her.

Innocence had the sense of a gigantic presence, scowling and leering, with eyes like red flames, before the stone entity retreated and Joy disappeared with it.

Just behind him, Huginn gasped. "The troll-jarl."

At last Innocence found his voice. "Joy!"

"Innocence!" came the voice of Persimmon Gaunt, for now she saw him. And even after the shock of seeing Joy taken away, Innocence wondered anew at Gaunt's presence. "Mother?"

She made to speak, but her form grew transparent and vanished from sight.

Innocence half-expected to disappear as well, or at any rate for the Straits of Tid to vanish back into whatever dream-realm they'd emerged from. But for now they persisted. Perhaps if he stepped into those waters, he could swim to where his mother and his friend were now. . . .

"Boy, what are you doing?" Huginn demanded.

"People I love are out there."

"Those are the Straits of Tid. They are the waters of time itself. What you've seen may just be echoes of the past or possible futures."

"No. They are my friend and my mother, and we shared the present moment. I can sense it."

"You're mad, boy, and while I admire mad—"

There was a commotion on the stairway.

Steelfox emerged, with Dolma beside her, conducting a fighting retreat. This time the Kantenings they opposed were armored men with shields and swords, and there seemed no end to them. Jokull Loftsson was in the second rank. Nine Smilodons and Red Mirror rushed up to assist as Steelfox and Dolma entered the old chapel; Huginn held back. Innocence stood at the magical gateway.

"They ambushed us," Dolma gasped.

Jokull said, "I knew of a secret passage . . . Swan preserve us, what is that?"

"My scribe has strange powers," Huginn said. "He's opened up the waters of time to claim the Karvaks. You can be rid of them! I never meant to betray you." Huginn winked at Innocence.

"What?" Steelfox snarled, fending off a thrust.

"I believe you," Jokull said. "Now that I've thought . . . I know you're not responsible. Hand your men over, Steelfox, the ones who slew my wife. Then you may go peacefully!"

Nine Smilodons and Red Mirror spoke in the musical-sounding Karvak language, but Steelfox cut them off. In Kantentongue she said, "Do you people know nothing of honor? They're my responsibility, and *I* will answer. And I answer this. Your wife's death is a sorrow, but she brought it on herself. My men stay with me. But you may have your Huginn. Such a wind-blown man is of no use to me."

"Then," Jokull said, "your companions will die, and you will be ransomed."

Innocence felt his anger rising up. As at the hall, it could no longer be contained. "No!"

The chamber shook. He didn't know how his power was doing this, but he didn't need too. "No! To hell with you barbarians! Steelfox, Huginn lied— this gateway isn't your doom. Follow me." He stepped into the Straits of Tid.

It was like walking into snow, for though cold the surf felt more like viscous fluid than water, and it tingled. A moaning wind rose up.

Steelfox and her escort bolted toward him.

"Boy!" Huginn called. "Do you want to live among aliens?"

"I *am* an alien. A child of the East!"

The Karvak party stepped through. The scene behind them, the wooden chapel and the incredulous Kantenings, disappeared.

Now they bobbed upon a silvery sea, strange nebulae overhead like rainbow bridges.

"Well," Steelfox said, "thank you. I think. Where to, child of the East?"

"To that mountain," he said, giving one last look at the wooden church from which Persimmon Gaunt had peered. It faded even as he decided. "For we have someone to save, great Steelfox."

CHAPTER 17

RUIN

Skiing compared favorably to riding an angry dragon. After Gaunt had buried herself in three snowdrifts, that was all she could say for it. The cold raised fresh aches in the spot where she'd hit a mountain rock that first day in Kantenjord.

"You are getting better," Vuk said, helping her out of the third snowdrift.

"I am glad you're preserving the honor of the family," Bone said. He was still sporting a purple bruise on his cheek from an encounter with a tree branch.

"Should we not press on?" Alder said. Despite his wounded hands, he was keeping up well, and Muninn Crowbeard for his part was an experienced "skier." There was a barely restrained glee about him that Gaunt would have found intolerable, were the bastard not so useful.

Muninn said, "We are deep enough into the forest that I think we can rest a short time."

"What was that?" Bone asked, looking around. "It almost sounded like an ocean wave. . . ."

"I heard nothing," Vuk answered. "But these woods are said to be haunted."

"And cursed," said Alder.

"And filled with wild beasts and monsters," Muninn said.

"Haunted, cursed, *and* infested?" Gaunt said. "This forest is a social climber. It collects bad reputations like a petty noble collects titles."

"Mock if you will," Muninn said, "but the Morkskag is no place to be wandering at night."

"Will our former masters share this opinion?" Bone asked.

"Very likely. But Skalagrim may press on in the name of vengeance."

Gaunt said, "Ah, vengeance. So satisfying to think you can set fire to your enemy, till you remember you share a hall."

"We are slaves," Vuk said.

"Were slaves," Bone said.

"Were slaves," Vuk said, "and as such we share nothing with our masters. They showed us some minor consideration when we were property. But now we are outlaws, and we've stained their honor. If only to save their reputations they'll slaughter us if they can."

"If it's returning you gentlemen to captivity or the unknown dangers of the woods," Gaunt said. "I'll choose the woods."

Vuk said, "Indeed."

"Nevertheless," Bone said, "let's veer away from that sound I heard. This way."

They proceeded at a gentler pace amid the great trunks of what Muninn called the Morkskag. Bone looked this way and that, every hooting owl and settling snowdrift rousing him to grim alertness. Gaunt wanted to soothe him, help him leave his captivity behind in mind as well as body, but she knew he'd refuse comfort. And sooner or later the dangers he heard might be real.

She glanced at Muninn, who seemed rejuvenated by recent experience. Alder noticed it too. "You've angered a powerful chieftain's son, Master Crowbeard, and left your home behind. I know why *I'm* smiling, but I have no idea why you are."

"It's a nice night," Muninn said.

"In the Morkskag!"

"Death is coming for me no matter what else befalls. Fate waits for us all."

"What of you, Persimmon Gaunt?" Alder said. "You're from my own homeland, aren't you? Do you believe in these Kantening notions of fate?"

Gaunt shrugged. "If you can't know your own fate until the moment of your death, then I say fate is no matter. I choose to believe I choose."

"So do we all," Muninn said. "But fate isn't just a road or a river. It's a seed within us, growing into the tree of our lives. At last we hang upon it."

"So cheery. Perhaps it's *my* fate to believe I have free will. If so, I shall not defy it!"

"And you?" Alder asked. "Do you agree with your wife, Imago Bone?"

"What answer do you expect," Bone asked, "when I walk beside her?"

She skied close enough to rib him. She was pleased with her balance, and it made her impish. "Your wife commands you to speak your mind. No harm will come of it."

"This is surely a trap. Nevertheless. If you say my fate lies ahead, then I ask you, what is the height of fate's walls, and how many guards does it have, and are any of them bribe-able? What traps lie within, what are the dispositions of its masters, and where does its treasure lie? Answer these questions and I can tell you whether or not I can overcome fate."

"You are as mad as your wife," Muninn said.

"I have a practical mind . . . wait."

Vuk, who'd been walking ahead of them, returned with hand raised. "I hear something. A large something. A bear, perhaps."

"I do not like bears," Bone said.

"Nor I!" said Gaunt.

"Well, don't look at me," Alder said.

"Bears are not much to fear," Muninn said, "if one walks in a large group. Even a big one will not want to tangle—"

A dark shape burst from the trees and tackled Muninn, who screamed. The beast was a huge brown bear. One eye flickered strangely with an eerie green radiance.

Gaunt let fly an arrow.

She hadn't considered that she was still on skis. Her motion sent her sliding backward, and her shot arced high into the air.

Bone threw a dagger, stumbling. It struck true, but the bear seemed unconcerned. Vuk grabbed one of Muninn's fallen "ski poles" and whacked at the bear, bellowing. Alder waved his hands and chanted something; a rumbling afflicted the ground, and now everyone's footing was momentarily lost.

Yet Gaunt had no time to think on this, for in the next moment, as she struggled to remove her skis, a clear, sweet sound echoed through the woods.

It was the sound of a bell.

At the sound, the green radiance within the bear's eye rippled as though it were moonlight in a windswept pond. The bear growled mournfully and leapt away, soon lost to sight.

The sound of the bell receded. The rumbling was gone too.

"You all right, Crowbeard?" Bone said.

"I . . . yes." The Kantening seemed just as surprised at Bone's concern as at his own survival.

"It was frightened off by that bell," Gaunt said.

"There must be someone living up ahead," Vuk said. "Let's be cautious."

"I suggest we remove our skis," Gaunt said, having already done so. As Alder untied his, she asked him, "Care to explain your connection with that tremor?"

"Ah," said Alder. "I was, for a time, a student of magic."

"For a time?"

"I'm simply not very good at it. I'm third son of a wealthy family back home. At great expense I was apprenticed to a wizard. I didn't want to enter the clergy, you see."

"You seem to have learned a thing or two—"

"Yes, yes, everyone's very interested in my magic, until they have to suffer through my miscastings. The wizard turned me out in frustration, and I . . . neglected to return home. Alas my wanderings put me in the path of a Kantening raid. I am beginning to think I'm unlucky. But that is surely premature."

"You may be poor at magic, but I think you're decent at dry wit."

"We shall see."

"Hush," said Vuk. "We draw near a fortress."

The gray preceding the dawn had crept stealthily through the trees, and mists swirled along the forest floor, but the outlines of the place came into view.

"No," said Muninn with a wondering tone. "It's a church."

The old church rose out of the forest and mists like a ship nosing through the fog of a narrow strait. For a moment, as the solemn wooden structure came into focus, Gaunt thought she'd been transported back to the distant East, for there was something in its many-tiered construction that recalled pagodas. Nearby rose a ruined windmill, evidence of a larger, abandoned settlement.

They crept closer. Wooden dragons grinned from various corners, and likewise signs of the Swan. The bell that had frightened the bear hung yet over the door. Gaunt found her lost arrow in the snow just below.

"Ha!" she said, picking it up. "I thought I'd missed, but I hit better than I'd imagined. My shot rang the bell!"

"Well done," Bone said.

"It's strange . . ." Alder said. "Like no church I've ever seen."

"It's a stave church," Muninn said. "The first Swan-churches built in these islands were stave churches, like this. For reasons no one remembers, they often got built in out-of-the-way places. Some of them still get used, but most have faded into the forests. Never knew this one was here."

"I've heard it said," Vuk mused, "the stave churches were built from ship planks, by foamreavers who gave up piracy."

Inside, the church was musty but not moldy, with neat rows of pews facing an altar carved with swirling scenes of the Swan and life in these isles, runic inscriptions, and ribbonlike designs reminiscent of knotwork patterns from Swanisle. The far wall was likewise thick with such designs.

"It's a place to get lost in just sitting down," said Bone, and he set out to test the thought. They all took places on one pew or another.

"This place," Muninn said. "It stirs strange feelings. . . . It makes me sorry to have betrayed you, Imago Bone. Thank you for helping me with the bear."

"Why did you betray us, Muninn, truly? Was it because you thought me a nithing? Were you trying to get back at time itself, by punishing a, ah, younger man?"

"Or," Gaunt said, "were you trying to prove you were a foamreaver still?"

"I . . ." Muninn shook his head. "There are too many reasons, and too few words. I am weary."

"We all are," Gaunt said. "I propose, gentlemen, we rest here for a time."

And so they did, Gaunt and Bone leaning against each other, Muninn, Vuk, and Alder nodding nearby. Gaunt seemed to be the last awake, and she was amused by seeing them, outlaws all, dozing like parishioners during an uninspired homily.

Her own head nodded.

The light changed. Suddenly it was dark. She snapped her head up and stared.

The altar was still there, but the far wall was gone, and beyond was a rolling sea, silvery under stars and moon and blazing nebulae.

She extricated herself from Bone, who still slept, and passed the others, who likewise did not stir.

She stepped beyond the altar and peered out. Two other structures floated upon the spectral sea.

One was a church, though of stone not of wood. The other was too large to fully see, for it appeared to be the side of a mountain with a great cavern opening upon the waters. A girl stood at the cavern's mouth, staring this way and that as though fearing something that pursued.

CHRIS WILLRICH   223

Their eyes met.

"Joy!"

"Gaunt!"

"What—what is this? Is it a dream?"

"I do not know! I must escape—"

A gigantic, gnarled, stony hand emerged from deeper within the mountain and snatched her away.

Gaunt would have cried out, but a voice from the other church shocked her into silence: "Joy!"

She whirled and saw a boy staring through a missing wall beside an altar, just as she did.

"Innocence!"

"Mother?"

"Gaunt?"

Bone's hands were on her shoulders, and bright sunlight streamed through the windows of a stave church that once again had all its walls. The strange ocean, the mountain, the stone church—all were gone. "Gaunt? I couldn't wake you. . . ."

"Bone? Bone, I . . . we have to find Innocence! And Joy . . ."

"I know . . ."

"No! It's more than that. There's danger."

"I know." He nodded to where their companions had taken defensive positions by door and windows. "Skalagrim is here."

CHAPTER 18

SKRYMIR

The balloon of the Karvaks approached, and Joy's hopes swelled as she recognized it as *Al-Saqr*. It had suffered somewhat and possessed wide patches of red cloth supplementing the blue that represented the Eternal Sky. But it still flew.

It was as though she'd wished for the perfect escape, and the universe had granted it.

Now she had to be worthy of it.

She whispered to her companions, "All right. Believe it or not there's a chance we'll be rescued."

"But what is *that?*" Inga asked.

"It's a flying craft," Joy said. "In my own language it's called a *qìqic*. In Roil, it's a *balloon*. I can't explain it all now. But there's room for us if we can somehow get there." She searched the terrain, nodded toward a high point. "There. I'll leap and carry Malin."

"Carry me?" said Malin.

"Yes. Inga, I'm counting on you to run like hell to catch up. From there my friends can get close."

"Sounds like a risky plan," Inga said.

"Better than what we had a few minutes ago."

"We should do it," Malin said.

"I may never learn the truth about myself," Inga said, and sighed. "But you're right. Trolldom isn't all I'd hoped for."

"You lot!" Wormeye called out. "What are you talking about?"

"Silence, you!" shouted Inga, imitating his tone. She ran.

Joy grabbed Malin. "Hang on."

"Hang on," Malin agreed. Joy envisioned energy flow flaring through the muscles of her legs. She leaped.

They landed and slid down a gravelly slope, just ahead of Inga. Now Joy leaped again, reaching the precarious summit of a rocky pinnacle.

Panting, muscles aching, Joy searched for the balloon. It was coming, but she might have leapt too soon. Pursuit was underway. Wormeye was repeating his maneuver of days before, when he'd hurled Claymore and Mossbeard.

The two hapless—but dangerous—trolls landed near Inga.

Inga spun and attacked, a furious grin on her face.

Claymore now had a new, stumpy arm to replace the one he'd lost and eaten. Inga rushed up, gave it a savage tug, and ripped it off. "Noooo!" cried the troll, as she battered him across the face and knocked him downslope.

Mossbeard grabbed her, raised her above his head.

It was a mistake. Inga Peersdatter had spent seventeen years trying to rein in her strength. Her look was one of glee.

Inga whipped her legs up and sent a series of hammering kicks against Mossbeard's eyes. Stony though they were, they were still a vulnerable spot. He shrieked his outrage and dropped her.

Inga scrambled uphill as far as a head-sized boulder. She snatched this up and threw it against the blinded troll. It collided with his head, and he toppled, cursing, after Claymore.

Inga jogged up the hill, shouting, "Did you see that! Did you see that!"

"I know a bard," Joy said when Inga arrived. "You're going to have a song!"

"See that?" Malin said, her voice tense. She was not echoing.

She pointed at Wormeye. He'd seen the balloon. He put his hands to his mouth and bellowed in a language Joy hadn't heard before. Even in the troll's guttural tones, it had a musical quality.

He was shouting at the balloon.

A further surprise met her, for a voice answered in kind from the balloon. Her hopes soared as the balloon descended. It was the voice of the inventor Haytham ibn Zakwan ibn Rihab.

Inga was still energized from battle. "What the hell is going on?" she said, sounding jaunty.

"Joy!" called Haytham, perhaps in answer. "I am attempting a prisoner transfer."

"What?" Joy answered.

"You are prisoners of these trolls. I will make you prisoners of the Karvaks. Trust me!"

"What are Karvaks?" Inga said dubiously.

"Nomad conquerors of the steppes," Malin said.

"How can you manage that?" Joy called up. "Oh, and I am so very glad to see you!"

"I am glad to see *you*!" Haytham called down, and she was delighted to behold his turbaned head and impish smile as he tossed down a rope. "And I can manage this deed because, you see, the trolls and the Karvaks . . . well, they are allies. Luckily my Karvak patron is in Kantenjord as well. I've learned Lady Steelfox is in Oxiland!"

"Steelfox?" Joy called back to him, feeling something slide beneath her that was not her footing. "What is she up to?"

"Let's not fret about details!" Haytham called. "You're not safe! The trolls aren't sure about the deal! Climb!" He began bellowing something new in the Karvak language.

Wormeye the troll bellowed back. His troll subordinates were still on their way. Joy sensed the negotiations were not on a sound footing either. "Inga, I need you to climb, so I can get Malin into the ger."

"The what?"

"Never mind. Will you do it?"

"Okay. What are you and the old guy up there talking about?"

"Um, how crazy trolls are."

"Okay, fair enough." Inga climbed.

"Malin, I will jump you to safety, if you do not mind."

"I do not mind," Malin said.

Joy got hold of Malin and leaped.

But she'd overestimated her strength. Her chi could not loft them all the way to the balloon. She and Malin plunged again.

Her skill allowed her to lighten their weight, so they didn't harm themselves in the fall, but they slid down the hillside into a shallow gully where Claymore and Mossbeard waited, nursing their wounds.

"Hey!" said Claymore, and Mossbeard said, "Them!"

"Uh-oh," said Malin.

They lunged at Joy, and Joy drove them back with a spinning kick. More trolls yelled invectives.

Joy knew Inga would jump down momentarily to help them, giving up her own safety. Joy had to get Malin up to the balloon first.

CHRIS WILLRICH

You are the land, and the land is you.

She didn't know how to call upon the Runemark, but she stared at it, willing it to bring strength to her body as it had before. Red light flared in the gulley. New vitality flowed into her, and a determination to use it. Grinning, she leapt again.

This time she nearly overshot. She hit the side of the ger and tumbled inside. She dropped Malin, bowed without really looking at the occupants, and leapt back to the hill to guard Inga's ascent.

Now Rubblewrack came at her.

She shifted, kicked, blocked, struck. The Runemark kept sending energy into her, power drawn from the Chain of Unbeing somewhere to the southwest, vitality claimed from the draconic essences of the islands themselves. Rubblewrack tumbled, screaming in rage. Joy began to laugh.

Wormeye shrieked, "Runemark! The Runethane has arisen! She must not escape! We must bring her to Skrymir!"

Once again, out the corner of her eye, she saw him prepare to hurl smaller trolls. She braced herself to dodge, but Wormeye's target was not Joy, nor Inga.

First one, then a second, then a third troll projectile was sent bursting through the canvas of the balloon.

The vessel careened away, dropping fast into the desolate hills. Inga was dragged along with it. She hit a hillside and dropped from the rope, out of sight. With a sickening crunch *Al-Saqr* came to rest. Trolls swarmed after it.

"You have an alliance!" Joy called to Wormeye.

"A treasure like you supersedes all alliances!" Wormeye replied. "Besides, you picked fights with my tumult. You must be brought before Skrymir!"

Her battle-joy had turned to ashes. Half her friends in the world might be injured or dead. The light from the Runemark faded. She was only herself. But she had to help them.

She scrambled over the jagged slopes, trolls bellowing behind her. She reached Inga. The changeling was bruised all over, with a dozen bleeding scrapes dirty with grit. But her wounds weren't all that had grit. She was already on her knees, and she smiled feebly at Joy. "Well, you gave it a good try," she said.

"Come on," Joy answered, helping her up, grateful that Inga forgave her this failure.

They reached the wreck of *Al-Saqr*. Its rent canvas was sprawled against a hillside, impossible to miss. In a rocky streambed the ger lay tipped on one side. The crash itself had been gentle enough that all seemed unhurt. There stood Haytham, gripping a huge brazier from which the smoky form of the efrit Haboob fluttered out like a kite, staring over the hilltops at the approaching trolls. Mad Katta was there as well, the monk standing ready, head cocked as he listened for the creatures' arrival. Northwing the shaman leaned against him, evidently exhausted from commanding the winds. And Malin rushed up to make sure Inga and Joy were all right.

Another figure was there was well, a striking Kantening woman of some forty years. She wore a narrow-brimmed black cap and a fine gray cloak, and she gripped a longsword as though she'd trained with one since birth.

"So," said the woman, "this is the Runethane whom we've come so far to rescue. I confess you are not the Runethane I was expecting, but I am pleased to meet you nonetheless. I regret we will be needing rescue ourselves. And you must be Inga, the redoubtable changeling." The woman bowed. "Pleased to make your acquaintance."

Joy didn't know what to say.

"Who the hell are you?" Inga asked.

"Inga," Malin said in a strangled-sounding voice. "Princess . . . Corinna . . . Soderland."

Inga's eyes widened, and suddenly she was on her knees.

"Rise, rise, rise," the woman said impatiently. "We aren't exactly in the Fortress in Svanstad. But it's true. I am Princess Corinna." She sighed. "And won't grandfather and Ragnar be pleased to learn about this."

Wormeye the troll, with some twenty of his compatriots, cleared his rocky throat behind them.

"Well, well, well," was all he said.

The trolls led their captives into the deep mountains, down tunnels and into gorges, up passes and through fissures. The journey took two days, during which gray spires ate more and more of the sky. In the nights, fires blazed from caves, and what had seemed an uninhabited realm revealed itself as the center of a trollish civilization.

"If I survive," Haytham the inventor said, staring at the fires, "I intend to make great contributions to Mirabad's travel literature."

"I can never tell," Joy said, "if you're happy or bitter."

"There's too much misery in the world for me to ever be entirely happy. And too much wonder to ever be entirely bitter. I sometimes envy those who can take their emotions raw, but I must have the meat roasted and spiced."

"I am afraid that may be what the trolls will do to us."

"You may be right! I haven't seen them eat—unless you count what Wormeye has done, in swallowing my brazier for easier transport. But I have heard them joke about roast human often enough that I'm convinced they enjoy the taste."

Late the second day, they found out.

They came to the great mountain of the Trollberg, rising just southwest of its subservient human community Jotuncrown. The mountain had no gate, carvings, or statuary, no markers of residence, only a roughly quarried gap tall as ancient pines. Inside, as their eyes adjusted to the darkness, the humans were grabbed and chained and led deeper in. Soon Joy was able to see the interior was just as rugged as the entrance. There were no crystal towers such as the delven once made, only a series of monstrous caverns lit by vats of green troll-fire and by gaps rent in the mountain rock, pale-blue sky beyond. Here, there, everywhere were hollows in which the detritus of troll life were strewn, giant daggers, mounds of straw, penned goats, treasure bags, cauldrons, roasting spits. Joy tried not to look at those last, for sometimes they were occupied. She wondered why vast animated mounds of rock or earth must eat, for their captors had not done so thus far. But it seemed eat they did. A great reek filled the mountain halls, a mix of meats, dung, soot, moss, pine needles, dust. It made Joy sneeze.

She was initially grateful to enter the last cavern. It had a tunnel leading to the open air, through which passed a clean, cold breeze. The path of the wind divided the chamber into halves, with scores of smooth boulders scattered on one side and a single monumental rock rising on the other. Set into this rock was a chair so big, Joy at first thought it was a small house. It was formed of a blue-white block of ice, inset with priceless gems of all colors. The various crystals all flickered in the green firelight.

Upon this chair sat a gigantic troll, perhaps twenty feet tall when sitting.

He was like a miniature version of the mountain, with two dark stony peaks for shoulders and a ruby-eyed summit for a head. The face was gnarled and fissured, with a prominent gash for a mouth. His arms were like promontories, ending in crystal extrusions that might have been claws. His legs were obscured by an axe big as a man, a black weapon crowded with red half-runes along the blade, the marks looking bloody, as though they'd been picked up from the murder of some old codex.

A great, gaping opening lay where the heart would be on a man, leading all the way through the troll-king's body. A fluttering carpet, swirling with intricate colors, was rolled up and stuffed into the gap.

Joy gasped when she saw the carpet, for she remembered it.

"Deadfall!" she cried.

"I have that distinction," hummed a voice from the carpet, a thin musical sound that recalled desert winds. "Long has it been since I traveled the Braid of Spice or plunged into the sea to seek out your Scroll of Years. I regret we must meet again in this way, A-Girl-Is-A-Joy."

Joy forced herself not to glance backward to see Mad Katta's reaction, for he and the carpet had once been friends.

A triumphant chattering erupted from scores of trolls filling the opposite side of the cavern; they dragged Joy forward first, even ahead of Princess Corinna. Joy kept her right hand firmly clenched.

"Kill her!" cried a troll. "A human child from beyond the sea has invaded our land and taught treachery to our changelings!"

"May I hack her fingers off?" jeered another.

And, "May I spin her head by the hair?" screeched a third, until the whole gallery joined in.

"May I bite?"

"May I boil?"

"Roast?"

"Or fry?"

But the great troll upon the throne of ice and crystal raised a hand with fingers that resembled stalactites, or else stalagmites. A voice filled the cavern; it was not a shout but a sort of sardonic purr. "Winter take your fury, ladies and gentlemen. These are strange, new times; Skrymir Hollowheart says, let us not be hasty. I sense we have an Easterner here, not unlike our friends the Karvaks."

"I am nothing like them!" Joy shouted, and the trolls around her shrieked and tugged on her chains.

"Do you truly wish to become stew? Be silent. I will speak first with Princess Corinna. After all, she's your superior in rank."

Corinna held her chin high as she was dragged before the throne, and though Joy barely knew the princess, it hurt to see Corinna's dignity scratched.

The troll-king snatched Corinna like a loaf of bread. His stony fingers enmeshed Corinna's skull. The princess bit her lip but did not scream. Joy's heart raced. A single squeeze would pop the princess's head like a cork from a bottle, yet Corinna studied her captor with an icy gaze. Skrymir said, "O princess, with my claws about you I could make Soderland cough up a great ransom. Yet I would rather wipe the contempt from your face and replace it with a portrait of my choosing. First I will scratch your right eye, so that a splinter of troll-stuff will enter it, and you will see the world as we do—that you may comprehend the Trollberg as beautiful. Next, I will with one of my fingernails carve away the window-pane of your left eye, but you will perceive it as no more than the shedding of a wart. All that will be left to you is troll-sight. As we render you to soup you will smile with glee. Thus do I show my love for the Kantenings! The manner of your death will terrorize your people for generations, and in between serving the Karvaks, parents will tell an eventyr about the horrid death of foolish Princess Corinna. But first of all, this will be known to your family in Svanstad. Hold still, my dear."

Like an unsheathed knife a crystalline fingernail shone in the cavern, but even as it plunged toward Corinna, rage quickened within Joy and she opened her hand.

The Runemark glowed a volcanic red.

Though she was chained, her legs were free. Her limbs tingled with strength, and she ran forward, scaled the throne, and kicked the outstretched hand.

A concussion like thunder exploded through the cavern. Crystalline fingernails snapped and scattered like glass. Skrymir Hollowheart roared, and Joy and Corinna fell to the cavern floor.

But they were not alone in the fight.

Mad Katta leapt forward, having slipped his bonds. His aim was perfect as he threw one of his blessed, discus-shaped sweetcakes. It hit Skrymir in the nose, and rock shattered; the troll-king hissed.

With a bellow, Inga broke her own chains and set about freeing Malin, Haytham, and Northwing.

Northwing, though still chained, closed her eyes while murmuring a chant.

Haytham shook his chains defiantly and turned to the onrushing troll Wormeye. "Haboob of the Hundred Hilarities! I ask you to interpret your mandate flexibly! In return I will reduce our agreement to six months."

"Eh?" said Wormeye, before the soil of his torso exploded.

The troll fell to the cavern floor in two pieces.

Joy absorbed all this while struggling to her feet and helping Corinna to hers. As she rose she noticed that the gaps opening on the sky seemed filled with stars and nebulae, as though night had suddenly fallen, though a more brilliant night than any she'd known.

She had no time to consider this, however. Corinna was saying, "While he's distracted! Move the axe! It is the work of Wayland, the Axe of Sternmark!"

Joy had no idea what that meant, but she could hear the capital letters. On a hunch she struck her chains against the blade. They split like kindling. Corinna did likewise, and together they grabbed the huge axe. Groaning, they shoved it out of reach.

Skrymir roared and slapped Joy across the chamber.

That she could roll with the blow was partly the result of Walking Stick's training and partly the strange power of the Runemark. She tumbled down the tunnel leading to the outside air.

As she rose, she could not help but gaze out.

What she saw was impossible. An ocean, lit by a silvery moon, lapped at the mountainside, its waters just a few inches below where she stood.

Almost as strangely, two structures bobbed in the waters nearby, one of wood, the other with a foundation of wood but upper levels of stone. The wooden one reminded her somewhat of her home pagoda, and her eyes studied it first. Even though her friends needed her, she could not look away.

A wall of the lowest level was missing, and out of that wall gazed a familiar face. Gaunt was there, calling her name.

Joy was so shocked she wasn't even sure what she said in reply. Then she gasped as she spied Innocence in the second structure.

Suddenly Skrymir Hollowheart grabbed her in one enormous hand, dragging her away from the tunnel.

"You have surprised me," the troll-king growled. "I had assumed the report of a Runethane false, but the power has truly chosen you. You have even awakened the forces of this mountain, opening the way to the World-Tree."

"Let us go!" Joy said. "What do you want with us?"

"A great deal! Behold!" As he wrenched her into the great chamber a mist fell over everything. She could no longer see her companions, nor any other trolls.

Now the mist cleared underfoot, and it seemed she floated high in the heavens over the Bladed Isles, looking down at a place where the two greatest landmasses met, as well as jagged, broken extensions of the next-largest isle.

"How——?" she began.

Skrymir laughed. "I am a lord of illusion, as well as of might." They appeared to descend. Where the two great promontories stood, there was an enormous chain wrapping about them, linking them to a barren island in the strait.

Joy beheld riders upon what she judged the Spydbanen side. Some wore byrnies, swords, and shields in the Kantening style. Others were archers of the steppes. "Karvaks!"

"Indeed," said Skrymir. "They have an interest in the human domains of these isles. I choose to indulge them, partly on behalf of the collegiality I owe the khatun. With my help they will conquer. This will make it much easier to achieve my true goal—control of that chain. With you, and that boy Innocence Gaunt, I can command the energies of the sleeping dragons of the isles and truly become myself. And what I truly am is a god."

"What you truly are is insane."

"Ah! You think so! Deadfall did at first! But it's his gift to siphon and sift magic. With him I can tap all manner of power, whether or not the source is willing."

"He speaks truly," came the thin voice of the magic carpet.

She could listen to no more of this. Her friends were struggling somewhere beyond this illusion. *Help*, she called out silently, not knowing whom she asked.

Help arrived.

Inga Peersdatter leapt through the mists, scrambled up the Skrymir's rocky body, and began smashing the troll-jarl's nose. Skrymir dropped Joy to swat at the intruder.

Joy staggered through the mists. She could see nothing now. "Inga? Where are you? I can't see—"

She felt a hand on her shoulder. Katta's voice said gently, "It can be frightening to go without sight. But you are not alone." He murmured a chant, and the fog dispersed.

The conference with Skrymir had taken only seconds. Her friends were not yet defeated but stared down the trolls, who seemed to easily match her companions but were unwilling to advance with their leader preoccupied. Inga was still scrambling around Skrymir's shoulders, avoiding his hands, kicking and punching when she could. At any moment the balance would tip, and they would rush forward.

"I . . ." Joy said. "I don't . . ."

"Carpet," Malin said. "Troll hearts very important. Eventyr Number Thirty-Six."

"Deadfall," Katta mused, "has the potential to become good."

"That's it," Joy said, and followed Inga's lead.

She leapt at the troll-king's chest, diving through the gap where his heart should be.

Power flared from the mark on her hand, and the carpet tore free of its prison. Together they landed hard upon the icy throne.

"Will you help?" she asked the carpet.

"Yes," it said.

"Help us escape."

Deadfall unrolled itself with a crack like a whip. She dove on, and it launched itself high, sweeping Inga away from Skrymir and into the air.

It swooped around the chamber and dove among the companions. Joy was amazed. In her elders' tales, the carpet had been described as spasmodic in flight. Clearly its luck had changed, as had theirs. They all got on.

But as the carpet rose to escape through the tunnel, Skrymir cried out, "Ah! To hell with it all!" The Axe of Sternmark was in his hands, and with its red runes blazing, he struck.

"No!" Inga was at the carpet's edge. With her own trollish strength she protected her companions, blocking the blow.

CHRIS WILLRICH   235

The axe chopped her arm clean off. She fell from Deadfall to the cavern floor, writhing there.

"No!" screamed Malin. "No! Go back!"

"Do as she says, old friend," said Katta.

"No," hummed Deadfall, "we are leaving this place."

"He is right," Princess Corinna said.

With a curse Northwing leapt off the carpet.

With a strength belying the shaman's years, Northwing tumbled with the fall and rose unharmed. "Get out of here!" Northwing shouted, before kneeling beside Inga, chanting.

"Deadfall, no!" said Joy. "Go back for them!"

But Deadfall heeded neither rage nor weeping and instead shot through a tunnel into what was now, inexplicably, a high alpine valley of deepening shadows, filled to brimming with the tents of the steppes.

CHAPTER 19

DRAUG

The Straits of Tid were star-domed and moonlit. Innocence, Steelfox, Dolma, Nine Smilodons, and Red Mirror swam to a skerry jabbing out of the water. The two Karvak soldiers took longest to catch their breath, as they were swimming in armor. At least the strange night was warm.

Steelfox's falcon circled the area and landed upon her wrist. "I take it you know something of this mad place."

"They're the Straits of Tid," Innocence said.

"To compound my ignorance with an unknown term is not entirely helpful."

"Apologies," Innocence said. "All I know of this place is that it allows a form of dream-travel through time and space. I didn't realize one could travel into it physically."

"Intriguing," Steelfox said. "So one could swim to days gone by, or days to come?"

"Yes, or to places far off." Innocence looked across the waters to the mountain rising into the night. "I want to get to that mountain. That's where I saw a friend, peering out."

"Liege," said Nine Smilodons. "Look at the stone of this tiny place." He gestured at the onyx-like stuff of the skerry. It was polished enough that in places one could see reflections, and Nine Smilodons' own reflection blinked back at them. But this Nine Smilodons looked leaner, more weathered, and stood beneath the sail of a Kantening ship.

Red Mirror pointed at another spot, where his reflection was of a gangly youth who could have been Red Mirror's younger brother. "That is I," said the warrior, "when I was Innocence Gaunt's age."

Innocence looked at the stone, and in place of himself there was a baby being jiggled by a red-haired woman. He looked down at his feet, and instead of his own reflection he beheld a white-bearded old man.

"I see myself," Steelfox said, "on the day I bonded with the egg of my falcon." Innocence saw a girl shaking in terror beside an egg. The flesh-and-blood Steelfox beside him noted him staring. He looked away. She said, "It is the way of my people not to record what is shameful, but it seems this stone remembers."

Dolma was studiously shutting her eyes. "This little island," she said, "seems not to access any particular time or space. Perhaps it is made of time and space."

"I wonder what becomes of us if we die here," Steelfox said. "At any rate, Innocence Gaunt, let's be off to your mountain."

It swiftly became clear swimming was something they were all rather bad at. If the mountain had been farther away, they might have drowned and discovered the answer to Steelfox's question. As it was, Steelfox and Dolma helped Innocence sputter onto the rocky slope to which they clung, gasping.

"I think—" Innocence began.

Something stung his ankle, grabbed his leg, and dragged him into the water.

He splashed and grabbed the shore. Nine Smilodons gripped his arm. Innocence looked over his shoulder at a nightmare.

A blurred sailboat rode on the moonlit waters. It looked to have been chopped in half lengthwise, yet it stayed impossibly upright. Even its mast and sail were split in two. The lone occupant stood whole, albeit monstrous. It was a shadowed shape covered with seaweed, carrying a spear in one hand, with a single blazing red eye in the dark mass of its head.

The hand without a spear held a rope, attached to a grappling hook now stuck to Innocence's foot.

"Draug!" Innocence cried, recognizing a description from stories.

Steelfox waded into the water, a risky business as the mountainous shore plunged sharply. She swung her sword and cut the line. Nine Smilodons dragged Innocence onto the slope and freed him from the grapple.

The Draug hissed. "Go back to your grasslands," it said in a voice like a spatter of surf. "These isles cannot be tamed."

"Whatever you are," Steelfox called out, "you are a corruption, and we are coming to cleanse you."

"We are eternal guardians of wyrd. Is it your fate to die?"

"I am a princess of the great Karvak nation. And this boy is under *my* protection!"

The Draug hissed again and raised its spear. But now the falcon Qurca screeched out of the sky and clawed the target of its red eye. It wept blood resembling molten metal. The Draug howled in fury, and its throw went wild.

"To me, Qurca!" Steelfox called, and she pointed her companions around the side of the mountain.

As she returned, Innocence said, "You were amazing."

"Don't waste breath. Where is that doorway of yours, Innocence?"

"It—it was right here!" He limped along a cliff, hands searching the stone, but there was not so much as a seam to show a tunnel had been there.

"Your time will run out!" called the Draug, for its half-ship still glided along the waters.

Steelfox said, "Keep searching. I will swim out to confront it."

"No, you can't," Innocence said, surprised how frightened he was for the princess of the steppes. "They are like embodiments of fate. No encounter with them goes well."

"Is that from experience or stories?"

"Stories," he admitted.

"My father was told stories. That he was unimportant, weak, of inferior blood, fit to be subordinate only—and for a time a slave! He never believed those stories, and one day he became the mightiest man in the world. I will fight this Draug."

Her words stirred something deep and angry in Innocence.

"No," he said, turning to face the blazing eye. "I will."

He raised his hand, and the mark on his forehead pulsed with pain. "Draug! I am Innocence Gaunt, chosen of the Heavenwalls of Qiangguo—a mightier civilization than you've ever dreamed! I bring the light of the East. Begone, horror of the West!"

Like a blast of wind, chi flowed from his hand. The waters split before the onslaught, and the boat buckled, groaned, and snapped along its width. Twice-rent, it sank into the waves.

The Draug bellowed its rage and fell into the Straits of Tid.

Innocence remembered his sensations when tearing the fabric of reality in Sølvlyss. Light flared in a huge circle upon the stone, and the stone within that spot faded away.

They tumbled into the tunnel.

When they regained their wits, the Straits of Tid were gone.

"You speak of amazing?" Steelfox exclaimed.

Innocence, shivering, no longer felt the power of the Heavenwalls. He swayed at the opening, beholding an alpine valley rimmed with ice and stone. Within its white-covered meadows were scores of farmhouses and a scattering of great halls. Beside them were thousands of the round tents of the Karvaks.

"What?" he said.

"We are back," Dolma said, her voice full of relief. "This is the valley of Jotuncrown, realm of the human vassals of the Spydbanen trolls, and the mustering place of the Karvaks. We are in the Trollberg."

"What?" he said again.

"Thank you for saving us," Nine Smilodons said, patting him on the shoulder.

A voice boomed in the tunnel, and a vast face appeared on its other end, a stern visage of stone and crystal. "Lady Steelfox! I am pleased to see you, though I am surprised to find you entering by the back door!"

"I had help, Skrymir!" Steelfox called back.

"I . . . see! Oho! The chosen of the Heavenwalls! You have delivered him!"

"He has delivered me, Skrymir. I am in his debt. He is under my protection."

"Of course!" the huge voice chuckled. "I will not challenge your authority!"

The great troll named Skrymir, whom Innocence instinctively feared, raised a vast hand, opened it.

"I have one here who is under your protection as well, and one who helped the other land-touched one escape. What shall I do with them, do you think?"

Within the hand stirred what Innocence took to be a young woman of Kantenjord and a hunter (man or woman, he wasn't sure) of the distant East. The Kantening was maimed, with the stump of a severed arm wrapped in rough bandages.

Steelfox gasped. "Northwing!"

The troll said, "I did not at first know the shaman was your servant. I think you should keep closer watch on your people! For another man of yours, one Haytham, helped the Runethane escape me."

The Easterner, the one who must be Northwing, said weakly, "Liege. You must understand . . ."

"We will speak later, Northwing!" Steelfox said. "You overreach, Skrymir! My sister will know of this!"

"All in good time," said Skrymir. "It is you and yours who've endangered our alliance. But fear not, I'm in a thoughtful mood. Rather as if the heart's been ripped out of me. You can make good by taking this Northwing back under your own wing . . . and by minding the chosen of the Heavenwalls."

"And what of the girl there?"

"This one? She is of troll blood. Years ago we dealt with the uldra of Svardmark, to place her among the humans. Part of a peace arrangement. We are welcoming her back to the fold, in our own way."

The young woman began saying something, over and over. It started inaudibly but slowly grew clear. "Kill you . . . kill you . . ."

"Yes, yes, yes," said the troll, "and a pony too. Now—"

"Now it ends," came a new voice.

A black-garbed human figure leapt into view and landed upon the great hand. Before Skrymir could react, the stranger grabbed both of the wounded people, one in each arm. With strength hard to believe in one so old, he leapt deep into the tunnel, all his actions scoffing at gravity.

But it was not really a stranger, and as soon as Innocence recognized him, it was no longer hard to believe. "Walking Stick!"

Walking Stick paused in shock.

Innocence Gaunt had waited years to do something that could truly surprise his mentor. Now that the moment had come, it was not quite as satisfying as he'd imagined. "Shifu," Innocence said. "I am under the Karvaks' protection. Join us!"

"What?" Walking Stick stared at Innocence, Steelfox, Dolma, the soldiers. "I come looking for Joy, and I find you? With Karvaks?"

"Oh, yes!" Skrymir bellowed. "Do join our party!"

But Walking Stick had sized up the opposition and did another unexpected thing. He swung a scroll into the air and with a flourish jabbed it at four spots around himself. The first two times he pointed, a warrior monk materialized in that spot. The third time it was a woman of Qiangguo who greatly resembled A-Girl-Is-A-Joy. She brandished a sword and said, "Who do I hurt?" The fourth arrival was a tall, light-brown man with a sword of his own, who said brightly, "I think there will be many options!"

"Toys!" chortled Skrymir, and grabbed.

In his grip one of the monks burst like an overripe melon.

"No!" Walking Stick said.

"Enough!" Northwing said, and from the open end of the tunnel, eagles with glowing green eyes winged forth to peck at Skrymir's eyes.

Skrymir slapped again and again, and red marked the tunnel walls. "No—these—are *my*—spies!"

"Northwing!" Steelfox commanded. "Your place is by my side! I invoke the pact between your people and mine!"

The shaman stood stiffly and walked to Steelfox's side.

"No!" said the Kantening woman. "How can you do this? I thought you were our friend!"

"I have old loyalties, Inga," said Northwing. "Just as you have yours."

"Traitor!" Inga rushed to attack.

Steelfox and Dolma got in her way, but Inga had appalling strength. She slapped the sword from Steelfox's grasp, backhanded the shocked Karvak princess into the stone wall, and kicked Dolma so hard the one-eared woman doubled over.

Red Mirror advanced. "Cease at once, or—"

She did not even let him finish. She punched.

Her strength proved what Skrymir had said about troll blood. His head left his body. Head and body tumbled out the tunnel opening, plunging thousands of feet to Jotuncrown below.

"Stop!" Innocence said. "They're my friends!"

"No," Walking Stick said. His group had advanced to Innocence's side. "They are Karvaks."

"They have honor. Unlike the Kantenings."

"Humans are a mix of good and bad."

"I think," Innocence said, anger bringing his power to life, "you may not understand which is which."

"Enough!" Northwing said. "Innocence Gaunt. Choose. You take my meaning?"

The mountain air made Innocence feel dizzy, giddy. Power crackled unseen within his hands. "I do. Leave us, Walking Stick, all of you. What will be will be."

"What are you saying, lad?" the tall man said. "Don't you realize, we could take you to your parents?"

"Innocence!" said the woman of Qiangguo. "I'm Snow Pine, Joy's mother. She will want to see you. Steelfox, what are you doing? What do you want with Innocence?"

Steelfox groaned her way to her feet. She put her hand on Innocence's shoulder. "He will help with the war."

"War?"

"Go."

"What will I tell your parents?" Walking Stick asked Innocence.

"Tell them to live happily," Innocence said, "far from Kantenjord. I have work to do here."

"The hell with you!" Inga said.

"Come," Walking Stick said. He tapped Inga with the scroll, and she disappeared, as did Walking Stick's other companions.

"I will not block you," Steelfox said, stepping aside.

"Stop him!" bellowed Skrymir, who was now finished with the green-eyed eagles. The stone hand shot forth. But Walking Stick leapt into the void. Unlike Red Mirror, Innocence thought, he would somehow land on his feet.

CHAPTER 20

WOLVES

"They are just waiting," said Alder. "Why are they just waiting?"

Bone wanted to reassure the Swanislander, but as he peered through the crack between the stave church's intricately carved doors, he wanted reassurance himself. The gigantic Skalagrim the Bloody, their former master, stood at the edge of the clearing. He was dressed for war, bearing a shield and axe, chain armor and helmet. This seemed like gilding the lily, since Skalagrim looked more than capable of slaughter with his bare hands.

Worse, he'd brought friends of similar armament and girth.

"We have the defensible spot," Bone said cheerily. At least, he hoped he sounded cheery. "They must consider their approach."

"Five of them?" Gaunt asked.

"Even two would be enough," Crowbeard said. "I know these men by reputation."

"They're five of Nine Wolves, then?" Vuk asked. "Which ones?"

"Well . . . the Wolves are accounted to be Skalagrim the Bloody, with whom we're all acquainted, and Rafnar Dragon-Axe, whose weapon I see gleaming in the sun, and Yngvarr Thrall-Taker, who seems to have other plans this fine morning . . . Ottmar Bloodslake, Arnuf Pyre-Maker, and Kolli the Cackling are three Spydbanen chieftains, and I think they remain in the north. . . . That leaves the Oxilanders—Arngrimur Townflayer, Muggur Barrow-Friend, and Einar Bringer of Wailing. Pretty sure we've got the Oxilanders with us today."

"How often do they all get together?" Bone asked. "The card games alone must be worthy of song."

"To my knowledge they have never gathered all at once but sometimes visit each other in dreams. They are not united in purpose, only in fury. They are often at odds. Each has long dreamed of becoming the Runemarked King."

"They may be disappointed in that," Gaunt said. "Let us disappoint them in other ways."

"How?" Crowbeard said. "Look at us! One good warrior among us, Vuk, and he ill-equipped. One palsied foamreaver. One maimed wizard's apprentice. Two thieves. Against five of the most powerful fighters in the isles."

"Five against five!" Bone said brightly. "Even odds."

"Our doom has come," Alder muttered.

"Speak not of doom," Bone said, "think always of odds. The odds could be better, but this is the only hand we've got."

"Eh?" said Vuk.

"All right, how about this. We're in a game of *hnefatafl*, and we're the king. Think of the glory if we win."

"I will play," said Vuk with a smile. "We will make them come to us."

"That's the spirit," Gaunt said. "You and Crowbeard—I suggest you guard the front door while Bone barricades the back. I will ascend to the balcony and see if I can get a good arrow-shot on somebody. Alder, find heavy objects to drop on heads, then join me. When you're at it, wrack your brains for any magic that might help us."

"I keep telling you," Alder said, "I wasn't much of a magician even with my pinkies. My spells tend to go awry."

"Keep asking yourself, *Is this worse than death?*" Bone said. "I find that question clarifying."

"Bone will join us on the balcony soon," Gaunt said.

"So it's just Vuk and me," Crowbeard said, "to stand against five?"

"When battle is joined inside," Gaunt said, "I will descend and join the fray."

"You will?" Bone said.

"I have Crypttongue," Gaunt said.

They were about their work. Bone had a bit of luck: in searching for things to block the back door, he found an old sword in an alcove (perhaps Kantenings stashed swords before services, along with cloaks.) He gave it to Vuk, who grinned.

Bone shoved loose pews against the back door, smacked his hands to clear the dust, and ascended the balcony. Gaunt had found a gap where a window had once been.

"It is strange," she said, "how long they're waiting."

"They're trying to inspire fear."

"Well, I'm afraid," she said. "But there is more to us than they imagine."

Alder joined them. "I know what I should do. My main area of study is called the Logic of Lithospheres—"

Gaunt said, "Is that related to the weather-manipulation art? The Algebra of Atmospheres?"

"Yes, but this affects soil and rock. It's less practiced because it's harder to control. But I can make the ground shake violently. If they're determined to stand in one spot like that . . ."

"Oh, please demonstrate," Gaunt said, preparing to shoot.

Alder murmured to himself, raising his maimed hands.

Bone's eyes widened as he saw a wave appear in the snowy ground, rushing upon the Wolves. They were all knocked over, snarling and cursing. Gaunt began firing arrows, concentrating on the nearest one, who, judging by the symbol on his weapon, was Rafnar Dragon-Axe.

At the same time, the stave church shook.

"That wasn't planned!" Alder said.

The light outside changed. Instead of dawn, it appeared to be sunset. Their surroundings changed as well; the stave church suddenly appeared new, with stained-glass windows and polished wood.

"What on Earthe?" Bone said.

"Time," Gaunt said. "We are beside the Straits of Tid, and Alder's magic must have set something off."

"Certainly!" Alder said. "Blame me! That's what I'm here for."

"Calm yourself," Gaunt said. "This may yet work to our advantage. There may be a path of escape. Vuk! Crowbeard! Do you happen to see a dimensional portal behind the altar?"

"Eh?" called out Crowbeard.

"Would a 'dimensional portal' look like an opening to a moonlit sea?" said Vuk. "If so the answer is yes."

"There is a new plan!" Gaunt said. "That's where we're going!"

They scrambled downstairs, and Muninn and Vuk joined them in regarding an opening to a bizarre body of water. Inexplicably, there seemed to be a stone church rising from the waves. Farther off lay a small, rocky island, and beyond that, a large one.

"Once we are through the portal," Gaunt said, "swim for that church."

"May we get an explanation?" Alder said.

"Gaunt said so," Bone said. "That is adequate explanation for anything. Now, who will be first?"

There was a moment of hesitation. Bone coughed. "Very well, I . . ."

The portal vanished. In its place was carven wood. The church again became ancient and dusty, and the ruddy light became bright and clear.

"I take it back!" Alder said. "I don't need an explanation!"

The doors burst open, and in came Skalagrim, Rafnar, Arngrimur, and Einar.

"Enough witchery!" Skalagrim yelled. "Our day is dawning, when we carve the isles between us, trolls and nomads at our side! But first we carve you!"

Alder muttered and raised his hands.

Muggur Barrow-Friend strode down the aisle. "Too late to surrender, slave."

But it was not a gesture of surrender. The wave in the ground returned, this time rushing through the structure of the church.

Everyone toppled, as did the altar, some statuary, and a few rafters. The light changed; aside from the fresh damage, the church again looked new. And the portal was open.

"The Straits of Tid," Muggur said, rising.

Vuk ran to him and hacked away with his old sword. It bit deep, but Rafnar countered with a blow that savaged Vuk, leaving a red trail in the sunset light.

"Go!" Vuk gasped. "Escape!"

"Move, gentlemen!" Gaunt said. "I'll get Vuk!" She drew Crypttongue, offering her other arm to Vuk. Skalagrim had reason to fear the blade, but Muggur had no knowledge of it. Thus he was startled to find Gaunt's sword jabbing at him everywhere he turned. He stepped back. Losing composure, he swung his axe wildly and destroyed a pew.

Bone shoved Alder through the portal, hoping the man could swim. He threw a dagger at Muggur, and it found a home in the man's ample gut.

"That tickles, fool," said Muggur. His fellows were advancing behind him. Bone knew a lost cause when he saw one.

"Let's be gone, Gaunt—"

"Come on, Vuk!" said Gaunt. "I've got you."

"Too late for me . . ." said Vuk. Yet some final strength took hold of the Wagonlord, and he lunged out of Gaunt's grasp and charged the Wolves.

Muggur and Skalagrim hit him with axes simultaneously, and Vuk fell.

"No!" Gaunt yelled.

"Go!" Bone said, tugging her toward the portal. Together with Crowbeard they stepped forward—

—and collided with the wooden wall.

"That's not good," Bone said, in the renewed dawn.

Skalagrim began chuckling.

"No," Crowbeard said. "No—laughing!"

He never could have managed the attack, Bone thought later, except that he'd caught them completely by surprise.

Crowbeard grabbed Crypttongue from Gaunt's grasp and rushed the Wolves. Screaming something about Torden's foul breath he drove the saber into Muggur's massive form. For all that the result was of benefit, it was sickening to see the powerful man fall dead from a single blow, a look of astonishment upon his face. Muggur fell backward into Skalagrim, and the Wolves' bulk worked against them as they stumbled against the pews and each other.

"Hahaha!" Crowbeard said, as he raced along the side of the sanctuary for the front door.

"Best we follow," Bone said, taking his own advice, stopping only to grab the old sword poor Vuk had carried.

"Absolutely!" Gaunt agreed, close behind. "The bastard took my sword!"

"I thought you were ambivalent about the thing!"

"Not when Crowbeard steals it!"

They exited the stave church. In the snowy dawn they ran for the treeline. Bone hoped they could stay ahead of the Wolves. Or that at least they could run faster than mad Crowbeard.

"Crowbeard, come back here!" Gaunt shouted.

"No!" Crowbeard called over his shoulder. "Muggur, Floki, the Charstalker, and I, we are going to escape to glory!"

"Charstalker?" Bone asked.

The four surviving Wolves burst out of the church.

Free of obstacles, their speed was obscene. Crowbeard, the old foamreaver freshly invigorated by the influence of Crypttongue, reached the treeline, but

Gaunt and Bone found themselves cut off by Skalagrim the Bloody, Rafnar Dragon-Axe, Arngrimur Townflayer, and Einar Bringer of Wailing. At least, Bone thought, their last moments would have made a good song.

"Gaunt—sword!" He tossed her the old, mundane blade, suspecting she'd make better use of it. He got a dagger in each hand.

"Thanks!"

"It's been fun—"

"Likewise—"

They began the fight. Bone expected them to last whole seconds.

Out of nowhere, Muninn Crowbeard returned, screaming, waving Crypttongue. This distracted the Wolves. They had come to respect the sword.

At the same time a shaking commenced, and the world changed.

Dawn turned to sunset, the clearing grew flat and well cleared, the ruined windmill rose whole and spinning, and a thunderous rumbling emerged from the church, amid a flight of startled crows.

Bone could not help but spin, as all the Wolves were staring that way.

Alder ran out, snarling, "Die, foamreavers!"

The church collapsed behind him, and as he gestured a wave of shaped ground rose ahead of him.

Gaunt and Bone dove to either side.

The wave hit the Wolves and shoved them, like a vast hand, deep into the woods.

Gaunt recovered her wits first, Crypttongue second. Bone helped Crowbeard up.

"I . . . was . . . magnificent," Crowbeard murmured.

"Of course you were." Bone led him on behind Gaunt to where Alder had fallen.

"Had to come back," the Swanlander was saying, shaking and pale. "The girl on the narwhal, the Chooser of the Slain . . . said if I turned back I belonged in the hall of heroes. Sounded like a turn of good luck. . . ."

"Alder?" Gaunt said.

"He's gone." Bone closed the eyes of the man whose life he'd once helped save, and who had now saved theirs. He made a fist. It shook like Crowbeard's.

"We must go," Crowbeard said, his voice subdued. "The Wolves."

"We should at least move Alder's body into the church," Gaunt said.

Together she and Bone got the unlucky magic-worker and settled him amid the wreckage, beside the bell. Now Vuk had a companion here.

The light returned to dawn, and the windmill joined the church in looking ruined.

"Now may we go?"

"Yes, Crowbeard," Bone said.

"Don't suppose you could loan me that blade?" After a pause: "I mean the other one."

"No, Crowbeard," Gaunt said.

They recovered enough skis to make their way north, sliding through long shadows.

CHAPTER 21

A JOURNEY TO KANTENJORD, CONTINUED

(As told by Northwing, Shaman of the True People)

Of the finding of the document

There are things that happen for a reason. And there are things that simply happen. I'm not sure which of the two best describes finding one of Haytham's notebooks lying on the floor of Skrymir's audience cave. The trolls had ignored it as so much garbage, and just between you and me, they're good at ignoring garbage. I knew at once what it was, however, for I'd seen Haytham's calligraphy many times. It was striking, precise, kind of fussy. Like him. But seeing it as I shuffled in the corner during the war council, feeling a trifle lonely, was like stumbling on an old friend. I snatched it up.

And so I discovered it was really like finding two friends. Flipping through the pages adorned with Haytham's flowing Mirabad script, I suddenly ran into words in another hand, this time using the script of Geam, which the Karvaks share. The language itself was Anokan, which I know, and there was something a bit off-kilter about the script and language, and I realized it was the work of Mad Katta, whom I'd seen scribbling aboard *Al-Saqr* with that noctograph thing as we flew from Svardmark to Spydbanen. I remembered him explaining his intent.

"It's a record of events, Northwing. What Haytham calls a 'vessel's timber.'"

"Ship's log," Haytham called out from across the gondola.

"Yes, that."

"Perhaps," said Princess Corinna, our not-quite-accidentally kidnapped royal passenger, "it will be kept in the Royal Archives."

"Sure," I said. "If you should perish in some bloodcurdling way, your family may indeed be interested."

"Then I hope," Corinna said, "Katta takes down everything in excruciating detail."

"You remind me of my patron, Lady Steelfox," I said. "Except that she doesn't just have a love for adventure, she has common sense."

"Oh, I have far too much common sense, shaman. It has kept me bottled up in Svanstad for more years than I care to think of. I've been entirely too safe. In our silver mines, there's enough unrest that people are willing to die defying the crown. Have I ever seen those mines? No. We upbraid the Gold-Jarl of Gullvik about the slave trade, but have I ever said it to his face? No. Many of our men go to Fiskegard to fish over the winter. Have I ever been there? No. I am a princess and must be safe. Such nonsense. What limited freedom I have, I maintain by keeping suitors at bay. My father, before his infirmity, trained me to fight, but I've never been allowed real combat. I've a man's heart, but I'm trapped in a woman's role."

I found her words interesting. "You say you have a 'man's heart.' What does that mean? Do you think only men's hearts crave adventure?"

"It's just how we speak of it. Men have one sphere, women another. But I am much more interested in the energetic—and, frankly, violent—aspects of *their* sphere. And I find prospective husbands pleasant enough. . . ." Here her gaze flicked to Haytham's, and his to hers, in a way each probably thought the other didn't notice. ". . . but I'm not much interested in marriage. Give me the hunt! The voyage! The battle! This balloon flight amazes me, and I'm prepared for the storms that will surely come." She looked down upon miles and miles of snow-covered pine forest. The view and her words took me backward in time.

In a forest not so unlike the one that passed below, I'd spent my girlhood. I say *girlhood* even though from an early age I felt uneasy being considered a girl. I didn't particularly think I was a boy either. Both ideas were like the big bucks leading trains of reindeer. Behind the beasts named Girl and Boy, let's say, were ones with names like Weaver, Gatherer, Hearth-keeper, Wife, Mother. Or else Hunter, Tanner, Warrior, Husband, Father. And each line of animals snorted and ran and ate in their own way, with customs peculiar to each. I didn't particularly see why we all had to hurry to get into one line or another, but that was the expectation.

Except among the shamans. We feared them but also respected them. And they had a strange way of living. Those of male sex would take the garb normally reserved for women and go about their duties with a feminine air. Shamans of female sex would take the clothes and manners of men. Eventually the womanish shamans might even marry an ordinary man of the tribe, or a mannish shaman might marry an ordinary woman. In rare cases two shamans might marry.

Not all the shamans felt quite as I did—as neither man nor woman. But their society was a haven for me. I wondered if Corinna felt similarly betwixt, with her possession of "a man's heart." Yet when I broached the subject she seemed confused by my words.

Life is crazy sometimes. We talk as though across a vast, snowy plain, tossing words at each other like clumps of snow. Sometimes they fall apart before they reach anybody. Sometimes they clump together all too well and hurt when they strike. Why did I imagine my experience would make any sense to Corinna? Mad Katta is my own countryman, and he studied with the shamans, and yet even he does not really understand me.

Ah, Katta—I hope you are well. We were comrades long enough that I think of you as a friend. Though I may never say that to your face.

Perhaps for that reason, I have taken up this document that I cannot read, adding to it my own "Secret History," in the manner of the Karvaks, using their script. Only the world-birthing spirit knows what will become of it, or me.

Of the beginning

This business of writing things is exhausting. Haytham and Katta are more mad than I thought.

Let us begin at "the beginning."

Not the before-time when the world-birthing spirit made the land and sea, nor the days in which the Wood-power and Blood-power made plants and animals. Not the days when the True People journeyed north and learned the ways of the reindeer and their migrations. Nor when the Karvaks took our land and named us the "Reindeer People."

No, by "the beginning" I mean the story Inga Peersdatter told me.

She was close to death when I leapt off that bizarre spirit object named Deadfall, and it took all my power to save her. Having an arm hacked off spells doom for most. But not every such victim has a shaman.

I ignored the surging mass of trolls except to exclaim now and again, "Back off! I'm saving her!" until I heard Skrymir Hollowheart say in Kantentongue, "Let it be. As she says." Furiously I bandaged the wound he had made and, leaning in, held it tight with my hands, chanting to her essence to remain in her body, and for spirits of light to chase out any infection that might come. As I did these things, it was as if the cavern was suffused with light. The trolls were like green flames in my sight, and Inga was a fluttering fire that mixed troll-green with the more usual orange-red human flame (for in my spirit sight humans look like the natural fire they've aligned themselves with for so long). My song captured spirits of the fresh mountain wind, blue-lit rippling things like blazing water snakes, and sent them flashing through Inga's body. From time to time a noxious thing like a deep-red smoky blaze sought to enter Inga's form, but the mountain spirits flashed them back.

I think over an hour passed. I sank into an exhausted sleep. In my dreams my own spirit floated above the mountain, and I saw the thousands of Karvak tents and the score of balloons among them. I saw pastureland in lower valleys where horses and sabercats were kept, and another valley with goats and cattle and other beasts of nomad life. I realized the Great Karvak Nation, the People of the Felt Walls, were in earnest about whatever they were about.

Far to the north, I had a sense of bright light, concentrated energy. There was a lot of spirit activity beyond these troll-mountains, but I had no idea what it represented.

I returned to myself when Inga shook me.

"Hello?" she asked, her voice gruff and a little frightened. I did not like anyone to be frightened (except of me sometimes), and I forced myself to return to myself.

"You. You're awake. Before me." I sat up. We were in a sort of stockade in a cave near the throne cavern. I suspected the trolls had snacked on the previous occupants. Inga was indeed awake, a little feverish but alert. I yelled at the trolls and bade them bring Khorkhog.

"Who's Khorkhog?" said the girl. "Do I want to know?"

"Not who, what. It's lamb or goat stew cooked with hot rocks. Hearty Karvak stuff."

"I could use hearty stuff. . . . You saved me, shaman. . . ."

"Just call me Northwing. Take it easy, Inga. That would have been a fatal blow for most."

"Well, I am a changeling."

"A what?"

"Oh, right, you're from far away . . . I'm really a troll, who grew up as a human. I think being among humans shaped me, made me look like them, grow like them. But I'm not. I feel my stump itch. I don't know how long it will take, but that arm's going to grow back."

I have to admit, I felt a little revulsion hearing this, when I should have been happy for anyone getting to grow back an arm. We're all narrow-visioned in our own way.

Khorkhog proved a good choice. Inga wolfed it down. "It's strange," she said when she'd half-finished it, "but good."

"I feel that way about Kantening food. The things you do with fish . . . gah."

Later, when she'd belched and leaned against the wall, she said, "Thanks for saving me. And getting me food. Not sure which one I'm happier about. What are they going to do to us?"

"I'm hoping they'll give us to the Karvaks. If they don't eat us soon that's probably what will happen."

"Well, that's cheerful."

"I'm not a very optimistic person."

"What happens if the Karvaks take us?"

"Depends on who's in charge. If my patron Steelfox is out there, we're fine. If it's her sister Lady Jewelwolf, we may be in for trouble."

"If a Karvak is your patron, what were you doing flying around in a Mirabad inventor's balloon?"

"That's a long story. If you're a troll, what were you doing growing up in a human village?"

"That's not a long story. Not much to tell."

"Then I suggest you go first. If the trolls eat us, we're more likely to have heard a complete tale."

"I'm starting to hate you, Northwing."

"It's a popular opinion. Talk."

She talked.

THE BEGINNING

In the beginning, the Creator took up Her brush and painted all the worlds.

That's the first part of Swan-scripture, one of the things we get from the People of the Brush, and it's the start of what my mother would read to me right after she swatted me with the Godbok, every time. Which was often. I think she was trying to calm herself down with the words, as much as she was trying to turn me into a good Swanling. Word had it that my mother had lost her real daughter by failing to keep steel and salmebok beside her crib—my crib—and trolls or uldra had crept in and snatched her away, leaving little old me behind.

Ulrike, my mother, sometimes seemed to think I must have known all about that scheme, but at first I knew nothing but fuzzy colors and sounds and shapes. I don't even really remember the first beating. I know how it happened, though. When Ulrike learned I was a changeling left in place of her baby, she asked the wise women of the village for advice, and they gave her the best they had: trolls or uldra will sometimes come back for their blood-child and give up their captive one if they hear the wails of their kin. I gather Ulrike snatched me up and made sure I wailed good.

The treatment would have killed a human babe. I was troll-stuff, though. You might think I'd have hated Ulrike. You'd be wrong. I thought my new mother was beautiful. She thought I was horrid. Though in truth I looked pretty much like any other baby, except for a bit of green light that spilled from my eyes now and then, and a thickness to my bones that she discovered with a *whoof* as soon as she tried to carry me.

Well, a fine mess we were all in, the priest's family and the changeling. But though they were hard people they couldn't just murder me. Guess I'm grateful.

My father, Mentor Peer, wasn't the one who'd strike out. Maybe it was all that Swanling teaching about taking a second blow before giving one yourself. Maybe it was that he could hurt almost as much with a hard word and cold eye as Ulrike could hurt with a hand or a wooden spoon. He could be kind, but even on a good day it was a pitying sort of kindness. And Ulrike, she had a good heart in her too, but sometimes after ale she'd grow sullen and red-eyed and remember what she'd lost. And then it was only a matter of time before I said or did something—break a cup with my strength or yell too loud when I bashed my head on a low doorway—and all at once I was the nastiest, most insolent, most ungrateful creature who walked on two legs, she who'd taken everything from her, and the hitting would resume.

I spent many years trying to reconcile all the terrible things she said into one consistent theory of my horridness. But in time even I realized I couldn't *simultaneously* be too thin and too fat, too loud and too silent, too aggressive and too scared, too worldly and too pious. I think it was when I was eleven, and realized she'd begun a meal by complaining I hated her cooking and ended by saying I ate like a hog, that I realized there was something wrong that wasn't me.

Now, I had options ordinary human children lacked. Even at eleven I could lift a boulder over my head. I was sorry for any child of a violent drunk who couldn't summarily crush all her mother's bottles of spirits underfoot. I was sorry for those children, because they needed protectors. But I finally realized my troll blood meant I could be my own protector. That same day, the wooden spoon, long unused, broke against my troll-bottom.

My father and I had a long talk at his church. I spoke to him while clutching the great icon of the Swan, pointedly showing that my skin did not in fact smolder. I said, "She will not hit me. You will stop talking to me as if I were a monster. And if either of you wants to get drunk, you do it in another town. Go without me. As the goddess is my witness, I'll be fine."

I know there are people in the world far, far worse off than I've ever been. But I had strength, and damned if I wasn't going to use it.

I am glad to tell you something. That was the worst of them. They actually got a bit better. Peer reached out to his superiors, and whatever one may say about the Swan-church, this time it helped. Instead of blaming me, my father's colleagues tried to change my parents. And because they got better I learned something strange.

To my eyes, Ulrike and Peer had been the loveliest people in the village, while most others were misshapen and ugly. Yet over the months as they struggled to become their better selves, they too became ugly in my sight.

I figured out the truth from Peer's books. I have troll-sight. People of good will? They appear ugly to me. Saintly people look horrific. People of evil intent look attractive to me. The truly wicked look beautiful.

(You, Northwing? You look like a plain old human being. It's kind of reassuring.)

I'm a good judge of character. It pays to hang around with ugly people. That's one reason I ended up making friends with Malin Jorgensdatter. She's hideous. To me. A-Girl-Is-A-Joy, she looked horrid too.

So, that's who I am. It's a lot like what you'd hear about me from Malin, except that I don't tell her how bad things sometimes got. Not everyone's ready to hear things like that. (I think you hear, and see, a lot.) And even though Ulrike and Peer became better people, it was never easy around them, which is why I jumped at a chance to get on the road. I can forgive. That's a choice. But I can't forget. That's a scar.

But there's one thing, something I rarely say out loud, something I'm doing for them as well as me. I'd like to find out just why trolls exchange their babies for human ones sometimes. I've been among trolls a while now and I don't see any humans. And is the original Inga Peersdatter still somewhere in the world? I'd like to meet her, if so.

So that's how I began. How do you think I'm going to end up?

Of Innocence

Well, I thought she might end up badly, which is why during her story I'd been reaching out with my perceptions to find some animal, any animal, who might consent to help us. This was difficult. The natural creatures of the area steered clear of these mountains, and with good reason. What birds and beasts remained in the area had bits of troll-substance stuck into their brains, twisting their minds, making them easier for the trolls to command. I started cajoling them, getting a surprise ready for the trolls.

Meanwhile I began to tell Inga my own story, or at least the part of it that began when my patron Steelfox ordered me and Haytham to hunt for Innocence Gaunt. We were rudely interrupted, in one of those events that the spirits themselves may have arranged.

Skrymir Hollowheart flung the cage's door open and grabbed us both in one hand. That stony cave of fingers shut out most of what passed for light. I lost my mental grip on the troll-addled creatures outside. Skrymir was not a gentle beast of burden. It was like being back on *Al-Saqr* during a storm.

There was some sort of commotion at the tunnel, the one leading to the cave where Skrymir could look down upon the Karvak army. Skrymir ran to the tunnel, and then his voice boomed, chattering our teeth, and hailing, to my surprise, Lady Steelfox. My patron answered.

Now, you should understand something. The conquering Karvaks set Steelfox over us by marrying her to our rightful ruler. As I'd been the best shaman in the land, I'd been advisor to them both. When my ruler died in the Karvaks' endless wars, I served Steelfox. I don't have much reason to like her. But, grudgingly, I do. She is a remarkably decent imposed leader, one who tries to understand our needs. And when I heard her voice, my heart raced. I have to admit I grinned.

Spirits grant she never reads this.

Skrymir's voice drove the grin straight from my rattling jaws. For he'd seen someone with Steelfox. "The chosen of the Heavenwalls! You've delivered him!"

This I certainly didn't expect. I did not know what would happen or whom to trust, but I wanted help. I reached out to the animals I'd sensed, eagles in the heights with troll-splinters in their eyes. I had the control I needed, and I set them winging toward this tunnel.

"He has delivered me, Skrymir," Steelfox said. "Without my shaman at my side, I needed his help. I am in his debt. He is under my protection."

Well, that was interesting.

"Of course!" Skrymir sounded like a boy persuaded not to be cruel to an animal. "I will not challenge your authority!" He opened his hand, palm up. I'd like to claim I was ready for action, but I was more interested in throwing up.

"Here is your shaman," Skrymir said, "the mighty Northwing, whom even we trolls fear. And also this troll-girl who helped the Runethane escape me. Shall I crush them?"

"Northwing!" Steelfox actually seemed to care. I vowed to throw up on her last. "What has become of you? What have you done to my friend, Skrymir?"

"I captured a foe. I think you should keep closer watch on your people. Another man of yours, one Haytham, helped the Runethane escape as well, though his contribution was minimal compared to Northwing's."

"Liege," I managed to say, "You must understand . . . I have tried to follow your commands as best I could, and I am not afraid to die. . . ."

It was all more eloquent in my head.

Steelfox cut me off. "I have absolute faith in you, Northwing! Your clutches overreach, Skrymir! My sister will know of this!"

"All in good time," said Skrymir. "It is your foolish inventor and your mighty shaman who have endangered our alliance, but you can make good by taking this Northwing back under your command . . . we surely cannot contain the shaman. And by minding the chosen of the Heavenwalls."

"And what of the girl, there?"

"This one? She is of troll blood. Years ago we dealt with the uldra of Svardmark, to place her among the humans. We are welcoming her back to the fold, in our own way."

Inga began saying something. It was, "Kill you . . . kill you . . ."

I wondered if it also sounded better in her head.

"Yes, yes, yes," said the troll-king, "and a pony too. Now—"

"Now it ends," rang out a human voice. I knew it. I didn't like it, but I knew it.

Walking Stick, of the wulin of Qiangguo, jumped onto Skrymir's hand. I have to give him credit for guts. And strength. He hauled me and Inga up and leapt deep into the tunnel. I got a fleeting sense of his power. You could say that we are both masters of spirit, but my focus is outward onto the world, and his is inward, giving great resources to his body.

Innocence gasped. "Walking Stick! Teacher!"

Walking Stick just stared. He was obviously surprised to find the boy here of all places. But he recovered quickly.

He snatched up the Scroll of Years and started jabbing here and there. Each time someone appeared in midair until he was accompanied by Liron Flint, Snow Pine, and two monks. It was good to see them, but I realized the feeling might not be mutual.

Skrymir laughed like a little kid before grabbing a monk and crushing him like a clump of snow.

This was too much.

I've long wandered the southern lands, the Karvak Realm, Qiangguo, the trading cities of the Braid of Spice, and now the Bladed Isles. And what I've seen everywhere is a disregard for life. You all see yourselves as so distinct from one another, but spilling blood is the sport you all share. My own people fear us shamans, because we remind them so much of blood and death. But among our own people we are reserved, even gentle. Down in the south I have cultivated a certain gruffness, acting as though I didn't care about the violence around me.

But this casual slaughter isn't the way we were meant to live. When my people hunt, we offer up prayers to the wild creature who has consented to be caught and eaten, so that when its spirit returns to its source, it will think well of us and come again. When a person dies we are careful to honor the essence as well.

Skrymir Hollowheart understood none of that.

When I became a shaman, I had a vision of climbing a tree around which the stars wheeled, going up and up to the place where the tree pierced the skin of the sky. Out of that gap roared spirits of power, shapeless and shining, and they slew spirit-me, cut me to pieces like a game animal. Down they brought a cauldron made of night and boiled me up. Out of the cauldron my spirit arose again, a thing of speed and cunning, like a waterbird of the northern seas, able to survive in two realms, water and air. So, too, I knew both the realms of flesh and spirit.

I was the shaman Northwing.

It is sometimes the burden of the shaman to speak to the mighty and say "enough."

"Enough!"

And my voice brought the troll-eagles to us.

They had no hope of slaying the troll-king, but Skrymir clearly did not enjoy the pain.

"Northwing, enough!" said Steelfox. "I need your power beside me! Skrymir is our ally!"

That was it. I obeyed.

"No!" yelled Inga. She rushed at me, killing one of Steelfox's guards.

Innocence was yelling at her to stop, while Walking Stick pleaded for him to come away.

"Enough!" I said, and told Innocence it was time to choose sides.

He chose the Karvaks.

Skrymir had destroyed the eagles. I might have felt guilty about that, but they'd been corrupted by crystalline troll-splinters already. Skrymir made a grab for Walking Stick, but the wulin warrior leapt from the tunnel into the high mountain air. He'd already magicked his companions—and Inga too—into the scroll. He dropped out of sight.

And so there I was, and there Innocence was, choosing one faction of a great struggle. I didn't like having some friends on one side and some on another, and I didn't think he would enjoy it either. But war is like that.

Of the War Council

And so I was alone, or might as well have been. My traveling companions were gone. Innocence Gaunt was busy being morose, stalking here and there among the caves. I had all the trolls and troll-twisted animals I could ever hope to talk to, of course. Ha. I glowered by myself in a corner of Skrymir's audience hall. I was back in Steelfox's service, but she was completely preoccupied with war plans.

It's been a long War Council. The Easterners are bad enough—the princesses Steelfox and Jewelwolf, the Karvak general Ironhorn, the crazy warrior Dolma (who seems to have glued herself to Innocence), all talking, talking, talking. And then there are the Kantenings—yes, Kantenings, ready to sell out their fellows, the chieftains of places called Langfjord and Grawik and Jegerhall, northern lords with long grudges against Oxiland and Svardmark. Those three are of monstrous proportions, big as any men I've ever seen. In the jabbering of the trolls, they're called three of the *Nine Wolves*, and they're supposedly more than human, something I'll have to investigate later.

Ah, the trolls! There must be thousands of them. You'd think they could overrun the Bladed Isles all by themselves. But I gather they're limited in some ways. They're none too happy with bright sunlight, and in some way I don't understand they're stronger on Spydbanen than elsewhere. Skrymir needs human help to fulfill his plan of claiming the Chained Straits. He'd like to slaughter as many humans as possible, naturally, but the Great Chain is what he really wants.

"Our riders have already secured the strait, great ones," General Ironhorn reported. "We've met no real opposition. We had to eradicate one village, but once the survivors fled with their tale, the others capitulated. We have encampments on both sides of the gap, and on the island in the middle. The Chain is ours."

"Mine, you mean," Skrymir said easily. It must be very comfortable to talk to your allies when they're human and you're big as a hill. "You Karvaks and hangers-on, you can have the land, as long as my trolls can ravage a bit. I want the magic."

"As long as I and our wizardly colleagues have access to it," Jewelwolf told him. She was ever a striking woman, both like and unlike my patron— younger, fiercer, more commanding. I understood that in their childhoods, Jewelwolf had earned her conquering father's respect. Steelfox had merely earned his love.

"Of course," Skrymir said impatiently. "If not for our association in sorcerous circles, Jewelwolf, this whole alliance would be impossible. You and the others may tap the power for your own purposes. There is plenty for all."

I kept my eyes low, scribbling. I would have to investigate that matter for myself.

"Tomorrow," Jewelwolf said, "we move the main force. Innocence will accompany us, so that at the right time he may master the Chain."

"I could take one of those balloons," Innocence said. "Isn't it true we could be there right away? Why wait?"

Dolma said, "Patience, great one."

"Indeed," said Jewelwolf. "It is good fortune we have you now, but there are those who might seek to snatch you away."

The lord of Jegerhall, a huge, fierce-eyed man named Arnulf Pyre-Maker, spoke up. "You're really planning to move a whole army down Spydbanen in the dead of winter?"

The equally big, many-scarred Ottmar Bloodslake of Grawik shot back, "We've sparred plenty of winters, we three."

"Skirmishes!" mocked mighty Kolli the Cackling of Langfjord. "With war-bands of twenty or less! That's a *real* army down there in Jotuncrown, with hungry stomachs."

General Ironhorn laughed. "You have no experience with us. On the steppe we learned to campaign in winter, bringing what food we needed on the hoof. We know how to use frozen rivers as roads. We know how to use snowfall to disguise our movements. Winter is our friend."

Steelfox said, "Nevertheless I fear we are overconfident. This is alien ground. And we campaign without a clear path home. My father never put himself in that position."

"I am not our father," Jewelwolf said. "And although a great strategist, he respected boldness above all else."

"We will use all our craft," the general said, seeming to appreciate his awkward position between contentious royals. "We have every expectation of victory, but we will not underestimate the Kantenings. Give the order, great ones."

I have caught up now, with the present time.

Jewelwolf looks across the gulf before the throne of Skrymir, into the eyes of Steelfox. Jewelwolf is khatun, the chief wife of the Grand Khan back on the steppe. This is truly her expedition, but she has chosen to involve Steelfox, whether as punishment or peace offering, it's hard to say.

It matters now, that the sisters agree.

Steelfox nods.

Jewelwolf smiles. "Begin at dawn, General."

And the trolls roar with satisfaction, and the Kantening barbarians shout with glee, and the Karvaks go about their business with the discipline that has shaken the world.

And I? I reach out to a natural world that will soon know much more pain and death than usual, and although I obey, I cannot celebrate. I wonder at the feelings of the many Karvak Wind-Tamers, shamans who are my almost-colleagues, who hear the roaring down in the valley and begin their own preparations. And beyond, far to the northeast, I wonder at the spirit energies I sense there, in a place no troll or Kantening has spoken of. And—

"What do you think you're doing?" Jewelwolf says, looming above me. "You should be helping my sister . . . you impudent Reindeer People savage, are you writing what I'm saying? How dare—

(*Here ends the portion of the* A Journey to Kantenjord *in the hand of Northwing, shaman of the True People. The bloodstain is presumed to be hers.*)

CHAPTER 22

PYRES

Gaunt, Bone, and Muninn Crowbeard emerged from the shadows of the Mork-skag and skied through high, snowy country, passing ruined farmhouses and copses of trees, crossing frozen streams and ridges that seemed to have strayed from their mountain parents.

"We're in the Gamellaw now," Crowbeard said. "The realm of the old ways. No nations up here. It's a rough place, but if you can lie low for a year and a day, Bone, most will agree you're free of your bonds."

"A year and a day," Gaunt said, the image of Innocence fresh in her mind. "We can't hide that long. We need to find that stone church."

"No stone churches up this way," said Crowbeard. "Not in Laksfjord. More a bunch of farms and a marketplace than a town. The chief thereabouts is Harald the Far-Traveled, a priest of Torden. He won't defy the Gull-Jarl, but news doesn't get here fast. We can probably stay a day."

At sunset they descended to a fjord with snowy white fields and farmhouses scattered throughout. They inquired at a longhouse near the green-blue waters, flanked by sentinels of bare trees. A nondescript guard let them in.

They waited upon fireside benches with other guests, for it seemed to be a time of good cheer. Someone played a fiddle, one with the same haunting sound as they'd heard in Gullvik. Soon a gray-haired man in a cloak of rich colors came to sit beside them.

"Can it be?" said the chieftain. "Muninn Sure-Hand, I am certain of it!"

"I'm glad you're sure, Harald, because I'm sure not. I go by Crowbeard now."

"You don't say! You have bones in your beard, like some sort of witch-man!"

"A wise woman told me they'd wing me from trouble. I think I want my money back."

"Ha! You were always a surly one. And who are your companions?"

"I am Lepton," Gaunt said, "and this is my husband Osteon. We are lately of Amberhorn."

"A long journey!"

"You have no idea," Bone said. "But we're glad to have arrived in such a hospitable land."

"Courtesy! Well, Muninn, or Crowbeard, I get few visitors from my old foamreaving days. You will stay in my hall. Share tales and good cheer. Or, if you are of a Swanling mind, their church is celebrating Saint Fiametta's night. Though I'll warn you they're superstitious about the Vestvinden fiddle, so you'll hear none there!"

"Why do they fear the fiddle?" Gaunt asked.

"It's said it attracts and enchants spirits, especially the fossegrim of the waterfalls. But then, it also attracts drunkenness and revelry, and the Swanchurch dislikes such things."

"I am no Swanling," Crowbeard said. "I would love to hear old tales, and a fiddle."

Gaunt saw an opportunity. "My husband and I, on the other hand, have been too long away from Mass."

"We have?" Bone said. Gaunt stepped on his foot. "We have!"

"You will want to leave that sword," Harald said, eyeing Crypttongue. "I don't mind folk going armed—indeed, the All-Father's sayings encourage it—but the priest is particular about weapons and armor in church."

"In the days of the stave churches," Gaunt said, "it was otherwise."

"Are you a historian of the Swan-church?"

"Not exactly." She and Bone shared a look.

"I give you my word," Harald said, "no one will touch your property."

"Very well," she said.

Leaving the hall several bits of metal lighter, Bone said, "Mind you, I have reason to doubt the honor of Kantening chiefs."

"I understand." She'd already spotted the church upslope on the northern side of the fjord and led Bone there arm-in-arm. The mouth of the fjord was glowing with rosy light, and her mood lifted. She laughed.

"What is it?" Bone asked.

"Me. Despite everything I've done, everywhere I've gone, I cling to an image of myself as a well-to-do farm girl of Swanisle." She gestured. "But the thought was occasioned by a setting my countrymen would call barbaric."

"I wondered why you were so eager to go to the church." He sighed. "I've been able to give you many things, but never normality. The demons and monsters and assassins may have gotten in the way of that." He paused. "Demons. Crowbeard talked about a Charstalker in the sword. That's a very *particular* term."

"Yes. It's true. There's an Eastern demon in there, and it's indeed the kind that nurtures hate over several incarnations. Previously it was in the body of Muggur Barrow-Friend."

"What is it doing here?"

"Its answers are evasive," Gaunt said, "but I gather it and eight comrades came out here because there is some sort of connection between the Heavenwalls in the East and the Chain in the West. They found the Nine Wolves congenial hosts and stayed around."

"Strange. I suppose having such a thing in church would not be in the spirit of the proceedings."

"No indeed. Thank you for coming along, Bone." She laughed. "If nothing else, perhaps the next time the priestess in Gullvik takes a reading of your soul, you won't end up with the slavers."

"Please don't joke about that."

She stopped and studied him there in the dim light.

"I'm sorry," she said.

He nodded.

She said, "Do you want to talk about it?"

"Want?" He chuckled. "You know . . . I've been looked at with scorn, derision, and hate, Persimmon." He put his hands around her face, as if he hoped to send the memories from his sinew directly into her bones. "But until now no one's ever looked at me like I was a human-shaped shovel or butter churn." He laughed, let go, turned away. "Think of people looking at you like that every day. Nothing personal, no malice, just the facts of life. Cows moo. Ducks quack. You're a slave. It gets into your head."

She reached out, put her arms around him. "Let me put other things into your head. If it takes a lifetime, we'll make those memories fade."

He said no more and followed her to the Swan-church.

This church was a much simpler affair than the old ruin in the Morkskag. There were some fifty worshippers, and Gaunt and Bone attracted stares. Of course they did. Even in Kantenjord the tattooed woman and the scarred man stuck out.

She held her head high, prepared to list their pedigree, references, and heists.

Then came the pageant, and her smile became more easy. Very small children played gingerbread men and tiny, helpful uldra. She could not follow the Kantentongue well enough to understand how these elements figured into a story about a saint who lived centuries ago and thousands of miles away. Maybe it didn't matter. Soon came older children playing some kind of star-wizard, and she did not understand that either.

She studiously did not laugh at any incongruities, stumbles, or miscues.

At last came Saint Fiametta herself, a freckled teenaged girl with lit candles in a wreath around her head.

"Gaunt," Bone whispered. "This is a dangerous land indeed. The girls light their heads on fire."

"Hush."

The congregation sang of Saint Fiametta's kindness, embodied as light. She could not follow the words, but she hummed the tune. She held Bone's hand. She thought of missing friends, of Alder and Vuk. Of Innocence. Candleflames danced and shadows swirled.

They returned under starlight to Harald the Far-Traveled's hall. They walked unspeaking at first, and it was satisfying to be silent together. Traveling with others they'd had little privacy, and much to say when they had it. She sighed, realizing she'd enjoyed the walk so much she'd forgotten her ulterior motive in taking Bone to church. "Bone. We must talk about Crowbeard."

"Must we?"

"He's been helpful, Bone. But."

"He sold me into slavery. Yes, I do remember that. That does erode my trust somewhat—"

He broke off. His face became red-lit. "Gaunt—"

She spun and saw a nightmare. Harald's hall was burning.

They ran, other men and women joining them. Fire flayed the darkness, shifting orange claws illuminating a column of smoke. Crowbeard lay sprawled before the burning entrance.

Another man raised a saber, glinting in the firelight.

It was the hall's lone guard, the nondescript man.

"Ah! Lepton and Osteon. Or should I say, Gaunt and Bone? For my late lord, my ring-giver, did recognize the woman with the rose-and-spiderweb tattoo and the man with the two scars on his face, one from blade, one from flame. You are not the most famous people who have fared along the world's roads, but you are hardly unknown, and Harald was indeed Far-Traveled."

"Was?" Gaunt demanded, staring at the sword that was recently hers.

"His body lies dead and burnt behind me. But his spirit dwells within this fascinating blade. Yes, he swore an oath, but Grundi serves mightier masters."

"Are you one of the Nine Wolves?" Bone demanded. "Did Skalagrim alert you?"

"Them?" Grundi laughed. "I care nothing for such rabble. I am an agent of the khatun Jewelwolf. She is marching even now. I was to smooth her passage, but she will understand my decision when I bring her this prize."

"Bring her this," Gaunt muttered, and hurled a fist-sized rock.

The man deflected it smoothly with Crypttongue, the magical blade shattering stone.

At the same moment, daggers flew from Bone's hands, for he'd covertly carried a pair. One was similarly knocked from the air, but the second sunk into the spy's side. Grundi snarled. "I have not yet mastered this weapon, but I shall! Kantenjord will burn!"

"I care little for Kantenjord," Bone said, "but that's Gaunt's sword you have there."

"I already know it better than she. Floki, Muggur, and the Charstalker send their regards."

With that Grundi rushed into the night, bearing Crypttongue and Gaunt's hate. Armed men tried to stop him. He slew two, barely breaking stride, and Gaunt's second stone missed. He rushed into the snowy night.

"We," Crowbeard gasped. "We must find him . . . he will leave footprints . . ." Warriors rushed off even as he spoke.

Bone knelt beside the old man. "Easy. We need to make certain you are all right."

"You'd do that for one who betrayed you?"

"Reminding me is perhaps unwise . . ."

"Bone," Gaunt said, her tone sharp. "Our gear. The *Chart*. We may need it to find Innocence."

They raced around back, found another entrance, dove into the smoky ruin.

It was a lavishly bad idea, Bone realized. Smoke from a burning wall was coiling along the ceiling and up through the openings in the roof, but quite a bit of the miasma was stubbornly staying in the building. Bone remembered a bit of lore from dead Master Sidewinder, his old teacher in the trade. *Never burn a building or be tempted to torch one. But if you find yourself in a burning structure, stay low, for smoke will rise.* He followed the advice, and Gaunt did likewise. The next part was *Then Get Out*, and he regretted not following that part.

Their armor and his pack were a loss, but Gaunt found her bow. He snagged Gaunt's pack. As they turned to go, Gaunt pointed to the body of Harald the Far-Traveled, dead from a thrust to the heart. It was not burned as the spy had claimed, though the night was young. Nonetheless, dead was dead.

A coldly practical assessment of a hot-tempered people made Bone take a risk. He gestured and Gaunt nodded.

They reemerged from the great hall dragging Harald's body.

The irony, Gaunt thought as they boarded the ship a week later, bags of Laksfjord gold in hand, was that Harald's heirs were going to burn him anyway, in a mock longship on a mound of earth. But it was the principle of the thing. Impressed by her and Bone's heroism, they'd paid a reward and arranged passage for Oxiland with a band called the Lardermen.

Crowbeard insisted on joining them in the search for Innocence, for he'd been to Oxiland—indeed, he'd seen a majestic church there that matched the one glimpsed on the Straits of Tid—and said he still had a debt to pay.

They berthed amid crates of victuals and barrels of liquor as the carrack *Raveneye* sailed down Laksfjord. Aquavit, it seemed, was a spiced spirit whose production, for inscrutable reasons, required aging aboard a ship. As a result the hold had a heady atmosphere. Crowbeard excused himself, for foamreaving days were thick in his mind, and he wanted to be on deck. Once they'd spread blankets, the rocking of the boat bumped them together. Gaunt laughed, and it cheered Bone to see her relaxed. He kissed her.

"My, sir," she said, nuzzling up to him. "You are forward."

"Yes," he said. He felt giddy, his desire stoked. "I realize this is no inn, but perhaps . . ."

"You do realize Crowbeard could show up at any moment?"

His hands ceased their explorations. "Damn."

She stroked his chin with her finger. "How about some fresh air?"

"Wise," he sighed.

On the deck, Captain Glint was studying the dawn, which had come red, illuminating a carpet of thick clouds. "I mislike this sky," he said. Glint was lean of face and thick of beard, with a protruding jaw and an expression that warned of impending bloodshed. "Storm is in our future. If it hits while we still sail for Laksfjord, I will take it as an omen and turn back."

Crowbeard said, tying knots, "I think it will be on the open sea, from the taste of the air."

Glint squinted. "You know all that, from the look of it and the taste?"

"It's only a guess, Captain. I've made many voyages."

"You tie a good knot too—" Glint's voice broke off as he saw a tremor seize Crowbeard's hands. "All you all right?"

"It's nothing," said Crowbeard, and nothing was what the captain said.

The journey down Laksfjord took a full day. The open sea was choppy but manageable, and Bone had wholly forgotten the rumors of storm. But at night the moon rose crimson, with ghostly red rings around it, as though it were a spectral archery target. The sea went calm.

"Pretty," Bone said.

But the crew murmured, and Crowbeard swore. "Not so pretty, landsman. That's what we used to call a storm-lantern moon."

Captain Glint shook his head. "Too many portents. I'll not make for Smokecoast now. We'll skirt back toward the Chained Strait and beyond that to the Meadow of Whales. I'll drop you three at Vinderhus. I'm loath to brave a storm so close to the Draugmaw."

"Fair enough," said Bone. "I only want to reach Oxiland and find our son."

"Ah," Glint said, voice warming a little, "so you are seeking family. I wondered what would bring you to that desolate, mad place. Did your son go there seeking employment? Adventure?"

"It's hard to say," Gaunt said. "We parted in anger."

"Well, I have no children, but I left my childhood home in Spydbanen and never looked back. The usual story, youngest son, no place for me on the farm. So I suppose estrangement is not so unfamiliar to me. Couldn't imagine my own parents come looking."

"It's unfinished business," Bone said, surprising himself with his willingness to speak. "He can hate us if he wants. But he's young yet, to be wandering the world alone."

Glint squinted at Gaunt and Bone anew. "This boy of yours. He wouldn't be perhaps thirteen or fourteen summers? Yea tall? With blue eyes and red hair?"

"Yes!" Gaunt said. "You have word of him?"

"Word of him? I've seen him!"

"Red hair and blue eyes," Bone cautioned, "must describe thousands of youths hereabouts."

"Nevertheless," the captain said, "I see it in your faces. The way he walks, the way she talks. The Swan's guided you here, or else the fate-weavers threaded us together."

Eagerly, as *Raveneye* scudded for Oxiland, they pressed him for everything he could remember of the boy Erik Glint knew as Askelad.

In time they passed the Chained Straits, and Gaunt and Bone beheld the Great Chain of Unbeing. Maps had not conveyed the unnatural nature of the place. The headlands of Svardmark and Spydbanen stretched far out over the waters, looking like they must surely crumble. It was easy to imagine a supernatural origin for the islands. Immense metal chains wrapped around each extension, linking them to a small, craggy island in the midst of the straits. From miles off they could see occasional flashes of lighting traveling along the length of the Chain.

They saw something else as well.

"Bone," Gaunt said, squinting. "Are those Karvak tents, there, and there?"

"There too. They're everywhere the Chain is."

"What are they doing here?"

"I wonder if Steelfox is mixed up in this," Bone said. "She was supposed to meet us in Fiskegard, originally. I wonder if we should pay the Karvaks a visit—"

"Ware weather!" cried a lookout.

There would be no visiting the rough coasts of the Chained Straits, for a new storm billowed grim, bearing down upon them from the northeast.

"Race to Fiskegard!" Captain Glint commanded. "That's our best hope for shelter!" To Gaunt and Bone he added, "We took your son there. They may have news. Now, I think you'd best get below." He turned to Crowbeard. "You, foamreaver, have acquitted yourself well, but I've seen the quiver that assails you. I'll think no less of you if you join them."

Crowbeard's tone held both pride and anger. But his words were merely, "Thanks, Captain. I'll stay."

Gaunt and Bone descended not a minute too soon. The calm gave way to choppy seas, then agitated seas, then mad seas, with waves half as tall as the masts. *Raveneye* heaved through the surge. Bone, tossed about like a rag in a dog's mouth, heaved in other ways.

"Sorry," he managed to say.

"Hang on, Bone," Gaunt said.

They were battered about by more shaking. Bone felt a little better now with his guts emptied. They tried to make jokes about it at first, but it was unsettling in more ways than one. "This is almost as bad," Bone shouted, "as the time we sailed the western ocean!"

"Was that when we sought the sleeping warrior or when we sought the ruins of the gods?"

"I get them mixed up! Getting old! Gah—damn! What does the world have against my nose?"

"For my part, I seem to keep bumping my head on the same spot as when I landed in the mountains!"

He wished he could have kissed that spot, but he'd only have smacked their skulls together.

There came a lurch greater than any before, and of a different character.

"What?" Bone cried out to the heavens. "What?"

"Bone! We've scraped something. An undersea rock formation. We must have gotten too close to the coast. We're taking on water. Look."

Indeed, water was gurgling up between boards like a delicate mountain stream.

They scrambled to find buckets, reeling their way up the gangway to the deck, screaming about a leak. Sailors joined them.

Existence became a nightmare of bailing, illuminated at times by lightning and moonlight, punctuated by the occasional fall. Bone did not look like an acrobatic walker of rooftops anymore. He would have reiterated his hate for the Bladed Isles, but he had no time for it, if he didn't want to feed its fish.

Once he spied another ship. "Look!" he screamed. The others looked, and Crowbeard cursed. Bone was learning to be discouraged when Crowbeard found something to swear at.

"Draug," the foamreaver said.

The ship was small and appeared sliced in twain from bow to stern, and upon its deck stood a shadowed, quivering shape, bearing a harpoon and a single, baleful red eye.

The Draug was not approaching them but rather racing *Raveneye*, and its impossible ship skipped gracefully among the waves.

Captain Glint, sounding like a man who'd seen his death, spat and commanded all aboard to hold their course or continue bailing.

"What is it doing?" Bone heard Gaunt say.

"It's herding us," Crowbeard said, "to the Draugmaw."

After what seemed hours, though it may have been only half of one, a cry rose up from the decks, for a man had been lost overboard.

When the second was lost, Bone was on the deck, and just before a wave surged and claimed the hapless sailor, Bone saw the Draug raise its harpoon and point at *Raveneye*.

"It's picking us off!" Bone cried. "We have to attack it!"

"You're mad!" Captain Glint said. "If we can ride out the storm, we'll escape!"

"He *is* mad!" Crowbeard said. "I'll attest! But look at that storm! We may have a choice between slow death and fast!"

Captain Glint narrowed his eyes and grinned a grin that unsettled Bone, for all that he'd prompted it. "Run up the colors," the captain said.

Soon the black flag of skull and crossed meat-cleavers slapped the air, and he bellowed their intent to ram. Crossbowmen manned their weapons, and Gaunt lay ready with her bow.

Bone, still bailing, had the notion the Draug was astonished. Contemptuous, but astonished. It raised the harpoon, and *Raveneye* nearly floundered, but the crew mastered the vessel and kept it bearing down at the half-ship.

"Aim for the eye!" Gaunt called.

Her arrow flew, and crossbow bolts followed.

It wept like molten gold, and its shriek was like all the seabirds in the world.

The Draug did not fall. It spread its hands, and a wind ripped the Lardermen's flag from the mast, as a wave big as five *Raveneyes* blocked out the first rays of the sun.

"Draug!" screamed Muninn Crowbeard, and off the deck he leapt, to bury his axe in the head of the shambling thing.

The wave crashed over them all, and *Raveneye* floundered at last.

Bone had only one goal. Doomed or saved, he must stay with Gaunt. He grabbed her as the surge hit.

The force of the wave made him lose her in the dark waters. But when he resurfaced, she was nearby, as was the broken mainmast. It was she who helped him clutch it. Other hands joined theirs.

"Is it—" he gasped. "Is it gone—"

"Bone."

He looked where she looked, and a gasp went up from the survivors aboard ship, for the half-ship approached, and the shambling shape in its midst had nothing but a ruined cave for an eye. It bore down on the mast nonetheless. Crowbeard was not to be seen.

He had his foamreaver death. Bone felt a tiny comfort at that.

But in the next moment a shape reared up from the Draug-ship, something Bone had taken for a collection of rags, and it seized the harpoon-arm of the Draug with berserker fury.

Muninn Crowbeard grasped the weapon with a howl of mad glee.

His hands shook, but they drove the harpoon true, stabbing the Draug through the ruined cave of its eye socket. The metal burst out the back of the seaweed-covered skull, spraying an ichor like molten gold.

It was as though the Draug's chilling screech sliced open the clouds, for light blazed through the storm, and the sun lit the rain to dazzling streaks. The Draug seized its harpoon from Crowbeard and jabbed the foamreaver through the heart, sending him at one stroke to the halls of the valorous dead.

But even in its victory it turned its cavernous eye-socket to starboard, as though in that blaze of sunlight even its wound could see.

There raced another ship, a vast galleon of cedar and teak, with golden sails and a flag of black with the sign of a prism splitting light into many colors.

The Draug hissed and shook its harpoon, and Crowbeard's body slipped into the sea; but the monster was at last broken, and with a final defiant stare at the ruin of the *Raveneye* it sank with its half-ship into the frothing waves.

Crowbeard's corpse bobbed in the forsaken waters.

"No, Bone," Gaunt said, but he was already swimming, getting his arm around the body of his betrayer. Soon Gaunt was there, and others from *Raveneye* helped, its captain among them.

"Hail!" Erik Glint shouted to the new vessel.

And an answering cry went up upon the galleon's deck, for they had seen the valor done upon the deep. Ropes were flung into the waters, and now Bone saw clearly the black, mighty mariners of faraway Kpalamaa of the savanna and jungle, come like something out of a fever dream, to their aid. And in their midst one he knew.

"Eshe," he said. "Eshe of the Fallen Swan. Priestess. Wanderer. Cook."

"Spy. We are in trouble, Bone," Gaunt said.

"That is for certain. But at least we'll be dry."

"I had some difficulty finding you," Eshe said as they sat with her and Captain Glint, nursing warm mugs of coffee in what Eshe called the captain's mess. Her voice sounded amused and a trifle scolding. Bone found that he'd missed that voice. Though he did not entirely trust it.

"Who," gasped the captain, bundled tight in intricately woven blankets, shivering. "Who are you? What manner of ship is this?"

"You are aboard *Anansi*," Eshe said, "a ship of the Kpalamaa Union. It's on a journey of exploration and cultural exchange."

"It's on a whatsis?"

"They're foamreavers, Captain, in a way," Gaunt said. "Only with rather more foam and considerably less reave."

"I'll try not to be insulted by the comparison," Eshe said. "My people are of the Southern Semidisc, and for the past decade we've been exploring the North, learning what we can, trading a bit."

"Kpalamaa," Glint mused. "I've heard of you, of course. Great power of the South. Just never expected to see one of your ships up close. This whole room is just for the captain to take meals in?" Glint looked around at the mess, with its wall hangings of maps, wooden masks, flags, spears, cutlasses.

"Be patient with him, Eshe," Bone said. "He just lost his ship to a Draug."

Captain Glint shot him a look of anger, before shutting his eyes and nodding.

"We saw," Eshe mused. "I don't know how to classify such an apparition, except, of course, as 'frightening.'"

"It was worthy of song," Gaunt said. "And there will be one, about *Raveneye* and *Anansi*, and Muninn, and Eshe, and Captain Glint."

Erik Glint smiled a little, though his hands shook, spilling coffee. "That is well said. So, Eshe. I'm grateful you're here. But why?"

"Allow me," Gaunt said. "Eshe is a wandering priestess of the Swan, allowed great latitude by the Brilliant Seat. But this is just a cover for her deeper role as an agent of Kpalamaa, traveling the world hunting evils to fight and heroes to fight them." She nodded to Eshe. "Bone revealed all this to me over time. And I think your arriving on this galleon pretty well gives it away."

"I'm not sure what you mean," Eshe said, though she smiled and sipped coffee. "My conversion to the Swan was quite sincere. And why not? Even though the goddess incarnated in one particular land—a necessary consequence of incarnation, I'd say—her message of love is universal. And, if my homeland's government occasionally finds my ecclesiastic station useful, well, that hurts nobody. Except the evils I track down."

"What evil are you tracking today?" Bone spread his hands and smirked. "I am very flattered if it's us."

"His name is Skrymir Hollowheart," Eshe said.

"The troll-jarl," Erik Glint said. "But he's a legend. And even if he's not, he lives deep within the Trollberg by Jotuncrown, brewing storms, not out here on the sea near Fiskegard."

"No," Eshe said, all seriousness now. "But for a time one of his targets was here. A target named Innocence Gaunt."

"Tell us everything," Gaunt said.

"I will do better than that. I will show you."

Anansi brought the Lardermen survivors to Fiskegard, a place looking more like a set of half-drowned, sky-lancing mountains than a proper island group. There lay one small harbor, with a fishing village called also Fiskegard. It was filled with itinerant workers from all around these parts, and the houses were fenced in by racks of drying stockfish.

And there on the beach before the tavern called the Pickled Rat, Captain Glint burned the recovered bodies of dead Lardermen and Muninn Crowbeard. Gaunt, Bone, and Eshe watched the foamreaver funeral and raised mugs to the dead. The others drank coffee, but Bone sipped aquavit, for he figured he was entitled. It was a little like tasting the funeral fire.

"I'll be glad to trade you a barrel of aquavit," said one of the proprietors beside them, a wizened, bright-eyed woman named Nan, "in return for a bunch of this Kpalamaa coffee. Seems to take a year off me, in the good way. If we can come to a fair arrangement, of course."

"I'll ask Captain Nonyemeko to speak to you," Eshe said. "Her business is the cultural exchange and trade agreements. Mine is the skullduggery."

"All right, then," said Nan, nodding as her companion Freidar passed by, tending to the other patrons. "What skulls need to be dug?"

"You say Innocence disappeared from this place?" Gaunt said.

"Yes," said Nan. She told the tale of his kidnapping by uldra, how Nan and Freidar failed to retrieve him, and how they followed rumors of his appearance in Oxiland. "We actually went there recently and learned he'd vanished from the basement of Saint Kringa's. Innocence seems to have a talent for disappearing."

"That's my boy," Bone murmured.

"I see the resemblance," Nan said, and her voice was sad. "I am so sorry we weren't able to keep your son safe."

"I am not certain anyone could," Bone said, moved. "We're grateful for all that you did."

"He is a good lad. Troubled, but his heart is good."

"It's good to hear that."

But Gaunt said nothing as she pulled out the *Chart of Tomorrows*. The heavy book thumped onto the table and silenced them, as though an ominous sixth person had come to the table. Gaunt opened the book to sea-charts of central Kantenjord. She lingered over an image of the Chained Straits and frowned at red ruins marking some sunken site on the island in its midst. Intriguing, but not useful to her.

She turned the page to an image of Fiskegard's main island. It was intricate, displaying hills and shoals, though not any of the modern buildings. She pointed at another spot marked in red runes. "There. Does that match the site of the Pickled Rat, Nan?"

"I think so. What's it supposed to be, here?"

"An old place of worship. A stave church." She flipped to maps of Oxiland. "This is Loftsson's holding, yes? And this spot, on the hill?"

"A stone church," Nan said. "Saint Kringa's."

"But the notes again indicate a stave church. And it was a stave church in which I had my dream of seeing Innocence." She flipped to a map of the Morkskag. "There."

"Our ancestors," Nan said, rubbing her temples, "built old wooden shrines to the Vindir, making the foundations resemble wooden ships. Some of the shrines even held ship-graves, places where chieftains and their families and slaves were buried. It's whispered that these first Swanlings saw something powerful in these old places and sought to top each of them with a stave church, a wooden building fashioned by Swanling shipwrights."

"You are saying," Eshe said, "they sensed these were places of power, and they built structures that would keep the power intact."

"Yes. Perhaps they're places where the might of the old dragons seeps through their petrified skin. Places where one can travel to strange realms." She looked directly at Gaunt. "That is why Freidar and I built our tavern on this spot. We are practitioners of Runewalking, a magical art. We thought the energies would help us in our researches. I think they have, and that we've done good for this village thereby. But I am so very sorry this power helped snatch away your son."

"Do you know how it is done, Nan?" Gaunt took the older woman's hand. "How to access this gateway? Please. If there is a way . . ."

Nan's face was solemn, but she squeezed Gaunt's hand in return. "My husband and I have been trying to open the way since the day your son disappeared. Without success. I think the key was not knowledge but your son's own power, and the desire of the uldra to reach out to him."

"I want to sleep here. Right out here where you say he disappeared. I reached him before, in the Morkskag. I must try again."

"Of course."

Eshe cleared her throat. "If it does not work, Persimmon, or even if it does, you will have my help tracking him down. Bluntly, as long as he bears this might, he is a lightning rod for any unscrupulous power. My country wants him found."

"And controlled?" Bone said archly.

"And with his parents," Eshe said, meeting his gaze. "I suspect any father would agree that's not quite the same."

Nan patted Gaunt's hand, smiled ruefully, and left to get more for the table, or so she said. She passed slowly by a line of shields.

"But I am in earnest, you two," Eshe said. "I care what happens to your family, but I'm more concerned about the world. The Karvaks and the trolls are up to mischief in these isles, and I think Innocence is mixed up in it."

Glint cleared his throat. "I understand little of this talk of strange powers. But invaders and trolls, that I understand. If there's a fight ahead the Lardermen are ready. We may partake of Kantenjord's squabbles, but this sounds like a threat to us all."

Nan returned with mugs, and Freidar beside her. "Erik Glint speaks for us all, I think," Nan said. "Sounds like mad, beautiful old Kantenjord needs us."

Bone thought of his enslavement and squeezed Gaunt's hand. She squeezed back, and he thought she understood, at least a little.

Kantenjord can burn, he thought. *The Karvaks can hang, and Qiangguo can twist in the wind. I just want my son.*

CHAPTER 23

CHOOSER

Gaunt sat in the darkened tavern and dreamed. She found herself drifting above a quicksilver sea, its sky awash with brilliant stars.

A young woman riding a narwhal swam that sea, bearing a spear. Seeing her stirred a memory, or a premonition. In this place it was difficult to tell the difference.

She called out, "I am Persimmon Gaunt! I seek answers! Can you help me?"

The girl laughed. "Most visitors to the Straits of Tid are terrified. Those who are not raise their weapons. You are the only one I've seen who responds by demanding answers."

Gaunt smiled. "That was not a much of an answer, you know."

The girl smiled herself, but it was the smile of one who was keeping a secret. She almost seemed not to have heard Gaunt. "But then, your dread weapon is gone, and you have not yet claimed your fiddle. You are betwixt and between, as is Imago Bone, who is now neither thief nor spy. I can help you—but only briefly. My substance is highly subjective at this juncture." And indeed, her aspect rippled as though Gaunt's breath had disturbed the reflection in a clear pond.

Gaunt remembered something. "Alder. He said he'd met a girl riding a narwhal."

"I think I remember him. Or foresee him. I have chosen, or will choose him."

Gaunt felt as though something cold brushed her neck. "You're an agent of the old gods of these lands. A Chooser of the Slain. Though I thought your kind rode flying horses."

"I could, if you wished it enough. The specific manifestation of time, and me, that you perceive is filtered through your preconceptions. The *Chart of Tomorrows* depicts time as a body of water, and so for you it is. Were you a Kantening warrior of elder days, you might instead perceive time as a battlefield, and free movement through time as flying over the fighting."

"You don't speak much like someone of elder days."

"In part that is also an effect of your perceptions. You are a learned person—well do I know it!—and I can explain matters in a way I couldn't to a frightened warrior fresh from the farm. For him I would speak simply and bravely, as a comrade, while there was any chance our conversation would be overheard by his fellows. When he had passed on, I would embrace him like a mother, that he might accept his fate. Then I would lead him to the hall of heroes, my hand in his like a lover's."

"I am glad you are not doing any of those things. Nonetheless, your thinking seems modern, almost familiar."

"I am of your time, Persimmon Gaunt—almost! The old gods reached across the centuries to name me a Chooser. It is easier to claim champions of this age if one has an agent of this age. But you are wasting time! I am enjoying meeting you, and I risk my future and your own by lingering. Ask your most important three questions—quickly! And I will answer, if my memory or foresight can serve."

"Where, right now, is Innocence Gaunt?"

"Too many assumptions! But if he is not with you, then he must be with Jewelwolf or Skrymir." She held out her hand, and with some trepidation Gaunt took it. The girl said, "I will take a risk and attempt to find *right now*."

Gaunt descended like a leaf onto the narwhal, and the scene flickered like a Swanisle windstorm in the autumns of her girlhood, all golden leaves and spears of sunlight and shadows at her feet.

Now they seemed to swim over the craggy island in the middle of the Chained Straits, in the place where the Chain itself wrapped around the rock, rising at an angle at either side toward the absurdly attenuated headlands of Svardmark and Spydbanen. There were domed gers all over, and many Karvak soldiers. The sky was gray-black with clouds, and sunlight seemed more of a pleasant idea than a reality.

She gasped, for what she'd at first taken for a huge boulder was a gigantic troll. Kneeling before the troll was Innocence. Despite everything, it filled her with astonished relief to see him alive and whole.

In the next moment, she realized he was not whole. Not quite. One of his beautiful eyes glowed green. Gaunt shuddered.

"Do you see well, lad," the rock-thing said in a startlingly quiet and intimate voice, "with the troll-splinter I've given you?"

"It's made me understand many things, glorious king. Now daytime seems dark, and nighttime bright. Now bloodshed seems heroic, and generosity weak."

"Do you see now," said the troll-king, "any difference between humankind and trolls?"

"I think you *do* all the deeds my parents' people only *think* of. But if thinking is what matters, then we're all the same."

"Fair enough! But there is a key difference, boy, that you'll understand in time. Humans say they must be their true selves. Trolls say that to be themselves is sufficient."

"That sounds like you're saying the same thing with different words."

"Ah, but Innocence Gaunt, chosen of the Heavenwalls of Qiangguo, it is not the same thing. You will know. Perhaps soon. Your enemy stirs."

"My enemy?"

"The Runethane."

"She is my old friend."

"A-Girl-Is-A-Joy, daughter of Snow Pine and Flybait, is your old friend. The Runethane is your enemy. Which is Joy's true self? I leave you with that question as I go to plumb the labyrinth of the Splintrevej. There is a haven of light and freedom there that has long vexed me. It is time I went looking for it. And I think soon enough you will go on your own errand as well. Meantime, seek again to unlock the power of this Chain, as we discussed. Bring on the Fimbulwinter, my boy."

"It resists me, Skrymir. I think it knows there is another with a claim on its power."

"But you are the stronger, Innocence. And now, with your troll-perceptions, weakness and mercy will not hamper you. In time you will suck its power dry, like a lamprey taking blood. Now I take my leave."

Gaunt watched the troll-king rise and depart. Sometimes he scratched the emptiness where a heart should have been. Once, as he did so, he looked in her direction, as if half-noticing something there. Gaunt tried to still her breathing, in case any sound of hers might somehow reach him from the Straits of Tid.

The troll shrugged and surged into the waves.

Innocence turned from the ripples of water to the whorls of power flickering like lightning upon the metal of the vast Chain. A woman walked up to him, someone who had but one ear. Gaunt recognized her as Dolma, a member of a group called the Fraternity of the Hare. They'd once protected the lost land of Xembala but had chosen to serve Princess Steelfox of the Karvaks. Why was Dolma tending to Innocence?

"What did he say?" Dolma asked.

Innocence chuckled. "Did he not bellow loud enough for the whole island to hear?"

"No, he whispered. What did he say?"

"Troll things."

"You have changed." Dolma, too, stared at the Chain. "You were kinder, before. More . . . innocent."

"Perhaps my name should be Lamprey."

"What?"

"Nothing." He smiled. "Do you still wish to serve me? You may be off if you wish. Or you may keep minding me if that is your and Steelfox's desire. I do not care either way."

"You need help. You need people who will stay by you."

"In the long run, no one can be relied upon . . ." He looked around. "Someone is spying on me. I know not how."

He seemed to look directly at Gaunt.

"Innocence!" she could not help but cry out.

"What is it?" Dolma asked.

"I . . ." He shook his head. "I could have sworn I heard my mother calling me. It is surely my imagination. I must be afraid of growing up." He turned to the Great Chain. "It is time to make a change in the weather."

"Innocence!" Gaunt called again.

"No," said the Chooser of the Slain. "You can do no more here. And I won't risk Skrymir Hollowheart sensing you and returning."

The world blurred, and again they floated in a moonlit sea.

"I could help him!" Gaunt said. "It's not too late. He's so lost, but I could still help him." It was like a stony troll-hand was constricting her chest.

"There will be many times," the Chooser said, "when he believes you do not love him. I wish I could put this moment in a bottle, bitter as it is, and give it to him, to open at those times."

"Who the hell are you?" Gaunt snapped. It was unfair—she needed this Chooser's help—but a dam was bursting.

"Too many possible answers. The question could destroy me. You may call me Cairn." Cairn's form twisted, blurred, grew transparent. It solidified again. "One more, then I must leave you!"

There was probably a perfectly tuned question, the right one to ask, but Gaunt's heart wasn't giving it to her. "Where are our friends," she asked, "*right now?*"

Cairn raised her spear and the sea blurred and the sky flickered.

CHAPTER 24

SETER

A-Girl-Is-A-Joy squinted at the mountains of Svardmark, blowing snow from her eyebrows as she trudged across an alpine pasture beside Corinna, Malin, Katta, and Haytham. Deadfall moved low to the ground, unwilling to bear them any longer until the snowstorm cleared.

"Could you not at least form a canopy for us?" Haytham asked. He was having a hard time of it, carrying Haboob's brazier, though at least the efrit was warming his hands.

"You do not understand," Deadfall hummed. "Skrymir's power grows. This must be his storm. He knows my essence and could snatch me back. I must be cautious."

"Please leave my fellow inorganic entity be, O glorious master of flight," came the voice of the efrit. "I have vast sympathy for anyone who's been magically trapped."

They had flown circuitously, at low altitudes, avoiding the Karvak army and Skrymir's unnatural weather. But this snowstorm was worse than anything before, and Deadfall claimed it could not stand against it. They'd come down for a hard landing here.

"I don't think this is Skrymir," Joy said, rubbing her hands together. "At least not Skrymir only. This feels like the power of the Great Chain."

"Can you combat it, Runethane?" said Corinna.

"I've been trying. But I still can't command this power. If we'd been able to land at the Chain—"

"We would have been captured by the Karvaks encamped there," Katta said gently.

"There's a dairy up there," Malin said, pointing.

She had spoken so little, it was startling to hear her. Joy squinted again and blew the snow from her eyes once more. "I don't see anything."

"Nor I," said Corinna.

Katta shrugged. "I don't notice anything evil that way."

"I don't see anything either," said Haytham. "But Malin is unusually good at discerning detail. I recommend we trust her eyes."

There was indeed a barn, but Malin halted them. "Uldra and trolls occupy seters in winter."

"Seters?" asked Joy.

"The high pastures," Corinna said. "Places like this are used in summer for herding and milking. She's right about the seters being abandoned by humans. As for trolls and uldra, that's what the country people say."

"Do we have flint?" Malin said.

"What?" Joy said. "Our friend Flint was left behind on Brokewing Island. How do you know him?"

"No, flint! Not a person. Flint and steel. Not Steelfox either. The other folk don't like flint, steel, and salmeboks."

"That's how the stories go," said Corinna. "I don't have a salmebok—a book of psalms such as the People of the Brush sang, long ago. It's part of our Swan scripture, and they say it scares off the otherworldly."

"I do carry flint and steel, however," Haytham said, "as you never know when you might fall out of a balloon."

They knocked at the barn, and Joy slowly opened the doors. There seemed nothing inside but a pile of hay.

"Well, that's a relief—"

The hay rose upward and sprouted a single eye. Earthen hands burst out on either side; legs of wood appeared at the bottom. The whole thing was the size of a hut.

"You don't even knock!" screamed the thing. "You don't even say, 'Hey, troll, Hay-troll?' You're worse than Skrymir's bunch. I don't want to be in any troll army, and I don't want to make room for *you*!"

The troll rushed her. Her action was instinctive. She raised her hands, and the Runemark blazed.

Fire engulfed the hay-troll. Howling, it blazed away into the darkness. In the distance they heard a splash and a groan of relief.

The remaining hay in the barn caught fire, and the barn itself was engulfed.

"You said you needed flint and steel?" murmured Haytham.

"Sorry," Joy said.

"So much for shelter," said Corinna.

"The elements are invigorating," said Katta. "We will be all right."

"Wait," Joy said, for when the power had risen within her, strange visions had crowded in her head. She had the sense of being watched by someone. She also had the notion that someone she loved was approaching.

She looked all around, and then into the sky, whence smoke was rising into the snowfall. There, in the distance, was the blue bulb of a Karvak balloon.

She closed her eyes, trying to concentrate on the craft.

Suddenly she saw the faces of her mentor Walking Stick and her mother Snow Pine and their friend Liron Flint.

"Mother," she said. "My mother is aboard that balloon."

"How can you know this?" Corinna said.

"How can they guide the craft?" Haytham said.

"Walking Stick is with them. He's said he can, at great wear to his body, use the breath of his essence to call upon the breath of the wind."

"I do not understand this," Corinna said, "but I hope it is true."

"Deadfall," Katta said, "will you not go to them?"

"I will not," hummed the carpet.

"Enough," said Haboob. "If you will not reach them, I will. Stand aside, O inventor."

"What?" said Haytham. "Yaaa—!"

Fire burst forth from the brazier. Haytham dropped it in the snow, but the blaze rose hundreds of feet, forming a highly attenuated, but very visible, image of a scowling man. The fiery figure made a thumbs-down gesture in the direction of the burning farmhouse.

The balloon descended.

"Never make me land in a narrow, forsaken place like this again," Walking Stick told them. "It is agreeable to see you," he added.

Snow Pine embraced Joy tightly, pushed her back to regard her daughter, and sternly said, "You are never gathering wood alone again."

Joy hugged Flint too. "Find any treasure?" she asked him.

"Considerable knowledge," Flint sighed, looking at Snow Pine, "but my only treasure is what I started with. Are you Malin? A friend is asking about you."

Within the captured Karvak balloon lay Inga Peersdatter, who to Joy's horror had lost an arm and gained a burning desire to fight Karvaks and trolls.

"Let them come!" Inga said after she'd gotten the startled Joy and Malin in a one-armed bear hug and explanations were made. "I've tangled with Skrymir himself. Bring them on!"

"I will fight beside you," Joy said.

"Like hell you will," Snow Pine said, following them into the ger. "If need be, you will hide in *A Tumult of Trees on Peculiar Peaks*, as you did once before."

"And will the mark upon me fade within the world of the scroll?" Joy replied. "I think not, nor will the memory of my duty."

"Duty? Your duty is to your mother, child. Did Walking Stick not teach you that?"

"Perhaps," Liron Flint put in, "we should simply be grateful for now that we have each other to argue with."

"Indeed!" said Haytham ibn Zakwan as he began shifting the balloon's brazier to one side to make room for Haboob's. "And for new help. How did you manage to command the Charstalker demon in its brazier?"

"It," said Walking Stick, "was difficult. I have learned that demons do not entirely lack pressure points. If I had not been able to steal and control a balloon, we'd likely still be on Spydbanen. I am surprised you are not at Svanstad already, as you travel with this princess."

Haytham sounded defensive to Joy. "We've done what we could!"

"Indeed," said Corinna, "I can fault no one. Deadfall has labored heroically against the influence of Skrymir."

"Thank you," hummed the carpet, sounding surprised.

"And everyone here has borne the journey well. My own knights could not do better."

Walking Stick bowed. "You are courteous, Princess Corinna, and I admire that. Alas, I cannot quite repay you in kind. Princess—your time is short. Sooner than you believe possible, the Karvak horde will be on your doorstep."

"This I believe," Corinna said. "But Soderland is strong, and surely we'll have allies. This Jewelwolf will find us not so easily swept away. We are Kantenings. Children of ice and violence. They will regret ever coming here."

"Those are fine words to spread among the people," Walking Stick said, "for their spirits will need it. But this will be the battle of your life."

"Then I wish to join it, not talk about it. If you ladies and gentlemen can get me back to Svanstad with this news, you will be well rewarded."

"Haytham?" said Walking Stick. "Haboob?"

"Ready."

"Ready, O superior man."

"Thank you, O ironic efrit," said Walking Stick. "We fly!"

Joy was glad to leave the seter behind. She winced for whoever's barn was burning, but as the blaze disappeared beneath a haze of snow, Joy feared much worse was coming.

CHAPTER 25

COUNCIL

When *Anansi* reached the harbor at Svanstad, the waterfront was full of soldiers, warships bustled with activity, and the piers were crowded with ships from all parts of Kantenjord. Nan, standing beside Gaunt as the Kpalamaa vessel took anchor, said she saw flags and shields of Oxiland, Ostoland, Gullvik, Garmstad, and many another places. "I've never seen it so busy. I suppose we'll have to wait to moor."

"It's a lovely city," Gaunt remarked, looking upon cheerfully-colored multistoried buildings rearing beside the water with snow-spattered orange roofs. Beyond rose a cathedral of gray-white stone with stained-glass windows flashing in the sun. Upon a nearby hill she saw the statue of a regal man lofting a book, not a sword. "It looks surprisingly un-barbaric." She added, "Excuse me. That was rude."

Nan laughed. "It was not so very long ago that Kantenings terrorized the region. And farther north, the game of foamreaving's not yet done."

Gaunt frowned. "Is slavery done, here in Soderland?"

"Princess Corinna has forbidden for Swanlings to be in a condition of slavery here, or for anyone to be made a slave here."

"Not quite the same as saying slavery is outlawed." Gaunt smirked. "Those have the vinegar taste of carefully chosen words."

"Indeed. But they are Corinna's words, not mine."

"Hm. I think I trust her. Mostly."

"You speak as one who's encountered her—Orm's eye, is that a flying carpet?"

It was. The twisting, colorful rectangle of the carpet rose from a fortress of orange stone and arced toward the harbor, bearing directly upon *Anansi*, with four people upon it. Gaunt didn't pause to squint. "Bone!" she cried as she ran belowdecks. "It's Deadfall!"

She found Bone playing a strategy game with Eshe, something involving wooden basins and beads, as many of the off-watch crew observed, offering tips.

"Bone!" Gaunt called. "Sorry, the game must end! Deadfall is coming!"

"What? The carpet?" He said to Eshe, "You win down here, because it's quite likely I'm about to lose up there. Deadfall's a thing of evil."

"It's more a divided thing, Eshe," Gaunt felt compelled to say. "Caught between bad and good."

"Few things are perfectly divided, as in a game of oware," Eshe said. "Interesting."

Anansi had a contingent of crew whose only business was fighting, and ten of these marine warriors were present as the carpet settled to the deck. They bore flashing longswords and bright shields in the shape of boats, with prows pointed upward, intricate carvings on the surfaces.

Gaunt found their presence reassuring, but most reassuring of all were the faces of the riders aboard the carpet.

"Snow Pine!" she called out. "Joy! Flint! Katta! It's so good to see you all in the flesh!"

"We share your enthusiasm," Katta said with a quizzical smile.

"We've all had narrow escapes," Snow Pine said, embracing Gaunt.

"We're all eager for you to turn them into epic poetry, Persimmon," said Flint.

"I will! But you'll have to wait in line." Gaunt's smile faded as she remembered the songs she owed the dead. She put her hands on her hips. "So. This is the flying carpet that freed Innocence . . . and who took him away from us."

"You are correct," came a humming voice from the carpet. "I have risked much flying from the Fortress, but I am told the need is critical."

The marines stepped forward, swords at the ready. But Eshe had arrived, and she spoke rapidly in the language of Kpalamaa. The ship's captain, a stern-looking, elderly woman in a uniform of yellow and green, intoned a command. The warriors backed off.

"It is very tempting," Bone muttered, "to fetch a torch."

"You are not the first to feel that way," said the carpet.

"We will have words, Deadfall," said Gaunt. "But I suspect that you haven't come here for a chat."

"We're inviting you to one," Joy said. She seemed well, but Gaunt noted that her hands were concealed by black gloves. "Princess Corinna wants you at a council, Persimmon and Imago. The Runewalkers Nan and Freidar too."

Gaunt squinted at Nan, and at Freidar, who'd come walking up to his wife. "You two are more prominent than I realized," Gaunt said.

"Well, likewise," Nan replied.

Captain Nonyemeko said, "For two days I have exchanged messenger birds with the princess. We seek cordial relations with your countries. Eshe is the one who suggested the four of you discuss recent events with Princess Corinna."

"Will you join us?" Gaunt asked.

Eshe shook her head. "We must remain neutral. This is a war council."

"That's right," Joy said, her face rueful.

Erik Glint coughed. "To which *I'm* pointedly not invited."

Freidar said, "Old friend, the Lardermen made their names breaking a Soderland blockade. I'm sure the royal family hasn't forgotten."

"Well, I hope they haven't forgotten I'm a Kantening," Glint said. "There's still some fight in my crew, and there are other Lardermen ships about. Remind them."

Nan squeezed his shoulder. "We'll tell them. They're in need of allies, it would seem."

Snow Pine said, "You're not kidding." She turned to the Kpalamaa crew. "Captain Nonyemeko? We're to show you this. A messenger brought it today." She held out a scroll. The elderly captain claimed it with a nod, untied and unrolled it. Scowling, she showed it to Eshe.

"It is worse than I thought," Eshe said. "This hour should not have come for many years."

"But what does it say?" Gaunt asked.

Eshe handed the scroll to Gaunt. "Read it to all, Persimmon. You have a good voice."

The letter was written in fully adequate, even graceful, Kantentongue, though it bore a signature chop in the manner of Qiangguo. Gaunt fumbled a bit with the vocabulary, but the meaning was clear.

"*'From the greatest of Kings, master of the four directions, the Grand Khan. By way of his representative, his chief wife the Lady Jewelwolf. To Corinna Olafsdatter of the Soderland Kantenings, she who fled our hospitality. You should consider the fates of other lands and submit. Word will have reached you of our conquest of the vastest empire under Heaven, and of our purification of the world's disorders. We have overrun nine times nine nations, massacring multitudes. The terror of our forces is inescapable. Where will you run? On what road? Our horses and sabercats are swift, our sky-craft tireless, our arrowheads piercing, our swords like lightning, our hearts as mountain rock, and our forces as many as the flakes of snow burying your lands. We do not fear warring in winter. Castles will not slow us. Armies will not halt us. Your foemen the Spydbanen foamreavers now serve us, your neighbor the Gull-Jarl has already submitted to us, and your rivals of the Five Fjords have pledged not to interfere with us. Your ancient enemies the trolls march with us. Your prayers to your Swan will not harm us. We are not stirred by weeping nor moved by wailing. Only those who submit to our protection will be safe. Reply swiftly before we kindle the fires of war. Only catastrophe awaits those who resist us. We will burn your churches and parade the weakness of your goddess and then we will slay your children and your old folk in one heap. At present Soderland and its vassals Garmstad and Ostoland are the only realms against which we must march.'"*

There was silence after she read this, leavened only by the lapping of waves against *Anansi* and the shouts and bustle of the harbor.

From a height Svanstad had the shape of a lumpy crystal, bounded by turreted stone walls, with a harbor enclosed by two arms of the wall. Outside the walls the buildings were predominantly of wood, but inside they were of stone. Prominent among the latter was a palace of orange rock. Unlike the city walls, this building seemed like an oversized home masquerading as a citadel. Clearly the royals of Soderland counted on the city walls defending them, not their palace.

They landed upon a balcony and passed through wide doors into a library that was also a sitting room. Most days, Gaunt would have been drawn to the many volumes displayed on three walls, not to the people in the middle. But not today.

"Haytham! Good to find you again! Inventing new flying machines for the Kantenings?"

Though Haytham smiled and embraced her, there was a troubled cast to his eyes. "I have broken faith with the Karvaks, for yes, I am indeed building vessels for Corinna. But there is very little time."

A regal-looking, fierce-eyed woman in blue spoke up. "Ah, the far-traveled Persimmon Gaunt. Please don't curtsey, it looks painful."

"An honor, Princess Corinna," Gaunt said.

"If you say so. Greetings, and to you too, Imago Bone. Nan and Freidar, I know your reputation, welcome." She gestured to a long, crowded table. "Please join this council, all of you. Others will be arriving, but I cannot wait . . . ah, Deadfall . . . I'm uncertain of the protocol for magic carpets."

Deadfall silently flew up to a wall and hung itself over the portrait of a king, hanging there in defiance of gravity.

"How amusing," snapped a man wearing a stiff-looking blue outfit, studded with medals, sounding rather unamused. "Do sit, all of you," he said, setting an example. "It's New Year's Day, by the Eldshore calendar, a good time for plans, I suppose. And I want to have the army in position by the Seventh." He gave a negligent, impatient wave. "Oh, and I'm Prince Ragnar, how do you do."

Corinna scanned the faces at the table. "Each of you has information valuable to me. Lord Klarvik and Lord Stormhamn, you are both critical to any defense." She nodded at a youngish man, tall, thin, and bald, with a cold bland stare, and an old man, short and possessed of a fierce gaze framed by white hair and beard. Corinna continued, "And Ivar Garm here is Lord Mayor of Garmstad, where it seems the blow will fall."

"Thanks to Soderland's distractions," muttered a black-haired man wearing a byrnie with a bejeweled golden necklace hung round it.

"Voice your grudges on the ride north," snapped Prince Ragnar.

"Oh, I shall," said Ivar Garm.

"Last of our happy band," Corinna said, "we have a special guest, Jokull Loftsson, known as the uncrowned king of Oxiland. He has led many chieftains here to help us."

An elderly man in a black robe and cloak, with a red woolen cap portraying horses and volcanoes, simply nodded. Yet he peered intently at Gaunt's face, and Bone's, in a way she didn't much like.

"Have we offended in some way?" Gaunt asked.

Slowly, Loftsson shook his head. "You remind me of someone. Go on, Corinna."

Corinna said quickly, "These travelers are caught up in all this. So too is Malin Jorgensdatter of Ostoland." Here she nodded to the willowy, dark-haired young woman who seemed intent on staring at everything in the room besides the people in it. "We are expecting Master Walking Stick for his advice on tactics, and Squire Everartson as a representative of the common people—"

"*That* will be entertaining," said Ragnar, sounding just as entertained as he'd sounded amused at Deadfall.

"—and our grandfather Hakon, the Retired King."

"So, is the impending fire and woe going to drag him out of retirement?" said Ivar Garm.

Prince Ragnar said, "My half-sister is in charge, as ever. We are glad to have Grandfather's advice. Now, Corinna, introduce these others."

The princess introduced the companions of *Al-Saqr* as a merchant company, which Gaunt found appropriate. She also introduced Nan and Freidar as if everyone seated should know them by reputation, and no one demurred.

This done, Corinna said, "We'll wait no longer." She pounded the table, an act of precise fury. "Invaders dare come to Kantenjord," she said. "I have seen with my own eyes their tents, their flying vessels, their horses and fighting beasts. I have seen the mustering of the Trollberg and Jotuncrown. I've heard the ranting of Skrymir Hollowheart himself. The battle of our generation has arrived."

And she described these matters in detail, aided by the others around the table. Gaunt had sympathy for Corinna, for events were drawn like a noose around the princess's neck.

Meanwhile an elderly man entered the room. He moved slowly and with great care. He accepted the help of Prince Ragnar and sat at the table's head.

"Granddaughter," said the newcomer, after he'd listened for a time, "if it were not you saying this, I could scarce believe it. A band of *herdsmen* rides out of the East to topple our kingdoms? Flying out of the air? And even if they have managed to cow our primitive heathen cousins and the feckless Five Fjords, this is *Soderland*, the high kingdom!"

"King Hakon," said Jokull Loftsson, the uncrowned king of Oxiland, "I have seen their airships for myself. I've witnessed their warriors in battle. I would rather face five Kantening berserkers than two Karvak archers."

Haytham cleared his throat. "Great King. I am Haytham ibn Zakwan, inventor of the airships the Karvaks employ. It is my sad duty to confirm these tales. The Karvaks are the terror of the East." He surveyed all the faces at the table. "And I think it likely you will face a full tumen of them—ten thousand."

"Ten thousand?" Prince Ragnar scoffed, clearly voicing the opinions of the other Kantening men. "I don't mean to suggest there's no threat, inventor. Far from it. But how do you come by that mad number?"

Haytham blinked at the angry men, but his voice was steady. "Weeks ago I saw a fleet of Karvak balloons on the continent, at Loomsberg. The passage from there to here is not so very long, by air. And I know the Karvaks; they do nothing halfway. They will have brought a large force."

"He's right," Snow Pine said. "I'm from Qiangguo. I grew up with tales of the Karvaks. Underestimating them is suicide."

Mad Katta scratched his chin. "Pardon my interruption. Matters of war are not my specialty; I am more of a baker. But something nags at me. What about horses? A Karvak would feel limbless without a horse."

"Horse thieves," Gaunt said, suddenly remembering. "We heard talk of horse thieves in Gullvik Town. If the Karvaks have been planning this for months . . ."

"Yes," mused Ivar Garm, fingering one of the gold bands around his arm. "Garmstad's been plagued by these thieves as well. You think this is the work of the nomads?"

Katta said, "It *is* the Karvak method to scout the lands they mean to invade, and to use local resources as much as possible."

"Well, what of it?" said bearded old Lord Stormhamn. "So they are many. So they are clever. Whatever their numbers, we will never surrender!"

"Indeed," said his young, bald neighbor Lord Klarvik. They glanced at each other as though surprised to be in agreement about anything.

"Aye," Jokull said. "Death comes to us all, and it will not come to me as a Karvak subject. I have come hither because my heart told me a fight was in the offing. My heart is rarely wrong. I will have blood-debt for the loss of my wife." His gaze flicked to Gaunt and Bone in a way that made Gaunt feel cold, though she knew not why. Jokull said, "But that is a tale for another time. So the odds are poor. Let us speak of how to best gamble our lives."

"Well said," put in Bone.

"Aye," said Ivar Garm. "Ragnar and I have been discussing this very matter. Now, it seems to us we've still an advantage in ships of the sea, if not the air. I think the Karvaks will send a land force through Garmsmaw Pass. That's where we have to meet them, where the high terrain can even the—"

"What fantasy is this?"

The new speaker who strode into the chamber seemed almost as out of place as Gaunt's companions. He was a blond, muscular man with a noble's bearing, yet his clothing was rustic. Underneath his bearskin cloak he wore a thin sword and a hand-axe.

Princess Corinna said, "I welcome your opinion, Squire Everartson, but—"

"Your Highness, you are welcome to call me simply 'Everart,' as the *common* folk do. I like to keep things down to earth. But your advisors' fancies seem to have flown to the clouds! Far Eastern nomads with flying machines? For years I've heard many excuses why ordinary folk's concerns cannot be addressed. Negotiations with the Eldshore! Madling dragons! Lardermen! And now it's *mysterious nomads*? What will you conjure next time? I await it with bated breath."

"Why," sighed Retired King Hakon, "do we tolerate this man?"

"Because he has a peasant army at his fingertips?" said Prince Ragnar.

"Because he has valuable things to say," Corinna said, tapping the table. "But it will be *more* valuable, Everart, if you will see reality. All those dangers you listed are real. As is this one!"

"And after them, there will be more," Everart said, "and still more. Oh, there is fire behind the smoke, I'm sure, but there is considerably more smoke. A pack of barbarians, primitives who drink fermented mare's milk, will not topple the mighty walls of Svanstad."

Gaunt was entranced. She saw in this Everart someone who could have been a bard.

She cleared her throat, raising her own bardic voice. "Squire, it's not so very long ago that your people were considered 'barbarians' by your southern neighbors—my people. Indeed, your cousins in the Gamellaw seem little changed. And did your grandfathers fear *our* walls, our coasts, our courage, our more sophisticated food?"

The young woman Malin spoke up. "There is a prayer of Swanisle. 'From the fury of the Northmen, Goddess preserve us.'"

Gaunt nodded to her, impressed. "I heard it this way:

The sea is calm today
Would there was storm and loss!
For the Northmen sail this way
Goddess save us.

"Indeed!" Everyone looked up again as Walking Stick strode in. "All of you—you cannot underestimate your danger. If you underestimate it, then my advice is to take a knife and cut your throat right now."

The royal guards snarled and began drawing their swords, but Corinna stopped them with a gesture. "Sir," she said, "say what you would. I would like Everart to hear it."

"The Karvaks," Walking Stick said, "are the most obedient folk in the world. Their soldiers follow orders without question. And yet their officers are given great flexibility in interpreting these orders. Their army rewards skill, and thus these officers are a match for any from East to West. They have been known to move a hundred miles in a day and are skilled foragers. Thus their army can surprise an opposing force. They choose their own moments to attack and deny the same pleasure to their enemy. Your defenses rely on your coasts, which they have bypassed, and on your footmen and heavy cavalry, which they can outmaneuver. You are on desperate ground, Princess Corinna."

"Granddaughter," said Retired King Hakon, "this bizarre outlander cannot simply walk in here and insult our prowess—"

"Insult?" Walking Stick growled. "Feckless fool! I am trying to save you all!"

The meeting dissolved into a torrent of shouting. Before long Gaunt and Bone withdrew with their friends into a corner. She made sure Malin came with them, as the discerning young woman was covering her ears, looking distressed.

In time Corinna shooed out all the mighty, who continued their arguments down the halls. Only Nan and Freidar were left, shaking their heads. Corinna gave a long sigh. "So much for men and armies. Luckily I'm in charge, and will decide matters. But this is not all about armies, is it? I have errands for you all. Especially you, A-Girl-Is-A-Joy."

Joy ripped off her gloves, raising the hand displaying the mark of three intertwined chains. "So I cannot choose to go with your warriors? Why is that up to you? Aren't I the Runethane? Or don't you trust me because I'm from far away and don't look like you?"

"Joy," Snow Pine warned. "You are young, and must not insult the powerful." She stared at Corinna. "That's my job. So how about it, Princess? Does my daughter have the wrong accent to be Runethane? The wrong skin color? Wasn't she chosen by the land?"

"By *my* land," Corinna said evenly. "Of which I am the most powerful liege."

"Skrymir Hollowheart might disagree with you," Flint put in. "The mightiest troll-jarl in centuries, I hear. And one who's recovered the Axe of Sternmark, one of Wayland of Baelscaer's weapons. You need a Runethane, I should think."

"You're no Kantening, are you?" Corinna said. "An Easterner? How do you know of Wayland?"

Flint laughed. "The Easterners think I'm a Westerner, the Westerners suspect I'm Eastern. I'm of the People of the Brush, who dwell in many lands of the Spiral and Midnight Seas. And even though I no longer believe in our God, I do share my people's love of learning. I know enough of Wayland to know his weapons are nothing to trifle with. You need the Runethane. You need Joy."

"And how well did Joy fare against Skrymir? Eh? I do accept you as Runethane, Joy, of course I do. But you obviously need time to master the power. Time you won't get marching to Garmsmaw Pass."

Joy folded her arms. "What do you want me to do?"

"Listen, all of you," Corinna said, though Gaunt noticed her eyes did not meet Haytham's. "We face a monster out of myth—Skrymir. Mortal armies can be met by armies. To deal with Skrymir will take heroes."

Flint chuckled. "Are you under the impression any of us fit that description?"

Corinna smiled a little. "A-Girl-Is-A-Joy does."

"I will concede that."

"But I will take everything I can get. You are all clearly bound up in this. I am a Swanling, but I am also a Kantening, and I know the strands of fate when I trip over them. If you will accept my commission . . . then seek a way of defeating Skrymir. In return I can offer royal gratitude. I might provide you homes, wealth, interesting work. Assuming, of course, I have a land when all is done."

Gaunt said, "Princess, Bone and I have a mission of our own, to find our son."

"We can't just go questing against every troll-king that comes our way," Bone said. "Majesty."

Nan spoke. "I have only compassion for what you are feeling. I've lost sons of my own. But from all we've heard, Innocence is likely to be found among the Karvak leaders. And thus near Skrymir."

Freidar added, "And indeed, if Skrymir understands Innocence's power, your son's not safe from him."

"In the meantime," Corinna said, "how will you seek Innocence when the land is torn by war? You will want a ship."

Gaunt glanced at Haytham. The inventor shook his head, looking at Corinna. "I'm sorry, Persimmon. Aside from the balloon Walking Stick stole from the Karvaks, I don't have anything now that can fly. And I've committed my work to the defense of Soderland. In any event, I think you will be less conspicuous at sea."

"You won't come with us?" Bone said.

"I am sorry."

You are smitten indeed, Haytham, Gaunt thought. Then she mused, "We have Deadfall . . ."

"You do have Deadfall," came the eerie hum of the magic carpet's voice, hanging there upon the wall. "And I would have my vengeance on Skrymir, who forced me to occupy the hollowness where his heart once beat."

"Heart," said Malin. "Troll heart. Eventyr Thirty-Six. A troll can escape mortal wounds by hiding his heart in an inaccessible location. If one finds the heart, one can destroy it, and with it the troll."

Corinna said, "I am learning to respect your words, Malin Jorgensdatter. But where could the heart be sought?"

"I have knowledge," Deadfall said. "When I plunged beside Innocence into the sea, he nearly drowned, but I was swept up by a supernatural vortex, magic calling to magic. I was pulled into it and knew it was too much for me, that I would never escape. I refused to be captive again. With all my strength I sought refuge and sensed another source of magic at the edge of the maelstrom. I found a barren island, in sight of a larger island dominated by a great volcano, and there I flopped down to rest. I never beheld the source of the island's magic. Before the day was out, a flock of green-eyed ravens landed beside me and snatched my edges in their claws. Too weak to fight, I was flown to what you call the Trollberg. There Skrymir examined me and chose to stuff me into the gap in his chest. He believed he could use me to absorb magical power from the world around him. He was right."

"This is fascinating, old friend," said Katta.

"I am not your friend. I am your namesake."

"I am sad to hear you speak so, but let it go. How does this information help us?"

Deadfall said, "While I languished in the gap, I sensed certain energies about it, having the same sensations, the same flavor, if you will, of the magic on the barren island."

Joy said, "You think the island is where Skrymir's heart lies?"

"It may explain why troll-birds came to collect the carpet," Freidar mused, "for such is what they were."

At once Corinna rolled out a map labeled in Roil. It seemed mostly accurate to Gaunt, though the Chained Straits had looked narrower in person, and she doubted anyone could know the disposition of the northern ice. She pointed at a set of islands in the group labeled Oxiland. Her finger landed beside the X. "These would all fit the description Deadfall gives."

"Could you fly us there, Deadfall?" Gaunt asked. "Because I am thinking that, with his heart in our possession, we might be able to bargain with Skrymir."

"Bargain and not destroy?" Nan said.

"If he has my son, I may want to bargain. But suppose his heart were a permanent trophy here in this palace?"

Corinna said, "I like how you think, Mistress Gaunt. Very well, you may decide how best to use it. But I urge you to seek it."

Gaunt looked at Bone. He nodded.

"All right," Gaunt said, feeling the world wheel around her. "Deadfall, can you take us to that place?"

"Yes," said the carpet, "but I will not journey by air. I fear the troll-jarl's power over the atmosphere, and he caught me once before. I will take ship, guiding you."

"I'm sure we can find a ship," Corinna said. "Your friend Katta will go too, I hope?"

Katta said, "Even as echo follows voice. Though he insists I am not his friend."

"None is," said the carpet, "for who can trust what is caught between good and evil?"

"Eventyr One Hundred ," said Malin.

"What did you say?" said Deadfall.

"Eventyr One Hundred. 'The Companion.' A bad dead man rises to help the hero who paid to give him a decent burial. Good and evil, side by side, working together."

"I will never have a burial," said Deadfall.

"Malin Jorgensdatter," Princess Corinna said, "I think the kindest thing for you may be to return you to our ally Ostoland, that isle of small villages and whispering forests. But if you wish it, you may stay in the Fortress beside your friend Inga while she heals."

"I will take ship," said Malin. "To find the heart. I will miss Inga, but my home will suffer if trolls and Karvaks aren't stopped."

"I request," Freidar said, "the ship be captained by Erik Glint. And crewed by those of his choice."

"I concur," Nan said.

"You drive a tough bargain," Corinna said, and there was silence. "Very well, let the Lardermen aid in this too, if they can. Nan and Freidar, you are among the last Runewalkers in our realm. I can't command you to help these people, but I would be grateful."

The two looked at each other. "We will help as we can," Nan said. "Starting with training you, Runethane, on this journey."

Joy shook her head. "I'm not going."

"What?" Gaunt and Corinna said, at nearly the same time.

"I was chosen," Joy said. "I've dreamed of this land and its people. I know what you're up against. I agree seeking Skrymir's heart is important, but I don't think that's what I'm here for. I think I'm here to fight."

"That's madness," Corinna said.

"Is it?" Joy said, and Gaunt wondered that the girl could hold her own, meet the eyes of this mature, royal-born woman. "You said I needed to train. To learn. I'll do that better here than on some ship. I was raised to do my duty. The sages say, 'To see what's right, and not act on the knowledge, that is a lack.'"

"Well," Snow Pine said. "For once I can't fault Walking Stick's teaching. I'll stay with you, Joy."

"And I as well," Flint said.

Gaunt hugged Joy, saying, "You're your mother's daughter, though I'm not sure either of you realize how much! Haytham, you have to watch over her too."

"You have my word," Haytham said.

Nan and Freidar shared a look. "And mine!" said Nan. "Freidar . . . will you travel with the questers?"

"Aye," he said slowly. "I don't like it, wife, but it seems necessary. And it's the privilege and curse of a married couple that they can divide their forces."

Nan squeezed his hand. "One Runewalker with the seekers of the heart. One with the Runethane."

"So be it," Corinna said. "I'm glad we'll have you, Nan. And I look forward to getting to know you better, Joy."

But as with the sidelong glances of Jokull Loftsson, Gaunt thought there was more to the princess's scrutiny than met the eye.

For that reason she said nothing about the *Chart*, even as she took Bone's hand and said, "We'll go as soon as possible," for she thought that it, too, might provide a road to Innocence. And she did not trust kings and queens, princes and princesses.

CHAPTER 26

WAR

After hard marching, the allied Kantenings reached Garmsmaw Pass on the fifth day of the new year. Prince Ragnar brandished the banner Landwaster as the army halted. Under its rippling colors his father and grandfather had united the southern realms—shattering idols, accepting fealty, giving gold rings and bright blades. He passed it to his herald with instructions it be kept high. His army encamped on rugged ground just before the pass's most narrow pinch, and Ragnar kept moving from band to band, making sure the difficult tenting was done, but also ensuring he was seen by all, and that his devotion was understood.

Such a diverse force needed to know someone held the reins. His strongest unit was five hundred horsemen, most of them in mail-shirt byrnies, though some poorer warriors wore leather armor, and some richer ones wore the plate armor that was becoming so popular in countries south and east. For these, Corinna had even created an order, the Knights of Saint Fiametta, in imitation of the fashion in Swanisle.

With them came fifteen hundred footmen with sword, spear, and shield, all trained fighters from the retinues of lords or the town militias. Ragnar also had, as an experiment, fifty longbowmen trained in the Swanisle fashion.

The rest of Soderland's force was a group of mutually suspicious non-combatants—Swan priests and Runewalkers, representing new powers and old. But he wanted them both at his back. The rabble-rouser Squire Everart had sent none of his peasant fighters, but that suited Ragnar. They'd win without Everart's help, tales of valor would fill the land, and the squire's position would be weakened.

They had better allies—two hundred Oxiland warriors, including some who still wore the bear-shirts, the sign of men who could enter a ritualistic battle frenzy; a hundred doughty men from rustic Ostoland, good with axes; five hundred well-trained militia from Garmstad Town.

They'd taken a position beneath Hel's Tooth, a promontory extending from the otherwise sheer granite wall of the pass's western side. As sunset gave its intimation of carnage to come, and campfires filled the pass, Ragnar ate beside the warleaders in a sheltered hollow beneath the Tooth.

With them was a portly but hardy old man attached to Loftsson's band, Huginn Sharpspear. The man was too garrulous for Ragnar's liking, but he told good stories—tales of blood-feuds in Oxiland, high-minded quests in Svardmark, encounters with the gods in Spydbanen. Ragnar detected a theme of meeting difficult odds.

"You must be a skald of old," Ragnar said, with a lift of his mug.

"I'm old, to be sure, young man," Huginn said with a wink, earning laughter.

"You," Ragnar said seriously. "I hereby charge you with observing all and making a song of it. I relieve you of all burden to stay and fight. If you feel it necessary, flee, so the song can survive us."

Ylur, a white-bearded Oxilander chieftain, spoke. "Our foes seem to command the winter. They've left this pass clear of snow, which proves they are coming. Do you have a premonition? Do you foresee death?" The notion lived in Oxiland that those on death's door gained powers of foresight.

"No," Ragnar said, knowing he should quell such thinking. The Oxilanders might enjoy a good doom, but his Soderlanders, at least, wanted encouragement. "Quite the opposite. After seeing this position I anticipate battle eagerly. A clear pass helps us more than the Karvaks. From Hel's Tooth the archers can spot and shoot anything coming through the pass, and once softened, the invaders can be ravaged by the horsemen. The horsemen can withdraw at need to the narrowest part, where the warriors on foot can hold the line. Here is a place where a few can hold out against a force of any size. No, I merely like the assurance of knowing we'll have our song."

"Even though Oxilanders bow to no prince," said Huginn, the mischief gone from his voice, "I respect your command of the army. You have some sense. But in this matter I am beyond your edict. I came out of debt to my benefactor, Jokull Loftsson. He had cause before to take my life. It is his."

"But Huginn," said Jokull, "Ragnar speaks true. There is none better than you to make sure this fight is remembered. I don't mock your service, or your valor. But perhaps you should face battle with the bowmen so you can watch from a height."

"I'll do as you ask, old friend."

Another Oxilander cleared his throat, a young chieftain named Gissur. "What of these balloons, Ragnar?"

"And the rumors of trolls?" said his big, red-bearded colleague Styr. The Oxilanders were garrulous tonight.

"For balloons we have the Runewalkers," Ragnar said, "who can change the weather. And for trolls we have priests, for accounts agree they fear the Swan and flee even from the mere sound of church bells." He smiled. "Thus our mutually antagonistic friends in robes are united in helping us."

"Well," Huginn said. "What now then?"

"Now we wait."

He'd been waiting all his life. Born illegitimate but called to serve, he'd needed patience. Options for honorable combat had dwindled since Grandfather Hakon's day. Soderland's neighbors had accepted the White Swan, and his family grew loath to slay Swanlings without severe cause. And the plague that had taken his mother and Corinna's mother both, and rendered their father a babbling madman, had left the countries nearby too depleted for conflict. Grandfather Hakon, his own mind shattered in a different way by the losses of war, would not reclaim the crown, and their grandmother was in the ground. Corinna had done what she could.

Ragnar had sought war among the Ursine Guard of distant Amberhorn. He'd fought pirates and nomad raiders and even his own cousins in the Ayl Corps across the Midnight Sea, and in between he'd sipped muscat wine and irony. He begrudged his half-sister nothing; what he hated were the mutterings that as a bastard, he was unworthy of his blood.

At last he was earning glory in his own land.

He just had to wait.

They waited two days, as scouts and travelers brought word of a fantastically vast force of alien horsemen that congealed and dispersed like smoke. None could be sure how many, for the Karvak horde seemed able to march and encamp across a wide area and yet maintain its discipline. But it was said the cookfires that appeared briefly in the gray after sunset were like the scattered stars. The Karvaks appeared true to their agreement with the Five Fjords, and the few Fjordland villages down in that rugged lowland between Gullvik's domain and Garmstad's went unharmed.

At dawn on the second day, Ragnar woke from a nightmare. He had dreamed that a falcon menaced a bear, and though the bear had seemed ferocious and unconquerable, the falcon, too fast for the bear's claws, slowly and patiently and beginning with the eyes pecked and clawed the beast to death.

Nothing in the pass justified his cold sweat. The sky overhead was a blue-gray to match the mountain rock, while southward there was blue and sunlight that illuminated the pass's few trees, making them green beacons against the gray. Ragnar had an urge to paint the scene. He kept it to himself. One had strange thoughts before battle sometimes.

Then he saw it: a dark circular shape in the gray sky to the northeast. Two, and three. Far off but unmistakable, for he had himself seen the fallen craft of Haytham ibn Zakwan.

"Awake!" he cried, and the heralds took up the command. But he also ordered that ale be given to those who wanted it, and likewise blessings from the priests.

Once armed and armored, and ready with reports from the lookouts, he saw his army ready, their murmurs conveying eagerness. The bowmen were up on the Tooth, Huginn among them. He spoke to his key warleaders, Klarvik, Stormhamn, Jokull, and Garm.

"We are ready," Ragnar said without preamble. "And we are fortunate, for the lookouts report a force of only three thousand."

"Heh," said Lord Klarvik. "Only."

"Nevertheless, our chances are less dire than rumored. I think our Karvaks are skilled at braggery. And I think our own ability to come together will have surprised them. Let's be ready to welcome them."

Two hours later the strange army arrived. Ragnar had never before seen a force that was entirely cavalry. Were they all nobles, then, and so many? And all bowmen? He marveled at these strange men in their tasseled helmets and their coats blue as a cloudless winter sky. All had swords, and some in the middle of the line wore armor, and in this they were like and yet unlike his own force. (Indeed, some of their horses looked of Kantenjord breed.) The swords were curved, and the armor was unlike either chain or plate, being a cuirass of rectangular metal strips. The saddles were more complex than the Kantenings' and possessed extensions to anchor the feet.

The Karvaks advanced with impressive discipline, each man keeping true to signalmen waving colored flags. Ragnar wished he could question one of these warriors as to their methods.

After he had slain or routed all that one's fellows, of course.

The Kantenings took first blood. The hidden longbowmen on Hel's Tooth loosed their arrows when the Karvaks were within a quarter mile.

Warriors died. A cheer rose up from the Kantenings.

Landwaster held high, Ragnar bellowed, "Hold! Do not advance!" The order was repeated, and his own horsemen kept discipline.

The Karvaks were in confusion for a short time, during which Ragnar wondered if he'd missed an opportunity. Many of them shot arrows in response to Ragnar's longbowmen. Their smaller bows and lower ground put them at the disadvantage; none of their arrows found the mark.

The confusion did not last, and the Karvaks pulled back and regrouped with admirable unity. Their loss of some twenty men and horses was more symbolic than meaningful, but first blood mattered. Ragnar smiled.

Now. What would I do in their place?

He saw signal flags waving, and answering flags from the distant balloons. The "Orb Dragons" advanced. *Of course.*

"Runewalkers!" he called out. "It is time!"

Jokull said, "I don't like using heathen spells. The Church forbids it."

"You are quite accommodating to heathen worship up in Oxiland."

"It's different, what people do in their own homes," Jokull said. "This is magic."

Ragnar frowned, watching gray-robed men and women behind his lines, bedecked in gold rings and bird-bone necklaces. They paced out broad designs upon the stone of the pass. Each one cradled under one arm a bladder made from the guts of a pig or goat, each filled with what Ragnar devoutly hoped was animal blood. The Runewalkers left red trails behind them.

"If we don't use it," Ragnar said, pointing to the Karvak balloons, "then our foe owns the sky."

Minutes passed and red runes filled the pass. They were the elder *hagalaz* rune, associated with hail.

Clouds rolled in, lighting flashed, thunder cracked. The balloons were obscured.

Now came another crackle, this time from the Karvak side of the pass. Ragnar could not see the cause, but smoke filled the gap, turning the enemy horsemen into shadowy ghosts.

The Karvaks again advanced, new crackles accompanying bursts of smoke as they went.

"Magic?" Loftsson said.

"I don't know," Ragnar admitted, as a first bit of hail iced his cheek, and then another. "The hail may disperse it."

"If the timing is right—"

"We can't rely on the longbowmen," Ragnar decided. "We will blunt their advance, before they can aim through that smoke. Horsemen!" he shouted, waving Landwaster. "Knights! Men of Soderland! Garmstad! Ostoland! Oxiland! Kantenings all! Men of ice and fire! Heroes of Garmsmaw! This is our moment! A day of hail and steel! All with horse ride forth! We will bloody them and return to our line! Ride!" He gave Landwaster to his herald, readied his spear, and joined the charge.

His instincts were correct. The Karvaks had meant by their smoke to evade his longbowmen and reach a range where their own bows could rain death. But it left them briefly vulnerable to a charge. Ragnar had noted a lack of spears or lances, or even shields.

It seemed that good fortune, the Swan, and even the old powers were with him. For even as the Kantenings rushed upon the foe, hailstones fell, dispersing the smoke. Visibility came too late to help the Karvak archers, but just in time to aid Ragnar's men. Fighting through hail wasn't easy, but at least they could see their foes.

Scores of Karvaks fell before that onslaught, and Ragnar's heart hammered, for his was blood of conquerors, foamreavers, and berserkers.

In what seemed in one sense moments and in another hours, the charge was done. The Karvaks pulled back, galloping down the pass toward the Fjordlanders' lowlands. Ragnar grinned and raised his sword, and beckoned his herald lift Landwaster high. He was glad Huginn could see all this.

Jokull Loftsson, crying, "Vengeance!" kicked his horse and gave chase, and all the Oxilanders followed. The knights of Saint Fiametta would not be outdone, and in the knights' wake other horsemen followed too. Battle-fury was upon them all. Ragnar was in danger of being left alone in the pass.

Perhaps it was the hail that cooled his rage, or perhaps it was that a leader instinctively mistrusts the excitement of his people. Something nagged at Ragnar. There were many Karvak dead, but not so many as to constitute a slaughter, not from a force of three thousand. And their retreat had been swift, but had it truly been a rout? Thinking back, it seemed as though the steppe warriors had fled all in one body, like a withdrawing wave.

"Stop!" he called out, ice taking his heart. Riding to his herald he snatched Landwaster and rode after the main body of horsemen. "Do not leave our strongpoint!" He shouted behind him, to any who would listen, "Keep the footmen there! I command it!"

He could not put a name to his fear, but the image of the bear and the falcon stayed with him. Riding as fast as he dared, he still could not see the horsemen up ahead through the hail. They were already dangerously far from their encampment, a mile now, a mile and a quarter . . .

He knew he'd found them by the screams of horses echoing through the pass. A minute later he saw them. He drew up on the reins. Ragnar could not believe what he was witnessing.

Leaping down from the heights on either side were dozens of giant cats, big as horses, with fangs like white, curved swords. Into the body of Kantening horsemen they ran, clawing, raking, biting. Horse-meat was their aim, and in their seeking they spread panic and despair.

Also on the heights were endless Karvak archers. The hail and sabercats made their shots difficult, but they had all the time in the world. The Kantenings had ridden into a killing zone.

"Go back!" he told his herald. "The army must hold."

"It's your death if you go on," said the herald, speaking like a seer.

"It's my duty. I must rally them if I can. Go!"

He took his horse into the madness, Landwaster in hand. "Kantenings! Retreat! Retreat!"

It was a worthy effort, and it was a shame the battle-madness was long gone. When the sabercat leapt upon him, he wished Huginn was there to see it.

Nine Smilodons might have wished for a better fight. He suspected the Bladelanders might have given them one at close range. But as his commanders had long instructed him, there was no good in anything until the thing was done. Evenly matched fights were for sport. Slaughter was for war.

He was pleased for his liege Steelfox, for this battle had been directed by her, a demonstration to her sister Jewelwolf that Steelfox could command in war. The Kantening weather magic had been a surprise and might have upset the calculations. Nevertheless, the balloons had done their most important work already, placing many hidden, dismounted arbans in the mountains days earlier, awaiting the moment when they could attack the Kantenings' back ranks while pretending to be a superior force. Even as the islanders' horsemen rode to their doom, the footmen were panicked by the sudden deaths of their magicians and priests. They lost their cohesion as a force, and soon lost their superior position as well, leaving themselves open to the return of the Karvak riders and, with the weather magic disrupted, the balloons.

At last Nine Smilodons had this moment to pause and survey the thousands of dead, even as balloon-borne archers slew the Kantening bowmen in their high redoubt. The screams were not pleasant, nor the stench—but victory was.

Many groups of Kantenings still held out behind their shield walls, able to stave off the arrows but not to escape. Given time to regroup they might yet cause trouble. Nine Smilodons, as a special servant of Steelfox, was bound to report his opinion. First he snatched up the many-colored banner the fallen prince had borne, carefully removing it from the dead hands. As he led his horse among the corpses, one proved itself still alive, calling weakly, "Vengeance . . . Torfa . . ."

Nine Smilodons narrowed his eyes and felt a moment of shame. The nearly-dead man was Loftsson, whose wife Nine Smilodons, along with dead Red Mirror, had killed. Nine Smilodons owed the man a word, so he paused. "Yes, I am one of her slayers," he said in Kantentongue. "It was an error."

"Kill you . . ." said the man. He was nearly pale as bone, perforated by six arrows, covered with his own blood. Nevertheless he tried to rise, gripping a dagger.

"A Kantening already killed Red Mirror," Nine Smilodons acknowledged. "Vengeance has been done. It may yet be done to me. But I can't allow you to kill me."

"Die . . ." Loftsson crawled to where he might stab Nine Smilodons' horse.

Nine Smilodons tucked the banner beneath one arm, carefully prepared his bow, and shot four arrows into Loftsson until he was sure the man was dead. He rode on to the war commanders. Soon he was in the presence of General Ironhorn, Lady Jewelwolf, and Lady Steelfox. Among the honor guard was the shaman Northwing, the stump of her lost hand wrapped in ironsilk.

"Why in the Eternal Blue Sky did you bother to kill a dying man?" Jewelwolf asked him.

"He was a noble of the enemy," said Nine Smilodons, eyes flicking toward Northwing. Jewelwolf was known for capricious violence. The Kantening spy Grundi, who lurked beside her, had even brought her a strange magic sword, which now gleamed at her side. "As I understand it," Nine Smilodons said, "these people believe it's possible to achieve victory with dishonor, and defeat with honor. It is an alien idea, but I wished to grant him the latter."

"I approve of your choice," Steelfox said. "Is that the emblem of the prince?"

"It is."

Steelfox said, "Drop it there. It may possess some totemic power, and I would handle it with care. I will order it burned, with respect."

Nine Smilodons did as she bid. He said, "It seems to me the battle is nearly won, but those Kantenings yet holding out should be slain now. Should we charge?"

General Ironhorn looked to the sky. Blue shone through the gray. "Princesses," he said, "I would advise conserving soldiers, and using the balloons."

"Do so," Jewelwolf said. "Also, insert into our dead men's eyes the crystals we obtained from the trolls. Grundi, proceed to Svanstad as we discussed, and prepare to spread terror."

"Sister," said Steelfox. "Their magic is vile—"

"Excuse me, elder sister," Jewelwolf said with a laugh, as if she had merely belched at the wrong moment. "This is your battle, of course. And you have done well! Now you can return to your preferred duties and claim you participated in the war."

Steelfox ignored the taunt, and Nine Smilodons took pride in her. "General, send the balloons," Steelfox said. "Finish this. Return to the front, Nine Smilodons."

Nine Smilodons rode back to offer what aid was needed, but there was little to do. The signals went up, and the balloons drifted over the pass. The simple expedient of dropping large rocks upon the clusters of Kantenings was enough to peel many men away from the shield walls. The archers in the air and on the ground finished those quickly.

At last the holdouts' endurance flagged, and they chose to make their slayers remember them. They charged the horsemen, their armor clinking and their voices echoing war cries through the pass. Arrows took almost all. But it happened that Nine Smilodons was near the point where a few Kantenings reached the horsemen.

The screaming islanders sought to bring melee to their foes. But on horseback evading them was like stepping aside for a blindfolded man.

The Karvak mounts swerved and ran, and Nine Smilodons and his horse joined the encirclement. It was like the end of the hunt, with great beasts of the plains brought down, ferocious, noble, and—in the grasp of the Karvaks—doomed.

Black birds descended in earnest to feast upon the Karvaks' labor and to return the stuff of fallen comrades to Mother Earth, beneath the approving gaze of Father Sky.

But Steelfox's light force had its victory, clearing the path for Jewelwolf's full tumen. The way south lay open.

CHAPTER 27

FOSSEGRIM

Captain Glint wasn't happy about taking his new longship *Leaping Bison* to Klarvik, Gaunt knew. After delays in Svanstad and bad weather leaving the city's fjord, he at last had a following wind and was eager to ride it into the Splintrevej, where he hoped to get more men and information. But Gaunt had other plans. She could wear down even a foamreaver when her mind was set.

Klarvik had mustered. Its nobles had taken most of the grown men north, so the questers were met by women, or else men of great youth or age.

"Are you here to protect us?" demanded the dockmistress, her voice implying Gaunt was responsible for all ills in Klarvik since the days of the Vindir. "Given we're now vulnerable to anyone who sails by?"

They were not actually at a dock, for a ship of *Bison's* ilk—a hundred feet by thirteen, single-sailed, of narrow draft—could be hauled by its sailors onto the sandy shore. There was indeed no way short of combat Klarvik could refuse such a visit.

Erik Glint waded up to greet the dockmistress. "Corinna's navy still patrols these waters," he said. "I don't think it's the sea you need fear."

"We're on a mission for the Crown," Gaunt added, showing the ring bearing Corinna's seal. "I require directions to Klarfoss, the great waterfall."

"A strange mission," sighed the dockmistress. "But these are strange times. My boy will guide you."

Gaunt glanced at Malin Jorgensdatter, who was examining the way the waves lapped against Klarvik's shore. Gaunt said, "Your knowledge may be valuable to us, Malin. Will you come?"

"I will come."

Katta, the man of the steppe and desert, and Freidar, the aging man who complained of popping joints, each enjoyed a chance to stand upon dry land. Deadfall remained hidden aboard ship. Captain Glint dealt with officialdom. Gaunt, Bone, and Malin bid them good-bye and followed a lad named Peik through snowy lanes. The intricately carved wooden buildings of Klarvik crowded on a headland between the sea and a great cliff topped with a turreted keep. The road inland was rough and winding.

"I can see why you didn't want Freidar trying to hike up here," Bone remarked, "but why not Katta?"

Gaunt considered how much to say around Malin. The young woman, though studying the boulders and trees they passed, surely heard all and remembered. "I'm not worried about Katta," Gaunt said, "but I greatly mistrust Deadfall. Katta seems to have some influence on it, so it's better for them to stay together. Beyond that . . . I am playing a hunch here, and I don't think a crowd will help."

"I hear nothing!" Peik broke in. "You can keep confidences around me, surely as Lord Klarvik could conceal his tryst with Lady Stormhamn, or the abbot his business ties with foamreavers. I am the soul of discretion!"

The terrain hid the waterfall until they were almost upon it. Within a hands-breadth of the path's tranquil snow, water surged downward to feed a river concealed among the white-dappled pines five hundred feet below.

"Well, here you are," said Peik. "Klarfoss. I could tell you lots of stories about it and the spirits hereabouts. My cousin Knute said he learned to play the Vestvinden fiddle from a fossegrim of the waters, in order to impress his lady love. But because the spirit songs made him strange, she wed my cousin Kjell instead."

Malin spoke. "No, that's a hundred-and-thirty-three-year-old poem written by Henning Ingson:

> I met the maestro of the water
> He spilled music into my mind
> My fiddle lured Lars' fair daughter
> But she became my brother's bride.

"All right, Ingson, sure," said Peik, "but it sounds better when it's about someone you know. You ever feel like nothing ever happens to you and yours? Like boredom is strewing cobwebs through the inside of your skull?"

"No," Malin said. "I'm never bored."

"Then you're lucky. Me, I want something big to happen."

Gaunt set down her pack, removed the *Chart of Tomorrows*. Turning to a map of eastern Svardmark, Gaunt said, "Fossegrim! Guardian of this place! I know this is a place of power, for I see it here in the *Drakkenskinnen*! Come forth!"

And the fossegrim came forth.

At first there was no distinguishing him from the froth, for he was white as the falls' heart, and his hair and beard were like the cloudy tendrils of water at the deluge's edge. Gaunt was put in mind of the efrit Haboob, formed of smoke where this entity was shaped by water. Then the fiddle appeared, or rather did not appear, for the suggestion of a musical instrument manifested as a gap, unaccountable, in the flow of the water.

The fossegrim appeared to fiddle, but its instrument was merely air. An eerie music manifested, beckoning them all to wander through the waterfall and onto trackless forest paths.

At last it seemed the shape would fiddle endlessly, so Gaunt called out, "Fossegrim! We mean no harm!"

The words "mean no harm" echoed all around them. The fossegrim appeared to set down its fiddle, for the gap in the waters flicked downward and sideways.

"Humankind is incapable of meaning no harm," it said. Its voice was formed of interruptions in the roar of the water, a kind of subtraction rather than addition of sound. The effect was jarring, and the words raised uneasy chills down Gaunt's back; at the same time, voice and speech were alluring. Something in her longed to walk into the waterfall, to know the fossegrim's heart.

"There is less and more harm, surely," she said. "We mean to find our son and take him away from conflict. That will mean less violence, perhaps for everyone."

"What does that have to do with me?" said the fossegrim.

"The *Chart of Tomorrows* shows Klarfoss to be a way into the Straits of Tid. Do you guard that portal?"

"I do. You stand beside one of the cool thoughts of an arkendrake, and I am a watery manifestation of that thought, just as the trolls are mineral manifestations of various obsessions. Beyond me lies the dragon's mind. Beside any of the great waterfalls of Svardmark, you will find a guardian so similar, we might be the same entity. Behind us lies the same mentality. And whether you dream your way into this gateway or walk forward boldly and bodily, there are but three ways to pass me. First, give yourself to me, woman, body and soul, and dwell with me always."

"Let's hear the other two," Bone said.

"Second, overpower me, a creature of the rushing waters, by force."

"And the last?" Gaunt said.

"Impress me with your fiddling. The Vestvinden fiddle will do nicely."

"I don't have a Vestvinden, or any fiddle," Gaunt said. "Nor do I know how to play one."

The fossegrim laughed. "Give me a song I have never heard. Open your thoughts, and I will know if you have one."

Gaunt closed her eyes and imagined all the lullabies and rhymes of youth, all the lore of the bards, all the strange things she'd heard on the road.

"You have nothing," the fossegrim sighed. "Kantenings have traveled far, and I know all your songs, skald. But return on Tordensday with a fiddle and a fat lamb, and I may teach you. For I sense tumult in the land, and a spirit of the waterfalls likes tumult."

"Our ship won't wait that long," Gaunt said. "Not when there's a good wind blowing."

"That is no matter to me."

"We're not letting you go so easily," Bone said, advancing, making Gaunt wonder what had gotten into him. "I've survived a dragon. I can face you, see what's beyond your gateway."

"Boastful," said the fossegrim. "The woman is at least intriguing. You I have no time for."

Before anyone could react, the water-spirit slapped Bone aside with an arm that seemed a sideways fork of the falls. The fossegrim fiddled as Bone plunged toward his doom.

Gaunt lunged for him, dropping the *Chart of Tomorrows* on the path. She had him by the arm, but he dangled over the abyss.

"Deserts," he was saying. "Much better than mountains. Flat . . ."

"Shut up," she said, pulling, straining, until she saw the brilliant burst of color below him.

"Bone, let go," Gaunt told him.

"I realize Katta's religion has been rubbing off on all of us," Bone said, struggling to get purchase on the cliff, "and I respect the outlook of the Undermined, but I'd rather not be plunging to my doom just yet. . . ."

"You're not doomed, Bone. Trust me."

And, closing his eyes, he did.

The flying carpet Deadfall caught him in his plummet.

"I had a premonition we were needed after all," said Katta, Freidar beside him, as Deadfall rolled Bone off onto a stony ledge beside the waterfall path.

"Be grateful at the risk I take," said Deadfall, "thief."

"Very, very, very grateful," said Bone, hugging the ground.

Freidar stared up at the waterfall in wonder. "The reality of the fossegrim overwhelms the tales."

As they watched, the misty figure began fading back into the falls.

"Wait!" Gaunt called out, pointing at Katta. "Behold this man. He's journeyed from hidden lands of the East. Search his mind for new songs, fossegrim."

The figure's sharp definitions returned. "I sense this is true. Speak, traveler."

Katta did not miss a beat, and Gaunt wanted to hug him. He said, "O spirit of the waterfall, I have come from far lands to tell you the ways of the Undetermined, who broke the chain of causes, and has had great effect. I will sing you a song of his teachings, and then speak of its meaning. For skilled as I am, I cannot match the songs of the Plateau of Geam to the tongue of Kantenjord. You must take sound and meaning as if they were two accounts of a deeper reality, like two blind men trying to deduce the shape of an elephant."

Katta took a deep breath and intoned low rumbling notes that astonished Gaunt, who hadn't heard a singing voice so deep since her time in a lamasery of far Xembala. Katta's words boomed slowly upon the face of the rock, and their strength and inevitability made even the doom-laden song of Wiglaf seem a lighthearted, ephemeral thing. If the Earthe itself had a heartbeat, it might sound like this.

It seemed a thousand years before the booming was done, and yet in its aftermath it felt like an isolated moment, a single thought.

She could see nothing in the waterfall now but sensed a presence there, listening.

Katta said, "That is a song based on a poem of a great teacher of Geam. I will try to render his words in Kantentongue:

Here is my place of meditation
Snowy heights rise high above
Far below, my patron village
Down the snow-edged rippling river.
The eagle soars between
Above the village meadows blooming
Below the wheeling clouds
And shepherds graze their scattered herds
Singing songs and playing reeds.
Yet all of it is as a mirage,
A reflection in the waters.
I am nothing much
Fathered by eagles, birthed by glaciers
I don't balk at the endless sky
Nor fear the constricted earth
It will all pass away
Like a magic trick, a dream.
How strange the phenomena of this illusory world—
Everything manifested from nothing.

The sky unexpectedly cleared, and sun blazed upon the waterfall. Within the spray the fossegrim's form had become dark, like a human-shaped portal into the underworld. Within him gleamed tiny lights like distant stars, or flecks of white in onyx, or fireflies of a distant summer land.

The voice of the fossegrim, gentle and sad, resonated like water striking rock. "You have given me a gift with these words, and especially with this song, a music unlike any I've ever heard. You have paid the price I demanded of the bard. So, poet of Swanisle, you who would learn the fiddle. Step forward."

She did so, shivering in the spray.

"Step into the water."

After a moment's hesitation she did so.

She should have been drenched, but what she felt instead was a rush of sensations pouring into her mind. Stars whirled, and meteors flashed, and worlds were formed from fire and died in ice. In between came the music, bright, bittersweet, rich with archaic echoes. She knew with sharp clarity how Kantenjord was but one era upon one tiny corner of Earthe, and Earthe was but one world of an unimaginably vast cosmos.

Yet all was connected, worlds linked by one fabric of space and time, landmasses rising from one lithosphere, beneath one atmosphere. She saw the connections could bring pain as well as joy, for she experienced Kantenjord erupting in fire and smoke, and the smoke covering the whole world, choking out light and heat.

The world died in endless winter: Kantenjord, Swanisle, and the Eldshore. Amberhorn, Palmary, and Qushkent. The Karvak Realm, Xembala, Qiangguo. All dead in a grave of frost.

And on went the sound of the Vestvinden fiddle. Even at the end of the world there must be music.

"Gaunt? Gaunt. Persimmon."

Now Bone had his hands on hers, and she realized she was facing away from the waterfall and whistling. She stopped.

"Persimmon?"

"I'm here, Bone." She met his gaze. She was hardly touched by the water, but the feeling of doom stayed with her. Turning, she saw the fossegrim was gone. Its insights would remain, however. She shivered. "I've learned how to play. I just need a fiddle. Imago. I can open the way with this. We find the right waterfall, we can find Innocence through the Straits of Tid. We can find our son."

"That can wait," Bone said. "We nearly lost each other, here. Let's get back to *Bison*."

"We should hurry," Freidar said. "Villagers are streaming into Klarvik from up Garmstad way. Something has happened."

Despite the news, Deadfall declined to fly them back to Klarvik but instead rustled down the path like a colorful serpent. Freidar and Katta looked thoughtful. Malin walked silently, bearing the *Chart of Tomorrows* and staring into it now and again. Peik, once voluble, looked lost in worry.

"If there are refugees . . ." Bone began.

"They are lost," Peik said. "The army. I know it in my gut."

"We have to get Innocence out of this," Bone told Gaunt.

"Yes," Gaunt said, but it was hard to hear his words over the memory of the music.

When they returned, Bone saw that Klarvik seemed on its way to adding a hundred more people, peasants fleeing word of the sacking of Garmstad Town and the burning or submission of the villages in the Karvaks' path. Folk were coming here because the Karvaks were ignoring Klarvik. The horde was headed to Svanstad.

Of Ragnar's army, there was nothing left but a few, many too shamed to speak of it. There was a new prayer in the air: 'From the fury of the Karvaks, Goddess preserve us.'"

"The wheel turns," Bone heard Gaunt murmur, as they loaded supplies onto *Bison*.

A boy approached the ship. It was Peik.

For a moment, Bone thought the lad was going to ask to sail with them. Instead he held out a fiddle, nearly the shape of a violin, with mother-of-pearl inlay.

"This is . . . was . . . my father's. He is not coming back. You're on a mission to kill Karvaks, yes? If giving you this fiddle will help you avenge him in any way, I am happy."

"I am honored to take this," Gaunt managed to say. "I will find a way to be worthy of the gift."

"Just kill Karvaks," the boy said, never leaving the strand. He was still there when *Bison* rounded the bay's edge.

CHAPTER 28

SIEGE

Joy was training with Nan when word of the disaster at Garmsmaw Pass came to Svanstad.

"Training" seemed an odd word for it. In the world of *A Tumult of Trees on Peculiar Peaks*, training had meant pugilism and swordplay, concentration exercises to cultivate chi, endless jogging regimens through mountain paths, and discussions of the body's energy flow and how to redirect it.

"Training" for Nan seemed to consist of learning strange old stories and a peculiar old writing system.

"I'm just not sure," Joy said in frustration one day, "how learning *about* something can teach me to *do* something."

"I understand," the old woman said, not pausing from the work she was performing in the Fortress courtyard, to the consternation of the guards and servants. They stood in a twenty-foot-diameter circle of white, for all the rest of the night's snowfall had been cleared at dawn. Nan was slowly tracing a pattern in the snow, using a knobbed wooden staff decorated with brass and gems. "The difficulty is, the only people with experience being a Runethane are long dead. I can't take you to the Great Chain of Unbeing. What I can do is tell you stories of earlier Runethanes, and help you to picture the Great Chain in your mind. It is marked with the elder runes of the Vindir. Know these runes and you can truly envision the Chain. Now then, behold the rune *raido*, meaning 'journey.'"

"So . . . you summon the power by tracing a rune?"

"Yes."

"Couldn't you save time by making it smaller?"

"Ha! Yes. There are Runewalkers who have spent days tracing out the patterns. Indeed, I suspect there are a few runes now activated in this city, writ in stone, barley, ash, or blood."

"Is bigger better?"

"A larger pattern carries more influence but is also less specific in intent.

The bigger the wish, the more likely the intent will go awry, or succeed in a fraught way."

"What have you wished?"

"That you might travel mentally. Close your eyes and spread-eagle yourself in the snow. Think of the Chain as I've described it."

She did these things, though she felt foolish.

"Do you see the Chain?"

"I see horses . . . they carry riders . . . they carry riders here!"

Hoofbeats echoed through the courtyard of the Fortress. Joy rose and dusted snow off herself. Ten men rode up to Nan, mistaking her for an authority.

"Well?" Nan said.

They were so distraught they had trouble speaking. A hairy teenaged boy and a bald teenaged boy each began speaking, each failing to get the words out, each vainly encouraging the other to talk. Yet if their tongues were still, their eyes spoke of horrors. At last a burly, florid-looking man spoke up. "I am Huginn Sharpspear, Lady. Kollr here, Rolf, the rest . . . we are nearly all that's left of Ragnar's army."

Protocol was lost. Joy found herself beside Nan and Corinna as the princess spoke with her grandfather upon a balcony, looking north at snowy farmland, blue mountains beyond.

"You will not claim the throne, Grandfather?"

"It belongs to the young. Our people will need your straight back and shining face. Ah, Corinna. How is it that Ragnar died?"

"Bravely."

"Do not humor me. How did his army, on which we've spent so much effort, perish so utterly?"

"By the Oxilander Huginn's report, the Karvaks are a force unlike any ever seen. Now our whole country lies open to them. We must assume Garmstad Town lost."

"They will come here. They must. To Svanstad. The walls must be our mountain now. And there may yet be time for alliances. Send to the Five Fjords."

"They have already stabbed us in the back," Corinna said.

"There's Swanisle, and the Eldshore. Mirabad. Kpalamaa."

Corinna nodded. "Haytham says he's completed a small balloon for us, one fit for two or perhaps three. I'll send him to King Rainjoy in Swanisle. Nan . . . you go with him. You're the best Runewalker we have now. He'll need you to command the winds."

"But Joy—" Nan objected.

"She may go with you, and you may instruct her as you fly."

Joy could not believe it. "Again you try to send me away when a fight is coming. Why, Corinna? Are you afraid of me?"

It was an ill-chosen word, but Joy saw it struck home. There was indeed a wariness in Corinna's eyes as her grandfather said, "You are an old power, Joy . . . your mother is Snow Pine, yes? Joy Snøsdatter, then. You are alien to our land, but you have power, and courage. Corinna has always liked being the toughest person in the room."

"Grandfather . . ." Corinna said, in a warning tone. "Joy, if you don't wish to go, by all means stay. We'll send one of those two Oxiland boys who survived, the hairy one or the bald one. They want to do me service, but I am tired of putting children at risk."

For the next few days Joy threw herself into her "training," trying to visualize the Great Chain of Unbeing as the Karvaks grew ever closer. She sparred with Walking Stick and attempted the visualizations of Nan. But Walking Stick was, it seemed, everywhere at once and only sometimes able to help her. And after the breakthrough that let her perceive the approaching riders the visions again eluded her.

Now she stood upon a turreted tower of the Fortress. From here she could look south down the fjord and to the sea, wondering when Haytham would return from Swanisle. And she could look north past the city walls and the wooden outer district, across the farmlands and woods, whence swift riders arrived from inland, crying woe.

In the afternoon light she saw why. The dark mass of the invading army filled the land to the northeast.

As the minutes passed she saw something she didn't understand. She'd been given to believe the Karvak army was a mounted force, but there were throngs of footmen. She slowly realized the mob in front of the horsemen were no warriors but rather captive villagers, prodded along by the Karvaks as living shields.

Rage filled Joy. She shut her eyes, shaking with it.

She saw the Great Chain, its vast metal links, its huge runes. She saw the island it wrapped around.

Upon that island stood Innocence Gaunt, and she sensed at once he was engaged in much the same project as herself. She saw him glance upward, left, right, as though hearing distant music.

A voice murmured in Joy's ear, though no one stood there. A cold, tight sensation tickled her spine. The voice was a woman's and young, but it was not her own, nor anyone's she knew.

Call to him, the voice said. *Let him know your anger, dragon-touched one.*

The voice worried her, but she decided to trust its advice.

Innocence, she thought. *Innocence Gaunt! My friend! How can you tolerate this? How can you work with Karvaks and trolls?*

What? came his voice, as the vision of him frowned. *Joy? Could it be?*

Your parents do not want this. Walking Stick does not want this. I do not want this. Leave that place, my dear friend! Come back to us!

You . . . Disbelief fled his face, anger taking its place. *You don't own me, Joy! None of them do. Not Walking Stick, not the Karvaks, not the trolls. But I've seen what endless fighting does to people. It warps them. It turns even wise men into traitorous bastards. It kills ten-year-old kids. The Karvaks didn't bring war to these islands; it's been going on for ages. The Karvaks just have a chance to stop it. For good. That's a cause worth fighting for.*

You're confused! You're bringing war, not stopping it.

I'm confused? You're helping a bunch of savages. The Karvaks are closer to Qiang-guo's civilization than these butchers.

This land chose me. I will fight for it.

The land? In her mind's eye she saw him kick dirt onto the dark metal of the chain. Upon that link she saw a rune resembling a flag on a pole, or an axe. *What chose you is an artifact of humankind, drawing on the power of dragons. Same as what chose me. It's no different, really, from some lord investing you with authority. You can be grateful, certainly. But the authority is yours, Joy. Take the power, and make it your own. You didn't ask for it. You have the right.*

Something in what he said stirred her. But she thought of Malin's determination and Inga's rage. She could never dismiss her friends as "savages." *Come tell me all that to my face, Innocence. Then I'll think about it.*

She willed him gone.

It was only after her vision ended that she realized the rune he'd stood before was *wunjo*, which could mean "joy."

Soon the invaders covered the nearer plains, and Joy could believe there were ten thousand. The front ranks were near enough that the wails of the captives reached the heights. They were being prodded toward the walls.

Her companions joined her. Flint gripped the turret stones. "I've heard of this. The captives provide cover. But also, they can be used to breach defenses."

"What?" Inga said. "How?"

Flint's voice was cold and steady. "They will be crushed against the walls to form a hill of flesh."

"No," Inga said.

"It won't be allowed to happen," Snow Pine said.

When the captives reached the abandoned wooden district outside the walls, explosions burst up in scores of places within the buildings. Soon everything was ablaze, including many captives. Thanks to their expedient of using human shields, no Karvaks were lost.

"Walking Stick's work," said Flint, shutting his eyes. "He has many more surprises. Most of them grisly."

"Are you all right?" Snow Pine asked.

"There is such suffering down there, and more to come. I wonder how I've spent my life. I don't believe in the Painter of Clouds, but I'm a man of the Brush yet. I've sought treasure instead of performing deeds of kindness, craved adventure instead of restoring light to the world."

"Surely that's not all on your shoulders."

"Some of it is. If we survive this I will use my rationality to help end human suffering." He stroked his chin. "Meanwhile, I may have an idea how to help matters here." He turned and looked out at the fjord, to where the vessel *Anansi* lay at anchor, watching, waiting.

As the stench of human burning reached Joy's nose and made her shudder, Flint said, "I think I know a way to tip the balance."

CHAPTER 29

SISTERHOOD

As she watched the captive Kantenings driven forward on Jewelwolf's order, Lady Steelfox could not help recalling her younger sister as a child.

It was even before Steelfox had bonded with the falcon Qurca. Steelfox had been eight years old and Jewelwolf seven, and one afternoon their father, the Grand Khan, had summoned them forth to ride. Of course they had no difficulty doing so, having spent much of their toddlerhood in the saddle.

The Grand Khan's personal forces had been encamped in a green region just north of the Qiangguo's Blue Heavenwall. The local tribes hated Qiangguo and its demands of tribute, so the Karvaks had taken the country without a fight. The garrison at the wall fired arrows and catapult stones at Father's riders now and then, and Karvak wheelships sometimes lobbed spiked wooden balls back at them. It was like boys at play, Mother would say. Father had no intention of attacking the Wall, but he wanted Qiangguo to seethe at his presence, even as his sons struck far away in Qushkent.

"If they feel threatened in their home territory," he told his daughters that day, "they'll worry less that we are testing the Braid of Spice like a musician plucks a tobshuur."

"Don't you want to claim Qiangguo?" Jewelwolf said, shaking a fist. "They are cowards, hiding behind their walls."

Father laughed. "You believe their own stories. The Heavenwalls are not the same as the walls of a town. I do not comprehend their magics, nor do I wish to. But I understand enough: through them, herds cannot pass. They are lines drawn against the Karvaks and against all those who move at will upon the land. They mark the end of the free world and the beginning of tyranny."

Steelfox frowned. "Then you think the Walls are an attack, not a defense."

"You begin to see! Much in the world makes more sense when you glimpse it topsy-turvy. Come! I have more to say about this."

Yet at first the Grand Khan seemed to forget everything concerning war and nations. Out of sight of the Walls and the encampment, they trampled over whispering green grass until they came to a stream winding its way through a stand of poplar trees.

There they began looking at clouds.

Their grave, imperious father, who had brought his clan back from the brink of destruction until it ruled the great Karvak nation, who had crushed the steppe under Karvak hooves and wheels, and who now set his sights on the whole vast world, this khan among khans now talked about wispy tigers and mastodons and steppe mice like a boy. For the moment Steelfox and Jewelwolf were no longer Karvak princesses, students of conquest, but little girls admiring billowing ponies and flying ships.

After they compared clouds in this manner for a time, the Grand Khan did something peculiar. He rose and climbed the tree. "Stay there," he told them.

Once situated in the branches he said, "Daughters, I want you to imagine something. I want you to imagine that up is down."

They'd giggled, for surely this was their father in a whimsical mood, such as they'd not seen him for many years.

"Daughters, I know this seems silly, but it is serious. Imagine that the world exerts an upward-pulling force upon you, and that you are looking down at the branches below you, down at the swirling clouds. Now, do you see your father? Look down upon him."

The Great Khan waved, and his daughters, despite his earlier words, laughed again. Then it was as if they'd offended him, for he shifted into more distant branches, out of sight.

But he had not been angry. "Daughters, you cannot see me, but you are still looking down at your father. You are looking down at endless Father Sky."

Moved by the words, they'd stared into that vast blue.

"We are taught," said the Grand Khan, "that Father Sky looks down upon Mother Earth, and has lordship over her. I tell you that is a trick of the mind, and it is just as valid to say Mother Earth looms over Father Sky, and envelops him. This is what I learned when I fell near to death at the battle of Mudwater Lake, staring up at the endless void. Earth and Sky are co-equal. This is something you must remember. I have, so far, two daughters and four sons. Tradition would say that it's a son who should follow me as khan. Yet I tell you in secret, each of you is worth any two of them. I do not know which of you will prove better suited to rule, but it is in my heart that one of you will succeed me."

Steelfox did not know what Jewelwolf was thinking, but she felt the blood pulse in her body. Were these forbidden words? They could not be, for they came from the Great Khan. Yet she felt as though it was a secret to be kept from everyone but Mother Earth and Father Sky.

Father said, "Mother Earth taught me to value the strength of women for a reason. But it will take all my will to make our people understand. Even your mother, the beloved khatun, has an older view and will make trouble. But this is as it must be. If this new empire is to flourish, it will need the best guidance—one of my daughters, with the other daughter as counselor. I have faith in you. For women are better than men at putting pride aside and working with shared purpose."

Steelfox could say nothing. But bold younger sister spoke sure and swift, as if she'd been waiting for such words her whole life. "We are grateful for your trust, Father. Whichever of us rules, we will always be loyal to each other. We will show each other love and our enemies despair. Our strength will drown the world in blood."

Even bursting with her father's pride, it had unnerved Steelfox how eagerly Jewelwolf dreamed of destruction.

It was almost a relief to see the Kantening trap go off, igniting the abandoned wooden perimeter of the city and burning the captive villagers in droves. Jewelwolf would have to pull the captives back.

Yet the signal flags waved, and the villagers continued to be fed to the fire. Steelfox frowned and rode to the hilltop position of Jewelwolf and General Ironhorn.

The general knelt, and Jewelwolf nodded to Steelfox, a faint smile playing on her lips. "Yes, sister?"

"You will not recall the captives? It seems wasteful to let them burn."

"You have a decent mind for tactics, sister, I will give you that. But you miss certain dimensions. The city-dwellers dared set a trap for us. Now they must watch as their countrymen are consumed by it. Now they must listen as men, women, and children scream in searing agony. The whole city will hear the sound. The whole city will smell the burning flesh. Terror will grow."

"Father would not—"

Jewelwolf frowned now. "Father is not here. And you have idolized him into something he was not. He invented the tactics of the living shield and the corpse-rampart. He would approve."

Steelfox was not so sure. Father would at least have offered Svanstad a chance to surrender, something Jewelwolf had declined to do. General Iron-horn, a careful subordinate, said nothing. "At least," Steelfox said, "consider sending trolls to breach the walls. They've so far been good for little."

At the mention of trolls, Jewelwolf's bond-horse Aughatai snorted. Did Steelfox note a dim green gleam in the horse's eyes? No, she must have imagined it. Jewelwolf stroked Aughatai's mane and looked to the gray skies. "I think the light is still too great for the trolls' comfort. Though I see a storm rolling in from the east, against the prevailing wind."

"Kantening magic, perhaps," Steelfox said. "My balloonists report high winds."

"Mine as well. It's clear they mean to give us a fight. General, we may be here some time. Send to our Spydbanen subjects that today is a good day to send their longships against the harbor. As long as Svanstad can feed its belly by sea, our task remains difficult."

"Of course," the general said. "I must remind you, however, there is a craft of Kpalamaa in the fjord, a ship big as a hill."

"I know little of this Kpalamaa. But what I do know says they are timid as steppe mice. Tell the foamreavers to ignore that ship, as long as it ignores them. Meanwhile, the army's engineers are free to cut down any tree, dismantle any building, to construct the siege engines. We desire the ability to rain death upon city and harbor."

"As you command—" the general said, tugging on his horse's reins.

A booming commenced from the city walls, and the three leaders turned their heads.

Fiery streaks flashed out from the walls, passing over the captives, terminating in explosions among the Karvak lines. Men and horses screamed.

"Fire-powder rockets," Steelfox said.

"That bastard from Qiangguo," Jewelwolf said. "Somehow this is his doing. I will kill him myself. General, pull us back. The captives too. There is no sense wasting human life."

"You mean Karvak life," Steelfox murmured, as the general rode to his task.

"Indeed. Sister, there is a thing I request of you, since the general is busy. Take charge of the Splintermen."

Steelfox gazed into the Karvak back ranks, where shambled green-eyed men who should have been fed to the birds days ago. She shivered.

"I can pass the task to another," Jewelwolf said, "if you are squeamish."

"Nonsense. What shall these fine young men do?"

Jewelwolf smiled. "I am giving them catapult duty."

The falcon Qurca searched the windows of the Fortress, seeking Haytham ibn Zakwan but finding him not. Steelfox, seeing through Qurca's eyes, wanted him to know she thought of him; seeing Qurca, he would guess the rest, how his betrayal stung, how it was unbelievable to her, how there might still be room for speech.

But not if the man was not here. Had he left the city?

She then sent Qurca to find familiar faces. The bird encountered the young woman Inga, she of the one arm. Qurca landed discreetly near where Inga stood on a balcony facing the north and the Karvak fires, and heard Inga say, "Soon, we will make an end, I think. It is not what I might have wanted. Still, it is on the Swan's wing, what will come. Good luck to you, Malin, my friend, wherever you fare!"

Elsewhere Qurca listened by an open window to the talk of voices Steelfox recognized as belonging to Snow Pine and Liron Flint.

"So you're set on doing this thing?" the bandit-woman of Qiangguo asked.

"I am," said the explorer. "I've ransacked Corinna's library, and I've a good idea where the swords fell when Wiglaf Sword-Slave and Eilifur Ice-Gaze slew each other, centuries ago. They met aboard ships, in a fjord whose description matches Svanstad's. The argument was nominally over a woman, but I think the weapons always hungered to destroy each other."

"Don't magical weapons always?"

"Not like this. Crypttongue was the work of the legendary King Younus, who was just possibly an ancestor of mine. It was a blade made to bind demons, jinn, efrits, that sort of thing. Wayland was envious of the long-ago king's prowess and sought to make a matching sword, something potent against uldra and trolls. But Wayland's envy corrupted the blade. While evil can be done with Crypttongue, Schismglass quite actively seeks to devour souls . . . and it's every bit as happy to consume a human as anything else."

"You're trying to convince me to help you? I'm not completely sure it's working."

"Listen now! The battle, as such things so often do, consumed the men but left the weapons intact. The swords fell into the fjord. Crypttongue washed up on the continent, but sailors have seen a bright object down in the fjord for years. *Anansi* has a contraption by which a diver can suck air through a flexible tube connected to the ship. I will seek the cursed thing, and you too, and together we may find the Schismglass of Baelscaer, hungry for souls other than those of fish."

"Good! I approve."

"You surprise me, Snow Pine. May I ask why? These are not your people. We may have sympathy for them, but why are you risking your life . . . and more . . . for them? I *think* I know why I'm doing it. But I need to know your mind, before we brave the waters."

"It's for her. You know, Liron, when I was her age I seemed to have no options but to claw and kick until the world bled me a path to follow. In those days I hated my homeland, and the whole world. Yet in time, as I found my way, I came to respect my homeland and be amazed by the world. And what might I have become, Liron, if I'd had someone, anyone, to reach out to me at Joy's age? To tell me, *You are important, you matter*. What might I have become? I, a woman with nothing but a bloodthirsty streak and a good sword arm?"

"Far from nothing," Liron Flint murmured.

"Who am I to take this from Joy—that a whole country reached out to her and said, *Help?* Do you see what it's doing to her? I fear it. Oh, gods, I fear it. But I also see how tall she stands. I'm just the vagabond Snow Pine, who used to be the bandit Next-One-A-Boy. But she's the Runethane. Somebody I respect."

He chuckled. "Well. I know how it is to respect someone. But know that this weapon is not a trivial thing. It hungers, as even Crypttongue does not."

"Oh, it worries me, Liron. But you've seen what the Karvaks are capable of."

"Yes. I have seen. . . . One way or another, this may be our last day together."

She gave a snort. "You're appealing to my sense of danger? We've had a barrel full of may-be-our-last-day-togethers."

"And they didn't sufficiently move you. So I arranged a nomad army at our doorstep and a mad quest for the morning. If that doesn't work, there are always earthquakes and meteors."

"Ha! Come here, you. Show me your earthquakes and meteors."

Steelfox sent Qurca on his way, not wishing to eavesdrop further. The notion of sex had stirred her a trifle. She'd enjoyed her late husband's embraces and had a time or two since taken lovers to bed and risked the burden of pregnancy. But desire didn't seem to weigh upon her as it did others. She wondered if that made her strange. So be it. It made her free, too.

She eavesdropped in many places in the city, learning fascinating things, though none so much as the plans of Snow Pine and Flint. At last she bade Qurca return, passing over the ditch and the engineers' ongoing work upon the catapults. She noted the hundreds of Splintermen, silently watching, patiently waiting for the nervous workers to finish. Patient as the dead.

"Ah, there you are," Northwing said as Steelfox entered the ger. The one-handed shaman sat cross-legged, with eyes shut. "I am struggling with the wind, but this is a trickier business than steering one balloon. These Runewalkers aren't as good as Karvak shamans . . . or me. But they are more familiar with the local spirits."

"Leave that for now. I want your council."

"Really! Someone check to see the moon hasn't plunged into Mount Mastodon."

"I am serious."

"So am I. Bah. Very well, give me a moment. All right. The spirits are dismissed. Talk."

"Northwing . . . I have misgivings about what my sister is doing. Not conquest. That is our way. But mad conquest, far from our heartland. Employing diseased allies and evil magic . . ."

"You have misgivings because you are sane. Well, basically sane. There are times—"

"The time may come," Steelfox whispered, "when I have to act against my sister, for the good of the Karvak Realm. Will you stand with me?"

Northwing looked down at a handless wrist, grunted. "I will. I have my reasons."

"Good. Am I correct that you can journey underwater, and take others? Or was that just boasting?"

"I'll take you to the bottom of the sea, if that's what you need. Just don't ask me to like it."

"Thank you. No woman has done more for our cause." Steelfox added quickly, "Or man."

"I am glad you would say this. But you're still unwilling to acknowledge that I am neither woman nor man."

Steelfox sat down beside the shaman. "I confess . . . it is an idea I've had considerable trouble comprehending. I can show respect without perfect understanding, however. And I should. I have at times treated you merely as an eccentric woman, rather than the individual you profess to be, one who walks between and beyond dualities. That ends now, my friend. You are Northwing, none other."

Northwing studied Steelfox in surprise. "You have changed."

"So have you. You've always seemed to dislike me. Yet you stayed by me when Haytham betrayed me."

"He had his reasons—" Northwing began.

"We all do, Northwing. We all do."

CHAPTER 30

LARDERLAND

When Bone first boarded *Leaping Bison*, taking note of its spaces for sixty rowers, its bright red-and-white sail, and its bull-shaped prow, Captain Glint had shown him and Gaunt a chart generously supplied by Eshe of Kpalamaa, whose people's cartography far outstripped the Kantenings'.

"As I feared," he'd said, "Deadfall's island, where we think the heart lies, is boxed in. The Draugmaw blocks the obvious path, and it has gained in strength; I'd not go through it with anything less than your Kpalamaa friends' galleon. Their map points out another worry. One could go around Oxiland proper—but it's the worst winter in years and the ice would grind us up. Likewise for passing around Spydbanen. That leaves only the Chained Straits, which the Karvaks hold."

"But?" Gaunt had said.

"And?" Bone had added.

"All right. The straits may be unavailable, but Lardermen know of many caves in that region, and rumor has it that some caves lead through to the other side. I know a woman who knows the way through. We'll find her in Larderland. The pirate port."

And so after their detour to Klarvik they caught the following wind toward the Splintrevej. Days passed, days of fiddling and language lessons, days of rowing and reading, days Bone learned to love the banter of the foam-reavers and the sunset on the waters . . . and loathe, with his beloved beside him, the lack of privacy.

At last the Splintrevej's thousands of rocky islands sprouted from the mists ahead.

Even the Kpalamaa chart did not account for every nook, cranny, islet, skerry, and seamount in that mazelike archipelago, where islands rose like wreckage, piney woods stabbing skyward, surrounded by high-cliffed shores. Here and there they saw chimney-smoke rising from unseen huts, or ramshackle docks with rafts beside. Deep into the Splintrevej the open ocean seemed far away, and the rowers were often needed. It was as though they passed through some salty, many-islanded lake.

"Legend has it," Freidar told them after they anchored one sunset in the shelter of a larger isle, "this was once a single land, in the days when only one arkendrake had settled and mineralized in these parts. It was a mighty dragon, that Staraxe, so great that its inherent power attracted two cruel younger dragons who contested for its carcass when they became arkendrakes themselves. It was a battle experienced by humanity as earthquakes and landslides and sea-waves. The younger arkendrakes began by slowly smashing the headland of the Splintrevej and consuming its powers. But a curious thing happened. The Vindir, who dwelled upon the body of Staraxe, forged and raised up the Great Chain of Unbeing, binding the three petrified dragons into a deep slumber, and draining their power for the use of the Runethane, their champion."

He fell silent.

Bone said, "I know you are worried about Svanstad. We have people there we worry about too."

Freidar nodded, "Nan will do her best for your friend Joy."

"I'm glad our son spent time in your care," Gaunt said. "You are good people."

"If only," Freidar said, "good deeds reliably produced good outcomes."

They traveled for two days through labyrinthine passages among the islands. Gaunt, practicing her fiddle, admired the setting, forests rising almost directly from the water to fill these rocky places, ranging in size from sea-stacks to massive islands, almost nations unto themselves. *Bison*'s mood lifted in this whimsical place. Early the third morning even Deadfall unrolled itself and began talking.

The carpet told a story of traveling with Innocence to many lands, and even to the moon, before crashing into the seas near the Draugmaw. "And so ended our companionship. But during that time, I continually fed his dreams of grandeur, telling him that his destiny lay not just in ruling Qiangguo but also the Karvak Realm and ultimately the world."

"Why would you tell an impressionable boy such things?" Gaunt demanded.

"Did you never sense the power within him, poet? I was fashioned by an unscrupulous wizard to tap all forms of magic and channel them into usable form. Corrupt magic in particular. I forever feel the call to become monstrous myself. Yet Innocence fed my need for power, and he was by no means evil. If he could embrace his full destiny, I thought I would have all the power I craved, without giving in to the cruel, murderous impulses within me. Without him I was lost. I did not want to be stuffed into the empty place where Skrymir's heart once lay, but once again I could not resist an evil power."

"You're a broken thing," Bone said.

"You should talk, thief."

Gaunt removed the *Chart of Tomorrows* from her gear. "And did you give us this, when we sought the Silk Map?"

"I did. It was on a sudden impulse. I knew it was a powerful thing. I wondered how you would react. I wondered if you would keep it to yourselves, rather than share it with your friends. You did. By this I knew you were essentially selfish people, a fact I shared with Innocence later."

Gaunt frowned. "Selfish we are, though not as regards him. But your reasons seem vague and strange."

If a carpet's ripple could be a shrug, Deadfall managed the trick. "I cannot fully explain my actions. Nonetheless they are my own."

A whistle cut through the air from a nearby, green-crowned sea-cliff. A young voice cried out: "Are you the Swan's friends?"

Gaunt and Bone stared at each other, for the question was most strange. But Erik Glint seemed to understand it as a passphrase. "Aye," he replied, his tone wary, "and the world's enemies."

"What shall be your share?"

"The equal of anyone's."

"Are there those among you who are not Lardermen? Are they prepared to blindfold themselves?"

"They are." Erik nodded to the passengers, as well as those few of his crew he'd recruited in Svanstad. He had warned them they could not see the final approach to Larderland. They all tied cloths over their eyes. Even Katta did this, not mentioning his blindness. Deadfall had previously consented to be rolled up and placed within an unlocked chest.

There came a swoosh and creak: Gaunt heard ropes swinging, straining branches. Footfalls hit the deck. There were perhaps a dozen people, half of whom she guessed were children.

This pilot crew steered them through the last channels to Larderland.

"You may remove your blindfolds," said the young voice, which by now was sounding a trifle familiar. Gaunt did so, and beheld the home of the Lardermen.

Bison might as well have drifted in a circular lake, surrounded on three sides by forested, rocky hills. Gaunt could not see any passage out. The fourth quarter possessed a small riverine valley with a dockland and rising rows of tall, snow-covered houses. Windmills rose on the heights, and waterwheels followed the serpentine twists of the river. It was a place for athletes or mountain goats.

"Welcome to Larderland," said the young voice, and Gaunt saw it belonged to a girl of perhaps nine, capped with an unruly tangle of dark-brown hair, dressed in a peasant tunic but with pants cut short, sandaled even in the snow, carrying a fine shortbow and a gnarled staff with a few carven luck-runes. "I'm Brambletop."

Protocol probably demanded Erik speak first, but Gaunt heard Bone swear, and she suddenly she understood why. She recognized Brambletop, and stepped forward.

"Hello, daughter of Yngvarr Thrall-Taker," Gaunt said.

"Hello," said the girl evenly. "I trust you won't break the peace of Larderland."

"I wasn't aware," Erik said, "you knew Yngvarr and his family."

"Only professionally," Bone said. "As his daughter helped cast me into slavery."

"Ah."

"No one is a slave here," Brambletop said easily. "Even my father obeys that rule."

"Is he here?" Erik said, not sounding pleased at the prospect.

"Oh yes. Many have come home to Larderland, as Fimbulwinter arrives."

Gaunt looked and saw that their pilot crew included adults and children of every hair color, with skin color ranging from pale peach to dark brown.

"I see eight ships at dock," Erik said, "and that one there's Yngvarr's *Iron-beard*." Gaunt noted the ship and its spiked iron barding at prow and stern, useful for impaling ships.

One of the adults spoke up, the one most girded for battle, with his byrnie, a round shield, and a sword that looked to be a khopesh, a hooklike blade from the far southern land of Ma'at. He had a wiry build, dark skin, curly hair, and an Amberhornish accent. "You won't know me, Captain, as I ate from the larder only in the last year. Tlepolemus, a member of the Likedealers."

Erik bowed. To his passengers Erik said, "That means he's a trusted member of the guards hereabouts. Larderland is as near an anarchy as we can arrange, but we need some organization to divvy things up and keep the work going."

Tlepolemus said, "It's also my duty to remind you, if you've a grudge with Yngvarr Thrall-Taker, you keep it to yourselves or settle it on the Hol-mgangway." Here Tlepolemus pointed his khopesh at a ragged-looking pier, shipless, meandering out into the water on the far side of the dockland from the lighthouse. It terminated in a circular platform on stilts, cut from the heart of some gigantic ancient tree, with plenty of room for a duel.

"That I know," Erik said.

"Then be welcome. Tie up at Southpier."

Gaunt was grateful to step upon something stable and was first on the pier, holding out her hand to Bone.

Where the town met the water, its houses looking ready to topple right over, a central square surrounded a vast, gnarled yew tree, supporting no less than four swings. Diving boards extended from all the piers and not a few of the waterfront houses. In the snow-swirled twilight, square and lanes were lit by lampposts stuffed with magical illumination-gems, such as in other towns would only be present in the richest quarters; and the docks were marked by a small lighthouse at the end of the longest pier, its mirrors flashing a fire-born glow onto the timbers, its top flying a black flag with skull and crossed cleavers.

"Pleasant," said Bone, looking around. "It reminds me somewhat of Deep-vein, the thieves' market of Palmary. Although that place is underground and gloomy."

Tlepolemus said. "Captain Glint, have you treasure?"

"Some," Erik said, gesturing, and his men opened chests.

Brambletop said, "You've been gone a long time. That isn't much."

"I lost *Raveneye* and all its goods by the Draugmaw," snapped Erik. "What you see here is everything owed me by every mariner in Svanstad, plus payment from Princess Corinna."

"You must have a good story," said Brambletop. "My mother will want to hear it."

"Your mother?" said Gaunt. She had trouble imagining the woman who would willingly share herself with Yngvarr Thrall-Taker.

"Lead on," said Erik.

And so they passed up the winding streets, past openings in the cliff-rock through which pockets of farmland nestled. All the while youngsters of the town followed them, and it seemed to Gaunt she'd never seen such brash children. Erik told his tale, and some within a pub (marked with the sign of a cleaver-brandishing mermaid) heard a stitch of it and peered out from the doorway.

The procession reached a four-story house of stone, roofed with glass so as to capture warmth for plants of southerly climes. Here they entered the presence, they were informed, of the Lardermistress, Ruvsa the Rose.

She was a short, strong-muscled woman nearing advanced years, dark-haired like Brambletop, and bearing a cruel-looking scar on her neck. She sat in her hothouse among emerald vines and flowers of all colors. Her wicker chair was not quite a throne, but it was elevated and allowed her a clear view of the town, the harbor, and the falling snow. (Gaunt noted that the egress from the harbor was still bafflingly invisible.)

"Welcome back, Erik," Ruvsa said, and her voice was warm as the chamber.

"Delighted to be home, Ruvsa," said Erik with a bow. "Though I'd be more delighted if *Raveneye* had made it back with me. These are my guests—Freidar, Gaunt, Bone, Malin, Katta. And there is a sixth guest whom I have reason to keep hidden aboard my ship, for reasons I will explain in private."

Ruvsa raised her eyebrow, but the Lardermistress merely said, "Welcome to you all, so long as you mind our rules. Freidar the Runewalker is known to me, and of the thieves Gaunt and Bone I have heard tales."

Bone coughed. "It's pleasant to know one's fame has swift feet, but we are not here in our professional capacity, ma'am."

"Good. Young woman, I do not know you, nor you, far-traveled gentleman."

Malin said nothing, her attention drawn by the many exotic plants and the insects buzzing among them.

"I am a baker," Katta said quickly. "I've also mastered caravans, and I know a sutra or two of the Undetermined."

"I feel I could spend many pleasant afternoons talking to all of you," said Ruvsa. "Such are the privileges of a retired pirate queen. My duty lies elsewhere, however."

"Ma'am," Bone said, for he was ever saying things that were unwise to voice, "you're in charge of this hideaway?"

"Larderland is the work of many retired captains," she said, "and we who hate kings and lords will accept none over us. But I admit I have some unofficial sway."

"'Sharpest among equals,' we call her," said Erik.

"And we call Erik Glint a rogue and a flatterer," Ruvsa said. "I would have words with him."

"And I with you, ma'am. *Bison* has secret ways it must travel."

"Indeed! We may find a price for this knowledge. My daughter will be your guide for now, guests of Glint. You may stay aboard your ship, or else there are homes that can serve as inns, if you'll pay in work or coin. I recommend the one they call the Outside Inn."

"Are there musicians?" Gaunt asked.

"There are, at the Mermaid's Cleaver," said Brambletop. "I'll show you there."

The others were more than happy to visit the tavern. The chill nipped them as they left Ruvsa's home, for the respite in the hothouse had lulled Gaunt into thinking the weather had changed.

"I don't like this snow," Freidar said.

"No argument here," Gaunt said, shivering, not saying how Skrymir had bid Innocence bring on the legendary Fimbulwinter, the final snow.

"It's more than that. I sense the North Wind's been riled up by something. This is unnatural. Troll-work."

"*Can* you rile up the North Wind?" Bone mused.

"A farm lad could, in Eventyr Seven," said Malin, looking at all the swings and ropes and even slides tucked here and there around the town.

Freidar noticed what she was studying. "Yes, Malin, this place has many youths. It's a safe place for the Lardermen to leave their offspring while on voyages. They will also bring orphans here, or abandoned children, for their adventuring often brings them to desolate places."

"I am not a child," said Malin.

"No, but you were one not so long ago. Brambletop, perhaps you could show Malin places where a young person can enjoy herself. I know my way to the tavern."

"Gladly," said Brambletop. "Come with me, Malin? I can send my brother, Taper Tom, to guide these worthies. Come with me."

"With me," said Malin, a little hesitantly.

"Is this a good idea, Freidar?" Gaunt asked, looking at Bone, for her memory of Brambletop's father was fresh.

"It is all right," Freidar said. "No harm comes to children here. I swear it."

Gaunt watched Malin and Brambletop head off toward the great tree.

Bone looked down upon swinging youngsters, tree-climbing youngsters, even youngsters diving into the icy water. "Looks like fun."

"Yes," said Gaunt.

The moment was so fresh, crisp, and pleasant, at first he disbelieved what he heard: Gaunt was crying.

"What," he said, "what—what—what—"

He had faced (as he often said to others) sorcerers, assassins, cannibals, demons, and supernatural swarms of bees. He had never been carefree about doing these things, had often been terrified, but he hadn't been at a loss. But Persimmon Gaunt's tears left him at sea. He did not know what to do. He could not throw a dagger at them.

He took her in his arms, tentatively.

Freidar and Katta gently informed them they were in search of beer, and left them alone.

Gaunt gripped Bone almost savagely, head against his shoulder.

"Persimmon," he told her, "it will be all right. Whatever it is. Tell me and I will loot its lair and stab it through the eyes."

A laugh cut through the sobbing. "Bone. Imago. It . . . it all became real for a moment. The absurd . . . the mad truth of our lives. Children. Over there. Playing. Laughing. So ordinary a sight. No? And we've crossed the continent twice, to know such things."

He did not know what to say. They stayed that way a long time.

A boy ran up to them, and Bone clenched his fist, for this gangly seven-year-old with unruly dark hair, a red cap, and a slingshot, was none other than Yngvarr's son.

"Ah," the boy said, "I remember you two. Well, I'm here to guide you."

"We tried to save you," Bone began.

"Taper Tom never needs saving!" the boy said cheerfully.

"It's not worth it, Imago," said Gaunt. "Boy, take us to the tavern. I need a drink."

When they got there, a brawl was raging inside. As they watched, Freidar was thrown out beside a pair of *Bison*'s crew.

"Fight!" yelled Taper Tom in joy and raced inside.

Helping the old Runewalker up, Gaunt said, "What happened?"

"There's a bit of a dispute between Erik's crew and Yngvarr's."

Bone clenched his fist. "You don't say."

Freidar said, "They say the Nine Wolves have declared themselves Skrymir Hollowheart's men."

"That should be Eight Wolves, by the way," Gaunt said.

"And they said many insulting things about the men of Soderland, Garmstad, Ostoland, the Five Fjords, and Oxiland."

"All *Bison*'s crew, in other words," Gaunt said.

Freidar said, "They were on the verge of blows when Katta tried to mediate. That was when Yngvarr backhanded Katta with a mug! Well, by now all in the tavern knew Katta was a blind man. Times may have changed in Kantenjord, but honest folk know you don't bring battle to the helpless."

"Katta's a long way from helpless," Bone noted.

"Shh," said Gaunt.

They slipped within, sizing up the brawl.

It was a fine venue for a fight, with three broad oaken tables to battle upon, weapons and shields hung on the walls, bottles of spirits to be grabbed from the bar, and a blazing fireplace to illuminate the manic scene. Upon the center table, Mad Katta swung this way and that with his staff, connecting with a familiar, massively built, thick-headed foamreaver with a scar on one cheek. Taper Tom was rushing to and fro, launching rocks from his slingshot at Katta. Somehow Katta was always somewhere the stones were not.

Leaping Bison's crew battled *Ironbeard*'s, and Bone wouldn't have been able to tell them apart if he hadn't sailed with *Bison* this long. The northerners, perhaps, wore more scars and furs.

"Enough!" rang out a voice.

Flanked by Malin and Brambletop, followed by some twenty Likedealers, was Tlepolemus, his face twisted in fury. "You break the peace of Larderland and your oaths!" He grabbed two combatants and knocked them together. As they fell in a heap, Tlepolemus bellowed, "Stand down!"

The crewmen seemed ready to settle down, and both parties hesitated. Yet Yngvarr seemed eager to finish Katta, and Katta was focused entirely on the foamreaver.

"You'd side with that nithing Glint?" Taper Tom shouted at Brambletop. "Against your own father?"

"You always take Father's side," she shouted back, "even when he beats you!"

"He made me strong!" said Taper Tom.

"You're no blind man!" Yngvarr said to Katta. "I say you're a liar!"

"Your stench fully compensates for my blindness!" said Katta good-naturedly, to the laughter of the tavern.

Erik Glint now burst in, followed by Ruvsa the Rose herself. "Well!" said Erik. "Yngvarr so fears me he must waylay my crew behind my back? Even one who is blind?"

"I will not speak to the nithing who'd cuckold me," said Yngvarr, still giving battle, still blocked by Katta's staff.

"Husband, cease!" roared Ruvsa, with a voice in her throat Gaunt could only envy. "Not in twenty years has Larderland been so upended! Cease! Or by the founding law your ship is forfeit!"

Now Yngvarr backed away from Katta. "You would not," the foamreaver said.

Tlepolemus broke in. "Is it ever said of Ruvsa the Rose that she speaks idle words?"

"No," Yngvarr spat, "it is not." And he threw down his sword. "If she chooses Erik Glint for her bed, I cannot stop her. But I demand satisfaction from him, for his men have broken the peace and wantonly attacked ours."

"We attacked?" sputtered Freidar.

"You are an idiot, Yngvarr," Ruvsa said. "We are estranged, but I keep my vows better than you keep yours—"

"I demand holmgang!" Yngvarr said. "Erik and I will duel upon the Holmgangway. Or else he must forfeit captaincy, by your precious law."

"We're to leave tomorrow," Erik said, eyes sizing up the younger, larger man. "By tradition a holmgang is fought three days after the challenge or more. I accept if we ignore tradition and fight at midnight."

Yngvarr smiled. "I agree. Midnight then."

Ruvsa said, "Very well."

Tlepolemus said, "On behalf of the Likedealers, I declare this agreed."

"Hold," said Katta. "I would take this challenge, on behalf of the captain."

"What is this?" said Yngvarr.

"Explain yourself!" said Erik.

Katta smiled. "I find this opponent fascinating. I do not fully understand him, and I do not like leaving mysteries behind me. Besides, *Bison* needs its captain. Do you know of one fit to replace you? I would act in your stead."

Gaunt said, "Katta, do you know what you're doing?"

"Usually not," the monk said. "But this time, I believe so . . ."

"I cannot gainsay your argument," Erik said, pounding the table. "If Yngvarr agrees."

"I do not!" snarled the slaver.

"So you fear to fight a blind man?" Katta said gently. "All of *Leaping Bison*'s crew will swear to my condition, having observed me over many days. It will be well known, thanks to the poet Gaunt over there, that Captain Yngvarr Thrall-Taker is afraid of fighting one so infirm. Even a self-proclaimed 'wolf' may not live that down."

"Let it be, then!" snapped Yngvarr. "You die at midnight!" He stalked back to *Ironbeard*.

"You are mad," Erik said, shaking his head.

"I come as advertised," Katta said.

CHAPTER 31

A JOURNEY TO KANTENJORD, CONTINUED

(As told by Haytham ibn Zakwan, gentleman-scholar of Mirabad)

I had eagerly accepted the commissions of Princess Corinna, both in preparing balloons for her use and in piloting one to the land of Swanisle in search of aid for her cause. Thus I spent considerable time in the company of Haboob the efrit, giving me cause time and again to prove I was a gentleman of great patience. Also accompanying me was the Runewalker Nan, who seemed rather constrained pacing out weather-runes in my craft *Rukh*'s gondola, and as man-at-arms a barbaric hairy seventeen-year-old Oxilander named Rolf, whose lord had perished at Garmsmaw Pass.

I would like to claim we made a happy crew, but I am a better inventor than a liar.

On the day I came again into possession of this document, we were descending into Svanstad Fjord, just out of arrow-shot of a blockading fleet of longships fitted with red-and-white sails. Grim weather surrounded Svanstad proper in a shroud of mist, but out here the waters reflected a clear blue sky and white-capped stone heights. It was beautiful. It also afforded me a look at an unexpected sight.

A Kantening longship had pulled up beside the grand, but assiduously neutral, Kpalamaa galleon of Captain Nonyemeko. I stepped carefully around Haboob's brazier, out of the path of Nan as she paced out a rune, through the stacks of yew longbows that were a gift from Swanisle's King Rainjoy, and beside the glowering Rolf, that I might look out the ger's window with a spyglass.

"What is going on?" the young man said. "Have King Rainjoy's ships preceded us to Svanstad?"

"They are days away," Nan said, "and we were lucky to get them at all."

"Thanks to the king's respect for you," I said, tightening the focus. "There. On the longship's deck I see the bandit-warrior of Qiangguo, Snow Pine. And there is Liron Flint the treasure-hunter. And a small crew of Kantenings. Also . . . Eshe, the Kpalamaa spy."

"She is a Swan priestess," Nan said.

"Did I deny it? There is something peculiar here. Snow Pine and Flint are wearing strange masks with flexible tubes resembling reeds . . . these are connected to some apparatus aboard the longship, which Eshe guards. Snow Pine and Flint are jumping overboard! It must be some manner of breathing device, allowing underwater exploration!"

"Do try not to drool over the longbows, O great ibn Zakwan," said the glowering, smoky presence of the efrit.

"That is what Princess Corinna will do," I murmured, knowing well how much Corinna prized these weapons, the only ones to sting the Karvaks at Garmsmaw. I swung the spyglass to peer at the surrounding waters.

"Do not speak that way of a Kantening princess," Rolf said, "infidel."

"Infidel," I said, now scanning the steep rocky shore. "Heathen. Pagan. Enemy. Corinna, whom I greatly admire, has never used those words of me, for she can appreciate the world beyond her nose. Which, I may add, is quite a lovely nose. Hold on, now . . ."

"Perhaps you admire her," Rolf said, "but you speak far too casually of her. I might challenge you for it, were you not essential to the working of this craft."

"I would accept your challenge, oaf, were you not essential to our amusement." It was a mistake to say this, but I was annoyed by the distraction, for I was focused upon three figures on the slopes. Shockingly, I thought they looked familiar.

"Enough!" Rolf drew a sword (a fine one from Corinna's armory, Tancimoor steel, or I'm a Swanling) "Runewalker, how long must we bear his mockery?"

"*His* mockery?" said Haboob. "You wound Haboob of the Horrid Harangues. Have I labored in vain?"

"Young man," snapped Nan. "If you cannot tell by now who deserves your sword-point, there's no help for you. Put that thing away before you hurt yourself. Inventor, what has you so preoccupied?"

I could barely say it. "Lady Steelfox of the Karvaks is on that shore, with her shaman Northwing and one guard."

Rolf said, "Good! We can slay them!" His enthusiasm for killing the nearer infidel seemed to be forgotten.

But I said, "Stop and think! What is their purpose, away from their main force? They must be interested in whatever Snow Pine and Flint are doing. And Steelfox would not endanger herself recklessly. Her shaman will be well-prepared with magics. No, we must press on, deliver our weapons and our news."

Nan said, "Rolf's words have merit. It may be the Swan, or the All-Now, as you prefer, has granted us an opportunity."

"Corinna placed me in charge of this craft," I said.

"And she put me in charge of this mission," Nan said. "And while I don't share Rolf's dislike of your people, Haytham ibn Zakwan, it is true you're no Kantening. The choice is ours. I will try to direct the winds closer to that shore. Rolf, you will prepare to slay the Karvak lady with one of these fine bows."

As we drifted closer to Steelfox, the falcon Qurca rushed by, and I saw upon its foot a message. Gently I opened the tent flap, and in it came.

The event was missed by Nan and Rolf, lost in their own preparations, and Haboob, uncharacteristically, said nothing. I untied the message and read one word in Karvak script.

Why?

I crushed the paper.

"Smoke," I told Haboob, tossing the falcon out the flap. "Hide the balloon."

The efrit seemed to swell and its darkness flowed through the opening in the ger and around the portholes.

"Inventor," Nan said, "you betray Corinna."

I said nothing.

"Infidel," Rolf said, "order your unholy monster to remove that smoke, or I will remove your head."

I drew my scimitar. "I will not murder my former patron. Let Corinna decide my fate."

"I may aid her," Rolf said, "but she is not my liege. For Oxiland, I strike."

Rolf rushed me. I defended.

With her staff Nan traced a rune within the smoke.

Wind rocked the balloon, and from time to time the smoke cleared, showing us careening toward the fjord's cliffs.

Rolf had a young man's reflexes, and I've reached an age when my joints creak even when all is well. Nonetheless his fighting style might be charitably described as rustic, all sweeps and stabs. My training was by contrast rusty, but it had focused on duels in the confined spaces of cities.

I slipped in under his guard, pressed my scimitar to his throat.

"Yield," I said.

He spat in my face.

At that moment I saw Nan aiming through a porthole with a longbow. The old Runewalker lacked the strength to pull it well, but she wasn't about to lose her opportunity.

I had to finish Rolf, but I was loath to kill.

A fresh gale shook the balloon, and I heard Nan gasp, "The shaman," before Rolf shoved me and cut my shoulder with my own blade. To avoid worse hurt I lurched sideways, and, locked together as we were, I and the Kantening fell through the ger's flap.

The fall, to my surprise, was only some twenty feet, for we were rushing close to the waters. I plunged in, losing Rolf in the impact.

In my sputtering and flailing, someone grabbed me from below and hauled me under.

The last thing I expected was to find myself breathing air, but so I was, gasping and dripping upon a muddy surface. At first I believed myself within a cave, but as my eyes adjusted to the rippling light, I saw fish swimming past the boundaries of a bubble of air about ten feet across. Rolf was coughing water beside me.

Above us stood Lady Steelfox, the shaman Northwing, and a Karvak soldier I did not know.

"Can you answer my question, Haytham ibn Zakwan?" said Steelfox in the Karvak tongue.

When I could manage to speak, I answered, "'Why?' I did it . . . because I am shocked by how swiftly your people are using my inventions . . . to conquer the world. And also . . . my head was turned by a woman."

"Honesty!" Steelfox said. "You amaze me."

"I tried to protect you, just now."

"Indeed, Qurca saw and heard. You gave Northwing time to speak with the spirits of these waters. I will spare you, Haytham, though you will now be my slave."

"Will you spare this Kantening warrior?"

"He meant my death. Yours too, I observed."

"He is young and can be a useful slave as well."

Northwing spoke up. "The pompous inventor has a point, Lady. This is one of those we saw in Oxiland. They're often at odds with Soderland. He might come around."

"We shall see. Nine Smilodons, bind them."

In this way we joined Steelfox and Northwing on their sloshing journey toward Snow Pine and Flint. I explained our situation to Rolf, who gave no response but to eye me resentfully. Northwing's bubble of air shifted along with us, and I resolved never to stray far from the shaman. It was awkward travel, trudging down the slope of the fjord bottom, and many times I slipped, fearing that I would pass through the barrier.

The surface we now traveled upon was brittle and variegated, filled with branching structures, and with a gasp I realized what we walked upon.

"What is it?" Northwing asked.

"We're on a coral reef. I never expected to see one so far north—"

"A what?"

"A structure built from the skeletons of tiny, sessile undersea animals—"

"Never mind. Even when you're speaking a language I know, I don't understand you half the time. Still, glad you're alive."

"Likewise."

Steelfox halted, raising her hand. "Something up ahead. Shapes approaching us."

"Fish?" I said.

"Do fish walk, slave?" Steelfox's blade was out, and I grieved that mine was lost somewhere in the waters. Indeed, I almost mourned the loss of Rolf's.

Shapes advanced through the dim green light, three of them. Gradually I made out the details of Karvak armor and weapons, and it dawned on me what the trolls had done.

"They've turned Karvaks into—"

"I know what they've done," Steelfox said.

The three troll-touched Karvaks came to the edge of the air shell and stopped. Green light glinted from what had once been their right eyes. Looking at them, I realized there was no life within the warriors, for two were slain by arrows, and another by fire.

"Warriors!" cried Steelfox, raising her arms. "Acknowledge me!"

The three dead men bowed.

Steelfox let out a long breath. "What is your business here beneath the waves?"

As one the three turned and aimed their swords the direction whence they'd come.

"Lead us there," Steelfox said. And so we followed the dead into darkness. I suppose we all must do so eventually, but this felt like unseemly haste.

We ascended a slope and the light improved, until we could see the sun perhaps twenty feet above. Seven more dead Karvaks gathered around a boulder surrounded by coral and undulating green kelp. Within a fissure in the stone was embedded a peculiar sword whose blade was a violet crystal mirroring its surroundings. So perfect was the reflection that until I recognized the violet tint I saw only a silver hilt hanging suspended in the water.

Beside the sword, seemingly unaware of their danger, were Snow Pine and Liron Flint, connected to the surface by ropes and rubbery breathing tubes. They were struggling to draw the sword from the stone.

"I've heard the tale," I murmured. "The Schismglass, lost here by the hero Wiglaf's fight with a troll-king. It can only be taken from its resting place by one of a ruler's bloodline."

"What does that mean, really?" snapped Northwing.

"I am an inventor. I do not write prophecies."

We watched Flint tug on the sword, to no avail.

The dead warriors advanced.

"Beware!" I cried out.

Snow Pine looked around, and her eyes widened as she recognized that the ten nearby shapes were not kelp, but flesh. She pushed Flint aside and pulled forth the sword.

"Her?" Northwing said. "Never heard she had royal blood."

Perhaps being the mother of the Runethane made her such by default.

"It was not your place to act, slave," Steelfox said.

"And will you act?" I asked. "Mistress? You seem displeased at Jewel-wolf's work." She did not reply.

The dead warriors advanced, and Snow Pine waved the unfamiliar sword, taking its measure. Flint grasped her shoulder, pointing upward. She nodded and shed a belt weighted with rocks, pulling on her rope; he did likewise.

They were hauled upward, but three of the Karvaks removed helmets and sword-belts and armor, rising toward the light. They swam with unnatural speed and grappled the swimmers, weighing them down, slashing with knives. The water darkened.

I could not let my companions—yes, my friends—be slain before my eyes. I strode forward. "Cut me loose, if you will not act!"

As I spoke, Snow Pine's new weapon slashed, and a peculiar thing occurred. The reflective blade glowed with purple light, and images of the three Karvak warriors appeared within it, furious and proud. The bodies, with their green troll-splinters in their eyes, slowly rose toward the surface.

Snow Pine and Flint swam after them, trailing blood.

"Northwing," Steelfox said. "I *must* have that sword. Can you retrieve it?"

"Maybe," said Northwing, and she raised her arms and shut her eyes.

A tendril of air extended from our bubble and lashed through the water. It engulfed the sword in Snow Pine's hand and sucked it away from her. I was obliged to leap away as the blade descended and buried itself in the coral. (Did it seem as though the coral darkened for a cubit all around? Perhaps it did.)

Steelfox tugged at it. It came free, but immediately its reflectiveness ended, and the blade became pure black.

"I see," Steelfox mused. "It does not want me."

"I suspect it's chosen," I said, hoping my old companions were safe aboard their boat.

"No matter," Steelfox said. "We've deprived them of this weapon, and that is enough. Let's head back, Northwing."

Northwing sighed and commenced walking—but soon she halted. The arban of dead warriors blocked their path.

"Stand aside," Steelfox commanded, "or walk with us. I am taking this weapon to the Karvak camp."

The warriors did nothing.

"Well," I said.

"This is Jewelwolf's work," Northwing said. "They must have instructions to claim the sword and nothing else."

"They should obey my commands," Steelfox said, "not Jewelwolf's alone. For in life they served the nation, not my sister."

"Be that as it may," Northwing said, "I can't maintain our air forever."

Rolf laughed.

"So what is it to you, Steelfox?" I said. "A weapon you cannot use. Surely it does not matter if Jewelwolf takes it."

"It matters, traitor," snapped Steelfox. "She's given too much authority to these trolls. She's used vile sorcery to animate the bodies of loyal men. She's usurped authority that belongs only to the khan. My father killed kinsmen for less."

I dared say, "Old friend, your father is not here. You are. What will you do?"

"Silence, slave." Steelfox shut her eyes. "Qurca. Show me what I need to know."

Minutes passed. Sweat beaded on all our faces, especially Northwing's.

"Lady," I began.

"Hush!" Northwing said. "Give her the time she needs."

Soon, Steelfox said, "I know what I need to know. Sister! I have overheard your words, and I know you watch me through your dead servants! They must let us pass! As the sword is of no military value, it will go from my hands to the master of loot, there to be allocated, as is proper, when all the treasures of Svanstad are taken." She laughed. "You cannot kill *my* spy, for he's already flown out of bowshot. I cannot hear your rantings now, sister, but you can hear me. Now you must ask yourself, will you do what is right? Or will you have me for an enemy?"

The dead soldiers moved aside.

"March," Steelfox told us.

At last we staggered onto the fjord's narrow shore. Northwing collapsed. I, too, wanted to rest, but a longship bore down upon us.

Steelfox showed us the sword of Baelscaer. It displayed glints of reflection.

"It is choosing you," Nine Smilodons said.

Steelfox shook her head. "It knows its chosen wielder is near. Snow Pine is on that longship. We need to go. Rolf! I can't trust you. You stay and greet the Kantenings. But cut Haytham's bonds, Nine Smilodons. You and the inventor must carry Northwing."

And so it was. We hurried from that place and ascended the least maddening of the rocky slopes, finding beyond it three horses. I rode behind Northwing to the Karvak camp.

"Thank you," Northwing told me.

I shrugged. "Whatever else happens, you are my friend."

"And I yours. What strange places the spirits have guided us! I need to return something to you. A document that you and Katta and I have all contributed to."

"Indeed! I must see this wonder."

"And continue it, I hope."

"We both will. There should be a record of these strange times."

We rode unmolested to the camp of the Karvaks, through the sea of their living warriors and past the pile of dead ones, some of their eyes faintly glowing, which rose beside the newly constructed trebuchets. Steelfox warily led us first to a tent piled with treasure. True to her word she left Schismglass there. As we came to Steelfox's own great ger, I wondered when Jewelwolf's reprisal would appear, and decided it would be a fine thing to continue our document. *God willing*, I thought, *I shall do so.*

(*As continued by Northwing, Shaman of the True People, though written in the hand of Katta, called the Mad*)

Of the Siege of Svanstad

Well. Easy come, easy go. I've lost Haytham once again. And so, here, despite my current condition, it falls to me to continue. One day the mix of narrators and scripts will drive a scholar mad. This pleases me.

I know, I know, you've heard about my lost hand, but now you wish to know how I sustained these other impressive injuries. Patience. You get beaten up as badly as I've been, you earn the right to a long telling.

So. Jewelwolf didn't retaliate against Steelfox until later that day. Having recovered some strength, I spied upon Svanstad through the eyes of crows, rats, chickens, and cats. In the narrow cobblestone streets, I saw fear everywhere. Now and again the catapults rained the dead upon the city, broken bodies with glowing eyes, corpses that raised themselves up, sometimes shambling or crawling owing to lost limbs. Once I saw a head rolling about in manic glee, biting at passersby till someone stuffed a torch into its mouth. The abler ones caused more trouble. They moved with purpose, setting fire to buildings, slaughtering families while they slept, making coordinated attacks on watchtowers. Sometimes the goals were military, but more often the objective was terror. The animals I inhabited could smell the stench of it, a city sweating with fear.

From time to time my beasts scuttled or winged past others that seemed more than usually aware of the war, for I was not the only shaman in the vicinity. Merely the best. If I was spying on the Kantenings, others were too. Steelfox needed the best information I could give her.

A raven watched a man named Huginn lead a group of Oxilanders from the walls, for their turn at watch was done. They entered a tavern and joined a nondescript Kantening man with a forgettable face. Now a mouse listened to their talk.

"This city is doomed," the forgettable man said. "It is only a matter of time before it drowns in blood."

"Aye, Grundi," Huginn replied. "We know it better than any. The Karvaks are too strong."

"Remember how they came to trade with us?" said a young Oxilander, the same Rolf we'd encountered earlier. "That Steelfox. She isn't so bad . . ."

"Not so bad?" hissed another youth, who'd gone bald early. "They throw captives against the walls, trying to make living ramps. We must kill our Soderland cousins or be overwhelmed."

"Courage, Kollr," said Huginn. "It seems to me we brought this on ourselves, when Loftsson's wife Torfa attacked me for talking peace. Well, Swan's peace to both of them." Here he made the sign of his goddess. "That act must have enraged the Karvaks. And Oxilanders have now warred against them. We can't assume our land will be spared."

"Perhaps," said Grundi, "if Oxilanders made a suitable gesture . . ."

"You mean surrender?" Kollr mocked.

Huginn stroked his chin. "I think I know a suitable gift. Ah, if we could only meet with them again . . ."

Grundi made to speak, but Rolf cut him off. "I know! The walking dead, with the troll-splinters in their eyes. The Karvak princess Jewelwolf can hear and see through them."

"You may be right," Grundi said thoughtfully.

"That's it, then. Listen closely," Huginn said, "we are Oxilanders, men of ice and fire, and we'll not perish here . . ." His instincts must have been good, for he spoke too quietly now for me to overhear.

But meanwhile a cat in the palace had loped near the chamber where A-Girl-Is-A-Joy tended to Snow Pine and Liron Flint, who bore many wounds from their encounter in the fjord. "It was in my hands," the cat overheard Snow Pine say. "I felt its power, rivaling the staff of Wondrous Lady Monkey herself. And I lost it."

"It's not your fault," Flint said. "You must believe me."

"Of course I believe you. Fault! Who cares about fault? I failed! I can't afford to fail in anything, anymore."

"It's because of me, Mother," said Joy. "You both think you have to defend this land because it chose me. It chose me, and everyone else is fighting and dying, but not me, because I don't know how to use the power."

Another spoke, and I shifted the cat to discern who. It was an old Kantening woman, and I realized I'd seen her before, when she'd fired arrows at Steelfox, Nine Smilodons, and me. "Girl, that is not your—"

"Fault, Nan?" Joy said, with a laugh bordering on the hysterical. "Mother is right. Blame doesn't matter anymore. It can all be my fault. I still have to act. Act first, speak later, Walking Stick would say." She strode from the room.

"Where are you going?" came the voice of another Kantening, the changeling Inga.

"To fight the walking dead. Because the only way the power's worked for me is when I've been in danger."

"All right," Inga said, "then I'm coming with you."

"No!" Snow Pine said. "I forbid it, Joy."

"Mother, it's *my life* . . ." Joy said. Yet her anger ended in a gasp.

"The Runemark!" Snow Pine said. "It's glowing. Was it your anger?"

"Partly, Mother. But I can also sense something. Innocence is coming here. To Svanstad. He commands the power of the Great Chain, and the Runemark responds. He's coming by balloon . . . I can see it in my mind. I have to reach him. If he's still the boy I knew, we can talk about this. About everything."

"What about the Runemark?" Nan said, doubt in her voice. "You haven't mastered the power."

"No. But I still have to do this."

"All right," Inga said, "walking dead, power-mad boy, either way I'm coming along."

"We need a balloon too," Joy said. "If there's a fight, I need to meet him away from the city. Nan, will you help us maneuver it?"

"I don't know that anyone can employ Haytham's new balloon," Nan said, "without Haytham. But Walking Stick once managed to use the captured Karvak balloon. And was he not teacher to both you and Innocence Gaunt? He will want to join you, I think."

"What are you doing, then?" Inga said.

"If I am right, I can use the collected troll-shards from the walking dead. I will use them to make a great rune to protect the city. I must try. If we do not meet again . . . it was an honor, Runethane. All of you."

All this needed reporting. But now my attention was drawn away to where a rat observed Princess Corinna leaning against a bookshelf in a library of the Fortress, Walking Stick beside her.

"Your city is doomed," Walking Stick said. "Your southern army, and your allies from Swanisle, will not suffice to break the siege. But there is a way to escape."

"I will not flee on a balloon. I will not abandon my people."

"You do not have to abandon your people. There is a way. But I will not speak of it here." He showed her the magical scroll of Qiangguo. "I fear spies."

"Are we not alone?"

"I wish I was certain. Come. From the point of view of the outside, we will only be gone a short time . . ."

They vanished, and the scroll fell upon the table.

Let it never be said I ignore opportunities. I had the rat leap upon the table and clamp jaws upon the scroll, so as to drag it into a hiding spot.

As it did so, however, its vision swirled, and soon I beheld a place like and yet unlike my homeland, for though covered in trees and mist, it was filled with spindly mountains, and there was no sign of the ocean. Below lay a peak with a crumbled monastery, and looking up at me was a strange gentleman of Qiangguo with a rumpled cloak and a hat made of bark.

"Ah," said the man, and somehow the rat and I heard him perfectly, "you must be the shaman Northwing. I am pleased to meet you. I'm sorry to learn you and Walking Stick are at odds. I confess I dislike the man, but when it comes to the enemies of Qiangguo we are on the same side."

I thought he was missing some essential points, and I tried to explain, but it came out as a squeak.

"Yes," he said, as I seemed to drift among the clouds, "I realize the Karvak nation is not currently attacking Qiangguo, but we both know what the future holds. I offer you two choices. The rat will stay within this scroll either way. You can choose to break contact now, or I will hold your consciousness here, so you will be useless to the Karvaks."

I broke contact. In so doing I lost my connection to the other animals in Svanstad as well.

"Wise . . ." I heard the voice trailing away.

I found myself back in Steelfox's ger, where my body sat cross-legged near the central cauldron. I heard a commotion outside.

Of Jewelwolf's Retaliation

"Are you all right?" Steelfox said. She actually sounded concerned. That was almost more disorienting than the loss of contact.

"I'm fine," I managed to say. "I've been in the heads of a dozen animals. I'd like to see these Karvak shamans try that. Listen, there's much to—"

Nine Smilodons rushed into the tent. "Jewelwolf comes," he said.

"Let her in."

It was just as well that I was not in some animal's mind just now. The Grand Khan's khatun must be greeted with all due respect.

Respect didn't seem to be on Jewelwolf's mind. When entering her sister's tent, even the khatun of all the people of the felt walls should wait patiently by the flap. Instead she left two bodyguards there and strode forward, two swords ostentatious at her belt. Sweeping the ger's interior with a disdainful glance, she pointed at Haytham. "What is this swine doing alive?"

"This swine," said Steelfox, "is the reason we were able to mount this expedition at all."

"He betrayed you."

"He was not then part of the great Karvak nation. Now he is—in the role of a slave."

Haytham bowed, though I didn't miss his scowl.

"Hm. Mercy. Your pattern of weakness is causing many to whisper, sister."

"Who is whispering? I have a sword to answer them."

"But not this sword," Jewelwolf said, patting one of the two she wore.

"So," Steelfox said. "You fail yet another test."

"What are you babbling about now?"

"You take loot on a whim, like a savage. You usurp authority that is not yours. You waste life and energy on cruelty. You sacrilegiously corrupt the bodies of the dead."

"Some saw your balloons as sacrilegious to the face of Father Sky. Every innovation in war seems cruel at first, but the worst cruelty is prolonging battle."

Jewelwolf unsheathed her two swords, and they were both disturbing yet unlike, the black sword Schismglass and the gray saber Crypttongue. "These weapons are said to be rivals, both takers of souls. Yet this is merely a challenge for a strong mind to overcome. As our father overcame the divisions between the nomad tribes . . ."

"Sister," Steelfox said. "I say truly, I fear what you are doing. Father never wanted us to dabble in wicked magic."

"You are narrow-minded. It's the courageous heart that seizes victory. Follow my lead or return home. I will not tolerate your interference again."

Another of Jewelwolf's guards appeared. "Great one. A balloon comes. Its flags claim it has Innocence Gaunt on board."

Jewelwolf sheathed the swords. "The whelp was supposed to remain at the Great Chain!"

Steelfox strode out to see, and I rose, painfully, to follow.

Jewelwolf had another idea. Hesitating at the tent flap, she said. "No, not you, shaman. It is you who empowers my sister to defy me, who turns her against me. I shall assign her a new shaman, a Karvak shaman. And you . . . you will serve me eternally."

I scowled at her. "You don't have the authority to do that."

"Here is my authority," she said, unsheathing Crypttongue and stabbing me through the gut.

Of My Bloodcurdling Scream

It went something like this.

Of My Unexpected Salvation

If you don't feel up to transcribing it, it's not my problem. See how you sound if someone stabs you through the middle. Yes, that's an impressive neck wound you have there, but did Yngvarr Thrall-Taker have a soul-stealing blade? Aha, I thought not. Jewelwolf had two.

And oddly, this saved me. For as I felt my spirit being sucked into one of the sword Crypttongue's many gems, I used every bit of shamanic will left in my wounded body to keep that will and body together.

Jewelwolf's murderous grin changed to anger, and she raised Schismglass. It was not all black in that moment, but reflective, like polished obsidian.

She plunged it into me, beside the first wound.

In addition to the excruciating pain, there was a peculiar relief—for it was as though some of the current sweeping me toward Crypttongue was diverted to Schismglass. Both blades wanted my spirit! They were contesting for it, dogs fighting over a bone.

I don't know what might have happened had the struggle continued. Perhaps my essence would have been rent, or one of the swords would have prevailed. Anyone but I, it's clear, would have been destroyed. Don't give me that look. You have no experience sending your spirit outside your body. I know all the tricks. Are you writing down *everything* I say? When I get my strength back, you're getting a drubbing.

My strength was giving out then. But with a resounding clang of metal, Steelfox knocked the magic blades from my gut.

They did more damage on the way out, but I figured, *Who's complaining?* Although it seemed clear I would die, at least I'd die as me.

Haytham was there too, desperately trying to bind my wounds and saying sweet stupid things about holding on. Such a boy. My vision swam with the sight of Steelfox and Jewelwolf with weapons raised against each other. I noticed Nine Smilodons beside my mistress and Jewelwolf's two guards dead upon the ground. My estimation of Nine Smilodons rose.

Steelfox screamed, "Our father's laws—"

"To hell with our father's laws!" Jewelwolf answered. "Nine Smilodons, subdue your mistress or die!"

"I respectfully decline, khatun," the soldier said.

The falcon Qurca screeched into the tent and savaged Jewelwolf's face. The khatun cursed and tried to skewer the bird with one magic blade or the other, but maybe she had too many options, for Qurca was already wheeling around.

Outside there were shouts of alarm. I heard talk of balloons.

Qurca alighted beside me and Haytham.

"Haytham," Steelfox said, "we're getting out of here."

Jewelwolf, face slashed and seeping in many places, laughed. "There is no help for you, sister. At last I have broken the ice-covered river of your heart, provoked you into violence. Now you are outcast, a traitor, and you have no companion but your own shadow."

"You are wrong," Steelfox said, and for all Jewelwolf's words, I had never before heard so much winter in Steelfox's voice. "I have companions. You have only servants. Even your husband the khan is only a servant."

"You say you have companions," Jewelwolf said. "I will remedy that."

And now I heard the cry of Jewelwolf's horse, Aughatai, the bond-beast who had always so agitated Qurca.

It burst into the tent, whinnying its madness, and as its hooves came down upon Haytham and me, I saw one of its eyes glowing troll-green.

CHAPTER 32

CHAMPIONS

"What are you all doing out here?" Walking Stick said, staring at Joy's right hand. They all stood in the snow-covered courtyard of the Fortress—Joy, Snow Pine, Flint, and Inga on their way to the captured Karvak balloon, Walking Stick on some unknown errand. The city seemed hushed, panic given way to exhaustion. They saw few people.

Joy explained about Innocence.

Walking Stick shut his eyes. He was silent a long moment. "I cannot come with you. I have a duty that I cannot deny."

"What is it, teacher?" Joy could see a weariness in him she'd never seen before.

"If you are going where you are going," Walking Stick said, "then I cannot tell you. May I dissuade you?"

Now it was Joy who shut her eyes. She had a vision of Innocence. He had landed upon the snowy fields near the tents of the Karvak princesses, and he was borne laughing in silk robes upon a litter. He shouted commands to cowled figures with shining serrated swords.

She opened her eyes, shocked by the twisted cruelty upon Innocence's face. Could he have changed so much?

"I have to talk to him," Joy said.

Walking Stick sighed. "All things have their roots and their branches. If you would go, then I suggest you seek out the efrit Haboob, for he may yet have some sympathy for you." He placed his hand upon Joy's head. "You are my beloved student, A-Girl-Is-A-Joy. Would that you had had better teachers. But I have done what I can."

With that he leapt to a nearby townhouse and let himself inside.

"What the hell is he up to?" Snow Pine said.

Some intuition made Joy cold, but it was the warmth building within her hand that she must obey. She'd seek the fire. "Let's find Haboob."

Jewelwolf was not in her tent, so Innocence and Dolma strode up to that of Steelfox. He heard struggle within and turned to Dolma and his escort. The six members of the Fraternity entered fighting stances. He was grateful for their presence. Two pulled the tent flaps aside, while four more slipped into the tent with weapons ready, stepping over the bodies of two dead soldiers.

Innocence could scarcely believe his eyes. Jewelwolf's horse Aughatai was trying to trample Haytham ibn Zakwan and Northwing, who rolled together away from its hooves. Northwing seemed to be unconscious, trailing blood. Steelfox and her bodyguard had swords raised against Jewelwolf, who bore two curious-looking swords in her hands.

"Innocence Gaunt!" Jewelwolf shouted. "Slay my sister."

Innocence could only stare.

"We are sworn to *your* service, Steelfox," Dolma said, though disbelief filled her voice. "What are your commands?"

"Subdue Jewelwolf," Steelfox said. "Do not kill her."

The Fraternity rushed in.

Jewelwolf lashed out with her blades, but now the odds were six to one. She slew two of the dexterous martial artists, one with each sword, but Dolma kicked and knocked one of the blades, a black longsword, out of Jewelwolf's grasp. Nine Smilodons scored a hit upon Jewelwolf's shoulder. Blood stained the khatun's deel, and she sagged.

"Aughatai, to me!" said Jewelwolf.

At once the horse, troll-light glowing from one eye, ran to Jewelwolf's side. Despite her wound, the khatun leapt upon the horse gracefully, and as she galloped out, Innocence thought he'd never seen anyone so beautiful.

Steelfox, for her part, looked very plain, with warts here and there. Gasping, she said, "Our lives are forfeit at this moment. Dolma, you say you serve me. Will you flee with me, though the Karvaks want us dead?"

Dolma hesitated only a moment. "We do not lightly give oaths. You gave us a haven when our land Xembala cast us out. But we also serve Innocence Gaunt."

The homely princess looked at Innocence. "Well?"

Innocence's world seemed to pitch and sway. All he knew at that moment was that while Jewelwolf was beautiful, he trusted Steelfox. "All right. Let's get aboard the balloon. But I don't think the Wind-Tamer on board will help us."

Haytham said, "Northwing will, if the shaman lives. I'm reluctant to move Northwing, but we can't stay here. Help me!"

Innocence helped Haytham, though the inventor's pleas were cacophonous to his ears.

The ragged group struggled toward the balloon, abandoning Innocence's litter. He regarded it as an artifact from ancient times.

An arban of ten Karvak soldiers was already positioned between them and the balloon. More were rushing toward them.

"Stand aside!" Steelfox shouted.

"I'm sorry, Lady," said their commander. "I do not think that would be wise."

Innocence was surprised how ugly the Karvaks all seemed; given his troll-sight he'd assumed men in the business of killing would have appeared more handsome. He raised his hands. "I am Innocence Gaunt, the chosen of the Heavenwalls of Qiangguo. You know of me. The trolls have helped me understand my power. I command you to step aside."

"I'm sorry, Lord Gaunt," said the man. "I can't do that either."

"Lord Gaunt," Innocence mused. "I like that."

He called upon his chi, and with a squint from his splintered eye, he drew upon the power from the distant East. It was as though he flung open a door, and a divine wind blasted its way from his hands to the arban, scattering the men with a thunderclap.

The balloon, too, surged off the ground, and its anchor cable flew loose.

Steelfox rushed forward and grabbed the cable, yanking it downward. Dolma joined her. "Get aboard!" the Karvak princess said.

Innocence weaved as though in a dream, watching the others climb aboard. There was a brief struggle and a Karvak Wind-Tamer was tossed out of the gondola. Soon, at Steelfox's and Dolma's urging, Innocence leapt into the craft.

They lofted skyward, arrows flying after them. Shafts stuck into the bamboo and felt, but the envelope itself was ironsilk.

Steelfox looked through a porthole, down at her people. "'Now you will have no companion but your own shadow,'" she murmured.

"What?" Innocence said.

"It is nothing. Lord Gaunt. We are quite the crew, are we not? I have betrayed my people, as perhaps was my fate all along. My friend and shaman lies dying. And you . . . you appear to be becoming a fine little overlord. Well, what are your plans? Do you think the trolls will give us shelter? I doubt the Kantenings will."

"I . . ." He looked down at the shaman. Northwing was a bloody mess, and while he was no expert on the human body, he'd learned a bit from Walking Stick. He doubted Northwing could survive these wounds.

He knelt, placed his hands gently upon the shaman and willed open the door to power. He stilled his breathing, remembering the frame of mind that went along with the exercises to unblock chi flow. He gently touched the thirty-six essential pressure points and let bursts of his power pulse from the distant Heavenwalls into his hands and thence into Northwing's body. Slowly, carefully . . . if he unleashed too much power it would destabilize things, stop the heart. But in the right measure, it might . . .

The shaman's eyes opened.

". . . Didn't think you had it in you."

"It's not me," he said. "It's the Heavenwalls. And a little of the Chain."

"No matter. Let me sleep. I know, I know. 'Northwing, we're on an out-of-control balloon. Help us steer, Northwing. We're all going to die, North-wing.' You deal with it." With that Northwing fell into a deep slumber.

"You still need to tend to those wounds, Haytham," Innocence said.

"I should do fine, in the absence of insane horses and vengeful Karvaks," snapped Haytham. More gently he added, "That was well done, whatever it was."

"Yes," said Steelfox. "I thank you. I cannot lose any more friends, just now."

"Maybe we should find Skrymir," Innocence said. "Maybe he can mediate whatever's happening between you and your sister—"

Nine Smilodons said, "Lady! Another balloon!"

"Whose?" said Steelfox.

"I'm not sure, but it comes from the city!"

"What?" said Haytham, peering out the porthole. "Yes, that's the one Walking Stick captured. Who is trying to steer it?"

Innocence looked, but he did not need to. "It's A-Girl-Is-A-Joy. I think that's her mother, and her mother's lover, beside her. And the troll-girl. They're coming for us."

Joy hadn't wanted really wanted her mother and Flint and Inga to come aboard the balloon—they were injured, all—but there was no stopping them. It was both a comfort and a worry. She was glad for their help, but there was a desperate edge to them that troubled her. The failure in the fjord weighed on her mother. Snow Pine seemed to channel that anger into a fierce desire to battle the Karvaks, a notion that suited Inga as well. Flint for his part seemed eager to demonstrate his devotion to Snow Pine.

A dangerous mix, all around.

Joy shook her head at them—and then at herself. Here she was, younger than any of them, acting as though they were all her responsibility.

She looked down at besieged Svanstad, with its walls and its burnt-out perimeter, and at the countryside filled with foes. Somehow all these people, so alien to her, were her responsibility.

Innocence, she thought, *what do you think you're doing?*

"Haboob," she said. "That's Innocence Gaunt out there in that balloon. I want you to take me to him."

"O dreadful and imperious girl," the efrit said, taking sooty shape before her, "I decline to do any such thing."

She raised her hand. "Walking Stick was able to control a Charstalker demon. I bet I can do the same to you."

Haboob laughed. "I am no bland demon, full of malice. I am an efrit, full of everything! But especially mockery. In truth, A-Girl-Is-A-Joy, I wish to comply, for my current master Haytham ibn Zakwan is also aboard that vessel, and I would speak with him. However, my skills do not extend to controlling air currents. Do yours?"

She hadn't thought of that. "The power of the Chain seems to enhance whatever I'm already doing. But I have no idea how to control wind."

"You can manipulate chi," her mother said. "I've never understood that craziness, but I've seen it happen. Maybe with the Runemark you can do what Walking Stick could do, and use your vital breath to shape air currents."

"Here goes," Joy said, and raised her hand. Nothing happened.

"It's the lack of fighting," Inga said. "I think you need to be fighting to make anything work. Here, I'll punch you."

"Argh! Hey! Let's see if there are any other options . . ."

Flint was staring through a spyglass at the city. "Something is wrong."

"What?"

"I know that face," Flint said. "Huginn Sharpspear. And some others from Oxiland. They are opening the gates . . ."

Joy's mother said, "Maybe they're coming out to fight."

Inga raised her fist. "At last!"

"No . . ." Flint said, his face pale. "No one is coming out." He swung the spyglass. "The Karvaks. The Karvaks are rushing into the city. As if it was all prearranged."

"He betrayed them," Joy said. "That Huginn, he betrayed them all."

Flint put the spyglass aside. "If they're true to their history the Karvaks will kill almost everyone."

"Take us back, Haboob," Joy said, clenching her fists.

Even the efrit sounded subdued. "I cannot, O child."

Below them the horde rode into Svanstad like a dark, diverted river.

"We can't go back, Joy," Flint said. "We would make no difference."

Joy turned to face the balloon where she knew Innocence flew. "There is one place we might make a difference. He's going to explain himself to me."

She raised her hand, and the Runemark flared red.

Wind gusted and swept them toward the other balloon.

"Do you mean to crash us?" her mother said as their quarry loomed larger. "I'm not complaining. I'm just wondering."

Joy raised her arm again, and the wind ebbed. "Just talk. At first. Just talk . . . Innocence!"

A stone's toss away, the ger's flap opened. It almost seemed a pleasant, ordinary visit in the skies, as people died far below.

"I'm here," Innocence said. His appearance shocked her. He was leaner, fiercer. Green light glowed from one of his eyes. A mark of two interweaving dragons was visible on his forehead. "Hello, Joy. I see we've both . . . changed."

"You more than I."

"I'm not so sure."

"Do you see what's happening down there?"

He lowered his gaze. "What always happens when people defy the Karvaks. But this is the worst of it. After this . . . they bring culture, civilization, peace. No more arguing about kingly succession. Or religion. And women are better off, Joy—"

"Shut up! I can't believe you're going along with them."

"The world's a broken place, Joy. That's not my fault. Maybe you don't know the Kantenings the way I do. Maybe you haven't seen them slaughter each other."

"I know the Kantenings! They're brave and loyal!"

"You're naive."

"Who is that with you . . . is that Princess Steelfox?"

"She's under my protection."

"I don't know you anymore. But I know what I have to do, Innocence." She lifted her hand. "I'm taking Steelfox hostage."

The Karvak princess chuckled. "That may not go quite as you expect."

"Shut up!" Joy raised her hand, and power flared.

Fire, she thought.

Smoke rose from the envelope of the other balloon. It was ironsilk, however, as were the cables beneath. They resisted her power.

The ger below was a different matter. Flame sprouted from its structure.

"No!" Innocence brought his hands together. With a thunderclap the fire went out.

"Fine, be that way!" Joy grabbed a rope and leapt across the gap.

She kicked him on arrival. Startled, he tumbled backward. The others in the ger were at first too shocked to respond.

Joy tied the rope to a bamboo strut and grabbed a sword from the wall.

"You've neglected pugilism," Joy told Innocence. "Shifu would be disappointed."

He wiped blood from his nose. "Never wanted to fight you . . . you've become a maniac, like the Kantenings." He leapt forward and delivered a spinning kick. Objects clattered in the narrow space. She dropped low, but his foot still clipped her head, and colors filled her vision.

She feigned incapacitating pain (it wasn't hard) and shot a punch at his larynx. He gurgled and twisted backward.

Her Runemark flared, as did the mark upon Innocence's forehead.

"Lord Gaunt!" Steelfox said. "Joy!"

"*Lord* Gaunt?" Joy sputtered.

"Both of you!" said the Karvak princess. "Cease! Other balloons come!"

"I think," Snow Pine said, having crossed the span on the rope, "that's a very good reason to take you hostage, Steelfox."

As Snow Pine entered the ger, the black sword in Steelfox's hand changed. Its blade shifted from onyx to a surface perfectly reflective, except for its violet tint. Steelfox raised it, but it seemed to resist her grip.

On instinct, Joy kicked at Steelfox's hand.

The blade fell, and Snow Pine snatched it up.

White-robed, cowled figures in the ger lashed out, but Snow Pine swung once, twice, thrice, and as the warriors fell, their faces appeared, purple and ghostly, as additional images within the reflective blade.

"Stop!" said the surviving white-clad figure. "I have lost too many friends already."

By now Flint had followed Snow Pine into the crowded ger, and he aimed a sword at Nine Smilodons. "Wise advice," he said. "That is Schismglass, now fully awakened in the hand of its chosen wielder, she who claimed it from the depths."

Inga arrived and raised her fist.

"Very well," Steelfox said with a sad smile. "I am your hostage. It will do you little good."

"We'll see," Joy said.

"You don't understand," Haytham said, "and maybe you will believe it from me. Those balloons are under Jewelwolf's command, and the soldiers aboard will kill us all. She and Steelfox have had a falling out."

Joy stared at Innocence, at Steelfox, then turned to her mother. "What do you think?"

"I think we cut our losses and get the hell out of here."

Joy guarded their retreat and was about to leap across when Haytham said, "Take me with you."

"What?" Joy said.

"What?" Steelfox said.

"You need me to handle Haboob. And there's a price. We're going to try to find Corinna. She's a survivor. If anyone lived through that, it's her."

Steelfox said, "You are as changeable as the wind, my inventor."

"I have always loved the wind. You did make me into a slave, Steelfox.

Take care of Northwing. Tell her I'm leaving the journal with her. She'll know what I mean."

When they were across, Snow Pine slashed the rope with Schismglass.

Arrows from the approaching balloons began streaking the air. One hit Snow Pine's hand. Crying out, she kept hold of the rope but lost the blade.

Schismglass fell to the battlefield below.

"Are you all right, Snow Pine?" Innocence called across the widening gap.

"None of your business!" Joy called back, as she helped haul her mother to safety.

"I don't want to be enemies!"

"I don't care about *want* or *fault*!" she shouted back. "Haytham, Haboob, give us altitude!"

"Yes. For now," Haytham said.

The doom of Svanstad fell below them.

CHAPTER 33

FATES

Nan walked a slanted route through the streets of Svanstad, scraping the snow, and sometimes the stone beneath, with troll-shards. She meant by this to begin a vast *odal* rune that stood for "family land" or "inheritance," so as to lend strength to the city's defenders.

As she walked it seemed strange she saw so few people. It was as though it was a plague year and everyone was shut up in their houses. Or as if it were her former house, not so far from Svanstad, the year the last of her and Freidar's sons died. In those days even a cairn would have seemed more companionable, for at least a cairn does not pretend to be a place of joy. She'd borne only a few months of it before asking Freidar if they might move somewhere far from Soderland.

When she was one-quarter done with the rune, she was near the north gate. And so she knew when the gate groaned open and riders began rushing through.

She knew there was no escape, not for most of the citizens, and not for her. There was no way she could complete this rune.

However, she was not wholly committed to a particular shape. A change of plan, and she could be halfway to completing the *kaun* rune, which could mean "torch." She would have to be careful, but it could be done.

Her path led away from the gate district, into a poorer region. The Karvaks would not come here first. The military targets, and the best looting, lay elsewhere. The royal family had demanded a certain amount of stonework in every structure, but here the regulation was often ignored, and so wooden and thatch buildings sprouted everywhere, or else stone buildings of haphazard and sometimes stolen materials. Whenever she glimpsed a rider, she did not stop to verify its identity but hid behind walls or dug into the snow. Whenever she saw someone on foot, Nan warned them to run.

Once an old man said, "I told the man in black, and I'll tell you, I'm not going anywhere!"

"Man in black?" she asked, pausing. "Dark hair? Yellow skin?" But the fellow was already ambling away. She heard screams in the richer districts. There were fewer cries than she might have expected. Perhaps the Karvaks were being more merciful than advertised. But her feet led her on. She had chosen a task, and she would complete it.

It seemed odd to her that in the end Freidar, on his foamreaving trip, had been in less danger than she. Or perhaps that was false, and his doom, too, had come. Then at least she might see him soon.

She saw a boy, with the look of an orphan or a runaway, spot her from a hovel window. "Flee!" she said. "Flee to the harbor and swim! This city is doomed!"

"I'm hiding from the man in black!" he said, apparently trusting her. "He touches people and they disappear! He's gotten everyone!"

She stared at him. Then she could only laugh like a madwoman. Of course. Had she returned to the Fortress, perhaps she too would have been made to vanish by the man in black.

Such was luck, or fate.

"Run!" she said, and she put all her experience of disciplining boys into her voice. "Doom has come to Svanstad! Run, boy! Run!"

He ran.

She could go to her grave in good conscience.

Boys, I will see you soon.

A dozen yards to go.

Jewelwolf rode Aughatai into the city behind the first wave of troops. She had no intention of disciplining them; her instructions were to kill everyone. Even her father had always spared people with useful skills, but Svanstad, and Kantenjord had already claimed too much from her.

Most of all, it had poisoned her sister against her.

She spotted an old man the riders had missed and fired an arrow through his head. A stray cat met the same fate, and a dog, and a bewildered toddler clutching a sword, separated in the chaos from his family. The exercise helped calm her. She reached the Fortress and joined the slaughter of the servants, but by then something was greatly nagging at her.

"There are not enough people, General Ironhorn," she said.

He frowned, as much at the killing, she realized, as at her observation. She resolved to watch him more carefully. But Ironhorn said, "I agree, khatun. We haven't found the princess, the Mad King, or the Retired King. But that aside, the Fortress and city seem nearly deserted. Most of the people must be hidden somewhere."

"Could they have escaped?"

"Our spies reported no escape tunnels. Our allies beyond the fjord have reported no fleeing ships."

Jewelwolf gazed toward the fjord, thinking of the galleon of Kpalamaa. But even it wasn't large enough to house a whole city. "Bring me the traitor," she said.

The Oxilander Huginn Sharpspear was brought before her, the spy Grundi in his wake.

"You have saved me a great deal of trouble," Jewelwolf said, "and you will be rewarded."

"Thank you, Great Khatun," said the stout Kantening chieftain. "We wished only to end the conflict."

"That is my wish as well," Jewelwolf said. "One thing I do not understand. This is a great city. My troops have put scores to death. There should have been thousands."

Grundi said, "I do not understand it, Great Khatun. There must be a hiding place."

Sharpspear seemed genuinely troubled. "Perhaps under the Fortress? That they did not share it with me saddens me greatly—"

A burst of red light blazed forth from the poorest part of the city, and a wall of fire a hundred feet tall began slicing its way through the town. Much of Svanstad was stone, but the flame was so overpowering that fire spread through all parts of the city.

"Up!" Sharpspear said. "To the rooftops! This place is all of stone, but we will need air!"

It seemed good advice. With three arbans beside them, Jewelwolf's company led the horses to the battlements. There they saw a fiery rune inscribed across the city, wreathed in smoke, like the burning shape of a bird. The screams of Karvaks and horses came to Jewelwolf's ears.

"A trap," Jewelwolf said. "Somehow they evacuated the city and set a trap. I have lost many men."

"They didn't tell me?" Sharpspear said. He seemed more troubled by this than by the death and destruction. "Why did they not trust me?"

"Khatun!" Ironhorn approached, ignoring Sharpspear. He offered Jewelwolf a black sword she'd feared she'd never see again. "This weapon was found outside the city gates. It fell from your treacherous sister's balloon."

"Earth and Sky smile upon me," Jewelwolf said. She claimed Schismglass and drew Crypttongue. "This is a sign that my plans are correct. Grundi, attend."

The spy came closer. "Yes, great one. I have wielded Crypttongue before, and if you wish I can do so again—"

His voice broke off in a scream, as she plunged both swords into his chest.

"Why?" he whimpered.

"You have been in the city for days, and somehow the whole population escapes without you knowing? You are either a fool or a traitor. If you are the first, I am rid of you. If you are the second, why, soon I will know all you know."

As Grundi died, Jewelwolf conducted the experiment she'd failed to complete with Steelfox's shaman. With great care she was able to precisely shred Grundi's essence between the weapons. She pored over the contents of his calculating mind and was surprised to see that he'd neither been lax nor treacherous. The Karvaks had simply been outmaneuvered.

She released the remnants of Grundi to the great beyond. The body slumped to the stones.

"I do not know where to search for the missing people," she announced to the grave gaze of Ironhorn and the bulging eyes of Huginn. "But when the flame dies, we will loot this city and raze it. It will be as though it had never been."

Walking Stick leapt through the snow amid the cliffs of the fjord's western side, carrying in his pack the scroll-painting *A Tumult of Trees on Peculiar Peaks*. With his command of chi, no man could follow him, even if they had seen him. With a great effort he jumped fifty feet from a narrow, crumbling ledge to the top of the cliff and looked out upon the ruin of Svanstad. He bowed to whatever departed Runewalker had laid a trap for the nomads.

There was no time to mourn the city. He had to reach the redoubt.

Walking Stick raced through forested country, bursting onto a road. A gaggle of armed peasants was headed north to the defense of Svanstad. "Flee!" he commanded them. "Tell others! Svanstad has fallen! If you wish to fight, take to the mountains and the Skyggeskag, and dig in for a long war. If you cannot do so, return to your homes and surrender as soon as the Karvaks come! There is no dishonor in this! Either way, turn back!"

He ran on into higher country, wreathed in woodlands. Here was a place empty of people, though soon there might be many here, taking up the life of bandits. He climbed a tree and paused for breath before withdrawing the scroll. It seemed no heavier than ever. Peculiar indeed.

The great snowy mountains swirled in his vision, and he looked down upon the tiny figure of the self-portrait of the sage painter. It seemed to Walking Stick there were throngs of other such tiny figures nearby.

"How do they fare?" Walking Stick asked, knowing his words would be conveyed to the guardian of the magic painting.

The self-portrait was stroking a pet rat he'd picked up somewhere. He said, "They are frightened, but they are well. For now. We have never had so many people here before. Thousands! Hunger is the great worry. Remember that time flows swiftly here." He cooed to the rat. "Do not worry, friend Xiao-huang, no one will eat you."

"Tell Princess Corinna they must keep hope. I have not rested since she agreed to have her people shelter in the scroll. I will still not rest until we reach the high pasture, the seter, she called it."

"You can find it?"

"I have a mind for detail, friend."

The self-portrait had to laugh. "That you do, Walking Stick."

"I will yet win this war, portrait."

"I admire your resilience, but how? All you have now is yourself, formidable as you are."

"I have the scroll."

"What you have is a handful of fighting monks and a mob of frightened refugees."

"What I have," Walking Stick said, and the barest hint of a smile crossed his face, "is thousands of trainable people inside a realm of accelerated time flow. Thousands of people who know at last exactly what is at stake. And that means, I have an army."

CHAPTER 34

REUNION

Torches blazed around the perimeter of the great tree stump in the harbor of Larderland. A handful of figures stood upon the meandering pier leading to it, and a crowd upon the shore, including the pensive Bone, Gaunt beside him. Mad Katta stood upon the timbers, and Erik Glint and Freidar the Runewalker beside him. There too was Yngvarr Thrall-Taker with Brambletop and Taper Tom and a few men Bone didn't know, presumably from Yngvarr's crew. A few steps back stood Tlepolemus of the Likedealers, and beside him Ruvsa the Rose.

Yngvarr called out, "To whom shall I pay the one-half man-price when Katta falls?"

"You may discuss rivers flowing upward and pigs flying when they occur," Katta said with a grin. "Now stop avoiding combat!"

"Nithing!" Yngvarr shouted. "Sorcerer! You die now!"

The two stepped onto the great trunk.

Gaunt pushed her way up to Ruvsa. Bone stayed close to Gaunt; he reflected it had been a good policy thus far.

"Must they fight to the death?" Gaunt demanded.

"It is not necessary," Ruvsa said, her face impassive, "but they have agreed to a combat with no surrender. The loser must be unable to respond."

"Let none enter or leave the circle of the tree trunk," called out Tlepolemus, "until the holmgang is done."

Yngvarr fought with an axe, Katta with a staff. Yngvarr, who had mocked Katta's claim to blindness, nevertheless took care to circle quietly behind the monk. Katta for his part took up a defensive posture and waved his staff as though tracing out seagulls' wings in the air.

Bone was about to shout, "Katta, behind you!" but Gaunt seized his arm. "No," she said. "Trust him."

Yngvarr advanced and swung, but Katta dropped low and savagely struck the foamreaver's arm. In what seemed a simultaneous motion, Katta slipped away from Yngvarr's second blow and backed up to the edge of the tree trunk.

Katta was smiling.

"I will end that grin!" Yngvarr said. He lunged.

Katta stepped sideways and again struck for the weapon arm. The foamreaver winced and nearly dropped his axe.

It astounded Bone that Katta could fight so well. Unless . . . yes, if the Nine Wolves (now Eight!) were agents of evil, perhaps Katta could see one, however dimly. But it must not be a sure thing, or Katta would be throwing one of his cakes.

Yngvarr rushed in and scored a blow to Katta's left arm.

The monk must have been in terrible pain; yet he took advantage of the connection to strike Yngvarr's face with the staff. As the foamreaver reeled, Katta brought the staff down upon Yngvarr's weapon hand, and this time Yngvarr dropped the axe.

Yet blood spattered across the great trunk, and it was all Katta's. The monk was moving slower now, and Yngvarr caught him barehanded, tried to choke the life out of him. Katta brought the staff against Yngvarr's neck and pushed back.

Now both men struggled to find their own breath and end the other's.

Katta's blood loss was deciding matters. The monk fell to his knees, still struggling. Now he pitched back. . . .

And out of the night rushed an amorphous shape, a nightmare beast with tassels.

"I respect no man's laws," said Deadfall.

The carpet engulfed Yngvarr, and the foamreaver kicked and struggled, but the life in him ebbed.

"Stop . . ." Katta said, rising to his knees, dropping his staff, and clutching his wound with his left hand. "Deadfall, do not take his life! That was never the goal!"

"As you wish." The carpet unfolded, and a gasping, retching foamreaver crawled to the trunk's edge. Now Deadfall wrapped itself around Katta like a cloak and, Bone suspected, stanched the flow of blood. "I will save yours instead."

"I thought you had not ceased being my friend," Katta said, crawling to Yngvarr's side.

"Was that the purpose of this?" said the carpet. "To draw me out?"

"Among other things." Katta put his hand on Yngvarr's forehead. "Charstalker! You will afflict this man no more! Faced with demons I will never waver; your illusions hold no fear for me! For *Being is as one with Nothing, Nothing is as one with Being, Being is Nothing, and Nothing is Being.*"

Out of Yngvarr's mouth and ears flowed a strange smoke, and within it coiled a fire that needed no fuel to burn.

"We've seen this before," Gaunt said to Bone, "far to the East."

The demonic Charstalker billowed over the dueling trunk, forming three blazing eyes. The Larderlanders gasped.

"Begone!" shouted Katta, and now he was throwing his enchanted cakes into the smoky mass. "You are less than an illusion! You are but the memory of a nightmare! You chased Wondrous Lady Monkey to this land in dreams, and once here you afflicted the Nine Wolves. But your time here is done!"

The Charstalker formed three of the ancient Kantening runes in the air. Bone was no expert, even after traveling with a Runewalker, but he thought they indicated fire, hail, ice, or other such woes. It was a fleeting gesture, however. The Charstalker's substance broke apart. Its smoke drifted away to the east. Katta chanted, *"Travel on, travel on, cross the river of perception, and know at last the other side."*

The demon gone, the Larderlanders broke into excited talking. Tlepolemus bellowed for the other bystanders to stay where they were, and amid the hubbub he knelt beside Yngvarr. "He lives!" said the Likedealer.

"Foul!" called out members of Yngvarr's crew. "Trickery! We have no result!"

Ruvsa said, "Erik Glint, this is all very irregular. Your crew interfered, and your champion used magic."

Gaunt said, "Ruvsa! The carpet Deadfall is part of our quest but hardly part of the crew. And you see the necessity of the magic!"

Bone thought it was a good argument, but Ruvsa raised her hand. "Nevertheless! I must rule that Mad Katta forfeits, and Captain Glint is the losing party!"

Gaunt spoke up. "Ruvsa," she said, "we all saw what Katta did for Yngvarr. For your husband! Does that count for nothing?"

"The holmgang is the holmgang," Ruvsa said. "It comes from long ago. Mercy has no part of it—"

A great booming silenced Ruvsa and the crowd. A splashing and surging rent the lake.

"What is out there?" demanded Tlepolemus. "Send to the lighthouse to illuminate the lake."

"Skrymir," Deadfall said. "He has found me."

Gaunt and Bone backed up a discreet distance from the water. They were not abandoning friends, Bone told himself. Merely getting into maneuvering room. And out of illumination . . .

The lighthouse beam swung to and fro and at last halted to light up a monstrous stony shape, a head and torso of house-like proportions rising from the water.

"Greetings, Lardermen!" boomed a sardonic voice. "I thought I smelled old comrades here. Much have I heard of your exploits, and now I will see your fighting prowess firsthand."

What Bone presumed to be Skrymir Hollowheart rose beside the piers, towering thirty feet above them all, revealing the gash within his stony chest. He looked among the ships and selected the proudest one, *Ironbeard*.

He stepped on it, breaking it in two.

The men still aboard screamed and fled to the pier or the water. Skrymir chuckled and snapped the mast, raising it over his head like a club.

Yngvarr Thrall-Taker, teetering, hauled himself to his feet. He sounded astonished. "Troll-jarl! But I am your *ally*! It is my ship you've destroyed!"

"I will compensate you," boomed Skrymir. He swung the mast onto the island of the holmgang.

The foamreaver stared stupefied at his doom, but Katta, still wrapped in a magic carpet, leapt and knocked Yngvarr out of the way, sprawling men and carpet into the water.

The mast shattered, and fragments sprayed among the onlookers. Some fell, and Bone feared for them.

Skrymir was saying, "Any others seeking compensation? No? Good! For I am Skrymir, and this is the end of the human age. Svanstad has burned, victim of the Karvaks and the death-rune of the Runewalker Nan. In this wolf-time human law is nothing. The codes of pirates and the edicts of kings are null. I demand the return of the entities called Innocence and Deadfall. They once were a set; they will be again!"

Gaunt strode into the torchlight. Bone would have covered his face with his palm, but it was his job to be pulped first, so he scrambled to get in front of her.

"Innocence is not here!" Gaunt shouted. "And Deadfall is a free being!"

"Not here?" Skrymir answered. "But I can smell his essence. Did I track him here, or was it a premonition?"

A boy's voice called out from the darkness above.

"It doesn't matter, troll-jarl! For I've come from the ruins of Svanstad, following *your* scent! I'm here!"

Bone saw the round shadow of a Karvak balloon overhead.

"Delightful!" Skrymir called out. "Now get down here!"

"Leave these people alone!" Innocence said. "Leave my parents alone! Leave Deadfall alone! I want nothing more to do with you! I am chosen of the Heavenwalls of Qiangguo. I am wielder of the power of the Great Chain! I will take no more orders."

"Defiance? Amusing! And pathetic. Come down from there!"

"Skrymir Hollowheart!" called Steelfox from the balloon.

"Ah," said Skrymir. "The elder sister, overshadowed by the younger. So sad. I am aware of your falling out. Do not fear. I will not antagonize the Karvak Realm by killing you. Every single other inhabitant of this island, now . . . well, that's quite possible. We'll see how matters stand."

"Innocence Gaunt is under my protection!"

"I alone decide who plays with my toys."

Skrymir raised a gigantic axe. "Wayland the war-smith made this, his price for our aid in driving the uldra into their retreats. Let us see how it fares against ironsilk." The air boomed as he hurled the weapon.

Bone felt like a mouse with a tiny hammering heart as the axe clove the balloon's gas envelope. With a vast hiss the craft settled onto the great tree in the town square. With a great crash the axe destroyed a house.

Yngvarr sputtered onto the shore. Deadfall, still wrapped around Katta, flew itself and the monk toward the balloon's wreck.

Skrymir stomped onto the boardwalk. Yngvarr shouted, "Arrows!"

"You heard him!" echoed Erik.

"Likedealers, to battle!" shouted Tlepolemus.

Arrows flew and impacted uselessly against Skrymir's bulk. Skrymir thundered up into the town square. He uprooted the great tree, hurling it through the air into the hothouse of Ruvsa, taking the balloon wreckage with it.

"No!" Bone shouted.

"Look!" said Gaunt.

"Mother, Father," said Innocence, and he rushed to them, leaping as they'd seen Walking Stick do in the past. A white-robed warrior followed him, and Bone recognized her as Dolma, of the Fraternity of the Hare. Meanwhile Katta, levitating with the assistance of Deadfall, carried the shaman Northwing to the ground. Steelfox too had survived, though her face was scratched and bloody.

Gaunt and Bone gripped Innocence's arms. He looked terribly changed, and Bone recoiled when he saw a green light emanating from one of Innocence's eyes.

"I know," his son said. "There is much to discuss. But not now. Now it's time to teach the troll-jarl his place."

Katta knelt. "Deadfall, go. I will tend to my own wounds and to Northwing." The carpet released him and shot toward Skrymir. Innocence broke away from his amazed parents and clapped his hands together.

A shockwave split the air, striking Skrymir and cracking his stony chest in tiny fissures. The troll-jarl howled his rage but did not seem otherwise troubled. His rocky hand shot out to seize Innocence, but Deadfall slapped itself against one of his eyes. The troll-jarl's depth perception was ruined, and Skrymir missed Innocence.

Bone and Gaunt shared a wondering look. "Let's help our boy," Bone said.

"Right beside you."

Gaunt, Bone, Dolma, and Steelfox took the opportunity to direct swords and daggers against Skrymir's hand, but it was the metal that fared the worst. Daggers bounced off with sparks, and Steelfox's and Dolma's swords shattered.

Skrymir roared and swatted; he caught Dolma squarely with the middle finger, and she tumbled head over heels into the pit left behind by the great tree.

Bone followed. He found her gasping, her breath ragged, and blood seeped from her in many places. "I am finished, thief," she gasped. "I may be able to fight yet, but I am broken inside. I hope my spirit will be welcomed back to Xembala, as my body was not."

"Dolma," Bone said, holding her hand. "Brave heart. I never understood you, but I know your intentions were good."

"Your son," Dolma said as Gaunt and Innocence arrived. "Teach him to use his power wisely."

"His empty heart," came a voice.

Malin Jorgensdatter arrived, beside Yngvarr and Ruvsa's children, Brambletop and Taper Tom. As Brambletop fired an arrow at the troll-jarl, and Tom followed with a slingshot, Malin added, "Skrymir. The place where his heart used to be. It is a void within him, and he will change depending on what is placed there."

"Like Deadfall," Innocence said.

"Yes. But it does not need to be a magical thing."

"I understand . . ." Dolma said. "For I can yet hear things through my lost ear, and I concealed it in the Trollberg, against the chance of treachery. . . . Often I have heard Skrymir speak of his heart. . . . Yes, I understand what you ask of me, girl. . . ."

"I did not ask anything," Malin said.

But Dolma found some store of strength within her and rose, advancing against Skrymir.

The battle had not gone well for anyone but the troll-jarl, Bone saw.

Scores of Lardermen had been crushed beneath his feet or swatted by his hands. Whatever Dolma planned, he did not think it likely to work. But it might give the others time.

He rushed forward, knowing Gaunt was cursing behind him and employing her bow to give him cover. He leapt upon one of Skrymir's hands, scrambling high so he might aim a dagger at one of the vast troll's eyes.

He threw true. With a burst of blue sparks, his dagger bounced off the eye and plunged into the water.

Skrymir sneered. "You are the one they call the greatest second-story man of the Spiral Sea?"

"No! That was my late cousin, uh, Illusio." He flung another dagger into Skrymir's voluminous mouth. The troll-jarl spat it back at him. Bone yelped and jumped, at the last moment aiming himself for a water trough below. The impact still hurt.

As he rose and shook the water from his head, he heard Innocence call out, "Deadfall! Let's use the trick we used upon the moon! My power and yours!"

Bone extricated himself from the trough, seeing Dolma scaling the troll-arm opposite the one Bone had climbed. Bone chose to be a nuisance, screaming threats at Skrymir, throwing his last daggers, insulting the troll's lineage and implying Skrymir was the son of dung-heaps, not mountains. In return Skrymir obligingly tried to stomp him.

But Bone was not the only threat underfoot. Freidar was running beneath the troll-jarl, a dagger in hand, trailing dark blood.

"Freidar," Bone called, "what—"

"With my own blood I have drawn the ice-rune *isa*!" shouted the Runewalker. "You will be frozen in place for what comes next! Destroy him, chosen of the Heavenwalls—"

In that moment Skrymir plunged down his foot, and Freidar disappeared beneath it. But the foot did not rise.

Bone, quaking, nearly collided with Innocence, who had his arms raised, Deadfall billowing before him.

A thundercrack resounded through Larderland, as Innocence conveyed his power toward Skrymir. The troll-jarl winced and staggered. He might have wished to move, but he could not. His foot seemed rooted in place.

Dolma leapt at that moment and filled the hollow space in Skrymir's chest.

"I die, troll," Bone heard her say. "Let your substance taste my death."

"Foul!" boomed Skrymir. "Such a deed is most foul." He made to claw her out of his innards, but Innocence, falling to his knees, blasted the troll-king once more with his unseen thunderous power.

Skrymir shook with the impact. "You have ceased to be amusing, human—eh?" A black, suckered tentacle whipped from the lake and snagged one of Skrymir's arms.

Skrymir's stony eyes looked toward the ground where Northwing lay. "Shaman, you think to command a kraken? You are mad . . . or you will be before you are done. . . ." Now Skrymir groaned and sagged. "And this one's death falls upon me. . . . Enough. You have won for now, Lardermen. Enjoy the brief victory. Next time I'll not come alone. . . ."

Skrymir made a supreme effort, and massive chunks of earth and stone came loose as he fought free of the island. More tentacles appeared and dragged him into the lake. The waters bubbled and closed over him.

The echoes of their disappearance faded, and there was only snow and moonlight and sounds of pain.

"I—" Bone began.

A stony hand thrust from the water and spread its fingers. A gigantic axe flipped head over handle above Larderland and came gently to the hand. Both sank.

Bone swore. Nothing rose again.

With a rippling in the air, Bone saw that some of the destruction was a mirage, for some ruined buildings stood restored, and some people who'd seemed dead rose to their feet.

Yet Dolma was dead. Freidar was dead. And many others.

Innocence helped Bone rise. "He has powers of illusion," Innocence said.

"He wanted us to lose heart," Bone guessed.

"He hardly needed to," Gaunt said. "Look."

Malin cradled the broken body of Tangletop in her arms, and the Likedealers were bearing away the body of Ruvsa, who had perished with splinters of *Ironbeard*'s mast in her heart. Taper Tom stood shaking beside Yngvarr Thrall-Taker, who stood unmoving as any statue.

"Thank you," Innocence said to Gaunt and Bone. "I brought danger to you. You fought to help me."

Bone stared. What do you say to the child you've barely met?

"Welcome, son," Bone said, and somehow made it sound dignified. The world was spinning.

Innocence sagged. "Father. I need . . ."

The boy seemed just as dizzy as he, and Bone took his arm. Gaunt took the other one. "Whatever you need," she said, "you'll have it."

She was the one good with words. He was glad she was here. They both were here. The world was mad and had trolls, balloons, and sons.

"Mother. I need . . . rest." Bone stared at the green troll-gleam in Innocence's right eye. "I do not know where to turn."

Bone and Gaunt shared a look. He thought she understood his mind, and he hers. They might not be able to trust him, but it did not matter at all. "Come with us," he said. There, adequate words. He could manage.

But not everyone would. Tlepolemus moved away from the funeral procession and knelt beside Malin. He took Tangletop's body from her and rose.

It was to Innocence Gaunt that he spoke. "You, and everyone associated with you, must leave. This place must be abandoned. But first you must leave."

"Yes," Innocence said. "Of course. But how?"

Erik Glint joined them, Mad Katta and Steelfox beside him. Northwing leaned against Steelfox. Erik said, "You will come aboard my ship *Bison*, which has withstood the assault. We will continue our quest to . . . to end the threat of the troll-jarl."

Yngvarr staggered over to them, Taper Tom beside him. "And I," Yngvarr said, "and the best of my men will join you. Mad Katta saved my life—and more—and I owe him blood-debt. Even if I did not, Skrymir broke faith. Let us burn the dead in *Ironbeard*, and sail on to burn Skrymir."

Erik grunted. "Shared hatred is no friendship. But if this is truly Fimbulwinter, shared hate may be like a warm fire. You may come."

Gaunt said, "Bone. Innocence . . . we're together again. We could escape together. But I think we must finish this thing. Is that a troll-splinter I see in your eye?"

Innocence nodded.

To Innocence, Bone said, "Son . . . we have a plan to thwart the troll-jarl. But as long as that splinter is in your eye, we dare not speak of it. Do you understand?"

"I think so," Innocence said. "I will come. I cannot trust my old allies now. I must be free. Deadfall?"

"Yes," said the carpet. "It is my quest as well."

Innocence said, "Steelfox?"

The Karvak princess, supporting the weary Northwing, was staring at the lake. "If my sister is ever to be freed from evil influence, this troll-jarl must die. I will join you—and Northwing, if she is able."

"Try and stop me," the shaman said weakly.

Tlepolemus said to Malin. "Girl. I spoke hastily. You alone may stay, if you wish it. Larderland has ever been a haven for children."

Malin's voice held winter in it. "There are no more havens. I will stop the trolls if I must walk all the way to the North Wind."

CHAPTER 35

PORTALS

Gaunt's heart felt like the strings of a Vestvinden fiddle, and she longed to play one. Alas, as they rowed *Leaping Bison* amid the thousands of rocky islands of Splintrevej, they dared not add any unneeded sound. The hush began as they rowed across the lake to the now-fallen gate of timber leading to a narrow channel with a rooftop of intertwined trees. She and the others often looked down to see if there was a troll, or a kraken, down there. The mood stayed with them over the days, as they passed among steep-cliffed islands in the endlessly falling snow.

She and her son said little. Her son, whom she remembered as a light burden in her arms or a whirlwind underfoot. Now he rowed like a man and brooded like a teenager, and in both respects he seemed to have lost his childhood.

She knew that was not true, however. It was she who had missed it. He'd had his childhood in the Scroll of Years.

Katta and Northwing had both looked at Innocence's troll-splinter, and each had confessed uncertainty as to how to be rid of it.

"It seems entirely fused," Katta had said. "I fear removing it could damage Innocence. Perhaps destroying sight, in one eye at least. I would not wish that on anyone."

"I say destroy the troll it came from," Northwing had said. "Is that possible?"

"It was the troll-jarl himself," Innocence had said. "So at least I am on the right ship." He'd said no more.

"We'll be in sight of the Chain today," Gaunt told him one morning when most of the others still slept at their stony anchorage.

"I know," he said, looking westward. "Mother," he added.

"Captain Glint thinks he can follow Ruvsa's instructions and get us into a tunnel. Then we can cross to the west without fighting anyone."

"I'll fight if I have to."

"I know. I saw. You were brave."

He shrugged, but she saw the words pleased him, a little. But words were failing her. If only she could sing or fiddle.

There was some entertainment in that Katta was transcribing a whispered account from Northwing, using a writing device Haytham had called a noctograph. What she could overhear was fascinating. At one point Northwing screamed, apparently for dramatic effect.

At day's end they did come in sight of the Chain, and its vast links again awed her. Other things had changed, however.

Spydbanen dragonships lay at anchor in the strait. They were roped together into a line, and the ships at either end were tied to sea-stacks rising flush beside the great cliffs of Svardmark and Spydbanen. A barrier of wood and steel and flesh lay between *Bison* and Ruvsa's tunnel.

Erik scratched his beard. "They guard the Chain well."

"I retain my link to the Chain," Innocence said. "I can stir up the atmosphere and scatter them."

"Do you see how they're lashed together? Can you wreck them all? Can you drown the Karvaks?"

"I don't know. Probably not."

Erik pounded the mast. "All that way to get Ruvsa's knowledge. All that death. And it comes to this."

"Then we fight." Yngvarr's serene smile worried Gaunt.

"If the Vindir are with us," declared Taper Tom, "they cannot stand against us."

"We Karvaks will not shirk from fights," Nine Smilodons said. "But let it be a wise one. Under cover of dark."

A thought came to Gaunt, and she rummaged through her gear.

Bone was saying, "Does Ruvsa's tunnel end beyond the second line of ships? If so we have a chance."

"I can't be certain," Erik said.

Steelfox said, "I'm sending my falcon through that tunnel."

"Thank you," Erik said.

Gaunt had their books out—the *Chart of Tomorrows, Lamentations of the Great Historian*, the maps provided by Eshe. "I think there is something—"

She was cut off by Yngvarr. "It's good to know the way, but battle is certain. We should pray to Orm for victory."

Erik said, "You are rededicating yourself to the Vindir, and I respect that. You were inhabited by some manner of demon. Of course you want a connection to the gods. But let those who follow the Vindir pray as they wish, and Swanlings likewise, and followers of Eastern ways in their own manner."

"That is wise, Captain," Steelfox said. "The Universal Khan insisted that no subject be compelled as to their manner of religion. That decision has brought us strength."

"Comrades—" Gaunt tried to put in.

"It will bring us doom," said Yngvarr. "I have fallen away from good clean ways. I have allied with trolls. My crewmates and I must return to the forthright worship of the Vindir. It would be better if all of us did."

"It's unwise to argue cosmic matters," Katta said cheerfully, "when we're all in the same boat. Let us not dwell on the infinities before and behind our present lives, but on this moment, in which we are all shipmates."

Yngvarr stared hard at the monk. "I owe you much. I would be remiss in not bringing you to the right path."

Now the many oarsmen were starting to wrangle, along the old theme of the Swan versus the Vindir.

"Gentlemen—" Gaunt said.

"If I may—" Bone tried to say.

"Enough!" shouted Northwing. The shaman had stayed quiet for most of the voyage, much weakened from a wounding at Jewelwolf's hands. The outburst was startling even to Gaunt. Northwing said, "The poet is trying to tell you something. Listen!"

In the silence, Gaunt coughed and said, "There is another path."

"Another way than the Vindir and the Swan?" said Yngvarr. "Or Katta's strange beliefs?"

"I mean another path for the ship. There is a place upon Svardmark, not so far from here. Lysefoss. It has a waterfall so famous it even appears in a text from Qiangguo. That waterfall plunges directly into the sea."

"So?" said Erik.

Gaunt pulled out her Vestvinden fiddle. "With this, I can commune with the spirit of the waterfall. The *Chart of Tomorrows* says the waterfall is a gateway to the Straits of Tid. We can sail into that realm and find a way to emerge in the seas beyond the strait. We won't need to fight our way through."

"Gaunt is right," Malin said slowly. "Stories say fishermen and their boats have disappeared into the falls near Lysefoss."

Steelfox said, "Qurca has reached the tunnel's end. It is not guarded, but there are ships positioned nearby."

"So," Erik said. "It's to be war or magic."

"If I may," Bone said. "We're on a magical quest already. Let us ante in."

"Ante in?" Erik said.

"A gambling term. Magic is the game we're playing. Let us play it to the full."

Erik nodded. "We make for Lysefoss."

At dusk her son summoned winds, how she did not know—enlivened chi, the Heavenwalls, the Great Chain—regardless, he was a mystery to her. *Bison* raced beyond the Splintrevej and steered by the stars and in the morning reached a high-cliffed place where nine waterfalls plunged into the sea.

From a distance the falls resembled lines of chalk exposed from the cliff-face by the claws of a great beast. Closer up she saw the whiteness moving, like frothy masses of white ants always marching downward to the sea.

"They call the falls proper the Stralendefossen," said Erik, "the glorious falls, or sometimes the Nine Sisters."

"Nine," Malin said. "Like all the worlds known to the Vindir. Ours is but one."

"One keeps us busy," Gaunt said.

"I like looking at them," Malin said.

"I don't," Innocence said unexpectedly. "What should seem beautiful, to me seems ugly. These seem like a mass of broken teeth."

"The troll-splinter," Malin said. "It makes you see the world askew."

"Sk—the troll-jarl. He said it would help me ponder the Great Chain of Unbeing. He was right. I can call upon its power and that of the Heavenwalls too. I'm like a god. A stupid god with a headache. Could I have some ale?"

"You're a little young, aren't you?" Bone said.

Innocence scowled. "I've been getting older as fast as I can."

Gaunt put in, "Maybe a little, Bone. They do start drinking early around here."

"I can't imagine why." Bone passed Innocence a flask.

Innocence winced as he sipped. "You have hardly been in my life enough to tell me what to do."

"Alas," said Bone, "because I would have told you not to insert troll-splinters into your eye!"

"It made sense at the time, O master-thief-father."

Steelfox said, "My sister and the troll-jarl are both members of a society of sorcerers, and they've been trying to influence Innocence in their own ways. It's no wonder he cooperated. He's seen much savagery. They convinced him that a Karvak conquest would improve this land."

Bone grunted, remembering his enslavement.

"Improve it by murdering its inhabitants?" said Gaunt.

"It's not that simple, Mother," said Innocence.

"Isn't it? Why does murder become noble when it's done by one army to another? Svanstad is destroyed? The graveyard is a path to a better world?"

"Please . . . I don't know. Dark is light and night is day. I want the troll-splinter gone. I don't know what I am anymore."

The wind died as *Bison* sailed close enough to be misted by the falls and deafened by the surge. The houses of the braver inhabitants of Lysefoss teetered at the edge of that cliff, and a stone stairway descended for the bravest—or perhaps the maddest—of all.

No one was there today.

Qurca circled high above them. Steelfox said, "Qurca sees an uninhabited town. There are signs of burning."

"Your work," Erik said.

"And mine," Yngvarr said, "it should be said."

"I do not know this town," Steelfox admitted. "It must have resisted."

Erik snapped, "Persimmon Gaunt, be about your work."

As Gaunt readied the Vestvinden fiddle, Steelfox said, "Qurca also sees dragonships on the horizon, heading our way."

"Be about your work quickly," Erik added.

Gaunt played a rendition of Katta's song from Geam, using flourishes picked up from a Kantening standard called the Stonemaiden Sequence.

She put into it her yearning for the distant boy beside her, her vexed but constant love for his father, her sorrow at war, her wonder at this wild landscape and the homesickness it inspired in her for the gentler shores of Swan-isle.

But she knew that an artist's feeling was less than half the game, and she put into her playing all the technical skill she'd been granted at Klarvik.

When she finished, she bowed.

Around the central waterfall, just before the prow of the longship, the spray darkened as though a cloud loomed above. An emptiness formed within that spray, big as a house, and it had the dimensions of a man.

Beyond the man gleamed a quicksilver sea and wheeling stars above it.

"It is worthy," came a whisper upon the wind. "A fitting song for the end of all things. Begin a voyage such as none have dared since the days of the Vindir."

"Thank you," Gaunt said.

"Aye, thanks," muttered Erik, and if ever a command to row was a hushed one, it was Erik Glint's.

Bison passed through the waterfall into the Straits of Tid.

The longship lurched upon a sea lit by two moons, pierced by skerries of melted crystal, adorned by swirling stars, and celebrated by squawking crows. The falcon Qurca shrieked as the crows hounded him, and with claws and beak declared which avian was master of the longship. As the crows veered off, Gaunt saw they had twinkling stars for eyes.

"The scenic route," Bone said.

At first they seemed to ride a shaft of rippling sunlight from the waterfall portal. As Bone spoke the light wavered, dimmed, and vanished like a snuffed sun. All that remained was the double-moonlight in its silver and blue, and its reflection in the skerries, and the star-streaks.

"Indeed," said Steelfox. "But where do we go?"

Malin surprised Gaunt by speaking up. "Spyglass," she said.

Erik gave her one. With great care she climbed the mast and tucked one arm into the lines lashed about it. She pivoted one way and another.

"Is snow falling even here?" Nine Smilodons said.

Gaunt put out her hand. It was indeed.

Northwing spoke. "Well, now. The end of the world, or at least its possibility, is at hand. The spirits here are jabbering about it. All around us, unseen, are men and women and stranger things who believed they lived in the wrong era, or who died well before their time. They all speak of where the current is leading us."

Yngvarr cleared his throat. "It is indeed a strong current. Where do you suppose it leads, witch-woman? Share with us your wisdom."

Even liberated from a demon there was something about Yngvarr that sounded insulting even when he tried to be helpful. But Northwing was surprisingly even-tempered. "Look on the horizon, foamreaver. See the fiery shapes that writhe upon the horizon? I see two dragons warring with each other, and the fury of their fight raises a smoke-cloud that blots the stars."

Gaunt squinted, and though she had to use her imagination, it might be as Northwing said. "Are those the spirits of Svardmark and Spydbanen? Do they struggle even now?"

"It's the image of their spiritual struggle, poet. But that is where the currents of this place lead us, so it will become a real, physical event before long."

Katta said, "Does this war awaken them?"

"Perhaps."

Malin descended the mast, returning the telescope to Erik. "I see many things. There are places that resemble old buildings, or waterfalls, or crystal towers of the uldra. I don't know if any of them lead back into our world."

"We can compare the details to the *Chart of Tomorrows*," Gaunt said.

"We're going to be fighting that current," Bone said. "I hope we have time."

"There's something else," Malin said. "One of the big skerries out there has a split tunnel big enough for a ship. In one direction I see a huge metal structure. In another I see a strange cavern with light of many colors."

"Does it have golden grass?" said Innocence.

"I think it may."

Innocence looked out at the warring dragons. "I know where that tunnel leads. On the one hand, the great structure you see is a stove on the island of Fiskegard, in the home of . . ." He did not finish the sentence.

"A stove?" Erik said.

"Size is distorted by this passage," Innocence said. "On the other hand you will encounter the otherworldly cavern of Sølvlyss. That realm of the otherfolk is somehow stretched between Fiskegard on the one hand and Oxiland on the other."

Looking at a map, Gaunt said, "I don't like the idea of this ship suddenly expanding inside a small building. Innocence, you've been to that other realm?"

He nodded.

"Can you get us from there to Oxiland?"

"Yes. The power is getting easier to control."

"And this time," said Deadfall, startling the crew, "I will be there. I can magnify your energies, Lord Gaunt."

Gaunt raised her eyebrows at hearing that name with "lord" attached. Innocence stroked his chin. "They'll be hostile in Sølvlyss. And when we come through to Oxiland, we'll be inland, near Huginn's place, called Sturla's Steading."

"Is there a river nearby, lad?" Erik said.

"Yes."

"Then we can move the ship by sweat and shoulder, and ride the river to the sea."

"Then let's be about the thing," Yngvarr said. "I don't like that current, and the witch-woman's dragons seem clearer to me."

After two hours of hard rowing they neared Malin's skerry and its tunnel. Taper Tom gasped and pointed.

Out in the strange sea was a silver chariot pulled by a frothing, tentacled disturbance in the water. The man aboard the chariot itself was tall and thin and had a white beard flecked with red. Gold runes covered his black robes like precisely cut bloodstains.

"I know him from descriptions," Gaunt whispered. "The Winterjarl. Author of the *Chart of Tomorrows*."

The chariot swung toward the disturbance on the horizon and was lost to sight.

In the uneasy silence, Innocence called out, "*Leaping Bison!* I have a sort of riddle for you. Imagine you can speak to yourself—a future self who has come to your time and place to talk with you. What is the most important question you can ask?"

As it happened they were a nervous band, and it was a good moment for a puzzle. There were glib answers—"'Where was the woman of my dreams hiding, anyway?'" "'Which town really had the best beer?'"—and funny ones—"'What's that axe doing in your head?'"—but most tried to be thoughtful. Gaunt sensed that despite her son's easy tone, Innocence was deathly worried about something. She thought upon the problem as others offered their answers.

Bone was quick out the gate. "'What moments should I savor?'"

Steelfox was almost as swift. "'What was my worst mistake?'"

Katta said, "'What can I do for you?'"

Northwing said, "'What can I do to make you leave?'" When everyone stared at the shaman, Northwing answered. "Who the hell wants their future ghost haunting them? The past ones are bad enough."

But Deadfall said, "'Who was worthy?'" and his tone raised prickles on Gaunt's neck.

Nine Smilodons replied, "I know who is worthy. But I would ask, 'What should I carry?'"

"That's a practical answer," Erik said with an approving nod. "Funny question, isn't it? It isn't like asking Heaven, or the dead, for answers beyond our ken. My future self. He'd be an ordinary man, wouldn't he, just like me. Only further along." Erik laughed. "I think I'd ask him what he'd ask *his* future self. That might be illuminating."

Malin said, "I would ask where Inga is."

"'Did . . .'" Yngvarr hesitated. "'Did I err?'"

Taper Tom said nothing.

There were some other intriguing answers from the crew—"'One more foamreaving?'" "'What is the most spectacular thing I will ever see?'" "'Has my best moment already come?'" "'Birgita or Eeva?'"—but Gaunt thought most about Nine Smilodons' and Bone's. Implicit in the first was a confidence that future information could be of specific, immediate value to the past. Underlying the second was the assumption that events would not change, that the best one could do was better appreciate them.

And why had Innocence asked in the first place? Because of the vision of the Winterjarl?

"Mother," Innocence said, "do you have an answer?"

Something came to her. "'Do you remember this meeting?'"

"What?" Bone said.

"I would ask her, 'Do you remember this meeting?'" Gaunt looked at their blank faces. "Because, you see, there are two basic possibilities about meeting your future self. If everything is fated, she must remember meeting you, because it's an event in her own past. But if she does not remember, then perhaps everything is not fated. Perhaps she brings news that can change the future. And maybe even she herself doesn't know which is the truth about time. It is something the two of you must decipher together." She shrugged. "I have probably missed something important. I've never met my future self. I hope she has reason to be proud of me."

"That might be what I'd have asked," Innocence said. "'What do you think of me?' But I like your answer better—"

"Beware!" called Steelfox. "Qurca sees something."

"More specifics, perhaps?" Bone drew a dagger.

"Difficult to say. A ship like this one, I think, but it lacks sails, and its construction is peculiar. It is built of many tiny, pale, jagged stones, I would say."

There was whispering among the crew. Malin said, "Do the tiny jagged stones look like fingernails? Or toenails?"

Steelfox stared at her and simultaneously at something else. "Yes. They might. But aboard it . . ."

"Tell us," Gaunt said.

"Aboard it is one who should be dead but isn't. Captain Glint, do you see the ship?"

"I do," Erik said. "And I hope it isn't *Naglfar*, the ship that sails at world's end."

"I do not know what it is," Steelfox said, "or what it portends. But I must go within shouting range, for the Grand Khan is on board."

"What?" Gaunt said. "Jewelwolf's husband is out there?"

"No, not Clifflion. The first Grand Khan. My father."

"Just to clarify," Bone said, "because I am sometimes slow-witted. Your father is dead, yes?"

"Yes. He should not be here in some far Western nightmare. His spirit should be in the skies above the Karvak Realm."

Nine Smilodons surprised Gaunt by speaking. "Then so he is, Lady. This is some apparition meant to trick us." He said more in the Karvak tongue, and she lowered her head.

But a voice called out across the waters from the ship, and Gaunt looked up to behold this *Naglfar*. It sailed silently nearby, a longship of similar dimensions to *Bison* but with only tattered remnants of sail. Its hull did indeed look like thousands of human fingernails all fused together. The agglomeration made her skin crawl.

"*Yngvarr, come to me,*" said the voice. "*Let me repay you your kindness. . . .*"

Yngvarr closed his eyes. "It is Kalim, my brother. The first man I ever slew."

Now came a voice Gaunt did recognize, and it troubled her greatly.

"*Erik,*" said old Nan the Runewalker. "*Erik, you must listen. . . .*"

Erik covered his eyes with his hand. "No! Rowers! Onward!"

Malin cried out, "Nan! Then you are really dead?"

"*We are,*" answered a different voice from *Naglfar*. It was Ruvsa, the Rose of Larderland. "*The ship has come for us, and we go to fight the Vindir, wherever they are. Will you join us?*"

Both Erik and Yngvarr looked stricken.

"No!" shouted Taper Tom.

"No." Malin sounded afraid, but she also sounded focused on matters more important than ships of the dead. "I go to stop the troll-jarl."

"*You're going the wrong way,*" came the voice of Briartop. "*Silly girl.*"

"I am going the right way, and I am not silly, and I am a woman, and you are not Briartop."

Gaunt shouted, "Malin has the right of it! Think! Even if this nail-ship had the power to gather the dead, why would it gather our dead specifically? Why would it take a form exactly the dimensions of our ship? It may be *Naglfar*, but it's our personal *Naglfar*, our nightmare. Something wants us scared."

"You're right, Gaunt!" said Bone. "Also, I don't think dead men's nails are really that reliable a construction material."

"*Clever, clever girl,*" sighed a voice from the nail-ship. "*You were always the brightest of my children.*"

"Father," Gaunt gasped. "You are dead?"

"*As I said, clever. And the most spoiled and selfish. When the monsters of the wizard Spansworth tore your younger siblings apart, did you grow up? No, you spat in the face of everyone who did right by you—your mother and I, your elder sisters, and the bards. Until you took ship to become a harlot of Palmary.*"

"Poet," Gaunt said, but her voice shook.

A new speaker said, "*You think you have a serpent's tooth for a child, Basil of County Gaunt? Look at mine—arrogant, murderous, useless. He turned away from the honest path of a fisherman to become a thief.*"

Bone twitched. "Fishermen drown, Mother."

"*And thieves hang. I never wanted such things for you, but when the sea took your brothers, you took to the road. Did you never wonder what happened to the rest of us, with one less able back?*"

"I . . . I always meant to go back. But years passed, and then decades . . ."

"*Listen to yourself. 'Years passed.' As if you were helpless before them. The truth is, you lived, day after day, each one deciding not to visit us. Until now, when we are all dead, O finest thief in the Spiral Sea.*"

"*At least he has a trade, Illudera Bone,*" called out Basil of County Gaunt. "*My daughter is just a pickpocket.*"

"Poet!" shouted Gaunt.

"*They shame us,*" said the voice of Illudera.

"*They compound their shame with each other,*" answered that of Basil.

"You two," Bone declared, though his hands were shaking, "are perfect for each other."

"Yes," Gaunt managed to say, "find comfort in each other. Do not mock the living. Especially the poets. You can ask Muninn Crowbeard about that."

"*We know all about Crowbeard,*" said Basil. "*How you mocked him into throwing his life away.*"

"He sold me into slavery," said Bone.

"*At least you finally did some useful work,*" said Illudera.

"Leave them alone!" Innocence raised his hands. "I've had enough of my elders telling everyone what to do! Let my parents live their lives. Go away!"

A crackle of unseen energy, and a path of displaced water roared from *Leaping Bison* to *Naglfar*, from the living to the dead. The nail-ship rocked, and as though a spell was broken *Bison*'s foamreavers rowed, putting distance between them. But the shadowy crew rowed as well, and the voice of Freidar called out, *"Beware your power, Askelad! It will eat you alive! We think we wield power, but more often it wields us!"*

And Nan echoed, *"Erik, steer your ship away if you can, but once you've roamed the Straits of Tid, part of you will always be here. Listen, that is the source of us . . . the memory of each of us that resonates within time. . . ."*

"Go!" said Innocence. "Away!" And with each word he sent more of his essence against *Naglfar*, rocking it with wind and wave.

Voices in the musical-sounding language of the Karvaks crossed the quicksilver sea between the ships, and Steelfox and Nine Smilodons looked at each other in anguish. Nine Smilodons rowed like a madman.

There followed voices in three languages Gaunt did not know, though perhaps she'd heard one of them in the marketplaces of the East. Katta and Northwing looked stricken. Yet there was a third mysterious language being called out, and there seemed no one left to be affected by it.

No, there was someone. Deadfall thrashed upon the wet floor of the boat.

"They will destroy us," Deadfall said. "They will weaken our resolve and attack when we are at our most disoriented. Some of them will claim to want otherwise, but they will still attack."

"How can you know this?" Innocence said.

"Lord Gaunt, it is my maker I heard, the evil sorcerer Olob. His shade understands the situation better than the others. They are summoned into being by the Straits of Tid themselves. For time resists alteration."

"We're not trying to alter time!" Bone said. "We're just passing through."

"Nevertheless. Our presence disturbs the forces here. We are confronted with our dead in response."

Innocence looked out into the waters. "Cairn! Do you hear me? You helped me once. Do so again!"

And Gaunt saw a narwhal leap out of the waves, and on it was riding a battle-decked young woman of perhaps sixteen. She raised a polished steel spear, and braided red hair flowed beneath her helmet.

"Ship of nails!" she called out, and her voice was accented with the lilts of the desert lands between the Eldshore and Mirabad. "You have your full complement of dead! You cannot dishearten me. Back! Back into potentiality, and harry this longship no more!"

She threw the spear, and the hull of fingernails and toenails was weakened, for the material shredded at that spot. *Naglfar* took on water and slowed. The warrior looked over her shoulder at *Bison*. "Go! I cannot travel with you, for there are those among you who would cast a shadow upon me. But I will keep your shades from destroying you. Go!"

"Row!" commanded Erik, and the strange warrior receded behind them.

"A chooser—" Yngvarr said, "a chooser—of the—slain. We are—favored—"

As *Naglfar* receded behind them, the dead aboard took on the aspect of shadowy creatures with one blazing eye apiece. They had been Draugar all along.

Bison reached a vast rocky islet with a sea-cave fit for sailing into. Gaunt felt a sickening disorientation as she saw the tunnel fork into two paths, one of which led to the base of a gigantic stove. She preferred to look down the other tunnel, for all that it led somewhere strange. It was easier to look at a different world on her own scale than her own world writ large.

She saw a cavern lit by self-luminous crystals in the primary colors, mixing to form every hue. Golden grassland filled the cavern floor.

In *Bison* went, rowing right down a frothing river, rushing toward a silver castle that made Gaunt think of vast drinking vessels, and daggers, and loot. She looked up at a dim, misty sky, for the cavern was huge enough to form clouds.

"Is this the place you remember?" Bone asked Innocence.

When Innocence didn't reply Gaunt touched her son's shoulder, wondering if she was really allowed to make such gestures, yet. He stared at her hand but didn't shake it off. "Are you all right?"

"I'm . . . all right. Truly all right. The troll-sight has faded." It was true. There was no green gleam in Innocence's eye. "Skrymir can't see through my eyes or hear my speech. Tell me, what is our quest? This may not last."

The other questers shared a look, and Gaunt nodded. It was Malin who said, "We are going to destroy Skrymir's heart."

"I sense where it is," Deadfall said. "Or rather, I did. We will have to return to our world to find it."

"All right," Innocence said. "I'll still help you. I like being free of Skrymir. I am my own master. Or I wish to be. . . ." He hung his head, shook it as if pushing through cobwebs.

"What is it?" Gaunt asked.

"*Naglfar*, if that's what it truly was, was hard to see. In my troll-sight it was beautiful. But it made me sick. Freidar and Nan were kind to me. And Cairn . . ."

"Who is she?" Bone asked. "Gaunt's met her too, but I do not understand what she is or what she wants."

"She claims to serve the Vindir. I don't know why she has an interest in me." He hesitated. "She once posed the question, of what should you ask your future self."

"We have more immediate questions," Gaunt said. "Look."

Riding up to them on smoky gray horses were a dozen warriors in translucent armor. They were what Gaunt's own folk called "delven," with translucent skin and organs beneath the armor. Ropes were thrown to *Bison*, and the riders' leader called out, "Humans! Tie off these lines and be taken to the castle of Sølvlyss. Else you will fight us."

"Go along with it," Erik commanded.

The riders brought *Bison* to the castle, and waiting for them were two mismatched figures. One was a short, wizened gray-skinned man in a brown robe and a wide-brimmed straw hat, who said, "Welcome, foamreavers! I am Earl Morksol, and this is my daughter—"

"Inga!" called out Malin.

Earl Morksol frowned. "Alfhild. Her name is Alfhild."

The second figure was the spitting image of Inga, if Inga had been shorter, slighter, less powerfully muscled. She wore a colorful bunad—a peasant dress—of red and blue.

"You are the girl who was taken," Gaunt said, "when the changeling Inga was left behind."

"Ah!" said the earl. "You know the troll-scion who was offered up, so I might claim a human as my daughter."

Malin said, "But you are not trolls."

"Indeed not! But we had a threefold arrangement with Skrymir Hollowheart. I gave him my daughter to be his foundling. She was before the age of Shaping, and so she took on troll-aspect. Her name is now Rubblewrack. Meanwhile Skrymir gave his daughter to the humans, and we took theirs."

Malin said, "Inga . . . Inga is Skrymir's daughter?"

"Yes," said the earl. "I believe I said that. The important thing is that you are wrong. My daughter is Alfhild. Not Inga."

"Hello, Alfhild," said Malin. "I have a friend who would like to meet you."

"You mean Innocence Gaunt?" snapped Alfhild. "He can't have me. He spurned me once, and I do not forgive."

"Ah," said Innocence in obvious mock sadness. "Well, that is as it may be. Our errand was fruitless. May we be gone?"

"Hold on now," said Morksol. "You've eaten of our food, lad. Maybe just a little, maybe not-quite-willingly. But enough to make you feel at home here, is it not? You should remain in my service, Innocence Gaunt, whether or not Alfhild wants you."

Gaunt saw worry in Innocence's eyes, and she gripped his arm. "None will keep him captive, Earl Morksol. Never again. I swear this."

"His mother, are you?" Morksol said. "And his father beside him too, eh? The familial bond in humans is strong. Perhaps because you're so short-lived. But you both feel great guilt for reasons unclear to me. Love and guilt! Two curses I am luckily spared. You swear to defend him?"

"We do," Bone said. "We will never be lost to each other again, except by death or his own choice."

Alfhild stared at them.

Morksol said, "So be it. But hear my rede. Your son will never feel fully at home, anywhere. The road will always call to him."

"I am familiar with that feeling," Bone said.

"You are a traveler, I see. Tell me your tales, then. We've heard much about the outside world since your son's visit piqued our interest. We know he's not the Runethane, for a Runemarked Queen has arisen."

"Does she live?" Innocence asked, and Alfhild frowned at him.

"Last we heard, yes, though time is strange in your world," said Morksol.

"We must find her," Innocence said.

"We have our own task, lad," Erik said.

"You need to be free of Skrymir," Gaunt whispered in his ear. He nodded.

Alfhild said, "Father, if they are to pass, then a suitable man must be left here to be my plaything." She searched the crew and pointed at Katta. "Perhaps that one."

Katta bowed, but he said, "I think I would disappoint."

Alfhild looked at Northwing. "You are interesting," she said.

Northwing laughed. "I would disappoint in a very different way."

"You people perplex me," Alfhild said. Searching the crew, her gaze settled upon Erik Glint. "You are old, but you might do."

"I am mourning a lost love," Erik said.

"He means my late wife," said Yngvarr.

"She did nothing to dishonor you," said Erik, "nor did I. Our love lived only in the days before she met you."

"Excuse me?" said Alfhild. "Why do you talk about this dead woman when I am here?"

Bone coughed. "Survival? Eh?"

Erik seemed to ignore him. "You do seem magnificent, Princess Alfhild. An exquisite beauty with a commanding mind."

"Yes?" she said. "And?"

"And rather spoiled. But you might grow out of it. I have a proposal."

"You are rather forward."

"It is not, perhaps, what you expect. Travel with us. See the world we mere humans struggle and toil within. Judge me the best way you can, by my craft and my courage. And I will see how you fare. We might come to approve of each other. Either way, we will have learned something."

"The insolence!"

Erik shrugged. "If you are afraid . . ."

"I fear nothing. Father, I shall travel aboard this ship of fools for a time."

"Daughter," said Earl Morksol. "I knew a time like this would come, when you were tempted to leave our domain and see the world of your birth. But I did not wish it to be a time of war. There are ice-gems to be savored and circlets of stolen sunlight, garlands of smoke and brooches of ash. The Whispering Games have yet to commence, the Ceremony of Blazing Frost only a cycle distant. I beg you to defer suitors for a time, and stay."

Alfhild blinked and lowered her head. "If I were uldra I would obey, Father. But I am human, and perhaps it is fitting I see my homeworld in a time of war."

"Then go, and begone from my sight. I will welcome you when you are wiser. You will have no help in the going, however."

Alfhild stepped aboard *Bison*, and Innocence pointed to the great rock around the far side of the moat, whence a stream emerged.

"We are rowing into that?" Erik asked.

"Into the portal I will make," Innocence said, adding, "I hope" in a voice only Gaunt could hear.

Leaping Bison's men threw off the lines and rowed past the stunned warriors on the shore, moving around the strange moat toward the mass of rock from which streamed the peculiar river. As they neared it, Earl Morksol appeared to take leave of his senses, or perhaps find them again. He screeched, "Stop them! Rescue Alfhild! Kill them all!"

Arrows were loosed, and men died from the elf-shot. Gaunt and Bone tried to shield Innocence with their bodies as he raised his arm and a bright light appeared in front of them, a swirling illumination with a ghostly, bleak plain lying at the center of it.

Bison plunged through.

CHAPTER 36

QUEENS

Joy's company flew into the mountains of central Svardmark, seeking shelter and a means of defying Jewelwolf. Among the remote villages and forests they heard rumors that Princess Corinna fought on, aided by a mysterious Man in Black.

At first she doubted these stories, as they often included tales of a Run-emarked Queen who battled Karvaks and walking corpses, who could destroy trolls with a kick, and who could fly. But Snow Pine pointed out to Joy, "There's something to those stories. We may find Corinna and Walking Stick out there too."

So they traced stories as though they were Spring Festival ribbons, moving up into the highlands.

Descending beside a familiar, burnt-out dairy, they encountered bandits by way of a sudden blast of air.

The wind moaned and lashed at them, throwing them toward a granite cliff-face.

"Haboob!" Haytham called. "We need to descend!"

"I know, O Mighty Changeable Inventor!" called the efrit. "You may be a man of shifting loyalties, but I am the polestar of your journeys, the one you may bellow at without fear! I will diminish our height as best I can!"

"Less talk! Less altitude as well!"

"Know that I will mourn your every toenail, cherish every jot in your manuscripts, speak well of you to the women who love you."

"Which women do you speak of?"

"A little focus, man," scoffed Flint.

"You're one to talk," said Snow Pine.

Grownups. Always finding time to bicker. And to talk about sex at ridiculous moments. Someone has to act. Joy felt the cold wind and behind it some entity directing it. She took exception to that.

She allowed herself to feel anger, raised her Runemarked hand, and willed a blast of heat to shred the cold wind.

The attacking weather died away.

The balloon came gently to rest, merely scraping against the cliff. The craft dropped as Haboob eased his fire.

Joy studied the snows beneath them, searching for the reason for the wind. Snow Pine and Flint peered beside her. "Well done," Snow Pine observed.

"Thank you, Mother."

"It seems wisest to stay on your good side, daughter."

"I was raised to believe in filial piety."

"So was I," Snow Pine said. "That didn't stop me from running away from home."

"Well," Joy said, "I seem to have done that already."

"Ha."

Flint said, "I see something in the woods, yonder."

"Your treasure hunter eyes at work?" Snow Pine said.

"Or my interest in self-preservation. There's a group of Kantenings in there."

Joy peered across the white fields toward the piney woods and did indeed see a group of men and women, thick-haired horses among them.

The balloon thudded to the ground beside a waterfall and the stream it birthed. "We had better make contact," Flint said. "Be careful, however! These are people of savage temperament in a time of tumult. And let's be honest, this land *is* a bit primitive. They may react with violence."

Flint's words seemed reasonable, and yet thinking of the Kantenings Joy had fought beside, she felt guilty dismissing them as primitive. She said, "Let's approach with hands open. I want them to see the Runemark."

"Hands open," Snow Pine said, "but weapons nearby. Haytham—"

"I know," said the inventor. "Guard the balloon."

Joy, Snow Pine, and Flint stepped out of the gondola. "You follow me and Flint," Snow Pine began, but Joy cut her off.

"I am the Runethane." Joy led the way.

As they passed the burnt-out dairy, there came a pounding from within the ruin, and a tinkle of laughter.

"Someone's in there," Snow Pine said.

"They can see us, certainly," Flint said, "but I can't see them."

Joy peered inside.

Immediately there burst out three beings who appeared to be young Kantening women dressed for a summer fair. Each had cow's tails. They were talking simultaneously.

"It's too early—this house is ours!"

"Come back in spring!"

"We don't want *you* in any case, girl!"

Joy supposed the open-handed gesture was worth a try.

The girls gasped.

"Is she the Runethane?"

"Isn't that supposed to be a boy?"

"She looks strange."

Joy said, "I am the Runemarked Queen. Who are you?"

"We are uldra," said one of the girls. "This place was occupied by a hay-troll, but he left. Maybe he joined the great troll army. Anyway, it's not yet spring, so humans don't belong up here, Runemarked Queen, if such you are."

"I broke your control of the weather, if you doubt me."

"It wasn't our control of the weather, human."

The Kantenings were approaching on skis. Their leader was a boy who skied with a heavy pouch around his neck. She wondered at his intent, but the uldra seemed sure of it. "He comes to drive us out with salmebok and steel," said the girl who'd spoken earlier. "Let us destroy him!"

Joy knew her loyalties. Yet something made her say, "I am the Runemarked Queen. I might be able to talk them out of it. I might be able to banish you myself. What can you give me to help you?"

One of the uldra hissed and attacked. Out of nowhere she plucked a sword forged of impossibly thin filaments, like a silver labyrinth or a platinum spider's web.

Joy leapt and kicked the sword from the wielder's hand. Next she hit the uldra with the flat of her Runemarked palm. Unseen power flowed forth and knocked the uldra back into her fellows, toppling them into the derelict structure.

The lead skier curved to a stop, his jaw dropping.

The uldra rose unsteadily. The leader recovered her sword and clapped it back into nonexistence. "We have emberfruits and stormberries, meat and milk from frostcattle, bread from dreamwheat. Our bounty can be yours."

The lead skier had removed his skis in order to walk close. He was little more than a boy, though he removed his woolen cap and bowed with ironic courtesy. "Begging your pardon, Lady, but I was passing through and could not help but overhear. Please know I am the soul of discretion and will tell nothing I shouldn't. But I must ask. Isn't it true that eating uldra-food binds a person to your subterranean realms?"

"Untrue!" said one of the girls. "Our realms are not subterranean!"

"They are, rather, extra-terranean!" said another girl.

"Therefore your assumption is all wrong!" said a third. "And furthermore insulting!"

"However," said the ringleader, "this enchantment fades if we bring the food into sunlight. You can then eat it without fear."

"I've heard stories like that." The boy turned to Joy. "I think it's a deal. But we need a lot of food." As more people on skis arrived, the boy bellowed, "The Runethane is here!"

"No time for another of your tall tales, Peik!" shouted a familiar-sounding older man. "You're talking with Karvaks and Karvak agents there."

"Untrue!" Joy shouted, displaying her hand. "I am no Karvak but a daughter of the great land of Qiangguo, the Karvak Realm's old foe! And like it or not, I am the Runethane!"

"She tells the truth, Squire Everart," the boy Peik said. "I saw her battle the uldra with moves no berserker could touch. And I think it was she who broke my Runewalked weather."

"That was you?" Joy said.

Peik bowed. "None other! So you see, we have to get her to the queen and the Man in Black."

"It is they we seek! But first . . . uldra, will you help these people with food? In exchange for the right to remain here?"

The girl said, "I must speak with those beyond. We will return." The cow's-tailed figures swished into the wreckage of the farmhouse. A cheery light glowed within.

"This is most strange," Peik said, "to negotiate with the uldra instead of banishing them. I don't think they'd have agreed without the Runethane. But it is a great boon. The army's greatest weakness is hunger."

"You have an army?" Flint said.

"We do! We let out the story that it's just a rag-tag bunch of bandits, but in truth—"

"In truth, Peik," said the older man, "the Man in Black wants the tongues of people who reveal military details. They will learn all soon enough." Everart bowed. He was leaner than when Joy had seen him at Corinna's council, but she did recognize him. He said, "I'm sorry I doubted you, Runethane. These are difficult times."

Joy bowed in return. "I take it you now believe the Karvaks are a threat?"

"Aye, and those who follow me are sworn to reclaim their homeland. Although after that, there will be a reckoning with the nobility. Things cannot remain as they were . . . ah, here we are."

The oldest uldra girl reemerged. "I am bidden to say, that for the Runethane my liege will provide enough food to maintain a host, in return for the right to inhabit this place for the winter . . . and further for driving out the Spydbanen trolls, who have no business stomping hither and yon over our favorite earthly places. The Svardmark trolls are bad enough but are normally much more tractable."

Joy said, "Tell your liege the Runethane hears and is grateful."

Peik said, "May we encamp in the forest yonder? Perhaps even build habitations?"

"That seems acceptable," the uldra said.

Snow Pine spoke up, "Are there other realms like yours who could help us?"

"They will make their own decisions, though none of them like Spydbanen trolls."

In two heartbeats Flint had a map out. "Show us."

A cow's tail swished and pointed to four locations.

Everart said, "The Skyggeskag, the Morskag, the mountains between Vesthall and Grimgard, and Fiskegard."

Peik said, "The Morskag's dicey, and Fiskegard's probably out of reach, but this gives us possibilities."

"We will bring food tomorrow," said the uldra girl. She turned to Joy. "Uphold your end of the bargain. The death of your kind means little to us. The life of the land means a great deal."

"I swear to fight the invaders," Joy said.

The uldra withdrew without another word.

"Whew," Peik said. "This would have been a tough one."

"I think," said Everart, "the rest of us can wait here for the promised food. You, Peik, had better get these visitors to headquarters."

"You're just tired of lye-fish."

"No true patriotic Kantening gets tired of lye-fish! But a little variety is welcome."

"Headquarters" turned out to be a seter, protected by high forests that could be skied, rope bridges that could be wobbled across, hidden tunnels that could be shuffled through. The balloon had to be left behind, after much argument, because Peik insisted no flying craft were allowed in Sky Margin, the secret redoubt of the resistance. But Haboob's brazier came along, for Haytham was reluctant to part company with it. Joy thought the inventor and the efrit were becoming an old married couple. They bickered enough for it.

"When I consented to joining you in the skies, O brilliant Haytham, I did not imagine so much walking would be involved!"

"If you prefer plummeting down a cliff, O Haboob of the Hundred Histrionics, that can be arranged."

Their voices echoed through the third tunnel they'd traversed. A voice ahead called, "The superior man speaks and everyone listens."

Peik replied, "No, the superior man waits for everyone else to speak, and in that way he learns the most."

"Welcome back, Peik. You bring recruits?"

"You could say that!"

They passed a guard post, a side-cave where twenty archers waved at them, and a pit trap where they had to carefully step single-file. Beyond that they blinked in the light at a collection of boulders primed to spill across the entrance. More archers waited on a cliff directly overhead and in nearby treetops. Joy marveled that they'd fortified so well, so quickly.

"Princess Corinna is not entirely trusting," Haytham said.

"That's Queen Corinna," Peik said. "The harsh conditions proved too much for the Retired King and the Mad King, Swan rest them. Come along, now."

They descended a narrow path, noting more traps and ambush points, and reached a modest pasture surrounded by cliffs. The rock faces bulged slightly outward as they rose, leaving a ragged gray rectangle of sky overhead. A pair of farmsteads shared the seter, one on either side of a stream. Some fifty men were busy with tasks in both locations.

"Bandit country," said Snow Pine. "It reminds me of home."

"Where is the army?" Flint asked. "Surely this is not all of them?"

"Can you guess?" Peik said.

"The scroll!" Joy said. "Walking Stick has them in *A Tumult of Trees on Peculiar Peaks*."

"That's it." Peik sounded pleased. "They say you were born in there. You and Lord Gaunt, vile son of the villains Gaunt and Bone."

"Gaunt and Bone are not villains!" Snow Pine said.

Joy said, "Innocence is confused, not vile."

Peik held up his hands. "I surrender, miladies. I don't have anything personally against them. The Man in Black is in charge of legends."

"Legends?" Flint said.

"The Man in Black says every army needs legends."

"I want to talk to the Man in Black," Joy said.

The Man in Black and the Mountain Queen dwelled in the farther of the two farms, in a simple thatch-roofed building with an iron stove. A Kantening girl served the newcomers drinks. Haytham took coffee, and the others had tea. The masters of the resistance came out to greet them.

"It is a pleasure to see you again," Walking Stick said.

"Likewise," said Corinna, and her eyes lingered on Haytham. "Inventor."

"Queen," said he.

"Let us sit." Corinna accepted coffee and Walking Stick tea. Corinna said, "Well. Welcome to Sky Margin. I cannot pronounce the name in the Tongue of the Tortoise Shell. Tell me of your journeys?"

They spoke of their adventures, and Corinna said, "This is wonderful news you bring, of the uldra and their offer of food. We have a willing army but a hungry one. We cannot do more than harry the Karvaks so far. And it's good that you found us, but even better that you didn't reach us in the balloon. We don't want Karvak observers spotting this place."

Haytham said, "We'd have had trouble landing a balloon here in any event. This is a wonderfully defensible position. My compliments."

Corinna smiled. "I enjoy your compliments."

Walking Stick nodded. "It is said in the *Classic of War*, 'The natural formation of the country is the soldier's best ally.' The Kantenings are fortunate in their terrain. And even this spot could fall to the Karvaks, with their shaman-guided balloons."

Corinna said, "We have few Runewalkers to repel the shamans, though we are training more."

"The queen handles the Runewalkers directly," Walking Stick added, studying his tea. "To understand the magics of a distant land is beyond me. But the common peasant is the common peasant. In some respects my people share more with the farmers here than with our nomadic neighbors. These are folk I can train."

Corinna said, "We have an army of thousands—people saved from Svanstad, warriors late to the siege, Everart's rebel peasants, and others who've joined us from the surrounding lands. Walking Stick and his chosen commanders train them constantly. At first I disliked his methods. He cares little for bravery or glory. But what we need is victory."

Walking Stick said, "The *Classic of Conduct* tells us, 'To lead an uninstructed people into war is to throw them away.'"

"So he instructs them," Corinna said. "By training them inside the scroll he swiftly builds a skilled force. But it's hard to feed them."

"It is a treacherous balance," Walking Stick said. "The accelerated time flow has given us a disciplined army, but the cost is an accelerated need for food."

"We've leaned on everything," Corinna said. "Stockfish, hardtack, winter berries. We slaughter precious livestock, gambling we can find more later. We even peel tree bark for our bread. The uldra's help could mean the difference between victory and defeat."

"I'll go to each of the uldra-places we can reach," Joy said. "They responded to me, or to the Runemark."

"I'm grateful," Corinna said.

"I wonder . . ." Joy looked at Haytham. "There were many more mountains in the scroll. We could never reach them. They were as untouchable as the dragons that would sometimes fly by in the distance. But perhaps a balloon could go there—and return with more food. And *you* could build a balloon much faster in there than out here."

Haytham scratched his chin. "I could do both. The difficulty is finding a safe, portable heat source. There is only one Haboob."

"And well do you remember it!" said a voice from the brazier, startling Joy.

"Karvak Charstalker-braziers will be a target of our raids," Walking Stick said. "Meanwhile I think your company should enter the scroll with us, to see what we've accomplished there. I am due to train fresh recruits."

The new men—and some women—were mainly Soderlanders ready to fight for their homeland, and folk from the Five Fjords who thought their leaders were mad to cooperate with the Karvaks. There were also a few Oxilanders who feared their land would be invaded next. Walking Stick struggled to forge them into a unit.

"These are raw recruits," Walking Stick sighed. "They will take time."

The recruits mock-fought with crazy ferocity. That was part of the trouble. They were eager for fighting, but not prepared for marching, maneuvers, or holding ground. They all wanted to be heroes, not soldiers. Some had somehow managed to get drunk. A certain Magnus—a young, powerful warrior and a natural focus for other fighters—openly mocked the trainers.

"Where is Queen Corinna? That's what I want to know!"

Walking Stick called out, "She has her duties and you have yours. Get into formation and learn to fight."

"I already know how to fight, old man! I don't need fancy philosophy to swing an axe!"

There were shouts of agreement.

Magnus grinned, sensing the tide was turning his way. "These new ways may suit *Eastern* men, whose blood is cold! But we Kantenings must return to the ways of our ancestors! The ways of hot fury!"

Others called out, "Our berserkers will destroy the invaders!" and "We will take to our dragonships!"

Walking Stick raised his namesake. He swung it above his head in a blurry circle. While this was not exactly an argument in itself, it did refocus the recruits' attention. He ceased the spinning and struck a rock with a disconcerting boom. "You will indeed need all your fury! Your berserkers and your ships will be needed before we're done. But fury alone will not save you. Discipline is what you need, and a sense of unity."

Magnus stuck to his theme. "Who is *he* to speak to us?"

"One who knows war! You speak of bravery as the greatest virtue? But I do not want warriors who will attack a troll unarmed or cross a fjord without a boat." There was laughter at that. "The greatest virtue in war is thought. There is art to war. But do not fear. You have the foundation. You love your land, you will fight for it. Fight for victory, not for show. Spare no thought for the songs of the skalds. In victory there is time for all that."

"We can't trust him!" Magnus yelled. "He's no Kantening!"

"He's an outlander!" another man called out.

"He looks like the invaders!" said another.

"I beg your pardon," Walking Stick fumed at that last. Joy knew the story of the War Sage who'd liberally decapitated recruits who wouldn't listen. These men didn't realize how easy they had it. But the beatings were about to start.

She put her hand on Walking Stick's arm.

"May I speak to them?"

After studying her a long moment he nodded.

She harvested her chi and reached Magnus's rock in two great leaps. The man stared at her, confounded.

"Warriors!" she yelled. "I am Joy. Daughter of Snow . . . Joy Snøsdatter! You may have heard of me."

There were mutters and scattered cheers of assent. "I saw her fighting in the sky!" And Peik shouted, "I saw her battle the uldra!"

"Listen to me! This man is a warrior and my teacher. He speaks the truth. You must train. You are already heroes. Simply by making it here you've proved that. But now you must become a unified force. An army for Kantenjord."

Queen Corinna had emerged from the monastery with Snow Pine, Flint, and Haytham, where they'd been discussing the building of balloons. Corinna bore a look of concern, but Joy's instincts led her on.

"Your land touched me before I ever came here! I believe it is my purpose to defend you! Unite as an army, and I will fight at your head!"

And she revealed her hand, turning so all could see.

"The Runemark!" someone cried. "Then it's true!"

Someone else said, "The Runemarked Queen!"

Beside her, Magnus scoffed. "How could this be our foretold champion? She is a child, an alien, an outlander! She looks more like the invaders than like us!"

Others took up the theme. "A girl? You would have a girl rule us?"

"Only a real Kantenjord *man* could be the chosen one!"

"This is some trick."

"The Easterners want to conquer us from within and without!"

Joy could feel the crowd's emotions shifting like a balloon lost in the wind. She looked to the queen, reading fear and dismay on Corinna's face.

The real question was, was it fear about fighting Karvaks and trolls? Joy remembered Corinna wanting to send her away from Svanstad. Despite her apparent friendliness, did the queen share the others' feelings? Did she need the Runethane to be a man? And a pale, native one at that?

Well? Joy silently mouthed the word at her.

A voice from the edge of the crowd turned all their heads. "Swan's Blood! Look at the sky!"

They looked and saw a pair of clouds swirling into complex shapes, shapes resembling winged dragons approaching each other sidelong. As the humans watched, the clouds touched heads, and a peculiar transformation took place. The two sideways-looking eyes seemed to become a pair of forward-looking eyes. Two toothy mouths seemed to become one much larger toothy mouth. Claws and wings now seemed frills upon an enormous face looking down on the gathering with an immense hunger.

"Taotie!" said Snow Pine. With astonishing bravery her mother grabbed a sword from a slack-jawed recruit and stood ready to confront the monster. "Everyone into the forest! I've seen this before. It will try to blast you with wind, knock you off the mountain!"

The taotie roared, and the echo reverberated through the mist-cloaked mountains.

Upon the boulder, Joy stared. She stood alone, for Magnus had yelped and ran.

She wanted to obey her mother's command, but she couldn't move. The entity had a perplexing beauty. It seemed to belong to both this world and another reality, one of pure form. The taotie's aspect shifted from one forward-facing being to two sideways-facing creatures in the blink of an eye and back again.

As the recruits dispersed, the taotie opened its titanic jaws and plunged toward Snow Pine. Flint was running toward her, shouting, waving a sword. Once, Joy remembered, her mother and her lover had wielded magic weapons. They had no such advantage now. Only courage. And love.

And me.

Joy's chi was already awakened from her leap. She used it to draw forth the power of the Great Chain. This time instead of blasting away with invisible force she wrapped that force around her body and leapt between the taotie's eyes.

Her energies tore asunder the cloudy head.

The concussion in the air toppled her hard onto the grass. Her side hurt. She hoped she hadn't broken a rib.

Above her the clouds composing the taotie split and retreated, two separate cloud dragons again, flying toward what passed within the scroll for east and west.

Snow Pine and Flint helped her up. Flint said, "I have no idea what just happened. But it was impressive!"

"It was a spirit of the scroll's reality," Snow Pine said. "I met one long ago. Maybe the same one."

"Why did it come here?" Joy asked.

"I think it may have been attracted by the new power within you."

"Look," Flint said.

Corinna returned, and shame-faced recruits shuffled back into the clearing, Magnus among them. Joy's eyes met Corinna's. At that moment, the queen of Soderland looked little more than a girl herself, despite the difference in their ages.

As Corinna ascended the boulder once occupied by Magnus and Joy, the queen's eyes showed the worry of one who wished her elders were still able to guide her.

But when she spoke, that was swept aside by the power of her royal voice. "Kantenings!" Corinna boomed, pointing at Joy. "Well do I know this girl!

Well do I know her courage! Now, you all do as well! Know this also! I choose her to be my champion!"

Corinna met the gaze of Magnus, and Magnus lowered his head. He was the first to raise his weapon. "Hail, Joy Snøsdatter!"

"Hail!" called out others, and "Runethane!" and "Soderland!" or "Five Fjords!" or "Oxiland!"

Someone cried out, "For Kantenjord!" and it echoed around the throng.

"Kantenjord!"

"Joy Snøsdatter!"

"Kantenjord!"

"Runethane!"

"Runemarked Queen!"

"Kantenjord!"

"Runemarked Queen!"

Even with her side screaming in pain, A-Girl-Is-A-Joy, daughter of Snow Pine, felt she was ascending like a pine indeed.

She hoped she would not end up breaking, and falling like snow.

CHAPTER 37

HEARTS

Innocence recognized the great boulder upon the barren plain. He had nearly frozen to death here.

It was colder now. The wind keened. White covered the brown scrubland and the mountains. Half the sky was thick with cloud, though no snow fell.

Leaping Bison leapt no more. It was landlocked beside the vast boulder, whose bulk kept the ship upright.

As they got their bearings and saw to the wounds of those who'd survived the uldras' arrows, Innocence felt a stabbing pain in his right eye. The troll-splinter there had awakened. At once his companions seemed to change.

Before they had seemed ordinary men and women or, in Northwing's case, neither. They'd been mostly no uglier nor comelier than anyone else. His parents commanded his attention because he saw himself in their faces, and because Gaunt in particular stirred his memory, but he did not find them lovely. He supposed some of the other men were handsome, but they made little impression on him. Malin he found pretty, though her lack of eye contact, and her unwavering focus, unnerved him. Steelfox's athletic body drew his eye, but she was a trained killer, and knowledge of that slew much of his appreciation. And Alfhild might have been gorgeous—he'd found her so on their first meeting—but her chief expressions were haughtiness, cruelty, scorn, and more haughtiness.

The transformation of his vision was even more unnerving now than the first time. Suddenly the crew of *Bison* transformed into extremes. Much of the crew became ugly. Katta and Malin were particularly hideous. A fraction remained plain—the crewmen Yngvarr had brought, Taper Tom, Erik Glint, and Innocence's thieving father.

Yngvarr retained his good looks, though it seemed to Innocence the slaver had been comelier when the demon was within him. Alfhild was even more attractive than before. He looked away from her, fearing for the captain, whose arm she kept touching.

He could trust his mother's ugliness. And his father—well, he wasn't a good man, but he wasn't so bad, and he was on Innocence's side. He understood that now. He didn't know where his path led, beyond freeing himself from Skrymir. But he didn't want to be their enemy.

Deadfall, meanwhile, was just Deadfall. In response to an argument between Erik and Yngvarr, the carpet said, "Cease. I will remove the five dead men and arrange cairns for them amid the rocks of the plain. I can do this swiftly. I can perform no rites; I feel equal scorn for cosmic beings as for earthly ones. But this minimal respect I can give."

"That is enough for me," Yngvarr said. "They have beheld a Chooser of the Slain. They will go to the All-Father's hall, or none will."

"Let it be done," Erik said, but he made the sign of the Swan over his heart and pounded the charm of Torden on his chest. As Deadfall began its work, Erik said, "Steelfox, can your falcon survey the area?"

"As we speak," Steelfox said. "We are in Oxiland. Not on the main island but on the outlier that holds Loftsson's Hall."

"And Huginn's," Innocence said, finding his voice.

Katta studied him. "Our companion's troll-splinter is awake again; his respite is over. Let us say nothing of ultimate destinations."

"Indeed," said Bone, putting his hand on Innocence's shoulder. "Steelfox, do you see that river?"

"I do," she answered.

"So," said Gaunt, "how do we move a longship?"

The answer was, on their shoulders. Innocence reflected that it was a great change from the moment when the Fraternity of the Hare had carried him on a litter. He felt guilt at the Fraternity's destruction, all to protect Steelfox and him. Power and guilt, neither one asked for, piled up upon him.

But everyone had something on his shoulders. Or her shoulders. No one seemed to begrudge those who stayed out of the work—Alfhild, Malin, Northwing, a few men who'd been wounded by uldra arrows. It made Innocence feel he was part of a true crew, that people pitched in, but no one was compelled.

It was hard work, but not quite as hard as it had first appeared. The structure of the ship was light. Still, he was glad after an hour when they reached a horse path and it became practical to pull *Bison* with a long rope, the crew rotating between the task of hauling and the job of keeping the ship balanced.

There was something satisfying in the work. Walking Stick had said, *A superior man would gladly work a hundred times harder than an ordinary man, in order to learn more.* Innocence had thought it rather a heavy-handed thing to say to a boy and girl who just wanted to stick-fight a little longer.

But leaving aside how he felt about Walking Stick, maybe a *not-quite-so-superior man* could work a little harder than an ordinary man. There was much to learn.

Such thoughts made his troll-shrouded perceptions a little lighter.

They caught sight of the river and also of a farmhouse carved from the side of a snow-covered hill. An armed band rode out to meet them. Erik called a halt.

"Who are you," called out the blonde-haired, hard-eyed woman leading the band, "and what is your business? Are you otherfolk, who come from the Moss-Stone with a longship?"

She and her men were ugly in Innocence's sight.

"We have come a long way," Erik said, "but we are human beings. I am Erik Glint, the Larderman, lately captain of *Raveneye*, now commander of *Leaping Bison*. We are on the business of Corinna of Soderland. And though we come peacefully, my ship is thirsty for your river."

Innocence bowed. "Hekla, companion of Huginn. Hail. We mean no harm."

"Innocence!" Hekla gasped, lowering her sword. "Innocence Gaunt! Why, I never thought to see you again. What . . . has happened to you?"

Innocence could not help but smile a little. "There are many answers to that, Lady, but I sense you wonder about my forehead and my eye. The one is a gift from Qiangguo, the other from Kantenjord. I am not altogether pleased with either. But it's said that a gentleman who loves comfort is unworthy of the name."

"Tell me, lad, have you word of Huginn?"

Innocence shook his head. "I know he was at Svanstad when it fell. That is all I know. I am sorry."

Hekla surveyed *Bison*'s crew. "You travel with Karvaks . . . and the boy has a troll-splinter. And yet you serve Corinna? This is a riddle."

Steelfox stepped forward. "My bodyguard, my shaman, and I are considered renegades. Yet it is my sister Jewelwolf who has truly betrayed our ways, by allying with trolls and using their cold magic. Speak what is in your heart, Kantening. Is Oxiland ruled by the Karvaks?"

"It is. My own bedmate, with his Oxiland volunteers beside him, opened the gates of Svanstad. In return for his treachery, this farm is allowed autonomy, in anticipation of the return of Huginn, the Crowned King of Oxiland." Her voice was not proud. "All this was six months ago. Yet the winter goes on. Fimbulwinter, folk call it. We are given supplies and promises that the cold will break soon. Such is my lover's work. We will have words one day, he and I. Meantime, I won't give you over to the Karvaks. But you had best be quick about your business." Hekla pointed her sword to the north, where a distant pair of balloons drifted above the horizon.

Innocence said, "Can you tell me if the Oxilanders Rolf and Kollr yet live?"

Hekla said, "The names of Rolf and Kollr have emerged as those of Huginn's scribes."

Innocence laughed, and the sound was bitter.

Erik said, "I can only guess at your worries, Lady. I don't want to add to them. Will you allow us to reach the river?"

"I don't think I could stop you," Hekla said. "That's what I'll tell the Karvaks when they come. For I doubt you'll long escape their notice."

Innocence said—and for this he needed all his courage—"I would ask you, Hekla . . . do you know the health of one Jaska Torsdatter? She lives on a farm north of here."

Through all her worry, Hekla's eyes widened a little. "Of course she is known to me. I have taken her into my service, for we are short-handed. She is well. Do you wish to see her?"

Innocence stared toward the farmhouse in the hillside, wondering if he would be disappointed or relieved if Jaska was peering out at the strange ship. He became acutely aware that whatever Jaska might be doing, everyone else was looking at him. "No. There is no time."

Hekla moved closer and put her hand on his shoulder. So only he could hear, she said, "Shall I tell her you asked after her?"

"I—yes. Please." He wracked his brains for something wondrous, brave, and memorable to say to the dark-eyed girl. But only Walking Stick's classical quotations came to mind. "A sage of Qiangguo once said, 'If I hear Truth in the morning, I'm content to die in the evening.' I feel this way about having met Jaska."

"They have the hearts of foamreavers in Qiangguo," Hekla said. "It must be. I will tell her."

Innocence retreated, feeling all those stares. Alfhild in particular watched him as he worked beside Kollr to get *Bison* to water. "What was all this about, Innocence Gaunt? This girl Jaska? Is she very beautiful?"

Alfhild herself seemed astonishingly beautiful in that moment, and Innocence tried not to look at her or at the jealous glance of Erik. "She was kind to me once. That is all."

Bison floated at last. Innocence's father was the one who tossed the rope up to his mother, beside the ox figurehead. They were graceful together, and Innocence felt a strange pride. He waded into the icy waters and boarded the ship.

They rode the river south in a meandering path. The banks became rocky, and the water became a frothing roil of white on blue. The ship sped. In an hour they were in a low gorge of white water, swishing between shores of pocked gray basalt.

"There's another gentle region beyond this," Steelfox said, looking through the eyes of Qurca, "but then there are more rapids and then a waterfall into the sea."

"We'll portage soon, then," Erik said.

"Beware," Steelfox said. "Karvak horsemen are headed this way."

"Why do they not use the balloons?" Persimmon Gaunt asked.

"To surprise us, I'd assume. They must not know about Qurca and me."

"Will we make it?" Bone said.

Steelfox shut her eyes. "I think it will be close."

"What's your sense of the ship surviving the falls?" Yngvarr asked.

Steelfox shook her head.

"We'll move *Bison* by land then," Erik said.

The rapids ended, but it seemed nearly an hour before a suitable landing shore appeared. At last they dragged *Bison* onto a bank of egg-sized rocks. There was salt in the air.

"Everyone who can, haul the ship!" shouted Erik. "The sea is our salvation!"

There was nothing pleasant about this second portage. They alternated lifting and hauling as befitted the terrain.

"The riders are crossing the river," Steelfox said as they could hear the breakers over a rise of black sand and gray stone. "But we are almost there." Qurca circled overhead, guiding them. "We should shift leftward, to easier ground—no! They have sabercats with them! The cats are lurching ahead. Captain, we have to go over that rise. It is steep on the other side, but we can manage it."

As they groaned and hauled *Bison* upslope, Bone in the lead yelped and looked back. "Are you mad?"

They looked down at a descent to the sea some three hundred feet long, pitched so steep that a man would have to race down it to keep his balance, or else slide.

"Perhaps!" said Steelfox. "Do you wish to face ten sabercats?"

"All right, all right," said Bone.

"Up and over!" said Erik. "To the water or to the underworld, down we go!"

It was like some mad sporting event, racing a longship down the rubble and sand, trying not to break it or yourselves. Innocence's father in particular was running with the rope quite aggressively toward the water, a giddily terrified expression on his face. Innocence was, for once, not entirely dismayed to have the man in his bloodline.

His mother called out, "They've come!"

Ten golden cats massive as ponies, with huge, curving canine teeth, reared over the slope. They leapt to the attack.

Steelfox called to her man, and together they faced the beasts. She raised a sword and barked a command.

A few beasts obeyed her and halted. But three veered to her left and four to her right. Two men were swiftly mauled. *Bison* went off balance and tumbled on its way, cracking its masts.

Nine Smilodons cut down one of the creatures that were his namesake. He might have had more trouble, but it hesitated at the approach of a Karvak. The deed done, the blood upon the snowy sand, now there were nine indeed.

"Innocence! Down here!"

His parents, along with Malin, Northwing, and Alfhild, had retreated into the freezing water, Gaunt readying a bow, Bone applying some sort of elixir to the arrowheads. Innocence ran toward them. The water numbed his feet as he stood within the gentle surf of the bay. Bone said, "If you can raise any power against these beasts, son, I would."

Innocence calmed his breathing, trying to raise the chi within him, unlock the powers given him by the Heavenwalls and the Great Chain.

Gaunt was loosing arrows now, and one beast had two sticking from its hide, to no apparent effect.

Strength awoke within him. As the combatants were of different species, he tried to push chi into the humans, enliven them, make them ferocious.

The Kantenings and Karvaks responded with unnerving eagerness. Some of them even frothed. They stabbed and hacked and leapt forward with no regard for their own lives. Mad Katta seemed better able to keep his wits about him. He backed away as the battle surged and his allies' swings grew wilder.

The sabercat targeted by Gaunt toppled, and she switched to another. Beside her Northwing concentrated and murmured, and all of the animals grew more sluggish. Soon more cats were falling. With unexpected speed, all the animals lay orange and red upon black-and-white sand.

Some of the enlivened Kantenings would not cease battle. Yngvarr, deranged, fell upon Taper Tom and split his son's head apart with an axe.

"No!" Innocence wailed. He dimmed the energies of the warriors. The battle ended, men at last slumping with their injuries.

Bison hissed into the sea.

They had lost eleven crew, including Tom. Face stony, Yngvarr gave to the waters the wreckage of his son.

"Just like Numi," Innocence murmured. "My fault."

His parents told him that was nonsense, but they could not comprehend his power. Only Joy could have understood.

They hadn't all boarded when Steelfox called out, "Karvaks!" and a force of five arbans, fifty of her people, reared upon the rise. Methodically, the Karvaks fired arrows at everyone but Steelfox and Innocence.

Erik Glint fell first, an arrow in his eye. He lay at the prow, dead instantly.

Nine Smilodons glared at a shaft protruding from his right arm. He snapped it and began rowing. Mad Katta took a shot in the back and nearly toppled from the craft, but Northwing caught him.

Bone stared at an arrow shaft in his stomach and stumbled into the bilge. Innocence heard his father saying, "Shoot them, Gaunt . . . don't waste the poison . . . Innocence, help me. . . ."

Yngvarr commanded oarsmen with a dread voice. Those who couldn't row held up shields to protect the rowers. Innocence helped Bone point a peculiar black baton. "Got this from Eshe . . . no, use *that* end . . . point that end at the Karvaks . . . and pull this thing, here. . . ." Innocence moved the metal lever, and the device delivered a kick that stung his hands. A rocket like the fireworks of Qiangguo shot upward past the Karvaks, briefly distracting their archer.

Deadfall was in the air, flying past the archers, slapping at their hands. Some dropped their bows.

Persimmon Gaunt dropped hers as well. She joined Innocence in tending to Bone's injury.

"Just a flesh wound," he said. "Perhaps a few more important things . . . but mostly flesh . . ."

"Shut up, Bone. Innocence, help hold him still. This arrow is coming out."

"Why must he help me hold still?" Bone complained. "I've had wounds befo—yeargh."

"There," Gaunt said, tossing the arrow overboard. She looked up, and Innocence followed her gaze. Deadfall was rushing back onto the ship, sometimes leaping skyward to slap arrows from the sky. The dark shore had receded, and *Bison*'s survivors were rowing as swiftly as possible.

Survivors—they had lost eight more crew to the archers, including the captain. *Bison* now carried eighteen human beings, a bird, and a magic carpet. The ship was meant for a crew of forty.

They had no mast or sail. Everything was now muscle. Bone insisted he was fine, and Gaunt's expression did not agree. But she protected him sternly, so Innocence felt free to row. He ached with the work, and with the draining effect of enlivening the foamreavers' chi, he was facing exhaustion. But he couldn't let others work themselves to death while his strength remained.

At any rate, the exertion took his mind off the dead.

At last Deadfall said, "Tie a line to me and secure me to the figurehead. I can tow the ship. Not at any great speed, but it will allow the rowers to rest. I will head in the direction that seems best."

"Thank you, creature," Yngvarr said.

"You are welcome, entity," said Deadfall.

"Before, you were reluctant to reveal your powers," Gaunt said.

"I think there is no question of avoiding detection," Deadfall said.

Steelfox said, "I would expect my people to send balloons now, there being no possibility of surprising us. Or Oxilander allies with ships. Yet I see no pursuit."

"You sound worried," Gaunt said.

"I am. They may have something worse in mind."

"Worse," Northwing said. "Ha. That would be something to see. I have rested as much as I dare. If no weather control is desired, I shall deal with the spirits to speed the healing of our wounded. Me first, of course."

"Of course," Bone said.

"You and Katta are next on the list. You were both hit badly."

"I can maintain myself for a time," Katta said. "Others may be healed first."

"Such brave nonsense ill-becomes you, monk. You are badly wounded. I'd prefer to have a proper gathering, with drums, an awestruck village, the whole performance. But your good wishes, crew, are welcome."

"I could send chi into their bodies," Innocence said. "It might help."

"Like it helped us?" Yngvarr said. "I sensed the power entering us, and for a moment I had visions of fiery dragons dancing in the air with similar creatures, misty and green. Then the rage came, and I saw a vision of Orm One-Eye and his golden hall, and fire danced before it. I have never walked the path of the berserker, one who enters a battle-trance, but you brought it on."

"Yes," Innocence said. "Tom's death . . . that is my burden, not yours. I didn't expect that effect. Maybe it is most potent for warriors . . . but the act was mine. My mentor taught me to address my mistakes. I'm sorry."

Yngvarr frowned. "Yes. I mourn Tom, as I mourn Brambletop. And Ruvsa. But the battle-fury is in me, boy, no matter what you did. Just as the foamreaving and slaving was my doing, before the demon ever had me."

Deadfall pulled them through the night. It seemed tireless, but in the morning, as they woke to the surges of the open sea on their left and rugged black cliffs to their right, Deadfall returned to the broken *Bison* and did not speak.

So they rowed and sometimes sang songs of people long dead, and when at noon they saw a rare stand of tall trees, they went ashore and chopped until they had a new mast. It was badly done, but it was done. With a spare sail they were moving at speed again. Innocence called upon his power, for Northwing was still silently imploring the spirits to help the wounded. A wind puffed the sail.

Alfhild was staring at him. She had been doing that more since Erik, her would-be paramour, had died. "You are a wizard."

"I'm nothing of the kind. . . ."

"You are modest."

"I'm not that either. I have power. I've learned from a wise civilization. I've come through great danger. But I'm not a wizard. The powers I have are a gift from nature, or else from the Heavenwalls or the Great Chain of Unbeing."

"I do not understand anything about this world. I followed a man into this place, and now his body feeds the fish."

"I do not understand this world either, Alfhild. I grew up in a different realm, as did you. Perhaps it is only in sheltered places that life makes sense."

His mother spoke up. "What you've seen, Alfhild, is a land at war. Once I might have believed that war was an adventure. It is not. It is the end of adventures. It shortens lives that might have gone on to see wonders."

Imago Bone groaned.

"He is getting worse, isn't he?" Innocence said.

"He may," Gaunt said.

Innocence thought about losing the father he'd so long avoided. Perhaps his mother too. He could not feel it as anything but a weight.

He tried to push *Bison* harder. They must find Skrymir's heart.

Days passed, and they followed a bleak coast where no farms stood. There were no good landings here, and rivers fell in surging waterfalls. To the south was a permanent storm bank, and Yngvarr informed them this was the Draugmaw.

The morning came when Deadfall refused to give up its dragging of the ship, for it said, "We are close."

An island loomed out of the gloom, right beside the storm clouds and churning sea of the Draugmaw, close at hand to Oxiland's coast.

The island bore a vague resemblance to a giant's foot a mile lengthwise, petrified and snapped off above the ankle. Snow covered its steep slopes except upon the sheer ridges between the shore and the jagged top. They came around to the north side, where the hypothetical giant's toes jabbed toward another grim island nearer to Oxiland. Ice linked them. Innocence had the impression one could walk between these islands upon the frozen sea, and then to a third, and on to Oxiland.

They landed *Bison* where the little toe might be, splintering ice as they pulled the longship onto the pebbly strand. Ahead, halfway up the island's treacherous slope, was a cave.

"Nice spot," Gaunt said. "A cold beauty to it. Suitable for witch's cauldrons, shipwrecks, last battles."

"You'll bring bad luck," Yngvarr said, "with talk like that."

"Not Gaunt," Bone murmured. "Thinking about doom makes her lucky. And me by association."

"You're staying with *Bison*," Gaunt said.

"You're thinking about doom again," Bone said, departing the longship, all stubborn purpose. "It's my lucky day."

There was no stopping him. The ten questers left the surviving crew of seven foamreavers to guard the ship, for the sailors had suffered much. Booted feet crunched snow, Bone looked out at the dark-blue sea and its white-streaked waves. "Anyone spy anything on the horizon?"

"Nothing new," Gaunt snapped. Others grunted agreement. "Should there be?"

"That firework-weapon was a gift from Eshe, a signal. Should have just shot it straight into the air. I was hoping she'd come sailing up to save us."

"She has her own priorities."

"True. I've always fancied we are among those priorities."

"You maybe. Me, I think she tolerates. She finds you appealing."

"Well, that appeals to my vanity. But she'd knife me in my sleep if it served Kpalamaa."

"But she'd feel very badly about it."

"I'd like to think so."

"Well, you're mine, Bone. If anyone gets to kill you in your sleep it's me."

"I think that was in our vows somewhere."

Innocence did not wholly understand his parents' banter, and he wasn't sure he liked it. The mix of love and aggression troubled him. But there was more passion in that love than for many a more tranquil couple.

They reached the slope and ascended a narrow path two-by-two. Yngvarr led the way, and his former enemy Katta insisted on staying near him. Next came Nine Smilodons and Steelfox. Afterward came Bone, leaning on Gaunt. Innocence followed, and Northwing leaned on him. Last were Malin and Alfhild, a strange pair united by Malin's absent friend—and Alfhild's doppelganger—Inga. An even stranger pair shared the skies, the peregrine falcon and the flying carpet, doing their best to stay out of each other's way.

Deadfall focused on leading the way to the cave, swooping forward, looping up, beckoning with a corner. Thus it was Qurca who saw the danger.

"Something approaches from the summit!" Steelfox said. "Like ravens, but larger. They have rocky extrusions for beaks and claws, and their eyes glow green."

"Troll-crows," said Malin, not looking at them. "Unique to Oxiland. Each great land has its flavor of troll. Spydbanen's are mighty and vicious. Svardmark's are shy and comical. Oxiland's are few but brood endlessly upon their hatred of men, and of the passage of time."

"There are six," Steelfox said, readying her bow. Nine Smilodons, Yngvarr, and Gaunt did likewise. Katta removed from his robes a disc-shaped cake. Northwing, leaning against Innocence, eyes shut, murmured in a language Innocence did not know. Innocence tried to prepare his mind for an exertion of chi.

The troll-crows swooped down with a screech like the torture of metal. They were as patches of darkness cut early from the oncoming night. Innocence found them weirdly beautiful, like dark angels. His heart pounded.

Four arrows shot from the path, and all found their marks. The troll-crows shrieked like a clash of shields, black feathers falling with the snow. Yet none perished.

The six swooped and clawed.

Nine Smilodons took a risk as they strafed him, dropping his bow, drawing his sword, and slashing. He decapitated one of the creatures, taking many cuts as he did so.

The head rolled down the slope, shrieking outrage. The body plunged into the sea.

Katta threw a cake, and the holy pastry sliced off a wing; a second troll-crow crashed into the snow, flapping spasmodically.

Yngvarr took a nasty cut to the shoulder and threw his axe. It buried itself in the skull of a third troll-crow. That one spiraled madly into the cold ocean.

Bone stumbled, for a wing had slapped him. Gaunt shot at the attacker as it passed. It spat and cursed, quivering, though it did not fall. Gaunt bent over her husband, but he gasped, "Fine, fine, never better . . ."

Alfhild had also been wounded. She clutched her shoulder, staring at her own red blood welling between her fingers. Malin tried to help her. "Unhand me," said the uldra princess.

"Malin," said Northwing. "Do those stories tell you if these things are mostly troll? Or mostly animal?"

"It is a mix," Malin said.

"Let's see," Northwing said.

Innocence didn't know what the shaman was doing, but lack of knowledge had never stopped him before. He envisioned the power of the Heavenwalls coiling within him like a braid of fire and air.

Three troll-crows remained able to fight, though all had arrows sticking from their bodies. They swooped to the heights and grabbed large rocks to drop upon their enemies. As they returned, the archers loosed more arrows, but the troll-crows kept coming.

Deadfall flashed out of the sky and grappled one. Together they careened over the peak.

The remaining two dropped their stones. Nine Smilodons was unlucky and went down in a heap, as did Malin. Alfhild stared at the fallen Kantening woman, whose red blood matched her own. But Innocence had no time for Alfhild's perplexity. With the power of the Heavenwalls swirling within him, he reached out for the energies of the Great Chain.

Beside him Northwing smiled.

One of the troll-crows shrieked as its aspect rippled, like something beheld beneath heaving water. It twisted and split. Briefly there hung in the air two entities, a crow and a humanoid of gnarled rock, blinking with green eyes. In the next moment the crow winged away, to all appearances an ordinary animal. The humanoid fell to the island's rock, shattering.

That left one. Innocence meant to finish it.

He combined the forces of the Heavenwalls with that of the Chain.

It was a mistake. While the Heavenwalls' energies were a balance of passions, the yang of the fiery dragons and the yin of the watery ones, the Chain's forces were entirely yang—and not a youthful yang but a power ancient and uncompromising.

The two powers fought within his body and threatened to tear him apart.

He collapsed. Snow steamed around him.

When the energies were purged, Innocence blinked at the setting sun. His mother helped him up. "What happened to you?" she said.

He shook his head; he could not explain. "How are we?"

Gaunt lowered her gaze. "We won. But Nine Smilodons will not share the victory. Nor have we seen Deadfall."

Steelfox bent over the shape of her servant, her body shaking.

Others had fresh wounds, though all were able to walk. Bone was looking particularly ragged, however.

"Perhaps," Gaunt said, "you should stay. You could build a cairn for Nine Smilodons."

Steelfox stood. "It is not necessary," she said, and her voice was cold. "Exposure to scavengers is our tradition."

"I am sorry," Gaunt said, "for forgetting your customs, and for your loss."

"So much death," Alfhild murmured, staring at a livid cut on her arm.

"He was a brave fighter," Yngvarr said.

"Take his sword," Steelfox said, "for you have lost your axe. He would want that. He was the best of warriors. All courage, no bluster. He was my last connection to home."

Northwing said, "I remain your friend, Lady."

"And I," Innocence said impulsively.

"Your loyalty went to Steelfox the princess," said the Karvak. "She is dead."

Innocence could not bear it. He bowed before her. "I am friend, then, to the one who stands in her place."

"And I," said Northwing. "You may break our bond, but events remain. The world remembers. As do I."

Katta knelt beside Nine Smilodons. "If you like, Lady, I can conduct a full sky burial, in the manner of Geam."

"It is impractical," Steelfox said with a sigh. "And he was a practical man."

They soon had to go single-file, and they fell into their own reveries. Innocence wondered what it meant that he gripped two incompatible powers. Gaunt and Bone's looks of concern were a burden he didn't want.

They reached the cave. Up close it was like a narrowed eye-hole sliced into the stony slope. The tunnel plunged down with a slope almost the mirror image of the one they'd ascended.

"Let us be about this," Innocence said. "I want to be free."

Abruptly Bone laughed.

"What is it?" Gaunt said.

"This is yet another occasion when it never occurred to me to bring a torch. I am slipping."

"Don't, love. It's a long way down."

"Do not worry," Katta said. "I can see very well."

"Now I *am* worried," Bone said.

"I find I can see as well," Innocence said. "It's the troll-sight."

"Go ahead, son," Bone said. "You two lead the way."

In troll-sight, the darkness swiftly became a dreamlike haze, and within it appeared various intriguing forms. Icicles big as swords hung beside walls of fractured stone that almost looked hewn and bricked but seemed too haphazard to be even the work of troll-hands. Treasure chests with locks in the shape of skulls grinned from the back of the cave, and as they stepped carefully across the irregular surface, Innocence saw five statues.

No, not statues.

Katta was first to understand. "We are not the only ones breathing in this place," the monk said. "And the evil that clings to the shapes ahead is distinguishable even in this accursed place. There are four men here."

"Four?" Innocence said, squinting. "But I perceive a fifth."

Laughter boomed through the cave. It was so hearty, Innocence could almost imagine the sense of danger that constricted his heart was a mistake. Soon these men would welcome them to a feast, and they would joke together about death and war.

"The fifth is no man!" said one of the figures on the cave's far side. "We are here to . . . protect her. But she is no man, nor even human. Welcome, warriors. I'm pleased you fought your way through the guardians outside, because taunting our charge is dull work. Do I perceive my sniveling slave, hiding there at the back?"

"Skalagrim," Bone said.

"Four of Seven Wolves greet you. Gentlemen, the scarred thief back there and his fiery-haired bride are key reasons why we no longer number nine. And look, there is Yngvarr, now among our foes. You will appreciate this, Yngvarr! By some wyrd we are confronted with nine opponents. I say, if we kill the men, brothers, we can each claim a woman. The redhead is mine. She has thwarted me too often, and she reminds me of the one who has haunted my dreams."

"In dreams your schemes will remain," Gaunt said.

"Your reckoning is off," said Northwing, "in so many ways. Give us Skrymir's heart and your spirits needn't leave your bodies. Pass over the chests."

The massive man named Skalagrim laughed anew. "The heart is no more in these chests than it's within Skrymir's. Isn't that right, companion?"

And now the fifth figure stepped forward.

She had the dimensions of a powerful woman of perhaps six feet, and she was made of ice. She resembled a one-headed troll, though cut and fractured and scarred all over her body. So damaged was she that at first Innocence did not recognize who she resembled.

"Skrymir?" he said aloud.

"No," said the being with a peculiar, gentle, tinkling voice. "I look like him, but I am very different. I am anima to his animus. I am his heart."

"What?" said Yngvarr.

"I am Skrymir's heart. Long ago, before he placed me here for safekeeping, he shaped me into a homunculus of himself. As he associated femininity with weakness, he made me seem female. Then he commenced tormenting me. In doing so he became strong."

"I don't understand," Katta said.

"The trolls are the solidified thoughts of the great dragons who sleep in these isles," said the heart. "They gain a sort of half-existence but will eventually, through violence or direct sunlight, be returned to the minds they sprang from. Only by summoning vast will, and obsessive ego, can they persist and become mighty. None has gone farther down this path than Skrymir, who has nearly freed himself from his parent, the dragon Moonspear, whose slumbering form birthed Spydbanen. Skrymir learned that cruelty is one path to bolstering will. When he reached the limits of what he could manage with the trolls, uldra, and humans within reach, he hit upon a great insight. He could externalize a part of his psyche, even as he himself was part of the psyche of Moonspear."

"And so he made you," Gaunt guessed.

"Yes. A part of him embodying all that was kind, merciful, selfless. A part he could torture at leisure. It made him mightier yet. But the time came when he realized I was a potential liability. Someone might shatter me and leave him without an easy source of ego. So he placed me on this island to retrieve should he feel diminished, always with some guardians to defend me, and to . . . remind me of my purpose in life. These gentlemen are but the latest in a long line of . . . protectors."

"If you die," Bone said, "what happens?"

"What happens to any of us when we die? Is there not considerable angst and disagreement on the matter? Ah, but you mean what happens to Skrymir. I suspect he becomes temporarily more powerful, utterly untouched by anything resembling gentleness. But brittle also. Something else might come to occupy his heart. Who knows? The right thing—or being—might change him. I will not know. Perhaps I will be absorbed in some manner back into him but too shattered to affect him. Perhaps I will enter the void or be blessed by a Chooser of the Slain. . . ."

"Enough," Yngvarr said. "Maybe killing you won't kill him. But it's clear he doesn't want you dead, and that's good enough for me. Stand aside, Four Wolves."

"Hardly," said Skalagrim. "Heart, give us a little light, if you please."

The heart, sad-faced, shed cold light upon the cave. The Four Wolves advanced.

"Heart!" called out Northwing. "I offer you another path. Somewhere in these isles exists a thing my friends name the Scroll of Years. It can sever magical connections between things. I've experienced this myself. You can be free of Skrymir. Surrender to us, help us defeat these Wolves, and we'll make it happen."

"You speak truly?" the heart said.

"Yes. Can you sense it?"

"You speak truly," the heart said, and the light vanished.

The Wolves cursed, and Innocence understood. They had not accepted troll-splinters and were at a disadvantage without the light. He and Katta could fight in this place.

But it was still four against two, plus whatever help the rest of the blinded voyagers could offer.

Katta flung a disc-shaped cake, and Skalagrim howled in pain as it connected with his face. Innocence saw the other Wolves advancing, and he brought his chi to full life.

This time he stuck with the pugilistic moves Walking Stick had taught him. He smashed the nose of one Wolf with the Snorting Buffalo Kick and disarmed a second with the Pain Blossom Strike. The two men were massive opponents however, and they grabbed at him. Innocence was able to unbalance the armed one, sending him with a grunt to the feet of Steelfox, who struck at him ferociously.

But the other man got Innocence in a hold. Innocence struggled but could not break free. He needed a stronger power. Briefly he envisioned the Heavenwalls in his mind, but he was too desperate to embody a balance of yin-yang forces; he needed the violence of the Great Chain.

Fire flowed around him.

The Wolf shrieked and released him. Innocence spun and struck out with a blazing hand. The Wolf fell. Innocence advanced upon the next man, who was blindly struggling with the adroit Katta. He kicked, and the volcanic force surrounding his foot vaporized the Kantening's midsection.

Innocence laughed.

Katta's look was one of horror. He stepped back.

A blazing nimbus surrounded Innocence, and he smiled at the freedom the power gave him. Seeing two standing figures who were not of his party, he raised his hand and directed gouts of fire outward. A human shrieked. Another voice seemed to sigh as its life was consumed.

Blazing triumphantly, Innocence looked upon his work.

"Innocence!" Gaunt called. "No!"

The Wolves were all dead, but Skrymir's heart was a shattered, melted ruin.

Far to the east, so thin he might have imagined it, there came on the wind a bellow of pain that became a shout of glee.

The island began to rumble.

It was all his fault. He had lost control, and everything was going to fall apart. He scrambled out of the cave, wanting only to escape the others and their accusing, horrified faces, especially his parents.

Pell-mell he ran down the slope, and it shook as he went.

The island was tearing itself apart. Stones burst apart, and steam or lava spewed from the new-formed pits. His flight was proceeded by tumbling stones. Far below, the seven men minding *Bison* shoved their craft out to sea. Of course. What else could they do? There was no escape for Innocence or his family and friends. At least these men could free themselves.

He sat down, covering his face with his hands, surrounded by a fire that would never burn itself out, and waited for the end.

The end did not come. Instead Deadfall did. The flying carpet, covered in black feathers and ash, scooped him up and lifted him above the nameless island.

"What have you done?" it demanded.

"I ruined everything, old companion," Innocence said. "Can you save anybody?"

"What do you think?"

Innocence looked down and saw only a cloud of ash, fires roaring at its heart.

CHAPTER 38

A JOURNEY TO KANTENJORD, CONTINUED

(being a section written by Katta, called the Mad)

Here, at what might be the end of the world, it falls to me to write. Readers from Geam, land of my apprenticeship, may assume that I am commencing an "inner" version of my account, filled with dream-visions and allegorical notions. I assure you this is still an "outer" account and contains only literal events.

I write this in a most unexpected place, bleak yet oddly reminiscent of home. There is snow, of course. There are reindeer. There are people doggedly confronting the end of all things, and I admire them, even as I try to regain my equanimity in the face of destruction. I write in the dark upon the noctograph, for night does not inhibit me. Even with the occasional shaking beneath me, I can form the letters with some assurance they will be readable.

But by whom?

As we raced away from the exploding core of the island, it seemed that Gaunt, Northwing, and I would perish. We'd been separated from the others and could only do our best to escape a lava flow. There was one slim chance: an icy surface leading to the nearest island.

Our survival depended on Northwing. Redoubtable as she was, Gaunt had just been torn from her husband and son, after she'd suffered so much bringing them together. Distraught, she could be led but could not guide. I, despite my many blessings, am hardly the best choice to lead others through a treacherous natural landscape.

So Northwing led us both, taking us arm-in-arm. The shaman's acerbic voice became stern yet soothing. I have never heard anything quite like it.

"Here we go. Onto the ice now. Move carefully but don't stop. . . ."

I was only a little less surprised when Haytham arrived.

I saw him first, or rather the demonic entity that flitted across my sight, the only thing I could perceive, an ember of hatred against the cool blackness.

"A Charstalker," I said. "Is there a Karvak balloon out there?"

This stirred Gaunt from her reverie. "It's not a Karvak balloon . . . that's Haytham in there."

"Haytham?" he said. "Why is he using a Charstalker and not Haboob?"

Northwing's usual voice was back. "That's not the question! Why is the mad fool landing on the ice?"

The shaman was right. I could see the Charstalker descend, and hear the balloon skidding and sliding. Haytham's usual emergency landing strategy, of hitting the ground very hard, was not going to work here. The craft was sliding at high speed.

"Fool! Fool! Fool!" Northwing was saying, not exactly the model of a grateful rescuee.

"He's throwing a grapple," Gaunt said. She sounded more like her usual self. "And another one."

"It's not enough!" Northwing said, trying to pick up our pace. "He's heading toward the edge of the ice floe! Jump, Haytham! Give up the balloon! Jump!"

I heard a thump and a scream of pain. I also heard something large hitting the water, and a great crackling noise.

The Charstalker descended. Its flames made a rude gesture as it dropped into the deep.

"The ice," Gaunt said. "The grapples didn't stop the balloon, but they cracked the ice. Haytham's still out there, in danger. I'm going after him."

"You mustn't!" Northwing said.

"I have some familiarity with ice," Gaunt said. "Let me try."

Northwing gave up. I ached to assist Gaunt but I could see nothing. Haytham was a man of basically good character, and I had no hope of seeing him. Even Gaunt, person of loose morals that she was, was invisible to me.

"What's happening?" I asked.

"She is creeping out to him. She is helping him up."

My stomach churned as I heard terrible screeches and groans from the cracking ice floe.

"They are shuffling this way," Northwing said. "Hurry, you two. . . ."

A savage rending sound announced the ice's collapse.

"They are here!" Northwing said. "I am so relieved to see you both. Come closer, Haytham, so I can beat you senseless."

"Northwing," Haytham gasped. "Delighted. Together again."

"It does seem to be our fate. Bah."

"Katta. How goes your war?"

"It produces attachment and suffering at a swifter rate than I would prefer," I said. "Thank you for coming to rescue us."

"You're welcome. The All-One sees fit to send lava against our ice as well. I think I can walk, with help. Shall we reach the farther shore?"

"That's what we were doing," Northwing said, "when you interrupted us."

"Why can't you be more like Katta? Katta is polite. Katta appreciates rescuers."

"Katta's tradition involves harmonious interaction with the universe. My tradition involves haranguing the universe to make it do what we want. Get moving."

"The universe would be wise to obey," Haytham groaned. "Thank you for the assistance, Persimmon."

"Slow and steady," Gaunt said.

At last we reached the next island, where we took shelter in a sea-cave. Months of Fimbulwinter had frozen much of the surrounding seawater, so we were in no danger from the tide. We slept, exhausted, all but Haytham, who did his best to peer into the mass of smoke and lava that marked where we'd come from.

Haytham explained he'd been on a mission to Fiskegard when he saw a strange flare on the horizon. Tracking it as best he could, he encountered the ship *Anansi*, and together they had tried to locate *Bison*. Bad weather had thwarted them until the explosion of the island of Skrymir's heart.

"So you found Bone?" Gaunt asked Haytham, her voice desperate. "But not Innocence?"

"I saw Innocence draped over the carpet Deadfall. I do not think he spotted me as they rose, and then smoke covered everything. It's likely your son lived. Your husband . . . I do not know. *Anansi* might have found him and the others. But I can't be sure. He was insistent that I find you." He sighed. "I succeeded in that much."

"Stupid," Northwing said. "You are too much the gambler, inventor."

There was much talk after that, of war and treachery. Reader, if you survived these days, you know something of the conduct of the war of Karvaks and Kantenings, so I will not dwell upon it here. At last human weariness overpowered human contrariness, and sleep came.

The ship from Kpalamaa did not find us, but neither did any hostile Kantenings nor airborne Karvaks. We were quite alone.

"Where to?" I asked briskly, over our morning fire.

Haytham said, "I suggest we take our chances trying to reach Oxiland."

Northwing said, "Oxiland is occupied by Jewelwolf's forces. The Karvaks have many ingenious methods of killing traitors."

"Kantenings may deal with us, if we are careful," I said.

"I am going for a walk," Gaunt said.

When she'd left us, I said, "I worry for her. She has a strong spirit, but she's suffered a great deal."

"We've all suffered," Haytham said. "She will recover."

"Everyone breaks eventually," Northwing said.

A strange, haunting melody hummed through the air from the direction of the beach.

"What on Earthe is that?" Haytham asked.

"A fiddle," I said. "A local instrument. She kept it, even when she left most of her gear aboard *Bison*."

"It is heartbreaking," Haytham said.

It was, but it also made me remember. As I fell into a reverie and then sleep, listening to the sound of the fiddle, I resolved to watch for waterfalls.

Days passed. Through snow and rough terrain we trudged. We crossed to another island over the ice, and with one more passage we reached Oxiland.

My companions spoke of a monumental bleakness about the snow-covered coast. I myself could attest to the endless moaning chorus of the wind and the odd rumbling from the great volcanic mountain Surtfell. No food presented itself, so Northwing trapped the minds of rabbits and birds, and we had a sparse supper, Northwing begging the patience of the animals' spirits for such an unsporting hunt.

"If they are dead," Gaunt snapped, "why must you apologize to them?"

"You think a rabbit is a rabbit," Northwing said. "But I think a rabbit is a part of the Rabbit, the essence of that shape in the world. And Rabbit itself is a part of the Blood-power that lies behind all beasts. And Blood-power is itself a part of the world-birthing spirit. So it is wise to acknowledge your food, if you ever want more."

"I don't understand," Gaunt muttered, her teeth tearing into rabbit flesh.

"You are a southerner," Northwing said patiently, "just as these men are. No matter."

We went inland, seeking farms. When we found one, the proprietress had a harsh voice. "I've already given you my tribute and my men. What more do you want?"

"We are not with the Karvaks, goodwife," said Haytham, because with Gaunt in her melancholy he was the closest we had to a diplomat. "We are renegades."

"Outlaws? Brigands?"

"We were lately on a mission from Corinna of Soderland," Haytham said, and there was a great conviction in his voice that might have been born of love.

"I'll give you food," the woman said at last. "That's all. Get gone quickly."

"Thank you. Are Karvaks camped nearby?"

"No, but their balloons appear at any time. We're like mice beneath hawks. Wait here."

We left with stockfish, bread, and directions. Footsore but with full bellies, we reached a ridge above a frozen lake, iced over save where a waterfall thundered into its midst, keeping a gap open.

Gaunt did not pause to explain herself but played a sorrowful tune on her fiddle.

In time a voice called out from the waterfall. "Go away!" it gurgled. "Go to my cousins in Svardmark or Spydbanen! Oxiland sleeps!"

"I can't go away." Gaunt's voice was nearly as sad an instrument as the fiddle, which she continued playing, slow and rich as a wide river. "My husband! My son! You must help me find them."

"Madwoman! This land has slept since long before the dragon brothers came to rob us of our power. Forever they fight over us, over the shattered headlands of the Splintrevej. If you want struggle and woe, go to them!"

"I will not."

"It is as it is, then. Bring on Fimbulwinter."

The roar of the wind overwhelmed the voice of the waterfall. Then all was silence.

"What has happened?" I asked.

"It's . . . frozen," Gaunt said, dropping her fiddle in the snow. "No. The waterfall. The lake. As though the fossegrim had killed itself." I heard the snow around her compress; she had knelt beside the fiddle. "Did it hate me so much?"

The three of us knelt beside her, as if gathering to protect a fire from the wind. "I've damaged my mind," Gaunt said, "learning to fiddle in a way that will please them. And now they shut me out. Where can we go?"

"We must leave Oxiland," Haytham said. "To find the Soderland resistance. Or perhaps . . ."

"To find shamans to help us," Northwing said.

"What?" Gaunt sounded incredulous, but at least she was breaking free from the ice of despair.

"Haytham and I have been talking," Northwing said. "Corinna told him of a people called the Vuos who dwell beyond troll country in Spydbanen."

"They don't like Kantenings," Haytham said, "but they like trolls even less." Northwing continued, "I've sensed powerful shamans that way. We need their help. But there's no way to reach them without a boat," Northwing said. "Or maybe a stolen balloon . . ."

Gaunt said, "There may be another way." I heard her tracing something in the snow. "I don't have the *Chart of Tomorrows* anymore, but I remember something. Here's Oxiland, and here's Spydbanen. The book described how the northern sea freezes over." I heard her draw another line in the snow. "It was shown as extending to here, I think, in winter. It's summer now. But with this Fimbulwinter lasting as long as it has, the ice is surely more extensive. Much of it will be fast ice, stuck to the land."

"You are joking," Haytham said, "if you are suggesting what I think you are suggesting."

"What is she suggesting?" I asked. "I can't see her map."

"She wants us to walk to Spydbanen!" Northwing said. "Over the ice. I'm not unfamiliar with ice myself, Persimmon. There is open water here."

"Frozen over," Gaunt said.

"Yes, but it won't all be stuck to the land. Somewhere out there will be great fissures where the pack ice detaches from the fast ice. It's there we might find ourselves plunging into water too cold to survive."

"It would be impossible without you," Gaunt said. "But you can see through the eyes of the animals. You can be a fish, a whale, a bird, a bear. You can find the fractures, the ridges that will mark the ice boundary. You can find safe places to cross."

"Bah," Northwing said. "Insanity."

"The alternative is for us to attack a Karvak position," Gaunt said, "and steal a vessel of sea or air. And escape to tell the tale. Perhaps we can do it. We are formidable, we four. But I won't hide as an outlaw in remotest Oxiland until winter kills me. Choose."

There was no denying her.

After many days of hiking, foraging, and begging, we reached the northern edge of Oxiland at last, taking note of the increasing tempo of smoke eruptions from Surtfell. My companions could not see the volcano but frequently glimpsed its plumes.

"I cannot tell where the coastline actually lies," Haytham said. It was a bright day, and glare afflicted my sighted companions. "Snow and ice seem to cover everything as far as the eye can see."

"I cannot tell either," I offered, smiling as I said it.

"I can," Northwing said. "The ice is indeed very thick, however, and that which is fastened to the land extends many miles. It is madness to consider traversing it. And yet less mad than I thought."

"Are you willing to try?" Gaunt asked.

As Northwing considered, there came a great conflagration far to the southeast.

"In the All-Now's name . . ." gasped Haytham.

"What do you see?" I asked, struggling to hear and to keep to my feet as the ground shook beneath me.

"Not . . . possible . . ."

"Tell me!"

Gaunt said, "Dragons. The arkendrakes. Spydbanen. Svardmark. They are rising."

Oxiland seemed quite tormented by the disaster as well. We heard Surtfell erupting.

Northwing shouted, "Trust me! Everyone! Onto the ice! Now!"

We hurried after her. For it seemed the only proper thing to do—to obey a snarling shaman when the world was coming to an end.

(Here ends the account of Katta, called the Mad.)

CHAPTER 39

GAMBIT

On a day that should have been high summer, a balloon named *Guraab* flew at an absurd altitude where cold hounded the passengers and the stars nearly ceased twinkling in their ink-black sky.

A-Girl-Is-A-Joy said, "I wish Haytham could have seen the success of your plan, Haboob."

"I too," said the smoky form of the efrit in the brazier, currently surrounded by many buckets of water. Sometimes lightning-tendrils flashed from efrit to pails. "Together we discovered this gas I can liberate from water—far more effective than hot air. I am tempted to name it in his honor, *haythamine*, perhaps. Or perhaps more aptly, in my own honor—*haboobide*. But Flint tells me natural philosophers have taken to using the Amberhornish tongue, so I suppose we'll use his term meaning 'water-creator'—*hydrogen*."

"When you unleash the gas's explosive qualities," said Walking Stick beside Joy, "we will tell the world the name." Her mentor moved as if performing morning exercises, but their purpose was to steer the balloon. For a time the Runewalker Peik had navigated, but as they closed on their target Haboob had lofted them into the highest reaches. Peik, afflicted by thin air, had returned to *A Tumult of Trees on Peculiar Peaks*.

"And then I will be free," Haboob said, "as Haytham agreed."

Joy breathed carefully, concentrating on her chi. She couldn't see the land below, but she knew Haboob's magical senses were focused upon the Great Chain. "I wish he could be here, Haboob. All our friends . . ."

And Innocence. There'd been no word of him since *Bison* had brought Steelfox, Malin, Yngvarr, and Alfhild to Svardmark, whence they'd come to Sky Margin. Even their uldra spies, who'd done so much to report the Karvaks' plans, had no word.

Haboob made a sound much like the clearing of a throat. "We are directly over the rock formation, O passengers."

"At last," said Inga. The troll-changeling's arm had regrown, her lungs were more than strong enough for the altitude, and with her friend Malin back she seemed ready for any challenge. Even her perplexing double Alfhild, carrying word of Inga's parentage, only spurred her on.

Haboob said, "Secure yourselves. We will descend. Silence now."

They plunged through darkness. Joy's hair flowed up and became a cloud around her. Her stomach wanted to depart her body, as an eerie whistling sound surrounded them.

At last Haboob's eyes flashed, and their descent slowed.

She untied herself, crossed to Walking Stick, and touched the Scroll of Years.

Suddenly she seemed to drift above the daylit, spindly mountain of the monastery.

"It is time!" she shouted. "Let the noble champions of the archery competition come forth! Let all the resistance stand ready! This snowy day is Midsummer. In years to come, all who survive this battle will look forward to the day, and roll up their sleeves, and say, 'Behold, the scars I earned on Midsummer's Day, the day we broke the Fimbulwinter!'"

A roar went up from the mountain.

Joy's senses returned to the darkened world. She put a finger to her lips, as one archer after another appeared beside Walking Stick, until the gondola was crowded with ten. Joy nodded to Haboob.

The efrit spread a smoky hand, and magical embers appeared in dozens of spots around the dark land beneath, hovering like fireflies.

The archers fired.

Karvak guards, awake or asleep, died in droves.

The Swanlings among the archers made the sign of their goddess, for the act of killing helpless men.

Whenever the efrit discerned a man had died, he snuffed that light. Wherever a man yet lived, the ember flickered. Not a single foe escaped.

Inga leapt over the side with rope and stake and secured *Guraab* to the battlefield.

Now Walking Stick leapt out, and there emerged from the scroll three members of royalty, Corinna, Alfhild, and Steelfox. Next came guards for Joy—Snow Pine, Liron Flint, and Yngvarr Thrall-Taker. Inga joined them.

Then came seven Runewalkers, half of all available, among them Peik and their newest member, Malin.

Malin hugged Inga. "This may be The End," she whispered.

"Don't think like that," Inga replied. "We will both make it. We'll fill our book of stories and greet the summer."

"Come on," Peik hissed. "We've runes to walk."

"Good luck," Joy told the Runewalkers.

Walking Stick paced out the battle formation, sowing warriors like seeds with the scroll. He would be at the task for a long time. He had six thousand soldiers to guard the rocky promontory where it descended to the mainland of Svardmark.

Now Inga let out the balloon's rope so the archers might rise to fifty feet. Haboob, fires dimmed, kept watch. As his hydrogen required no heating of the air (indeed, fire would be quite unwise) *Guraab* could stay hidden.

Joy turned away. Where the Great Chain wrapped around the promontory's lip was a narrow spit called the Giant's Tongue. She stepped onto that extrusion, an icy wind whistling around her. She could not begin until the army was in position.

She waited.

In the first hint of gray light, with the white tops of distant mountains illuminated but the world still dark, a wreath of fog and howling winds rose up to surround their position, though all within was clear.

Walking Stick stepped beside her. "As you see, the Runewalkers shield us. All is ready."

Joy approached the nearest of the huge metal links.

She touched a rune, *wunjo*, which could mean "joy." Why not?

Crimson energies leapt from the Chain, like a wildfire spreading across shapes of ice. A cold flame of blue rose in response. The cold was not just visible to her eyes; she could feel it within her skin, a slowing, freezing compulsion laid upon the Chain and the land.

Her power flowed down the links leading to the small island, still shrouded in darkness, that was the Chain's midpoint. From there it rushed up the far side and touched Spydbanen.

And not just Spydbanen. The vast dragon whose body had been the beginning of that land stirred, just as beneath her a sleeping dragon trembled within Svardmark. There was a hint of a third dragon-presence, older, more deeply asleep, beneath the island in the strait.

Everywhere the red-orange fire of her power spread, the blue fire was there to resist it.

She realized now the challenge was less wrenching the Chain from the compulsion Innocence had laid upon it, and more not awakening the dragons. They must retain a spirit of Unbeing.

Her perceptions were everywhere around the straits. And now she knew Innocence was down on that island, stirring. He was not alone but in the company of Jewelwolf, the troll-jarl, and the magic carpet.

Her army awaited the counterattack bravely, filling the narrow space of the promontory. A thousand hand-to-hand fighters stood shoulder to shoulder and four lines deep. Five thousand archers, armed with yew longbows in the Swanisle style, stood behind these fighters and in wings to either side, the abyss at their backs.

Now the Karvaks came.

Their balloons arrived first, but the cold winds shaped by the Runewalkers repelled them.

Next came ships—but they were over a thousand feet below. The Three Wolves' fleet, supplemented by the Gull-Jarl's, would have to find a landing and send men up the paths.

Third came a small group of Karvak scouts from the garrison at Lysefoss. They were fast, but by the time they arrived the sun was well up, and Joy, struggling with the Chain, could see everything down in the strait. As the scouts' horses reared, Walking Stick bid the archers wait. By now their position was known, but not necessarily the reach of the longbows. Best not to make the truth obvious.

The outnumbered Karvaks sped back to the garrison. More would be coming. Many more.

Now, near Joy, Princess Corinna ordered flags raised. This unleashed a hundred volunteers, berserkers all. They were to march downslope, guarding the sea approaches to the promontory and causing as much destruction as possible. Joy's heart ached for these men, for most were heading out to die. Guarding the approach was only their secondary purpose. Their primary role was to convince the enemy that Joy's force was an undisciplined rabble, as Walking Stick's rumormongers had told the tale for months.

They meant to lure the enemy into a killing zone.

A wave of cold hit Joy's mind. Innocence was fighting her actively now for the Chain.

She kindled her anger and flung it back at him.

Red-gold and silver-blue energies contended all along the links.

Joy. Stop this. The voice was bleak and tormented. Innocence.

She answered with a fresh blaze of power. There was a tremor underfoot.

Joy. This will wake the dragons.

She kept fighting. She was the fighting daughter of a fighting mother. She would never give in.

Joy, listen. I'm trying to help these people.

She felt a sob beginning inside her and willed it to become fire.

Who are you trying to help? she demanded. *Jewelwolf? The beautiful conqueror? Or Skrymir? Poor misunderstood killer?*

You don't see them as I do. They took me in when I was lost, after nearly killing everyone at the island. No one is really a villain when you see them close up. Those two are broken inside. When Jewelwolf gets the victory she needs, she will change. When Skrymir is at last able to feel himself an independent being, he will stop being cruel. We need to help them reach their destinies. Then they will become better beings.

O, my friend Innocence! You are so well named! These entities loom so large in your sight you can see nothing else! You choose to ignore how they trample thousands of other beings—each one equally worthy of your concern! But because they lack power these victims don't snare your imagination.

Never mind. You can't win. But we can both lose, if the dragons wake. That will mean death to us. And to everyone else. Your mother. My father.

What?

Imago Bone is here, on the island. Jewelwolf brought him upon Deadfall. She threatened war with Kpalamaa if the mariners didn't give him up. My mother is probably as dead as your father, Joy. So you see, we are in the same longship today. Do you not care?

Where before she'd fed raw anger into the Chain, now something changed. It was not a burst of fury but a sudden clarity of purpose.

Through her power, she sensed the main Karvak force from Lysefoss on its way. She perceived the little figures of Innocence, Bone, Jewelwolf, Deadfall down on the craggy island. She could indeed have a degree of pity for them all.

But she did not just see Bone down there; she saw bones. Bones of people lost at sea. Bones of people slain in combat. Bones of people who'd simply had mishaps in this treacherous landscape.

There was a past, and a future, and yes, in the present it all hinged on her and Innocence. And yet in a way it wasn't about them at all.

I care. Oh, my friend, I care. But I care about many other things too. I wish you were on my side, Innocence. I need you, in the time of my greatest fight. But you have chosen what is glittering and mighty over what is plain and loving. I am so sad for us, and for you. But I will fight on, for all the other people I love, and for the land that chose me. If the Kantenings survive I will urge them to abandon slavery and cruelty. If they do not survive they will join the bones of their ancestors, as is the fate of all flesh. But either way, they will not be enslaved, not by each other, certainly not by you.

There had been a hint of passion in him, but now the cold was back. His voice was nearly a monotone. *You cannot understand. They were right. You are too bound by Qiangguo's ideas of honor. I play the game of life at a higher level.*

Shut up and fight.

Her renewed conviction coiled down the Chain as weaving fire. She pushed Innocence's line of silver-blue back to the central island and beyond. She sensed his surprise. He gathered strength and shoved back.

But she realized something: she was better at this. Against an equally powerful foe she'd have won. But he also hadn't been lying about her chances. The Heavenwalls gave him greater strength. He didn't need her skill.

Qiangguo's bastion of mystical power slowly ground down Kantenjord's.

But she wasn't done yet.

"A-Girl-Is-A-Joy," came a voice, and then another: "Joy!"

She kept struggling with Innocence but allowed her attention to return to her body. Beside her stood Snow Pine, Flint, Steelfox, Corinna, Alfhild, Yngvarr, Inga—even Malin, resting after her Runewalking. So many personalities, so many energies.

"I'm here," she said.

"What can we do, Joy?" her mother said.

"Is there . . . a way to distract them? Down on that island . . ."

Steelfox said, "The winds will foil arrows or rockets. If we send our balloon, my people's balloons will swarm it."

"What of the balloon's explosive gases?" Alfhild asked.

Joy said, "Walking Stick . . . wanted to hold that in reserve . . ."

"Everything depends on the Chain," Corinna said.

"She's right," Snow Pine said. "If Flint and I get aboard that thing, we can just lower it into the straits until Haboob's ready to light."

"Yes," Flint said, "and we jump into the water at the last second. All should go swimmingly."

"Take me with you," said Yngvarr. "You may need a warrior."

"Flint and I are warriors," Snow Pine objected.

"But you're most welcome to come," Flint added quickly.

Joy said, "Mother . . . too risky . . ."

"No," Snow Pine said, "everything now is too risky, my brave girl. I am here to help you."

Corinna said, "I have the authority to release that balloon, and so I will. But Malin should go also. You need a Runewalker."

"No," said Malin. "I will find Peik. He is better rested."

"Very well," said Corinna.

Joy knew there was no stopping Snow Pine when she was set upon a goal. "Mother . . ." Joy said. "Be careful."

Snow Pine put her hand upon Joy's head. "You make me proud." She, Flint, and Yngvarr were gone without another word.

Joy hoped their mission would help, but she still needed a distraction now. "Is there anything else? Give me something else. . . ."

Steelfox held up a burnt, reddened hand. "While you've been talking, I've tested the energies of the Chain. . . ."

"Because she's a *lunatic*," Inga put in.

". . . And they cause intense pain. I don't think anyone is going to climb down it."

Joy said, "I didn't . . . ask anyone to!"

"I'm not just anyone," Inga mused. "I can handle a lot of hurt. And I can carry one person."

"I'll come with you," Malin said, returning from her search for Peik. "I can do something."

"You'll get killed," Inga said.

"You'll get killed," Malin replied.

"It has to be me," said Steelfox. "In all modesty, I am the best archer in five thousand miles. And you've been muttering, Joy. I heard you say my sister's name. She's down there, is she not? We have business."

Corinna said, "Steelfox is right. But the risks are great."

Inga and Steelfox looked at each other and nodded.

Malin walked away. Joy hurt for her.

"Go," Joy said to Inga and Steelfox, adding, "Imago Bone is down there too. Try not to shoot him. He may be of help."

They looked surprised but nodded again. Inga crouched, and Steelfox climbed her strong shoulders.

"Joy," Steelfox said. "What of Innocence? What is your word? Does he live or die?"

The world seemed to spin. Duty to the past . . . at odds with duty to the present and future.

"If you can take him in the arm or leg," Joy said, "do it. That should break his concentration. But one way or the other . . . you have to put an arrow in him."

"It will be done."

Now the troll-changeling stepped onto the links of the Chain. Inga grimaced, saluted her companions, and began the long descent to the island.

It was a mad plan. But everything was mad.

Joy's focus now was the point of contact between her energies and Innocence's. She had to keep that conflagration ahead of Inga and Steelfox.

It all seemed to take hours.

A shout arose from her army. Her enhanced senses couldn't help but flit to that location. The berserkers had led the enemy en masse onto the promontory, where maneuvering was tight and the Karvak horsemen lost much of their agility.

Before the Karvak shortbows were in effective range, five thousand Swanisle-style longbows let loose. The screams of men and horses ripped through the misty heights.

The Karvaks rode on, determined to reply. Their precise shots felled many a Kantening. They shot twice before switching to spears and closing on the Kantening lines.

But in the last moments before contact the Karvak commander grew unsure. For he saw that the Kantenings had planted thousands of wooden stakes into the ground here, in the place where the stone of the promontory gave way to the inland soil, ground now soft and pliant from the Runewalkers' mist and rain.

The commander gave a sudden order to turn.

It was a worse mistake than the charge would have been. The horsemen had little room to maneuver, and worse, the less-disciplined Spydbanen and Gullvik foot troops, eager for battle and glory, were close on their hooves. Some Karvaks broke free by trampling their allies. Others were stuck in confusion and mud.

The Karvak-led force was twenty-five-thousand strong, and its vanguard of a thousand horsemen were from the best fighting force on Earthe. But they were mired in a killing zone.

In the midst of the battle, the exiled lord of Laksfjord, Jon Haraldson, screamed for vengeance for his father and led a manic charge. The Gull-Jarl, burning with the desire to avenge his son Skalagrim the Bloody, met him head-on.

The two gutted each other and fell to the red mud, but now the men of Gullvik and Spydbanen faltered in the soggy ground. With a roar the Free Kantenings began slaying every warrior they could find.

I should not enjoy this slaughter, she thought. She was no Kantening. She was a civilized person. But her heart raced. She poured her excitement into the struggle with Innocence and pushed his influence back halfway to the Spydbanen heights.

Then all at once, when her mother's balloon emerged into sunlight, and Inga and Steelfox were two hundred feet above the water, Innocence's power slammed into hers with desperate force.

He knew Joy's companions were coming for him.

He kept nothing in reserve, pushing her back, back to the island and beyond. Steelfox and Inga saw it. Inga descended as fast as she dared, and Steelfox aimed at extreme range.

Answering arrows from the island's Karvaks flashed toward the two women, but at least the nimbus of energy where Joy's and Innocence's power intersected threw these off course.

Impossibly, one of Steelfox's arrows found Innocence—just as the nimbus hit Inga.

Inga and Steelfox fell toward the sea, but Innocence's power faded.

Joy's fiery energies claimed all the Chain. Light blazed through the strait. With a ferocious shout she strangled the supernatural winter.

It was cold there on the Chained Strait, but summer had come at last. She had won. Not the war, just a crucial battle. Yet she had won.

But she did not know if Innocence lived. And her friends would surely die. She had to—

A jabbing pain wracked her.

She looked down, stunned, at the two bloody wounds in her side. Her vision blurred.

She looked up and saw Corinna and Alfhild beside her, their faces stony, their daggers red.

"What," Joy gasped, falling to her knees, "what?"

"It is not personal," Alfhild said. The mask of womanhood had slipped and an inhuman uldra soul looked out, cold and disdainful. "You have served your purpose. We must not be ruled by someone alien to these shores."

Corinna by contrast was shaking, but her voice was firm. "I cannot accept you as queen of my homeland. You, an outsider. You can never be one of us! My folk are impressionable and already imitating your ways, learning your language, asking about Walking Stick's philosophy. Inevitably your culture will overwhelm ours. We'll forget our traditions, our language, our very souls. Did my brother, my father, my grandfather die for that? It is nothing personal, A-Girl-Is-A-Joy. This is how it must be."

Joy tried to respond but only coughed out blood.

Then Malin Jorgensdatter was at her side, drawing the sword that lay forgotten on Joy's back.

"This is how it must be!" Malin screamed.

"Little halfwit," Alfhild said, stepping forward. "You cannot possibly fight me. I am the image of your only friend in the world, the closest thing Inga has to a sister. If you kill me, she will hate you."

"Hate you!" Malin answered, and struck.

Their struggle took them away from Joy, but Malin had given her the time she needed to respond.

Her only hope was to draw upon the power of the Chain, and as Corinna advanced, bloody dagger shaking in the royal hand, Joy threw herself onto the Chain itself.

I die, Great Chain of Unbeing, she thought. *Betrayed by the very people I came to help. Save me—*

Joy?

Innocence?

He was still connected to the power. She'd thought he was defeated, struck down even as she was. But as her strength failed her she heard a shout of incoherent rage fill the air of the strait. It held the fury of a boy on the verge of manhood and the despair of a lost child.

As the dagger came down, the power echoed by that shout rushed up the Chain.

Everything was flame. Then all was blackness.

CHAPTER 40

YESTERDAY

Bone awoke in the sunlit infirmary of the vessel *Anansi*. He knew this because he recognized, though he did not understand, the language of the sailors hereabouts, because the fine construction of the ship spoke for itself, and because Eshe of the Fallen Swan was leaning over him.

"You were ranting in your sleep," she said, "about a woman of ice and a boy on fire."

"We failed at the island of the heart," Bone managed to say, trying to sort out his dreams. Or were they premonitions? "Or succeeded. They seem like the same thing. Where are my wife and son?"

"I don't know. We found your longship and its seven crew. Between us we recovered five more—yourself, Princess Steelfox, Yngvarr Thrall-Taker, Malin Jorgensdatter, and a peculiar young woman named Alfhild."

"That's all?" He racked his memory. "Innocence's power got away from him. He ran. The island fell apart. I remember Malin and Alfhild dangling from a cliff. Steelfox, Yngvarr, and I tried to haul them up. Then another tremor. We all fell."

When he'd looked back up at the clifftop, he'd seen Northwing surrounded by a glow, and within that glow were Katta and Gaunt. Gaunt was calling his name. Then smoke covered everything. "I lost consciousness at some point. Eshe, you must not give up searching."

"We have not given up. But you should be prepared for the worst. You five are lucky. Haytham ibn Zakwan had a balloon in the vicinity, searching for you. *We* did not see your flare, days ago, but he had."

"Ha . . . I'm glad to know he's still around."

Eshe frowned. "He is among the missing now."

"Tell me."

"After finding you, Haytham searched for more survivors. His craft was small, and too many people would overload it. You were unconscious at the time. He never returned."

"And Innocence?"

"He and the carpet Deadfall were never seen."

Bone made a fist. "Hours ago I had a family."

Eshe hesitated. "We are restoring *Bison*. It can transport survivors to the Five Fjords, which are relatively safe."

"How goes the war?"

"Rumors fill the isles of a Runemarked Queen who commands a rebellious army. In many a town this symbol is carved into trees and buildings, stone and snow."

Eshe held up a bark fragment that had a character in the language of Qiangguo. It was hard to decipher, because the renderer clearly did not know his or her strokes.

"Does that say 'happiness'?" Bone asked.

"It could. But the Kantenings are calling it 'joy.'"

"Do you mean to send me to the Runemarked Queen?"

"I think your companions will go, though Steelfox wavers."

"Not my problem, in any case. If we can't find Gaunt, I have to look for Innocence."

"Imago Bone, you are not going anywhere. You have a deep arrow wound, scratches, a blow to the head, a broken ankle, and superficial burns. The captain has agreed you may stay aboard *Anansi* to heal."

Bone sat up. "I'll be the judge of . . . ooph." He lay down.

"You see?"

"I beg you, keep looking for Gaunt."

"We will. For now. Now rest. You're no use to anyone if you fidget there, tormenting yourself."

"It's time, and its changes, that torment me. Time . . ." He looked through the portal at a dark wall of storm cloud, silver curtain of rain underneath. "The *Chart of Tomorrows*. The Kantening tome Gaunt and I carried from the East. It was aboard *Bison*. Was it found?"

Eshe smiled. "We are studying it even now."

He smiled back. "I keep making the mistake of thinking you're altruists."

"We are altruists. Altruism is motive, not method. Would you like to see the book?"

They brought him his and Gaunt's belongings from the ship. He noticed the fiddle wasn't there. He hoped she still had it, somewhere.

He studied the *Chart* until his strength gave out, puzzling out the runes, frowning briefly over passages in the languages of Mirabad and places farther east, scrutinizing maps, squinting at sea serpents, giant lobsters, wrecked ships, toothsome dragons, and sometimes useful information too. At last he nodded off.

A boom of thunder jarred him awake. The pitching of the ship didn't help matters. The Draugmaw must be near.

Hands shaking, he found Gaunt's wax tablet and stylus. It was she who'd encouraged him to record dreams to better understand himself. He looked at what she'd last written, something she hadn't had the opportunity to transfer to paper. It might be the final word he had from her.

With one wing, O Swan, you show me the Painter's canvas, and an ache rises within my chest, to paint likewise with words, to celebrate sea, stars, family. Yet with the other wing you show me the sick, the suffering, the enslaved. It seems that to follow the calling of one wing I must turn away from the other. For there are not enough hours in the day, nor enough of Gaunt, to follow both. How can this be, O Swan?

She hadn't spoken aloud of these feelings. He stared at the words, unable to move.

Write quickly, he seemed to hear her say. *Don't lose it. . . .*

He tore wax from the corners and patted it over Gaunt's words, hoping they could be preserved if he wrote gently over them.

Dreamed I was dying, he wrote.

The tablet lacked space for his whole tale. But with a few words and many murmurings, he recited a story into his memory.

THE CHOOSER OF THE SLAIN

Dreamed I was dying (he wrote).

And drowned within a sea like smoke (he murmured.) Red light faded, and blue and white light washed over me. I thought of the many years of my life, and they seemed short. A flicker. A blood drop in the ocean. What had I really learned?

Someone pulled me from the waters.

I saw her red hair and thought for a moment she was Gaunt. She was too young, though. "Who are you?"

"You can call me Cairn," she said. "I am risking a great deal speaking with you now."

It was the Chooser of the Slain.

"Am I a warrior, then?" I had to laugh. "You would want me in the golden hall of battle?"

She laughed back. "You would steal the golden goblets. You would run across the green pastures, and the chosen warriors would catch you and chop you to pieces. The next day you would reassemble and steal the golden platters. It might be amusing. But it is not to be."

She said it wasn't my time.

"I fully agree," I said. "I will always agree. This is a dream, eh?"

"Yes," she said. "And you may not always agree."

"As regards the dream or my time?"

"I cannot be with you for long, in this place. Listen."

She said I can't die till my daughter is born.

"I don't have a daughter."

"Then live, Imago Bone, and listen. This conflict is not just about nations. If it were, this would be but a minor skirmish on the grand scale. But this time it's different."

She told me, time itself is being rent.

"Great powers are involved. It is not just that the isles are formed of arkendrakes, whose thoughts spawn trolls and whose power raises such distortions of reality as the Draugmaw and the straits. The Heavenwalls of Qiangguo are involved too. So much concentrated power can shatter everything. Along one path lies the end of the human world. Along the other lies much conflict still, but a chance for better days."

"I will have no better days unless I can find my wife and son. Where are they?"

She told me to come to the Straits of Tid.

"You want what?" Captain Nonyemeko said.

"*Anansi* to go to the edge of the Draugmaw." Bone pointed to a map. "Here."

After exchanging further words with Eshe, the captain asked, "Why?"

"I will dream my way into the Straits of Tid. I think at this particular node of power, I can find help."

Eshe said, "In your condition, Bone, even a bad dream could kill you."

"I have to try."

Eshe and Nonyemeko consulted. Eshe said, "For this service, we will need to ask you a thing in return."

He laughed. "I find that reassuring, Eshe. All this help with no price attached . . . it was unnerving."

"Your worries are at an end. In a month, regardless of what transpires, I want you to serve Kpalamaa."

"You spoke of employment to me before, a long time ago."

"You could be a useful agent. Gaunt too, if we can find her."

"I can't make promises for her." But if she and Innocence were lost, a grim part of him thought, then he would need something to occupy him. Something that would keep him from destroying himself. "I can only speak for me." He hesitated. "And I won't ever kill for you. I've had enough of that."

"Noted."

"I will spy. I will steal. For you. Now do this thing for me."

He dreamed he floated above *Anansi* and the endless whirling storm, but that the surrounding realm had changed. Stars wheeled visibly, nebulae stretched across much of the blackness, a blue moon joined the silver. A blue-white ocean washed ghostly all around him, and Bone bobbed within it. He did not believe he could drown, but he sensed that enough damage to his dream body might cause him to awaken and forget anything he'd seen.

Cairn and her narwhal leapt out of the spectral waters, splashing beside him.

"You are here." She reached out and hauled him up, demonstrating unexpected strength. But perhaps strength of mind was all that mattered here.

"What do you wish of me?" Bone asked. Though the air was cool, he already felt dry.

"The currents of Tid are flowing to two destinations, Thief with Two Deaths. You must help make them one."

Now that he'd a better view, he beheld a fiery shore in the distance, dotted with volcanoes. There was also a shore with dark forests, cheerful firelights, and snow-capped mountains. Nearer at hand was a coast with castles and villages, piers and knarrs. Though he saw no people, now and again he heard the whinnying of thousands of horses.

"It's been a while," Bone said, "since anyone called me that. And despite my many talents, I don't see how I'm qualified to shift the currents of time."

"No one is skilled at first; nothing can replace experience. But you are already involved. Your family is already buffeted by the flow."

"I can't argue the point. So is this a strait? It looks like a river."

"Some say the straits resemble a river, and others have visualized it as a great tree. Some say its branches lead to three worlds, or nine, or more. Many say the world of humans, the Middle World, is but the easiest branch to reach, the main one. But it is simply that humans occupy the *present*. The past speaks to them but cannot be spoken back to. The future beckons to them but cannot speak for itself."

"Are you trying to befuddle me? Because it is working."

"I am explaining too much! Your own path is simple in idea, difficult in attainment. Find a way to make the Middle World, the main branch of time, flow to a place where life endures."

"I am just a thief."

"There is a story that the All-Father was a thief. He stole the very mead that gives visions and poetry."

"Say, would that mean my wife owes her art to the work of a thief? That amuses me."

"I'm not sure it would amuse her. But listen. Now I must leave you; for reasons I cannot explain, your presence is disruptive to me. You may ride this narwhal, however. His name is Drømlanse. He is gentle, unless you are evil."

"I have had varying luck with riding, and being good."

CHRIS WILLRICH   463

"I know. Not-evil is good enough for Drømlanse. He will take you where you need to go."

"Where is that?"

"Your intuition must guide you, Imago Bone."

"Gaunt is the one with intuition—"

Cairn leapt from the narwhal, and Bone carefully hauled himself onto Drømlanse. He raised his hand in a tentative farewell to the girl, but she was gone.

"Drømlanse," he sighed. "If I'm to divert the flow of time, I suppose I should have begun yesterday. Swim against this flow that leads to what-do-you-call-it. Ragnarok. We'll figure out the rest as we go. It's what I usually do."

The narwhal rushed ahead. They raced alongside the spectral shore.

A vessel crossed their path. It seemed bigger this time.

"*Naglfar*," he said aloud.

"True, nithing," came a voice from the ship. "And this time you are alone." It was the voice of Skalagrim. He recognized others on deck. Crowbeard. Nine Smilodons. Erik Glint. And many others whom he'd met in his travels.

"Persimmon Gaunt is not among you," he observed. "She lives."

"Not for long," Skalagrim said. "The end comes, sweeping us all toward it."

"I've been outmaneuvering the end a long time. Ha!"

He gently kicked the narwhal's flanks, in the same way he'd tried and failed to control horses before. The narwhal was more cooperative. They charged *Naglfar*, attempting the same strike Cairn had once made against it—or its previous avatar.

But there sprang up from the water his two brothers who'd drowned long ago. They clutched at him, barnacle-faced, seaweed-draped, pearls in clammy eye sockets.

"Be at peace, brothers," he rasped. "I love you. Dive, Drømlanse."

They ceased their clutching and stared. The real Bone brothers had never heard him speak thus.

Down Drømlanse went, through what seemed more fog than water. The world became blurred light.

They drifted in the midst of a sunken citadel, one filled with books. Sunlight streamed through windows, and an eel-like thing twisted from floor to floor, seeking something.

No, not an eel. A flying carpet.

"Deadfall?" Bone said aloud.

He realized three things. First, speaking beneath the time-flow was like breathing mist. Second, the tower was not truly drowned but a place under the desert sun. Third, the carpet almost seemed able to hear him, for it twitched a little in response.

Was this the past, when Deadfall had dwelled in the great desert? Or some future in which Deadfall had returned?

The carpet ascended to a set of books arrayed in a pattern of black, with one white-colored book in the middle. Bone recognized it.

Deadfall hovered there, contemplating.

"The *Chart!*" Bone tried to call, sudden instinct taking him like a wave. "Psst! The *Chart of Tomorrows*! Take it! Give it to Gaunt and Bone!"

The carpet twitched. At last it extricated the book from its place and carried it downward.

"What have I done?" Bone said to himself. "Or had I already done it?"

Drømlanse swam them through a window into bright sunlight. It seemed he was a sort of ghost while he wandered the Straits of Tid. Even in this brightness he was wrapped in a nimbus of blue-green, a pocket of the waters of time. He didn't know how to navigate. Yet a way of influencing the past seemed open: to speak and plant ideas into minds.

They hovered now over the cliffside city of Qushkent. "Drømlanse, can you take me back to the Bladed Isles?"

The narwhal rushed west, and reality blurred around them. For a moment he thought they'd gone east; the place they encountered seemed a part of Qiangguo. Then he recognized the mountain of the Scroll of Years and saw how Princess Corinna called upon warriors to accept A-Girl-Is-A-Joy as her champion. It seemed there was one there who'd been especially recalcitrant. Bone shouted in his ear, "Joy! Joy is wonderful! You like Joy!"

"Hail, Joy Snøsdatter!" the man yelled, raising his axe.

"That's the spirit," Bone said. "This is fun. But Drømlanse, perhaps I need to be more direct. Take me to . . . Ragnarok."

Again, the blurring. Now all was fire and ocean and ice. They hovered high above the sea. He thought he recognized the islands of the Splintrevej below him and Oxiland in the distance ahead. But that meant Spydbanen and Svardmark should be to his right and left.

Instead there was only a series of new volcanic islands belching fire and smoke into the atmosphere. Oxiland seemed intact, but its own volcano was doing its best to keep up. The sky was dark, and snow was falling everywhere.

They drifted down to a little island bearing remnants of a vast metal chain.

"This was it," Bone said, sliding off Drømlanse. "The heart of the Chain. The dragons woke up. What made it happen?"

"I did," came an ancient voice.

Bone spun and saw a tall, thin, white-bearded man, the white flecked with red. Blood-gold runes covered his black robes.

"Winterjarl," Bone said.

"I have used that name, traveler. Do you come from the past or the future?"

"The past, or so I believe. I have made use of the book you made."

The Winterjarl looked confused. "I made a book? You must be from the future then."

"I am growing less certain. What has happened in this place?"

"The battle of the dragons was renewed. The ash blotted out the sun. The final frost is upon the world."

"Cheery."

"I've changed my mind. You must be from the past. Even your dream-form is making me feel more tenuous." The Winterjarl turned transparent as he said this.

"Don't go! I must change all this! Where do I start?"

"It's surely futile! The only path I see is to change the hearts of those who struggle. Make them see peace as a victory, not a defeat."

"Who? Who must I change?"

"Alas, I do not know. I have forgotten so much. You seem so familiar. . . ."

The Winterjarl faded from sight.

Bone sat beside ash-colored waters.

"Drømlanse," he said in time. "Will you take me to me? Somewhere in the past. Sometime between sleeping and wakefulness."

He rode the narwhal through dark seas and shifting stars. Now they were above a desert rooftop before dawn, in the thousand-towered city of Palmary. There a younger Bone stirred in his sleep.

As the future Bone descended from the narwhal and stepped forward, two figures rippled and shimmered out of the gray. To the left stood a thing of dust and spiderwebs resembling a tall, hooded figure, one of whose hands was a pair of sharp pincers, the other a dark scythe. To his right was a being of fire and smoke, its eyes and mouth like rubies glowing in the sunset, and it clutched what resembled at times coiling flame, and other times a burning cat-o'-nine-tails.

"Of course," said the future Bone. "I must be challenged by the powers who accompanied me in the old days. Angels of death, hear me. I am but a shade of a reflection of a dream. I will change nothing of substance."

"We know not what you are, spirit," said the dark one, "but you cannot take his life. That is given to me."

"He means, to me," said the fiery one. "But I sense you mean no harm."

"I assure you," Bone of the future said, "I would never harm him. Would you leave us?"

"Since I concede you intend no harm," the grim death said, "very well."

"I will kill him later," said the bright death, and faded along with his counterpart.

Bone shook his head and knelt beside Bone.

"Thief. Wake up."

Without warning the younger Bone somersaulted to a crouching defensive position, knife drawn. The older Bone envied the younger man's reflexes. It hadn't been so many years, had it? He was road-worn. His younger self had paler, smoother skin and darker hair. No moustache either; he'd forgotten that.

The younger Bone also seemed more focused, and desperate. Perhaps, under all the swagger, even sad. Curious. He hadn't remembered it that way.

As he assessed his younger self, his younger self likewise assessed him. At last the younger Bone sheathed his dagger and crossed his arms.

"Bloody hell!" said the younger man. "Time travel!"

"Yes," said his elder, nearly laughing. "Sorry."

"I've heard of it but never experienced it."

"I have," said the older one. "You're right to want to run."

It didn't seem possible that the younger Bone's eyes could widen more, but it happened. "So you remember this meeting?"

The older Bone shivered. Did he? The memory was tentative, dreamlike. Perhaps it was something the mind-assassin Hackwroth had taken from him in Qiangguo, only now coming back to life? Or was history subtly changing around them?

"Perhaps I do."

The younger man scratched his chin. "Then you're genuinely me, and history is inviolate."

"I hope not. A terrible event is coming I'm trying to prevent. It will destroy quite a lot of things. Possibly everything."

"Bloody hell! I'm listening."

"Good. But you may forget. This whole experience is dreamlike. In fact I'm counting on that."

"How so?"

"I think you will lose the memory of this," the older Bone said. "Because I feel certain now I did. But I'm hoping the sense of it will return when you need it. Listen. Your son may appear to you one day. Perhaps aboard a flying machine . . ."

The younger Bone shook his head. "Son? I was not sufficiently careful, was I?"

"He does not exist yet, for you. He . . . he needs your love. And his mother's."

"Such cryptic instructions. And yet somehow so alarming."

"Deep down, Bone, you need to understand . . . even if a day comes when the boy seems dangerous, you are his father, and he needs love. He will need your mercy and your help, even if he seems to be sliding into evil. Promise me you will help him."

"Love. Mercy. Evil. I change considerably in the future, don't I?"

"I had not considered it before now. But you may be right."

"If it were anyone else, self, I would reject what you say. But very well. I promise. Whether or not I remember, the promise has been spoken."

"Thank you."

"It's a small enough gesture, I suppose, phantasm of the future. Safe journey to you . . . unless you care to tell me the trap details and guard rotations of the Tower of the Four Faces, or the secret call signs of the Lords of Cups, Wands, Coins, and Pentacles . . . ?"

"I recall planning that caper, but none of the details. Frustrating, no?" Indeed, as he spoke, Bone felt his senses blurring.

"Alas!" The younger man laughed, his voice dimmer. "But at least you haven't materialized just to toss me a dagger, a parcel, and a mission, monstrous enemies at your heels."

"Give me time."

"Heh. Well, if we are done, specter of tomorrow . . . are you all right? You seem to be turning transparent."

"More experienced time travelers than I," Bone said, the words sounding distant to his own ears, "have said that speaking to people in the past can be disruptive to one's substance. Farewell."

"Farewell then! I need my sleep to be ready for the job and for an assignation with a lovely poet tonight, which the job will fund."

"It is that night?"

The younger Bone's eyes widened. "My son . . . is she . . . ?"

He shouldn't have said it, but the older Bone said, "She is a good one, thief. Better than we will ever deserve. Farewell."

He ran to the narwhal and climbed, feeling that he was becoming threadbare as he moved. Reaching Drømlanse solidified him, and the past blurred around him.

Now he should find Gaunt. Give her the same message and hope it did some good.

They seemed to be swimming above the Straits of Tid again, and still the fiery conflagration appeared on the horizon. "Can you find my wife, mighty one?"

Again a blurring, nights and days flickering past.

Now they were in a cold sea not at all unreasonable for narwhals. Icebergs drifted about them, and an icepack lay ahead.

"She is there?" Bone asked.

The narwhal did not answer, but another voice did. "It doesn't matter, son," said a rasping voice.

Ahead of them drifted a half-ship of the Draug.

But no Draug was aboard, just a man Bone recognized. "Father," Bone said.

"What you said to your younger self, it's the truth," said Effigy Bone. "You do not deserve that woman out there. What you deserve is oblivion. The people of Qiangguo are right to venerate the old, and parents most of all. You've begun feeling it yourself, haven't you? The pain of a son who wants nothing to do with you. How I felt it! You abandoned the family calling, for what? For a dream of travel? One that swiftly became the fact of thieving?"

"I have done many bad things in my life," Bone said. "The time you speak of . . . I am not proud of it. But the life of a fisherman would have killed me."

"Ha! Coward!"

"Killed me," Bone repeated. "Maybe drowned like my brothers. But even had I lived to your old age, I would have been dead inside. Here in this clear air, I see many things. I might have found another path. I might have found my way to a life of travel that was not a life of theft. I might even have stayed with you a year or two, to see you and Mother better settled. But I was not strong enough to contend with you. I had only the strength to escape."

"Weakling!"

"Your son! What did that ever mean to you? Another pair of hands! Another body to fish, and mend, and perhaps to avenge! Proof of your virility! Legacy!"

"Of course you would mock legacy."

"I understand it! Here on the Straits of Tid I know I'm but a bubble on the river of time, waiting to burst. I want my son to live after me and think well of me. But not at the cost of his own happiness. It all ends, Father, for all of us, so let's try like hell to be kind to one another in the meantime. I cannot be a better son to you. But I can be a father to my son."

When he looked up the half-boat drifted by itself. Bone stared at it a long time.

"Take me to Gaunt," he bade the narwhal.

They dove underwater, and ice rushed by overhead, and suddenly they burst through a gap in the sea's blue ceiling and slid over white ice beneath a gray sky.

Before him he saw Persimmon Gaunt, and Mad Katta, and Northwing, and Haytham ibn Zakwan. They were trudging across the ice, bundled up and roped together. Northwing saw him first, spearing Bone with that disconcerting gaze, yet Bone was glad for it now.

He waved.

Northwing swore. "Katta, you see that?"

Katta said, "A little specificity, while it can trick us into disregarding the Absolute, is sometimes desirable—"

"Imago bloody Bone! Right in front of us! There!"

"What?" Haytham said.

"Oh no," Gaunt said. "Does that mean he's dead?"

Bone smirked and shook his head.

"No, he's saying he's too annoying to be dead," Northwing said.

Bone glared at the shaman.

"I see him!" Gaunt said. "Imago!"

"Strange," Katta said, "I do not."

"Well, good," Haytham said. "I was feeling a bit left out."

"But then," Katta mused, "he only skirted evil. I tended to exaggerate my perception of him in order to keep him more honest."

Bone folded his arms and glared now at Katta.

"Imago, can you hear us?" Gaunt said. "Are you sending a message?"

"I'm here," Bone said.

"He's talking," Northwing said, "but I can't hear him. Bone, get closer to Gaunt. You and she have a connection."

Bone dismounted the spectral narwhal and joined Gaunt. He tried to embrace her but couldn't. He wondered why he was so much more insubstantial here than elsewhere. Then he looked south and saw the many volcanoes in the distance.

"Gaunt," he said. "Persimmon."

"I hear you!" she said. "I see you. I'm so glad you're alive!" She squinted. "Are you on the Straits of Tid?"

"That's it! My dream form is there. My body is healing on Eshe's ship. I, uh . . ."

"Spit it out."

"I agreed to serve Kpalamaa, for her help."

"Well, I didn't."

"She may consider it a package deal."

"We make these decisions together, Bone."

"You were not exactly in reach."

"Well, I'm here now."

Northwing said, "Thank you, both of you, for reminding me why I have never tried to marry! Take note of the southern fires and say what matters!"

"Gaunt," Bone said, "we have to prevent . . . that."

"You are traveling in time . . . Swan's blood, Bone, you said you're on a ship, but that . . ."

"Spit it out . . ."

"Maybe you are dead, Imago, in this moment, and are speaking with me from the past."

"You have a talent for stating uncomfortable things."

"You love it," she said but did not smile. "Can you take me with you?"

"I don't think so. Can you reach the straits?"

"We're not on land anymore. We are hoping there are shamans of the Vuos people out here. Northwing senses they survived. Maybe they know how to reach the straits."

"Listen," he began.

He woke in the cabin of *Anansi*, the Draugmaw's storm still raging outside.

"No!" he yelled at Eshe, who gripped his arm. "No! I was talking . . . talking to Gaunt. . . ." His memories were a jumble. He knew they'd been on the ice together. He knew they'd talked about time. Everything specific was lost. The rest of his journey, too, was only a blurry set of impressions.

"I am sorry, Bone," Eshe said, "but something has happened you need to know."

"Volcanoes?"

"What? No. Jewelwolf is here."

CHAPTER 41

TOMORROW

They trudged for many days over the ice, terrified by roaring winds, booming volcanoes, and the crackling of the ice. All the while Gaunt dwelled on Bone's last words to her.

Listen. The past can be changed. But the changes that endure belong to the mind only. Memories. Insights. Perceptions. You can plant seeds that will bloom in the present. Find Innocence. Tell him you love him. Tell him love and peace are what truly matter, not power, not control. And that the piling up of power does not lead to freedom, but to chains. But most of all, that you love him.

"We are near," Northwing said, interrupting her thoughts. "Reindeer. I'd know the sound anywhere."

Soon the animals snorted close, pulling two sleds that resembled at first glance a pair of giant shoes. In the sledges were people garbed in colorful leather and cloth, easily seen against the white. Some wore circlets of metal shaped into complex patterns. They bore curved daggers and beaded belts. They also had bows. These they did not aim at the travelers but kept in easy reach.

Gaunt raised open hands. "Hello!" she called. "Do you speak Kanten-tongue?"

The oldest man said, "Some of us do. Greetings. What brings you out this way?"

Gaunt, at a loss for words, gestured toward the volcanoes of the south.

"Ah," said the man. "It's the same for us. We wondered if any more southerners survived."

"Southerners?" Northwing asked.

"Everyone south of the Country of the First. You with your wars and your unhealthy magics."

"Do you have any idea who you're talking to? *I* am a shaman of the taiga of the continent."

"Interesting, as that's where the community is going. Climb aboard, if you would."

The Vuos camp spread in either direction as far as Gaunt could see. It was as if several villages had been uprooted, except that instead of houses there rose conical tents. Reindeer, sheep, goats, and other animals roamed about, tended by herders. Small children chased each other, like kids on a holiday. There were hundreds of people here, and aside from a few guards, all were engaged in labor—herding, tanning, sewing, slaughtering, cooking, or, in the case of one group, gathering around a map sketched into the ice.

When the sleds stopped, it was toward this group that the wanderers were led.

Many people stared. Gaunt was fully aware she and her friends were true outsiders. They were introduced to a group of elders, including a few old men carrying flutes, sitting beside ornately carved drums.

An old woman in a deep-blue garment, fringed with geometric designs of many colors, nodded to them. "Welcome, travelers, on this bleak day. My name is Aile. The shamans warned of your coming."

"I would love to speak with these shamans," Northwing said, bowing in the direction of the old musicians and getting nods in return. "I sense we have techniques in common."

"There are stories," Aile said, "that in long-ago times we were able to travel to the continent, and that we learned things from the people there, and they from us. Now share a meal with us, and then we will speak."

The travelers shared their meager stockfish and bread, and gratefully accepted fresh fish taken through holes in the ice. They also ate dried reindeer meat and a stew of potatoes and carrots, followed by a dessert of one cloudberry apiece. These resembled miniature strawberries and had a taste like sour and sweet apples mixed together.

The shamans sung a low-toned song that reminded Gaunt of the arctic wind. She studied their drums, whose skins were covered with pictograms. Gaunt recognized symbols for humans, reindeer, and the sun and moon, but the rest were mysterious. The symbols mostly treated the edge of the drum as "down," although a good many figures seemed detached from gravity, floating in the middle.

A shaman noticed her looking and spoke to Aile. She said to Gaunt, "You are curious. The drums help connect one to the many forms of the universe. The ripples and creases that appear on the fabric also help foretell the future."

"I also use a drum," Northwing said. "Or I did, before it was lost in my travels. Do they send their souls to ride within animals?"

Aile relayed the question and answered, "Their method is to send forth their souls and spin temporary animal-bodies out of the elements. Or else to move spiritually beside animals but not inside them. The difference is interesting."

Haytham spoke up. "I mourn the urgency that brings us. I wish Northwing could spend months discussing the fine points of shamanism. But you said there might be a way to respond to the destruction. I hope you did not mean simply running away."

Aile frowned. "No one is running away. We migrate as best we can. We knew of the war in the south, and our far-traveled hunters and our shamans watched for any rumor. We experienced the cold that stretched through the reindeer's calving time and beyond. We had some warning of the calamity. When the shamans saw the signs most of us came, as many as could be found. The Coastal Vuos, the Mountain Vuos, the Forest Vuos, the River Vuos, the Reindeer Vuos. We set aside all differences to survive, even as we have in the past, against foamreavers and trolls. Together we will cross the ice to the continent and find a way to survive. In such a journey there is no running away."

Katta spoke. "My friend did not accuse you of cowardice, Aile. He speaks of us and our bitterness at having been removed from the struggle in the South. We took it as our task to contend with this war. If there is anything we can do, we would be grateful to know."

Aile replied, "The shamans say there is a way to reverse what has happened. It comes at a price. A sacrifice of being. If you succeed, these past many days, with their deeds of courage, will vanish as ice disappears in the sun. For that reason we will not send any of the Vuos with you. All our energies must go toward survival. But we agree your quest is worth doing."

Aile drew her knife and scratched out a drawing of a human figure beside a reindeer. "For whatever valor we manage in the future, whatever great tales, we will never see the lands of home again, nor the great rocks our ancestors worshipped beside, nor taste cloudberries once the last are gone. And too, you may call back to life many who have died, and this is no small thing. For this we are willing for these days to vanish, to exist, perhaps, as a half-remembered dream."

She drew a line across her image.

"Hear me. What you call the Straits of Tid, our shamans experience as the Axial Tree, reaching up from the world through spirit country, to touch the North Star. The North Star represents time future; the great roots are time past. You must descend to the roots, you four. You may not like it there. The Tree will raise images of the dead to bar your way. Are you prepared?"

Gaunt and the others nodded.

Aile said a few words to the shamans and elders, then, "You will travel with the survivors of Larderland who managed to reach us. With luck, you may attain the nearest point that you may reach the Tree."

"Where is that?" Gaunt asked.

Aile directed her dagger point to a sketch upon the icepack. It represented the landmass of Spydbanen and its merging with the ice. There were wedges upon Spydbanen, and Jaska tapped the metal to the largest of these. "It is the place Kantenings call the Trollberg. The great mountain of Skrymir Hollowheart."

Gaunt was pleased to see the Likedealer Tlepolemus had survived the conflagration, along with some hundred of Larderland's inhabitants. "We'd been on the move already," he said. "That was lucky, in one sense. Our elderly will remain here. And the children are already becoming Vuos. How can it be otherwise? But for me, and some others, there can be no more discarding one identity after another. I am a man of Ma'at who became Amberhornish, an Amberhornish man who became a Larderman. I tire of change. A raid on the Trollberg sounds like just the thing I need."

"We can oblige."

They hauled the longship *Little Dragon* for hours, at last reaching a fissure like an ice-choked river. Carefully they lowered the ship and even more carefully got aboard.

They rowed. Northwing, seeing through the eyes of fish, assured them the way was open, but as the ocean neared a cold blast hit them. The shaman said, "Beware! The fissure is sealing up! The water at the mouth is freezing over! Row! Row!"

When they reached sight of open sea, the end of the passage had indeed been covered with a layer of ice. Gaunt joined Tlepolemus at the dragon prow, furiously hacking with axes.

"I will never again underestimate the strength of your arm," Tlepolemus said as the ship broke free.

They raised sail and entered the iceberg-clotted waters called the Ocean of White Knives. Tlepolemus judged it unwise to sail directly among the new volcanic islands that marked the grave of Spydbanen, so they took a round-about way.

After two days of difficult sailing they saw the peak of the Trollberg rising steep from the waters. The valley and settlement called Jotuncrown were drowned.

"See there?" Northwing said. "That cave used to be thousands of feet up. Now it's just hundreds. We can climb."

"No trolls," Haytham said.

"They may have perished with the dragon-mind that formed them," Gaunt said.

"I perceive no supernatural evil," Katta said.

"The difficult part will be mooring," Tlepolemus said.

In the end they had harbored a quarter mile from the cave. Roped together, Gaunt, Northwing, Haytham, and Katta, along with Tlepolemus and ten warriors, leapt onto a ledge. Gaunt feared for Katta, but a series of instructions and tappings gave him the information he needed to make the jump.

The Trollberg's surface was full of handholds, crevices, and ledges, so the climb was not too difficult. A worse danger was the cold. Gaunt was having trouble feeling her fingers by the time they neared the cave.

Thus they were in a vulnerable position when the madman peered out and sent them a magical gale.

Two men slipped, and the whole line nearly gave. They hauled the victims up, and Tlepolemus bellowed a challenge. "Who are you, wizard?"

"I am cold itself! My heart is ice!"

Innocence, Gaunt realized as soon as she heard the voice. She called out to him, but her voice was lost in a fresh moaning of the wind.

With great difficulty she readied her fiddle. As the fossegrim had taught her, she put all her sorrow into music.

The wind stopped. "Mother?" called the wild man.

Soon they reached him, clad in ragged furs and living amongst the bones of birds. He had a thin beard and countenance and wide, mad eyes. His forehead was still marked with the sign of intertwining dragons.

"Mother," he said. "I killed you. I killed my father too. You are a shade."

"No, I am real. And you are real."

"Stay back! I hurt everyone who comes close."

"Innocence, what happened?"

"I killed Joy. I killed them all. Steelfox. Inga. Jewelwolf . . . Father."

"You didn't kill your father, Innocence. He survived the quest for Skrymir's heart."

He sobbed. "He was with me at the Great Chain, when . . . Mother, I did it. I woke the dragons. I meant to save Joy, but I killed her, and everyone, everyone . . ."

"It can't be all your fault. Young people sometimes think they are responsible for everything."

His cackle frightened her more than his sobbing. "I'm not 'young people.' I'm Lord Gaunt. Dragonlord. So much power. The Heavenwalls and the Chain. Even with the Chain gone I'm still too strong for control. You don't know. None of you understand. Only Joy could and she's dead."

"Innocence," she said, pleading to herself as much as to him. "You must have hope. There is a way. The cave opening. We can open the gateway to time, change what happened."

"You think I haven't tried? When I go there, I see the dead! All my dead. Thousands of them!"

Gaunt saw the truth of it in his eyes. Yet she said, "I know you haven't given up. You are still living here, beside this gateway. And this time you will not be alone. I will be with you."

"And I, boy," said Northwing.

"And I," said Katta.

"And I," said Haytham.

lie that I was greedy. I sought a life of harder toil than you could imagine. You, clutching at coins and jewels, pomp and show! I saw it all, Mother. Not just the hollowness of our lives but where it ended, in the grave. Everything ends eventually. I made peace with that, built my poetry around it. But you—you hide from it. Cowards! As if shoving your head under fancy pillows will distract the reaper. Well, that was your business, Mother, but mine was living."

The image of Olivia of the Sorrowdowns screamed, "I have had enough! I will give you something to cry about!"

"I'm not crying." Gaunt took up her instrument. "I'm fiddling."

And she played.

It seemed as though pain was a string on a Vestvinden fiddle. The specters hesitated, as though no longer able to perceive Gaunt. The warband passed them by.

As they came over the next ridge, the journeyers saw the way ahead barred by a curtain of fire. They stepped forward and peered into it.

Within the fire wavered the image of a small island wrapped in a titanic chain, links stretching at either hand toward cliffs flanking a white-waved strait.

"This is it," Gaunt said. "But we are barred."

"So you are, Gaunt," Imago Bone said, stepping from the flames. He was a charred travesty of himself. Beside him walked two angels of death, one shadowed, one fiery. She knew their names, for they'd accompanied Bone of old: Severstrand and Joyblood.

Gaunt trembled and played her fiddle.

"Alas, it won't work on me," Bone said, "or these night angels."

"You're not the real thing, any of you," Gaunt said. "You could not be."

"You are correct. But the tree is raising whatever defense it can."

Northwing said, "The tree is dying!"

Bone shrugged. "It does not realize that. It is not truly a thinking entity. It only tries to protect its integrity. Beyond here is the key moment that can be changed, to restore what was lost. But I cannot let you pass."

"You are not my husband," Gaunt said, playing her tune.

"No," he said, and his voice was sad. "But I am enough like him that you cannot resist. Your own tune coils back upon itself."

It was true. She could not defy him in that way.

Tlepolemus and the other Lardermen simply shouted, "Aye!" and the cavern echoed with their voices.

Innocence did not look consoled. But he said, "I will try."

He walked to the cave and reached out, closing his eyes.

The daylight vanished, and outside lay a moonlit world.

Gaunt peered out and did not see the Straits of Tid. Instead, a gigantic tree filled her view. Its upper reaches rose to the sky, and around it stars wheeled. Below, its trunk faded into silver mist. It was so large that its bark imitated the handholds and ledges of the Trollberg. They could climb it.

The trunk just below the cave was living, healthy bark. But at eye level and above it looked charred and dead.

Northwing stepped beside Gaunt. "The Axial Tree. Our discussions with the Vuos inspired us to see it as a tree. Who knows what we're actually doing when we go out there."

"Well, I recommend ropes, shaman and gentlemen."

They descended through peculiarly warm, misty air, moving like ants down the tree.

After a long interval the slope bent and became walkable, like a mountain trail. They collected their ropes and carefully picked their way down.

Now shapes emerged from the mists, shambling corpses with moonlit eyes.

"No," Innocence said. "No."

Joy was there, a dagger sticking from her chest, her limbs moving far too freely, her face a travesty of burns. And now came a blackened skeleton in a charred Karvak deel, and a large woman with the skin half-melted from her bones. A monstrous troll figure loomed up, his thousand fragments seemingly held together by malice alone. After them, scores more.

"No," Innocence said.

"Bone?" Gaunt called out. "Bone?"

But she did not see him.

"Innocence!" she said. "Your father is alive. Time would torment us with him if he weren't! There is hope even now!"

"Oh, I feel so *very* hopeful!" Haytham said, sword drawn, voice shaking as he did. But now there came the corpse of Corinna, a mass of burns recognizable only by her crown.

"Yes, have hope, my dear," said Corinna. "We'll be together soon."

Haytham stood as though turned to stone. He murmured something in the tongue of Mirabad and followed in Kantentongue: "May the All-Now grant me life if that is best . . . and death if that is best."

"I have an opinion on the matter," laughed Corinna, advancing with a bloody dagger.

"So do I," said Katta, and blocked her thrust with his staff.

The start of combat broke Haytham free of his paralysis. But on impulse Gaunt drew not her daggers, sword, or bow but her fiddle. Why not? The odds were overwhelming, and the poetic precedents were good.

She played for the dead.

And the dead paused, hearing the music of the fossegrim in the hands of a poet who'd suffered. Northwing began drumming in accompaniment.

The dead stood transfixed, their attention momentarily frozen. She sang whatever doggerel came to mind:

> Come my friends, let us go past.
> Let us see, if luck can last.

Down they went.

In time the fog cleared. The slope became easy to walk. They moved through fissures in the bark as big as riverbeds. The roots of the great tree, like the crown, spread among the spinning stars. There was one of the titanic roots, however, which lay twisted awry, off in its own direction and far from its companions. That mammoth root seemed, at its distant tip, wreathed in fire.

Gaunt turned back, though the poetic precedent for that gesture was not so good. Many of their number had fallen, but Innocence, Haytham, Northwing, Katta, and Tlepolemus, and five more of their band remained.

"I regret our losses," Gaunt said to Tlepolemus.

"They hearkened to old Kantening ways," Tlepolemus said. "It suited them to battle the dead at the end of the world."

Haytham stared back at the mists where the shade of Corinna lay. "Onward then," he sighed. "Onward to destiny."

They walked on, and time seemed a distorted, dreamlike thing. The fire-wreathed root loomed big as a ridge of hills, and now they had to ascend. As

the fiery nimbus glowed over a ridge, the dead returned. These wer of figures only, but they seemed ravaged, twisted, bloody.

"No," Gaunt said. "Not them."

Her grandparents, along with her younger brothers and baby sis had been ripped to pieces in Gaunt's girlhood by a wizard's beasts.

"Persimmon!" they wailed. "Persimmon!"

She hadn't been known as *Gaunt* until later, in the distant city of when she'd styled herself "Persimmon of County Gaunt," and event "Persimmon Gaunt." When these siblings were alive, she'd been n the family holding, the Sorrowdowns.

Katta asked, "Who are these shades?"

"They are members of my family, slain by creatures of Spawr a wizard who was a bane to Swanisle for many years. They died whe young."

"Why didn't you help us?" the dead ones said. "Why weren't you

"I was with the bards," she found herself saying. "I was learning and poetry. . . ."

Now, "Selfish! Selfish!" came the voice of her mother. Olivia of th rowdowns followed the rent ones. She was in one piece but emaciated ar

"Mother? You are dead?"

"When your bastard son slew summer in the Bladed Isles," Olivia "it chilled Swanisle as well. We were starving. Then he loosed the dra and the sun was blotted out. I could not survive. Maybe your older sister I can't say."

"Oh, Mother . . ."

"What do you care? You were off on your adventures . . . just as w these little ones died, you were off with your music! Family was never eno for you!"

Gaunt reeled, dropped to her knees. Katta took her arm, and Hayth too. Northwing stood beside her. And Innocence too came between Gau and the shade.

Gaunt rose.

"Weren't we rich enough for you, spoiled girl?" the shade said. "Did y abandon us because we found hard times?"

"I didn't care about your wealth! That was your obsession, Mother! It's

She dropped the fiddle and drew and threw a dagger. It caught him in the shoulder.

"Well done!" Bone smiled. He and the night angels advanced.

Northwing said, "You men! These are Gaunt's shades, and maybe we have a better chance of defying them than she. Are you with me?"

Katta, Haytham, Tlepolemus, the crew of *Little Dragon*, and even Innocence roared their assent. They met the attack of the thief and his two deaths. Katta flung the last of his enchanted cakes, and Severstrand hissed where they connected. Haytham and Tlepolemus faced Joyblood, saber and sword flashing as the cat-o'-nine-tails lashed. Innocence leaped and kicked at Bone, and Gaunt joined them with daggers drawn. Northwing chanted and slapped a Vuos drum, and Bone became slightly transparent as the shaman did so. The five remaining men of *Little Dragon* guarded Gaunt or looked for places to surprise the enemy.

At first it seemed strength was on their side, but then Severstrand and Joyblood both vanished and appeared beside the men of *Little Dragon*. Scythe and lash cut the air, and two men fell dead. Katta raced to continue his attack on Severstrand; Haytham did the same with Joyblood, though Tlepolemus turned to Bone. Northwing continued the chant.

Bone regarded the shaman with an insolent smirk and threw a dagger. It missed Northwing and slashed the drum. Eyes narrowed, Northwing hissed her response. A cold wind rippled the curtain of flame, and Bone briefly faded from existence.

It seemed to Gaunt that Joyblood and Severstrand flickered out of sight at the same moment.

Before Gaunt could voice her insight, Severstrand's pincers closed around Katta's staff arm and severed his hand. The wanderer's scream echoed around the Axial Tree. "No!" Gaunt cried, as Severstrand's scythe finished off a warrior from the ship.

Gaunt slashed at the doppelganger of her husband, and Innocence whirled and kicked, distracting Bone. Gaunt shouted, "Kill Bone! The deaths are linked to him!"

Out the corner of her eye she saw Haytham try to obey, though Joyblood's lash cracked the air. Another sailor lay dead beside the fiery angel. Tlepolemus's sword cut at Bone; the thief's shade was hard put to escape it. But

Bone's concerns were elsewhere. He threw a fresh dagger at Northwing, and this time he caught the shaman in the throat. The chant turned to a bloody gasp, and Northwing slumped down, head bleeding onto the drum, covering the pictograms there.

At once Bone became more solid, more agile. He slashed and drew blood from Gaunt; but it was a feint that allowed him to impale Tlepolemus in the eye.

For a moment it was mother and son battling the father. Then Bone jabbed a dagger deep into Innocence's gut.

"Father," the boy said weakly, slumping onto the ground.

"No!" Gaunt drove Bone back from Innocence, seeking vital points. Now Katta was there, somehow fighting despite the blood spurting from his stump; and Haytham was there, saber flashing. She heard a scream and knew the last survivor from *Little Dragon* was trying to hold the night angels off. The scream ended.

They had to finish Bone now. She feinted, blocked, lunged. . . .

Severstrand removed Haytham's head. Joyblood's lash turned Katta's face into a mass of fire.

In the last moment, Gaunt thought of Innocence lying injured behind her. She remembered the real Bone's words: *Tell him you love him.*

I love you both, she thought, and stabbed Bone through the heart.

He dropped to his knees and turned to mist, blew away into the stars.

Beside him the two angels of death faded from view.

Innocence moaned and breathed. No one else lived.

She grabbed him. "I have you, son. I will bandage you. We will make it somehow."

"You are bleeding too. . . ."

"The wounds of my spirit are far worse."

She bound his midsection tight, and her arm, and they staggered forward to the flames.

"In a just world these would have faded," Gaunt sighed.

"There are many cloaks here, and we can soak them with the water we've carried."

"You think like your father. The real one. Just take care not to empty the flasks of alcohol."

"I worked in a tavern. I know the difference."

While he worked, she made one more hopeless check for life among her other companions. Hands shaking, she took the strange manuscript that Katta, Haytham, and Northwing had worked upon. It seemed wrong to leave it here, in limbo.

She kept one arm around it, one around Innocence, as they ran through the flames.

Coughing, smoking, they fell into cloudy daylight.

It was the same island they'd seen through the curtain of fire, but now it possessed only blackened, broken fragments of the Chain. And there stood the Winterjarl.

"Eh?" said the strange wizard, stepping toward them. "Are you with the thief?"

"Thief?" said Gaunt. "Was Bone here?"

"A familiar sound to that name . . . who are you?"

He was staring at Innocence as he said it.

Innocence dropped to his knees. It looked like supplication, but she knew it for pain and exhaustion.

"You," said the Winterjarl.

Innocence gasped, "Do you remember this meeting?"

The old wizard blinked. "I do not."

Innocence, tears streaking his face, began to smile.

The Winterjarl said, "But I . . . recognize you. Though I have never spoken to you. Except, perhaps, when muttering at a pool of water."

"I'm you. And now I'm sure history can be changed."

"We all have our fates."

"But you don't remember this conversation. There's a chance. This is where we have to fix it, Winterjarl. We have to witness that day."

"No!"

"Can you bring it to us? Bring us to it?"

"No!"

"I love you," Gaunt said, putting her arms around the Winterjarl. The wizard gasped, stiffened. "You are my beloved son."

"No . . ."

"Yes! Please. Let me help you by taking away the worst day of your life."

"No," he whispered. "It's all coming back. . . ."

Now a great conflict came rippling into view. A storm shrouded the cliffs of Svardmark and Spydbanen. Balloons filled the air. Trolls rose from the water. Upon the part of the Great Chain linking the little island with Svardmark, Inga was carrying Steelfox down the Chain. Bone, the real Bone, lay beside Deadfall, near Jewelwolf. And Innocence, a third, ghostly Innocence, had his hands upon the Great Chain.

It seemed that time flowed slowly in the vision, perhaps ten seconds there for each experienced by Gaunt.

"There," the Winterjarl said. "I have done it. But I cannot bear to look upon it. Let me leave. Your presences may destroy me."

"All right," the Innocence beside Gaunt said. "Thank you."

"Wait," said Gaunt, an intuition seizing her. "Take this." She passed the Winterjarl the manuscript of Katta, Northwing, and Haytham. "This is a collection of writings that may shed light on many secrets of the Bladed Isles."

The Winterjarl flipped through the pages. Considering the manuscript seemed to calm him. "It needs a cover. And maps to give context. And some commentary. Hm."

He walked away, through a curtain of ghostly fire.

"Mother," said the bleeding Innocence beside her. "I have little time, in either the mystical or physical sense."

"Whatever messages we deliver, we must give them now. I'll whisper in your younger self's ear. My son, please give some encouraging word to your father."

They stepped to their tasks, Innocence rising painfully. He chuckled. "Peace and love, is it?"

"Swan, Undetermined, All-One, spirits of the sky . . . isn't love at the heart of all of it?"

"So easy to say," Innocence said. "But it's all confusion once we take one step beyond that."

"Well. Half a step then?"

They advanced.

They whispered.

They vanished like water drops upon a sword pulled fresh from the forge.

CHAPTER 42

TODAY

Imago Bone felt cheated. For the second time he'd flown a significant distance on a flying carpet, but he couldn't remember any of it. After he'd willingly left *Anansi* with Deadfall and Jewelwolf—wanting to see Innocence and not wanting to bring trouble to Eshe—his consciousness failed. His battered body remembered, however, with aches and chills. He woke on an island in the Chained Straits, upon a litter, covered in a blanket. He'd been placed where he would have a good view of the Great Chain of Unbeing, whose vast dark links covered the island in this spot. Thoughtful. The gray before dawn had only just started revealing the heights above. He'd awoken several times before, to see only darkness.

A shadowy figure slept beside the Chain, not far from Bone.

Two Karvak soldiers stood near, and one shouted something as their eyes met.

The shadowy shape rose and stretched and stepped beside Bone. "Father," it said.

"Innocence."

"Leave us," Innocence told the guards. Innocence knelt and said, "I'm glad you're alive."

"Likewise." Bone hesitated. "What I mean is, I am glad you're alive. Well, I am glad for myself, too."

"It's all right, Father. I understand. I nearly destroyed you. I don't blame you for being uncomfortable around me."

"That's not it—"

"I may have killed Mother too. The Kpalamaa crew said she might have survived, however, so Jewelwolf relayed."

"Son, I know more than Jewelwolf. Your mother is alive, somewhere far north."

"I am relieved to hear it. I will send Deadfall to find her."

"Deadfall serves you, then? Not Jewelwolf? Or Skrymir?"

There was a moaning of the wind as he said the second name.

As if summoned by the sound, the humming, disconcerting voice of the carpet rose from the ground near Bone. It said, "Lord Gaunt understands what it is to be torn between good and evil, to seek a path that surpasses both. Once again I serve him, he who will be Emperor."

"I will no longer hide from what I am," Innocence said. "In my hands I have the strength to unite the world. To end all wars."

"Do Jewelwolf and . . . the troll-king . . . know of your exalted plans?"

"Of course not. They each think they're in control. But Jewelwolf is mortal, and holds no fear for me. And in the disaster on the island of the heart, I was freed from Skrymir's influence. At heart they're both broken, and they need me to take charge."

Bone said. "Innocence. Son. Let me say what I'd say. I forgive you for what happened at the island. I would forgive you even if your mother had died. You never chose to be shackled to some bizarre power. We never wanted that for you. Do me a favor and open that pack on my left?" Innocence did so. "Now, unwrap that cloth there, the purple one."

Innocence revealed a strange contraption of rusted brass. "What is this?" the boy said. "Is it some magical weapon?"

"No. It's the Antilektron Mechanism, and no one's really sure what it is. We're only sure that it isn't magic, and that it's meant to calculate numbers. Perhaps it aided in navigation, or in crop planting, or in party scheduling. It's anyone's guess. What we do know is, in a past age, sages were able to construct such things without benefit of magic. There are many wonders possible in the world, Innocence, that have nothing to do with dread dooms or higher powers."

Innocence set the mechanism on the stony ground. "I don't understand why you're telling me this, Father."

"So many people believe you've been given a blessing. But I know not every inheritance is welcome. To be footsore and free can be a finer thing than to have your toes massaged in a bejeweled palace. You speak of power, and you think you're being strong. But what I hear is a lost boy, grasping at what looks like gold but is really straw. Leave it, son. Enough of this nonsense of empire. We are together, and we have a magic carpet. Let's fly!"

Deadfall said, "You presume much."

"Be silent, Deadfall," said Innocence. "You too, father. I realize now I don't know you. You're a mediocrity."

Innocence stepped away, pacing before the Great Chain.

"You know I'm right," Bone said to Deadfall. "Your whole existence has been a struggle against confinement, compulsion."

"All the more reason to ally with power. Speaking of which."

The ground shook in heavy pulses. On a sudden impulse, Bone tucked the Antilektron Mechanism under his pallet. It was treasure, after all.

"You," said the troll-jarl. "I know not whether to squash you or thank you. You helped destroy my heart, a deed I could never nerve myself to do. I never knew if such an act would destroy me or free me. It seems it is the latter! I have come to embrace the hollowness of my being. I have peeled away the onion of myself and found a great nothingness at its heart. Where is myself? The emptiness!"

"I suggest," Bone said, "your true self lies in that noxious stuff that sprays from the onion and stings the eyes."

"Do I make you cry, thief?" Skrymir laughed. "I see the world for the hollow lie it is. My one regret is that my new clarity has robbed me of my power of illusion. All that is left is to amuse myself with the pain of more ignorant beings."

"I am certainly ignorant, and in pain. I see there is a small gap still, in your substance?" For Bone had seen the sky through Skrymir's chest.

With a rumbling of grinding stone, Skrymir patted the spot. "It is much smaller than before," the troll-jarl said, "but it persists. Curious. I suppose I must have a reminder of my empty nature."

"Are you not still an extension of the dragon that underlies Spydbanen?"

"My new perspective will soon free me of that ground. I will hang within the void."

"What if something filled that gap?"

"My heart?" Skrymir chuckled. "My emptiness would consume anything that presumed to claim my center. Even the carpet beside you would perish, now."

"I was not offering," Deadfall said.

"Too bad," Skrymir said. "It's tempting to pay you back for leading them to the heart."

"What do you want, Skrymir?" Bone said.

"I want only to see your face when I do this." Skrymir raised his foot, and Bone could not summon the strength to roll away.

The foot came down and crushed Bone's pack. Skrymir caught an arm-loop in a little toe and flung the pack into the waters of the strait.

"There," said the troll-jarl. "Enough of this nonsense of the *Chart of Tomorrows*. Whatever the Winterjarl is, or that Chooser of the Slain I've sensed nosing about, they won't stop me."

"There was no need to do that. I can't hurt you."

"Perhaps it just amused me. Rubblewrack! Attend!"

Now a troll-woman like a congealed avalanche stepped up to Bone's left. "What is your bidding, O great one?"

"First I bid that you improve your sarcasm. It does not cut me at all. Second, keep an eye on this thief, this dabbler in strange doings, this Bone. I don't like having him here. Guard him."

"He is spent and wounded. I smell his death close by. Perhaps twice over."

"Guard him, Rubblewrack."

"I also smell the coming of two other girls. The human who thinks she's an uldra. The troll who thinks she's a human. They are out there."

Skrymir looked pained. "You are always imagining that you smell them. Serve me, Rubblewrack. Guard Imago Bone."

"The sun is coming to this place, the sun that evaporates soul from troll, and leaves them piles of stone."

Skrymir swatted Rubblewrack. Bits of stone fell upon Bone, and a cloud of dust.

"I will do worse to your soul, uldra-changeling! You have the guise of trolls, but you are of otherfolk nature and can abide the sun. Why else would I have adopted you?"

"Out of love?"

"Aha! You have obeyed my earlier command. Your sarcasm is improving. I leave you now, for I must yet be careful of the sun. I will wait beneath the waves."

As Skrymir rumbled off, Rubblewrack crouched and became indistinguishable from a pile of boulders. Bone knew what a mouse feels like, helpless between the cat's claws. The light improved, and Innocence did not return, but the Karvak guards did, keeping a discreet distance from the new boulders. Deadfall said, "Jewelwolf comes."

"Lovely," said Bone.

"Why thank you," said the Karvak khatun. She was riding a steppe horse with one eye blazing green. Huginn Sharpspear walked beside her, and with him two young Oxilanders, Rolf and Kollr, Bone presumed. "I trust your accommodations are pleasant, thief?"

"A fine seaside vacation, khatun! Ah, Huginn! How is the treachery business?"

"I will never cease to be amazed," Huginn said. "No matter how low my critics—thieves, murderers, scum of the land—they still presume to judge me for looking after my own interests. I am no worse than you. Just perhaps more honest, quicker to reach conclusions. After all, thousands of my countrymen are now under the Karvak yoke and yielding to the inevitable. Are they traitors too? They came to the same decision as I and showed as much loyalty to their homelands."

"They didn't open the gates of Svanstad."

"Enough," said Jewelwolf. "What matters, thief, is that those gates were opened, those people were yoked, and Kantenjord is all but in Karvak hands. Your allies from Kpalamaa have sailed off. Your friends are dead or scattered or trapped in the mountains. And yet you may live, first as a hostage, then as a servant."

"I do have a few skills. Would the khan take me on, then?"

"Ha!" said Huginn, with a triumphant laugh.

"My husband!" laughed Jewelwolf. "Clifflion is irrelevant. Let him gobble up a few countries back at the continent. In time I will return in glory. He can have the title of Grand Khan; I have the true power." She dismounted and unsheathed the two swords she carried, the gray saber Crypttongue with its jewel-studded pommel and the straight black sword Schismglass.

The blade points hovered for a moment near Bone's throat.

He forced himself to smile. "Ah, I could be your servant? Remember? Highly skilled? Bargain price?"

"Jewelwolf," Huginn said. "Your point, or points, are made."

Jewelwolf sheathed the swords. "You may have an opportunity as a clown, thief. Just as Huginn has." She walked off to speak to Innocence. The horse cast Bone a speculative look, as though considering just how much effort it would be to crush the thief's skull. Nonchalantly, it followed its mistress.

Huginn lingered to say, "When you are ready to drop the superior airs, friend thief, I can advise you on serving the Karvaks."

"Well, she did say there are openings as a clown. You're just the person I'd consult."

Huginn shook his head and followed Jewelwolf.

Though the light improved, Bone's feelings darkened. Jewelwolf wasn't wrong. Battered as he was, he was fit only to be a hostage.

He recalled his long-dead mentor Master Sidewinder. *Do not be tricked into thinking that rest and contemplation are a waste of time. It is often while apparently doing nothing that something becomes clear.* Very well. He rested.

After a time he heard distant shouts in the direction of Svardmark. Those cliffs had a peculiar look, for a strange foggy weather clung to that side, but the rest of the strait was entering sunlight. And . . . was that a balloon rising from those mists? It seemed of different design than the Karvak type, smaller of gondola. . . .

There was a rumbling beside him. The boulders shook.

"What is the matter, Rubblewrack?" Bone said. He let intuition guide him. "Could your changeling sisters be out there?"

"Silence, human."

"That's it, isn't it? They *are* out there. Perhaps Karvaks or foamreavers have captured them. What would you say to them if you could?"

"I would say nothing. I would crush them. They disturb my thoughts, simply by existing."

"It is cruel of them," Bone goaded. "Taking up space like that. Mocking you with life and breath."

"Yes! You understand. Some would say that they're innocent, for they have done nothing overt to harm me."

"Nonsense. It is what you feel that matters. There is no such thing as objective innocence or harm! If a man a thousand miles away from me lives a happy existence, and I suffer, and I choose to feel that his happiness mocks me, why surely he is at fault. Who can gainsay my sovereign feelings?"

"Yes! You are wise, thief!"

"Why, thank you."

"If only I could go look for them."

"Skrymir is not here, is he? Who is he, frightened of the sun as he is, to bind you here? I am no threat, and here are these soldiers, and Deadfall too will guard me, no?"

"I suppose so," said the carpet.

Rubblewrack rose. "Thank you. You are the only one who understands."

"Don't let anyone hold you back!" Bone said. "The hell with the rest of the world."

"You would make a good troll," said Rubblewrack and lumbered off.

"I have the feeling I may have started an avalanche," Bone muttered.

Deadfall said, "Why did you do this thing?"

"Where stasis does not serve, perhaps motion will."

Jewelwolf ran up to them. "Where did that troll-thing go?"

"Into the water, it would seem," Bone said.

"Did she say where she was going?"

"She smelled the blood of a human. And a troll, maybe."

"I do not like this. Deadfall, if he so much as twitches, strangle him."

"As that would prevent him from further speech," Deadfall said, "I am willing—"

"*Joy!*"

The voice that silenced them was Innocence's.

As he shouted, the Great Chain shone with a cold blue illumination. . . .

Except in the Svardmark heights, where a fiery power was moving down the Chain toward them.

Jewelwolf took in the whole scene, the fog, the anomalous balloon, the Chain.

"I have been a fool," the khatun said. "I thought they would play the turtle, not the wolf." She drew the two magic blades and cursed anew.

Schismglass was changing. The tip of it was now a reflective violet, as though shadows were peeling away, revealing a tinted mirror. "It prefers another hand," Jewelwolf said, "that I will have to hack off. This will be a day of blood."

She moved to Innocence's side.

Bone dared not move, for he'd seen Deadfall's homicidal inclinations at first hand. He did notice a pair of tiny figures, one on the shoulders of the other, walking down the Chain. He couldn't tell who they were, but if he could trade Deadfall for a hat, he'd tip it at them.

He shut his eyes. *What now, Master Sidewinder?*

And it seemed that somebody answered, then. But it was not Master Sidewinder's voice.

It was a hoarse echo of his son's.

We have come a long way together, it said. *We are both broken things. But it is possible that nothing in this world is truly whole. I have said before that I wanted to grasp power. I was a fool. What I truly want to grasp is life, and I now understand that is not necessarily the same thing. There are people up on the Chain who are about to die. People whom my prior, power-grasping self is about to kill. People who in another life could have been my friends. Make that other life possible, O companion. You, ambiguous champion, mix of good and evil—do a good deed today. Save them.*

"How?" Bone gasped. "How can I—"

Deadfall leapt upon him. It surrounded Bone, and he knew his life would be crushed. He saw Gaunt's face and ached with the feeling he'd missed ten thousand chances to caress it.

And yet he was not smothered. Instead the rolled-up carpet, levitating with Bone inside it, whacked one Karvak soldier and then the other. He heard them *whoof* as they fell over.

Now Deadfall rushed into the sky, opening up a little to allow Bone air.

"You must let me know," said the carpet, "if you are strong enough to clutch me. Babying you like this makes me less agile, and I have more people to catch."

"Not yet . . . you overheard him? And you chose to help?"

"Fool. It was you who overheard. He wasn't talking to you. It is I who must prove myself today."

In one moment Innocence exulted in his power. In the next moment an arrow struck him in the shoulder. Pain and outrage exploded through his mind. He lost control of the Chain.

Huginn Sharpspear crouched beside him. "Hold still, boy. I know a little about arrows. . . ."

"Leave it in!" Innocence said. "No time for healing."

"Keep him there, Huginn," said Jewelwolf, and her face glowed with the light of the Chain. "This is the moment. The Runethane commands the Chain. The chosen wielder of one of the swords is nearing. And my sister approaches. I may not have another chance."

"Chance for what?"

Jewelwolf only laughed as she raised the swords. Innocence desperately tried to rise.

The Chain flared with light once more, and the energies of the Runethane faded.

"What?" Jewelwolf said. "No . . . I need the power. . . ."

But Innocence saw it all. His sense of his old friend still persisted, and he winced as he perceived two figures stabbing A-Girl-Is-A-Joy. And he heard her voice calling for help.

"Joy," he gasped, and everything, his hopes for power, his defiant scheming, collapsed like a melting ice cave. In its place was rage. The Kantening barbarian and her accomplice had dared betray a daughter of the greatest civilization on Earthe . . . and his friend.

He would destroy them all. He would blast the Svardmark highlands apart.

He lurched up, shoved Huginn aside, and toppled over the nearest link of the Chain.

Power blazed forth, and it was not the yin that he expressed this time, not the disciplined cold of his supernatural winter, but the yang aspect of the Heavenwalls, tapping the energies of fiery dragons, rushing up the Chain.

"No!" said Jewelwolf. "Not now!"

He ignored her. But there came another voice he could not dismiss.

Innocence, came the voice of Persimmon Gaunt. *Son. There is so much I wish to say to you, and I may not have another chance. But it must all boil down to one word. Love. I love you, my beautiful child. I am so sorry your father and I were away for so long. Do not hate us, and the world, for that. You are in a moment when hate can wreck everything that is. I know it is the hardest thing I can ask of you, but I ask you to act in love. You have too much power to indulge hate now. Remember the boy you were. Remember what still could be.*

For an instant he was no longer Lord Gaunt hurling power at hated savages who'd felled the Runethane but Innocence Gaunt leaping about a boulder garden with A-Girl-Is-A-Joy, whacking sticks with her, ferocity giving way to anguish whenever one or the other thought they'd truly given a bruise or poked an eye.

Joy.

I'm . . . here . . . I'm alive . . . help!

He checked his power as it sped.

He did not destroy the far side of the Chain. In his mind's eye he saw another reality, where the promontory exploded, killing Joy and her would-be slayers, making him the slayer. He even imagined he saw more, a great earthquake ravaging Svardmark and Spydbanen.

But that was not this life. In this life, his mind reached Joy's. *I can't strike them without hurting you! I'm sorry!*

Despite the helplessness, time seemed to crawl in his vision. He saw Corinna's dagger taking forever to fall, as he beheld it in Joy's sight.

She answered him, *I'm sorry too. But I am glad you care.*

I always cared. I have been a fool. If only there was a way.

Kantenings talk about fate a lot. Maybe this is fate, Innocence. I'm just glad you're here, really here again, at the end.

Joy . . .

His thoughts raced, like a desert whirlwind, like a maelstrom. *Act in love,* his mother had said. *Leave it,* his father had said. He saw images flash by like shapes glimpsed by torchlight in a shadowy cathedral—the Swan sacrificing herself, Torden facing giants at the end of time, the Undetermined renouncing the world, the sage of the Garden seeking right relationships, the sage of the Forest seeking spontaneity and the dance of opposites. All these teachings, seemingly so incompatible as to rupture his brain. Yet here in the heart of the whirlwind they suddenly, impossibly, seemed like the same message.

I can't stop them without killing you, he realized. *But there's another way. A-Girl-Is-A-Joy, I name you the bearer of the power of the Heavenwalls.*

What?

But he had made his choice, and instinctively he knew how to act upon it.

He screamed as the power rushed out of him, all along the Chain, glowing blue and red, dance of contrasts, yin and yang, everything and nothing.

The dragons faded from his forehead and his mind.

He fell over, Innocence, merely that, at last.

The power of the Heavenwalls rushed into Joy, and the power of the Chain quickened in response.

They were not opposites, not amenable to balance. The Heavenwalls had tapped the desperate energies of generations of mating dragons, Eastern and Western, and combined these chaotic forces in a monumental, delicately synchronized storm of chi.

The Great Chain of Unbeing had instead tapped the energies of ancient Western dragons beyond the age of mating, solemn fiery power drawn forth to empower the Runethane, and to keep these elders sleeping.

Harnessing these two powers was akin to wielding a sword and a lasso at the same time. The thought processes involved were very different. But Innocence had given her a chance at life, and she would use it.

Corinna's dagger fell. Before it could strike, Joy raised her left hand and with it shaped a blast of chi.

Backed by the power of the Heavenwalls she knocked the ruler of Soderland head over heels.

Joy rose to her feet, teetering. She saw that Alfhild had felled Malin Jorgensdatter and was preparing a death-blow. With her right hand Joy blasted a gout of fire at the changeling, and Alfhild screamed and fell, rolling on the stony ground.

Malin got up and rushed to Joy's side. She said, "Thank you" and stared at Joy's forehead.

"What's wrong?" Joy said.

"You have dragons on your head."

"In my head too. Malin, you were ready to ride on Inga's shoulders. I'm not as strong as her, but would you link arms with me? I have to get down there, to that island. I think I can survive the trip down the Chain. I think I can protect you too."

"I will do it," Malin said. "But what about the battle here?"

Joy saw Kantening soldiers rushing to their position. Corinna was groaning and trying to rise.

"It may take too long to explain things," Joy said. "There's a limit to the harm these two can do, for now. . . ."

There came a roar from the cliffside. A troll-woman hauled herself up, ignoring the sunlight.

"Changeling sister!" she called out. "Let me embrace you!"

Alfhild, who had just extinguished herself and risen, screeched, "Rubble-wrack!"

She ran through the Kantening troops, and the troll pounded after her.

Joy turned to stare at Corinna. Corinna said nothing.

"I go now to save your country, murderer," Joy said.

If Corinna replied, Joy spent no time on it. She and Malin leapt upon the Chain and descended it as fast as Joy dared, riding its power like an icy slope. She hoped they could retain their balance, in every sense.

Snow Pine watched the sky darken overhead as their balloon descended. Peik endlessly paced out a rune. "I cannot lie," he said, "though I may embellish. Every Karvak shaman in the world is now working against me."

Flint frowned. "And yet they are spending considerable energy on blackening the sky with thunderheads. Why is that, I wonder?"

"Don't wonder," Snow Pine said. "Just look."

Troll after troll reared from the waters, no longer fearing the day. They climbed the cliffs toward the army of free Kantenjord.

There were thousands.

"My people will be slaughtered," Yngvarr said. "The ultimate battle is there, and I am missing it."

"There'll be plenty of targets to go around," Snow Pine said. A shadow flitted across the sky. "What? It's Deadfall—"

As if Deadfall had expected it to happen, Inga and Steelfox were blasted from the Chain by a burst of fiery power. Deadfall caught them, nearly losing Bone in the process.

Deadfall's next destination was their balloon. Without ceremony it dumped its three passengers into the gondola.

"Excuse me, O exalted transportation method!" Haboob said. "But this gondola has its limits."

"It takes one to know one, efrit," Deadfall replied. "Are you not trying to land? I am merely offering ballast."

"The astonishing nerve of some supernatural entities . . ."

"You have my full agreement. But only for a moment. I have places to go."

Bone managed to say, "Did . . . he . . . give you more instructions?"

"No, these instructions came earlier. Eshe of the Fallen Swan spoke to me briefly when I carried Jewelwolf aboard *Anansi*, to claim you. Eshe made me an offer. I initially thought I would decline, but I have reconsidered. You are not now the only agent of Kpalamaa in this fight, Imago Bone."

"I'm not an agent of Kpalamaa," Bone objected. "Well, not yet . . ."

"What are you going to do?" Snow Pine said.

"Little enough," said Deadfall. "I am going to end a war."

And with that, the flying carpet shot off toward the East.

Down Joy went, riding the power, and a grin flitted across her face.

Jewelwolf of the Karvaks waited for her with two swords drawn. Innocence lay beside her, bloody from the arrow in his shoulder. Near them, Huginn Sharpspear and his Oxilander assistants had axes out, though they seemed dubious as to whether to use them.

Jewelwolf shared no such doubts. She looked upon the approaching Runethane, chosen of the Heavenwalls, with a knowing smile.

"You can't stop me!" Joy roared. In the midst of her anger was a bit of sincere concern for the Karvak. There was vast power crackling around her and Malin. "Get out of the way!"

"You are not my prize, Runethane!" Jewelwolf shouted.

She drove both blades into the Great Chain.

Joy was startled to see the metal planes stay intact as they struck the massive artifact. Rather, they sank into the substance of the Chain as though carving meat. Fiery energies rushed up the blades.

"She is eating dragons," Malin said beside Joy.

Jewelwolf screamed as the power spilled over her hands, but she did not relinquish her grip. She staggered backward, laughing between sounds of agony.

Where the blades had pierced, molten metal flowed out like blood.

A tumult of forces flowed through the Chain and blasted Joy and Malin off, onto the stony island. She had the wind knocked out of her, struggled to rise.

"Joy!" Innocence got unsteadily to his feet.

Joy saw Jewelwolf rushing upon her. She barely rolled in time as two fiery blades scorched the rocks where she'd lain.

"I have it!" Jewelwolf shouted. "The power of dragons! A force to master you, Skrymir, or even the Archmage of Ebontide!"

The ground shook.

"No!" Innocence said. Wounded though he was, he helped Joy up, and then Malin. Even with their support Joy had difficulty with her balance, with Heavenwalls and Chain roaring together in her mind. "It's happening! You're disrupting the Chain, waking the dragons."

"What do I care?" Jewelwolf said. "I can simply draw enough power to silence them. And you."

"Ah, Torden's balls!" Huginn snarled. "No one is ever going to trust me again, are they?"

He hurled his axe at Jewelwolf. After a moment's wide-eyed hesitation, his companions did likewise.

She laughed and caught the first with the swords, like a morsel between chopsticks. The axe head melted; the handle burst into flame.

With precise swings she destroyed the two axes that followed.

"There is an experiment I would like to try again," Jewelwolf said, striding toward him. First she caught the two young men from Oxiland, one with each blade.

Each fell at once.

"Kollr!" shouted Innocence. "Rolf!"

"Ah, Skrymir?" Huginn bellowed, running away. "Where is a troll-jarl when you need one?"

Jewelwolf whistled, and her troll-enchanted horse raced up to bear her.

"Too many bodies in his wake," said Innocence to Joy and Malin, "including those who might have been friends. But he saved my life, and gods help me, I'll repay him. I no longer possess magical might, however."

"I have a bit too much," Joy said. "What if I give yours back?"

He shook his head. "It was a gift I can only refuse once."

Huginn ran through a line of Karvaks. The soldiers let him go, looking upon their cackling khatun with confusion. Huginn was trying to reach the spot of ground where the new balloon was now landing, hard.

He almost reached it.

Jewelwolf rode past him, guiding her horse with her legs only. Leaning over, she hacked Huginn down with two simultaneous slashes.

The great storyteller and jurist fell burning at the horse's feet. Jewelwolf's laughter scoured the wind.

"We have to stop her," Innocence said.

Another tremor rippled through the ground. "No," Joy said. "My mother, your father, they have to deal with her, somehow. I have to heal the Chain. And you have to stay by me, my friends."

"My friends," Malin repeated. "Inga is over there, at that balloon. I have to help her."

"Go," Joy said. "Be careful. Innocence . . ."

They leaned on each other. "I'll stay by you. All the way from here to Ragnarok."

"Thanks. I think ten feet will do."

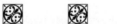

Bone saw Huginn fall just before the balloon came to a thudding stop.

Peik stared at the burning Oxilander. "I am open to a change of plans—" he began, but the impact cut him off.

Steelfox said, "Jewelwolf is my responsibility."

"You can't fight her alone," Snow Pine said.

"At last," Yngvarr said. "Battle."

Jewelwolf was grinning as she rode over Huginn's remains.

"Begging your pardons," Flint said, "but you have all forgotten something." He pointed up at the envelope of the balloon. "Natural philosophy? Eh?"

"Oh," said Bone. "Everybody out!" Peik was already gone by the time he added, "Ah, could someone carry me?"

Snow Pine and Flint hauled Bone out, and their easy teamwork made him miss Gaunt as much as he missed his own health. He looked up and saw that Steelfox, Inga, and Yngvarr were still in the gondola.

"Come, sister," Steelfox was saying. "Face me."

"Come out of there," Jewelwolf replied, laughing. "You were always a coward."

"Enough," Yngvarr said. "I will fight on your behalf, Steelfox. You must go. You too, changeling."

"I'm staying," Inga said.

"It's not your fight, Kantenings," Steelfox said. "You need to be ready for Skrymir."

That was something Inga could accept, and reluctantly she joined the others.

"It's not yours either," Steelfox told Yngvarr.

"Of course it is," Yngvarr said. "My crimes. My family. Of course it is my fight. And you are the best hope for setting things right. You know this. Yield in this one thing. Go."

Steelfox looked at Yngvarr and at Jewelwolf. It seemed to Bone that fleeing the gondola harmed Steelfox to the core.

But she leapt after the others.

Yngvarr departed the gondola in the other direction, toward Jewelwolf and the mad horse. "I spit at you, nomad! Your war has destroyed my family! I have the fury of my ancestors burning in my blood! The spirit of the berserker screams within me!"

"Interesting," said Jewelwolf, dismounting. "I merely have power."

Stepping forward she blocked his sword thrust with one blade and stabbed him through the heart with the other. He burst into flame. Screaming the names of Torden, Arthane, and Orm, he tumbled backward into the gondola, flames leaping upward.

Wide-eyed, arms gripped between his friends, Bone saw Haboob reach out a smoky hand to Jewelwolf. "O mighty khatun," it said. "I have a secret to tell you."

"What is that—" she said merrily, stepping forward.

An explosion burst the balloon's envelope, raining gouts of fire everywhere.

Jewelwolf cursed and raised the swords in an effort to block the destruction. And indeed much of the conflagration was absorbed into the weapons. Nevertheless she dropped the blades and fell backward onto the stones, her deel smoking.

Her horse was not so lucky. Its screams would haunt Bone for the rest of his days. The last he saw of it, it was like a blazing comet, streaking for a watery grave.

Guraab rose blazing into the air, twisting and tearing. Yngvarr Thrall-Taker had this distinction; he was the first foamreaver to have a balloon as his funeral craft.

Steelfox raced to her sister's side, while nearby Inga and Peik knelt beside the swords. Soon Bone arrived with Snow Pine and Flint. "Just set me down," Bone said. "Nice and warm here."

"Where is Gaunt when we need her?" Snow Pine lowered him. "You need kicking."

"Enough taunting the thief, my dear," said Flint. He pondered the swords. "Schismglass is mirror-like again. It knows you're here. Are you prepared to wield it?"

"We don't have a choice, do we?"

"No, I don't think so."

Snow Pine raised the blade, a length of reflective crystal, within which Bone perceived writhing purple fires. Huginn Sharpspear's face sometimes appeared, screaming something inaudible. Bone looked away.

"I think I can manage with it," Snow Pine said. "What about you? Are you willing to wield Crypttongue again?"

"I am a man of natural philosophy," Flint said, "a rejector of gods, and I dislike magic. After all we've been through, it seems to me supernatural forces are unhealthy for humanity. Both the religious man I was and the rational man I am can agree on that. But there is need. And I do have experience with this blade." He picked up Crypttongue, swung it. "There are many Kantenings in here . . . Muggur . . . Floki . . . they want revenge against what brought chaos to their lands, even if they participated themselves. And Yngvarr too. He warns us to watch for Skrymir."

"That can be my job," Bone said. "I'm not going anywhere fast."

"Huginn is in my blade," Snow Pine said. "Along with many of the Fraternity of the Hare. They tell us we can defeat Skrymir by placing something we value in the cavity of his heart. Friend Peik, I know you must be tired. But can you walk a rune for us? Keep the balloons at bay at least?"

"I will try," said the boy, staring at the fiery wreck of their craft.

"Inga, you guard him," said Snow Pine.

"All right," Inga said. "But if Skrymir comes, I'm in that fight."

"Steelfox?" Snow Pine asked.

"My sister lives," Steelfox said, "though I know not how. The power in those swords must have saved her. Her hands are burned and need attention. She sleeps. She can't harm us for now."

"I won't ask you to kill her," Snow Pine said. "I should, but I won't. But we should truss her up."

"I can do that," Bone said. "You need Steelfox to talk to the Karvaks."

As he worked, the others spoke with the soldiers, who backed off. Jewelwolf had thoroughly terrified her honor guard.

Joy was exerting her powers on the great Chain. The ferocious play of magics, resembling fire and mist and molten rock, made Bone highly sympathetic with Flint's opinion of magic, but her efforts might keep them all alive. There was still considerable rumbling in the strait. He did not know if she was succeeding.

He missed Gaunt. She should be here. Then again, perhaps not being here would keep her alive.

"The ice is indeed very thick, however," Northwing said, "and that which is fastened to the land extends many miles. It is madness to consider traversing it. And yet less mad than I thought."

"Are you willing to try it?" Gaunt asked. She felt a strange sense of familiarity as she said the words.

As Northwing thought it over, there came a dim rumbling. It seemed strongest far to the southeast.

"Strange . . ." murmured Haytham ibn Zakwan.

"What do you see?" Katta asked, inclining his head.

"Did you notice it?" Gaunt asked Haytham, for she had glimpsed something peculiar in that direction.

"I think I did. . . ."

"Tell me!" Katta said.

Gaunt said, "For a moment I saw a gigantic conflagration, as though the dragons underlying Spydbanen and Svardmark had arisen. . . ."

"I too," said Haytham.

"And I," said Northwing. "But it was all transparent, like a reflection on dark water. And now it is gone."

"A vision?" Katta said. "A premonition?"

"I don't know," Gaunt admitted. "But I do think we need to reconsider our journey onto the ice. It may be critical we reach the Chained Straits."

"It will take a long time to get there," Northwing mused. "Weeks. Hm."

"What is it?" Gaunt said. "Don't hold back."

"I've been struck by those soul-eating swords, Crypttongue and Schismglass. They tried to claim me. Well, turnabout's fair play, and I've felt a connection to the swords since that time. Maybe I could make a spirit journey to their location."

"Do it. Please. I need to know what is happening. I feel certain Bone is mixed up in this. Innocence too."

Walking Stick allowed himself to be pleased. The army had fought well and had so far defeated a superior force. The unnatural winter had been broken. The time had come to evaluate their position, choose to retreat or hold.

Then messengers came reporting disaster. Walking Stick left his commanders in charge of chaining of prisoners and securing of the battleground. He turned to the former agitator, Everart, who had become a valued aide. "You will accompany me." He grabbed Everart and focused his chi, leaping through the field.

"Eh—ah!" said Everart.

They reached the Giant's Tongue, where Joy should have been.

But she was not there. Instead they found calamity: the queen of Soderland bound in ropes, and a troll chasing the princess of Sølvlyss. "Keep Corinna here," he told the warriors, and leapt to face the troll.

He jumped onto the creature's back and began pummeling it in the places where paralytic points lay upon a human. He did not expect it to work, but the attack might yield information.

Surprisingly, the troll slowed. Either this was no normal troll, or he'd been misinformed about troll nature. Either way, the entity fell over.

"Truss it with heavy chains," he told the nearest warriors. He looked to Alfhild. "You. What is happening?"

"Joy Snøsdatter went mad! She said she was in league with the trolls. Corinna and I tried to stop her."

"Someone bind her too." He gestured to the men holding Corinna. They brought her closer. "What has occurred?"

"What you should have realized would occur," Corinna said, back straight. "When Joy succeeded in purging winter from the Chain, I tried to purge her from my lands. I will not accept an alien leader."

Everart said, "Alfhild told it differently. She said Joy turned against you."

Alfhild fought and kicked as she was chained.

Corinna scoffed. "Alfhild is a little fool, too frightened to be honest. I say it to all of you—we are in danger of being overwhelmed by Easterners. Being absorbed by Qiangguo is little better than being conquered by the Karvaks. Ask yourselves, why do we need an Eastern girl to save us? How long until she rules us?"

Walking Stick sighed. "You are deluded. Qiangguo will not conquer you. You are simply too far away to be considered important."

Corinna shook her head. "The world is changing. Air power makes everything closer. One day you will understand. So what will you do with us, sir?"

"Put them with the Karvak prisoners," Walking Stick commanded. "Let Corinna be reminded what Joy was saving her from."

As Corinna and Alfhild were led off, Everart said, "Strange. In some ways she was the best of the royals, the most compassionate toward ordinary folk."

"It is a human failing everywhere that sometimes we can be profoundly loving toward those akin to us and murderous to those who . . . look!"

"Swan's blood!"

Beneath darkened skies, a horde of trolls burst over the cliffs.

As Steelfox bent over her sister, bandaging Jewelwolf's ravaged hands, the voice of her father came to her, as he'd seemed to speak from the ship *Naglfar*.

You may become a bataar *yet, daughter, a hero. But you must first prove yourself able to act in a time of crisis. You must be ready to slay your kin. For you are right that*

Jewelwolf has strayed from my edicts. You must kill her, as I once did the half-brother who stood between me and leadership of my clan.

"Who . . ." Jewelwolf moaned. "Who is there?"

The old khan's voice still echoed in Steelfox's mind. *I misjudged you. I know you can handle yourself in battle, and you have kept honorable ways. Now end the disease that afflicts my nation. Kill your sister.*

"Is it Skrymir?" Jewelwolf said. "Clifflion, have you come? The Archmage? Who will care for me?"

"It is I," said Steelfox.

"You . . . get away from me, traitor . . . always a coward . . ."

"That is what our grandmother told our father, the day he slew his half-brother."

"She thought it was a crime . . . but Father had strength."

"And so do I. The strength to renounce your ways—and his. I am strong enough to find my own path. I give you your life, Jewelwolf. But you must leave these lands, which will become my home."

"You . . . you'd become one with these muck-dwellers?"

"Perhaps."

"Run!" came a new voice. "Run!"

The sisters turned to see the distant figure of Malin Jorgensdatter, sprinting across the rugged face of the island, pointing at something over their heads.

"How charming."

At the sound of the second voice both nomad princesses looked up.

Skrymir loomed over them. Black clouds swirled above him, covering the sky.

"I think," Skrymir said, "you've outlived your usefulness, Jewelwolf. My army is destroying the Kantenings as we speak, so my strength will be well-demonstrated among your people. Who can resist killing two birds with one foot?" Boulder-sized toes reared above them.

"They want to awaken, Innocence!" Joy said as she gripped the blazing Chain. "The dragons of Svardmark and Spydbanen. I am trying to stop them, but the power is so hard to control."

"I'm here," Innocence said. "I have no power, but I won't leave you."

Snow Pine saw the troll-jarl preparing to crush Steelfox and Jewelwolf. She acted without hesitation, rushing forward with Schismglass. Flint ran beside her.

Together they slashed at the heel of Skrymir. Snow Pine felt a certain exhilaration as her blade, so glasslike and fragile-looking, sliced through rock.

The troll bellowed and stumbled backward. Steelfox lifted Jewelwolf and tried to escape. Skrymir grinned down at Snow Pine and Flint. "Little fools! Your soul-stealing weapons may hurt me, but they cannot finish me! For my soul is linked to the dragon Moonspear, and you cannot take it."

"Well, take this!" yelled Inga Peersdatter.

She began kicking at Skrymir's feet, using moves taught her by Joy and Snow Pine and Walking Stick.

"Little changeling," Skrymir rumbled. "You fled before we could properly welcome you into the family of trolls."

"Oh, I know we're family," Inga said, commencing a spinning kick, "Father!"

A voice wracked with pain whispered into Snow Pine's ear. *Listen. Bandit. Let an old fool advise you.*

"Huginn?" she whispered.

"Ah!" Skrymir told Inga, as cracks developed on his heel. "You have discovered my and Morksol's little arrangement. You, whom I sculpted from stone, took on human aspect, and there is much I would learn from you now. The day is coming when I will fear nothing, not even the sun. I am heartless. Soon I will be free of any weakness."

Skrymir raised his hand. Bursting from the waters came his gigantic axe, spraying droplets everywhere as it flew to his hand. "Now. Serve me or be broken."

"I'm already broken, Father. I have the strength of someone's who's broken and fights on. You may have shaped me at the beginning, but I'm my own person now."

"Well spoken, Inga!" Flint said, swinging Crypttongue.

"Yes," Skrymir said. "Lovely. Disarming even." He swung, but this time Inga was ready for him and leapt aside. The isle's rocky surface shook and shattered.

"Understand!" Malin said, rushing up to them.

"Malin!" Inga said. "Be careful!"

"Careful, yes!" Malin said. "But you must understand! How to beat him!"

Snow Pine wanted to listen but couldn't avoid the voice of Huginn.

Aye, it is I. Who piled up lies and foolishness until I was crushed beneath them. I, who told stories of brave heroes, was myself terrified of death. Out of fear I clutched the hem of anyone powerful. By turns I told myself I was patriotic, or godly, or astute, or forward-looking, but I was simply a coward. Now I am dead as I always would be, without deeds to my name. . . .

Snow Pine slashed and leapt out of the way of Skrymir's clomping foot. "Listen, I understand you have things to say, but I am rather busy—"

"Eh?" said Flint. "I didn't say anything!"

"Sorry," Snow Pine said. "Someone else—"

"Oh! Yes, I understand. There's a bit of a racket in my blade as well—"

In her mind, Huginn moaned, *You must listen. Thanks to Jewelwolf these swords have sipped the energies of the arkendrakes. If both are shattered, by striking the Axe of Sternmark, the released energies should destroy the axe, and wound Skrymir as well.*

"Flint! We must hit the axe at the same time!"

"That strikes me as quite dangerous!"

"This dance strikes me as dangerous too!"

"All right! Will you marry me?"

"Aiya! Idiot! Romantic fool! Business first! Then we talk!"

"Very well!"

They rushed beneath Skrymir's feet, and when next Skrymir swung the axe, they simultaneously struck.

Light filled Snow Pine's brain.

Bone sensed more than saw the explosion of magic. The three enchanted weapons shattered, fragments of metal flying in every direction. Snow Pine and Flint collapsed, and Skrymir clutched his charred hand. Inga staggered also, for she'd shielded Malin with her body. But the changeling lost no time in pressing the attack against her father.

Bone, for his part, felt weirdly invigorated by the conflagration. He staggered to his feet, dazed, and helped Steelfox drag Jewelwolf farther away. They found a set of boulders that offered a little shelter. Karvak soldiers were approaching, their discipline momentarily shredded by wonder at these strange sights. Bone was relieved to see motion from Snow Pine and Flint.

The falcon Qurca circled near him.

At first he thought he imagined the voice. *Bone! There you are!* The tone was unmistakable.

"Northwing?"

"Qurca?" Steelfox said.

Good, you can both hear me. I'm using the peregrine as a vessel. Don't worry, Princess, it won't hurt him. I was always able to ride within his mind, but I thought it rude. My spirit tracked the two swords to this place. Just in time, too. Good riddance. Listen! Haytham, Katta, and Gaunt are apprised of the situation.

"Tell Gaunt hello!" Bone said, grinning despite everything.

She says shut up and focus, man.

"Tell her I love her too."

Katta suggests Skrymir is weakened and might accept a new heart. Haytham says look for an object of significance. It needn't be magical. It might change his character for the better, whatever it is. Gaunt asks if you still have the Chart of Tomorrows.

Bone said, "That is lost."

Steelfox said, "What about that strange artifact over there?"

He followed her gaze to his pallet. With all the disturbances, the Antilektron Mechanism had rolled back into view. Bone, feeling a tingling within him, left Steelfox and hobbled toward it.

"You know, don't you?"

He looked up, startled to see Malin beside him. "That is it," she said, "how to beat him. I've learned to study faces. I watched him up close until I knew where he was looking. He's afraid of something about this object."

"When he stomped my pack . . . he was hoping to crush it too. It's a relic of a people who got by without magic."

"Maybe that's why he fears it. The trolls are undone by the ordinary. Sunlight. Bells. Love."

"And rationality too?" Bone mused. "Help an old man and bring it to the fight, would you?"

Knowing he was damaging a still-fragile body, but buoyed up by the energies unleashed by the blades, Bone staggered toward Skrymir. Qurca landed on his shoulder. *Gaunt says she thinks you're on the right track*, came the voice of Northwing. *But she thinks Flint should be the one to get the heart into Skrymir's body.*

"Yes, I'm feeble! I know!"

It's not that. Flint is the rationalist of your group. The one who dismisses gods and avoids magic. Gaunt says he's the champion you want right now.

Malin caught up to him, helped him reach Flint and Snow Pine. They had gotten to their feet, bodies slashed by fragments of the exploding swords but luckily quite alive.

"Bone, what—" Snow Pine said.

"I need help, Flint," Bone said.

"What?" said Flint.

"Behold Skrymir's new heart," Bone said. "A relic of a more scientific age. Gaunt suggests you are the one to place it in his chest. You are the natural philosopher. Perhaps someone should speak a few words."

"What?" Flint said again, then: "I'm not a lawspeaker or loresinger. All right, I studied for a time, but was cast out—"

"To business, fiancé," Snow Pine said.

"What?" Bone said. "Congratulations."

"Shut up, Bone," Snow Pine said. "I will bless it if you won't, Flint. 'The Way that can be spoken is not the true and eternal Way. The name that can be named is not the imperishable name. Nameless is the origin of Heaven and Earth, but with names we bring forth the ten thousand things.' Now be a good heart."

Flint said, "In the name of the Circulation, the Musculature, and the Skeleton, may all things fit together. I witness that the human world is rational, even if the human heart is not." He took the Antilektron Mechanism. "Snow Pine, Bone, Malin, I'll need a distraction! Inga! Can you boost me?"

"Busy!" Inga yelled from where she fought with the wounded Skrymir. "Oh, all right—"

"Well," Bone said to the Mechanism, "whoever made you, I hope they don't mind how you're going to be used. Skrymir! Over here!"

He lacked the strength to do anything but throw rocks. But he still had good aim. Malin and Snow Pine joined him.

Inga rolled to Flint's side. "Get on! If you think you can do something, I'll get you up there!"

Inga scrambled up her troll-father. Bone remembered Gaunt describing how Innocence would climb her as a little boy, and something in him ached. "Watch out!" he yelled.

Skrymir grabbed Inga and Flint with the same grasp, but Flint was not entirely trapped and wiggled free. He crawled along the arm. The burned hand reached for him, but a peregrine falcon flew at stony eyes.

"I will crush you all! I feel nothing for . . . what is that sound? Is it fiddling?"

"Gaunt," Bone whispered. Just as Northwing's voice had emanated from Qurca, now the shaman was somehow conveying Persimmon Gaunt's music. It held all the long anguish of the winter and the war. Even Skrymir paused when hearing it.

Inga said, "It doesn't have to be this way. We don't have to hate each other. There's plenty of other stuff to smash in the world."

No sun touched Skrymir. But whatever the music and the conflict had awakened in him all but petrified him. Liron Flint held tight, reached the gap in Skrymir's chest, and shoved the Mechanism inside. As though some not-magic, some anti-spell had been completed at last, the stone expanded to seal the device tight.

Flint, his energy spent, toppled. Snow Pine caught him, or rather let herself be sprawled by his fall.

Bone and Malin hesitated in their stone-throwing.

"I . . . see," Skrymir said. "Daughter . . . I see. It's as though a veil is lifted. I see an interplay of forces giving rise to all things. The fundamental question of my consciousness is not so different from your own, after all."

"Oh, really?"

"All of us arise from something larger. All of us have changeable natures, until at last we meet that great change which is death. My quest to forge meaning by destroying others . . . pathetic. Unworthy of my majesty."

He set Inga down. "Now, perhaps, I will find meaning in creation. I will be constructive, as you were, Inga, and maybe that will let me keep my autonomy, as you have yours."

"But I don't build things," Inga said. "I like to smash them."

"Indeed. But have you not built friendships? Farewell, daughter, and assorted fools."

Skrymir strode toward the waters.

"Wait!" Inga called out, and Skrymir paused. "Your army! You have to call it off!"

"They will no longer listen to me, changeling," rumbled Skrymir, "for I have changed. No longer can I say, 'To myself be enough.' Now I know I have a real self—as real, or as hollow, as anything else—to which I must be true. You must cope with trolldom as best you can. One way or another, our age changes."

So saying, Skrymir surged into the sea.

"One down," sighed Bone. "Ten thousand to go."

Screams descended from the Svardmark promontory.

"Let's go," Flint said, supported by Snow Pine. "It's time we found Snow Pine's daughter. And your son."

Bone nodded.

"Here we are," said Haytham. He'd helped Katta carry Northwing to another frozen waterfall. Gaunt walked ahead, fiddling.

They confronted a wall of icicles, glistening like bright pillars, ingots, fangs.

Gaunt played on.

"This seems a somewhat futile gesture," Haytham said. "This is not truly a waterfall. More of a water-fell."

Katta said, "It is the middle of summer. The sun is bright. The enchanted winter is broken."

Gaunt paused in her playing. They heard a single droplet fall with a *plink*.

"It's a waterfall," she said. "Aren't you? And things are changing for your land. Awaken."

She played.

The trolls were ripping Walking Stick's army apart. His beautiful instrument, forged out of frightened refugees and transformed into a force to topple even Karvaks . . . it was now like a collection of porcelain sculptures under falling rocks.

Walking Stick leapt from one troll to another, his focused chi knocking heads from bodies. But many of the trolls had multiple heads. Others were not discomfited at lacking any. He could escape, but he would not abandon his people.

It was time.

He leapt once, twice, thrice, before reaching the Great Chain. He knew others had descended it, and he tried the trick himself. He was by no means immune to its energies. He hopped from link to link, despite the pain it caused. Some would think he'd fled, and indeed he heard triumphant guffaws from the trolls. But he was implementing his most desperate plan.

Even as he moved, he pulled forth *A Tumult of Trees on Peculiar Peaks*.

In his mind's eye he hovered over misty spires and saw the tiny figure of the self portrait of the Sage Painter, he who was often called Meteor-Plum, after the original.

Meteor-Plum said, "You do not look as if you bear good news."

"I must implement the last contingency," said Walking Stick.

"I still do not advise it."

"Nonetheless. Gaunt, Bone, Snow Pine, and my experience at Penglai proved that a young Western dragon could awaken a sleeping Eastern elder. It is time to test the reverse."

"She is ready."

Bone, Snow Pine, and Flint reached Innocence and A-Girl-Is-A-Joy. Innocence had his arm around Joy, but it was clear to Bone that Joy was the one whose power was at work.

"Daughter?" Snow Pine said.

"Mother," Joy said. "Innocence gave me the power of the Heavenwalls."

"He what?" Bone said.

"I'm not certain that was a good idea," Joy said. "Because I'm still the

Runethane. I'm having difficulty reconciling the powers. Let alone quieting the arkendrakes."

"I did what I had to do," Innocence said.

Bone put his hand on his shoulder. "I know, son."

Snow Pine took up the side opposite Innocence. "I believe in you, daughter."

There came a blast of cold wind, and raindrops hit their faces. They all looked up, even Joy.

Walking Stick was descending the Great Chain.

"At this rate," Bone said, "they should really add a rope bridge—"

"Look," Flint said.

Insubstantial at first, but gaining solidity as it flowed forth, an Eastern dragon coiled up from Walking Stick's location. She was a thing of beauty and majesty, green and blue, scales like river stones, wings like clouds. Her eyes were wise and bright, like pools of moonlit mountain water.

And she had doomed them all, Bone thought.

A renewed rumbling commenced beneath their feet.

"What?" Snow Pine said.

"You should know," Bone said. "We've seen this before. A young dragon awakening an arkendrake of the opposite sex."

"Oh," Snow Pine said. "We're dead, aren't we?"

But the Eastern dragon spoke, its voice falling like soft rain, and it was not speaking to them. *You who are called Staraxe, I am Yewan Long, and I have come to stir you. For many centuries, little beings have warred over your broken isles, and even your younger brothers Sunsword and Moonspear still hope to claim your energies. It is time to end their conflict. Rise a little and join me in the sky.*

Gaunt, Northwing, Katta, and Haytham fell as an earthquake rocked the land, and the volcano Surtfell roared to renewed life.

Gaunt said, "What has happened? Are the dragons awakening? Is everyone dead?"

"Can't tell you now!" Northwing said, for the shaman's spirit was back in its true body. "Someone's using a mastodon to crush a sabercat. We need to move inland. Do you not sense it? Death hanging near us?"

"I do," said Katta. "As if in a nearby reality we had already perished."

"It changes . . ." hummed a voice, echoing amid hundreds of crystals.

A shadowy figure appeared in the mass of icicles, surrounded by a border of rainbow reflections.

"He awakens . . ." said the voice. "Fiddler, you may pass."

Joy said, "I've been trying to calm the Svardmark and Spydbanen dragons. But Yewan Long is waking up the dragon of Oxiland! I don't think I can control it. . . ."

Suddenly Walking Stick was there.

"Nice to see you," Bone said. "Are you trying to kill us all?"

"No," Walking Stick said. "Not us. All depends on Yewan Long—and on you, Joy. You have the power of the Chain."

"And the Heavenwalls," Joy groaned.

Walking Stick's eyebrows rose. Bone was not above enjoying seeing the man shocked. "Indeed?" Walking Stick said. "That should make matters easier. . . ."

"It doesn't!"

The island rose beneath them.

Bone fell to his knees and looked all around. The many islands and skerries of the Splintrevej were all rising, water rushing away. The coast expanded, revealing mud, silt, and starfish. He noted the barnacled ruins of a stave church upon the sunken headland.

Indeed, it was a headland in more ways than one. Bone registered a terrifying image of a vast draconic skull rising from the waters.

Walking Stick said, "Calm yourself, Joy!"

Innocence said, "Surely you're joking, Shifu!"

"No! Yewan Long is calling to Staraxe only, making him rise for a singular purpose. You must help keep the other arkendrakes subdued."

"Ah," Flint objected, "I am not certain a gigantic draconic landmass is a precision instrument. . . ."

"I can't control the two powers!" Joy yelled. "They're getting away from me!"

"Then . . ." Innocence said, taking her hand. "Give one of the powers to someone else. It can't be me, anymore. But we know it can be done. Give it to someone you trust, someone who can help you."

Hand shaking, Joy reached out and grabbed Snow Pine's arm.

"Mother," Joy gasped, "Snow Pine. I name you the bearer of the Heaven-wall Mandate."

"What—" Snow Pine shrieked as power flowed into her.

Gaunt, Haytham, Katta, and Northwing emerged from the Straits of Tid in the ragged remnants of a drowned stave church. The whole world was shaking, and the land was rising into the storm-choked sky.

"You were right," Northwing told Gaunt. "That sunken spot of power isn't sunken anymore."

"What have they done to my balloon?" Haytham demanded.

"I do not perceive the efrit," Katta said. "This island is remarkably free of anything sinister, let alone evil."

"That will be comforting when the earthquakes kill us," Northwing said.

"Let's get to the Chain," Gaunt said.

They ran as fast as they could manage, ground trembling underfoot.

"Gaunt!" Any relief Bone felt evaporated with the knowledge Gaunt would share his fate. They were rising into the sky, toward the clouds . . . any more shaking and they would all topple into the sea. He craned his head and saw the slaughter over on Svardmark pause as trolls and men stared up at doom incarnate.

"Gaunt!" he cried, embracing her. "What are you doing here?"

"How can we help?" she asked. "I have this feeling I am supposed to keep the dragons from rising."

"That's what Snow Pine and Joy are attempting. Or rather they are trying to calm two out of three."

They joined the group at the Chain.

"I . . ." Snow Pine said. "I can't do it . . . it's too much. . . ."

"We have to . . ." Joy said.

"Mother!" Innocence said.

"I feel as though we were just together," Gaunt said, smiling weakly at him, "and nearly lost each other. I remember music." She raised her fiddle. "I was trained to play by a fossegrim. Perhaps it can help."

She played. She improvised a song that seemed to Bone all about loved ones united, mates, friends, mothers, and children, here at the world's end. And whether it helped calm the dragons or simply inspired the Runethane and the chosen of the Heavenwalls, Joy and Snow Pine took heart.

"Mother," Joy said, new confidence in her voice, "you tame Moonspear. I have Sunsword."

"Yes . . ."

The arkendrake Staraxe breathed. As with a voice of ten thousand thunderclaps, Bone heard two words.

NO.

MORE.

The Chain broke. Its rings flew across the waters, and its energies across the sky. The thunderclouds of the Karvak shamans were rent.

Sleep now, Staraxe, sang Yewan Long, *and dream of love. I may yet come to you, one day. . . .*

They were descending now, but Bone could see the promontory of Svardmark as they sped past.

The clouds were gone. The summer sun blazed upon the army of trolls.

In one heartbeat the trolls became inert, and the once flat-topped promontory now resembled a quarry, filled with thousands of piles of rubble.

Staraxe returned to the sea.

Gaunt awakened, waterlogged fiddle in hand, on the slopes of a spindly mountain. Far above, she saw a monastery wreathed by mist.

"What?" she said, coughing. "Here?" Her retching tasted of salt.

"You are all right, Mother!" said Innocence. "Father pulled you out?"

"*I* did!" said Peik, whom Gaunt remembered from Klarvik. "She did such honor to my father's fiddle, I had to help her. I fought off sharks and men and shark-men. I never lie."

"Peik never gave me any credit, either," Imago Bone said nearby, squeezing water from his clothes. "But he did help," Bone added.

Gaunt groaned, seeing more companions approach. "We . . . we are all right?"

"Yes," Walking Stick said. "I was quite thoroughly busy rescuing as many people from the island as I could. Inga and Malin helped, and Joy, despite her exhaustion. Steelfox rescued her sister, for reasons I cannot understand—"

"Don't forget me, Katta, and Northwing," Haytham said. "We did our part. As did Haboob, I understand, before we arrived." He carried with him a charred, cold brazier, dripping with seawater.

"Be happy for the efrit," Northwing said. "It's free."

"I seem to be losing all my companions," Haytham sighed. "After what you told me about Corinna . . ."

Katta said, "There is a great shadow upon her, which falls upon many with power. She may never escape it, my friend. But we are with you."

"You've got friends, Haytham," Northwing said. "I feel like I've been to the deepest underworld beside you."

"They're right," Gaunt said. "You are not alone, Haytham." Gaunt looked past him to see Snow Pine. "Wherever fate, chance, or bad weather take us, we are all friends. . . ."

The former bandit, she who was once called Next-One-A-Boy, was staring up and around in wonder at the monastery. And at more than the monastery, Gaunt realized. Flint sat beside her upon a boulder, holding her hand . . .

. . . And the boulder sat at the edge of steel-gray waters, flowing in the midst of craggy straits. This mountain was an island now, and the other Peculiar Peaks were gone. Familiar-looking coastlines rose in their place.

"She . . . this place . . . what has happened?" Gaunt said.

"Let me try," Innocence said. "The convulsion of forces destroyed the Scroll of Years, Mother. But Snow Pine, with her new powers, was able to rescue part of the world inside . . . or perhaps that world still exists, and she dragged over a fragment of it. The difference is academic now. The monastery now exists *here*, in Kantenjord, at the site of our battle."

"Snow Pine's powers?" Bone said. "So it's true—she's empress of Qiangguo now?"

Walking Stick said, "*Rightful* empress of Qiangguo. But there will be others who disagree. It will be a great struggle, making her reign possible."

"Is that what she wants?"

"Think about it, Imago," Gaunt said. "However it came about, who could be a better choice? She grew up a common woman, suffering what ordinary people suffer. She's seen much of the world. She is fierce in doing what she thinks is right. What pampered prince could serve better?"

"I once told somebody," Bone said, looking at Innocence, "that to become a ruler wasn't necessarily a blessing. But I agree. If Snow Pine wants the job, there couldn't be a better choice."

"We may not live long enough to worry about it," Innocence said. "The trolls are gone, and the Karvaks are distracted. But they still have a vast army, and Kantening allies. And the Chain was shattered, so Joy has lost her draconic powers, just as I have."

Walking Stick said, "I go now to rally my own army. We have this new defensible position to retreat to—one they're quite familiar with."

"Let me go with you," Inga spoke up.

"And me," Malin said.

"And me!" Peik said. "I could fight a thousand Karvaks, and often have. Though there's at least one," he added with a glance at Steelfox, "I would fight beside."

"I will go as well," Katta said. "Northwing and Haytham, I suggest you rest. But a swim sounds invigorating."

"All right," said Walking Stick. "You four will be useful, if you are up to the swim. I will help you cross safely. Innocence?"

"Master, I prefer to stay with Joy . . . and my parents."

Walking Stick nodded. "That is most proper."

Once Walking Stick's group plunged into the waters, Bone said, "Go talk to her, son. I'm sure she needs you. She's gone from being godlike to becoming an ordinary human being. Well, mostly ordinary. Just as you have."

Innocence nodded. Then, suddenly, he hugged Bone. "There is no one who is truly ordinary. You have taught me that."

"I, ah, well, I am glad."

He pounded Innocence's back and let the boy go. Gaunt put her arm around Bone, eased him back down. He was clearly in bad shape but would recover. There was so much to worry about, and their reunited family was only the most immediate item. But looking at the sun spearing through the last of the Karvak shamans' clouds, she could not help but smile.

There would be a tomorrow. Her family probably would be in it. That was enough.

CHAPTER 43

CHOSEN

Arnulf Pyre-Maker, Ottmar Bloodslake, and Kolli the Cackling strode through the army of Free Kantenjord like mowing farmers, a dwindling trail of Spydbanen warriors in their wake. The devastation of their forces was unexpected, the earthquakes uncomfortable, and the trolls' sudden petrification unfortunate, yet the Three Wolves slaughtered merrily on. They'd come too far to do anything but enjoy the mayhem. And who knew what a few ferocious men might yet accomplish?

Yet now, as they tore through a batch of Ostoland irregulars and hacked down a gaggle of longbowmen, time seemed to slow for the Wolves. The sky changed, showing a rich scattering of stars and an aurora rippling skyward like a bridge. Soaring through that sky was a spear-wielding girl riding a narwhal. Shadowy shapes followed, riding flying horses with far too many legs. Attending her were two ravens.

Fierce-eyed Arnulf said, "What apparition is this?"

"Do I see Orm himself?" many-scarred Ottmar gasped. "And Torden and Verden? Do they come to aid us or challenge us?"

"And who is with them?" laughed Kolli, for either possibility amused him.

The voice of the Chooser of the Slain rang out. "They are the ones I chose, Wolf, to defy this Wolf-Time! I was called from across the centuries by the Vindir to be the final Chooser, a daughter of a time-flow in which Fimbulwinter was foiled. For even as a young child I had an imagination for dooms and battle. A natural inheritance, you might say! As Chooser I claimed these spirits and brought them backward in time to join the Vindir. Now they are here to fight this would-be Ragnarok. Among them are Nan of Love and Grief, and Freidar of the Sunlight! There are Alder of the Earthquake and Vuk Horsemaster and Havtor the Brave! There are Erik the Bright-Eyed, Ruvsa the Rose, Tangletop the Trickster, and Taper Tom the Clever! There too is Yngvarr the Blazing! So many others. And watching all are Huginn and Muninn, raven servants of Orm himself!"

And the Three Wolves saw the gods, and as one they ransacked their memories. For a fleeting moment it seemed to them that not all these names were those they'd heard 'round the crackling hall-fires. The moment passed; they recognized all and knew their end was come. And Arnulf roared, and Ottmar grinned, and Kolli cackled. For they were as Kantenings of old that day, and even against gods they would fight on.

"You see, Rolf, old friend," declared Kollr, Friend to Ravens' Hunger, as the last Wolf toppled below the stars, "wherever your Swan keeps you. Our gods *are* violent."

As screeching Charstalkers rose from the bodies and were speared and hacked by weapons full of starlight, Jokull the Vengeful said, "And now I am fulfilled."

And Torfa the Wrathful smiled, and said, "But where is your friend? The Sabercat Warrior?"

"He sleeps in a blue sky above a green place," said the god, "and may his days be as peaceful as our nights are bloody." And he rode laughing after the Chooser toward the glittering place that was the past, and also home.

CHAPTER 44

THE MIDDLE

I remember how we arrived that noontime, amid the rock piles that once were trolls. Men and women were disassembling them to make barrows for their own dead. There were so many. Even the Spydbanen lords had fallen, though men whispered there was not a mark on them. So many cairns. Yet there was always more troll to go around.

They are now calling that promontory Trollhruga, by which I think they mean "troll-heap."

But there was one troll who hadn't perished from the sun, and one troll-changeling who had never feared it.

"Hello, Rubblewrack," said Inga as I climbed down from her back.

"Hello, Inga Peersdatter," said Rubblewrack, still chained. "Would that I could destroy you, and Princess Alfhild there. Your existence mocks mine."

"There's been too much destruction," Inga said. "Listen! You and I may be the only trollish folk left in a thousand miles."

"I have no troll blood! I am a mockery. Look at us! An uldra who took the shape of a troll. A troll raised as a Swanling human. A human raised as a haughty uldra. There is no true place for us."

I surprised myself by moving into the middle of them all. I spoke. "There is a true place for us. It is with each other. I am human, raised human, yet many would consider me broken in mind. But I will not give up. Nor should any of you. Broken we may be, in a broken world—the middle world, between the godly and the hellish. But we can work together and put a little of it back together."

I took Inga's hand, placed it on Alfhild's, and put both of theirs together on Rubblewrack's. "Make this promise. Not to kill one another for a year. Give yourselves that long to become friends. Or if not friends, then people-who-will-not-kill-each-other."

"Is that a word?" Alfhild sniffed.

"It should be," Inga said. "I agree. What about you two?"

"Very well," Rubblewrack said. "A year."

"At best," Alfhild said, "I will indeed become *people-who-will-not-kill-each-other*. I think the uldra would do well to stay out of human business. But . . . we will see."

I asked Walking Stick to undo the chains. He consulted Squire Everart, who looked suspicious but in the end gave his consent.

Together we joined the procession of rafts the army was making to take us to the monastery on the cold mountain, there in the middle of our isles.

For this reason, when Inga and I make our final book of stories, I will put this in the center. The stories should speak for themselves. The end is already written. But sometimes it's good to know why people put stories together, why we need them so much. So we can meet in the middle.

CHAPTER 45

PEACE

Clifflion, Grand Khan of the Karvaks, looked with satisfaction upon the siege of Maratrace. These people, dwelling on the border between the Wheelgreen and the Efritstan desert, were said to revere both beauty and pain, and well could he see it, with their lovely adobe buildings amid the twisted towers made by the torment-worshipping Comprehenders. The Lady of Thorns, their young ruler, had a philosophy that braided the good and the bad in life, but Clifflion knew it was destined to be replaced by simple, clean Karvak rules. She and the other rulers would be purged, the population ravaged, and those who had useful skills taken as servants or slaves.

The Maratracians had good fighters, and they had magic—Clifflion's army had been savaged by efrits and night angels and more disturbing things. The Grand Khan had long since put aside his scruples about retaliating with human sacrifices from among the captives. Indeed, their screams, greeting the purple dawn, had a certain music. Of course, unimaginative gods like Mother Earth and Father Sky had no love of such offerings, so he had to make them to such entities as his resourceful wife had made him aware of, the Herald of the Red Fountains, the Eye in Nightmares, or that which dwelled in the Pit Where Light Screams. Their services were even now in play. Above the city walls swirled heads severed from their bodies, singing sweetly eerie chants. A vast orb hovered above the largest tower, tendrils descending into windows, vaguely manlike shapes sliding gently up through the pulsing extensions to vanish into the eyelike mass. And now and then a warp in reality would open, dark like infinite space but with misty nebular teeth, to snap up one citizen or another. Clifflion sometimes wondered why Jewelwolf, to all reports, rarely employed these entities, preferring to let her husband practice the summonings. He also wondered why he never felt rested and could no longer remember his dreams.

When the strange, twisting shadow dropped out of the skies, Clifflion at first assumed it was something he had summoned, and so he paused upon his horse, squinting, raising his hand to forbid his bodyguard from loosing an arrow. Was it a mockskulk, a lostbeast, a reality scar?

He was disappointed to see it was only a magic carpet.

"You have my gratitude," it said in the language of the Karvaks.

"How so?" the Grand Khan asked.

"Ultimately you are merely a pawn. But as a creature torn between good and evil, I have long sought a path in life. And now I have it, as a playing piece in the great game. You have my gratitude—for you are the first pawn I've removed."

The voice was so chilling and yet so calm that Clifflion had no true sense of danger until the carpet engulfed him. Distant shouts of alarm reached his ears, but these did not prevent him from knowing sleep at last.

CHAPTER 46

SUMMIT

What Joy decided to call a "summit meeting" occurred one week after the battle at the Chained Strait, and one day after word came of the Grand Khan's assassination. A rider had arrived bearing General Ironhorn's message that he and his forces would withdraw to the continent, and that he would offer no battle if none were offered him. Steelfox had replied that when all the invasion force had either departed—or defected to Steelfox's personal banner—Jewelwolf would be released.

Peace had come, but like many a peace, it was near to boiling into fresh conflict.

So Joy had invited them to the summit of the monastery's mountain.

Here was a grotto just beneath a snowy peak, with little waterfalls of snowmelt from the fledgling summer. Standing in that peaceful place, Joy studied the Runemark upon her hand. It had not faded, though her dragon-fueled powers had. Now she was just a pugilist with classical training. Yet it seemed the land still wanted her to play a role. Perhaps the dragons knew her now. Very well. She would decide for herself what it meant to be Runethane.

Meteor-Plum offered her a cup of tea.

"You don't need to do this," Joy said.

"It is my pleasure to serve tea to our guests," he said. "It is my pleasure to do anything at all! By rights I should have ceased to exist. Yet by some miracle I now am corporeal. I have aches and pains! This tea scalded me! I am destined to become old and decrepit. Truly it is a time of wonders! Now I will leave you alone."

The gathered leaders were Joy, Snow Pine, Steelfox, Corinna, Alfhild—and Hekla, lover of Huginn Sharpspear, robed in black, sent as a delegate from Oxiland.

Rubblewrack was an unofficial voice of trolldom. Eshe of the Fallen Swan was present as an observer for Kpalamaa. The team of Peersdatter and Jorgensdatter was there, Inga to keep the peace, Malin to record events.

"Well, here we are at last," Snow Pine said, raising her tea, vapor rising from the cup. "Six leaders from East and from West, arranging the peace."

Steelfox said, "Joy, where you see six leaders, I see five town-dwellers arrayed against a Karvak. Where you see East and West, I see nomad country ringed around by sea-going powers. We have hard matters to discuss."

"Well," Joy said, staring back at her, at the others, particularly Corinna and Alfhild, who'd so recently tried to kill her. "I see we have a lot of ground to cover."

In the end no one wanted war. Not even when Steelfox announced her new khanate.

"I have made up my mind," the Karvak princess said. "My father's empire is in chaos. With the death of the Grand Khan we will have years of squabbling over succession and perhaps open war. But I want no part of that. I no longer wish to follow in my father's footsteps. Yet to those Karvaks willing to join me, and to Northwing's people, who've always stood by me, I have an obligation." She made a fist. "So there will be a new realm, along the seas of the north. The Khanate of the Endless Ice. It will extend from Spydbanen to the Mirrored Sea, and beyond to the realm of the True People. It will be my realm, and I will guard it well."

"You can't simply carve Spydbanen away from us!" Corinna said.

"That's Kantening country!" Hekla added.

"No longer," Steelfox said. "Their jarldoms submitted willingly to the Karvaks, and I claim them. I think the surviving trolls will cooperate."

Rubblewrack grumbled, "I think you're right."

"And," Steelfox said, "Northwing is learning that the Vuos shamans in the farthest reaches of Spydbanen have much in common with the True people. An alliance seems only natural. No, respected Kantenings, much as you would like to see my people vanish, we are here to stay. In time you may be grateful. For my first enemies are likely to be fellow Karvaks."

The rest was detail. The Karvaks would depart Svardmark and Oxiland. Alfhild announced the uldra would be disappearing from human affairs. Corinna's standing as mightiest ruler of Svardmark was unchallenged, and Oxiland wanted a closer alliance, much as the idea pained Hekla. Corinna herself owed a great deal to Squire Everart and his peasant army. Much was going to change.

That led to Joy's own announcement. "There is one more thing I would say. It is a thing Innocence Gaunt, Persimmon Gaunt, and Imago Bone have asked of me, and I owe them too much not to bring it to your attention. It is about slavery."

"Thralldom?" Hekla said. "What of it?"

"It should end."

"As I thought!" Corinna said. "You are imposing foreign ways on us. Soon you will have us kowtowing and reciting your Eastern classics morning to night. You should know, Runethane, that Soderland has led Kantenjord in diminishing slavery, and that process will continue."

"Diminishing," Joy said. "Not eliminating. And you have influence over your neighbors."

"Ah, so you are ready to trample those smaller realms."

"Aiya! You immediately see all proposals as hostile! Why? Do you hate me so much?"

As if Joy's anger proved some obscure point, Corinna seemed serene. "It is because I have an obligation to see the future." She gestured to Snow Pine. "You are the daughter of a mighty power, Joy. Perhaps," Corinna continued, with a slight nod to Eshe, "the most powerful on the Earthe. And we were nearly conquered by other Easterners, the Karvaks. We will have to tread carefully. Even if you come in friendship, you may overwhelm us."

"You misjudge us," Snow Pine said.

"Intention is not all that matters. Potential must be weighed. Nevertheless, if you are merely advising that slavery be ended . . . I agree. But it will happen when *we* decide."

Hekla said, "I lack Corinna's fear of you, Joy. I hear your words. But thralldom is essential to our livelihoods. Oxiland lives on the edge of poverty as it is. We cannot give up our farmhands."

"Don't give them up then!" Joy said. "Free them! Pay them!"

"You make it sound so easy."

"Perhaps. It may be the Runethane's job to be naive." Joy took a deep breath. "Nevertheless, any escaped slave who reaches my island will be considered free and under my protection."

The meeting broke up with a silent, stony sipping of tea.

Eshe came to Joy afterward. "You have the wolf by the tail."

"You think I shouldn't have pushed?"

Eshe shrugged. "I'm just a bureaucrat. I do what people tell me."

"Including assassinating the Grand Khan?" Joy whispered.

"There are many conflicting accounts of that event."

"Some of which you authored?"

"If I did have something to do with that," Eshe said, looking directly into Joy's eyes, "I hope the Runethane would note the positive effects. Any other way of ending the war would have cost even more lives. That is the burden of knowing things, and in a way I grieve for you, that you will share that burden. I have studied the *Chart of Tomorrows*, which might aptly be titled *A Journey to Kantenjord*, and I had the language skills to fully understand it. I have thus perceived how fragile the world really is, and how many alternate timelines lead to doom. I will give my agents their respite. But sooner or later, I will have work for them."

Joy stared after Eshe as she left, wondering. But Snow Pine joined Joy and hugged her, dismissing thoughts of dooms.

"I am proud," Snow Pine said. "And afraid. You don't have to come with me. You've made a challenge you may have to back up."

"Life is short, Mother. I want to help you get to Qiangguo. I want to see it at least once."

"Well then, I will not presume to argue. On this matter. I look up at the moon over Kantenjord and know it for the same that shines upon our homeland. And I, who once hated Qiangguo, long to return. I hope Corinna's fears are true in one respect, and that this truly is an Air Age—or Aeolian Age, as your stepfather-to-be would have it. Then we may see each other often, after you return."

"Agreed."

They descended the path. Looking down to the newly constructed harbor, they saw *Anansi* readying itself for departure.

"What?" Joy said. "So soon! They wouldn't!"

"Go," Snow Pine said. "You can get there much faster than I."

Joy quickened her chi, leaping downslope as fast as she could.

She passed Eshe, glaring at the spymaster as she went.

She passed Steelfox, who stood beside Jewelwolf on a cliffside, Karvak soldiers thick around them. She couldn't linger to discover the meaning of the gathering.

She passed Corinna, who had met Haytham ibn Zakwan. Joy nodded curtly and continued. She would always dislike the queen of Soderland, but from now on she would have to control her feelings.

Except with Innocence. *He* was about to get an earful.

"You will not stay with me, inventor?"

"I am tempted more than I can say, O queen. But I fear—"

"Yes? I think there is no fear we could not face together."

"My fear is of a different nature than you think. There is a quote of a distant land that keeps ringing in my ears. 'I am become death, the devourer of worlds.' It was my inventions that brought war to these lands."

"And your inventions that can ensure the peace! I will need vessels of the air to guard against those of the Karvaks. And sooner or later such craft will arrive from elsewhere, the Eldshore, Qiangguo, Kpalamaa. . . ."

"Yes. That is exactly it. I developed my balloons for exploration, and I dared hope they would bring a perspective that would literally elevate humanity. Instead they've become tools of death. I do not know how to respond. But building more warships is not the way."

"Then do not build warships. Build art. Build toys. Build castles in the air. But build them near me, my dear inventor."

"I . . ."

"I see. I am surrounded by people who now think I'm hateful. I'd hoped you were not one of them."

"I . . . have wondered what you really think of me, Corinna. For I am, from a certain point of view, also an 'alien.'"

"No one understands. . . . I saw the destruction of my land, Haytham. Not from any fault of ours. Because foreigners were simply much stronger. I do not fear Easterners for being different. I fear being erased."

"Please try, Corinna, to see them as people, with their own quirks, wants, and needs, not simply as a threat."

"If I can do that, will you stay?"

"Whatever I may feel, whatever my admiration . . . you tried to kill my friend. She who only wanted to help you. I am going, Corinna. For a long time. But I will listen for word of how you deal with matters in Kantenjord. Perhaps, one day . . ."

"I understand."

"You got your way. You've come to gloat."

"I've come to talk, Jewelwolf."

"I will inevitably return to the homeland, sister. I will inevitably come out on top. I'll determine how you killed Clifflion."

"I had nothing to do with that."

"And I will come for you and your rebel khanate."

"That is what I get for sparing you. But I would do it again. You are my sister."

"You are a fool."

"Perhaps. I am summoning delegations. Swanlings. Followers of the Undetermined. Scholars of the All-Now. Many others. I think it's time I considered the world's faiths."

"You abandon tradition."

"No. But I am open to new ones. I need a way forward that includes mercy. I cannot do without it."

"It will be your undoing."

"Perhaps. But it seems to be working so far. We will speak again, sister. I will never give up on you."

Gaunt saw Joy approaching through a spyglass. She passed it to Innocence.

"She looks angry," he said glumly.

"I would be too," Gaunt said. "I warned you."

"Women," Bone said, "in my experience, do not like good-byes. But they hate vanishings much more."

"I was *not* vanishing," Innocence said. "I was respecting her new station."

"You are in trouble," Bone said. "I promise to morally support you, in silence."

"Don't taunt him, Bone."

Joy leapt onto the ship's deck. "You!" she said to the three of them. "You were going to leave without saying good-bye."

Bone said, "It was actually all his idea."

Innocence sputtered. "You said you would be silent!"

Gaunt said, "Innocence truly didn't want to hurt you, Joy."

"It is hard to say good-bye," Innocence said. "I thought you would feel the same way."

"Yes, I do. But—it's all so much, Innocence. We never asked for those powers to toy with us. I don't know what they wanted with us in the first place. Why choose champions from beyond their borders?"

Gaunt said, "We might never know. But good came of it, I think. At any rate, Joy, our family needs time to itself—away from powers, empires, wars. We are going to Oxiland. We will try farming for a little while, until Eshe decides to send us on a mission."

"Which will probably be all of three days," Bone said.

"Why Oxiland?" Joy said. "You spent some time there, Innocence."

"I like the scenery. It suits me."

"Is there a girl there?"

"Bone," Gaunt said, "let's go check in with Eshe."

"But I still see her up on the mountain. . . ."

"Walk with me, Bone."

They walked.

"There *is* a girl . . ."

"I knew it."

"And I do want to speak with her again. Maybe it is something, maybe it is nothing. But that's not the main reason."

"I understand. I shouldn't feel . . . jealous. It would be strange . . . if you and I . . ."

"We grew up together. I want my friend to remain my friend."

"Then why do you want to leave, Innocence? Do you think we can't be friends anymore, if you lack power?"

"Nonsense, Joy! I have all the power I need."

"You speak of your bad breath?"

"Ha! Joy, we will be friends always. And we will meet again. But I have been driven near to madness. I need to be . . . just me. You know your mother in a way that I do not know mine. And my father is practically an imaginary figure for me, still. I need this time."

"Promise me you will come back to the monastery, if you hear that I've returned."

"I promise. The uldra-earl may be right; I will always be traveling. We will stick-fight on the heights again. And I promise more. If you do not return, I will come looking for you, all the way to the fairy isles."

"They would make a good couple," Gaunt said. "When they're a little older, of course."

Bone shook his head. "I'm fond of Joy, but it would all be doom this, empire that. He's had quite enough of such things."

"You mean *you* have."

"And you haven't? Aiya, Gaunt! All this time, trying to find Innocence again, and by some astonishing stroke of luck he's free of this power that's haunted us—"

"I know, I know . . ." She looked up at the mountain peak, remembering when she'd first seen it, desperate to hide from a then-sinister Walking Stick. "It's just that, there they all go. Snow Pine to her empire. Flint, Walking Stick, and Joy the Runethane at her side. Northwing to the Vuos to become even more powerful—and believe me, the idea of a more powerful Northwing is frightening. Katta will help train the monks into a fighting force to ensure Joy's dream of a haven. I think he's taken a liking to a monk or two, but that's Katta for you. I don't know where Haytham is going, but I know he'll keep inventing. And Eshe, quietly playing her chess game." She gripped the railing, remembering a much rougher trip aboard a junk of Qiangguo, when they'd first gone East. "All these heroes, legends, queens . . ."

He put his arm around her. "You are wistful, my love."

She leaned into him. "A little. I know. I shouldn't envy the lot of champions and rulers. What looks exciting from a distance is probably brutal and sordid up close. But it's hard not to feel as if the great events are passing me by."

"You wrote once you felt the Swan had called you to create poetry, but also to be of use to those in need. That the contradiction hurt."

"You saw that?"

"I had a good excuse."

"Hm. It's true. I feel torn at times. Thinking I might do more."

"It seems to me that if we are not on the road, constantly, you might find this conflict less acute."

"You might be right." She sighed. "Let it be. I will leave the grand stage. The spyglass of history will follow Snow Pine to the East." She laughed. "Well. I hear Oxiland is violent. Perhaps we'll stumble into a saga or two. Or have a child or two."

"Sagas. Children. I have been thinking about the Chooser of the Slain, you know."

"Yes, Cairn. Beinahruga."

"You know, Persimmon, that name Beinahruga means the same as Cairn, more or less. Or so I've learned. 'Bone-pile.' So in a sense . . ."

She stared at him. "She told us her name was Bone."

Riding the Straits of Tid, she who'd called herself Cairn watched Deadfall flee the vengeance of the Karvaks into the Efritstan desert. Suddenly a whirlwind rose up beside it.

"Ah, there you are," said the whirlwind. "We have had little chance to talk."

"Who are you?" asked the carpet.

"Did I stay so long in that brazier that people and carpets no longer recognize Haboob of the Hastening Horizon?" The whirlwind assumed the form of an imperious-looking gentleman. "Is that better?"

"Oh, you."

"Yes, I! We nonorganic intelligences need to stick together! I have found companionship agreeable and find I would like a friend. I have chosen you. Rejoice! There is much I could tell you!"

"I'm sure Haytham ibn Zakwan would be glad to see you. . . ."

"Oh, no! He is a fine person for a mortal, but one wrong move, and bam, I will find myself in a brazier or a lamp or a snuff box. No, it is you, O amazing assassin, I would regale with my tales."

"It might be interesting at that. I am to gather as much knowledge as possible on the players in the great game."

"What is that?"

"A pastime of the humans. I think it will be diverting. I have found my calling, efrit. Eshe has given me a long list of powers, creatures, spirits, and demigods to press for information. My next stop is a certain stone monkey."

"Oho! I have heard of that one. . . ."

The entities passed out of sight. Cairn shifted directions and traveled homeward, many years into the future. She paused beside a troll dwelling underneath what used to be called the Chained Strait.

"There you are," said Skrymir. "I have been thinking, and listening to the whispers along the Straits of Tid. Tell me. Innocence Gaunt was bait for us, wasn't he? Me and Jewelwolf, and the rest of our cabal, hiding in shadows. The Heavenwalls and the Great Chain, they consulted together and realized the Karvak Realm would threaten both lands. They came to a wordless conclusion to unite East and West against the nomads. Even though their plan was ultimately the death of the Chain. And thus an exchange of champions came into being. Innocence and Joy. We thought we were tangling them in our web, but we became caught in theirs."

"There is that," said Cairn. "Though who can be sure about the thinking of such powers? But consider also . . . they chose children of humble—even criminal—origin, and outsiders to the lands they might champion. Two lands that both could be called isolated. In an age when it will be dangerous to be so."

"Every age is dangerous. I know this, having done my share to make this one such. Be careful out there. For I know all this had a bit to do with you, too. And I almost care."

"I will. I have ridden the Straits of Tid enough. It is time to return home."

She passed unseen by airships and galleons and junks to find a green farm in Oxiland, well-tended young trees growing around it. Her parents and her brother were calling to her, worried that she hadn't yet woken up. It was time she told them the story they thought they already knew.

ACKNOWLEDGMENTS

Thanks to my wife Becky, as always, for her love and support. For giving Gaunt and Bone a chance to tie up loose ends, huge thanks to editor Rene Sears, to my agent, Barry Goldblatt, and to Lou Anders and Joe Monti for making the series possible. I'm grateful for the careful copyediting of Julia DeGraf and for the advice of Carla Campbell, Andrew McCool, William Rucklidge, Subrata Sircar, Scott Stanton, Becky Willrich, Sarah Willrich, and Michael Wolfson. For inspiration for Vindir, foamreavers, trolls, dragons, and hidden folk, I owe a great debt to Snorri Sturluson, H. Rider Haggard, Henrik Ibsen, Lucius Shepard, and Peter Christen Asbjørnsen and Jørgen Moe. Gaunt's rendition of the story of Wiglaf is inspired by *Beowulf*, which I know mainly from the translation by Seamus Heaney. Her satirical song is adapted from a praise-poem in *Egil's Saga* by Snorri Sturluson, as translated by Hermann Pálsson and Paul Edwards. Katta's song by the waterfall is inspired by works of the Tibetan poet Milarepa (eleventh to twelfth century), which I'm fortunate to have encountered in *Sixty Songs of Milarepa* by Garma C. C. Chang and *Tibetan Civilization* by R. A. Stein. Other books consulted include Nancy Marie Brown's *Song of the Vikings*, Jason Roberts's *A Sense of the World*, Jack Weatherford's *Genghis Khan and the Making of the Modern World*, and Anders Winroth's *The Conversion of Scandinavia*. Any foolishness in how I've used these sources is entirely my own.

ABOUT THE AUTHOR

Chris Willrich is a science fiction and fantasy writer best known for his sword-and-sorcery tales of Persimmon Gaunt and Imago Bone. He is the author of *The Silk Map*, *The Dagger of Trust*, and *The Scroll of Years*. Until recently he was a children's librarian for the Santa Clara County Library System in the San Francisco Bay Area. His work has appeared in *Asimov's Science Fiction*, *Beneath Ceaseless Skies*, *Black Gate*, *Fantasy and Science Fiction*, *Flashing Swords*, *The Mythic Circle*, and *Strange Horizons*. Find the author at his website, http://www.chriswillrich.com, on Facebook, https://www.facebook.com/pages/Chris-Willrich/407088872710511, or on Twitter @WillrichChris.

Photo by Richard McCowen, Maritime City Photography

DISCARD

DISCARD